Threshold

to

Eternity

Richard D. Green
and
Anita (Green) Johnson

THRESHOLD TO ETERNITY

by Richard D. Green & Anita (Green) Johnson

Threshold Publishing
SLC, UT 84171

Cover design/layout by Emily Roeder
Creative Contributions – Bill Green

For inquiries contact: thresholdpublishing@yahoo.com

Available on Amazon
ISBN-13: 978-0-9915163-0-46

List Price $19.95

DEDICATION

To Grant and Norma Green (Mom and Dad) for the foundation they instilled within all seven of their children. Even though both of us chose paths contrary to their direction when we were young, the teachings they provided while we were children and the continued example they set provided the base upon which we built our individual testimonies.

TABLE OF CONTENTS

PREFACE

This compelling story takes you on a journey from the beginning of time, a time when a war in heaven determined the fate of so many, to a final judgment of the world. The characters' experiences make the major points on the timeline of man tangible, and illustrate how prophecies play out even as people are still waiting for those very events to take place. After reading this book, you will view mortality and your eternal existence in a new way. The fear that is heaped upon us each day by the world we live in will be replaced with hope.

It is our prayer that our book will help you understand that relationships with Jesus Christ and God the Father, as well as the members of our Earthly families, are actual bonds of eternal love. Even though they have been temporarily forgotten, those bonds may provide encouragement and support during our short mortal existence. They will be remembered when our test on earth is complete, and we will understand how they form threads that connect each of us through all time.

Each person's belief, level of spirituality, and life's situation is unique. Some are new to religious study, some may be struggling for understanding, others may have a firm grasp of basic beliefs and are trying to expand their testimony and understanding, while many have devoted years to study and religious development. Regardless of a person's status, everyone shares one common goal – making the scriptures, prophecy, and those on the other side of the veil real and tangible.

The stories within the scriptures are played out in ancient cultures with characters that often interfaced with a caring and involved God; who, directly or through angels, created outcomes that fulfilled His desires. The characters may seem fictional rather than someone you may know or associate with. Sometimes it is not easy to feel as loved or as valued by God, in our day, as those enduring characters within the scriptures.

It is difficult to benefit or find guidance from the prophecies and warnings within the scriptures when it is uncertain what country or dispensation they are intended for. Even end-of-time prophecies are sometimes difficult to place in chronological order because references to them are spread throughout the scriptures. Our environment causes us to be reluctant to speculate and place ourselves in the most exciting times ever prophesied.

When those on the other side of the veil are contemplated, ancestors often come to mind. However, we often fail to include those we knew before we came to Earth; which may include both those who have and have not yet experienced mortality. Have you ever wondered if guardian angels could be friends with whom you created eternal bonds of friendship and love?

Returning to dwell with those we left behind should not create gloom and desperation. There is a beginning and an end to our time on the Earth, and all aspects of this life should be cherished. We can find comfort in knowing that this life is only a short portion of our existence, the middle portion. We existed as intelligent, spiritual beings long before we came here, and we will have life without end after this life ends. Our sincere desire is; by evaluating your mortal life with the fresh perspective offered in these pages, it will ease the weight of trials, remove the fear of the unknown and reduce the shadowy darkness of losing loved ones who return home before we do.

We hope the fictional characters we have created will help make the scriptures, prophecy, and those on the other side of the veil real and tangible for you

Richard D. Green
Anita (Green) Johnson

THE GRAND DESIGN

There was no indication the afternoon would be any different for Elias and his dear friend Shroba as they returned from their art class. They shared many common interests, and spent a great deal of time together. Conversation was easy between them, but not necessary. Elias smiled to himself as he listened to Shroba's frustration at only being able to reproduce what he saw when he painted, rather than having the ability to reach people's emotions so he could share what he felt when he painted. *I would be content with just having people recognize what I was trying to paint,* Elias thought to himself with a chuckle.

They left the shade of the wide tree-lined walkway and stepped into the warm sunshine as they turned to follow the short cut through the central garden. Benches lined each side of the path and Elias could hear lively conversations taking place as he and Shroba walked. However, on one bench there was a woman sitting alone. Unconsciously he slowed his pace as they neared her. Shroba's voice faded from his ears, and he was startled when he felt a tap on his shoulder.

"Are you coming or not?" Shroba asked.

"I think not," Elias responded without looking away from the girl. However, when Shroba did not respond, he wondered if he had spoken to himself or aloud. Turning toward Shroba, he said, "No, I'll be fine. You go ahead and I will see you in a while. Okay?"

Shroba shrugged. The confusion was apparent on his face, but he slowly turned and walked away. Elias watched him for a moment, and then looked back toward the girl. Slowly he walked toward her as though it were not a choice he made, but simply the only action possible. It was easy to see that she was deep in thought. The most beautiful blue eyes he had ever seen seemed to be focused on something far across the garden, and the girl seemed completely unaware of him staring at her, or anything else occurring around her. She seemed to be debating with an invisible partner. He would have liked to watch her for hours, but felt compelled to find out why she seemed so troubled.

"Excuse me, but do you mind if I sit down?" he asked.

She was startled, but then smiled and apologized for ignoring him.

"You seemed to be totally lost in your thoughts. I just wondered if . . ." He realized he had no idea what to say, and wondered for a brief moment if she would think he was rude . . . or crazy. However, she softly laughed and lowered her eyes as she drew in a deep breath.

"It's the upcoming changes in our lives," she offered, and then raised her eyes to look at him. With a quick shrug of her shoulders, she seemed to relax. She extended her hand toward him and smiled. "I am Sarah."

"Elias," he answered as they briefly shook hands.

For the next several hours, Elias was engaged in the most unique conversation he had ever experienced. As Sarah told him of her concerns, he was so engulfed by her beauty he had to keep pulling himself back into the conversation. Her soothing voice and the fragrance of the beautiful flowers that surrounded them distracted him completely. All too soon, she indicated she must leave.

"Oh, of course," Elias said as he looked around him, wondering how long they had been speaking. "Would you like to talk again tomorrow?"

She slowly stood and looked quickly at the people sitting across from them, then looked back at Elias and smiled. "I could meet you at the south gathering place," she offered. "There is a reading in the afternoon. Maybe we could listen to it together?"

"Good." Elias stood and took her hand. "I'll be there."

The next day, Elias arrived at the south gathering place long before anyone else, and found a marble bench wide enough for only two to occupy. The solitude left his mind free to replay scenes from the day before. When people began to gather, he watched for her, trying to ignore the panic that began to settle in his stomach when he allowed himself to wonder if she had been serious about meeting him.

"Hello, Elias."

Warmth flooded his entire being when he heard her voice. He quickly stood and said, "You came. I'm glad."

Sarah smiled at him as she nodded and they sat down together. Elias was surprised how comfortable he felt with her. He was both happy and relieved that Sarah seemed to feel the same.

"I've known the departures were rapidly approaching," she said, again looking concerned. "It is a good thing, and I'm excited. But . . ." Her voice faded, and she again seemed to be lost in thought.

"Personally, I'm glad you feel some inner turmoil," Elias said. When she looked up at him with a perplexed expression, he continued. "If you had not been so deep in thought yesterday, just as I walked by, I may have missed this opportunity to get acquainted."

Sarah laughed softly and Elias was pleased when she leaned slightly closer to him. She softly laid her hand over his, and slowly raised her eyes until she was looking directly at him. After a moment of silence, she asked, "Don't you worry at all about leaving here? Aren't you concerned about the challenges Great Father has set before everyone?"

Elias took her hand in his. "I do have a bit less enthusiasm about leaving than I had yesterday."

She squeezed his hand, and there settled between them a comfortable silence that neither felt compelled to fill. After several minutes, Elias turned so he could watch her face as he asked, "What exactly concerns you about leaving her?"

Sarah looked down. "What if I never get to come back?"

"If you love this place so much, why do you think you would ever do anything that would prevent you from returning?" Elias also had concerns about that very scenario, but he wanted to comfort Sarah.

She slowly shook her head. "I don't know, maybe just fear of the unknown."

The conversations around them quieted, and Elias looked toward the speaker's platform. He could sense Sarah's apprehension return when the reader began to speak. He explained Great Father's concern about the increasing contention among His children since the Grand Council had taken place. Elias' memory was filled with the glorious events that occurred during that Council when the Great Father had asked, 'Whom should I send to the New World to fulfill the responsibilities of your Savior and Redeemer?' Many of those present had automatically focused on their eldest brother, Jehovah, because there was no other consideration for most of the souls gathered there. Jehovah had assisted

Great Father in creating worlds without number and had already been chosen to serve as the Savior and Redeemer for those worlds even though He had not yet lived as a mortal. He had already proven himself, and it was known that He would obtain His mortal body and experience mortality on the Earth being prepared at the current time. The shout of confirmation that had rang out as a single cry was an opportunity for each spirit to confirm their acknowledgement that Jehovah was the only being with the authority to act as their Redeemer. Elias' entire being was again filled with the certainty of that fact as he recalled the wondrous event. The sound of Sarah's voice returned his attention to the speaker.

"I agree," she said quietly.

Elias looked at her and asked, "What?"

Sarah chuckled. "You must have been thinking happy thoughts because you were smiling. Did you hear the reader explain that we should carefully weigh what is spoken by those who oppose Jehovah being our Redeemer?"

Elias shrugged and smiled. "I'm afraid not. I was remembering how incredible the Grand Council was."

"Do you agree that Jehovah is the only person who has the authority to be our Redeemer?" Sarah asked.

"Of course," Elias answered.

"Then you didn't need to hear what the reader said, anyway. Somehow I already knew you felt that way."

The reader began answering questions from those gathered, and Elias listened intently. When the questions ended, Sarah said, "There's one thing I can say with absolute certainty. This New World will be interesting."

The tone of her voice indicated to Elias her continuing concern. "I'm glad we can discuss these things with each other," he said, carefully watching Sarah's expression. He was surprised how comforting it was when he saw her smile.

During the following days, while much time was spent discussing how things would soon be changing, Sarah seemed to fit in easily with Elias and Shroba. Although nothing was ever discussed, Shroba seemed to seek out Elias less often. In spite of this, the bond between the two was not diminished.

The relationship between Elias and Sarah could not be described as something that started small and grew. It seemed to be strong from the beginning. For Elias, it began as a slightly tense venture out of his comfort zone and grew into a familiar, comfortable necessity. He hoped Sarah felt the same way.

Those who opposed the Great Father's plan seemed to be consumed by their anger and discontent. They coerced and bullied those who did not agree with them, and the intensity of their negative feelings grew stronger. Although their actions never directly affected Elias or his friends, he was relieved when the Great Father called for another gathering of His children to address the situation. At the appointed time, all of Great Father's children gathered together.

Shroba made no attempt to hide his frustration and annoyance with those who felt everyone should accept their opposition to Great Father's plan. Speaking loud enough for everyone seated nearby to hear, he proclaimed, "Is anyone else as confused as I am about why some oppose the Great Father's plan? He knows all. I just don't understand their thinking."

Elias thought about that for a moment, even as he also thought how silky Sarah's hair felt against his hand that rested on her shoulder. His thoughts and awareness of her had been separate and consuming at the beginning, but now they seemed to be part of the whole that was his being. Thinking of her or noticing things about her were no more distracting than noticing that his ear itched. "I can see why you're confused," he told Shroba. "Have you tried to discuss the issue with any of them? They don't seem to be interested in that. All they want to do is shout at anyone who opposes them."

Sarah said, "If they are interested only in arguing and disagreement, I wonder how things can be resolved?"

"Good question," Shroba said.

"It makes no sense to me," Elias sighed, "but they seem to be gaining new converts to their way of thinking.

A sudden silence brought everyone's attention to the Great Father who was now standing in the midst of the multitude.

"My Children," He began. "Opposition grows to the plan presented at the Grand Council. The leader of this opposition desires to take away your individual agency while you are in the New World. He desires to reign over all of you as your ruler and king."

The leader of the opposition stepped forward and reassured in silken tones, "My plan will ensure that not one soul will be lost and each one of you that the Great Father has personally raised and loves will return to live with Him. I will take full responsibility in making sure that you return. I will remove any chance that you could fail."

Cheers instantly arose from the throng, making it apparent there were many who supported the opposing plan.

Elias let his thoughts wander to what life in the new existence would be like without personal agency. Everyone would be forced to make correct decisions. The Father of All had stated that too much would be lost if personal agency was withheld, but Elias could not understand what difference it would make. After all, nothing could be enticing enough to tempt someone to make a choice that could result in not being able to return home. But, if there was any chance of that happening, withholding personal agency might not be such a bad idea.

Jehovah stepped forward and addressed his Father. With great humility in his voice he said, "There may be some very dear to us all who choose not to return. However, those that do return will do so because of their own efforts and love for Thee. And Thou wilt reign over all that return as their God and King, for all glory is Thine." He then stepped meekly back into the crowd, and the crowd once again erupted into great cheering.

The Great Father expressed His desire that each of His children would see the wisdom in the plan that included individual agency, but assured them that He would not force anyone to abide by that plan if they could not accept it of their own accord.

Sarah laid her hand on Elias' arm. "Both of our brothers are great leaders and have achieved wide recognition, but they are very different."

"Very different," Elias said as he smiled at her.

Shroba seemed to exhibit a waffling acceptance as he spoke. "The one that vowed to make sure everyone returned to live with the Great Father was very convincing. If the purpose of this new existence is to help each of us learn about sacrifice, and loss, and all those other New World things, it would sure be nice to know that we will all return when we have gained that knowledge."

"Yes," said Sarah, "but there is something about our eldest brother that made me feel comfortable and I felt . . . admiration for him. As I listened to him speak, my faith was increased that Great Father's plan would be better for us in the long run." She continued to look at Shroba but her eyes lost their focus, and when she continued it was as if she were speaking only to herself. "And did his words about those who returned reach out and grab your very heart? I can still visualize him saying, 'Those that do return will do so because of their own efforts and love for Thee.' That really touched me."

"Leave it to you, Sarah," Shroba said as he smiled at her. "While we're trying to compare the merit of two very different theories, you make that decision based on which one grabs your heart."

Elias, acting as though he had not even heard Shroba's comment, spoke directly to Sarah. "Even the manner in which they spoke was different. The respect Jehovah has for Great Father was apparent when he addressed Him. But the one who opposes Great Father's plan spoke directly to us as though he were already trying to replace Him."

Elias pondered the many things that had been presented. Slowly he again became aware of nearby conversations. He looked around for Sarah, but she was gone. A sudden smack to the back of his head ended his introspective mood. He looked up to see Shroba standing overhead, laughing down at him.

"Marash and Ribiab are already on their way to the falls," Shroba exclaimed.

"Why are we still here, then?" Elias stood and followed Shroba, but it took a few seconds for him to shake off his sober mood and redirect his thinking to anticipate diving from the rocks around the falls with his friends. *I wonder when Sarah left*, he asked himself.

Rather than quiet the opposition to His plan, Great Father's counsel seemed to increase the intensity of the debate. The differences in the two ways of thinking became increasingly divisive. Emotions ran high and several people who had been numbered among Elias' closest associates for a very long time, refused to talk to him.

"Before Great Father presented His plan, had you ever seen anyone this angry before?" Elias asked Shroba one afternoon while they were at the falls painting. When I watch someone actually try to convince another person that their opinion is the only correct opinion, that makes me feel things I have never felt before."

Shroba stopped mid-stroke and held his paintbrush slightly away from the canvas. "What do you mean? What does it make you feel?"

"Well," Elias said as his eyes moved to the soft white clouds high above them, "I guess I feel . . . I don't know. I see that they're angry and that they're trying to impose their opinions on others, and it makes me . . . it makes me angry, too." He stopped and looked at Shroba for a long moment, and then continued. "It makes me want to tell them they are wrong for acting thus, and I want them to have the same opinion I have. It makes me want to act exactly as they are acting. I want to force my opinion on them!"

Shroba laid his paintbrush down and looked intently at Elias. When Elias saw the confusion on his friend's face, he asked, "What?"

"You're right. That's how they make me feel, too. That is the main reason I like to come out here where it's quiet," he said, waving his arm to indicate the peaceful meadow surrounding them. "I hadn't really thought about it like that, but I know that when I hear them raising their voices in contention to express their opinion, I want to get one notch louder in hopes that they come over and confront me. They never do. Have you noticed that once I raise my voice they seem to cower down? It amazes me how quickly those feelings come and how strong they are. Sometimes I'm afraid of what I might do if I were provoked further."

"Strange, isn't it," Elias said. "We're all at a point where the Great Father says we need to proceed to the New World and gain experience so we can become more like Him, and as a result of Him wanting to help us advance, some of His children are becoming less like Him."

"Quite a bit less," Shroba said.

"If this is one of the new experiences we're going to face in the New World, I can hardly wait," Elias said as he shook his head. "We haven't even left our world yet. We are all children of our Great Father, and yet those who oppose Him are arguing and becoming filled with hatred toward any of us who will not agree with them."

"Makes me wonder what other new character traits we will encounter when we're out of Great Father's presence. Maybe this is going to be a harder test than we think." Shroba sighed and turned toward the roaring waterfall, seeming to forget the picture he had been painting.

Elias stood and began collecting his supplies. "I wish Great Father would do something to put an end to all the arguing and anger."

"I agree, but I have never known Him to force His will on anyone." Shroba sighed as his eyes followed the tumbling waterfall. "Do you think the New World will be as beautiful as this?"

"I don't know. But I do know that no matter what it looks like, or how long I'm there, I will miss this place very, very much."

"Agreed," answered Shroba. "Are you going to the Great Gathering with us or Sarah?"

Elias laughed softly, looked at Shroba, and said, "Yes. We'll meet you in the usual place and we can all go together."

"So you like her."

Elias drew in a deep breath and said, "I guess. It's not so much that I like her. It's more that it feels comfortable to be with her. I like to talk to her, just as I like talking to you. But, well, yes, I guess I do like her."

The appointed time for the Great Gathering arrived. Elias and his friends wandered through the crowd until they found a place large enough for all five of them. After a short time Sarah whispered to the others, "It's starting."

Three figures stood together on the platform: Great Father in the middle, Son of the Morning who lead the opposition to His plan stood to His left, and Jehovah, Father's firstborn, stood on His right side.

The Great Father spoke in a quiet but firm voice that was heard equally as well by those sitting near the platform or at the outer edges of the gathering. "My children, some of you are fearful of the experiences awaiting you in the New World. Each of you has learned much, but it is not possible to progress any further if you remain here. Your time in the new existence will provide an opportunity to receive increased knowledge and understanding."

He turned to the son on His left side and gently hugged him. Speaking to him in a soft whisper that only he could hear, He said, "My Son, I love you, and although I will not force you to renounce your opposition to the plan that will provide further growth for my children, I cannot allow you to continue spreading contention that will cause further unhappiness and sorrow. I admonish you to change and follow my counsel."

He next turned to His firstborn and gently hugged him. To him He whispered, "My son, I love you and appreciate your devotion toward providing the opportunity for your brothers and sisters to advance and gain further knowledge and understanding. You alone have the ability and authority to serve as the Redeemer for all of my children. The time is near when you will descend to the new existence and live as a mortal amongst men."

Great Father then turned to the multitude. "My children. You will soon begin your individual testing in the new existence as mortal beings, unable to remember your life here in my presence, and your eldest brother will descend to live amongst you as a mortal being, providing the ability for you to overcome physical death and return to live in my presence." There was a heavy pause, "You *will* retain your personal agency during your mortal experience."

An audible sigh spread through the assembled group. It was interspersed with several surprised gasps from those who had been totally convinced their opposition would sway the Great Father's decision. All sound ceased instantly when the Son of the Morning dramatically demonstrated his anger of being rejected by storming from the platform. As he reached the crowd, he turned and loudly shouted directly toward the Great Father. "You had better change your mind or you'll be sorry!" His supporters erupted into loud emotional yelling.

When the Great Father attempted to address the group, He was drowned out by disrespectful outbursts. After numerous failed attempts, His face showed extreme pain and disappointment, such as those present had never before witnessed. Tears slid down His face as He looked out over the scene of rebelliousness. He slowly walked away from the gathering. It was incomprehensible to the majority that anyone could show such a total lack of respect toward the Great Father.

Elias and Sarah looked at each other in stunned silence. The shouts of disagreement escalated. Sarah gently put her hand on Elias' arm and leaned toward him. As if instinctively reaching out to protect her, Elias put his arm around her shoulder and tried to comfort her. Those who opposed the Great Father's decision repeatedly dashed toward the small group, shouting angrily and condemning them for being willing to go along with whatever Father chose for them.

Elias and his friends stood to leave, positioning themselves around Sarah to provide what protection they could. They slowly pushed their way through the multitude, but those demanding they change their opinion constantly blocked their way. Even though there were fewer dissenters than those who accepted Father's decision, they appeared to feel they had a right to force the majority to agree with them, and they seemed determined to continue intimidating and threatening until that was accomplished.

Elias' forward view was suddenly blocked as Shroba stepped in front of their small group. With arms extended wide, Shroba ran directly into a group of those attempting to block their escape, knocking them to the ground. Shroba rose to his feet and his stature seemed to increase in both size and confidence. Others attempting to leave the area gathered behind Shroba as he walked through the opposition, denouncing all their threats. Elias could see that they actually cowered as Shroba displayed an incredible presence, causing them to shy away from him. When they finally escaped the toxic environment of the protesters, they found a quiet place and fell on the grass in dazed wonder.

"I was afraid," Sarah said after a short time. "I've never been afraid before, but I was very afraid."

"What was that?" Marash asked Shroba.

Shroba started laughing, nearly uncontrollably, and then simply replied, "I'm not sure where that came from, but it seemed to shut them up. Honest though, I don't know who was more shocked, me or them."

WAR IN HEAVEN

The coming days did not lessen the efforts of those who opposed Great Father's decision. Elias was sickened as he observed the irreparable damage that occurred, ending many relationships thought to be everlasting. He felt heated debates over something Great Father had already decided were meaningless, but the situation continually worsened.

The Son of the Morning organized those who followed him, and segregated them in an uninhabited area he named the Camp of Isolation. Attempts to convert others to his cause through intimidation and threats had not satisfactorily increased their numbers, so he taught his followers to implement a plan of control. He promised his glory would be greater than that of his eldest brother, even superior to that of the Great Father. He promised to reward his followers by allowing them to reign over those that opposed his plan, in his kingdom.

The most powerful and dedicated followers of the Defiant One were organized into small attack groups. They were trained to infiltrate Great Father's followers and maneuver small groups into locations where they could be overpowered and taken prisoner. Using carefully orchestrated methods, the hostages were systematically terrorized; if they accepted the teachings, they became a member of the opposition. If they did not, their 'indoctrination' continued and they were kept prisoner.

Despite the danger of the roaming attack groups, the small group of friends frequently sought out the solitude of the waterfall. One afternoon Ribiab came to swim alone. He had much to think about as he had just learned from the Great Father of when he would be sent to the New World. It would be much sooner than any of his friends. Father also promised that he may assist his friends during their mortal experiences should they need help and be willing to accept it.

"It will be fine," he reassured himself as he stretched out on a warm rock so the sunshine could dry him. He closed his eyes and breathed in the fragrance that filled the air. He was aware that a shadow had fallen across his face, and when he opened his eyes, he saw Sarah standing between him and the sun.

"Have you seen Elias?" she asked.

"No, I'm not sure where he is, but I'll gladly help you look for him."

Suddenly, several faces appeared behind Sarah. Ribiab jumped to his feet and discovered eight men surrounding the two of them in a tight circle. He suddenly felt very uneasy. "Can I help you with something?" he asked, trying to keep the concern from his voice.

"No, we just want you to take a little walk with us," one of the men jeered as the group began pushing and shoving the two of them.

Ribiab instinctively tried to resist, but he was severely outnumbered and his actions proved futile. He could see the fear in Sarah's eyes and he protectively put his arm around her shoulder. After being continually nudged and shoved during a very long walk, a large encampment came into view and the two were separated. Sarah found herself in a large group of female hostages, while Ribiab was added to an even larger group of male hostages.

As the attack missions became increasingly successful, the dissenters became emboldened. Their attacks became more frequent, and their increased numbers allowed them to overcome larger groups.

The Great Father called for His son, Michael the Archangel. All of Great Father's children knew Michael had been chosen to be the first man on Earth, the first to receive a mortal body, and would be known as the Ancient of Days because he was the father of the human race. He stood next to Jehovah in authority and had been ordained to direct all dispensations of the gospel ever to be given to mankind.

"Michael," the Great Father said, "I can no longer allow those who have chosen to follow the Son of the Morning, to wage uncontested war upon those of my children who are obedient. Many of them have been taken hostage and are even now being subjected to vile tactics in an attempt to force them to reject my teachings. I ask that you go amongst the loyal and seek out those willing to stand against the opposition, train them and lead them in battle so that the dissenters are unable to take additional hostages. The fear and unrest they have created must be eliminated. This will be a short confrontation as I have decided to end this very soon."

"I will do as you wish, Great Father."

Michael and his army secured the unoccupied area between the obedient ones and the opposition. His army was successful in preventing any further interaction between the two groups. However, when Michael led his army into the Camp of Isolation to retrieve the hostages that had been taken, many fierce battles ensued. After several attempts, Michael returned to the Great Father to make his report.

"Great Father, I have tried to enter the Camp of Isolation from three different sides. Each time we penetrated their lines, the followers of the Son of the Morning rallied and drove us back. I was unable to discover where the hostages are being held, and I fear they may be deep within the center of their community."

"I understand, my son. In your battles, did you sense any remorse in those who were fighting against your army? Did any of them appear to regret fighting against their own brothers?"

"No, Great Father. I searched their faces as wave after wave of those who oppose Thy plan came against my army. I have known many of them for as long as I can remember and have fond memories of shared experiences. I have embraced them in friendship and love. Yet, when I looked into their eyes, they were vacant. Could my face have changed so much they knew me not? I recognized *their* faces, but their hearts were that of a stranger, filled with anger and bitterness."

"My heart is likewise filled with sadness," Great Father lamented. "A portion of my children have been deceived and now they have forsaken the very opportunity wherein I could bestow upon them all that I have. In their ignorance, they have turned away from my teachings, and yet they still believe they have free entitlement to that which they must earn. Oh, how could the Son of the Morning have fallen so quickly? How could his brilliant light turn to a darkness so absolute it engulfs even the slightest hope within those around him? Their vacant eyes are as such from the loss of their agency, for he has taken it, and they are his. They have chosen their master, and he provides their light, which light is darkness, for he is fallen and has no light."

"Great Father, even though the battle became very fierce, the greater battle was waged within my heart. My weakness caused me to wonder how the hearts of those who have been so valiant could so quickly become strangers, filled with anger and bitterness. How could darkness consume them so completely that they have become strangers to their own expectations for eternal exaltation?"

"My son, there is no weakness within you. It is not weakness that has bruised your heart, but love. The same love has prevented the tears of mine eyes to cease these many days. Even I, the Father of my children, do find it difficult to watch one as valiant as the Fallen One descend from such a position of respect to become the usurper of free will amongst my children. What began such a short time ago as only a war of words has escalated into a great battle for the very souls of mine offspring. Yet, you report you find no hesitation in any of their actions. Great is my sorrow."

"I pray I will never forget mine own brothers as thoroughly as they have forgotten me. I fear they consider not how they break the hearts of their parents, and their brothers and sisters."

"Michael, my son, I ask that you perform yet another task. I pray thee, go amongst the dissenters and find the Fallen One. Do not allow my message to be relayed to him, but insist on speaking to him directly. They will take you to him and cause you no harm for they will feel a great power within you. Tell the Fallen One that I accept his refusal to abide by my plan, and will remove him from the requirement of accepting his eldest brother as his savior. This will I do upon the condition that he and his followers come to a gathering of all my children, and bring with him all hostages he now holds. Inform him, at that time, I will provide an alternate option to him. Tell Lucifer that he may retain the spirits of all those who have chosen to follow him."

"I will do as you ask, Great Father," Michael answered.

To Elias' great relief, an announcement came that another gathering was to take place, and all those who had been kidnapped by the armies of the opposition would be returned immediately preceding the gathering. Sarah and Ribiab had been missing for some time, and Elias had been greatly concerned for their safety. On the morning of the gathering, Elias, Shroba and Marash arrived at the meeting place very early, hoping to find their missing friends.

"Looking for us?" a familiar voice asked.

"Ribiab," Marash exclaimed as he spun around. "Oh! You look terrible. Are you alright?"

Elias breathed a sigh of relief as he turned and saw Sarah. With no hesitation at all, he wrapped his arms around her and hugged her tightly. "I was afraid I would never . . ." He couldn't bear to speak his deepest fear. "I'm so glad to see you. Are you okay"

"I'm fine," she whispered into his chest as she embraced him.

"My injuries look worse than they are," Ribiab declared. Both Marash and Shroba looked very upset. "Let's find a place to sit, okay?"

"I'd like to sit as close to the platform as we can. After my experience in that dark camp, I would like to be as close to the light of Great Father as possible," Sarah said.

"I'm glad you're both back," Shroba said. "I don't think Great Father would have called for another gathering if He didn't have a plan to end the division between His children once and for all."

"I hope you're right," Ribiab said. "**I will never again be held against my will or be dominated by such vile darkness.**"

"Follow me," Marash said. "We'll get as close to the platform as we can, and we'll all sit together so we can watch out for each other."

As their brothers and sisters began gathering, it became apparent emotions had not cooled. The conversations amongst brothers and sisters evolved into arguments, and then escalated into angry outbursts.

Great Father walked to the center of the platform, but the ever-increasing volume of the outbursts continued. Disrespectful shouts rang out in an attempt to overpower Great Father's words each time He began speaking. Slowly, His countenance changed to one of visible strength and resolve. When He finally spoke, His thundering voice caused everyone to tremble, and there was immediate silence. This was yet another aspect Elias had never experienced from his Father. He desperately hoped the Great Father knew him well enough to know he supported His decision.

Great Father's voice pierced the thick silence. "No one is to speak. If you accept my plan, fall to your knees, lower your head, and close your eyes. If you do not accept it, stand on your feet."

Elias immediately fell to his knees and kept his eyes tightly closed. Judging from the sounds he heard, he guessed many people were rising to their feet. He did not believe any of his friends would stand up. He refused to believe Sarah would stand either, but he found himself silently pleading that this were true. He wanted to open his eyes and look for her, but he squeezed his hands into tight fists and concentrated on keeping his eyes tightly closed. *Please, please, please*, he kept repeating to himself. The sound of his heart pounding in his ears grew louder.

The Fallen One's angry voice rose as he threatened to steal all those that followed the Great Father's plan. The hate in his heart could easily be heard as he proclaimed he would become their ruler and king. Elias pressed his eyes shut even more tightly as he wondered how his own brother could exhibit such open defiance against the Great Father.

Suddenly, there was a flash of light so intense Elias could see it even though his eyes were still closed. Then there was again silence. The harder he listened, the stronger he felt the silence press against his ears. After what seemed a very long time, he heard his Father's voice.

"My children, arise and open your eyes."

Elias stood and looked around, barely daring to breathe. He was filled with joy at seeing his three friends still at his side. He could not see Sarah, and turned to search for her. She was standing slightly behind him, her deep blue eyes filled with tears. He gently took her hand as he began to comprehend that the crowd around them had diminished considerably. How . . . where had they gone? He looked at those standing nearby, trying to determine who might now be missing.

The anguish apparent in Great Father's voice captured everyone's undivided attention. "I have cast nearly one-third of mine own sons and daughters into another realm, even though it pained me deeply to remove them from my presence. The growing hatred was spreading quickly and consuming many; there was no other way. The disobedience had to be stopped before I lost all of you, my dear children."

The sobering comprehension of what had happened was hard to understand, but then the Father said something that stunned Elias even more. "Many more will be persuaded to follow the leader of the opposition in the New World; because, at this very instant many among you are wondering if you should have stood up and joined your dear loved ones that have been removed from our presence."

Elias had heard the Great Father's voice tremble. However, even though this day had brought incomprehensible sadness, Elias could also see a soft joy radiating from His face. He could feel Great Father's love and appreciation for his own obedience. Warmth filled his heart as he realized his Father knew him personally and that he did not oppose the accepted plan.

The feelings of darkness that had swarmed around him during the past several contention-filled weeks were swept away, replaced with an intense feeling of love. It was the same precious feeling he always felt when he conversed privately with his Father, but standing amongst the endless multitude of his brothers and sisters seemed to meld their joy to his own, and the result was a feeling more intense than he had ever experienced previously.

Naturally, little else was discussed during the following days except the unbelievable loss of a third of their brothers and sisters. Still, everyone appreciated the restored peace and contentment.

To help everyone understand the next phase in their advancement, classes were held to help each individual understand that every world the Great Father had directed to be created followed exactly the same path of progression. Teachers from a world that had completed the entire cycle shared their experiences of living mortal lives with no memory of their pre-mortal existence, explaining it was necessary so they could learn understanding and compassion for one another and accept their Savior through faith.

It was explained that all the dissenters and their leader had been sent to the New World. They had not passed through the portal and veil of forgetfulness, and would never receive the blessing of a physical body. Elias was concerned when he learned that his physical eyes would not be able to see them, but they would see him. His physical ears would not be able to hear them talking to him, but he would be subject to the thoughts they whispered to his mind. Since some of those spirits were former friends who knew him very well, they would remember where he excelled and where he was weak. The battle that had turned friend against friend was not over; it was just on hold until Great Father's obedient children began arriving in the New World.

Elias found himself questioning the purpose of the class. If he were able to retain the memory of what he was learning, he would be assured of returning to live with the Great Father – everyone would. To Elias, it seemed as if he would be facing the most important test of his entire existence, but every possible hope for completing it successfully was being removed.

Finally, hope emerged. While his physical body would prevent him from remembering his Great Father, he learned that the knowledge he possessed would remain within his inner being, and he would instinctively have a desire to communicate with the Great Father.

With these thoughts swirling through his mind, Elias went to his favorite spot near the falls and stretched out on the soft grass. The joyful sound of the birds mixed with the background of falling water, creating an almost hypnotic and serene feeling. It was a perfect place to let his mind contemplate life in the New World. Would he be a teacher that helped others understand what Great Father expected of them, or would he succumb to the whisperings of the Defiant Ones? How could a veil remove every memory of his current beautiful home? How would he be able to exist if he could not be near his Great Father? What if he made choices that placed him in a realm different from Sarah after the test in the New World was complete?

Some aspects of life before the great gathering seemed to proceed much as they always had. Elias and Shroba still attended their art class, and the four friends found time to seek adventure, whether it was diving from the cliffs by the falls or trying to discover a new species of fish in the deep lagoons where they swam. However, these activities seemed to be shorter in duration, and always ended in a group discussion about the new things they were learning.

Individual agency and the purpose of Jehovah being the Savior for all of Great Father's children were discussed at great length.

"I know everyone will make mistakes in the New World," Elias said to his friends one afternoon, "but if we make a sincere effort to overcome them, we can be forgiven. I know Jehovah has accepted the responsibility of being our Savior, but I don't completely understand how that works."

Ribiab answered slowly, as though he were reviewing his own thoughts as he spoke. "Justice requires that someone pay the price for sin, and Jehovah has agreed to pay for our mistakes. If no one accepted that responsibility, none of us could return to live with Great Father because we would forever be stained by our sins."

"It's comforting to know that the Holy Ghost will be able to talk directly to our souls while we're in the New World," Marash said.

"We've been promised help from those who have gone to the New World before us, too," he nodded in Ribiab's direction.

"I finally understand the importance of personal agency," Shroba said. "It allows us to choose which voice we'll follow."

"Right," Ribiab said as he smiled. "Once you understand that the Great Father's plan is perfect, it removes a lot of worry. But we have to remember that although our test in the New World will be brief, the consequences can determine our state for the rest of eternity."

Elias breathed deeply. "It seems obvious, sitting in this world we call home where there are no problems, that only a fool would attempt to make it through life in the New World without seeking guidance from the Great Father. What I'm afraid of is that it may not seem as obvious once we live there."

Nearly every conversation amongst Great Father's children was about life in the New World, and then something happened that changed everyone's focus. They were given a worksheet and asked to make choices regarding their Earthly parents.

"When it says to list one man and one woman that we admire and revere, above all others that we currently associate with, does that mean I have to choose one of you?" Shroba asked. He and his three closest friends had gathered near the falls as usual, but the group had grown; Stephan, Sarah and her friends, Bethany and Elizabeth, were usually included. "How to choose? How to choose?" he chuckled.

"My intent is not to be rude," Ribiab said quietly, "but, although we have fun together and I love each of you, when I hear the words admire and revere, your names do not come to mind. The man I have chosen as my father seems to expect more from me than any of you do, and, as a result, I find myself acting differently when I am with him. He seems almost like a teacher to me."

"I have a question," said Sarah. "We are all children of the Great Father. If we become the children of someone in the New World, will we have two fathers?"

"I wonder about that, too," Stephan replied and continued, "What if Elias and I chose different Earthly parents "Would that mean we were no longer brothers when we return home from the New World?"

"Personally, I think you all analyze things a bit too much," Elias said. "I simply wrote the first two names that came into my mind."

Sarah smiled at Elias and quietly asked, "Weren't you just talking about the importance of studying a situation thoroughly rather than making decisions based on our first impression?"

"Here we go," laughed Shroba as he jumped to his feet. "Analyze the worksheet and then analyze the discussion we had about analyzing the worksheet. That seems to be a common characteristic among females. Perhaps if you take a female with those traits and add a male who has none of them, they balance each other out."

"What? Serious thoughts coming from a man?" Bethany asked as she laughed.

"It happens, sometimes," Shroba said. "I'll see all of you later." He quickly stood and began to walk away.

Ribiab slowly stood and said, "Shroba, wait for me. Until later, everyone." He hurried to catch up with Shroba.

"Farewell," Elias called after them. He caught Sarah's eye and with a quick tilt of his head asked a question, which Sarah answered with an equally quick nod. "We're leaving, also," he said as both of them stood.

"Have you chosen a name to write on your worksheet for a father and mother?" Elias asked while walking with Sarah.

"Yes. It seemed an easy choice. How about you?"

"Yes, I've made those choices."

They walked in silence for some time. Elias began to feel an uneasy quiver developing in the pit of his stomach. He slowly asked, "And what of your other choice?"

"That also seemed like an easy choice," Sarah said without looking at him.

"It did? An easy choice?"

"Yes, there is only one person that comes anywhere near filling the requirements. You're the only one I confide in and I'm certain I will never grow tired of spending time with you. But I haven't written your name on my worksheet."

Elias stopped walking. He slowly turned, but could not make his voice ask the question.

"I couldn't write your name without knowing who you would choose," Sarah said.

Elias realized he was holding his breath, but in one long sigh, he slowly exhaled. "Oh." He smiled and noticed the sparkle in her eyes as the familiar sweet smile spread across her face. "Well, here, you can use my writer as soon as I put your name on my worksheet!"

Jehovah and Michael organized the New World under the direction of the Great Father, with the help of others who assisted them. Jehovah was now referred to as Jesus Christ, Savior of the New World. While the creation continued, a new gathering place was revealed – those going to the New World had not been aware of it. It contained a portal that allowed travel between their home and the New World. Everyone was excited to visit the facility, and Elias and Sarah decided to go together.

Upon their arrival, they received a diagram that directed them to the Assembly Area. The instant they stepped through the doorway, the beauty of the room filled them with awe. It was a very large circular room surrounded by twelve panels of gold-veined marble; in each panel was an ornate door decorated with gold and pearl leaves that formed a vine which cascaded down the front of the door. An immense chandelier hung from the center of the room and cast an amber light on every surface, making the gold in the marble and on the doors appear to twinkle. The door directly in front of them, on the opposite side of the room, was decorated differently than the others – the cascading vine that covered it was made of silver.

The floor was an iridescent marble that reminded Sarah of the inside of a clamshell. The light from the chandelier made the interwoven patterns of silver and blue seem to undulate under foot as they crossed the room.

The purpose of this room came into their minds as clearly as if a guide were moving through the rooms with them. When a person was summoned to the New World, their associates and those that had been assigned to the same New World family unit could gather in this room to bid them farewell.

"This is the most beautiful room I have ever seen," Sarah said in a hushed whisper. "There will probably be so many emotions felt here.

Happiness, sadness, and hopefulness." Together they moved to one of the doors decorated in gold and opened it.

They slowly entered and walked across the room; the floor covering was so thick and plush it seemed to caress their feet. The room was small and felt very private. The only furniture, a lamp and two chairs that faced each other, was situated toward the center of the room, making it possible to view the paintings that hung on every wall. The large murals were so lifelike Sarah wondered, at first, if they were windows that revealed beautiful vistas. It was made known to them that the murals portrayed scenes from the New World, and each depicted a decidedly different terrain. They sat in the chairs and leaned toward each other, holding hands.

"Look at that lamp," Elias said. "It looks like a twisted Melaleuca tree trunk and every leaf seems to be giving off light. It's incredible."

Sarah reached out and touched the lamp, and then stood and felt a leaf. "I think it is a Melaleuca tree, Elias. You can smell the leaves."

"That is amazing!"

It was revealed that this room was where the departing person and his chosen mate could share a private farewell with each other.

Elias chuckled quietly. "I can imagine each couple who comes to this room spending their last few moments together, trying to devise some way to recognize each other when they meet in the New World." Suddenly he knew exactly how he would feel when it was his turn to leave. "Any suggestions?" he asked.

Sarah shook her head and looked down.

Elias saw a tear slide down her cheek. "I'm positive that when we meet in the New World, there will be something about you that looks familiar to me – probably your beautiful eyes. They mesmerized me the first time I saw them, and I can just imagine the same thing will happen when I see them there."

Sarah slowly looked up at him and tried to smile, but it never reached her sad eyes. After a moment, they left the room and returned to the Assembly Area. They walked toward the door covered with a silver vine and Elias slowly opened it. They both felt the sacred reverence that filled the room. The marble walls were the color of wet sand faintly grained with gold. The floor was also marble, gray with large feathered sections of white. Their attention was drawn to a wide staircase made of the same marble as the floor. Short granite walls on each side of the stairs supported ornate black balusters topped with a polished walnut railing. At the top of the short staircase was a foyer, leading to a pair of walnut doors that were closed, concealing what lay beyond.

As in other rooms it was revealed; when the person going to the New World had ended their farewells, they would enter this room for a final visit with the Great Father. The departure portal was behind the walnut doors, and when a person stepped through the portal, they traveled directly to the New World.

Elias and Sarah returned to the Assembly Area. It was made known to them that a similar set of rooms at the opposite end of the building served as the Arrival Area for those returning from their test in the New World.

They followed the diagram to the Observation Area, and passed through a large, bright hallway; the walls, ceiling, and floor were made of a lustrous material that flowed from color to color in large random, dynamic patterns.

"This is like walking through a moving rainbow," Elias said. "It seems as though the moving colors are playing with us."

The hallway widened and opened into an immense area – viewing portals lined a wall that seemed to extend endlessly in either direction. The portals would be available to those wishing to watch the creation of the New World. The person using the portal had only to think of what they wished to view, whether it was general viewing of the creation process, or a specific element. Once the first parents had departed for the New World, permission would be required to enter the viewing areas.

"I wish we could see our friends while they're in the New World," Sarah said.

"I don't know that I would want everyone watching me," Elias said. "What if I lost my way and made a lot of mistakes. If I repented and those mistakes were washed clean, I would prefer that those who knew me here never knew about it."

"You won't make mistakes," Sarah assured him.

"That's what we all think, now," Elias answered. "But there wouldn't be any need for the ability to wash away our mistakes if no one ever made any."

"Oh."

As they walked back toward the entrance of the building, it was revealed to them that those sent to the New World to perform intervention and assistance assignments would also use the departure and return portals.

When they stepped into the warm sunlight following their tour, Elias said, "I can hardly wait until we are allowed to use the viewing portals. I want to know as much about the creation of the New World as possible."

"If the New World is as beautiful as the murals we saw, I think I will miss this place a little less. Well, I guess I won't miss it at all since I won't be able to remember it, but it appears the New World may be almost as beautiful as our home."

When the timeline for the New World was posted, Elias and his three friends were amazed to see that major events involving celestial phenomenon were the result of natural principles that had been used to develop the planet. They discussed the timeline and tried to imagine what it would be like to live in a physical body when things like famines, wars, and earthquakes were taking place.

Finally, the last step of the planning process was posted – each person's assigned time to go to Earth. It was finally possible to determine what would be happening when an individual stepped through the portal to begin their life on Earth.

FIRST FAREWELL

"Do you remember when life seemed to be unchanging, as though it had always been and always would be the same?" Elias did not look at his three friends after asking the question, but continued to stare at the white birds overhead as they glided on the updrafts from the waterfalls that plummeted over the edge of the cliff and crashed into the water far below.

"No one says that any longer," Shroba said as he began laughing.

"The only thing I don't see changing is this spot. Our spot," said Marash. "Maybe that's why we all like to come here, because everything else has changed."

Ribiab reached out from where he had been laying on the grass and touched Marash's forehead. "I think the sun has blinded you, my friend," he said. "Other than being allowed to tour the Gathering Place, I can't think of anything else that has changed. But, if you're talking about our brothers and sisters," he said as he laid back down on the grass, "I have to agree. Not one of them is the same."

Ribiab would be the first of the four to go to Earth. Next would be Marash, much later. Then Shroba and Elias would go at approximately the same time, many Earth years later. The only thing their experiences on Earth seemed to have in common was that each of them would live in roughly the same area; however, they learned that Earth, at those three times, would be so changed it would be nearly impossible to recognize any similarities.

As fun as it was to guess about the situations they might face while on Earth, and try to weave tales about how their heroic efforts against the Defiant Ones would become legendary, they remembered being taught that they would all face the same basic temptations. They each vowed that no matter what awaited them, they would make it back to this place they loved so much, and return to live in the presence of their Great Father.

Elias began to notice a feeling of aloneness, and this new feeling seemed to creep over him without warning, even when he was with Sarah. He had always been able to shut his mind to things he chose to not think about, but he could not shut out the awareness that time spent at the falls with his three friends would forever change once Ribiab departed for the New World. While walking alone, deep in thought, he wondered if such feelings were part of his progression. When he became aware that he had arrived at the falls, though unplanned, he stretched out on the grass and let his mind wander where it pleased.

He wished he could memorize every detail of the majestic falls, a place he loved above any other. The water thundered over the face of the cliff and crashed to the rocky shore below. He concentrated until he was able to push the deafening roar to the background of his hearing. Then he focused his mind on the myriad of small gentle waterfalls on either side of the larger falls; the water seemed to roll off the edge of the top rocks and gently slide down the face of the cliffs until it slipped silently into the pond below. The blue mist from the bottom of the falls drifted across a patch of yellow and red flowers growing along the bank.

He diligently tried to focus on the faintly audible sounds the birds made as they expressed their enjoyment at flying through the sprays and mists created by the falls. Their beautifully colored feathers reflected the vivid colors all around them. Some of their flocks had been sent to Earth and Elias wondered if those who had been left behind missed those that had gone. Did they feel sorrow? If they did, it was certainly not apparent by their actions.

On this day, Ribiab had also walked to the falls, and when he saw Elias, he had silently laid in the nearby grass with no words of greeting. After watching Elias for some time, he reached out and touched his friend's arm. "I thought I was supposed to be the first to go to Earth. Judging by the forlorn look on your face and the distant look in your eyes, I'm wondering if you have left without me."

Elias laughed and tried to express just how important his friends were to him and how much he would miss this special place. Neither he nor Ribiab seemed able to find the words to describe their feelings about their changing world, but each seemed to understand what the other could not verbalize.

When Sarah told Elias she would be going to the portal area with Bethany when Ribiab's departure day arrived, he was surprised to find he did not mind. When he walked toward the gathering place with Marash and Shroba, it was obvious none of them were prepared for the changes that were about to occur, changes which threatened to make it impossible for them to disguise their feelings. When the four friends stood together in the Assembly Area, no one seemed able to communicate with more than a partial smile and a nod. There was a great deal of nodding.

Elias wondered if Ribiab was experiencing the feeling of loss more or less than the three who would be left behind. At least the remaining three would still have each other and an unchanged environment; Ribiab would lose his three best friends, and all memory of his current existence.

The Great Father stood by Ribiab and said, "You are one of the elect among my children, Ribiab. I am well pleased with thee. Mighty works will result from thy actions on Earth." The tears of those who thanked Ribiab for his untiring service to them testified of his complete dedication to serving his Father and those around him. The Great Father's words to Ribiab helped Elias feel confident that his friend would return with honor.

Father put His arms around Ribiab and said, "Come, after you have said your farewells." Then He turned and walked toward the door covered with a silver-leafed vine.

Ribiab shrugged as he looked at the faces of all those he had loved for as long as he had been and said, "I guess I need to say goodbye for now. Thank you so much for coming to let me know you will miss me while I am in the New World. I hope you will forgive me for not missing you."

Everyone laughed softly as they slowly turned and began to leave the room.

When Ribiab turned to his three friends, he inhaled deeply as his expression returned to the fixed smile and he slowly nodded his head.

Marash stepped forward and embraced him. "I know you will do well."

"Thank you," Ribiab said.

They released each other. Then Shroba stepped forward and wrapped his arm around Ribiab's shoulder.

"Never forget, well, for the next little while remember that we could be watching you at any time," he said, trying to smile. "I'll save your spot by the falls until you return."

Shroba stepped away and immediately turned and walked toward the exit to leave the building. Elias stepped close to Ribiab and hugged him warmly.

"You've always been a good example to me. Thank you."

Ribiab caught a stray tear with the back of his hand. "I'll be back before you leave for Earth, so we'll see if you still feel that way when I return."

"I already know what the answer will be," Elias said as he released Ribiab. They nodded at each other and then Ribiab turned and walked to the door where the Great Father was waiting for him. As he turned the knob to open the door, he waved a final farewell to Elias and Marash.

The sand colored walls with the green, gold and gray tones made Ribiab feel as if he had suddenly returned to a quiet place near the falls. The scene visible through the open doors at the top of the stairs captivated him. The majestic Earth radiated with brilliance against the darkness of space.

"My son," the Great Father said, "Your character and personality will be unchanged in the New World. The mortal body and unfamiliar experiences that await you there will not alter your valiant character." He asked Ribiab to kneel before Him, and then administered a blessing upon him. "My son, Ribiab, I bless you with the rights and privileges you have earned through your obedience during your first estate. I promise unto you great protection in the New World from the evils that will be abundant around you during the days of your mortal life. You will have great powers to lead others in truth and righteousness. Your Earthly parents are very special souls, and I bless you with the strength to care for and defend them."

After conferring several additional promises upon Ribiab, the Great Father concluded the blessing. As Ribiab stood, his Father softly uttered His final words of council and they shared one final embrace. It was time. Ribiab walked up the stairs and turned for one last look at his Father, then stepped through the open doors.

Elias, Marash and Shroba had hurried to the Observation Area to watch Ribiab's arrival in his Earthly home. The opaque viewing panel cleared and they could see Ribiab's Earthly mother lovingly holding her tightly bundled infant. The soft words of love she expressed to her new baby son made the three friends forget their resolve to hide their emotions. Ribiab's Earthly father knelt and softly stroked his son's dark hair and soft cheek with the back of one finger. It was easy to see the great joy that Ribiab had brought to his new family merely by the act of arriving. Ribiab's New World mother softly began singing a lullaby to her baby. The observation panel began to grow dim and again became opaque.

Esther held her newborn son in her arms. "You have arrived in a world filled with fierce wars, my precious son. It is a constant struggle for your father to obtain sufficient food for your two sisters and I, but I thank God for your presence in our lives."

Zara placed his palm on his wife's cheek and said, "Lydia and Phebe are so happy to have a baby brother." He took his son into his arms and smiled. "Our son."

From the day I learned I was with child, Esther thought, *I have been blessed with the knowledge that you are destined for great things, my son. That inspiration fills me with peace.*

Zara studied the face of his son, and slowly smiled. "I feel strongly that this child will be great among his people. I think he should be named Alma, in honor of his Great Uncle Alma who performed many baptisms and was known throughout the land as a marvelous teacher."

"Alma is a fine name," Esther agreed.

"My son, this tent is your home and you belong to a family of nomads. We travel from place to place and you will see the many beautiful things our God has created for us." Zara lifted his eyes and turned toward his wife. "How I wish I could provide a life free of the danger here in the north country for our children. My greatest desire is to provide this precious child with a world filled with peace. I tire of the increasing danger here in the north that makes it necessary for us to flee from the large cities and more populated areas. How can so many people have become more concerned with their own comfort than that of their fellow men, even to the point of being willing to take a life for a small gain. The wickedness is spreading to every corner of our world and even the rural areas are no longer safe."

"We pray constantly, and God will help us preserve the lives of our children," Esther said soothingly as she stroked her husband's arm.

After seven years had passed, protecting their children was still the major struggle Alma's parents faced. "In less than a year, our son will celebrate the birthday of accountability," Zara said quietly one evening. "Alma has spent his entire life wandering in the land, never knowing peace. We have taught him the stories of his Great Uncle Alma, of his Nephite ancestors, and the goodness of their God. I have felt the promptings of the Spirit telling me that we must leave this area and go to the lands of our ancestors in the south country, to the home of our fathers at the Waters of Mormon. I pray it will be safer for our children there."

Their journey was grueling. For many months, they traveled south-west, tarrying in a place only long enough to accumulate the supplies necessary to continue traveling. They crossed steep mountains, their clothing was reduced to little more than rags as they trudged through thick jungles, and their prayers were constant and sincere for protection from the beasts and snakes they encountered. Many nights, their conversations were all they had to distract them from their growling stomachs due to the lack of food. It was only a few days before Alma's eighth birthday when they reached the white sandy beach of a massive lake they knew was close to their destination.

Zara fell to his knees and wept for joy. "Thanks be to God for helping us reach our destination. You will see the Waters of Mormon on the morrow, my son. Tonight we rest."

"Come, my daughters," Esther said. "We will gather fresh fruit and celebrate our arrival in the land of our ancestors."

The next morning they traveled along the shore of the lake. The sound of falling water could be heard even before the waterfalls came into view, and they saw a large garden surrounded on two sides by natural stone walls.

"The flowers are beautiful," Phebe said as she walked among them, breathing deeply.

"It feels peaceful, almost sacred," Lydia said quietly. "The way the water falls over the edge of the cliff makes it seem as though the water were falling down from heaven."

"Streams high in the mountains feed the waterfalls," Zara said, "but I like your version more, Lydia."

"How do you know about the streams, Father?" Phebe asked.

"Because heaven may be the source of living waters; however, not these waters," he answered. "Children, we have reached our destination. These are the Waters of Mormon."

The gently curving face of the stone walls was smooth and seemed to act as an amplifier for the splashing sounds of the falls. As Zara and his family spoke to each other, it amazed them that their voices were being magnified; they could hear each other no matter how far apart they were.

"Come, children," Zara said after they had explored the gardens and falls. "Look upon the words carved into the walls by your ancestor, Alma."

Alma moved his hands along the worn engraving and then said, "I wish I could have been here when Great Uncle Alma wrote this."

Zara's voice was filled with emotion as he spoke. "It's easy to imagine Uncle Alma preaching to all the saints hiding in the forest. I can almost imagine how it felt to sit in this beautiful setting and listen to Alma's fiery testimony."

"You are very blessed to be baptized in this place," Esther said.

"Just like when Great Uncle Alma baptized people here," young Alma said with a quick smile at his mother. "Do you think he is sitting up in heaven watching us since we have come to the place where he lived?"

Zara stepped close to his son and knelt in front of him, then embraced him warmly. "I think your Great Uncle Alma and your Heavenly Father are both very happy that you're going to be baptized. We will fast and pray that we might feel the Spirit of God in our hearts on this special occasion, and on the morrow I will take you into these waters and baptize you."

That evening, they sat together, close to the stone walls. "Alma, my son," Zara said, "I pray that you will never forget the feelings in your heart when you enter the sacred water, and begin a new life, free of sin."

Alma entered the Waters of Mormon with his Father the next afternoon. His mother and two sisters watched as he was immersed beneath the crystal blue waters. When he emerged from the water, he felt happy and was warmed from within by feelings he had never before experienced. He felt lighter, as though he could float upon the air and look down upon his family.

It had been an exceedingly long time since Zara and his family had felt so comfortable or protected, and they were not anxious to leave the safe haven of the Waters of Mormon. During the next few weeks they prepared clothing and food to sustain them during the final leg of their journey. During the month-long trek to the great city of Xenas, they told and retold of the spiritual feelings they had experienced while at the Waters of Mormon, helping to fix them securely in their memories.

On the day they arrived in Xenas, they could hardly believe their eyes. Zara and Esther led their children through the streets.

"It's hard to believe that such a civilization could exist in the same world as the warring armies we left behind a year ago," Zara said as he marveled at the myriads of people bustling around them. "There are buildings as far as I can see in every direction. I hope that means I'll be able to find work."

"What kind of work are you seeking?"

"Greetings," Zara said as he reached to shake the hand of the man who had spoken to him. "I am a skilled stonecutter. Do you know if there is work available?"

"I didn't really need to ask your skill after shaking your hand," the man replied. "Follow me. The King has authorized numerous new buildings to be constructed, and skilled stonecutters are in high demand."

Zara soon acquired a position and was able to secure housing for his family. They quickly settled into the daily routine of Xenas. During the next four years, they enjoyed a prosperous life. Zara taught his skills to Alma, which resulted in Alma being as skilled and as muscular as young men several years his elder. Their lives were filled with more peace than they had dreamed possible.

The years passed, and Lydia grew into a fine woman and was married. Soon Zara was blessed to watch his loving wife enjoy her first grandchild.

"Your skill as a stonecutter brings much praise to me," Zara told his son. "I am honored that you have grown into such a fine young man. You have the same dark hair and eyes, and the sun has tanned your skin nearly as dark as mine. You've grown to look just like me."

Many of the young stonecutters that Alma worked with spent the leisure time and money their profession provided seeking things that were far from uplifting. Even though Alma was introspective and observant by nature, his quick smile and obvious acceptance of others drew people to him; he never lacked for friends. However, his passion was not in idle recreation. He spent much time with Lemhi, a young man of his age who was also a stonecutter. They shared the same love for spiritual teachings and a desire for increased learning. In the evenings, they studied to become architects and analyzed the design and artisanship used in the country of their ancestors. Even though they were a long distance from the banks of the Nile, cities close to Xenas were filled with architecture influenced by those unique structures.

Alma and Lemhi also began learning the order of the Priesthood. Their fathers taught them the sacred ritual of offering a sacrifice to God in the recently completed temple. They learned the importance of offering only the first or best when selecting an animal for sacrifice, and realized that God the Father would someday offer His first born, His best, to be sacrificed upon the Earth. Alma and Lemhi spent many late evenings discussing how wonderful it would be if they could be on the Earth when the Savior was born.

Alma grew in stature, physically as well as spiritually. He was taller than many, and his muscles were more developed than most. He had been chosen to be an architect on many buildings, and Lemhi was progressing in equal manner. On the occasion that Alma was chosen as chief designer for a new building project, his entire family gathered for dinner to celebrate his accomplishment.

"Have you ever seen such a sweet little girl?" Esther asked Alma as he bent to take Lydia's second daughter from his mother's arms.

"Yes, I believe her older sister is equally as sweet," Alma said with a smile.

"Thank you," Lydia said as she set a tray filled with food on the table. "And when might you be looking for a wife to provide grandchildren for our parents?"

Alma breathed deeply and noticeably winced as he quickly looked in the direction of his mother. "I have never found the girl of my dreams." He walked to a lounge on the other side of the room and sat down, then began gently bouncing the infant in his arms. "Plus, I no longer have any free time to seek a wife. I used to have ample help in the evenings from my friend Lemhi, but lately he has been unavailable."

Lemhi, who was sitting in a chair next to the lounge, said, "I apologize if my priorities are more correct than your own."

"First I am in trouble because I have not found a wife, and now my best friend tells me my priorities are not even correct. This is too much criticism to hear on this day when we celebrate my new position as chief designer for the King."

"My poor son," Zara said. "Married or single, I applaud your advancement. Such a position may help to ensure my ability to find a position as a stonecutter on this new project. Yes?"

"I think that can be guaranteed." Then with a wink at his father, Alma added, "It is a large project and will require the skill of many stonecutters, even those who can think only of becoming a husband."

"Then all in this room are equally blessed," Zara said, returning his son's smile.

Phebe placed a large platter of spiced mutton on the table, where heaping dishes of vegetables and fruits of many varieties provided mouth-watering aromas. Everyone sat around the table; Lemhi sat next to Phebe and they smiled warmly at each other. Many compliments were offered to those who had prepared the wonderful food.

When the meal was nearly finished, Lemhi self-consciously cleared his throat and said, "I would like to make a small announcement, please. I have spoken with Zara and asked permission to marry Phebe, and she has accepted my proposal."

Alma rose from his chair to give Lemhi a tight hug. "Congratulations, my friend. I cannot think of anything that could happen that would make me happier on this day of celebration. I welcome you to our family as a brother."

"Thank you, Alma," Lemhi said.

"I have a feeling you will continue to be as unavailable for work in the evenings when you become a husband as you have been while you were endeavoring to become a bridegroom," Alma said, while smiling at his best friend and his sister.

"It is my good fortune that my boss will soon be my brother," Lemhi returned in like fashion.

Lemhi and Phebe were married and life moved forward. The building project where Alma had served as chief designer was very successful, and he continued to serve the King on one temple after another. The only change occurred when Lydia, her husband and their two daughters left to live in the north country. They were greatly missed at first, but the arrival of Lemhi and Phebe's first child seemed to be a blessing sent to ease the absence of older grandchildren who now lived far away.

Nearly overnight, the entire political atmosphere in Xenas changed as rumors of the King's failing health spread throughout the land. His illness was sudden, and reportedly grew worse each day. Zara and his entire extended family gathered daily to pray for the King.

"I pray the Lord will answer our prayers," Zara said one evening. "The king is loved dearly and respected by all his people."

"He has earned that respect," Lemhi offered. "If he dies, Sham will become King. We all know him well enough to realize he will increase the taxes and institute worship of pagan gods. That could change everything about living in Xenas."

In three short weeks, the citizens of Xenas watched as a great procession slowly carried the body of the King from the city to the temple where he was laid to rest high above the common ground of the city. The following week, the King's son Sham was crowned as the rightful heir to the throne.

"You were right about how things would change, Lemhi," Alma said to his brother-in-law as they worked. "Last night Father told me Sham has declared a tax of one third of all we possess."

"I'm sure you've heard the rumors that implicate him of having arranged his father's death so he might become King. I know rumors require no real proof, but he certainly didn't waste any time declaring the new tax."

"That's not all," Alma said quietly, leaning close to Lemhi. "He has expelled all the high priests and replaced them with people he personally selected. That does not bode well."

"I wondered how he would achieve acceptance of the new statues he has commissioned. They are of pagan deity and I was told they will be placed at various spots throughout the temples, and the citizens of Xenas will be required to worship them. The high priests would never have allowed that to happen, so it seems their removal was required."

"I will never worship statues," Alma said.

Shock spread through the community when people who refused to worship the pagan deity were killed. Fear replaced the peace that had been enjoyed for many years.

Zara's family spent each evening together, praying for guidance from God. "It seems impossible to me that Sham is the King's son. How could he be so wicked when he was raised by such a righteous man?" Zara asked.

"It's one thing to not believe in the one true God, but to punish those who will not bow to the new gods by sacrificing them in such unimaginably horrible bloodletting rituals is beyond comprehension." Alma sighed and shook his head. "And to do it all within the walls of the temple is unbelievable."

"Yesterday I was told that King Sham's blood is given to each of his priests and chief warriors. They drink it and believe it gives them protecting power." Lemhi stood and inhaled deeply in an attempt to calm himself. "I don't know whether the new beliefs are being accepted out of fear or willing agreement, but it's incomprehensible how corrupt the majority of the people in Xenas have become in such a short season."

"All we can do is continue praying," Esther said quietly. "Sometimes I am filled with fear that the wickedness is growing so quickly we will soon be affected personally."

Several days later, Esther's worst fears were realized when she answered her door and found two royal guards glaring at her.

"In the name of King Sham," one of them said, "your son Alma has been commanded to appear before the King on the morrow."

Esther was unable to speak, and watched as the two guards turned and left. Eventually, she managed to close her door and walk to the chair that sat near her cooking stove. She was filled with fear and sat, unmoving, until evening when Zara returned.

"What has happened?" Zara asked as he knelt in front of his wife.

"The peace and safety we have enjoyed these many years has ended," Esther said without looking at her husband. Her eyes slowly filled with tears as she continued to speak. "Two of the King's guards came to our door today. Our son has been ordered to appear before the King. I fear someone has noticed that he does not bow to the false gods."

"Did they hurt you?" Zara asked.

"What's wrong?" Alma asked from the doorway.

Zara stood and said, "I found your mother sitting here when I returned. She said two of the King's guards told her you must appear before the King tomorrow."

Alma knelt beside his mother and tried to comfort her obvious agitation. "Why are you crying, Mother?"

"I have tried all afternoon to think what the King might want from you. I am filled with fear that someone has noticed you do not bow to worship the false gods in the temple, and now you will be punished."

"My wife," Zara said as he pulled her to her feet. "I am certain the King has been aware from the beginning that we do not worship the false gods." He led her to the lounge in the living area and helped her sit comfortably. "Yet we continue to work on his building projects."

"Why would he suddenly command our son's presence before him?" Esther asked.

"Mother, perhaps it is to commission another project," Alma suggested.

When Phebe's family came to visit in the evening, they quickly joined in the speculation concerning the King's purpose.

"There are many who do not worship the new gods," Phebe spoke aloud.

"True," Lemhi agreed, "but they are not as visible and well known by the King as is Alma."

"My son," Zara said, "Sham has grown up seeing me working with you and Lemhi on his building projects. We have been guests at his father's home on many occasions throughout the years. I am greatly concerned . . ."

"I demand that none of you worry for me," Alma said, as cheerfully as he could manage. "I know God will protect me and that Sham will not harm me, not after all I have done to help build the kingdom he now possesses."

"You built the kingdom for Sham's father," Zara reminded him, "the father he murdered. Do you think he would hesitate to murder you when his blood runs so cold he could take the life of his own father?"

Alma searched his mind for words that would comfort his family, but found none. "If things turn out as you fear, you must leave the city. If my faith does not protect me, as I believe it will, you must promise you will depart. Whether I am jailed or put to death, no matter what, you must leave."

The following morning, with his family's disturbing fears echoing in his ears, Alma walked to the King's residence. He was immediately taken to stand before King Sham, who was sitting upon his throne of judgment in the room where Alma, his father and brother-in-law had been made to feel welcome so many times in the past. He listened as the King spoke in a cold, detached voice.

"Have you worshiped the new gods that have granted blessings to everyone within the city, or do you still believe in the god of old?"

Alma was saddened to his very core when he realized his family's fears had been well founded. Still, his faith filled him with conviction, if not peace, as he spoke. "I will never denounce my God, and I will not worship any gods fabricated by men."

The King looked stunned and glared at Alma. All conversation in the room ceased; the people had heard such refusals before and knew the fate of those who had spoken thus. After remaining silent for many minutes, the King stood and began to speak.

"Alma, you will be taken to prison, and will not receive any food or water. You will have three days to decide your fate. If you do not change your mind, you will be offered as a sacrifice to the god's you refuse to worship."

Alma was thrown into a dark damp cell. He found it difficult to understand how Sham could treat him like a common criminal without the smallest degree of guilt; they had socialized with each other since they were children. He prayed fervently for direction about what he should say or do when the three days had passed. He prayed for the safety of his family. Even in such dire circumstances, the forced fasting created a setting where he felt extremely close to the Spirit of God.

After two days, the heavy door to Alma's cell opened, and Sham stood before him. "Have you made a decision?" the King asked.

Alma steeled himself against the wrath his words might cause. "I have not changed my mind."

"You have one more day to decide your fate."

Alma stood motionless as the King turned and stormed out of his cell. The heavy door was pushed shut and silence returned as the voices in the hall quickly faded. That night, Alma pleaded in prayer for direction that he might know what to do. He told his Father in Heaven he was not afraid to die, but felt there must be something he could do that would allow him to remain and be of service to his family. He fell asleep on his knees.

Whether it was a visitation or a dream, Alma was not certain; however, he was certain he had received his answer. He knew, without a doubt, that he must not worship any other god, and in holding to his belief he would be given the opportunity to survive, for he had a great work still to do.

The next day the King again came to his cell, alone, and asked one question. "Have you decided to live or die?"

Filled with conviction that his action was what God wanted him to do, Alma said, "I will not worship any other God, but I do not want to die." Alma watched as the King drew in a deep breath, and then stood silently watching Alma for a considerable time.

"Alma," the King finally said, "I came here alone, without witnesses, because I know you well enough to assume that would be your decision. However, I desire you to continue your work in designing and building my kingdom. I cannot allow anyone to know that you openly refused my command to worship the new gods. You may worship however you want, as long as it is in private. Be warned. Even though you will not be required to worship the new gods, you must not show openly that you oppose their worship. Moreover, you will be required to design temples that include such gods. If you agree to this, I will let you and your family live."

"I swear I will tell no one but my mother and father of the agreement, and I swear to you my continued and complete loyalty."

With no further conversation, the King turned to leave. He stopped in the open doorway and turned back to face Alma. "Know full well, Alma, that your life, as well as the life of each member of your family, depends on you fulfilling your agreement, and also upon keeping the agreement confidential." Without waiting for a response, he turned and pushed the door shut, locking it behind him.

Alma fell to his knees and thanked God for His intervention in softening the King's heart. He prayed for continued blessings upon his family in the midst of raging wickedness. Later that evening, the door to his cell was again opened. The guard looked at Alma for a moment and then turned and walked away without uttering a single word, or closing the cell door. Alma was reluctant to leave at first, wondering if a trap had been set for him. After a few minutes, he cautiously departed, and discovered no one between him and his freedom.

When Alma stepped into his home, his family seemed stunned. He was expecting questions from everyone, but no one spoke a single word. "I've been released!"

His mother suddenly burst into tears and ran toward him. "I thought you were a spirit and that my son had been killed," she said through deep sobs. "I am greatly blessed by God." She hugged him tightly, and then Zara wrapped his arms around both of them.

"The Lord has answered our prayers," Zara exclaimed.

Alma explained to his parents the terms of his release and his promise to never reveal the details to anyone other than them. The three of them knelt to thank God for His blessings.

Alma returned to his duties, aware that most people would assume he had agreed to worship the new gods. His friends and extended family members never asked what he had done to get out of prison; they knew his undying loyalty to his family and God had not changed, so there was no need to know anything more. Interest in the situation quickly waned.

"Your faith has been an example to our entire family," Zara told his son. "By following the inspiration you received from God, you have been allowed to design and supervise the building of many new cities over the years, ensuring continued income for me and your brother-in-law."

"It has been a great blessing from God," Alma agreed, "but knowing that I help King Sham expand his kingdom every year weighs on my conscience. Knowing how much of the taxes paid by the people is required to build a palace in each new city for the King and his wives is sobering."

"You have never worshiped the pagan gods, and your faith has helped protect your entire family," Zara reminded his son.

"I know, Father. I acknowledge that God gave me the answer that has allowed us to survive. However, each time I hear the King addressing the inhabitants of the city from the tower that I helped design, I feel badly that I have helped make it easier for him to control his subjects. I hear him remind everyone how lucky they are to live in a city where their gods protect and bless them. He never tires of telling them of the many great things he personally provides for them."

"These are stressful times, and yet you design the magnificent temples of the God of Sun in each city. They are a testament to your knowledge and skill. When the first rays of the morning sun light up the tall temple spires before touching any other part of the city, it astounds me. The way the sun shines directly through the eastern window and aligns with the small opening on the western wall of the temple on the first day of summer is a testament to your superior skill. Never have I seen a building designed to allow the sunlight to stream through the building and light up the stairs outside that lead to the temple doors. Those are all amazing feats."

"Thank you, Father. If only those who worship in the temples were not so deceived, I would find more satisfaction. Do you find it as hard to understand, as do I, how anyone can accept the teachings that man was originally made of clay and can be perfected until he becomes made of corn? I know the priests helped the King contaminate the truths of our religion, because there is no other way that beliefs accepted by generations of families could be forgotten and new altered beliefs accepted in a few short years with little objection, simply at the command of the King. To believe that man lives on the Earth many times until he is perfected, and to believe that by offering themselves up for human sacrifice by fire could hurry that process of perfection is laughable. Being told that ancient priests did so certainly could never convince me that it makes sense."

"There are enough who do not believe such falsehoods that it is still necessary for King Sham's armies to conquer outlying villages and bring the entire population back as captives so they will have enough sacrifices for their *festivals*. It makes me wonder how sad God must be when he sees hundreds of people being sacrificed in such a manner."

Alma sighed and walked to the window, silently staring out into the night. "I am sickened by what our friends and neighbors have become. Each time the great carnage takes place, it becomes more difficult to block out the sounds of the horrible celebrations. It is difficult to stay, but I am required to remain faithful to the oath I made to the King. I also remember the revelation I received while in prison, that I have a great work to do."

Before long, Alma was called before the King. "I have received word that our ancient enemies, the Lamanites, are marching from the north toward Xenas, conquering every city in their path. They are advancing in a southeast direction in their pursuit to control all cities to the south. You will devise a way to fortify my many cities."

"I will begin immediately to find a way to defend your cities," Alma promised, and began at once to experiment with various methods until he found one that succeeded.

For many years, Alma's fortifications proved successful in preventing the Lamanites from conquering King Sham's cities. Even though a few cities were defeated, the colossal loss of warriors and resources suffered by the Lamanites for each conquered city convinced them it was in their own best interest to work their way around the King's cities and avoid further confrontations.

One evening as Alma and his parents sat together discussing their growing concern about the increasing corruption and violence, Zara said, "Again your skill and knowledge has provided safety for your family. The fortifications you designed allow life in Xenas to continue with little concern for the advancing armies of the Lamanites. Yet, lately I notice that the people have begun to feel superior to the Lamanites and become complacent. With no need to spend time and resources defending themselves, the once thriving cities King Sham has established have become focused on their blood thirsty traditions. They continue to worship idols and increase the persecution of those who believe in the one true God."

"But the people are not happy," Alma said. "I do not understand why the once proud Nephite people now controlled by King Sham would choose this life over the years of happiness they enjoyed while Sham's father was their King. The wickedness that abounds on every side reminds me of my childhood, a time that remains vivid in my mind because of the stories still told and retold by our family."

"My son," Zara exclaimed. "Is it possible that I am witnessing the fulfillment of the long-awaited prophecy that foretells of a night when darkness will not come, and of a star that will appear and be bright enough to be seen in the daylight. Do my eyes deceive me?"

"I know of the prophecy," Alma said as he turned to look at the sky, "but I always imagined that the Savior of the World would not be born when corruption was so rampant."

"There is no mention of the righteousness of men contained in the prophecy," Zara said. "But I see that darkness has not arrived this night, and now I see a star brightly visible in the light. I find no other explanation than the fulfillment of the prophecy that the Savior of the World has been born."

"God has finally sent the Savior, His Son, to save all that dwell on the Earth?" Esther softly asked.

"If it be true, how I wish we could live where the Savior is born so I could worship Him." Alma tried to envision the baby being held by his Earthly mother. "I wonder if those who know of His birth are aware of the changes He will bring about. How miraculous it is that this prophecy has been fulfilled during our lifetime."

"Can you hear the cries of fear outside?" Esther asked as she gazed out the window. "You have become aware of the fulfillment of prophecy, my husband, and it sounds as though others cry out in astonishment and beg God for forgiveness that they might be spared."

Some change was evident as early as the next morning. Many people had been convinced by the lack of darkness during the night that a time of accountability had arrived, and they withdrew from persecuting those who believed in the God of their ancestors. It was an immediate change that quickly spread; as one man gained the faith to proclaim his newly restored faith, several others would take notice and gain courage from his actions. The cycle repeated and peace spread. Alma was so happy to see the people and the cities throughout the land begin to gain some of the glory they had once possessed.

The changes lasted but a small season, however. When the people began to see that the arrival of a Savior had changed nothing in their world, they slowly became afraid again of King Sham. Once the wicked and corrupt decided there was no real change, and therefore no threat to them, they began to be bold once again. As they had quickly turned to righteousness, they now returned to wickedness even more rapidly. Within a few years, they seemed to exceed their former lust for wickedness and iniquity. Violence once again began to thrive.

"Is it true that the Lamanite armies are again attacking the fortifications you designed?" Zara asked Alma one evening. "I hear reports that war covers the face of the land in both the north and in the south."

"I hear the same reports, Father. I also hear rumors that attacking armies are not our biggest threat. Persecution of those who believe in Jesus Christ has been increasing and is now greater than it has ever been. Rumors abound that when spring arrives, the Christians are to be exterminated."

"Your mother's health is beginning to fail as the quickly spreading upheaval and persecution again become part of our lives. Since both the north and south countries are equally filled with wickedness and persecution, we both have a strong desire to return to the north where your life began."

"Perhaps we would be able to find Lydia. I'm sure Mother misses her and her family greatly and is very concerned since we have not received any word of her since the fighting peaked."

"I have spoken to Phebe and Lemhi. They have decided to remain for a while longer, but they also feel it would be good for us to leave and travel to the lands in the north. Will you take us there, my son?"

"Of course I will," Alma answered. "We will make preparations in secret, and leave the city during the cover of night. We dare not travel through the narrow neck of land, as the Lamanites have secured much of that area, and their treatment of the Nephites is well known. Instead, we will travel northeast by boat. The journey will be difficult and our progress will be slow, but I will do all I can to help you reach the north country."

After tearful farewells, the tiny group spent months traveling in constant fear of being detected. They reached the place where the great river that flowed from the northland emptied into the sea. People in this area were friendly and, since there was much trade up and down the river, they showed no surprise at seeing someone new traveling in their area. Alma and his parents were able to travel freely up the river without causing suspicion, making a portion of their journey surprisingly easy. When they reached the split in the large flowing waters, they had to occasionally travel overland on foot. Perhaps it was because Alma was a grown man, but this journey seemed much less difficult than the trip he recalled from his childhood.

They finally arrived at the valley where his parents wished to dwell during the remainder of their days. As they entered the valley, Alma turned to his father and said, "I feel a sacredness in this land that I have not experienced since I was a child when we were at the Waters of Mormon. Has it always been thus in this land?"

His father spoke in a very reverent tone as he answered. "This is the valley of our first parents."

As they moved up the heavily treed valley, Alma felt dwarfed, as if giants sitting on countless rows of thrones on each side of where they walked were watching him. He could feel a tangible silence. Although there were birds and squirrels making their usual sounds, the silence was that of complete reverence. Even though he was in the great expanse of the valley, he whispered as he talked to his parents, and felt guilty as the twigs snapped beneath his feet.

Alma was amazed that the animals in the valley had no fear of the three humans walking in their midst. As they passed a small herd of deer, Zara spoke to Alma.

"Choose a young deer and slay it. It will be needed for a sacrifice."

Alma crept quietly toward the deer and soon returned with an animal that was suitable for sacrifice to the Lord.

"The sacrificial alter is near the top of this small hill," Zara directed as he held Esther's arm and began the gradual ascent up from the valley. "Place the deer on the altar, my son, and we will make an offering to God, according to the Law of Moses."

After the ceremony was complete, Alma sat with his parents in the grass on the hillside. "This valley is beautiful and there is a feeling of calmness."

Esther smiled at her son. "The way the sun touches everything in the valley with a golden color makes it even more enjoyable."

"I feel very blessed that I have been able to help you return here. Looking at the ancient burial ground near the sacred alter reminds me of when I was baptized and we felt the engraving on the stone walls. It makes me feel that our ancestors are close by."

"From the time your mother and I left this valley to find a safer place to raise you and your sisters, we have had a strong desire to return here. This valley has been sacred since Adam, the Ancient of Days, lived here with our dear Mother Eve. This is where I want to end my days on Earth."

Sadness, greater than anything Alma had ever experienced, filled his heart when only two days later his father's mortal life drew to a close and he laid him to rest in the ground on the hill above the valley. Unable to console his mother, he desperately wished one of his sisters were there to provide comfort for her; women seemed to be able to find precisely the right words to convey deep feelings of sorrow. All he could do was repeat that he loved her very much and pray that her grief might be eased. In spite of his efforts, the loss proved too much for her, and barely a month later she also took her last breath of life. She had lived a full life, and when she lost her lifelong mate she lost the desire to remain on the Earth.

Alone. Burying both of his parents was the hardest thing Alma had ever been required to do. He felt totally alone for the first time in his life. He sat for days without eating, praying that his father and mother would be welcomed into the Lord's presence and receive His care. He realized the Savior was about five years of age, and he wondered if the saints would be able to continue fighting the spreading wickedness until the Savior was old enough to begin His ministry and spread the word of God to the inhabitants of Earth. Alma prayed for a long time that he would be blessed with hope and faith. Mostly he prayed that he could find the necessary strength required to leave the valley that contained the graves of his parents.

The silence and calm that had been such a balm to him when he arrived with his parents soon became too much for Alma to bear alone, so he left the valley and his parents behind, and traveled on alone.

THE GUARDIAN

After traveling for some time, Alma felt impressed to return to the city at the junction of the two large flowing rivers. That feeling grew stronger each day he traveled, and he was certain God was directing his path. When the city finally came into view, he was in awe of both its size and appearance. It was a city of mounds, too many to be counted, which rose up from streets and walkways. Other than some individual homes, every structure in the entire city was built on the top of a mound.

The city was made up of small communities gathered together in close proximity, each with a unique feel and appearance. Alma stopped at a trading post and asked if there were a specific location where he could seek work.

"Have you recently arrived in our city?"

"Yes, I have been traveling, but I feel I have reached my destination. I am a skilled stonecutter, but I have designed many different types of structures. Is there a need for my skill in your city?"

The man laughed and said, "This city is made up of many different cities. Somewhere there is a need for every skill. From where have you traveled?"

"I lived in the great city of Xenas far to the south. Many years ago my sister and her family came north and I have hopes of finding them."

"Come, my friend. I will show you our great city and help you find a place to stay." He motioned Alma to walk ahead of him. "Each community in our great city maintains its own identity, and each contains mounds of differing sizes with structures that range from simple dwellings or small shops to a variety of community enterprises, trading posts such as mine, a general council building and a charnel house. I would describe the people who live here as guarded, yet friendly and hospitable. Each separate community is based on a matriarchal order of rule that has been unchanged for generations."

The walkway they were following began to rise at a steep incline, and as their vantage point got higher, the size of the city became even more apparent. "From this point, I see your great city is even larger than I imagined." Pointing to the east where the sun had begun the day, Alma asked, "What is the mound that appears to be higher than any other?"

"That is the King's personal dwelling and a temple."

"The architectural style looks familiar, but it is not made of stone as in the south country."

"There are no stone structures in our lands. Our city is constructed of timber and clay."

"I am impressed with the organization of your city. It looks very safe and peaceful,"

"I must admit the peaceful appearance is deceptive. There is much violence and corruption, much wickedness, but those of us who believe in the one true God pray continually for peace."

"I also believe in the one true God, and I have fought for peace and freedom amid violence and wickedness my entire life. Tell me, my friend, is there a place in your city for another man of God?"

The smile on the man's face answered Alma's question. "Come, I will take you where you can find lodging and work."

Alma's physical stamina and large stature made it easy for him to find ways to be of service to the citizens of the city, and he soon dedicated his efforts to defending and protecting their freedom. However, even as his days became busier, his mind often reminded him how much he wished Lemhi and Phebe had left the south country with him and his parents. He longed for Lemhi's friendship and the support of his sister.

Alma found new concerns in his life when he began hearing rumors of approaching enemies. His concerns were confirmed when Lot, one of the city's leaders, sought him out late one evening.

"Alma, I recall your stories of building fortifications that were able to preserve entire cities. Is such a thing possible here?"

"Yes. I believe we could protect both our army and citizens if we were able to gather into a smaller location within the city that had been made strong." Alma replied with slight hesitation, not knowing the size of their opposition.

"Hmm. I fear we lack sufficient materials to build fortifications."

"We can combine our limited reserves of timber with large amounts of clay and straw to build defensive walls around a portion of the inner city. That will increase our defensive strength. Although construction of the walls will be considerably different than I have seen before, the strategy of war is universal."

"Then you have complete control of our protection. You will have the required resources and workforce at your command." Lot's words trailing off as he hurried away to report on his discussion.

By the time their enemies attacked, the people had gathered together within the fortified walls. The invaders could not penetrate the walls, and their losses were great. The archers, stationed within the shooting towers strategically located along the walls, sent waves of arrows, rocks, and hot tar down upon the enemies outside the walls. The effective fortifications convinced the Lamanite army it was not worth the loss to attack the city. However, they made temporary encampments a short distance away, causing uneasiness in the day-to-day life of the city's residents.

"I do not understand," one of Alma's friends said. "You have been chosen as a leader in the army because of your knowledge of tactics. You have dedicated years to helping people in the southland. You use your charisma and physical stamina to persuade warriors to follow your command, and yet you persuade no woman to be your wife?"

"I am alone. My parents dwell with God and my two sisters have families, but they live a great distance from here."

"But what of a wife? You have become greatly respected for your leadership abilities, as well as your knowledge and skill of war. You need only ask and any available woman would gladly become your wife."

"I seek the woman I knew long ago, but I have not found her. Until then, I am content to be of service."

"We cannot expand the city beyond our current boundaries due to enemy camps that surround us. Although grateful for your willingness to help us protect our communities, we both know that will not hold off our enemies for long."

"My friend," Alma said, "we both know the people choose to close their eyes to that fact."

When the actions of the Lamanites could no longer be ignored, the need for a stronger army was finally addressed. Even though they successfully fought many battles against the Lamanites, their primary responsibility was to venture out of the city to help defend people in the outlying villages. It was usually executed as quick sweeps through the surrounding villages so they could escort anyone who desired to move their families into the city. However, each rescue mission became increasingly more difficult as the Lamanite armies were also becoming larger.

Alma knew the tipping point had been reached so he gathered his leaders. "This is the largest battle we have ever fought. I fear our defeat is certain."

A messenger arrived on horseback at that instant, abruptly stopping in front of the leader's tent. "Word has arrived that armies from nearby cities that have withstood enemy advances are on their way to help us complete our rescue operations."

The news was as welcome as manna from heaven, but Alma spoke before anyone had time to enjoy its sweetness. "This means an increase in the number of those who will die on both sides of this cause, for this morning I received word that reinforcements from the Lamanite armies are coming against us."

"We have something the Lamanites do not," a warrior said with obvious admiration for Alma. "We have you as our leader, and your ability to plan successful strategies has become well known among our enemy."

"I thank you for that compliment, but the only result of that knowledge will be a change in the primary target. It will greatly increase the danger to those who fight close by my side."

"We will not fail you," several soldiers said together.

As the great clash began, losses were heavy on both sides, and the dead and wounded covered mile after mile of blood soaked Earth.

Defeating Alma soon became more important to the invaders than winning the battle. They were willing to sacrifice as many men as it took to eliminate him. Alma's companions knew the enemy's intentions and a large group of warriors fought close by him rather than disbursing loosely among their troops.

The invading army finally trapped Alma, but his followers fought valiantly to protect their leader. Word quickly spread among the invading army's ranks that Alma had been trapped. Many ran to where the battle was ensuing, each hoping they would be the one to finally eliminate the great warrior. The intensified battle raged on at a furious pace and many of Alma's protectors were slain or injured. Although he wore armor, Alma received a blow to his helmet that dropped him to the Earth.

Alma slowly became aware of conversations around him. He slowly opened his eyes, wondering if he were among members of his own troop or had become a prisoner of the invading army, but he discovered he no longer had his sight. While he struggled to accept the fact that he would never be a defender of freedom again, he realized he could hear the familiar voice of one of his protectors nearby. Alma was able to visualize his second in command describing the details of his escape to a group gathered around him.

"When I went down, I thought I was a dead man, but I was mostly stunned. By the time I was able to get up, I saw Alma fall to the ground. I knew if he were not already dead, he soon would be, so I took advantage of the surrounding chaos and signaled our troops. With the help of God, we were able to remove him from the immediate battle area."

Alma listened with a heavy heart. He was grateful to be alive but deeply saddened to hear of the heavy toll the day's battle had taken on his troops.

The second day Alma spent in the tent of the injured brought the realization that his sense of hearing was increasing, as if to make up for the loss of his sight. In the afternoon, he thought someone was pulling at the blanket he was laying on, as though they were trying to pull it out from under him. He called out but no one answered. He soon realized the ground under his blanket was trembling, and it quickly increased until it was pitching and rolling. His increased sense of hearing brought sounds of destruction to his ears. People were screaming and he could hear them running past his tent.

"Watch out, the rocks are falling!"

"Help me, I'm trapped!"

"The Earth is opening. Look out!"

He heard the panic and could hear the groaning of the Earth shifting, rising and falling around him. Death seemed to be marching through the area and the cries for help quieted long before the rumbling of the Earth ceased. Then, all that remained was a deafening silence.

After a very long time, Alma began to hear the cries of those around him, and their words made him aware that everyone was enclosed in darkness, nearly equal to his own. Although the darkness Alma experienced did not increase, he could feel a vapor press against the ground from above. No one came to comfort him, no one brought food for his growing hunger, and no one spoke words of comfort to help him deal with the darkness that surrounded him. Occasional moaning and cries of loss continued around him until he lost track of the passing of days and became part of the darkness.

A sound of joyous cheering and open praise awoke Alma as those around him once again saw the morning sun begin to rise. Fellow members of the army helped care for him and he listened to the horrific accounts of the earthquake that caused great crevices to swallow entire buildings and camps.

For several months, Alma remained dependent upon the care of others as he slowly recovered from his injuries. Those he had served so unselfishly came to repay his kindness to them. They repeatedly expressed their gratitude for the things he had taught them and his efforts to preserve and protect their freedom from enemy armies. When he protested, they told him it was their honor to serve and care for him.

One day as Alma lay considering the burden he must be putting on those caring for him, the silence was broken by a wonderfully familiar voice.

"Phebe," he called out, and then he felt her hand softly touch his arm. Her tears gently falling on his hands filled him with emotion as brother and sister sobbed uncontrollably.

"We have been traveling since the first morning of the new sun," Phebe explained when they had cried themselves out. "Even though we survived, we could not rest until we found you and discovered how you fared the three days of darkness."

"How did you know where to look for me?" he asked.

"I would not tell this to most people, but you will understand. We had no idea where to begin looking for you, but we always seemed to know the direction we should travel. Once we neared this place, it became very easy to find you. Every person we asked knew exactly where you were and expressed great concern for the injuries you received in the battle."

"What of your little son?" Alma asked.

Phebe chuckled softly. "Our son has grown to manhood, was married and has blessed us with three grandchildren. I know there is no way you could know, but we have two daughters who are also grown and married. I am sad that we could not bring them with us so you could meet them."

"You have remained a young mother in my memories, and now you are a grandmother. Where is the grandfather who is your husband?"

"Lemhi is outside. He's trying to make arrangements for a place where we can stay."

"You can stay at my home. And if you don't mind taking care of me, I could stay there with you."

"I have a little bad news for you, Alma," Lemhi said as he entered the tent.

"Lemhi, my friend, nothing you could say to me would be considered bad news. I am so delighted to hear your voice."

"Concerning that home you offered for accommodation. I am told it no longer stands."

"Oh, I had not heard that news. Oh, well, I wouldn't be able to see it anyway, but it makes me sad that you will not have a place to stay."

"Alma," Phebe said, "There are many empty beds around you. We will stay here and help take care of others who are not yet healed."

"I have longed for your companionship for so many years. It seems like a dream that you are now here with me."

"What of our parents?" Phebe asked quietly, gently squeezing Alma's hand.

"The journey to this land seemed to drain the last of their energy from their bodies, and they died a short time after we arrived. And what of Lydia and her family?"

"I am sorry to say we have no idea if they are living or dead."

Alma, Lemhi and Phebe tried to make up for the many years they had been apart, and the months passed quickly. It became obvious that Alma's health was not improving.

"Lemhi," Alma asked one evening while Phebe was away from the area, "I have a great request to make of you."

"Anything," answered Lemhi.

"We both know my health is failing. I wish to be buried near my parents. Will you take me there so I can also end my days there?"

"I will inquire about directions to the area if you will tell me what it is called," Lemhi offered without reservation.

"Inquire at the temple to learn the location of the valley of our first parents on the Earth."

"I will."

Shortly after Lemhi left, Phebe returned. "Phebe, I have sent Lemhi to make some inquires for me. While he is away, might I share with you a concern that weighs heavy on my heart?"

"Of course, what is troubling you, dear brother?"

"Do you remember years ago when you would often tease me about seeking the praise of King Sham more than the love of a wife?"

"I do remember. Many women were worthy to be your wife, but you always said you had no time for such things. I remember well how feeble your excuses sounded." Phebe lovingly squeezed Alma's hand.

"I never told anyone, but I was looking for a wife. I wish to share something with you that I have held in my heart since I was a young man. I would have liked to share this with our parents, and our sister, also, that each of you might know my heart in this matter."

"What is it that bothers you so?"

"The decisions I made during my life make me fear meeting my Maker. It is my prayer that you understand why I go to my grave, never having felt the love of a wife or children, something I have longed for all the days of my life."

"Oh, Alma, you have no need to fret over a single moment during your lifetime. God will be there to greet you with open arms. You have dedicated your life to service of your fellow man, and given all you have to help them, even your very life."

"I had a dream when I was a boy, and the same dream came to me many times until I was a man. In my dream, I was a warrior in a battle more fierce than any I have ever seen. However, I was a prisoner in this war, and with me was a beautiful woman. I still remember her vividly. Her blue eyes were filled with fear, and even though I was unable to protect her, I felt total acceptance from her. We were held hostage by a force darker than any I have ever battled, an army that was so great in number I feared they could not be overpowered. I saw the leader of the massive army as he passed by our prison one day. I prayed to God for strength to burst the gates of the prison and allow me to stop the assault that was about to begin. But the bars remained and the battle raged on without me."

Phebe gently wiped the tears from Alma's face. "It was a dream."

"Each time I had this dream I awoke trembling. It seemed so real, as if it were a memory of an actual battle or a vision of events yet to happen. I spent a lifetime preparing, so I would be ready to meet that great dark leader and his terrible army. I trained to become strong enough to prevent anyone from ever taking me prisoner, and vowed to fight to the death when I came against that evil army. I never wanted anyone I knew to become subject to their dark smothering power or fall under their evil control. Did I take pride in being a warrior so I could gain power? Now I am blind, and I have seen so many faces pass before my darkened eyes. I fear I have wasted my entire life preparing for the massive battle that I will never fight. Now that I lay waiting for death to swallow me up, I fear that the darkness I have spent my entire life preparing to fight is what awaits me when I leave this world."

"Your life has not been wasted. Such a fate may await wicked men who fight against God all the days of their life, but you have selflessly served your fellow man. That will not be your fate. It pains me to see you distraught over a perceived failure that is not real," Phebe choking on her tears.

"Never, in all my days, did I meet the goddess that was taken hostage with me, or I surely would have married her and protected her with my life. I searched for her face in the crowds, among the families of my fellow soldiers, and among those that I helped defend, but she was never to be found. Did I fail to find her because I was too busy looking for war? Her face haunts me and now I will never have the opportunity to free her and remove the fear that filled her eyes."

"You seem to be unaware of the many women you have saved from a life filled with fear and pain. That is what soldiers do, and you have been a great warrior. You have prevented many, many people from becoming prisoners, from having their lives ended by the armies of their enemies."

Alma paused and began breathing deeply; trying to reset emotions that he had restrained for a lifetime. "Your words are meant to pacify my soul, but the opportunity to have the family I longed for is no longer possible. Each child that came to you and Lydia brought conflicting feelings to me; sincere happiness for you and Lemhi, for our parents who found joy in being grandparents, for Lydia. But I also felt sadness for I knew you all enjoyed a life I was missing, a life I will never have."

Phebe's tears fell uncontrollably as she buried her face in her brother's chest. Alma caressed her hair as he also cried. Slowly her emotions calmed and she raised her head. "Alma, how has this short curse of darkness caused you to turn your selfless life into guilt? Our family would have surely been sacrificed many times if you had not gained favor with the king by your absolute obedience to God. Every army you fought was an army of darkness. Your dreams were surely only a catalyst to cause you to become the defender of freedom that has saved so many righteous lives."

"Phebe, I have held this secret within for so long, but I am sorry that sharing it causes you such pain."

"I truly wish you could regain your sight for but a moment so you could see that my tears are because of my love for you, not because you have caused me to feel pain. Do you now forget that life continues after you close your eyes here? Your bride surely awaits your return, and longs for the children you will yet have. When you join our parents and your eternal love in the glorious paradise that awaits you, you will understand the purpose of your dreams and the great value your life has been to those you have served. Yes, you will definitely be able to hold your head up when you meet your God. There are not many that have lived with as much honor as you, nor that will deserve His embrace as you do."

"Thank you for your words of reason, my sweet sister. I truly have walked with God and He has often provided an unmistakable light for me to follow. His bringing you to me is a miracle in itself. For that I am so thankful. Your kind words have brought peace to my soul once again."

Phebe placed her hand on her brother's cheek and gently kissed his forehead. "I am the blessed one, to have enjoyed the privilege of sharing your life and feeling the acceptance you have extended to me and my husband. The memories we created while we journeyed with our parents, and the peace-filled years we enjoyed while you created lasting edifices that were testaments to the power of the one true God, and even now when you have shared your fears and concerns with me. All these things will I treasure in my heart until the end of time because I love you."

As preparations were made for the journey the next morning, Phebe expressed great concern that Alma was not strong enough. He lovingly convinced his sister that it was the same desire that caused their parents to make the journey, and she agreed to help him in every way she could. The journey was difficult, not only because Alma was blind, but also because the terrain had changed so drastically during the massive upheaval. Finally, after many trials and disappointments, Alma announced they had entered one end of the great valley.

"You have regained your vision?" Phebe inquired.

"No, nothing so miraculous," Alma answered. "But I can sense there is a great crowd of souls present. So many, in fact, I think we may have great difficulty finding a way through them."

Lemhi and Phebe exchanged concerned looks, and Phebe hesitantly spoke to Alma. "I fear this journey has taken a great toll on your health, for I can assure you we are the only ones present in this valley."

"Can you see an alter at the top of the hill about midway through the valley?" Alma asked, unconcerned at her opinion of his mental state.

"I see it," Lemhi stated. "Come, I will lead you to it." As far as Lemhi could determine, there had been no upheavals or turmoil to this valley during the three days of darkness. The ground was smooth and the vegetation appeared to have been unchanged in the recent past.

"Reach out," Lemhi directed. "The alter is directly ahead of you."

Alma carefully extended his hand until he found the edge of the stones. He used his hands to determine the appearance of the sacred spot. "This is where our father instructed me to make a sacrificial offering of a small deer. Look to your right and you will see the burial ground."

"Yes, I see it," said Phebe.

"Then please lead me and we will find our parents' graves."

After spending several hours sharing tears and memories of their parents, Lemhi pitched the small tent they had brought with them and helped Phebe lay down the sleeping mat for Alma. They did their best to make him comfortable and shared a meal of fruit gathered from the trees growing in the sacred valley.

As Lemhi and Phebe knelt beside Alma's sleeping mat, they joined in a prayer of thanksgiving that they had been guided to this sacred place, and asked the Lord to protect them and their families, wherever they were. They expressed gratitude that the three had been allowed to spend time together and express their love for each other.

The following morning when Alma awoke, he opened his eyes and was amazed to see the lush green valley sprawling from the base of the hill. It was exactly as he remembered it, but the trees seemed a little denser than he remembered. He turned to look for Phebe and Lemhi, but instead saw his parents sitting on each side of him.

"My vision has returned," he announced happily. "But where are Phebe and Lemhi?"

Phebe and Limhi sat by Alma's bed the entire day, watching him slip away. At times, he muttered to himself in unintelligible words and sounds; other times he spoke very clearly and seemed to carry on a conversation with someone.

"I fear he is becoming delirious," Phebe said sadly, silently crying.

"He was weak last night, but today he seems much weaker and further removed from us." Lemhi placed his hand on Alma's chest and softly said, "Stay if you can, my brother. We have only now found you again."

Alma asked his parents many questions, and spent the entire day in conversation with them, until the sun began to set. When the sun reached the top of the hills on the west side of the valley, Alma rose to his feet, as did his parents. He was suddenly able to see Phebe and Lemhi, and his mind seemed to clear as though he were waking after a long night's sleep. The strength and vitality he once possessed when he was a young stonecutter coursed through his body. As he began to rise from Earth, he bid farewell to Lemhi and Phebe. His eyes were able to see the great city and the innumerable people he had sensed when he entered the valley with his sister and brother-in-law the day before. Looking upward, Alma found the return portal directly in front of him.

As he stepped through the opening, Ribiab was embraced by his Great Father, and all his former days before going to Earth returned to his memory. Excitement filled his entire being.

"Tell me of your time on Earth," his Great Father invited as they sat together in a room similar to the one from which Ribiab had departed.

Ribiab felt his Great Father's approval as he described all he had learned. He found it hard to believe that he had forgotten how much he loved his Great Father. When they were finished with their conversation, they both stood and warmly embraced each other. With His arm still around Ribiab's shoulder, Great Father walked toward the door and opened it.

Ribiab was extremely surprised when he looked into the Return Gathering Room and saw it was filled with people. He knew most of them, but even those he did not recognize indicated they had come to pay their respects for his efforts to protect the freedom of all while they had been on Earth.

He stepped toward his parents and hugged each one warmly. "You look so young," he said as they continued their long embrace. "Thank you for coming to get me. It seemed so natural to leave Earth with you showing me the way."

Ribiab had a hard time adjusting to the change in their appearance. When they had sat by his bed and visited with him, they had seemed old, stricken with the years of their Earth life. Now they were the youthful couple he had chosen to be his parents. They were renewed with vigor, just as Ribiab had experienced. Even though they seemed to be of an age equal to his, Ribiab held them in great esteem over himself.

"Amanda," he said as he moved to hug his oldest sister. "I still think of you as Lydia, but I'll get used to it. I've missed you for so long. I was hoping to find you when I took our parents to the north country, but I could never discover where you had gone. It is so good to see you."

"I missed you too. You were so young when I left with my husband. He was extremely concerned for our children and wanted to find a place where they would be safe."

"You look so happy," Ribiab said. "Is your family still on Earth?"

"Yes," Amanda answered. "When you are accustomed to being back home, we will go to the observation portal and I will request permission so you can see them. I am so proud of my children and grandchildren."

"I would love to see them," Ribiab said warmly. He hugged her and marveled at the strong bond of love and respect that had developed between them during their journey together on the Earth.

Ribiab felt an arm around his shoulder and then his Earthly father said, "Your Great Uncle Alma has come to greet you."

"Ribiab, I watched with pride the many great things you did while on Earth. You served and protected many, and you were a man of your word. I am proud you were named after me."

"Stories of your life were a great example to me while I was on the Earth," Ribiab said as he embraced the man. "My favorite stories when I was a child were about you, and I will never forget the feelings I experienced at the Waters of Mormon. I am glad my actions pleased you. I remember our life together before I went to the New World, and I am so happy to see you again."

"Sharing your return is wonderful. I see there are many hoping to speak to you, but we will visit more at a later time."

"I look forward to that." Ribiab said.

"Are you only greeting people you spent a few short minutes with on Earth?" Shroba asked as he stepped toward Ribiab. "What about the three of us who have known you forever?"

The familiar voice filled Ribiab with joy. Seeing his dear friends, he spread his arms wide and gathered all three within his hug. "What do you mean a few short minutes? I have been gone long enough to grow old on Earth."

"Funny," Marash said, "You don't look a day older than when you left."

"You should have seen me this morning," Ribiab returned. "I was blind and too weak to even walk without help. I was injured in a war and . . ."

"So you were a soldier?" asked Elias.

"Yes, and an architect and a builder. I trekked half way across an entire continent, and back again. I saw the star in the sky the night the Savior was born. Our eldest brother," he said as the realization suddenly occurred. "Jesus, the author of the plan that included personal agency. He was on Earth the same time I was. I remember the night He died. I was blind by then, but Earth was nearly torn apart with destruction that night. I have so many things to share with you."

"We look forward to that," Marash said.

All four friends started laughing and hugged again. "How is it possible that I forgot you while I was on Earth? But no matter, now we are reunited." Ribiab said.

"I've been saving your place at the waterfall," Shroba said.

"Oh, the waterfall! I look forward to being there again."

"I knew you would not change while you were gone," Elias said.

Many attended the celebration of Ribiab's return. As people he had known while on Earth repeatedly thanked him, Ribiab experienced a growing sense of satisfaction concerning how he had conducted himself during his brief departure. He felt he could have done a number of things better while he was there, but generally, he was proud of the things he had accomplished.

Ribiab soon learned his life would not return to the carefree leisurely pace he had enjoyed before going to Earth. He now had responsibilities to help those who were preparing to go to Earth, and assignments to teach those who had lived on Earth without receiving the opportunity to learn of the one true God.

Will I have time to be with my friends? Ribiab wondered. *I have so many things I would like to share with them.*

Ribiab took special notice, after that, of what his friends were interested in. Mostly they asked questions, endless questions, but he did notice that Marash never tired of the stories he told about the great valley.

From time to time Ribiab was allowed to go to the Observation Area to observe the mortal state of mankind. He observed that knowledge and development of new ideas nearly stopped after Christ was crucified, and little, very little, of what the Lord and His apostles had established remained. Myriads of churches were established on Earth, but none of them relied on the authority of God to direct their organizations. In most cases, corrupt kings or government officials who controlled the country decided upon the rules and doctrine of the churches. The incredible irony was obvious; the Defiant Ones controlled much regarding the manner in which men worshiped the Great Father.

Over time, Ribiab became an instructor to those the Great Father had chosen to restore His true gospel on the Earth. Those great souls were chosen because of their valiance and selflessness. The things they were taught would cause them to have a remembrance when they heard God's word on earth. Then they would help organize the restored gospel and spread its teachings across the face of the Earth.

The days seemed to fly by for Ribiab because he was always extremely busy. Yet, those same days passed at a snail's pace for his three friends, as the day of departure grew closer for Marash.

MARASH DEPARTS

Marash and his mate walked slowly toward the Departure Building. Deborah was trying to be positive and share in Marash's excitement, but he could easily read the sadness apparent on her face.

Deborah had been a close friend to Marash as long as he could remember. His friendship with her had been very different than with his male friends. He never invited her to go anyplace with him, as he did Elias or Shroba. He had not felt drawn to her the way Elias had seemed to be drawn to Sarah. However, when he was in a group that included her, he tended to migrate to where she was because he felt totally at ease with her. He never felt the need to impress her, and never tried to hide anything about himself from her. He remembered well when that changed. He had been with a large group of friends, and for some reason he noticed when she walked away from the group. For the first time, he felt the need to go with her.

"Deborah," he called after her. She slowed her walking a little, but did not turn to wait for him. When he finally caught up with her, he asked why she was leaving.

"No reason, I guess," she said. "I just thought I would walk for a while."

"Can I join you?" he asked, almost surprised when he heard his voice ask the question. Something about the way she stopped and looked up at him permanently burned that moment into his memory. He especially remembered the slight movement of her lips that made him think she was going to smile, but then changed her mind and looked away.

"I don't mind."

They walked a little ways without speaking, but Marash felt more uncomfortable every moment; the silence felt like an uninvited guest between them. "Do you have a favorite place you like to walk?" he finally muttered.

She looked at him with that same almost-smile and then said, "I think I prefer walking in the sand at the edge of the lagoon. I know the view is beautiful from the top, by the falls, but . . ." and she did not finish her sentence.

Once again, he felt compelled to think of something to say. "I spend a lot of time at the top of the falls with my friends." Even as he spoke the words, he realized he did not want her to think she was not one of his friends. "Just spending time with Elias and Ribiab . . . and Shroba," he added. Every word he spoke made his explanation sound worse.

"I see," she answered quietly.

After he was no longer able to stand the silence that again loomed between them, even though he had not thought of a single thing to say, he heard himself verbalize the one thought he never planned to discuss with her. "So did you get your handout completed?" He shut his eyes and wished he could somehow retrieve his words.

"No, I haven't."

He would never forget the amazing sense of relief that washed over him when she spoke those three little words. At that second, he realized he desperately wanted her to choose him as her mate; but couldn't push those words from his mouth. "Have you chosen your preference for parents?" he asked.

"Yes, I have made that selection."

Again, there was silence, and he wondered why she did not say something. Why did he feel it was his responsibility to put his thoughts into words? "And the other choice?" Again, he shut his eyes and waited to hear her answer. However, she did not answer.

He opened his eyes but she was not there. He turned to look behind him and found her standing a short distance away. "What's wrong, Deborah?" he asked as he walked back to where she stood.

She remained quiet for a moment, and then slowly began. "Marash, I have known for some time that I . . . liked you. You have never given me any indication that you liked me. Nevertheless, I have been trying to turn in my hand-out with no name indicated for my preferred mate, and I can't. Tonight while we were all visiting, I made up my mind to go get my handout and turn it in because there was no reason to keep hoping that you . . . might feel . . . might want . . ." She cleared her throat and turned to face Marash and then said, "I am going to turn in my hand-out with no mate indicated because you are the only one I feel that way about and you do not feel that way about me."

She immediately started walking very quickly away from Marash. In three long strides, he caught her by the hand and asked her not to do that.

"I can't believe this day has finally arrived," he said, obviously excited. When he looked down at her face, he quickly added, "I don't think I am totally ready to say goodbye, though."

She looked up at him and tried hard to smile. "Once we say goodbye, the time we are apart will begin growing smaller. That's something to look forward to, right." She responded.

Marash smiled and slowly nodded. They walked a little slower as the Departure Building came into view. "I thought I would feel a little more prepared. Here it is, nearly time to step through the portal and I keep thinking of things I should have asked, or things I wish I would have studied a little harder."

"You'll be fine," Deborah said with a chuckle. "You have questioned every person you know when they returned from Earth."

A voice behind them quickly changed the mood. "I wonder if you will be as cute a baby as Ribiab," Shroba said. "His Earthly mother held him and sang to him. Now it's your turn."

"I'll try to remember to smile for you," Marash answered as he put his arm around Deborah's shoulder. "Yes, it finally is my turn."

When they entered the Assembly Area, Marash was surprised to see how many people had gathered. Besides his close friends, several people slated to go to the same place in the New World came to share in his excitement and speculate as to whether or not they would recognize each other's physical bodies.

After the farewells had been expressed, Marash and Deborah slowly walked to one of the doors covered with golden cascading leaves. They sat in the chairs that faced each other and held hands.

"This is it," Marash said. "But it won't be long before you come through the portal."

"I know," she said, pressing her lips into a thin line in an effort to control the loneliness she was already beginning to feel.

"Then we'll both be in the New World, and each passing day will bring us closer to meeting each other."

She nodded but quickly looked down at her hands. "I know."

Marash reached across and put his hand gently under her chin. A nudge forced her head up and he looked into her light brown eyes. "I love you, Deborah. Don't be sad. We'll be together soon."

Deborah smiled but surrendered to her emotions as tears slid down her face. "I love you, too. Now go speak to the Great Father."

They stood slowly, hugged each other for a long moment, and left the room. Sarah was waiting for Deborah in the Assembly Area.

"Farewell, my love," Deborah said, and then turned toward Sarah.

Marash watched Deborah until she and Sarah had left the room. Then he opened the door to the portal room where his Great Father was waiting. He slowly inhaled, trying to clear his mind of everything but the experience that was upon him.

"My son," the Great Father said as Marash sat across from Him.

"Father." Marash smiled as the familiar warmth spread through him. Then he sighed. He would certainly miss his Great Father.

"I am pleased with your efforts. I know you have done everything possible in order to be prepared. Your skills and assistance will be a great help to the followers of the restored gospel and will make it possible for many of the saints to join in a cross-country trek who otherwise would not be able to go."

"I pray that I will not let You down, Great Father."

"Your spirit is strong. You possess a purity that will allow you to understand and accept the simple truths of the restored gospel."

The Great Father stood and laid his hands on Marash's head. The words He spoke increased Marash's faith in his ability to succeed in his Earthly mission.

"I bless you with endurance until your assigned duties have been completed, and bless you with the ability to be aware of those from the other side of the veil who assist you in your journey . . ."

Marash stood and they embraced; he hoped he would never forget the love he felt at that moment. He saw complete acceptance in his Father's eyes and was filled with confidence. They smiled at each other and then Marash stepped to the portal.

The instant he stepped through the veil, a flash of light startled him. He was very aware that he was now in the New World, but he could still remember everything that had just occurred. He remembered all that happened in the Departure Building: saying farewell to his friends, the difficulty he experienced watching Deborah walk away with Sarah, the blessing and encouragement he received from his Father.

I thought all memory of our life with the Great Father was gone once we passed through the veil, he thought to himself. Many of the things he learned while preparing for this experience flashed through his mind. Then he realized that he was trapped in his new physical body and had absolutely no control. He was totally at the mercy of those around him, but had no way to communicate with them. His tongue would not function enough to allow him to talk – he could only cry out in frustration. He recognized the mother and father he had chosen, but he could not understand the words his Earthly mother was saying to him.

Marash could see many people around him. His Earthly parents possessed bodies much like the one that had suddenly immobilized him; however, they were much better at making their bodies function correctly. He was sure Shroba must be amused that he could not control his new body enough to even smile for him.

His parents were totally focused on their newborn baby and were unaware of the other people Marash could see in the room. He noticed that everyone but his parents seemed to belong to two very different, but similar, groups. Unlike his parents, the other people were all able to move freely in any direction they chose, and they seemed to easily pass through solid objects like walls and furniture. All of them hovered around his parents, constantly talking to them, in a language Marash could easily understand, even though his parents did not appear to be hearing a single word they said.

There the similarities ended. One group uttered words of encouragement and love, and the glow around them was pleasant to look at. The other group had an odorless visible stench surrounding them and their words were filled with hatred, anger and lies.

Marash found it hard to continue watching the agile beings because his parents were constantly talking to him, but they must have thought he could not hear them because they put their faces very close to his and were speaking quite loudly. One word was spoken repeatedly, and Marash began to realize that word was the name they had decided to give him – Daniel. That seemed strange to Marash because he knew his parents. He remembered choosing them to be his parents on Earth, but it was apparent they had forgotten his name after they passed through the veil.

The agile people surrounded by the soft glow did remember his name, and they sometimes talked directly to him. Eventually Marash learned to laugh as they lovingly teased him about the way his arms and legs were flailing uncontrollably, or the fact that he was drooling. The dark ones were not allowed to go near Marash. For this he was grateful.

The next several months passed slowly and Daniel spent most of the time feeling very frustrated. No matter how hard he tried, he could not gain control over any part of his new body. When the frustration became more than he could tolerate, he threw fits of rage and his arms and legs would thrash around as he cried.

He noticed that his memory of life with his Great Father became harder and harder to recall. Maybe it was simply too painful to remember a life where he walked and talked with his friends when he now could not even lift his own head. The agile people continually talking to his parents became harder and harder to see. Each time he understood a new word his parents said to him in their strange language, he noticed memories of his previous life became more difficult to recall. By the time he had the capacity to speak a few words using his parents' language, he found he had forgotten most of the things he had been trying so hard to tell them. Sometimes, even though he could remember something very clearly, he had lost the desire to tell his parents about it.

From the time Daniel was a small child, he helped his father, William, with the chores on their farm in New York. Most all of Daniel's friends were also the sons of farmers, but his father was the only one that had a woodshop. Before Daniel was ten years old, he had already learned to build tables and chairs.

About that same time, in the year 1828, preachers started coming to town every weekend, putting up big tents in the fields. They invited everyone in town to come listen to them preach. Daniel and his parents went to several different revivals, as they were called, but then they quit because his parents felt there was more emphasis on competing with each other for new members than for providing truth and knowledge.

William's neighbors became involved in a new church that did not hold revivals. Their church had a different outlook about life on Earth and professed to have an exciting new spirit of authority. Each time Daniel's father visited with his neighbors about their newfound religion, he became more excited.

"I have prayed about the things this new religion teaches, and I have a strong desire to be baptized to become a member." William was happy and excited as he sat with his family and expressed his joy.

"I have seen a change in you since you started going to their meetings, William," Daniel's mother said. "What have you learned that makes you feel certain their teachings are truthful?"

"Oh, Mary," William said as he smiled. "They have taught me that God is a real person who loves each of us more than we can comprehend. He wants us to be happy so He created a plan that will help us find peace and joy, not just while we live here, but for all eternity."

"That does not sound very different than the other churches we have attended," Mary responded.

"This new church teaches what the Bible says, that God never changes, and since He called prophets when Noah and Moses lived on the earth, He will call prophets today so He can tell them what He wants us to do. Today that Prophet is Joseph Smith, the Church's leader."

"I think what you have described sounds wonderful. But, couldn't any preacher tell you God had called him to be a prophet?"

"Yes, I suppose he could. However, Joseph Smith has translated a book that was written by people who lived on the American continent hundreds of years ago, when Christ was on the Earth. It's called the

Book of Mormon, and Mormon was one of the men who wrote it. I have read it, and there is a promise written at the end of the book that says if you want to know if the book is true, pray to Heavenly Father and ask Him. I did that, and I received a strong spiritual confirmation that the book is true."

"And you believe this *church* is true?" Mary asked.

"I do. I would like you and Daniel to read this book, Mary, and ponder over the words, and then pray about whether or not it is true. If you receive the same witness from God about its truthfulness, then I would like all three of us to be baptized and become members of this new church."

"Okay," Mary answered. "Daniel and I will read it together every evening after dinner."

"Joining this church won't be the same as joining the church on the corner. There is growing opposition to this church and to young Joseph Smith, so we may run into some difficulties. That's one thing that convinced me it is true. You see, I believe that the people who have always rejected, harmed and even killed God's Prophets must have been doing the work of the devil. And if this church is God's true church, I'm sure the devil is not going to stand by and let it grow without trying to destroy it."

"We'll read the book, and if the Lord tells us it is true," Mary said while looking at her son, "then I guess we can stand up to the devil, can't we son?"

"Yes," Daniel answered with feeling.

Every evening Daniel and Mary read the Book of Mormon. To Daniel, the words were as hard to understand as those in the Bible, but every evening before they started reading, they prayed that God would help them understand the words. When they finished the entire book, and read the promise, they knelt and prayed that they would know if the book was true. A week later, all three were baptized.

Their membership in the Church brought many blessings into their lives, along with some unexplainable behavior from their neighbors.

"I was prepared for some of our customers to stop buying their tables and chairs from us, but I didn't expect them to begin telling others that my furniture was overpriced and of very poor quality," William said one evening as he talked with Mary, after Daniel was asleep.

"Would you forsake your new religion to regain your customers?" Mary asked.

"You know I would not," he answered. "I don't care half as much about my lost customers as I do about the way you have been treated, Mary. I will never understand why merchants would tell you they no longer want your business simply because we have joined this church."

"I don't mind. There are other shops. What I find amusing is that some of our oldest friends suddenly feel the need to cross the street in order to avoid the courtesy of speaking to us when we meet."

"Amusing is not the word I would choose. You are very forgiving, dear."

"I am less forgiving when it comes to our son," she quickly replied. "Some of his friends can no longer spend time with him because their parents don't want them associating with members of the Church. How does that behavior teach their children to follow the example of our Savior?"

None of them ever dreamed their very lives would be threatened. However, the persecution became so severe it was decided that all the members of this new church would have to leave the area. Their leaders decided they should move west to Kirtland, Ohio. That was the first of what Daniel's father called moving from city to city; Daniel thought moving from city to nothing was a better description.

William and his family left their farm in the midst of February's raging winter storms. Months traveling in freezing winter temperatures and waiting for ice to melt so they could continue their journey severely tried their conviction to the Church. They finally reached Ohio in early summer, and their faith had grown immensely. The members of the Church built their new homes on the outskirts of Kirtland and kept somewhat to themselves, hoping that whatever had caused the persecution in the east would not be repeated.

"I think we could make a fine living building furniture," William told his wife and son one afternoon as they ate dinner. "We don't have enough money to buy another farm, and there are so many people arriving who had to leave their furniture behind, I think we will have plenty of customers."

"We could build wagon wheels, too," Daniel said.

"Good idea," William answered. "How would you like us to build a whole house full of new furniture for you, Mary?"

"I don't think I would complain about that, but how will you make any money if you build new furniture for me. I can assure you I don't have a can full of money hidden away to pay for it." She laughed warmly as she saw how excited her husband and son were becoming about their business venture.

"I have a plan," William said. "We will build our woodshop big enough to build the furniture, and we will use our house as our display area. That way you could use the furniture and we wouldn't have to take up any space in our shop to store it."

"I see," Mary said. "I think it sounds like a fine idea."

Daniel loved working with his father to build their woodshop. He especially loved discussing the teachings of their church while they worked. Once they began turning out furniture, word quickly spread and Mary happily welcomed new customers into her home.

"Father," Daniel asked one afternoon, when they were quietly working. "When you first heard the teachings of the Church, was it hard for you to believe them?"

William reflected back to memories of the discussions at his neighbor's home. "I remember that they sounded strange at first, and I read and prayed a lot, but I don't think I would say it was ever hard for me to believe them. Why do you ask?"

"One of the fellows working at the sawmill is Charles Smith. He is Joseph Smith's cousin and sometimes we talk about the new things Joseph has been teaching. He said several of his friends have a hard time believing them, but I find it very easy to believe what the Prophet teaches. I wondered if you ever had trouble believing what he said."

"I see. Even when you were first learning about the Church, you never seemed to have any trouble accepting the teachings," William said as he put down his tools and leaned back against the wall behind his bench. "Whenever the Prophet receives revelation and teaches us something new, some people seem to wait and see if others will accept it before they make a decision. But you have a real gift for understanding and accepting the simple truths of the restored gospel."

"Are you like that, too?" Daniel asked.

"I guess I would say I'm willing, but sometimes it takes me a while to understand what I'm being taught."

Daniel turned to face his father. "Sometimes when I listen to the Prophet teaching, I feel so warm inside, and my heart feels as if it's going to burst. I love listening to him."

"I've been told the Prophet will be talking tomorrow about why we should build a temple. What would you think if we closed the shop and went to listen to him?"

"I think that would be wonderful, Father. I'll even work late tonight and get these chairs done."

William smiled and said, "I'll stay and help."

The next morning William watched his son during the discussion, and said a silent prayer of gratitude to his Father in Heaven that Daniel had the opportunity to personally associate with the Prophet of God.

"I know we can't work on the temple all the time," Daniel said later that evening.

"Is that what you would like to do?" William asked.

"Yes, but I know we still have to run the shop and fill our orders. I know we can't just leave and work full time on the temple."

"I think we could help and still run our shop," William said. Then he laughed at the impatience shining from his son's eyes. "They will need a lot of things we can make in our shop, and we could work on them when we're not busy with somebody's order."

"That sounds great," Daniel nearly shouted.

"And," William continued, "I think we should take turns every morning working on the temple until noon."

"Oh," breathed Daniel. "Father, can you believe how blessed we are? If we had bought a farm when we got here, we wouldn't have as much time to help work on the temple, and now we can help even when we're working."

"Yes, I certainly do feel blessed," William said, *to have a wonderful son and a thriving business that allows me to help build the temple.*

Several days later, William returned to the shop after working on the temple all morning. When he stepped through the door, Daniel looked up and said, "Look what I found on the door this morning," He held a wrinkled piece of paper toward his father.

"Cease your participation in the construction of your temple. It is a mockery of sacredness. Stop or face severe consequences," William read.

"I don't understand why people are so upset, Father," Daniel said, shaking his head. "How does our temple even affect them?"

"The devil always tries to stop God's Prophets, Daniel. Here we are, trying to keep to ourselves and not bother anybody, and still they seem to be stirred up against us building a temple. That tells me it's the devil that doesn't want us to build a temple."

"But aren't you afraid they will break in and destroy our shop, or do something to hurt Mother?"

"Yes, just like I was afraid when we lived in New York. However, we have chosen to join this Church, and I have faith that God will protect us. I'm going to keep doing what the Prophet tells me to do until I can't do it any longer."

"Good advice, Father. I'll try to remember that the rest of my life."

"So what are you working on?"

"We got an order for four wagon wheels so I started working on them," Daniel answered, feeling peace replace the anxiety he had been experiencing all morning.

"Okay, let me help you." They worked in silence for some time and then William said, "I think we need to make a change in our schedule. The Prophet asked for volunteers to stand watch at the temple at night from now on, and I volunteered us."

"Guards? At the temple? Why?"

"There's been some setbacks recently. During the night people are doing whatever they can to stop the work, so it has been decided that we need to post guards at the temple throughout the night."

"Unbelievable! So what is our schedule going to be?"

"I think we should continue working at the temple every other morning, and then three times a week one of us should help stand guard during the night."

"Maybe I should stand guard at night so you can be with Mother," Daniel offered.

"Thanks, son, but she won't be alone. I'm sure she'll feel safe with you in the house when it's my turn to stand guard, so I think we could take turns."

The unrest continued to escalate. Several shop windows were broken one night. A small group of men from town stopped Daniel on his way to the sawmill one afternoon and threatened him. Each act of persecution was met with increased determination to continue doing what the Prophet asked of them.

One night when Daniel and William were working late in the woodshop, someone knocked at the door and Daniel looked at his father in alarm.

"Don't worry, Daniel," William said as he reached to open the door. "I'm sure it . . ."

The instant the door opened, three men carrying torches pulled William out into the darkness.

"Father!" Daniel yelled as he ran toward William, but one of the men stepped in front of him and pushed his blazing torch close to Daniel's face. Two men ripped the shirt from his father's back and knocked him to the ground. One man put his foot on the back of William's neck and forced his face into the dirt. The other man slowly poured a bucket of hot tar on his bare skin. Daniel's fear was forgotten – he ducked under the torch and ran toward his father.

"Watch it, boy!" one of the men yelled as he grabbed Daniel's arm. The other two men rolled William over, forcing his tarred back into the dirt and gravel. The screaming agony of his father was barely heard above the raucous laughter and cheering from the three men. Daniel heard his own voice begging the men to stop, and he wondered how people who did not even know his father could do this to him. As he looked into the eyes of the three men, he realized they were not strangers. They were prominent, religious men from town who were very much aware of William's work at the temple. How could such a cowardly act of violence result in extreme pain and suffering, while at the same time produce feral delight from men who professed to believe in God?

After several additional shouted threats, the men rode off on their horses, filling the night with frenzied laughter and gunshots aimed at the sky.

"Father! Father!" Daniel called as he tried to help William get to his feet. By the time Daniel helped him stumble to their house, William was nearly unconscious. Daniel and his mother spent the remainder of the night pulling blistered skin and dirty tar from his father's back. William passed out several times from the extreme pain, and his agonizing cries made Daniel's stomach twist into a knot. He was sure it would be a very long time before the sounds of that night stopped playing repeatedly in his head.

Daniel worked alone in the woodshop the next few days. Even when William recovered sufficiently to sit at his workbench, it was evident he was far from recovered.

"I think you should still be home," Daniel said when his father inhaled deeply as pain twisted his face. "I can see that you're still hurting."

"Daniel, did you know that when Joseph Smith was tarred and feathered, he showed up the very next morning to preach, and never mentioned a word about the incident the night before?"

"Really? How could he do that?"

"I'm quite sure he was in even more pain than I am. Being a Prophet did not keep him from hurting, but it did seem to keep him from quitting. I have been home for three days and I do not want those men to keep me from helping build the temple."

"Do you know who they were?" Daniel asked.

"Yes, I know who they were. Good God-fearing men who seem to be listening to the devil these days."

"I don't understand how they can do that," Daniel said. "How can they believe in God and do that to you?"

"I do not believe for one minute that they feel they did this for God. I believe they want the world to think they did, but their actions tell me they were satisfying their own heart. Now, son, I want you to go to the temple and work for the rest of the day. I'll tend the shop."

Daniel looked at his father. Love and admiration filled his entire body, but all he could say was, "Yes, Father." He hoped that someday he would be as valiant in serving God as his father.

◆◆◆◇◆◆◆

Charles Smith and Daniel sat in the shade of a large tree not far from the temple. They had attended the dedication earlier that morning and felt so spiritually overwhelmed there was now little conversation between them.

"I didn't ever think we'd get the temple done," Daniel said.

"I thought for sure the men from town would burn it to the ground before we could ever finish." Charles sat as if lost in thought for a long time and then he said, "Isn't it amazing that no matter how hard they tried, they couldn't stop us from doing what God wanted us to do?"

"That is amazing," Daniel agreed. "Something else I find amazing is how much every single person sacrificed to get the temple done, and yet I never hear anybody complaining. I've never heard my dad complain about his back hurting, and I've never heard my mother complaining about giving up her China so they could grind it up."

"It sure makes the outside of the building sparkle when the sun shines on it," Charles commented.

"Yes, it does. It's beautiful!"

"Every single sacrifice was worth it when you think about what happened today," Charles said.

"Oh, I still cannot believe it. I wish we had been inside to see some of the heavenly visitors, but seeing all those angels standing on the roof is something I will never, ever, ever forget," Daniel said while looking at the roof as if he could still see them.

"And the singing. It was so beautiful."

The two boys never spoke for a long time.

"Charles, do you think the people in town will leave us alone, now that the temple is completed?"

"I don't think so, Daniel. I wish they would because I really like living here now that most everyone has a real house to live in and it seems like a regular city."

"Sure is different than when we first came, isn't it? I feel like we are part of civilization again."

"It seems strange to be moving without you," Daniel said. "I have no doubt the Prophet has a reason for sending me to Independence, but I'm sure going to miss living in this beautiful city."

"I think it's quite an honor to be asked to travel to Missouri with this group since you're barely fifteen, Daniel," William said. "Maybe it's because you are young and they need your strong muscles," he chuckled when Daniel laughed self-consciously, "but I think it's because you have a willingness to serve wherever you are needed."

"I think you learned that from your father," Mary said as she leaned a little closer to her husband. "But we will miss you very much. And I have to admit that I worry about you being so far from home and living in the wilds on the edge of the new frontier."

"Mothers are allowed to worry a little," William said, with a quick wink at Daniel. "One thing for sure, though, son. You will quickly become a man since there are no comforts or benefits awaiting you."

"One good thing, Father. It will be a relief to not continually see those men that have put our family through so much sorrow and pain."

"I know you struggle with bitter feelings," William said, "but I heard you say you always try to do what the Prophet tells you to do."

"Yes, and I know he has told us we should forgive those who have persecuted us. I want to do as he asks." Daniel looked down at his hands. "And I think it will be easier to forgive them when I no longer have to see them." He slowly looked up at his father and smiled.

"Yes, I'm sure it will be," his father agreed.

"But I will miss seeing the beautiful temple. We all worked so hard to help complete it, and I love the peaceful feeling there. I am thankful we were able to work on it together. I'll miss both of you so much, and . . ." Daniel stopped as he endeavored to control his emotions. "And I will miss working with you Father." He could say no more, but hoped his parents knew how much he loved them both.

A few days later, Daniel kissed his parents goodbye and went to the temple one last time. His heart was filled with peace and the beautiful woodwork stirred feelings of joy and pride knowing he had been able to contribute to the temple's magnificence. He stood hesitantly in the doorway, but forced himself to leave the temple's sweet sanctuary. He prayed it would not be long before he saw his family and friends again.

By the time the small group arrived in Independence, Daniel had become well acquainted with everyone, and discovered they all shared his sadness at having to leave the newly completed temple. For five years, Daniel helped each family build a new home, and then worked with the other men in the group to build the shops that would help provide each family's income. He became an adopted son to most families, even though he had become a very independent young man. He became especially close to Frank, who was several years older, married and raising three children.

"Think we'll be here long enough to enjoy what we've built?"

"Funny you should ask that," Frank answered. "I hear that question often these days."

"I remember how I wanted everything to be perfect when we were working on the temple in Kirtland. I don't feel that way about the homes here. Oh, sorry, I don't mean to imply that I didn't give a hoot how your house turned out," Daniel quickly added with a short laugh.

"Don't worry. I know what you mean. I hear some of the men wonder if they should finish the inside of their new houses or just sit back and make do until we're told to move somewhere else. Some grumble because they had to leave everything behind in Kirtland and start from scratch here while their neighbors back in Ohio are sitting pretty in their nice houses, taking it easy and enjoying the temple."

"I don't feel that way," Daniel said, slowly shaking his head. "I just wish I could make myself put more effort into the work I do here."

"Hey, have you heard?" Frank asked. "Brother Joseph is coming to Independence. Seems he's heard about all the grumbling and discontentment here, and is coming to address our concerns."

"Don't you just love to listen to him?" Daniel asked, remembering how strongly he could feel the Spirit when he was with Joseph.

"It will be interesting to hear what he has to say," Frank said.

The tone in Frank's voice made Daniel feel uneasy. He had never openly complained, so Daniel tried to refrain from reading too much into his comment.

Knowing the Prophet was coming to Independence provided all the incentive Daniel needed to, once again, put his heart into everything he was asked to do. When Joseph finally arrived, Daniel took advantage of every opportunity to hear him speak. On a warm afternoon, he listened as the Prophet spoke to a group of people on a little hill in the western portion of the city, not far from the post office.

"Brothers and Sisters," Joseph said, "The Lord has instructed me that we are to build a temple on this spot. He has called Independence the center place. This temple will establish the New Zion. Jesus Christ will visit this temple with a pillar of fire, as spoken of in prophesy throughout time."

The reaction was not the same as when the temple in Kirtland had been announced. Then, every single person Daniel knew had been very grateful they had the opportunity to help build a temple of God, and they were willing to sacrifice everything they had and all their time to make it happen. Even though Daniel found great joy in the Prophet's words, he heard murmuring from some who thought they had sacrificed enough for this new church.

As he wrote a letter to his parents to let them know what Joseph had said, Daniel longed for the enjoyable discussions they had shared before he left Kirtland.

"I wish you could be here to hear the message I heard from the Prophet Joseph yesterday. I personally heard him tell us there would be a temple built here. He told us Jesus Christ would visit the temple with a pillar of fire, and he said that event had been told about in prophesy throughout time. Sometimes I think living right now, when we can personally hear Brother Joseph speak to us and teach us must be a little like how people felt that were living on the Earth when Jesus Christ was alive. I can feel the Spirit so strongly whenever I am around Joseph Smith. It would be wonderful if you and I, Father, could again work together to build a temple of God.

I recognize that I have to depend on my own spiritual strength now that I am grown. Please do not worry about me, but there seem to be many members here who are tired of sacrificing and being asked to rebuild. I remember how many blessings our family received when we made sacrifices to help build the Kirtland Temple, and I hope to experience that again when a new temple is begun. With no shop to help operate, I could work on a new temple pretty much full time.

You should see how Independence is growing. Every day more people come into town and start looking for a place to build their new home. Because there are so many people here, a new town has been established to the north called Far West. I may move there if it gets any more crowded here in town.

Mother, I want you to know that the family who runs the boarding house where I live fixed me a birthday cake, but it wasn't nearly as good as the ones you make. Now that I am 20, I guess I should be looking for a wife. Maybe then I would not miss you and Father quite so much. I miss both of you and hope to see you again soon."

CRITICISM AND MOBS

"I have decided to move to Far West," Daniel told Frank one afternoon.

"I'm not surprised. You've been talking about it for a while, so I thought you might be moving. My family is going to miss you very much. I think my oldest boy will try to talk you into taking him with you."

"I'll miss you, too, but I need to go. Not sure why. I tell everyone it's to get away from all this hubbub and bustle, but, truthfully, I can no longer ignore this strange feeling that I must move there."

"You're not moving to a new settlement, just a little ways north. I'll bring my boys and we can all go hunting together. I probably won't have any choice anyway, once they find out you're moving."

"Do that. Bring them, and come any time you can."

"Do you need help moving?" Frank asked. They had reached the corner where Frank turned to go to his house. "Glad to help."

Daniel laughed. "Let's see, if all five of you came over, you might be able to find one thing each to put in my saddle bags."

"You can laugh now, my single friend, but as soon as you get married, you will know exactly why I asked the question. I can't even remember the last time I could fit everything I owned into a wagon, let alone my saddle bags."

"Thanks for offering, anyhow," Daniel said as they clasped each other by the arm.

As Daniel rode his horse toward Far West several days later, he began thinking about how the people in Independence seemed to be changing. The houses were big and spacious, some even more luxurious than those he remembered in Kirtland. Businesses were prospering –

how could they help but succeed when there were so many new people arriving every day, needing every service being offered. "What's changing?" he said aloud to himself. *Maybe it's just me*, he thought, *but I sure don't seem to remember so much griping and complaining in Kirtland*. After a few minutes, he smiled at his own thoughts. "You were a kid living with your Mom and Dad, then," he said, speaking only to himself. "You never heard anyone complaining because you were just a kid."

Daniel quickly fell in love with Far West, and the only time he spent in Independence was when he was helping build new homes. He found a place where he could board and met a new friend, Josh. They were both young and single, and loved to explore the surrounding countryside and hunt wild game. A spark of competitiveness developed as they endeavored to prove who was the best shot. The result was time spent doing something they loved while providing many hungry families in Far West with meat.

"Josh, I think the Johansson family could find a use for this deer meat. And I think you should take it to them."

"Why should I take it?"

"Because I'm not the one that's kind of sweet on that girl of theirs."

"I'll take it, but you don't need to be saying anything about this, to anyone," Josh said, trying to sound just a bit threatening.

"Don't worry," Daniel said as he laughed. "I won't."

As much as Daniel loved living in Far West, the bickering and unrest that seemed to increase daily saddened him. Conversations he heard while walking down the main street in town brought back memories of hateful talk when his family lived in New York. There was a big difference, though. In New York, men who were not members of the new church criticized the leadership – now members of the Church condemned their own leaders.

Daniel thought a good hunting trip would clear his head, so he found Josh and they headed to the outskirts of town. It was difficult to enjoy the silent beauties of nature with Josh talking non-stop about Missy Johansson and her enchanting way of talking, and her beautiful blond hair, and her meticulous hand writing, and . . .

"So are you going to ask for her hand?" Daniel interrupted.

"I'd like to, but her father doesn't seem to want me spending time with his precious daughter. But the real problem is that he thinks nobody should criticize the high and mighty brethren in Kirtland."

"Josh, I've never heard you talk like that before. Sure, I've heard you criticize things the Church leaders have done, but it sounds like you don't even respect their authority as leaders of the Church. Is that really how you feel?"

"I just don't think they are any better than the rest of us," Josh answered defensively. "They act like they're so perfect. Messengers of God's will. Well, I know things about some of those high-ups in the Church, and they are no different than you and me."

"Nobody's perfect, Josh. Not me, not you, and not them. But they have been called by the Spirit to positions of leadership and we should respect that."

"If you want to close your eyes to what's going on, fine. But I'm not going to pretend they're good enough to be telling the rest of us what to do with our lives. If Joseph Smith chooses that type of men to be leaders of the Church, it makes me wonder whether we should keep listening to what he says. Maybe it was a mistake to listen to him in the first place."

"You can't mean that, Josh," Daniel said in stunned amazement. "You left your home and came here to be with other members of the Church. How can you feel this way about the Church leadership?"

"Don't get all goody-two-shoes on me, okay, Daniel? I have a right to think how I want. I'm not leaving the Church. I just wonder if we should have different leadership, that's all. I'm entitled to my own opinion, you know."

"That's right, you are." They spent the rest of the afternoon hunting, but the divide between them was obvious to both. Daniel tried to make small talk as they returned to town, and uttered the expected 'let me know when you can go hunting again' when they parted, but he found it hard to comprehend how his friend could have changed so completely, so rapidly.

Grumblings and challenges spoken of in private conversations quickly escalated to open dissention. Some questioned whether Joseph Smith should continue to be the Prophet of the Church. This left the people of Far West in a fragmented disarray of emotions.

Daniel was surprised when Josh sought him out and asked if they could talk – he had some questions he wanted to discuss. The two men walked away from town without speaking. Daniel expected to hear more criticism of Church leaders, and kept telling himself to listen and think before he responded because arguing would not help Josh in any way. He was not prepared for what Josh said.

"I'm confused and I don't know who to listen to any more."

Daniel waited for a moment, but Josh did not continue. "How can I help you, Josh?"

"Tell me why all that has been said and done doesn't bother you."

"It does bother me, a lot. I don't understand how people can . . ."

"No," Josh interrupted. "Tell me how you can still believe Joseph is a Prophet when there are so many people who don't accept his authority to lead the Church. How can you not be confused?"

"Because Joseph Smith is not the one who changed, Josh. He is the same as he was when I was first acquainted with him in New York. Every time I'm around him I can feel how strong the Spirit is."

"But what about all those who don't feel that way about him anymore? Doesn't that make you wonder if you're right about him?"

"No," Daniel answered. He watched the expression on Joshua's face and could see confusion. "Have you prayed about this? Have you asked Heavenly Father if Joseph is His Prophet?"

Josh slowly shook his head and shrugged. "If I can't figure out what I should believe by talking to you, how could I ever figure things out by talking to someone who doesn't say anything back?"

Daniel spent many hours trying to help Josh understand the source of the contention. The on-going confusion and doubt weighed heavy on Josh, and he finally informed Daniel he was going to leave the Church and move back East in a couple of months.

The next week Joseph Smith came to Far West to organize a survey party. Daniel knew nothing about surveying, but attended the meeting anyway, just to be close to the Prophet and again feel the Spirit.

"Brethren," Joseph Smith said, "There is a beautiful valley northeast of town and I need people who can help survey the area. I would like to establish a community there, much like this one here in Far West. Are there any who would volunteer to go with me?"

Several people raised their hands and indicated they would help with the endeavor.

"Daniel," the Prophet said, "I would like you to accompany us."

"I would be happy to," Daniel quickly answered. At that instant, he was sure the Lord had heard his prayers about finding a way to help Josh. He knew he would get an opportunity to ask the Prophet for advice during the trip, and he anticipated getting away from all the turmoil in Far West for a few days.

As the survey party entered the valley the next day, Daniel became very confused. He had a strong sense of familiarity and felt he was returning home after a long journey. He studied the terrain and was confident he had never been there before, not even while hunting. Stranger still, although they were there to possibly lay the groundwork for a new community, he felt no desire to live there in the future. Somehow, he knew he would never live there.

As Joseph approached the top of a small hill overlooking the valley, he stood quietly for a moment appearing to be deep in thought. After a time, he slowly walked a short distance and stopped next to a pile of rocks. Daniel and the rest of the group followed the Prophet.

Turning to face the men, Joseph said, "You are standing in a very sacred place. Adam built an alter here to make a sacrifice to God. This location was later used by the Nephites for sacrifices and as a burial ground."

The Spirit was incredibly strong; the entire group slowly got down on their knees and began to pray. It was not a group prayer, but like Daniel, each individual felt compelled to offer their own very personal prayer to their Father in Heaven. As Daniel prayed, he felt as if someone as dear as his own father had suddenly sat down next to him. The Spirit was intense and tears quickly began streaming down his face. He briefly opened his eyes, amazed to find no one there. He continued praying for his family and his dear friend, Josh. They had shared so much. He could hardly bear the thought of Josh leaving the Church. After a considerable time Daniel ceased praying and sat quietly on the hillside, something many of the others were doing.

Joseph again spoke. "This is such a special place in a blessed country. It was the location of our first parents' home on Earth, Adam and Eve. It will be the location of a great meeting where father Adam will present the keys and records of all the Earth to Jesus Christ, the Son of God. It is called Adam-ondi-Ahman."

Everyone could sense the solemn sacredness of the valley; it was peaceful and beautiful. They sat in silence for some time, contemplating Joseph's remarks.

That evening after dinner, Daniel sat alone on a large rock a short distance down the hill from where the ancient altar was located. Still laboring in his mind over the situation with Josh, he was mentally fatigued. Joseph was suddenly standing next to him, and startled Daniel when he spoke.

"Would you mind if I sat with you and talked?" Joseph asked.

"I don't mind at all. I would be very honored to have the opportunity to talk to you."

As Joseph sat down, Daniel thought how amazing it was to have the opportunity to visit with a living Prophet of God, one-on-one, in an environment so filled with power and peacefulness.

"What's bothering you, Daniel?" Joseph asked.

Daniel explained the situation that had developed with Josh, and described how he felt at the prospect of losing that friendship. Joseph listened, without speaking, occasionally nodding. Daniel left nothing out, feeling as if Joseph could see into his soul and was already aware of the entire matter. When he finished, Joseph did not immediately speak, but let a little time pass with no words spoken between them. Daniel was surprised how peaceful he felt, even as he wondered why the silence did not make him feel awkward. They sat together, both looking across the valley as the sun began to slide behind the trees.

Without looking away from the setting sun, Joseph talked about his childhood, very slowly at first, as if he were narrating past events of his life while watching them play out before his eyes. He had been raised on a farm and didn't have a care in the world. Then, like Josh, he became concerned about all the turmoil created by religions challenging each other's validity.

"The debates became nearly violent and seemed so ungodly," Joseph said. "Feeling great concern, I slipped into the woods one afternoon and asked God, in a prayer, which church I should join. After a violent struggle with a very real and evil power, God the Father and Jesus Christ appeared. They told me to join no church, as none of them offered the correct authority or doctrine."

Joseph was silent for a moment and then continued. "Not really understanding what I should do, I went to the minister that had told me to pray for an answer about which church to join. I hoped he would be able to explain this event to me. To my shock, he told me the visit was evil and God did not appear to men on Earth any more. I was confused and somewhat embarrassed. It had been quite hard for me to tell the minister of the visit, as I knew it probably sounded like a tall story. The result was worse than I had ever dreamed it could be. The minister became a sole crusader against me, trying to publicly discredit and humiliate me."

Joseph slowly shook his head and sighed. "To this point, I had always been well liked and couldn't really think of a person I didn't get along with. Suddenly people were making fun of me and actually began doing destructive things to my family and me. Even people that had been good friends to us were suddenly joining in the persecution. I recall wanting things to return to the way they were before I talked to the minister, but knew I could not deny what I had been shown. Every aspect of my life began to be scrutinized and challenged. Even when I got a job and worked harder than anyone around me, they found some way to discredit my performance. It seemed to be a losing battle. As the years passed, however, there were those that gave much and some that gave all to further my efforts. Some of my greatest sorrow came as I watched people endure persecution or die because they followed my teachings. How I wished, at times, that I had fabricated the whole doctrine, for then I could have just disbanded the group when close friends began to lose their lives over it. But many of them had received the same witness to the truth that I had experienced, and that allowed them no more of a chance than I had, to turn from the truth and escape with a clear conscience."

Joseph paused, then turned and looked directly at Daniel. "You have a great work yet to do. I have seen what lies ahead. Troubles abound, and your road will be rocky, but you must do what is in your heart and not be pulled from your destiny by someone else's uncertainty. You need to talk to Josh, but dwell on where you need to go, not on what he may do."

Their conversation turned to idle exchanges about the beautiful evening and the impressive valley. Too soon, in Daniel's opinion, Joseph stood to leave, but then he turned and firmly gripped Daniel's shoulder, "God knows you, Daniel. He loves you, and needs you." Then he smiled and walked away.

Daniel spent ten days with the survey party, working closely enough to a Prophet of God to feel the spirit that emanated from him. He was impressed at how humble this great man was, and witnessed how easily he mingled with common, every-day men. Then Joseph returned to Far West.

The survey party finished their work and prepared to leave the valley, but Daniel decided to stay one more night. In the late afternoon, he watched the survey party disappear over a hill, but was surprised that he did not feel alone. He sat on the hillside and watched the sun slowly set as he replayed the events of the last ten days in his mind. "You worked one-on-one with a Prophet of God for ten days," he said. *And that Prophet said God loved you, Daniel,* he reminded himself. *That is a lot more than you prayed for.*

Several times during the early part of the night, Daniel had a sensation that someone sat down next to him. He thought someone from the survey party had come back, but when he turned to look, no one was there. The presence did not make him feel uncomfortable, but instead he felt a little sad that he could not see the person he knew was there. He finally decided he was experiencing the after-effects of feeling the spirit that exuded from Joseph Smith for so long. *I wonder what he saw in my future.* "Your road will be rocky. You have a great work to do," he quietly said aloud to himself as he spread his bedroll on the ground near the alter on the hill. Exhausted from the day's work, he drifted off while wondering whether he would want to know what his future held.

Daniel stood on the hillside in the late afternoon. He recognized the valley, and knew it was where he had been sleeping. He saw a young warrior kneeling in front of two graves a short distance away. The warrior was very sad and Daniel knew he had just buried someone he loved very much. A man and woman appeared, one standing on each side of the kneeling warrior, and all three rose from Earth toward the heavens. After watching them ascend, Daniel looked back at the gravesite where the warrior had been kneeling – an aged body now lay dead upon the ground. The scene in front of his eyes quickly changed to a strange wilderness, rugged and covered with snow. Daniel now saw himself pulling a large cart of some type through knee-deep snow, bent and shivering, cold and exhausted. He saw the same warrior descend from the heavens and step to the back of the cart, and then watched as the magnificent man lowered his shoulder to the edge of the cart and pushed with all his might.

Daniel awoke with a start. He quickly looked around, but he was still alone. He lay down and looked at the expanse overhead filled with glorious, twinkling stars. The dream had seemed very real; he knew it was a message of some type, but he had no idea what it could mean. He thought perhaps his mind was trying to resolve the questions he had been curiously considering. He felt the interpretation of this dream was lingering just beyond his fingertips and if he could just try a little harder he would understand it, but his body was too fatigued to think logically and too sleepy to focus clearly.

The next morning he awoke with no resolution to his dream, and no restoration of his energy due to the restless sleep. He rolled up his bedding and saddled his horse. As he rode back to Far West, he allowed his mind to replay the dream. There seemed to be no connection between the dream and his life, no matter how he tried to make sense of it. Finally, he told himself it had to be the result of comments Joseph Smith had made about the valley they were surveying and what lay ahead for Daniel in the future.

After several months, Daniel received a letter that made all concern about his future immediately cease. His parents were in Independence, and in less than a day, he was headed there. Life was sweet; he helped his father build a house and then another woodshop. Soon the comfortable routine he had missed returned; days were spent in the woodshop helping his father build furniture, anticipating the scrumptious dinner his mother prepared for them. He thanked God many times for the assignment in Far West, which had made him more appreciative of every moment he spent with his parents. However, as if the joy of being reunited with his parents had blocked out the grumblings and criticism that had disturbed him before he moved to Far West, he gradually became aware that it had intensified, as had the contention amongst their neighbors. Mob violence threatened the very stability of Independence.

Bursting through the door, Daniel shouted, "Mother, there is a big mob headed here! They have already entered the outskirts of town."

"I know, Daniel. Your father came in a few minutes ago and told me the unbelievable news. He just went to get a few things from the shop and then we'll be ready to leave."

Daniel looked around the room and saw that many things had already been removed, but there was still so much furniture he and his father had recently finished building. He could hardly believe they were now being forced out by approaching violence.

"I thought you would be devastated at having to leave like this," Daniel said, looking intently at his mother.

"Son, even now I have my husband and you. I cannot stop thinking of poor Emma and Sister Lucy. I don't know how they can carry on, the constant worry, the threats and violence . . ." Tears began to fall from her eyes, even though Mary was trying to smile.

The front door opened and William rushed into the room. "Oh, Daniel, I'm glad you're here. We must hurry. I've put the last of our tools from the shop into the wagon, and it's full. We really need to be on our way." He hurried to his wife's side and put his arm gently around her. "Mary, my Dear, are you ready?"

"Yes," she said.

"Then we must hurry. I could hear shots being fired and people crying out even as I rode home from the shop. Daniel, let's get out of here." William pulled Mary close to him and then opened the front door. "I'm sorry, dear. I thought you would have a little more time to enjoy our new home."

Mary had been about to give in to the wave of sadness that swept over her as she realized her family was leaving yet another city and heading for the frontier where they would have to begin again, from scratch. However, hearing the concern in her husband's voice steeled her resolve in an instant.

"William, I'm taking everything that's dear to me and you've no need to be sorry." Her voice was so firm and resolute she surprised herself. She pulled the door shut behind her and did not look back.

Daniel climbed up into the wagon and extended his arm to help pull his mother up. William mounted the horse he had ridden home from the shop, and rode close to Mary's side of the wagon as they slowly left town and headed east to Illinois.

"We are so blessed to have a wagon and not be leaving our home on foot," Mary said as they traveled. "It's going to be hard to survive the winter in Quincy, but we may be able to help a few. Some have been forced out by the mobs with no provisions at all. That would be hard anytime, but will be especially difficult in November."

William reached out and reassuringly patted his wife's knee. "We have funds to establish ourselves in Quincy, Dear, and we'll help as many as we can. We'll find a group of wagons and join them tonight, and then we'll decide how we can help those who are on foot."

The first night, families gathered around large fires to prepare their dinner. People continued to arrive late into the night, but eventually it became very quiet. Daniel and his father sat close to the remains of the fire, wrapped in heavy blankets in an attempt to stay warm.

"Can you believe it has come to this?" Daniel asked.

"It seems only yesterday your mother and I finally arrived in Independence. We missed you so much when you were gone. Every time we heard of another conflict brewing between members in Independence or Far West, we feared that something would happen to you before we could be reunited."

Daniel chuckled and smiled at his father with a shrug. "When the members started having disputes among themselves, my best friend was one of those that left. I remember thinking that having friends who shared our belief in this Church and then turned on each other and defied the authority of our leaders was the worst thing that could happen. Now that seems pretty mild."

"Yes, it does. The mobs have progressively become more violent, but never would I have believed the Governor of Missouri would order the extermination of every member of our Church."

"You know, Father, sometimes I think the devil got a foothold in our midst when we quarreled and bickered amongst ourselves. Then the hatred started spreading to the people who lived in the surrounding communities. Once the anger and distrust took hold with them, our quickly increasing numbers panicked them."

"It is unbelievable how fast that hate can spread and turn into bloody battles where people end up dead." William shook his head and studied the glowing embers of the fire without speaking for a time. Tiny snowflakes began slowly descending and he pulled the back of his blanket over his head. "It's as though the hatred takes on a life of its own. When we first arrived in Independence, little disputes grew with each telling, and soon we would see a communication from the Governor's office citing an incident that had been so distorted we could hardly recognize it. After so many one-sided versions of such stories, I'm not even surprised the Governor issued his extermination order."

Daniel took a deep breath before he spoke. He admired his father for his self-control, but Daniel could not be as accepting of the Governor's actions. "But, Father, it's nearly impossible for me to believe that, in a country established on freedom and the right to worship God as its citizens choose, such an order could be issued to remove a group of people whose only focus is on pursuing God's kingdom. It was appalling when the military came into our town and arrested Brother Joseph and other Church leaders. Then to take our guns and tell us to leave the state or be exterminated! Sometimes I feel like I'm stuck in a terrible nightmare that I hope will end soon."

"I know, Daniel, but just when it seems we are all doomed, God sends us a miracle to help us remember that He is aware of our situation. Remember when an order was issued to execute Joseph and his co-leaders, and then Captain Doniphan refused to carry out that order? He stood up to his own commanders and told them it would be cold-blooded murder, and he would have no part of it."

"The best part," Daniel added, "was when he said that if any of our leaders were harmed, he would follow up with a tribunal of his own. Yes, I can definitely see the hand of God intervening on our behalf."

William spoke so quietly Daniel had to lean closer to hear him. "Son, I feel the membership of our Church is either not doing what we have been commanded in a manner that pleases God, or . . . or we are being refined somehow by this constant tribulation and persecution."

"Really?" Daniel asked. "It seems as though losing our firearms is rather severe testing. We cannot even defend ourselves or hunt for food to feed our families. I remember the boys and men who were slaughtered at Haun's mill, the women who were raped, and people whose cattle were stolen or farms were burned. That seems a little brutal to me." Daniel stopped and filled his lungs with stinging cold air. "I'm sorry, Father. I don't disagree with what you said, but I do get a little upset when I think of Mother being forced to leave her warm house on a night like this, and how many others don't even have . . . ."

"No need to apologize, son," William interrupted. "I can handle what comes my way, but it is harder to watch my sweet Mary be tried when she has been so willing to do whatever is asked of her. But I think if we're not expecting her to drive the wagon by herself tomorrow, we had better get some sleep."

"I agree," chuckled Daniel. "I love you, Father, and I am so grateful that we're all together. It will be easier to begin our lives again as a family. Good night."

Daniel listened as his father's breathing became even and eventually transformed into soft snores. He pondered the things his father had said; he had never voiced a single word of doubt concerning Joseph Smith or his teachings. Daniel shared that belief, and acknowledged it was a great blessing to be personally acquainted with a Prophet of God.

Daniel's family was among the first to arrive in Quincy, Illinois. The entire community spent the winter struggling to survive. In the spring, they continued on to Commerce, where they hoped to find peace and acceptance. Instead, they found new trials – swampy ground that had to be drained before they could build a new community. There was no energy left for quarreling with one's neighbors. During the first summer, many died from diseases spread by mosquitoes; at times, nearly a third of the community was incapacitated by fever. When entire families were too sick to take care of themselves, others in the community nursed them back to health, and every sickness delayed the badly needed progress on improving their precarious living conditions.

After two very long years, the city was renamed Nauvoo. Each newly-completed home or business increased the hope that this place would be where lasting family roots would be established.

Once again, William and Daniel completed a home to live in, then built a woodshop to provide their livelihood. They again used their home as a display area for their furniture and wood items. This provided two things for Mary, a house that was quickly furnished with beautiful new furniture, and a steady stream of potential customers to visit with.

"You should have seen Mother's eyes when she saw the new bed," Daniel told his father.

"She liked it, huh?" William asked.

"She loved it, and there were two families at the house who also liked it."

"That sounds encouraging. And," William said, watching his son's face, "while you were gone, we had a visitor stop by with great news."

Daniel looked up at his father and asked, "Is it the news we've been hoping to hear?"

William laughed. "Yes. We have been asked to build all the spindles and railing for the two spiral staircases in the new temple."

"Fantastic!" Daniel shouted.

"And," William said, and then again paused, "we have also been asked to provide much of the woodwork for the upper level and spiral tower."

"What an honor!" Daniel said, slowly sinking onto his workbench. "I had hoped we would be asked to help, but to have an entire project we will be responsible for. How wonderful!"

"It will mean long hours of work, son. If furniture orders keep us busy during the day, we'll have to make the woodwork for the temple at night. I hope you will remember how blessed you feel right now."

They both laughed, but were equally proud that recognition of their artisanship in woodworking had provided this opportunity.

Many long days and nights were required, but they took great care to ensure every detail on the spindles and railings was perfect. At the end of each week, they loaded the completed items into their wagon and delivered them to the temple.

"Every time we make a delivery, it seems there are more and more people here working," Daniel said to his father as they left the temple and walked back to their wagon."

"It brings back memories of helping with the Kirtland Temple."

Daniel smiled and tilted his head in greeting toward a group of people passing by. "I don't know which I enjoy more, building things to make the temple beautiful, or feeling the spirit of reverence and gratitude every time we make a delivery."

"It sure helps bring the scriptures to life when we're doing the same things that we read about our ancient ancestors doing," William said. "Think of all the people who have lived on the Earth, and we are among a very small percentage who have been privileged to help build a temple where God can communicate with His children."

"I love listening to Joseph talk about the ordinances we will be able to do after the dedication," Daniel said. "It's hard to imagine, but we get to perform sacred rituals lost to Earth so long ago. I wonder if the dedication of this temple will be as magnificent as the Kirtland . . ."

William stopped and turned around to see why Daniel had stopped in mid-sentence. He was standing completely still, his mouth appeared to be frozen as it had been when he stopped speaking, and his eyes were focused on a family who had just walked past them.

"Daniel? Are you all right?" William asked. Daniel did not respond. "Daniel!"

Daniel blinked his eyes and said, "Did you ever hear anything sound so elegant?"

William shook his head in confusion and asked, "What are you talking about, son?"

"Didn't you see her, Father? She was talking to her mother and her voice was so beautiful. They must be from England. Got quite an accent, but did you hear how . . ."

"Elegant?" William finished for Daniel. "How elegant she sounded? No, I didn't notice, but I can see that she made quite an impression on you."

Victoria was the most beautiful woman Daniel had ever seen. Her long hair, usually braided and wound around her head like a crown, matched her golden brown eyes. However, something he could not specifically define drew him to her – something familiar that nagged at his mind as though trying to jog his memory. He spent several days trying to obtain an introduction to her father. Although his efforts were obvious to all of his friends, Victoria never seemed to notice.

It was fortunate the woodwork for the temple was nearly finished, because once Daniel *was* introduced to Victoria, he found it difficult to concentrate on much else. Her family had recently arrived from England with a group of new converts. Daniel soon became familiar enough with her accent to understand what she was saying, but still found himself distracted by the sound of her words rather than what she was saying.

"I can hardly believe the hardships your family has been forced to deal with, all at the hands of your fellow countrymen," Victoria said as they walked through the woods near town.

"How did the people in England treat you when you joined the Church?" Daniel asked.

"Most of the people in our congregation joined the Church the same time we did," Victoria said, "so I didn't have many problems, but I know Father had a difficult time with his employer. I believe if we had not left England, he may have lost his position."

"So instead of staying in England and becoming a threat to anyone, new members are coming to America. When members gather into a large group here, it seems to make the people in nearby cities very nervous, and soon problems arise. We're all hoping that won't happen here in Nauvoo."

"Many of those who join the Church in England are so poor they cannot find money to book passage for America. I am very lucky because my father is not poor, and he helped as many people in our congregation as he could. I'm pretty certain you have never met many of the poor who arrive from England because they cannot afford to have you build fine furniture for them."

"Why do the missionaries encourage new members to come to America if it is such a hardship for them?" Daniel asked.

"They said it would make the Church stronger if all the members were together in one place. I know that when we prayed about coming here, we received a strong witness from the Holy Spirit that we should. Even when people are very poor, they will sacrifice everything they have in order to accomplish what God wants them to do."

Daniel listened to the way her accent made every sentence sound magical. Her description of the Spirit's confirmation that they needed to come to America created a vision in his mind of an angel whispering in Victoria's father's ear, saying over and over that there was a man waiting in America for his daughter, and it was very important that he take his family there so the two could meet.

"Are you hearing me speak?" Victoria asked.

"Of course I am," Daniel answered. "You were talking about your father feeling it was very important that he bring you to America."

Victoria laughed and blushed lightly. "That's silly, Daniel. That's not what I said."

"Are you glad you came here and that we met each other?"

"Yes, I am. You are very interesting."

"That's all?" Daniel asked. "I'm just interesting? We've known each other for two months, and you only find me interesting?" He watched as her face reddened, and felt his heart race as he hoped he knew what that meant. "Do you like me, Victoria?" he asked, suddenly a little afraid of what her answer might be.

Without looking up, she nodded her head.

"Victoria," he said, and waited until she looked up at him. "I think I'm in love with you. Do you feel the same way or do you only find me an interesting person to spend your time with? I need to know."

"I have known from the first time I saw you that I would marry you, Daniel." She took a deep breath and continued. "The day you and your father were leaving the temple and I walked past you with my family? I saw you the moment you stepped out of the temple and I walked very slowly so we would not pass before you reached the sidewalk. I knew you felt the same way because every day you tried to find a way to be introduced to my father."

Daniel was fascinated at the way her eyes held his as her words settled into his mind, and then into his heart. Could it be this simple? He had met many girls who had become very good friends during his lifetime. Not one of them had made him feel more than friendship. "Victoria, will you marry me?"

"Yes, Daniel, I will."

Life sped by in a blur. The two families became acquainted, and plans were made for the wedding. A small house was found, and Daniel and his father worked together to make furniture to meet their needs. Then, on a warm evening, in a simple ceremony held on the bank of the Mississippi, Joseph Smith married Daniel and Victoria.

Life seemed perfect. Nearly every evening, as the day settled into a quiet peacefulness, Daniel and Victoria strolled through the streets and looked at all the beautiful brick homes, talking of their plans to someday have a fine home of their own.

One evening they walked down Main Street, looking into the shop windows as they slowly made their way toward the river. When they reached the end of the street, they stopped near the Nauvoo House and held hands while watching a riverboat make its way up the river.

"Won't you join us?" a voice asked.

Daniel looked toward where he thought the voice had come from.

"We have a beautiful view and would love you to share it with us," Joseph Smith said.

"Thank you," Daniel said, and he opened the gate for Victoria.

"Thank you for the invitation," Victoria said. "I have admired your beautiful yard many times as I've walked by."

"I hope we're not imposing," Daniel said, as they sat down on the blanket Emma and Joseph were sharing.

"Not at all," Joseph said. "It's nice to see you two."

"We have a wonderful vantage point where we can watch the activity on the river," Emma said. "We have a beautiful community in the most wonderful place on this Earth. Our temple is nearly complete and we have finally been left alone to enjoy a life that contains some joy and comfort."

No one spoke as they all looked toward the river. Daniel was a little surprised that he felt so comfortable sitting with his new wife, sharing a blanket with the Prophet and his wife. He had no idea what everyone else was thinking, but Emma's expression of gratitude seemed to leave no need to say anything further.

Daniel looked up at the temple that was close to being completed. It was as if the full moon's sole purpose that night was to relay the sun's light onto the temple; the temple seemed to light the community. The locust filled the night air with a slow calming rhythm that was in accord with the pulse of the flowing river, or the slow, deep breathing of the Earth. Daniel felt himself sliding into an hypnotic state as everything around him joined together to become a single, soothing cocoon that encircled the four of them.

He looked at Joseph, whose arm was holding Emma tightly to his side. It was something he had never witnessed before. They often seemed almost distant from each other. Joseph was normally in a constant rush to answer questions or give direction for an entire struggling community and developing religion. Emma, running in the opposite direction, seemed engulfed in the service of the thousands of sick and hungry immigrants who lived in temporary conditions on the banks of the river. They had willingly accepted great burdens. It was not until that moment that Daniel saw them as a couple, the same as he and Victoria, with real feelings for each other. He could feel their great love radiating between them, and felt they were desperately trying to absorb every ounce of beauty and healing replenishment the moment could provide.

In an attempt to express his feelings, Daniel said, "Victoria and I walk nightly and try to imagine the house we might someday have. It's nearly impossible to believe what a safe and beautiful community we have managed to develop on this swampy ground no one else wanted."

Before he could continue, Joseph said, "Because it's calm now, don't believe that trouble . . ." Looking at Emma, he stopped mid sentence as he saw the look that only a wife could give her husband. It seemed they held a sad secret about all their futures, holding it within, not wanting to burden anyone else with their awareness. Joseph continued then, with simple advice. "Enjoy every minute you have together, and find joy in the growth that lies in the challenges and struggles ahead."

It was not hard for Daniel to understand that the advice Joseph Smith gave him and Victoria was probably advice he lived by every day of his life.

Daniel spent most mornings working in the woodshop with his father, and in the afternoon, he made the deliveries. This was, by far, the most enjoyable part of each day because he stopped and picked up Victoria as soon as he left the shop. He hated to be apart from her; hours spent working in the shop, or any activity that did not include Victoria, seemed to be an interruption that he almost resented.

"Did you get the chest in the back room?" William asked Daniel as he was preparing to leave the shop one afternoon. "I finished rubbing it with oil this morning and can't remember if I told you it was ready to deliver."

Daniel turned back toward his father. "Yes, you did mention it. Already have it loaded." Rather than turning to leave, he sat down on his workbench and said, "It's a beautiful finish. That oil brought out the pattern of the grain. I think they'll love it." All morning long, William had seemed deep in thought and Daniel wondered if there was something on his mind he wanted to discuss.

"Yes, the grain was rather pretty, wasn't it? You know, son, I wish you would ask for payment when you deliver that chest. Most of our customers pay for their order before we ever start building, but the Haggerty family makes me uneasy."

"What do you mean, Father? Was something said?"

"No," William said, still looking down at the rocking chair arm he was shaping. "I have noticed lately that people are quick to find fault with others and I don't want to have troubles with the Haggertys."

Daniel took off his jacket and leaned toward his father. "What's bothering you? You have seemed occupied all morning."

William stopped pushing the plane along the edge of the wooden arm piece and looked up, sighed deeply, then looked through the window facing the street. "I see things changing, little difficulties within the community do not get resolved but grow into serious arguments.

Your mother told me a man and woman were at our house looking at furniture, and then another man came in, but he wasn't looking for furniture – he wanted to continue some previous argument with the man who was already there. He became very agitated and ended up making outright threats. That sort of behavior brings back too many ugly memories from Independence and Kirtland." He stopped and looked at Daniel. "I thought I could provide some safety for your mother here. I'm worried now about who might come to our house while she's there alone. Do you think it possible that we will have to leave our beautiful Nauvoo?"

Daniel was not prepared for the tears that suddenly spilled down his father's face. "Father, why didn't you speak of this earlier? I didn't know such things were happening. I can spend more time in the shop so you can be at home with Mother. Will that help?"

William wiped his face with the back of his sleeve and softly chuckled. "Since you met Victoria, you have moved through your days in a private world that contains only the two of you. It's wonderful to see you so happy. It's only that I am concerned about your mother." He raised his hand and motioned toward the door. "Go, make your deliveries. I'm sure Victoria is wondering what's keeping you. We can talk later."

"Are you sure?" Daniel asked.

"Yes, yes," William answered. "Put on your coat and go get Victoria. In the morning, we will talk. Now go."

Daniel sat for another moment watching his father's face. Whatever had been on his mind seemed to be gone for now. "Okay." He stood and put on his jacket. "But tomorrow I won't make any deliveries and we can spend the whole day here talking about what changes we need to make so you won't have to worry about Mother."

"That will be fine, son. Now go, enjoy the afternoon with your beautiful bride."

Daniel began spending the entire day at the woodshop. His father worked with him in the mornings and began working at home during the afternoon; a schedule was established with specific hours each afternoon when people could look at furniture in their home. Daniel made deliveries after the shop closed each day. Once Daniel began noticing those around him, he saw small violent actions beginning to happen in Nauvoo, exactly duplicating the same pattern of escalation they had experienced in Ohio and Missouri.

"How can this be happening again?" Daniel asked Victoria one evening. "Everyone has worked so hard to build this beautiful city, years of hard work so we could live in peace."

"But why would anyone want to make us leave this area? It was a swamp where no one lived. It makes no sense to me." Confusion spread across Victoria's face.

"Do you remember the man I told you about? The one who purchased the rocking chair yesterday?"

"Yes, you said he was not satisfied with it."

"That's right. When we offered to refund his money if he returned the chair, he still wasn't satisfied. Father offered to make whatever changes he felt were required, but that did not satisfy him either. He came into the shop and started yelling at Father, and telling customers in the shop that they should not buy from us because our furniture was not good, our workmanship was poor, and we cheated our customers by charging too much. It was so upsetting to Father! Once rumors begin, there seems to be no way to stop them." Pausing, Daniel got up, put another log in the fire and quickly returned to the extra wide chair he had built to share with Victoria. He wrapped the quilt she had made snugly around both of them and again focused on the hypnotic flames dancing in the fireplace.

"I worry about your mother," Victoria whispered. "She seems so fearful."

Daniel was quiet for a moment. "My father was pulled out of our shop one night, when we lived in Kirtland. Men tore his shirt off and poured hot tar over his back, and then rolled him around in the dirt and gravel. I was young, but we spent the night pulling that mess off his back, along with half his skin. It was a nightmare, and I'm sure those memories are very vivid when she sees the increasing contention."

"I didn't know that," Victoria said.

"What I find hard to believe is that some of the people who are causing trouble here are the same ones that stirred things up in Missouri. What would make them hate us enough to follow us here?"

"Perhaps they want to stop anyone new from joining our Church," Victoria said. "I have heard some people saying that if Joseph Smith were killed, we would all go back where we came from."

"Oh," Daniel said under his breath in a long sigh. "Remember the night Joseph and Emma invited us to share their blanket?"

"Yes, that was a perfect evening."

"They're just like us, a young couple that loves their children and wants a safe place to raise them. The devil must be very afraid of Joseph and the Church he has restored. Why else would he chase him all the way from New York?"

"That's an unsettling thought," Victoria said.

"I'm certain Joseph is aware of what's coming. He constantly tells us we need to be patient with our neighbors, and several times I've heard him tell people how important it will be to keep precise and accurate records."

The ungodly actions in Nauvoo continued to escalate, often performed in the name of God and religion. Daniel became bold in defying men who hid behind the cover of night to smash windows and destroy businesses. He asked them what kind of a god would direct them to do such things, and what god would pour hatred over men to turn Christian against Christian. His defiance resulted in black eyes and bruised ribs, and seemed to make the culprits even more angry.

One evening while Daniel and Victoria were visiting with his parents, Daniel said, "The day before yesterday while we were at the temple, Victoria heard Joseph had said his work was completed, and he was now as vulnerable as any man to the evil doings of unrighteous men."

"Daniel," Mary said, "did you know that charges were filed against Joseph and several other leaders of the Church a few days ago?"

"I am sure they will prove to be false, as they always are," Victoria said.

"There is one difference this time," William reported. "In the past, Joseph has stayed among us and fought the charges through the courts. Yesterday, Joseph and the other leaders decided to leave Nauvoo in hopes that their absence from the city would end the pain and destruction that the mobs have been inflicting upon us."

"When did that happen?" Daniel asked. "False charges being filed against Joseph have become commonplace, but this time he felt it necessary to leave his followers?"

"They left yesterday morning. I'm surprised you had not heard about it," William answered. "Sadly, the rumor mongers in our own ranks are saying Joseph has abandoned us because he is a coward and is afraid he will finally be caught."

"I'll bet they are afraid that the angry mobs will turn on them when they discover Joseph is not here to satisfy the arrest warrant," Daniel said, the anger apparent in his words.

"I have a question, and I don't want any of you to think I am losing faith in Joseph or have become afraid for my own safety," Mary said. Her words instantly had everyone's undivided attention. "I would like to know if any of you feel we have reached a point where we need to begin making preparations to leave our homes again."

Daniel quickly looked at his father. They had discussed that very subject recently at the shop. William reached out and took Mary's hand as he began speaking. "Daniel and I have discussed this, and we feel we should wait until we receive some direction from our leadership. Whatever the Lord counsels us to do, we will do."

"Good," Mary and Victoria said at the same time.

William looked at his son for a quick second and then looked back at his wife. "We have also discussed something that will need your approval, and yours, too," he said as he looked at Victoria. He took a deep breath and continued. "We are so richly blessed from our woodshop. We have both felt, for some time, that we should endeavor to help those who are unable to afford a wagon if we are asked to leave this beautiful city and move elsewhere. It's not something we can undertake until we know how you both feel about it."

"Are you suggesting that we give wagons to those who cannot afford to buy one?" Mary asked, all the while smiling at her husband.

"Maybe not *give* it to them, but accept whatever they can pay."

"And if they cannot afford to pay anything?" asked Victoria, also smiling.

"Then I guess we would *give* it to them," William said meekly.

"Then we both agree," Mary said while looking at Victoria. "You see, my sweet husband, Victoria and I have been discussing ways we can be of more help to those who are poor and cannot provide for their own families. We can take them a basket of food or help make clothes for their children, but we have been praying that, as a family, we could find a way to share our abundance with those in need."

"And the Lord has answered our prayers," Victoria said.

"And here we thought it was our own idea," Daniel said.

"Now Daniel and I have something to say," Victoria said as a smile spread across her face. William and Mary both laughed softly and waited to hear what they were sure would be announced. "You will be grandparents, soon."

"Wonderful," Mary said. "It will be good to hear the laughter of a little one in our home again. And Christmas will be so special when our grandchild's excitement fills our home."

"Congratulations, my children," William said, and the twinkle in his eyes confirmed he shared Mary's feelings on the subject.

The next morning Daniel and William were busy working in their shop when voices becoming steadily louder caught their attention. They hurried out to the street to see what was happening.

"It's Joseph," William said flatly. "He's returned to the city."

A crowd was forming behind the Prophet and other leaders who rode on horseback through town. They were moving slowly enough that people could walk comfortably and keep up with the group. William pulled the shop door closed, and he and Daniel joined the growing crowd that followed the Prophet. When Joseph reached an open space near his home, he dismounted.

William and Daniel were too far away to hear everything Joseph said, but then they saw him raise his sword above his head and the words he spoke were loud enough for them to hear.

"I am fully aware of what lies ahead for me. My life is of no value to myself if it is of no value to my friends. I would willingly lay down my life for the truth of the gospel and for those that have supported me through the many trials and much suffering we have been forced to endure."

Daniel felt himself grow angry that God would allow this to happen to Joseph, but the warmth of his father's hand on his shoulder instantly removed his agitation, and he felt only sorrow that such an act of surrender would be required from Joseph. Daniel saw Emma standing near Joseph, and he heard enough of their conversation to know Joseph was begging her to go with him to Carthage. Daniel's breath escaped in a gasp as he saw that Emma was carrying a child and obviously not feeling well; he could only imagine the worry and fear that she was experiencing. Joseph disappeared into his house, explaining he wanted to tell his children goodbye.

Most people in the crowd showed little concern. Joseph had been arrested over forty times before and he always returned. Most of the charges had been frivolous and were quickly dismissed. Other times he had been kept in jail for varying lengths of time, but in the end, God always protected him and he was allowed to return home and resume his leadership over the Church.

Daniel felt this situation was different. He had seen a change in Joseph, and found it amazing that anyone could not see the deep sorrow so clearly displayed on his face. When the Prophet hugged Emma and told her goodbye, Daniel was overwhelmed with emotion and turned away from the crowd. Tears filled his eyes as he walked back toward the woodshop. *Will I ever see him again?*

SACRIFICES

"Hyrum, I want you to leave me and return to Nauvoo."

Joseph and Hyrum were riding close together headed for Carthage. Ten men rode close behind them.

"No, I'll not be leaving you alone. I have never allowed wicked men to use false charges to separate us in the past, and I won't be letting that happen now."

"Well, then, let's just turn around," Joseph said, "and go back and grow old together in Nauvoo."

"And wait for your accusers to come drag you to Carthage? Let's get this latest issue resolved and then we can return to the city together."

There was no further conversation between them. The entire group continued in silence – the only sound made by the men riding behind the Prophet and his brother, as well as the members of the Mormon Battalion riding behind the group, was the steady rhythm of the horseshoes hitting the road and the occasional creaking of the leather saddles and gear.

Turning to face Hyrum, Joseph said, "If this group enters Carthage, there will be bloodshed. The Battalion is larger than any government military force in the entire state. Even if we were to win the battle, it would only lead to greater bloodshed later." Joseph stopped and turned his horse to face the men behind him.

"I appreciate each one of you who has visibly expressed your love by coming with us to Carthage," Joseph said. "I order you to now return to Nauvoo in order that deadly violence can be avoided, for if you follow me and the rest of the men in this group into the city, that is the only possible outcome."

Daniel, sitting on his horse in the third row of the Battalion, could hear the Prophet's words clearly. Not a single member of the Battalion moved or uttered a sound. Daniel could feel the farewell Joseph had just spoken settle into every fiber of his soul, and he realized his only course of action was to obey the Prophet. He listened as the words Joseph had spoken were repeated in hushed tones, being passed rearward, row by row, like a dark wave. He watched as Joseph slowly turned his horse and began moving away from them. Daniel heard his own voice utter, "Joseph, don't leave us," in quiet words he was not aware he had spoken. For a short time, the men in the group spoke with each other, debating whether they should follow their leader or obey him and return to Nauvoo. With subdued spirits and heavy hearts, they returned to Nauvoo in silence.

Daniel's mind was filled with memories of a happier day when he sat with Joseph in the sacred valley of Adam-ondi-Ahman. He realized he had never thanked him for the kind assuring advice he had received that evening. *I hope I will have the opportunity to tell him how much I appreciated his kindness*, he thought, even while he feared that would never be possible.

"The mobs have killed Joseph and Hyrum! The mobs have killed Joseph and Hyrum!"

Daniel was working late in the woodshop when he heard the words and recognized the voice shouting them. Porter Rockwell was known by nearly everyone in Nauvoo, and his sobbing voice announced to the town the death of Joseph and his brother Hyrum. Daniel felt his breath escape in a long sigh. He looked down at the spindle he had been sanding. The farewell he had heard from Joseph as they approached Carthage replayed in his mind. Both Joseph and Hyrum? Gone?

When Daniel suddenly realized he was cold, he turned toward the wood stove in the corner of the shop and saw that the coals were nearly black. He slowly pushed the spindle away from him and stood up. "I must go tell Victoria and my parents," he said quietly as he reached for his coat. Victoria and Daniel had moved into his parents' home when Daniel began working late into the evening and worried about his wife being alone. He walked slowly, unable to keep Joseph's final words from repeating in his mind. When he found himself on the front porch of the house, it took every ounce of will in his entire body to make his hand turn the knob and open the door.

His parents were seated in separate chairs near the fireplace in the living room. His father was reading his scriptures by the light of an oil lamp sitting on a small table beside his chair. His mother was tatting a delicate edging for the long white dress she had made for her expected grandchild's blessing day. Victoria was sitting alone in the extra wide chair he loved sharing with her. He wished he could erase the terrible news from his memory and simply enjoy one last evening of peace and contentment with his family. However, his sorrow must have been visible on his face, because they all three stood and stepped toward him.

"Porter Rockwell just brought news of Joseph and Hyrum." His voice caught in his throat as he tried to form the words, but he knew there was no easy way to tell them. "The mobs have killed them both."

"No," his mother cried as she buried her head against William's shoulder.

Daniel took Victoria in his arms and could feel her silently sobbing.

"So it has finally happened," William said. "Brother Joseph's trial is finished, and ours has just begun. Hyrum and Joseph were inseparable to the very end."

"Their poor wives," cried Mary. "What can we do to help them?"

"I believe their large extended families will be providing for their temporal needs," William offered. "Let's give them some time to accept their loss, in private, and then we will help in any way we can."

"Perhaps we could each pray for guidance in how to help?" Mary said quietly.

William smiled and hugged her quickly. "Of course, Darling."

Life in Nauvoo stood still during the next few days. The painful realization took time to set in, but everyone also recognized that the reality of the situation must eventually be faced. The saints had been through struggles that refined them, but nothing that prepared them for the crossroads where they now stood. William and Daniel worked at their woodshop each day, but most of the time was spent talking to their customers who seemed more interested in the details of what had happened in Carthage than what they were ordering.

"We should have gone into Carthage with Joseph," an angry fellow Battalion member said to Daniel. "I feel like we deserted him."

"No," Daniel said softly. "Joseph told us to return. We did not desert him. He even sent eight of the men who went with him away before the mobs arrived. I think he must have known . . ." Daniel could not bring himself to put his thought into words.

"Did you hear that the jailer and his wife had left and told Joseph he and the other men could spend the night in their quarters on the second floor?"

"Yes, I heard that. I also heard that Joseph asked John Taylor and Willard Richards if they wanted to remain in the jail or return to Nauvoo, but they refused to leave."

"I would have stayed with them," Daniel's friend said, a little less angry.

"Any of us would have," Daniel said softly. "Every single member of the Battalion would have gladly gone with Joseph to protect him. We both know that, but I also think that if there were more that God needed Joseph to do, He would have protected him. My father said Joseph's trial is over and ours is just beginning. I think he's right."

Daniel and William sat in the living room, waiting for Victoria and his mother to join them. "I think your mother is nearly ready to go view Joseph and Hyrum. It wore her out yesterday to stand in the hot sun waiting for their bodies to be brought home."

"I know she had to stand in the heat for a long time. I never realized how many of us lived here in Nauvoo until everyone lined the street to watch the two wagons pass by. It made me realize how much the Church has grown in fourteen years."

"I hope we won't have to wait long at the Mansion House today. I do not believe Mary can take another strain like yesterday. This has been very hard on the women in town. I think they identify with the pain that Emma and Mary and all of their children are going through."

Both men stood as they heard their wives' approaching footsteps. "We are ready to go," Victoria told Daniel.

"Okay. How are you doing, Mother?" Daniel asked.

"I'm fine," Mary said, even though it was obvious to anyone who looked into her eyes that the opposite was probably more true.

They walked to the Mansion House where Joseph and Hyrum's bodies had been taken. Throughout the day, the mourners had silently been filing past the caskets.

"There is still a line of people waiting to pay their respects," William noted.

"But it appears to be moving rather quickly," Mary said.

They slowly moved toward the house as the line inched forward. When the two coffins came into view, Daniel heard his mother's muffled sobs. None of them spoke as they filed past the two brothers lying in unadorned caskets. Then they followed the slow-moving crowd to the cemetery, the only sound being an occasional sniffle or quiet sob.

"I see John Taylor walking down from the Mansion House and I know he's going to give the eulogy," William said to Daniel. "But if your mother gets too tired, I'm going to take her home."

"Okay," Daniel answered.

"You two stay as long as you want. Don't worry about us," William said as he smiled at Victoria.

The crowd drew near to John Taylor, who was beginning to speak, and Daniel pulled Victoria close to him. "Are you all right?" he asked.

Victoria nodded and snuggled a little closer to Daniel. "I'm fine."

The mood was solemn as John Taylor delivered his moving words. When he finished, William Phelps began speaking, but even though the heat of the day was beginning to diminish as evening arrived, Daniel decided to take Victoria home. When she did not protest, he knew she was much more tired than she was willing to admit. They slowly walked home with little conversation.

"Very sad day," Mary said after they had all gathered around the dining table. She placed some bread and cheese on the table, with a cool glass of lemonade for each of them.

"Yes," agreed William. "And already I hear people voicing their opinion about who is to succeed Joseph as our Prophet. I don't understand why there is any concern because this is a decision that should be made by the leadership of the Church."

Victoria stirred slightly, and then said, "Have you ever heard anyone speak of passing the position of Prophet from father to son?"

"Yes," answered Daniel. "I have heard much talk of this lately, and I do not understand where it comes from. Some people feel the successor should come from within the leadership of the Church. But I agree with Father, we should just wait and see what they decide."

"The contention borders on ludicrous," William said as he reached for another slice of cheese. "Some of the same men who now profess that the authority to lead the Church should be passed to Joseph's son are the very men who have long been shouting that Joseph did not have any authority to be our leader in the first place. If a man does not seek guidance from the Spirit, he will bend the truth to fit whatever he wants at the moment."

"The people in Nauvoo have seemed unable to agree on much lately, and now we are hoping they can come to a consensus regarding Joseph's successor? I am sure it will be very interesting to see what happens in the near future," Daniel said. "Brigham is said to be due back from his mission within a few weeks, so perhaps his arrival will help quiet things down."

It was well after dark when William and Daniel hurried home, returning from a meeting the brethren had attended. "When we tell our wives of this great news, I think they will feel as confident as we do that Brigham is to succeed Brother Joseph," William said.

When they stepped into the living room, they discovered their wives were not alone, but had been joined by several other Sisters.

"We were anxious to hear what was discussed at your meeting," Mary explained, "and we realized several of our Sisters had no way of hearing this news since they do not have husbands who can bring word to them."

Daniel and William smiled and greeted the women sitting in their living room, then Daniel sat next to his wife and everyone's attention was turned to William.

"Very well. This is what we have learned. At the meeting, we received a report from Orson Hyde. He told us of a miracle he experienced when he listened to Brother Brigham speak to a group of people. He said as soon as Brigham opened his mouth, he heard the voice of Joseph through him. However, it was not only the *voice* of Joseph, he also saw the gestures and features of Joseph's countenance. He felt a spiritual conviction that Brigham was the man to lead this people."

Victoria asked, rather timidly, "And do both of you believe his words?"

"Yes," they answered in unison.

"In the past," William continued, "many of the saints have openly challenged the words of the Prophet. Joseph's mantle of authority has always proven sufficient in settling such disputes. Without his direct guidance, we must all depend on the still small voice of the Holy Ghost to confirm that what the leaders of the Church tell us is true."

Daniel's entire being filled with love for his sweet wife as he saw her expression visibly display her acceptance. He knew her well enough to know she had received confirmation from the Holy Ghost.

"Before his death, Joseph said the saints would someday migrate to the west, and he made a sketch of the area he had seen in vision. He said it was located in the shadow of the Rockies, within the Salt Lake Basin. Brigham knows the place Joseph sketched is awaiting us, and he announced that the members of the Church will begin leaving Nauvoo in the spring."

"Will we be safe until spring?" one of the Sisters asked.

William smiled and said, "The mobs *are* becoming increasingly violent. They have destroyed homes and attacked some of the saints. But Brother Brigham has indicated that we need the personal endowment Joseph taught us about. It will only be available to us once we have completed the temple, so the focus from this point on will be to finish it as quickly as possible. We must depend on each other, as well as God, for protection, and pray we will be able to leave before the violence becomes intolerable."

Daniel stood and said, "If any of you need help preparing to leave Nauvoo, please come talk to me or my father. We won't leave without making sure each one of you is ready to leave."

The smiles and sighs of relief confirmed to Daniel that the small feeling growing inside his chest indicating that he should help these Sisters and their families was spiritual direction from God. He resolved to dedicate himself to that until each of them were able to leave Nauvoo.

Mary and Victoria soon began the process of sorting through their belongings to choose those most important to them. "I am surprised how little it bothers me to once again be leaving everything behind and heading into the unknown," Mary said as they worked together one afternoon. "When Daniel was very small, we left New York and moved with the saints to Kirtland. William said we were moving from city to city, and I remember Daniel saying, 'Father, don't you mean we're moving from city to nothing?'"

Both women chuckled at the image that came into their minds, and then Victoria said, "I've never moved to a place where there was no established city. When we left England and came here, Nauvoo was already a thriving city. I feel you have had to prove your faith in this restored gospel time after time, and I have never really had to make much of a sacrifice. My life since coming to Nauvoo has been wonderful. Well, maybe not totally wonderful every minute, but mostly wonderful."

"This time it's different for all of us. Each time we moved before, there were mobs on our heels, and we fled with what we could salvage. Some had nothing but the clothes they wore, and they were pulling their little children along with them. It was heart breaking. Now we have time to prepare and instructions about how much we will be allowed to take with us. We have been told room in our wagons will be needed for supplies rather than household belongings and keepsakes." Mary smiled sadly as she reverently folded a tatted tablecloth. "This belonged to my great grandmother. It has been passed down to me so that I can protect it and keep her memory alive by telling the next generation about her when I give this tablecloth to them." She carefully rewrapped her heirloom and said, "I will teach you to tat, as my mother taught me, and then this precious gift will be yours to treasure and someday give to your daughter when you teach her to tat. It is a blessing that this priceless keepsake is small and can be taken with us. I love the rocker William made for me, and all the beautiful furniture he and Daniel have made, but they are too large to take with us."

"At least we will have plenty of time to prepare," Victoria said, trying to comfort her mother-in-law. "If we leave in early spring that will mean we can travel during the summer. I am very glad because our little one," and she patted her swollen belly, "is due at Christmas time. Spring will arrive very quickly once the baby gets here."

Completion of the temple became of utmost importance. In addition, preparations began in earnest to leave the city. It became apparent much more was involved than gathering personal belongings, purchasing food, and heading for an unknown destination someplace in the west. Homes were converted into workshops and much of Nauvoo became a huge outfitting city. Daniel and William stopped making chairs and beds, and began making wagons in their shop.

"How are we going to help those in need without making them feel indebted?" Daniel asked his father one afternoon while they were working.

"Can you tell me the exact price of a new wagon, son?" William asked without looking up from his work.

"No, it all depends on the price we pay for wood and what the iron for the wheels costs us."

"Exactly, so if we never know the exact cost to build a wagon, how can our customers know the price?"

"Oh, so whatever we tell them the price is, they will assume they are paying our full price," Daniel said.

"Right," William said, "And who is to know if someone makes us a gift of some wood or has extra fittings they purchased but no longer need."

"You are a smart man." Daniel worked in silence for some time and then asked, "Have you had any success finding a buyer for the house or shop?"

"Things do not look very promising in that regard," William answered. "When people know they can wait until we leave and take our property for free, there is very little incentive to offer much for anything. And more than a thousand homes will be empty when we all leave."

"So I guess you're saying we should continue to pray for someone to make us an offer, right?"

"Pray hard, my son."

"Daniel, I am so afraid for our son," Victoria said. Their first child had arrived just days before Christmas and they named him Thomas, after Victoria's father. Victoria was lying on her side on their bed, and Daniel was facing her, as both of them touched the tiny fingers and button nose of their son nestled protectively between them.

"He is healthy. That is a great blessing," Daniel said. "And we have about nine weeks before we have to leave. I'll make sure every possible effort is made to keep him warm in our wagon. I know it's hard, Victoria, but we have to trust in the Lord that he'll be safe."

"I know," she answered quietly. "I wish I had your simple faith and trust that everything will turn out perfectly." She breathed deeply and smiled at Daniel. "It was much easier to have faith when it only involved you and me, but now we have this special little spirit to be responsible for. That makes it much harder for me."

"You will have plenty of time after we leave to worry about Thomas. You might as well relax and enjoy your warm house and new baby for the next few weeks, and not waste a single moment fretting. Father and I have been very busy making our wagons extra strong and reliable. You and Mother have weeks to purchase supplies and decide what we're taking with us."

"I will consider myself reprimanded," Victoria said, and then laughed. "I admit I am greatly blessed. I won't let you down, Daniel."

When Mary gently knocked on the door, Daniel stood and reached for his jacket. "Come in, Mother. Lunch break must be over." Mary handed him a covered basket containing William's lunch. "I'm off," he said, and bent to kiss his wife's cheek and his son's forehead.

"Dinner will be waiting for you when you close the shop," Mary said as she accepted his quick hug before he left.

Daniel stepped out into the cold wind and tightened the woolen scarf around his neck. He bent his head low against his shoulder as he walked to the shop. When he pushed the door open, the wind scattered the sawdust that covered every worktable.

"How is your little family?" William asked. When the cold air reached him, he stood and rubbed his hands together.

"Doing fine. Here's your lunch. That little boy is so precious, Father. I've seen little babies, lots of them, but there are no words to describe the feelings when it's your own flesh and blood."

"I know," William said with a broad smile. He loosened the cloth tucked tightly around his lunch and said, "I'm starving."

Daniel resumed the work he had left before lunch. "Victoria is getting a little worried about taking the baby on such a journey into the unknown. I try to put on a strong face and tell her I'm not worried, but I am. I know there's no choice, we will follow our leaders, but I am worried about it."

"Of course, you are, son," William said reassuringly. "You wouldn't be much of a father if you weren't concerned. You must pray for the strength to convince your wife that she does not need to worry. We have moved from city to city many times, and I trust this journey will end as successfully as each previous journey has ended."

"Right," Daniel said with a laugh. "Again with the 'from city to city' speech, huh? However, I *will* pray that I can be stronger, for Victoria's benefit. Thanks."

"I have news," William said. "While you were gone, a man I have never met before came into the shop and said he is interested in purchasing it when we leave. I told him I also have a house, and he said he would also like to buy that."

"That's wonderful, Father. I thought for sure we would have to walk away with no income from either place."

"That's still close to the reality of our situation," William continued. "The price he offered was nearly insulting, but it may be enough to buy more warm blankets to keep our wives and that grandson of mine warm. I saved the best news for last. He wanted to know if we would be leaving our furnishings in the house, and when I told him yes, he said he would add a little more to his offer for them."

"A little more, huh?" Daniel laughed. "Maybe it will mean our house will not be torched by the mobs as we leave town. That would be some consolation, right?"

"Some," agreed William. "I'll tell your mother we have sold the house and shop, and all of her prized furniture, and I will evade a discussion about the amount offered. That will make her happier. Also, have you purchased the iron for the wheels we are making for the Snyder families' wagons?"

"Yes, I'll pick up the iron and the fittings after work this evening. The wood is nearly dry so we can begin building it the day after Christmas. They're not able to pay enough to even cover the cost of materials, so that means I can't buy you that new team of horses for Christmas we saw parked in front of the Mansion House last week."

"That is surely a blow. That would have been a lovely present, son, but I wasn't aware they were for sale."

Daniel smiled. "They aren't for sale, but it really doesn't matter since I cannot afford to buy them for you anyway."

Five years of dedicated work finally resulted in the temple's completion. Daniel and Victoria were able to go with Daniel's parents to receive their personal endowment. They could feel the reverence and warmth of God's spirit the moment they entered the attic of the temple. They signed their names in a logbook that would serve as a lasting record of those who performed the Earthly ordinance. The ceremony was filled with symbolism and helped them understand that life on the Earth was part of their loving Heavenly Father's plan, providing experiences that helped them mature as they exercised their faith in Him. It was especially sweet to be together to share that precious experience; each of them overflowed with gratitude for the sacrifices Joseph Smith had made to restore that knowledge to the Earth.

The persecution had become unbearable, so Brigham Young directed that the temple be open day and night for eight days, during which time thousands and thousands of sacred ordinances were successfully completed. On February 4, Brigham directed the first group of Church members to leave during the night. It was an unusually cold night, and the wagons began lining up on Partridge Street, overflowing onto streets throughout the city.

Daniel's wagon and his father's wagon were packed and ready to begin the trip west. The entire family was in the house, making sure Thomas was wrapped warmly, and bidding a final farewell to their warm home.

"I am so thankful we will be making this journey together," Mary said. "I remember when you left Kirtland, Daniel, and we were so lonely there when you were gone. I did not mind leaving Independence quite as much, since the three of us left together. And now, here we are, three generations, all traveling together." Her eyes filled with tears and she shook her head slightly in an effort to gain control of her emotions. "I love each one of you more than I can say."

"Oh, Mother, I love you, too." Victoria sighed as they warmly embraced each other.

"Let me take one last look at my rocking chair, and I'll be ready," Mary said as she quickly stepped into the bedroom.

"I can make you another one as soon as we are settled in our new home," William assured her.

"We'll go ahead and get Thomas settled in our wagon," Daniel said.

"I'm sure she just wanted to wipe away her tears," William said. "I'll get her and then we can begin our *great adventure*."

Daniel watched Victoria spread out the new quilt his mother had finished a few days earlier for her first grandchild and wrap it securely around their tiny son.

"Ready," Victoria said as she held Thomas closely against her. "Let's go." She smiled at Daniel and stood on her tiptoes to kiss his cheek.

"Daniel! Come quick!"

Daniel felt a sudden tightness in his chest. He had never heard his father sound so alarmed. He bounded to the bedroom doorway and saw his father kneeling before the rocking chair where his mother sat.

William was sobbing and Mary looked as though she had fallen asleep. "Mary, Mary," he cried. "Don't leave me, Mary."

Daniel knelt by the side of the chair and touched his mother's hand. It was warm and she looked so peaceful. "Mother."

"She's gone, Daniel." William laid his head in his wife's lap and his shoulders heaved as deep sobs racked his body. "She's gone."

Victoria stood in the doorway holding Thomas, and closed her eyes tightly as immense sorrow washed over her. Tears flowed freely, even as the wagons began to slowly move past their house. Passing friends, seeing the two wagons still waiting in front of their house, smiled and commented how the new baby must have slowed them a little; not one of them realized that the journey Mary had just begun was not an Earthly one.

"I've just been to see the man who had purchased our home and shop," Daniel said as he took off his coat and hat and shook the snow off them. He hung them on the hook near the fireplace and held his hands close to the fire in an attempt to warm them. "He accepted the return of the money he paid you, Father, and said he was fine with the whole thing because he would just wait until we snuck out of town some night and he could get it all for nothing. But then, before I left, he said he might still be interested in buying it because that would eliminate the need to duke it out with someone else when it was empty."

"Well, at least we still have our home," William said softly from where he sat near the window.

"And our shop, Father," Daniel reminded him. "And there are still lots of people needing wagons before they can leave here."

"That's good," his father said quietly.

Daniel looked at Victoria and she shrugged her shoulder. William had been overwhelmed with sadness since Mary's death, completely inconsolable.

"I'm going to re-open the shop in the morning and see what business I can stir up. Will you be going with me, Father?"

"I don't know, son. I would like to walk over to the cemetery. Will you go with me?"

"Yes, of course I will," Daniel said. "We can go right now."

They put their coats and hats on and went out in the freezing wind. Victoria watched them from the front room window until they disappeared in the blowing snow. She sighed and went in the kitchen to start preparing dinner.

It had taken two days to unload their wagons, even with the help of the people who bought them. Mary's funeral arrangements had kept their minds occupied for a few days, but dealing with their grief now seemed to be the only thing any of them accomplished. Every place they looked, everything they touched, every time they held Thomas – it all reminded them of Mary.

William went with Daniel the next morning, and they spent several hours returning everything to the same spot it had occupied before they sold the shop. At noon, they were preparing to leave and go eat lunch when the door swung open and an old friend entered. "Good morning, Andrew. What can we do for you?"

"Are you still making wagons?"

"Yes. Are you ready to leave Nauvoo?"

"I'm hoping to be ready in a week or two, but I don't have a wagon yet. I don't really need a fancy wagon, just . . ."

"We can make just what you need," Daniel said. "You tell us how much money you have to spend on a wagon and we'll build you a sturdy wagon that will fill your needs. How does that sound?"

"Sounds perfect," Andrew said as he pulled a roll of paper money from his pocket and laid it on the worktable.

"How many people will be traveling in your wagon," Daniel asked as he counted the money.

"Five, and a small baby," Andrew answered, patiently waiting for Daniel to finish.

"Okay, you have more than enough to buy a wagon." He handed a much smaller roll of money back to Andrew, who made no move to take it. "You still have enough to buy a few more warm blankets."

"But I was sure I had the right amount. Brother Singleton told me how much his wagon cost and . . ."

"The price of each wagon depends on how much we have to pay for the materials, and we just got a great price on wood and an even better price on iron the blacksmith left behind," Daniel said.

"Oh, well, thank you. Can you tell me when it will be ready?"

"I'll have to go through my inventory and make sure we have everything we need, but I should be able to give you a good estimate tomorrow. Will that work for you?"

"Sure. Thanks. Oh, and I am so sorry to hear about your mother . . . your Mary," Andrew said to William.

"Thanks, Andrew," William said.

After Andrew left the store, William asked, "How is it that I never heard anything about iron the blacksmith left behind? And, uh, where have you been hiding all this wood you got for such a great price?"

"Father, I'll show you that wood, just as soon as I get back from the sawmill. You'll see what a great deal it is."

William laughed, and this time his smile reached his eyes. "Let's go eat lunch," he said.

Business at the shop was not as brisk as it had been before the initial departure early in February. However, it was steady and kept William's mind occupied, at least part of the time. Each week or so another group departed, leaving more houses abandoned. The mobs did not seem to think departures were happening quickly enough, however, so there were constant reports of families being pulled from their houses during the night and attacked, or a specific neighborhood being targeted for days in a row.

Daniel and Victoria spent a lot of time at the Mansion House. Emma had chosen to stay in Nauvoo; Joseph's mother lived with her in the Mansion House and was too frail to make the trip west. In addition, the group that could not accept Brigham Young as their new Prophet felt Emma's son should become the successor to Joseph, and they provided constant help and support for her. For some unknown reason, those that aligned themselves with this new group seemed to pose less of a threat to the mobs. Since Daniel and Victoria's home was not far from the Mansion House, they benefited from the decline of violence in their area of town.

With each passing month, Daniel could see his father's will to live fade. He grew quieter, and the loneliness that emanated from him saddened everyone who knew and loved him. Still, he got up each morning and went to the woodshop with Daniel, and each day he helped build wagons for those who lacked the necessary funds to leave Nauvoo.

The warm fall afternoon allowed Daniel and Victoria to stroll along the edge of the river. "Did you hear that news has arrived from Salt Lake?"

"Of course I heard," Victoria answered with a quick laugh. "News travels very fast among the Sisters. But surely you know that by now."

"Just checking," Daniel said.

"Do you regret that we didn't leave earlier?" Victoria asked. "We could be in Salt Lake, strolling along the edge of a salt lake, whatever that is, rather than the river?"

"No, no regrets. I feel very strongly that Father and I were supposed to stay behind and help those who could not leave on their own. What about you? Do you regret that we are still here?"

"No. I'm happy I've had time to spend with Emma and help with her mother-in-law. Plus, with another baby coming, I'm happy to be in a nice warm house now that winter is approaching."

"I pray every day that we'll be allowed to stay and not be forced from our home in the midst of winter. And every day I wonder if Father can make the trip."

"Then, for now, we will concentrate on enjoying this beautiful evening and leave the future in God's hands," Victoria said.

All winter Daniel watched his father's health deteriorate. When the weather became warm enough for some of the poorer saints to contemplate departing Nauvoo, William seemed to perk up as he realized his skills were still needed and would make a difference in their chances of survival. He asked every customer if they knew of others who were too poor to consider leaving. When word of his willingness to help began to spread, he and Daniel were busy all day long, six days a week. The only drawback was that every wagon they built depleted their personal funds.

Daniel held his new baby daughter in his arms and seemed unable to remove the smile that spread across his face. "She's beautiful, Sweetheart."

"Emma seemed pleased when I told her we had decided to name our baby after her. Have you noticed that Thomas seems to love everything about having a baby sister? I was so afraid that a two year old would feel a little jealous of a new family member, but Thomas loves to sit on the little wooden stool his grandfather made for him and tickle her toes or giggle at how tiny her little fingers are."

"Maybe it's time for us to consider leaving Nauvoo," Daniel said as he rocked his daughter. "Emma is strong and healthy, and Father seems stronger and finally able to move forward without Mother."

"I hope we can wait at least a few weeks," Victoria said. "I know I sound ungrateful since we've been so blessed, but that is my hope."

The sound of the front door opening brought excited greetings from Thomas as he ran toward William. "Grandfather! Grandfather!"

William bent to swoop Thomas into his arms and walked into the bedroom. "And how is your new little sister doing?"

"Emma," Thomas said as he smiled.

"How are things at the shop?" Daniel asked. "Anything new?"

"The new residents of Nauvoo are getting restless."

"The new residents?" Daniel asked as he stood and delivered Emma into Victoria's waiting arms. He sensed that Victoria could easily survive without hearing what did not sound like good news. "We'll go in the living room so you can rest," he said, bending to kiss her.

"Come on, little man," William said as he carried Thomas out of the room. "Mommy and Emma need a nap."

Daniel pulled the bedroom door shut behind him and followed his father into the living room. "What are the mobs up to now?"

"It seems they've reached the end of their patience. They have issued a deadline. They say that anyone still in Nauvoo after that time, who will not denounce the Church, will be killed as soon as they are found. There are still saints living in town who have no means available to leave. I think we're going to be very busy if any of them have a chance to get out of here with their lives."

"When is the deadline?" Daniel asked, wondering how they could possibly help anyone else and still have enough to provide for themselves.

"October. That only gives us two months. We usually have good weather in August and September, so that is a blessing. Then we'll have to pack up and be on our way, too."

"I'll find a sister that can help Victoria for a few days and we can start right away." Daniel took a deep breath and looked directly at his father. "You know we don't have any resources to spare. We barely have enough to get ourselves provisioned and on the road. But we'll do what we can."

"The Lord will help us find the resources we need. I'll talk to the man who paid us for the house when we were going to leave . . . before . . . and maybe that will give us a little extra money to work with."

The weeks flew by. After helping everyone they could, all efforts were turned to building their own wagon. The man who had originally wanted to buy William's home and the woodshop was still interested, but not willing to pay as much. The small amount offered was genuinely appreciated, and by the first week of October, they were packed and ready to leave.

Two difficult goodbyes remained: one last visit to Mary's grave, and hugging Emma one last time. She had become a very dear friend, and they were saddened that they would never see her again. The goodbyes were completed shortly after dawn, and emotions were at the breaking point by the time Daniel's wagon reached the far side of the Mississippi River. He pulled to a stop so they could bid Nauvoo one final farewell.

"The sunrise makes the temple look as though it's on fire."

"The sun has long since risen, my Dear," Daniel gently corrected. "I believe the temple is on fire."

"No," gasped Victoria.

William never said a word, but took Victoria's hand and squeezed it tightly. Daniel sighed as he watched the entire temple roof blaze. Years of work and sacrifice were destroyed in only moments. Even as he watched the fire spread, he felt a sense of pride knowing the spindles and railings he had helped his father build were of the best workmanship they could produce. Victoria remembered the sacrifices made by the Sisters who saved pennies to purchase nails and imported glass. No matter how many days the temple had been in use, it had been built for the Lord; it was a tribute to the efforts of the saints that it had been worthy of His presence.

"I see other fires," William said quietly.

As the temple burned, fires began burning in some neighborhoods, and gunshots could be heard. They hoped the shots were celebrations, rather than fulfilled promises.

Daniel turned the wagon away from Nauvoo. It was too late in the year to start for Salt Lake so they decided to make their way to Iowa City. Emma was not quite three months old and they did not have enough money to provide shelter for the winter unless Daniel could find work.

After becoming accustomed to the gradual decline in Nauvoo, they were all shocked to see that Iowa City was a thriving town. There were many members of the Church in the area, but since they were only passing through and purchased supplies when they arrived, no hatred or persecution was experienced. "Lots of work and no mobs? I like this place," Daniel said.

"There seem to be lots of wagons parked over there," William said. "Some are in need of repair, and there are some for sale."

"There are families living in that one," Victoria stated.

"I think I'll be able to find work, so you don't have to worry about spending the winter in a wagon, Sweetheart."

Daniel temporarily worked for a furniture maker until he was able to establish himself as a wagon maker. He made wagons all winter long in preparation for the steady flow of saints that would begin passing through on their way to Salt Lake beginning in the spring. He found a small house where his family could be comfortable until warm weather arrived, and worked hard to replenish their reserves.

By Christmas, it became apparent that circumstances beyond their control were again in charge of their lives. William's health again began to fail. Daniel and Victoria determined they were content to stay in Iowa City as long as God allowed William to be with them.

The huge migration of people from Europe that wanted to become pioneers of the American West caused the accepted mode of travel in slower, more expensive wagons to shift to quicker and less expensive handcarts. Consequently, Daniel shifted his efforts to the building of handcarts. He established a growing business and the years quickly passed; his family grew with the addition of their third child, a boy they named William but chose to call Will.

William's health seemed to improve and decline on an unpredictable schedule. After seven uneventful but comfortable years had passed, William went to sleep one evening and never woke up. Even though he had been in poor health since they left Nauvoo, his death was unexpected.

"Remember how overwhelmingly sad we were when Mother died?" Daniel asked his wife the evening they buried William.

"Yes, I remember. I thought I would never be able to stop crying."

"I know Grandpa and Grandma are together now, but I'm still sad," ten-year old Thomas said."

"It is sad that we won't get to see him every day," Daniel told his son, "but it's only sad for us, and sometimes it's hard to remember that."

"Is Grandpa young again?" Emma asked with the simple faith of an eight-year old.

"Yes," Victoria answered. "He is young again, just like your daddy. Grandma is young, too. And now they get to be together forever and live in heaven with Heavenly Father."

"Well," Emma said as she sniffed, "I guess I should be happy then, but I miss Grandpa too much to be happy right now." She immediately burst into full-fledged sobbing and ran to her mother. Victoria quickly handed Will to Daniel and pulled Emma into her lap.

"You just go right ahead and cry, Honey," she soothed as she ran her fingers through Emma's long brown hair and rocked her slowly back and forth. "I think we should cry whenever we feel sad. Pretty soon we'll be able to remember Grandpa without crying, but for now, you just go right ahead and cry.

ASSISTANCE FROM ANGELS

"We have a big decision to make," Daniel said to Victoria after the children had gone to bed. "I know we thought we would be spending the winter here in Iowa City, but today I heard there will be two more handcart companies leaving this month."

"Isn't it too late for companies to be leaving?"

"As a rule, that has been the case," Daniel agreed. "But a missionary named James Willie has brought a huge group of converts back from England, and they're in a real bind. They are like the people you told me about in England, who used every cent they had to get here. These people are all using the Perpetual Emigrating Fund to get to the Salt Lake Valley."

"I know many of the people you have helped during the past few years have used that, but I don't understand how it works."

"It's a great idea," Daniel explained. "I'm not sure if their railroad passage was provided as part of this fund, but I know that some of the handcarts I made in the past were purchased by the Church and given to those who were sponsored by this fund. They also receive the provisions they need, and then when they reach the Salt Lake Valley they repay the Church in whatever way they can: cash, commodities or labor. That money is then used to help another convert."

"That's wonderful. Otherwise, those poor souls would never earn enough money to pay their own way to the Valley."

"Here's my concern. Some of the handcarts are being built with green wood, because there's no more dried wood available, and they cannot wait until more wood can be dried. These people need someone traveling with them who can repair their handcarts as they begin to dry out and break apart."

"And you can certainly do that," Victoria agreed.

"Since they have no money for provisions to winter over until spring, I don't see that they have any choice about leaving this late in the season, no matter what. They left England a little late and have run into one delay after another, and these unseasoned handcarts are going to do nothing but slow them down once they begin traveling."

"What is the decision you're trying to make, Daniel?" Victoria felt a little knot begin to grow inside her chest.

"We can stay in our warm house this winter where our children will be safe, and we can wait one more year to leave for the Valley. Or," and Daniel reached out and took his wife's hand in his own, "we can help them the only way I know how to help them. If I had enough money to feed all of them this winter, that's what I would be suggesting to you, but we have spent our money helping those we could, and now all I can offer is my knowledge to help keep their handcarts in one piece so they can make it to the Valley."

"This is a big decision. Have you prayed about it, Sweetheart?"

"Yes, but I'm asking you to pray with me tonight so we can make this decision together. This involves you and every one of those sweet spirits God has entrusted to us. I want to help, I think it's the right thing to do, but I don't want to put any of you at risk."

"Daniel, I'm not trying to make up your mind for you, but ever since the sad day when your mother passed away, I've watched as everyone around us has put their faith on the line. They took their newborn babes and headed across the frontier. Some put their aging parents and their frail, weak family members in covered wagons and followed the Prophet's counsel to move west. I know you've been placed in a position where you could better help people by staying behind, and I'm not saying you ever made a single decision so we wouldn't have to test our faith in that manner. All I'm saying is that if this is the time we need to put our complete trust in God and take our family to the Salt Lake Valley with the poor converts who have no choice but to leave, even though it would be better to winter over somewhere, then I accept that. I already know you're willing to do that, and I want you to know I'm willing to do that, too."

Daniel let his tears fall unchecked and slowly shook his head. "I have no idea what I ever did to deserve having you as my wife, but I am very grateful that you are. You are amazing. No matter what I ask of you or what the Lord asks of us, the only thing you ever ask is have I prayed about it. I love you more than I can ever put into words, and I will love you until the end of time."

The confirmation they received from the Holy Spirit was undeniable. Twice they had built a wagon, filled it with provisions and a few precious possessions, and committed to head west. But now that they finally were going to complete the journey to the Salt Lake Valley, they would be traveling with a handcart, a wooden wheelbarrow with a box that measured three-feet by four-feet, with eight-inch tall walls around the edges. The box was centered over a single axle with wagon-style wheels. A cross bar extended from the front of the box, and the cart was moved forward by a person leaning forward against the bar and pushing. Their handcart was covered with a bow-frame canvas assembly, much like a miniature covered wagon. Daniel's family of five was allowed 500 pounds of provisions and possessions, which included seventeen pounds of clothing and bedding each for Daniel and Victoria, and ten pounds for each of the three children. That meant they would be limited to 435 pounds of food, which they immediately began to purchase.

On July 15, 1856, Daniel and his family left Iowa City with the other 120 handcarts that made up the James G. Willie Handcart Company. The company's tents were carried in five wagons. The country between Iowa City and Florence was flat and relatively easy traveling, and they covered it in less than four weeks. By that time, they had become acquainted with a large portion of the 500 people in the group. The heat and dust did not seem to dampen spirits in any manner. That is not to say every member of the Company was happy in spirit.

"Papa, I am ten years old and I don't like to be called Thomas. My friends make fun of me. Can't you please call me Tom from now on?"

"I think I could get used to that. Your mother might have a problem with that, though. You see, there is something inside a woman that makes them call you by your full given name whenever they want to get your undivided attention. So, just be prepared for that, all right?"

Tom laughed, and then said, "Okay."

"And," said Daniel, "I understand you are unhappy about something else. Anyway, that is what I heard from your little sister. I believe it has something to do with your chores."

"I don't like my chores, Papa. Can I do something else?"

"Well, let's see. If you were still four years old and we were still calling you Thomas, I suppose you could just ride along in the cart, like

Will. If you were a few years older, you could be helping pull the cart. However, you're right in the middle. Do you think your friend James would like it if you got to do different chores than he does?"

"Probably not," Tom agreed, "but he's only eight and I'm ten. Isn't there something else I can have for a chore?"

"How would you feel about helping the girls collect buffalo chips to use to build fires. No wait, I think they also have to help their mothers cook dinner and you probably would not like that."

"No, I already have to help dry dishes every time we have a meal."

"So what exactly is this terrible chore you hate so much?"

"You know, Papa. I have to clean the dirt out of the livestock's nose at night, and it's a terrible chore. I think about it all day, and I feel like I'm going to throw up every time I have to do it."

"Well, maybe we could teach those animals to blow their nose. I'll make a deal with you, son. If you can teach our animals to blow their own noses, you won't have to clean them out ever again. Deal?"

"Papa, how can I teach an animal to blow their nose?"

"I don't know, Tom. That's why you have to clean it out every night, so they don't suffocate and die from walking all day in that dust. I bet if you think about it hard enough, you can figure out a way. Maybe you will decide it's just easier to clean out their dirty noses than work for hours trying to train them. You decide, and let me know."

Tom sighed and shrugged his shoulders. "Okay, Papa. But I still won't like having that as my chore."

Daniel told Victoria about his conversation with Tom, and during the next few days, they watched Tom examine the livestock's noses and try a few ideas of his own about alternate ways to perform his chore. After a while, they noticed he hurried to get his chore done as soon as they stopped for the day.

It was not long before Daniel could see the importance of his decision to come with the company. Some nights, so many handcarts needed repaired that he had to recruit help to get them all completed. One or two of the older boys became permanent helpers and that allowed Daniel to sleep some.

When they reached the Missouri River, they crossed it on a steam ferryboat and camped at the town of Florence, six miles from Omaha.

They were delayed there almost a week making repairs and final preparations before crossing the plains.

Daniel and Victoria, and every other member of the company, were aware of the growing division in the Company about whether or not it was too late to begin crossing the plains. Daniel spoke with many while he repaired their handcarts, and one afternoon he met a man named Levi Savage.

"I've made the trek to Salt Lake City several times and I know the dangers of leaving so late in the year," he told Daniel.

"How is it you have made that trip so many times?" Daniel asked.

"I've served a few missions. Even went to Burma once, and lots of places. But a body does not need to be a world traveler to know leaving this late in the year is foolish. Do you have any idea why so many are opposed to wintering over?"

"I know they don't have enough money to feed their families through the winter, so that may be a factor," Daniel said.

"I understand their plight," Levi said. "But I myself am not in favor of, but much opposed to taking women and children through when they are destitute of clothing, when we all know that we are bound to be caught in the snow and severe cold weather long before we reach the valley."

Daniel stopped working and sat up to face Levi. "Is it that dangerous? I knew the company was leaving a little later than most do, but you sound sincerely concerned."

"Each is entitled to their opinion, and that is mine," Levi answered.

Daniel had prayed fervently before joining the company. He had specifically asked if his service was needed badly enough by this company to warrant taking his family and traveling with them. He and Victoria had both been certain of the answer they received. They had been concerned, but he was confident that it had been the Lord's wish for them to join the company.

When Captain Willey called a meeting of the entire company, everyone was anxious to hear both sides of the debate. Captain Willie exhorted the Saints to go forward regardless of suffering even to death. Then he asked Brother Savage to share his thoughts.

"Brother Willie. If I am to speak, I must speak my mind, let it cut where it will."

"Please do so," Captain Willie responded.

"Very well. Brothers and Sisters. If we proceed with this journey, we should expect to endure hardships. We are liable to have to wade in snow up to our knees and lay ourselves in a thin blanket and lie on the frozen ground without a bed. Traveling with handcarts is not like having a wagon that we could go into and wrap ourselves in as much as we like and lay down. No, we are without wagons, destitute of clothing and could not carry it if we had it. We must go as we are. The handcart system I do not condemn. The lateness of the season is my only objection to leaving this place for the mountains at this time."

Captain Willie again exhorted the group's members to have faith.

Elder Atwood asked to speak. "I exhort you to pray to God and get a revelation and know for yourselves whether you should go or stay, for it is your privilege to know for yourselves."

When Levi Savage again addressed the group, Daniel and Victoria were taught first-hand the courage of a true disciple of Jesus.

"Brethren and Sisters, what I have said I know to be true, but seeing you are to go forward, I will go with you, will help you all I can, will work with you, will rest with you, will suffer with you, and if necessary I will die with you. May God have mercy, bless and preserve us."

After praying and wanting to follow their leaders, the majority of the Saints decided to make the journey. On August 18, the Willie Company left Florence. The trek became more difficult each day.

"You look so tired, Daniel," Victoria said when he finally came back to their camp after helping make repairs until late into the night.

"I am tired," he answered, "but so is everyone else. Have you seen how people are discarding things from their cart to lighten the load?"

"Yes, I have also seen many of the younger children being set down to walk during parts of the day. Everyone is growing tired."

Daniel continued, "We are still averaging between fifteen to twenty miles each day. However, the stragglers used to arrive in camp before those who arrived first had finished gathering firewood. Then I noticed they were not arriving until after the livestock had been watered and the fires had burned long enough to already have coals ready to cook on. Each night, the last group drags into camp later and later. Some are already becoming too weak to walk the entire day, and you can hear more people coughing and having accidents because they are so exhausted. The handcarts are constantly breaking. We are already so late to be crossing the Rockies, and yet we have to hold camp so people can regain the strength they need to continue."

"I am hearing many women express their fear that their husbands will drop dead because they're so tired every night. I try to encourage them, but they are so tired themselves it's difficult."

"That is concerning," Daniel said, already nearly asleep.

Since the children had to walk most of the day, they were also becoming exhausted. If they were old enough to help, they had daily chores that kept them busy until bedtime each night. One evening as the children began their chores, Emma teased Tom about the undesirable task he was required to perform every evening.

"That's pretty funny," Tom returned, "since you're headed out to pick up buffalo chips." He laughed as he watched her walk away.

Emma realized he was right and it made her start thinking about what it was she piled into her apron each evening. Feeling a little sorry for herself, she wandered from the other young girls as she began to look for the desired fuel. Raising the bottom edge of her apron, she began filling it with dried chips. Suddenly her worn apron ripped and the chips dropped to the ground. For the first time, Emma actually looked at the condition of her apron. Then she looked at her filthy yellow dress showing through the hole in the apron. Looking at her sleeves, she noticed the once beautiful white lace was now dirty and brown, torn, hanging in places and missing in other spots.

Little Emma slowly sank to the ground. This had been her favorite dress because it reminded her of the fresh spring morning when her mother had given it to her. She always wore it to Church. She remembered walking past yards filled with gorgeous blooming flowers. Wearing her dress had always reminded her of her favorite flowers, yellow and white daisies.

She began to cry as she realized how far away from her home she really was. She had only been allowed to bring the dress she was wearing, and all the others had been left behind. She wished she could again smell the beautiful white and yellow flowers that always brought her such joy. Now all she could see were weeds, brush, and dirt. She looked back down at her torn apron and began to sob uncontrollably. She closed her eyes tightly so she could not see the ugly prairie. She slid down and laid on the warm ground, keeping her eyes squeezed tightly shut so she could pretend she was back home in her bedroom, enjoying the smell from the kitchen when her mother was cooking. Maybe, if she tried hard enough to remember every single detail, she would magically be back there again, lying on her bed.

Victoria noticed the young girls returning to camp but could not see Emma. "Margaret, where's Emma?" she asked one of the girls.

"Over there," the girl answered, pointing toward the prairie.

Victoria was immediately filled with fear for her daughter and began running through the brush, calling her daughter's name. *Dear Lord, she's only eight years old. She's alone and probably scared. There are wild animals and ... Please, Heavenly Father, help me find her.* Through the brush ahead, Victoria saw the familiar little yellow dress lying in a heap on the ground, unmoving. She felt her heart race and began running toward her daughter. *Please, God, don't let anything be wrong!* She pushed the unbidden but gruesome thoughts out of her mind and kept praying. When she reached the spot where Emma was laying, she scooped the small body into her arms. "Emma! Emma!" When she saw Emma's eyes slowly open, she cried, "Thank you! Emma, I found you!"

"Mommy."

Fresh tracks of clean skin made by tears that had washed a trail through the dirt on Emma's cheeks made Victoria smile. "What's wrong, Sweetheart?" she asked as Emma began sobbing.

Nothing Victoria said could convince Emma to talk. Each time Victoria tried to set her down, she wrapped her arms tightly around her mother's neck and refused to let go.

Neither Victoria nor Emma ate much dinner. As Emma sat cuddled in her mother's arms next to the fire that evening, she finally began telling her about all the things she missed so terribly. Her words became slower and slower as she drifted off to sleep. Victoria rocked Emma back and forth, as she had done when she was a baby. *Could that really have been in the same lifetime,* Victoria wondered? It seemed impossible that she had once held her tiny baby girl in her arms, sitting in the comfort of her home, watching her fall asleep while they slowly rocked back and forth.

I have to be strong for my family or they might not make it to the Valley. Looking down at Emma, she remembered the morning she had given her the yellow and white dress, and now it was tattered and worn. As she ran her fingers through her daughter's long dark hair, she felt the gritty dirt in the tangled mass. She remembered sitting on the porch, brushing Emma's hair as sunlight reflected from her flowing curls. How she ached inside as she realized that her little girl could no longer be the carefree child she remembered. Victoria's tears now began to wash the day's dirt from her cheeks also.

It was late when Daniel and Tom returned to their campsite. Daniel pulled a couple blankets from the cart and placed them around his wife and daughter. Tom got a blanket and curled up against his mother's side. He was exhausted from the day's work and was asleep in minutes. Daniel was exhausted but sat looking at his bedraggled family. *Every day takes its toll. Please watch over my family, God.*

He stood and walked a short distance into the dark night and fell to his knees. He wanted to pray to his Father in Heaven but he did not know where to begin. So many memories of the past and questions of the future raced through his mind. He sat for some time before simply asking his Father to protect his family and relieve their sorrowful hearts. Daniel felt he should say more, but could not seem to organize the words. Then a strong awareness washed over him that his Father knew the feelings of his heart and of his family's plight. Exhausted, Daniel, too, returned to his family and was quickly asleep.

"Everyone knows our supplies are alarmingly low, but each day we get closer to Fort Laramie in Wyoming. There we can pick up the remainder of the goods needed to sustain us until we reach Salt Lake."

Daniel looked up from the wheel he was repairing. "And you believe we have sufficient to get us there?"

"We have no choice but to believe. Every day we see miracles happening all around us. Look how you've been able to keep our handcarts patched together."

Daniel replayed that conversation in his mind when the handcart company finally arrived at the post in Casper. He was in the group of men who went directly to the dry goods store. When they entered the building, he could not make himself believe what his eyes were seeing.

"A wagon train came through several weeks ago," the store manager tried to explain. "No one knew you were still coming west. The wagon train believed they were the last group for the year and they filled their wagons with nearly all the food that remained on the shelves."

No one spoke, or moved, as though none of them could accept the reality of their situation. "It's already the end of September," someone said. "The Salt Lake Valley is at least two full months away, and someone else took all the food?"

"We'd better go find Captain Willey. This is going to be hard news to hear."

Surprisingly, the news was received without any visible emotion. "There are only two choices available," the Captain said. "We can stay at the settlement and starve during the winter, or we can continue on and hope we reach Salt Lake before our remaining meager supplies run out. With luck, maybe we'll get some wild game along the trail."

If there is one thing the Willie Handcart Company has not been, Daniel thought to himself, *it is lucky.*

Captain Willie called a meeting of the entire company so everyone would be aware of their present condition and future prospects. "There is only one possible solution. At our present rate of travel and consumption, our flour will be exhausted when we are still about 350 miles from the Valley. Our rations need to be reduced again, from one pound to three quarters of a pound per day. I am well aware that is barely enough to keep a person alive. That is our only alternative. At the same time, every effort must be made to travel faster."

No one voiced any complaint. Many fainted along the trail between Laramie and Independence Rock due to the lack of nourishment, and those who were too weak to make the required crossings of the North Platte River had to be assisted. When the wind blew a tent down during the night, it remained leveled until the next morning, as no one had the strength to fight the elements during the night. Each morning, Daniel and the other men collected the frozen bodies for burial, while family members sat physically and emotionally numb.

Victoria no longer had enough strength to help Daniel push the cart, and she had to put their infant son in the cart, as she was not strong enough to carry him. She felt guilty that her weakness caused additional concern for Daniel, but she was nearing the end of her ability to put one foot in front of the other and push forward. She watched as Tom and Emma began pushing from the rear corners of the cart to help their father, and felt even more guilt because she could not help them.

One night while they slept, the temperature began to drop. The first snowflakes of winter began falling on the high plains, and quickly covered the ground. Many members of the company were weak and became ill; some were forced to stop traveling while nursing the sick, or to bury those that died. Others pressed on, nearly unconscious, feeling the dangerous threat of winter nipping at their heels. Their supplies were nearly gone, and the plains did not provide any trees for shelter – even Daniel did not have enough energy to stalk wild game without trees for cover.

As the early winter storm continued to blanket everything in snow, Daniel slipped into a nearly hypnotic state, focusing every ounce of strength he possessed on pulling the cart. He could hear panic-stricken screams but they seemed far away. Eventually he recognized the cries were coming from his two oldest children.

"Papa, come help Mommy," Emma was pleading.

"Mom! Mom!" Tom was bent over Victoria, tears streaming down his face.

By the time Daniel pushed through the snow to reach them, he was nearly too weak to pull his wife to her feet. He pulled her arm across his shoulder, and she rallied enough to walk with his help. "Tom, can you push things aside in the cart to make room for your mother?"

"Yes," Tom said, as he hurried ahead. "I'll get Will out so there will be room for Mom."

"What's wrong with Mommy?" Emma cried.

"She's hungry and tired and very weak," Daniel said, "but she's going to be okay. We'll just let her ride for awhile." He laid her in the cart and reached for Will. After snuggling the baby close to her chest, he draped her arms around him and pulled her knees up, tucking her clothing around her legs and feet. Then he covered them with anything he could lay over them. Most of their clothing was completely worn out but he hoped they could share a little body heat.

Daniel once again began pulling the cart. He was not sure how much farther he would be able to pull considering the added weight. The snow was nearly six inches deep, but he could no longer feel the cold sting of the snow against his bare skin through the holes in his boots. In fact, his feet no longer seemed to be sensitive to the cold at all. He closed his eyes much of the time as he pulled against the blowing snow. He let his mind wander to earlier days and events in his life. His mind passed from one scene to the next. He remembered the warm days he spent with the survey party in the valley of Adam-ondi-Ahman and his visit with Joseph as the sun was setting. He felt warmth begin to flow through his body as if the sun were shining on him.

The weight of the cart brought him back to the present; it seemed to grow increasingly heavy. Daniel opened his eyes; the sun was definitely not shining on him, and directly ahead was a hill with a rather severe increase in grade. The cart felt so heavy that Daniel was afraid it was going to pull him backward. He leaned forward on the push bar and, with each step, pushed off with his toes, fearing it would be the last step he would be able to take.

Closing his eyes again, he returned to thoughts of better days. He began remembering the evening he and Victoria had spent with Joseph and Emma in their yard. A brief sadness came over him at the thought of all that had happened since then. Joseph and Hyrum had been killed, and Emma was left alone after having been through unbelievable amounts of persecution and fear. Joseph had been her anchor and her strength, and he was gone. She had been torn between friends and family who could not agree with one another. Even the leaders of the Church pulled back and forth, arguing about who should take Joseph's place as the Prophet and leader of the Church. She was so afraid that his entire life's work might have been in vain if those who followed him became fragmented and could not agree among themselves.

Daniel's mind instantly became clear on a matter he had long pondered. It was as if someone was walking him through the entire situation, making each point clear in his mind. He remembered the love that he had felt radiating from Joseph and Emma that night. Their love was eternal and undying, a love that he had not only seen, but had felt. Emma had proven herself through service with Joseph. People criticized her for not moving west with the rest of the saints, and others made excuses for her when she chose to stay in Nauvoo. Daniel was sure of only two things. The love shared by Joseph and Emma was incredibly strong, and the personal strengths each possessed made a whole unit that was instrumental in bringing the restored gospel back to the Earth. Secondly, even though he could never imagine anyone in heaven with Joseph but Emma, he was certain God knew their hearts and would reward them for their desires and intentions, as He does for each one of His children

Suddenly Daniel lost his footing and started to fall forward. The push bar no longer offered the resistance it had the moment before. He thought, perhaps, he had miraculously made it to the top already, but when he opened his eyes, he found himself still near the base of the incline. Unsure how he had acquired this new strength, he found himself struggling to keep up with the cart, as it seemed to be rolling up the hill as easily as it normally rolled downhill. Soon he crested the hill and found no difficulty continuing through the snow that was nearly to the top of his boots. He walked along the river to where many of the company had stopped.

"No need to set up camp," someone said to him. "It won't take long to eat what little food remains."

"Good," Daniel muttered in return. He sank under the push bar of his handcart and slowly trudged through the snow to the back. "Victoria," he said as he gently moved the rags covering her and Will just enough to feel their skin. "Victoria."

"Is she okay?" Tom asked, as he and Emma neared the handcart.

"Yes, you two need to get in and help keep her warm," Daniel said. "Will is nice and warm, and you should lay next to him, Emma. He'll help keep you warm too. Then you can lie on your Mom's legs, Tom. Here, tuck your hands under Will so they will stay warm. I'll cover you all with these rags." Daniel pushed the rags tightly against them and scoured the handcart for anything he had previously missed that could be used to help protect his family from the cold. He slid to the ground and leaned his head against the box of his handcart.

"Keep breathing," he said to himself and to his family that he loved so dearly. "Just survive."

The snow continued falling until it was a foot deep, even though October was only half over. Many who drug their handcarts into the camp after he arrived moved a short distance further to a natural cove in the rocks, hoping to find a little additional protection from the wind. Daniel pulled his coat tighter around him and tried to pull his shoulders up to better shield his head and neck from the howling wind. He could not tell if the temperature was dropping or if he was just getting colder because he had stopped walking.

The night was unbearably cold, and occasionally the shuffle and creaking of another straggler arriving at the camp would shortly register with Daniel, but he quickly returned to the solitude of his fitful sleep interspersed with vivid flashes of memories and moments of fear and concern for his family.

When daylight arrived, Daniel joined the men who worked their way through the camp in order to determine how many of their number would require burial. There were ten, five men and five women. With no materials or energy to build coffins, Daniel and another man made every effort to dig a shallow grave. The ground was frozen, so they scraped it as clean as they could, laid the bodies together, and covered them with rocks or whatever could be found under the snow to provide as much protection as possible against wolves and coyotes.

Daniel was one of the few healthy enough to perform ordinary camp duties and look after the sick. Little could be done, as there was no food to nourish them, and no possibility of taking them closer to their destination. He resumed his vigil at the back of his handcart, checking often to make sure everyone was still breathing. He sank to the ground and waited for his breathing to slow down – the exertion from caring for the dead had left him gasping for air.

Daniel looked to the west. Was their final destination just beyond the edge of the place that faded into a white blur of snow, or was it days and days further away. When they reached the Valley, would people be lined up on both sides of the group as they slowly entered the city? Would the new arrivals be welcomed and fed? Would they be able to see the city when they were a mile away? Half a mile?

"Do you see that?" he heard someone ask.

He slowly looked around to determine who had spoken.

"I must be seeing things," someone else said.

A person nearby stood and touched Daniel's shoulder. "Look."

Daniel looked toward the man to see where he was looking. Then he turned toward that direction, but all he could see was snow blowing in the air, snow covering rock formations, snow swaying back and forth on bushes blowing in the wind. "What is that?" He grasped the edge of his handcart and pulled himself up. He could see something dark moving in the snow, but he could not determine what it was. "What is it?" he asked the man standing close to him.

"Deliverance."

No one near Daniel moved, other than to stand, as if standing would bring a clearer view of whatever continued to approach their camp. It slowly became apparent it was two men on horseback heading toward their group. The horses stopped directly in front of Daniel, and still no one near Daniel said anything or moved in the direction of the two young men.

"We have brought a little flour for you."

"Are you from Salt Lake?" someone behind Daniel asked.

"Yes, we're a day or two ahead of a rescue party. Do you think you can press forward toward them?"

Captain Willie stepped past Daniel and reached to shake hands with the two men on horseback. "Some members of my company are so weak they cannot even pull themselves through snow this deep. I will take one man and search for the rescue party in order to direct them to our aid as quickly as possible."

"We didn't bring much," one rider said as he pulled a sack of flour from his horse and let it drop into the snow. "I hope it will be of some help until the rescue party reaches you."

"It is much appreciated," Captain Willie said. "We are eating the last crumbs of what food we had left. Each morning we collect the souls who did not make it through the night, and I believe this will mean the difference between death and survival to some of the members of my company."

"We have to leave now. The Martin Company is behind you yet. They left two weeks after you did and we fear they are in even worse condition." The two young men climbed back onto their horses and headed toward Independence Rock.

Many shouted a hearty "God bless you" or "thank you" as the riders disappeared in the distance. Captain Willie and Joseph Elder rode in the opposite direction in search of the rescue party.

The flour was received with grateful hearts and those that were able filled cooking pots with snow and built small fires, sharing the precious flour amongst everyone.

Two days later, hunger returned. Some found it hard to remember if they had actually held warm bowls of broth in their hands or only dreamed of it. Nevertheless, spirits that had begun to lose their newly found hope were buoyed up when the supply wagon arrived. One of the wagons stopped near where Daniel was slumped to the ground in front of the handcart that held his entire family. One of the rescuers reached into the wagon and pulled a stack of blankets over the side. He offered one to the man standing by Daniel, and it was accepted in silence.

"We have blankets and warm clothes for all of you," the other young man said, as he, too, began pulling bundles of blankets and coats from the wagon.

"Let's get you warmed up," the man said as he handed a blanket to Daniel. When Daniel turned to lay the blanket over his family, the young man asked, "Is there someone in your cart?" He stepped to one side and slowly moved the rags. "Oh, my," he said. He laid down the stack of blankets and bent to pick up Emma, wrapping one of the blankets tightly around her as he gently rocked her and rubbed her arms and legs through the blanket. "Here, little one," he said as he secured the blanket and laid her back in the cart. He threw a large quilt over Victoria as he leaned down and lifted Will, immediately wrapping him in a small wool blanket. "Is this your son?" he asked Daniel.

"Yes," Daniel answered. The question seemed to pull Daniel from the dream-like vision he had been watching, and he reached out to take Will.

"Victoria. Victoria," he said, and she slowly opened her eyes. "Help has arrived," he said. He pulled her toward him until she scooted a little ways and stood. She hugged her tattered quilt to her chest, and Daniel quickly wrapped another quilt around her and pulled her close, nestling Will between them.

"Daniel. Are you all right?" she asked weakly into his neck.

"Yes, and we have food and warm clothes. The kids all seem fine," he reassured his wife. "Our prayers have been answered."

The tiny groups that were spread out from Daniel's handcart to the rocks that provided some shelter slowly began to stir and show signs of life. The two young men were trying to encourage them to move, to gather round the fires they had built, and to eat the food being handed out.

More blankets were unloaded and food was stacked near the fires where people were gathering. A large barrel was rolled off the wagon and placed a short distance from the fire.

That evening the rescue party built large fires and made sure everyone was fed and settled in for a warm night's sleep. The rescuers were overwhelmed at the condition of the Willie Company and spent most of the night going from individual to individual in order to make sure each person had eaten something – they fed those that were too weak to feed themselves.

"Victoria, are you well?" Daniel asked the next morning as he held a bowl of warm cereal toward her. "Someone fixed breakfast for us all and brought it right to our tent."

"I'm much better. Amazing what a little food and a warm blanket or two can do to change one's outlook on life," she said warmly.

"I'm certain the entire camp slept well last night, knowing we're going to be okay," Daniel said. "The sad thing is that several people think we'll be arriving in the Salt Lake Valley day after tomorrow or the next day."

"I have no idea where we are," Victoria said. "Are we close to the Valley?"

"It's a thirteen-hundred mile trek from Iowa City to the Salt Lake Valley. We have come about nine hundred fifty miles, so we still have about three hundred fifty miles to travel."

"That far," Victoria said faintly.

"That far," echoed Daniel. "If we average fifteen miles a day, like we have been, we still have about twenty-five days of travel ahead of us. It's the twenty-first of October now, so that would mean we should reach the Valley before Thanksgiving. They brought wagons to carry those who cannot walk, so maybe we'll get there sooner. So many are weak or injured that it's going to be a very hard trip on them. Even if we arrived in the Valley tomorrow, some would not survive. It's been a heavy toll laid on this company."

"To come so far, through such suffering, and then die before reaching the Salt Lake Valley? That seems very sad to me," Victoria said.

"So many little bodies laid to rest out here on the desert," Daniel said slowly while shaking his head. "Very sad. You know, other than us, I hardly know of a single family that has not lost someone during this journey. We have been so very blessed."

"Remember Tom's little friend James?" Victoria looked up at Daniel and continued after he nodded his head. "He's going to lose his hand. His fingers have been so badly frozen the skin is falling off the bones. They have to amputate his hand. And he's only eight years old."

"We have to keep praying, very hard, during the rest of our trip that we will all arrive in the Salt Lake Valley safe and sound. We've already endured such suffering, and survived, that I'm very optimistic we can complete our journey," Daniel said with a smile.

When Victoria and the children had finished eating their breakfast, Daniel stood to gather up their bowls, but fell to the floor in pain.

"What is it?" Victoria cried out.

"What's wrong, Papa," Tom said as he jumped up and ran to kneel by his father.

Daniel could hardly focus on anything but the pain. "My feet, they feel like they're on fire," he said as he forced himself to remain calm.

"Let me see," Victoria said. She pulled Daniel's pant leg carefully away from his feet. He had removed his boots before going to sleep the night before, and it was the first time he had taken them off in a very long time. As she gently rolled down his sock, she saw the blackened skin where his feet had been frozen. "Daniel, your feet have been injured." She looked at the pain in her husband's eyes and tried to not let herself think of what he must be feeling.

"I haven't been able to feel my feet for several days," he admitted softly. "I guess there's nothing to do for it now." He looked at his children, who were quietly crying. "You know what, Tom? I think I'll let you take care of us until we get to the Salt Lake Valley, and I'll just lay around in the wagon and ride the rest of the way."

"Tom, we can get the tent folded up, can't we, son?" Victoria quickly wiped the tears from her face with the back of her hand and gathered up the bowls that were scattered on the ground.

"You ready to go, Daniel?" one of the young men from the rescue team asked as he neared the tent.

Daniel sighed and then pulled his shoulders back and said, "I think we'll need a little help today, Isaac."

Victoria pulled back the flap on the tent and stepped out. "Daniel's feet are frostbitten. I think he's going to have to ride in the wagon."

"How can I help?" Isaac asked as he stepped into the tent. He bent in front of Daniel and carefully lifted one foot at a time as he examined them. "Not an uncommon sight, but it does get you a permanent place in the wagon for the rest of the trip. Let's wrap this quilt around your feet and I'll carry you to the wagon. Then I'll be back to help get things packed up." Isaac wrapped Daniel's feet loosely and then picked him up and left the tent.

Victoria knelt down and pulled Tom and Emma close to her. "Your daddy's feet have been frostbitten, just like your friend's hand, Tom. He can't walk on them until they are healed up a bit, and we have to keep his feet warm. Remember how James cried because his hand hurt so badly? That's how your daddy is going to feel, so we have to help do his work. I know Heavenly Father will bless us and I know both of you will help me with Will. Let's ask Heavenly Father to help us and then get things packed up and be on our way."

Since no one knew if Daniel would ever be able to walk again, Isaac took it upon himself to be Daniel's constant assistant. He carried Daniel from his tent each morning and placed him in the wagon, and then in the evening, he carried him from the wagon to his tent. This proved to be harder for Daniel than anything he had faced during the entire trip. He had to watch as Isaac cared for his family's needs, and as he taught Tom how to serve others that needed help. Daniel felt proud and sad, both at the very same time.

Each day Daniel rode in the wagon with Emma and Will. Victoria became strong enough to help Tom push their handcart. When they got to Rocky Ridge, it was snowing and the wind was blowing hard from the northwest. It was decided to make camp and wait until morning to trek the five miles to the summit.

"I am so sorry I can't help you get the cart over the ridge," Daniel told Victoria that evening. "The wind is blowing so hard, not to mention the snow is pretty deep."

Victoria sank to the ground next to Daniel and took his hands in hers. "I'm not going to be alone. Isaac and Tom will both be helping, and we'll all be rested in the morning. I'm in much better shape than some of the Sisters who have lost their husbands, and we have been so blessed. Don't worry. Just pray for us all."

"Captain Willie has assigned several members of the camp to travel at the rear of the company so there's no chance you'll get left behind. And I'll be praying every minute that you'll receive help from God to get to the top." Daniel's helplessness and sense of defeat could be heard in his voice.

The next day dawned to a continuing snowstorm and biting winds. When the wagon stopped at Rock Creek to make camp that evening, Isaac carried Daniel to the tent while telling him that Tom had helped many people that afternoon. There was already a fire burning down to coals in front of the tent, and Victoria and Tom were inside the tent preparing dinner.

"You must have been praying very hard," Victoria sang out, "because it only took us ten hours to get across. Did you stay warm today?"

"Yes. You look well, considering the difficulty you must have endured today," Daniel said as he wrapped his feet in a quilt.

"It was not as hard as I feared, and Tom was so much help to me. He helped a lot of people today."

"Is that right, son?"

"It was mostly Isaac," Tom said with a shrug.

"Tom and Isaac together," Victoria said while she continued to cut pieces of meat from a slab in front of her. "You're growing up fast, Tom. You worked very hard today, and I'm extremely proud of you."

Daniel knew his prayers had been answered, and he smiled at the realization that his own son had provided the divine help he had prayed for. He smiled and said, "Good job, Tom. I heard the men that were sent to the rear of the company today are not all back yet. They already gathered up three wagons, eight handcarts and about forty people. If you hadn't helped, they would have had even more."

"Every day we get closer to the Valley," Victoria said, "and yet the weaker members of our group continue to fail. We still have to cross the Sweetwater River and get over one more mountain pass, but then we're home free."

Two days later, the company approached South Pass. They came upon an encampment of brethren from the Salt Lake Valley who had been bringing more meat to the stranded travelers. Several quarters of good fat beef hanging from the tree limbs proved to be a very good distraction, and it helped the weakened people focus on something other than the last hurdle standing between them and their new home.

"Can you feel the temperature getting warmer, the further down we go?" Victoria asked Tom as they descended from South Pass.

"I hate winter," Tom said. "Look, Mother, here comes another team from the Valley."

Victoria and Tom watched the wagon as it approached them.

"Running low on any supplies?" someone in the wagon asked.

"Do you have any salt?" Victoria asked, deciding it could not hurt to ask. Salt would greatly improve everything they ate.

"Surely do," came the answer. "Is that all you need?"

"Yes," Victoria said as she laughed and walked toward the wagon. "You are like angels who continually come to offer assistance." She accepted the bag of salt and then watched as the wagon moved east.

That evening while the family was enjoying their dinner, Daniel said, "This stew is so delicious."

"The angels in one of the rescue wagons gave me some salt. It's amazing what a difference it makes."

The next day, as Daniel rode in the wagon with Emma and Will, he allowed himself to feel positive his entire family would survive their journey. "Do you think you will have any happy memories about our trip to the Salt Lake Valley?" he asked his daughter.

"I think so," she said as she smiled at him. "Riding in the wagon with you is fun."

"A lot warmer than when you were riding in the handcart," he said, mostly to himself.

"Who helped you push our handcart?"

"Your mother helped, and I know you and Tom helped sometimes."

"But I mean who was that man who helped you push the handcart through the snow, remember? When it was really deep and it was cold."

Daniel wondered what specific situation Emma might be remembering. "Was it Isaac?" he asked, thinking she was a little confused.

"No, the man that wore white clothes and shined like the sun. I saw him come out of the sky and put his hands on the back of the cart, and he helped push until we got clear up to the top of the hill."

Daniel's mind flashed to the dream he had years earlier while he slept in the great valley. He wondered if he had ever told her about his dream. He felt the warmth of the Spirit wash over him. His daughter's words were not those of a confused little girl, but those of a child still pure and innocent enough to see through the veil.

"I think I remember what you're talking about, Emma. The man dressed in white who bent down and pushed the wagon to help me get over the hill."

"Yes, who was that man?"

"Emma, I think that was an angel who came down from heaven to help our family. I hope you never forget that special memory, Sweetheart, because as long as you can remember that man helping us, you will comprehend that Heavenly Father knows when we need help, and if we pray very hard, He will help us. That's a very happy memory."

Later, when Emma had succumbed to the gentle rocking motion of the wagon and fallen asleep, Daniel turned to face the wall of the wagon and poured out his heart to God. The tears flowed freely from his eyes. He knew that, for some reason, the Lord had provided him with exceptional strength and angelic help. Through this ordeal, his entire family was aided and allowed to survive. Why that had happened when so many others around him had died along the way, he knew he would probably never understand. However, he knew he would always be grateful for that.

He realized that when people learned of the many hardships endured and the staggering number of people who died along the way, some would say they should never have left that late in the season. Although he could never deny there had been overwhelming hardships during their trek, he knew he would never doubt God had been with them every step of the way.

"We made it," Daniel said softly to himself.

"I didn't think I would live to see this sight," a woman sitting close by said through the sobs that shook her frail body.

"But you did," Daniel said, gently patting her shoulder. "We might not be able to walk into Salt Lake, but we survived. And what could be better than to arrive on the Sabbath."

"And it's still twelve full days before Thanksgiving," uttered another of those riding in the wagon. "We have so many blessings to be grateful for this year."

When the wagon stopped, Isaac carried Daniel to where Victoria and Tom were standing by their handcart. "I'll sit you here in the cart, if you promise you won't walk."

"I promise," Daniel said. "Isaac, I would have never made it to the Valley if it weren't for you. I would have been one of the sixty-six souls who never . . ." Daniel had carefully planned what he wanted to say to Isaac when they reached Salt Lake; he had searched for exactly the right words so Isaac would understand how much he appreciated his help, and what a blessing he had been to his entire family. However, nothing could get past the lump in his throat and he could not stop the trembling of his lips. He could only look into Isaac's eyes and try to blink away the tears so he could see him clearly. "Thank you." was all he could say.

"Daniel, I didn't even come close to making the sacrifice you've made. I have been blessed to know you and be able to help you just a wee bit. I'll stay in touch to see how you're making out. Oh, and welcome to the Salt Lake Valley," Isaac said with a bright smile. "Welcome home!"

Isaac hugged Victoria and said, "I'll find you in a few days and see if I can be of help. Good luck."

"Thank you, Isaac. You have been an angel who came to save our family. Not one of us will ever forget you."

"The feeling is mutual, I assure you," Isaac said. Then he grabbed Tom in a warm hug. "You're nearly a grown man now, Tom. Thanks for all your help out there. You take good care of your mother and help your father, okay?

"Now where's my best girl?" Isaac said, as he pretended he could not see Emma standing right in front of him. "Oh, there you are." He swept her up in a big hug and sat her back down on the ground. "I hear you're going to get baptized pretty soon. Will you invite me?"

"Yes," Emma said. "Maybe I'll have a pretty new dress."

"See you later, little guy," Isaac said as he ruffled Will's hair.

The entire family watched as Isaac turned and walked away, quickly disappearing among the people that surrounded them.

"I can't believe all these people have come to greet us," Victoria said. Daniel could not help but smile because his wife sounded so happy.

"We made it," Daniel kept repeating. "We made it."

There were so many people swarming around the new arrivals that Daniel's senses seemed to be on overload – his eyes could only see a blur of faces, and his ears could not separate individual sounds, so he only heard a jumble that occasionally produced a recognizable word. He looked up when he realized someone was saying his name. He looked from face to face of those closest to him.

"Daniel."

He turned to the left where the voice was coming from.

"Daniel, I can't believe you're here. Where is your father? Daniel, are you all right?"

Daniel looked at Victoria because he did not recognize anyone in the crowd, but Victoria was smiling and hugging a woman that she obviously knew very well.

"Daniel," Victoria said excitedly. "It's Andrew and Lavinia. From Nauvoo, Daniel. Can you believe it?"

Daniel looked at the man who was quietly standing next to the woman Victoria was hugging. *I don't know you*, he thought to himself.

"Daniel," the man said, as if he had heard his thought. "You probably don't remember me, and even if you remembered me, it's been ten years since I've seen you. You helped me when we were leaving Nauvoo. You and your father made me a wagon, and you only charged me about half of what I'm certain it cost you to build."

"Andrew?"

"Yes. Andrew. Where is your father, Daniel?"

Daniel shrugged and looked down. "He died in July. We were living in Iowa City and he just didn't wake up one morning."

"I am so sorry to hear that. He was a great man. Have you been building handcarts in Iowa City all these years?" Andrew laughed and grasped Daniel's hand warmly. "I think you built my brother's handcart a few years ago. He told me about a man who built a very solid handcart for him and only charged him what he could afford. You must be the Daniel he was telling me about!"

Daniel could not keep up with the quick conversation and just nodded his head.

"Come with us," Lavinia said. "You need a good meal and a place to sleep, and we want you to spend Thanksgiving with us. Come." Lavinia was leading Victoria by the arm and two young women that seemed to be with Andrew were helping the children out of the wagon and ushering them toward Victoria.

"Here, Daniel, let me pull this thing for you," Andrew said as he walked to the front of the handcart and slid under the push bar. Daniel scooted back and pulled his feet into the cart. As the cart slowly moved, a scene from what seemed like a lifetime ago played across his mind. He remembered Andrew giving him a roll of money to pay for a wagon so his family could leave Nauvoo, and he remembered giving part of the money back. He smiled, as he seemed to hear his father kidding him for telling Andrew the price for the wagon would be less than expected because they had obtained the materials at a savings, when the truth was they were using their own funds to help Andrew's family.

Daniel smiled and leaned forward. "Andrew, I can't believe you even remembered me. How long have you been here?"

"We came here in August of 1847. There were not very many people here when we arrived, but they have been pouring in ever since. It's been the most amazing thing. Nine years of peace and harmony, and now the man who helped make it possible for me to bring my family here has finally arrived. We can help you get settled, and you can stay with us as long as you need to."

Daniel never did regain his complete health after arriving in Salt Lake. His severely frostbitten feet eventually healed enough for him to walk for limited amounts of time, but he had continuing pain and problems with his feet the rest of his life. He also developed a heart condition during the trek that made him somewhat feeble, preventing him from ever doing anything physically challenging, such as teaching his sons the noble heritage of woodworking that he had learned from his father.

"Will you help me blow out the candles, Grandpa?" Will's four-year old son asked.

Daniel leaned close to the birthday cake sitting in front of his youngest grandchild. "Yes, I will." Daniel chuckled and drew in a deep breath. "Ready?" he asked.

"Go," someone said.

Everyone clapped and cheered when the candles were extinguished. Daniel leaned back in his chair and watched the delight that filled the little birthday-boy's. "Good job, Grandpa," Victoria said as she leaned close to Daniel and covered his hand with hers.

"He looks exactly like Will did when he was four," Daniel said.

"He surely does," Victoria agreed. "Hard to imagine that Will was that age when we arrived here in the Valley. Four years old. Sometimes it seems like that was a different lifetime, and other times, like now, it seems it was just yesterday."

"Here you go, Father," Emma said as she slid a plate containing a slice of cake in front of him. "Your favorite. Chocolate cake."

"Thank you," Daniel said, smiling up at his lovely daughter. "You always make the best chocolate cake."

"Thanks," Emma said, "but I didn't make this cake. My girls are getting old enough to do the baking, and their dad cannot tell any difference between what they bake and what I bake. Your recipe, Mom, so it's been enjoyed by three generations."

"Six generations," Victoria corrected. "I got the recipe from my great grandmother when I was just learning how to bake."

"I didn't know that," Emma said. "I think that's pretty amazing to think that my great, great grandmother could have spent a day just like today, celebrating a four-year-old's birthday, maybe eighty or a hundred years ago. When their dinner was over the birthday cake that was served would have been made using this very same recipe. That's hard to comprehend!"

"I guess you could say this cake recipe has become a family tradition, and a mighty sweet one, too," Daniel chuckled.

"Can I talk you into posing for a picture with us, Father?" Will asked Daniel. "I made arrangements for a photographer to come take a picture of three generations of our family: you, me, and the birthday boy."

"I would be delighted," Daniel answered. "Where do you want to take the picture?"

"He's already got the camera set up on the sidewalk," Will answered. "Mom's favorite rose bush will be the backdrop."

"Perfect," Daniel said. He slowly walked to the steps of the porch and leaned on the railing as he descended to the front yard. On one side of the gate at the edge of the front yard was a beautiful pink rosebush that Victoria had planted when they first moved into the house where they had raised their three children, who now were all married and raising families of their own. "How is this?" he asked.

"Good," Will said as he guided his son to stand between him and his father. "Be sure to smile, you two."

As soon as the picture was taken, Tom took his mother's hand and said, "Now before anyone runs off, how about a family picture? We need a picture of Mother and Father, and the three of us. Emma, come join us."

Emma shrugged. She never liked having her picture taken, but followed Tom and her mother as they walked down the stairs.

As soon as everyone was in position, Tom looked at the photographer. "How does that look?"

"Very nice," he answered. "Now everyone hold very still, please."

The camera clicked and Emma immediately asked, "Are we finished?"

Everyone laughed at her. "You are beautiful, Emma," Daniel teased, "and the only one who hates getting her picture taken. Someday your grandchildren will look at this picture we just took, and you will be able to prove to them that you have been beautiful your whole life."

Emma wrinkled her nose, but then smiled and gave her father a warm hug. "Thanks, Father. I love you."

"I love you very much, Sweetheart," Daniel said.

Everyone started back to the porch. It was a warm afternoon and the porch that ran the length of the house was lined with big, comfortable chairs that looked out over the field Tom had recently planted. It had been such a blessing to Daniel and Victoria that one of Tom's crop fields was next to their house. They had been able to watch his children grow and share so many special moments with his family. Tom loved being a farmer and was quite successful at it. He had worked very hard over the years and his skill was widely known and respected across the Valley.

Daniel decided to take a quick look at Tom's field to see if any of the new plants had started to come up. Walking in the freshly plowed field was something he always enjoyed because he loved the smell of the newly turned soil. He stopped and bent down to get a better look at the little spots of green pushing through the rich brown earth. He touched a new leaf that had not quite made it all the way through the ground yet, and suddenly felt a little dizzy. He stood up and turned toward the house. The house appeared to swing around in front of his eyes as though it hung from a string. His left arm became numb as he staggered toward Victoria. He wanted to call out for help, but the growing pain in his chest had nearly locked his jaw. Suddenly it felt as if a flaming arrow passed through his heart.

In an instant, the pain was gone and his vision was normal. A familiar voice behind him spoke. "My dearest Marash."

Daniel turned and found Ribiab looking at him. "My dear friend," he said, "I'd forgotten all about you. And here you are."

They embraced, and the veil that had hidden Marash's memories of Ribiab and the days they had spent together was gone. "You've been so close to me, but never on my mind. How could I have been so careless to forget you?"

Ribiab's eyes showed no resentment, only love and happiness that they were now reunited.

"It was you," Marash said. "The man in my dream when I was in that sacred valley. And you who helped push my handcart when I couldn't take another step."

Ribiab smiled and began to speak. "The place in the great valley where you prayed and slept, that was the place I took my Earthly parents and laid their mortal remains in the ground. That was the place I spent my last day of mortality. I sat with you during the night. And now I come to greet you at the end of your Earthly test."

Marash quickly turned to look at Victoria. She was sitting on the porch with her children and grandchildren gathered around her. Their happy voices floated to where Marash was standing and he hesitated.

"If I leave my wife and family, who will protect them?"

Ribiab spoke gently, "Many constantly stand watch over your family, even as when I helped you push your family to safety through the snow. You can be proud of each member of your family, and your efforts to prepare them for your departure. They will now be able to carry on the work in this valley that you helped to establish at its beginning. Your sweet companion, Deborah, will rejoin you very shortly. Your Father is waiting for your return."

Ribiab extended his hand. Marash accepted his invitation and followed him toward the open portal.

I WILL FIND YOU

Elias studied the brilliant colors of the area around the waterfall. This was the last time he would be able to let the beauty fill his senses. He remembered when the Great Father had first explained that each person would experience life as a mortal human being in the New World, and it had seemed his turn would never arrive. Now, finally, it had.

In the beginning, he had no fear of going to the New World. He could not imagine anything that would cause him to deviate from his Father's teachings and risk his eternal estate. However, as he watched close friends return after their time in the New World, his confidence had slowly grown thin.

Some had returned and told of wonderful experiences that had filled their time on Earth, and they glowed with great joy. However, others had returned, appearing defeated and ashamed, with little they cared to share about their experiences. Most disturbing were those who were nearly unrecognizable when they returned. They were filled with hatred toward the Great Father and loudly complained that their Earthly existence was unfair and they did not deserve to be punished. It was shocking that they had become so much like the Defiant Ones that had been cast out of Great Father's presence. Those individuals had been taken immediately to prison when they returned. Elias wondered what could have happened to cause such a change in them, so he visited with them in prison hoping to gain insight, but there was not even a spark of their previous friendship remaining. That caused him to feel confused and sad, and a little fearful.

Nevertheless, his departure day had arrived. He walked hand in hand with Sarah. They had walked through this garden so often, sat together on their special bench, and promised they would find each other and share their time on Earth. He heard himself laugh, even though he felt anything but jovial.

"What's so funny?" Sarah asked.

"I just remembered all the things we've talked about that we could use to recognize each other when we meet on Earth, desperately hoping at least one of them will work." He looked down and saw her big blue eyes looking up at him.

"We'll find each other," she assured him.

They both stopped mid-stride as a gentle breeze blew the intoxicating fragrance from the flowerbeds across their path. Elias closed his eyes and slowly inhaled. "It smells so wonderful I am always amazed that the fragrance cannot be seen. It reminds me of the first time I saw you. That was long ago, but at this moment it seems as though it happened very recently."

They spoke little as they approached the Departure Building. When they walked through the main entrance, Elias was surprised to see so many waiting in the Assembly Area. Even though there had been large numbers of people who gathered to bid farewell to others in their immediate circle of friends, Elias did not expect it would be the same for him.

He moved among his friends, expressing his appreciation for their encouragement. As each person wished him luck and bid him farewell, he quickly became aware that he received two distinctly different types of hugs. Those that had not been to Earth themselves hugged him quickly, and he could sense they were excited for him. Those that had already returned from their experiences on Earth hugged him a little longer and a little tighter. When he looked into Ribiab's eyes, he saw the same fear and uncertainty that had begun to grow within himself.

Ribiab couldn't conceal his concern, wondering if Elias would be changed for the better or for the worse by his experiences on Earth. The one thing he was not confused about was that he *would* be changed.

"Do you think we will know each other?" Shroba asked Elias, for at least the third time that morning.

"No, I don't think we will have a clue we ever knew each other, even if I do see you on Earth."

"I'm sure I'll find you." Shroba insisted with a private smile.

The two friends laughed with each other.

"It will be a few years before you can begin looking for me, you know," Elias said. "You've seen how helpless everyone is when they first arrive."

Yes, that has been pretty entertaining. But how do you know for sure that we won't know each other? Do you remember how excited we were to learn we'd be in the New World at the same time? I can't imagine not knowing you if we do happen to meet each other," Shroba said again, more confidently.

I guess we'll know soon enough," Elias answered. "You'll be stepping through the departure portal not long after me."

"I can't wait to see it. Ribiab has tried to describe it to me, but no one's description quite matches another's," Shroba said and then moved to where Ribiab was standing, allowing others to wish Elias farewell.

"So did you tell him?" Ribiab asked.

"No," Shroba sighed. "I kept debating with myself over whether it would be beneficial for him to know I'll be his mortal son and if such knowledge would even mean as much to him as it does to me." Shroba looked down, wondering if he had made the right decision. Should he have told Elias?

"I overheard you ask him several times if he believed you two would know each other. How did it get away from you to share something so special?" Ribiab waited for Shroba to meet his gaze. "Come on be honest with me."

Shroba's tone was subdued, "I am being honest. At first I thought it was funny that I knew we'd be in the same mortal family when he didn't. I thought I was making it so obvious that he would ask me, but then it seemed the joke had gone too far. He's already worried about how or if he will recognize Sarah. It just didn't feel right to tell him something else important that he won't be able to remember when he passes through the veil. Then I noticed others waiting to talk to him, and I felt I had already taken too much of his time. Maybe I will tell Sarah and she can tell him when she gets to the New World." Shroba joked and shrugged nonchalantly, but his short laugh seemed to still hold more regret than humor.

Ribiab heard the regret and reached out to squeeze his friend's shoulder, "Hey, I think you were right to not tell him. I'm not sure what benefit it would serve to have told him, anyway. Don't give it another thought."

A small group now approached Elias consisting of longtime friends and others he had only just met. The common element amongst the group was that they would all be departing for the New World in the next several days. One man, who Elias had long admired for his leadership and charismatic personality, stepped forward, naturally becoming the voice of the group.

"Elias, we are all so excited to be going to the New World with you. It is hard to believe in a short time our experiences here will be sealed in an unobtainable portion of our minds. We just want to tell you, now, how much we admire you and are pleased that we will be sharing this experience together." Stephan nearly lifted Elias off the ground with his enthusiastic hug.

Elias replied, "I was so pleased to learn that you and I will be sent to the same location and at the same time. It will undoubtedly feel strange when we meet, but I'm confident there has to be some element of our relationship here that will come to the surface in the New World. Surely you will continue to influence me with your greatness as you have here. I have always admired your courage, especially as some of our friends were debating which side to follow in the recent conflict. I'm sure I'll see you in a flash." Both laughed as they wrapped their arms around each other again in a last farewell embrace.

After all the goodbyes were said, Elias took Sarah's hand and they walked toward one of the doors covered with gold leaves. When he shut the door behind them, he felt his chest constrict. He sat down across from Sarah and said as much to himself as to her, "Great Father has assured us that if we choose someone here to be our eternal mate, we will find each other in the New World. I have faith that will happen for us."

Elias wanted to say so many things to Sarah, but struggled to find many words, so instead they looked into each other's eyes settling on communicating silent messages of love. Then, as if an unspoken command had been heard, they both knew it was time to say farewell. He studied her beautiful face a moment longer before standing and pulling her to his chest, hugging her tightly. "If I don't know it's you, but you know it's me, will you promise to give me a kick and remind me who you are?"

"I promise," she said with a laugh, and when they walked back into the Assembly Area, he was pleased to see that she was smiling. Sarah left him and had nearly reached the exit before she stopped, turned, and drawing in a deep steadying breath said, "I will find you."

Elias entered the portal room where the Great Father was waiting. When he had been there with Sarah on the tour, the dark wooden doors at the top of the staircase had been closed. Now, they were open nearly all the way. Between them, floating against the blackness of space, the vivid blue and white of the New World hung as if suspended in mid-air in the opening between the doors. "It's so beautiful," Elias said in an awed whisper.

His Father greeted him and asked him to have a seat. He put his hands on Elias' head and gave him a powerful blessing. Then he sat down and smiled warmly. "You are filled with anxiety and uncertainty, but you will do fine, my son." His smile made Elias' fears disappear. "Always listen to the whisperings of the Spirit of Truth, and never let the Defiant Ones pull you away."As the Father spoke, Elias felt a burning within his chest.

"The veil you will pass through is very powerful," the Great Father continued. "All memory of your home will be removed from your mind. However, your true nature and strengths will remain a part of you. As you heard during your blessing, I have placed some weaknesses upon your head. The weaknesses will serve to keep you humble in the new world and cause you to approach me in prayer for help in overcoming those weaknesses. Many experiences will also aid you in directing your life toward me. The things you have been taught in your preparation classes will remain buried deeply within you. Your teachings here and your natural being will become part of your soul. As you call to me in prayer and contemplate my ways, your inner being will offer up these teachings as the Holy Ghost gently raises them to the surface. The burning you now feel in your bosom will be a sign unto you that I hear your prayers, and I am with you. I will be with you whenever you allow me to."

"Thank you," Elias said softly.

Great Father continued. "There will be many in the New World to help you. You have chosen good and wise souls to be your parents. They will be able to assist and teach you, and you can learn from their mistakes and successes. Learning from your own experiences as well as the experiences of others will continue throughout your mortal experience. There will come a time when you will be responsible for your own actions and decisions, regardless of what your parents or others have taught you or done to you. You alone are responsible for your own destiny. There will also come a time when you will be a parent, trusted to teach and care for more of my beloved children. These children will also teach you much."

Elias could feel the love radiating from His Father.

"My truth will be on the Earth during your life. You will be part of those preparations that have been prophesied since my First Born was crucified. You and those in your immediate family have been reserved to participate in the glorious events that will unfold and usher in the great time of peace. Your family will receive unimaginable blessings because of your righteousness and the great support you have provided in this existence and that you will continue to provide to your brothers and sisters in the New World.

You will see firsthand how many challenge that truth, even as my plan was challenged in this existence. Some sources of truth in the New World were once pure and true when they were first received, but have since been distorted and changed. It will require much prayer and pondering to discern the errors in those teachings. If you ask whether a principle is true, I will cause your bosom to burn in answer to your prayers. The Holy Ghost will testify to you the truthfulness of all things."

For a short time, the Great Father was silent as he looked deep into Elias' eyes. Then He spoke again. "Elias, you go when the Prophets I send to carry my word to the New World are preaching that the end of time is close and all must repent. Whether a man hears the voices of the Prophets or reads their written word, the warnings are true, but no man knows when the Savior will return to the New World. Therefore, the Prophets will not preach of the end of time to confuse or mislead, but to warn of the inevitable end for everyone's experience in the New World."

"The tragedy of a man's life ending when he is unprepared to return," the Great Father explained, "is that justice must be served. Even though he can repent and progress after he returns, he has lost the opportunity to gain all that I have, for mercy cannot remove the requirements of justice, except when there was no law. Where there was no law, the Savior to all mankind's infinite atonement will meet the demands of justice. But where there was a law, on that day when they return from mortality they cannot ask for immediate and full repentance, for the same spirit which doth possess his body at that time is the same spirit that will have power to possess his body in the eternal world."

His Father stood and embraced him. Elias still clung to Great Father as he turned and looked at the New World through the open portal. He was filled with both fear and excitement as he reluctantly released Great Father's hand, stepped into the portal, and passed through the veil. In an instant, a blinding flash of light wiped everything and everyone from his memory.

◆◆◆◇◆◆◆

"He is so tiny," the dark haired woman said to her husband. "It's hard to remember the other kids were ever this tiny. They grow so fast."

The baby's father was smiling as he softly stroked the tiny fingers that were pulled into a tight little fist. "What shall we name him?"

"I have been thinking about that. We have already named sons after your father and my father, so I thought this time we could use my oldest brother, Mark's name. What do you think?"

"I like it."

"Good. Welcome to our family, little Mark," she said softly.

"Can I borrow him for just a minute? There are a bunch of kids waiting downstairs to catch the first glimpse of their little brother," he said as he picked up the tightly wrapped bundle that contained his new baby son and walked to the window. He held the baby up so the children standing by the family car parked below the hospital room could see their new brother. They all started pointing and jumping up and down in excitement, but their shouts of excitement could not be heard through the hospital room window.

"I think that's her baby," Mark's mother pointed excitedly. "She told me to be sure to stop by the nursery on my way out and look for him."

"Whose baby is he?" Mark's father asked.

"He belongs to the woman who shared my room."

"That's amazing," Mark's father said, slowly shaking his head. "Two babies come to Earth within two days of each other. It makes me wonder if they knew each other in the pre-existence before they came here."

"I think about things like that sometimes, too," his wife said. "I wonder if you and I knew each other before we came to Earth? Did our kids know each other before we all became a family?"

"Hmm. I guess we won't know for sure until our time here is done," her husband mused.

CHOICES

Tony's family moved into Mark's neighborhood the summer before Mark started fifth grade. The two boys met at church the week before summer scout camp. It was tricky to meet someone new at church because parents always seemed to assume that their children would automatically accept each other and become friends just because they went to the same church every Sunday. Both boys knew it did not always work out like that, so they sized each other up as they engaged in a short conversation, not wanting to give the other too much information. Neither boy wanted to get locked into an "expected" friendship until they knew the other was not some boring momma's boy.

On the first day of scout day camp, the two boys got a little better acquainted when they both ended up on the same team during some group challenges. A shared desire to cause the leaders as much grief as possible quickly moved their new relationship into true friendship. Tony seemed to be a natural-born leader; he was one of the larger boys in camp and jumped at the chance to be the captain of his group. Mark was okay with that – Tony seemed to have enough spunk to make their team number one.

To win the first challenge, theirs had to be the first team to identify two kinds of rocks and four kinds of leaves. They quickly scattered into the surrounding woods and within moments, had discovered a beaver pond. Less than a minute later, everyone was in the water swimming, and the contest was forgotten.

A large barrel floating in the pond quickly became the center of everyone's attention. Tony, acting as team captain, decided he was *king of the hill* and used his size to his advantage. Each time the other boys tried to get on the barrel, he knocked them off and held them under the water. He seemed to get some kind of thrill out of watching the smaller boys panic. When Mark tried to get on, Tony leaped from the barrel and threw him under the water like he had the others, but he quickly discovered size alone did not always guarantee success. Mark began thrashing and moving in all directions at once. He finally got a firm grip on the bottom of the pond with his left foot and sprung to the surface. As he shot out of the water he smacked Tony in the jaw. The two of them began rolling in the water, throwing ineffective punches, until they were exhausted. Then their competition evolved into a verbal bout that lasted until they realized neither one was winning.

By the time Tony's and Mark's team returned to camp, the flag ceremony was underway. They tried to sneak from the trees and form the back row of the assembly, but their instructor noticed them, immediately.

"You seem to be the only team that looked for rocks and leaves under water," he said as he shook his head disapprovingly at the soaking wet boys. They did not receive any trophies for the first challenge, but were successful in not missing lunch.

The heated exchange from the pond turned out to cement rather than undue the boys' friendship. Tony and Mark became partners in crime, and by the time they returned from scout camp they were inseparable. If Tony did not find a way to create chaos and disaster, then Mark did, and they continually tried to surpass each other in finding or creating mischief. Once home, they even found ways to continue their antics at church. After causing their Sunday School teacher to leave the room in tears after just four weeks; they applauded each time a new teacher escaped to the Bishop's office to resign his or her calling.

Scout leaders were not spared their antics, either, and soon months would pass with no scout leader at all.

"There's no reason we should miss out on fun times just because we don't have a scoutmaster," Tony told the other boys.

"Right," Mark quickly agreed. "We should plan our own activity."

"Doing what? Sleeping on the lawn at the church?" someone asked. "There's snow on the ground." Everyone started laughing and offering suggestions.

"No," Tony said, again taking control of the group. "We can figure out a way to get our parents to take us up the canyon and then go hiking by ourselves."

"Sure," Mark chimed in. "Me and Tony will get there early, and then when your parents bring you, we'll tell them that our chaperone had to run back to town to get something he forgot."

"We always meet at the church. It's going to seem suspicious if our parents have to take us up to the canyon."

"No problem," Tony responded. "We just tell them some guy in the ward volunteered to be our chaperone, but he doesn't have a van big enough to hold us all, so our parents have to drive us up there."

Soon, the rest of the boys in the group began believing it could work. The next few weeks during scout meeting, the boys planned what food they would take and exactly what they should say to each of their parents.

On the scheduled day, Tony talked his older brother into taking him and Mark to the mouth of the canyon. When there was no chaperone to meet them, they told him he was probably running late, and innocently asked if he wanted to stay and wait with them. Tony's brother did not. Each time a questioning parent dropped off their son at the mouth of the canyon, Mark or Tony relayed the same story – their chaperone had run back down the hill after one of the boys who needed a ride. Each family was given a different name when they asked who the chaperone was.

When the last parent had gone, the boys all cheered. Their plan had worked without a single glitch. The snow was deeper than the boys had anticipated, so they didn't arrive at their camp until nearly midnight. Most of them were exhausted and many of the younger ones were frightened. As usual, Tony took charge, demanding that the boys set up their tents, get out of their wet clothes and into dry ones, and put two people in every sleeping bag to get warm.

Tony set out to gather what little dry wood he could find while Mark set up their tent. Mark was so tired and cold he wondered how Tony still had enough energy to be out in the snow dragging wood around.

Mark removed his cold wet clothes and crawled into his sleeping bag. After dozing for a short time, he was awakened by laughter. He could see the flicker of a fire through the wall of the tent. He was again impressed by Tony's courage and ability to take control of a situation. Tony had managed to not only get the boys warm, but to get them laughing and telling stories around the fire.

When it got light the next morning, the boys once again followed Tony's instructions and soon had hot cocoa, bacon, and French toast sizzling over the fire. Everyone cooperated when it came time to break camp and clean up the dirty dishes.

As they hiked back to meet their parents, Tony started coaching the boys. "When your folks pick you up, make sure you start right in talking about how much fun you had and tell them every detail of how you helped build the fire in the snow, and then tell them about how you fixed your own breakfast this morning over the campfire."

"Should we tell them how Marty accidentally dumped his breakfast in the fire?"

"If you want to," Tony replied. "The point is you keep talking so they don't start asking questions. If they ask who the chaperone was, act like you can't remember his name, and then start talking about something else that happened."

"When they start talking about our campout at church, somebody's going to find out we didn't have a chaperone."

"I have this all planned out," Tony said. "The day before yesterday was Thanksgiving, remember?"

"Yeah, what's that got to do with anything?"

Tony slapped the boy who had asked the question in the back of the head. The smaller boy flinched away, "What'd you do that for?"

Tony just laughed at him. "The Sunday after Thanksgiving is the big Thanksgiving program. Everybody will be talking about what they ate, what game they watched on TV, and how they dozed on the couch all afternoon. They won't even think to ask about our little over-nighter. And make sure none of you bring it up to anybody, either."

"Good thinking, Tony."

"It's a cinch," Tony bragged. "By next week at church, no one will even remember we even went on a hike. So if you little girls can remember to keep your mouths shut for a couple days, no one will ever know anything about what we've done."

Tony was right, mostly, but Mark's mother turned out to be a little more persistent. Luckily, under Tony's tutelage, Mark was getting pretty good at fibbing.

"Did you ever remember the name of your chaperone at the scouting activity?" his mother asked, for at least the fifth time.

"Yeah, I thought I already told you."

"No, you could never remember his name."

"Well it was, uh, shoot, I forgot again. You know him, Mom; he's the guy that just moved here. I think he works at the University. He's got dark hair, pretty tall, and he's in good shape for someone his age."

"That just doesn't ring a bell, Mark. Is he married?"

"I think so, but I really don't know. I'm pretty sure you've met him though", he answered, vaguely.

"Oh, really? Why do you think that?"

Mark could hardly keep from chuckling because he was describing the principal at his school. "Well, because I'm pretty sure I've seen you talking to him."

"But you can't remember his name? How about next Sunday you point him out to me?"

"Sure. No problem, Mom."

Mark just made sure he did not feel well enough to go to church the following Sunday, and the entire subject was forgotten just as Tony had predicted.

After a year of friendship, Mark was pretty impressed with what Tony, and by extension: Mark, could get away with. Halloween had been filled with the new pranks Tony dreamed up, all of which had been pulled off with complete success. The very large stash of candy they scored would last at least until Christmas.

"You should hear what's happening to my dad at work," Tony said one evening while they were picking through their candy stash."Some guy my dad trained has decided he wants Dad's job, and he's been shooting down Dad every chance he gets."

"Isn't there anything your dad can do about it?" Mark asked around a mouthful of chocolate.

"Last night he told us he talked to his boss and tried to explain what was going on, but his boss told him this other guy had talked to him the day before and told him the same story, but in his version Dad was the one trying to cause the problems."

"So what's he going to do?"

"Dad said there's nothing he can do. He knows the creep is spreading lots of lies behind his back, but every time he says anything about it, the jerk goes running to his boss to complain. It makes my blood boil to think somebody is getting away with that crap."

"Can't your dad just tell the guys he works with what's going on?"

"No. Every time he says anything, the jerk makes it look like my dad is picking on him. Dad can't do anything. But I can do something, and I'm going to make this guy pay big time!"

"What are you going to do?"

"No, it's 'what are *we* going to do.' I'm not going to have all the fun alone. You will love this."

"Maybe you should lay low, Tony. If you do something and get caught, your dad might get in even more trouble. What would you do if he got fired because of something you did?"

"Oh, c'mon. Have we ever got caught? Don't worry. I have a great plan and besides, I need your help. You know all that paint your dad keeps in his shed? I need you to find one of the brightest reds, and bring it down to my house, tomorrow."

"What for?" Mark asked hesitantly.

"Will you stop looking so worried? We aren't going to ruin his truck or anything like that. We're just going to pull a little joke on him. Now, don't forget to bring the paint when you come over tomorrow."

Mark rummaged around through the shed the next day. Some of the cans looked brand new and were nearly full. He knew he couldn't take those without his dad noticing, so he moved all the cans in front out of the way, and clear in the back, he found a gallon of red that was about half full. Then he found a forgotten can that looked like it had been there a long time. It was golden yellow and nearly full. *This must be something he never uses*, Mark thought. He restacked all the cans exactly as they had been, hoping his dad would never miss the two he'd taken. He put the cans in a brown grocery sack and took them to Tony's house.

"Perfect," Tony said gleefully after he opened the cans. "In a couple hours, the fun begins."

When it was dark enough to remain somewhat hidden, but light enough to still see what they were doing, Tony grabbed the cans. "Follow me."

They walked along the line of trees that stretched from Tony's house to a field, being careful to stay in the shadows. Once they got to the field, Tony asked, "Do you see those horses grazing over there?"

"Yeah, why?"

"They belong to that jerk who's trying to get my dad's job." Tony set the two cans of paint on the ground.

"What are you going to do with the paint?" Mark asked nervously.

Tony pried off the two lids. He handed the small can of golden yellow paint to Mark and grabbed the larger can of red for himself. He walked to the fence surrounding the field and whistled softly. The two horses walked to them, probably thinking they were about to get a treat. Tony reached through the fence and petted the horse on the head then started walking along the fence while he kept petting her, working his way toward her rump. Without any warning, Tony raised the bucket of paint up and quickly poured it right on top of her back.

"Give me that," Tony said as he jerked the can of golden yellow from a dumbfounded Mark. He managed to dump the yellow on top of the red, just as the horse bolted from the fence. He threw both cans at the horse, barely missing the colt that was trying to keep up with its mother.

Suddenly, Mark felt as though he were the colt too, running and trying to keep up with Tony's much longer strides. The two boys did not stop running until they had returned to the darkness of Tony's backyard. Sprawled on the lawn, gasping for air, they laughed as they replayed the scene in choppy gasping sentences.

Finally, Tony said, "Thanks, Mark. It sure feels good to balance the scales of justice for my dad just a little bit."

"After all the things you've told me about that dirt bag, I'm glad I could help," Mark said, feeling much braver now that it was over and they were safe in Tony's yard.

The joy of delivering revenge was short lived. A couple days later, Tony walked up to Mark at school first thing in the morning looking very worried. He pulled a wadded up piece of newspaper from his pocket and began reading it aloud to Mark.

"Mr. Olsen contacted the authorities after finding the paint-covered horse in his field. The veterinarian who treated the horse determined that the colt might suffer long-term health problems due to paint it licked from the sides of its mother. The colt, having been bred for success on the racetrack, constitutes a sizable loss if it dies or does not develop wholly. Mr. Olsen found the empty paint cans the vandals left behind in his field. He turned them over to the police in hopes they will be able to find fingerprints that will lead them to the culprits."

Mark felt the earth sink under his feet. A wave of heat rolled over him, unlike anything he had ever felt before.

Tony leaned close and said, "You should have seen my dad last night at the dinner table. He held up the paper and read it aloud for everyone to hear. Then he looked right at me and said, 'You don't know anything about this, do you, Son?'"

"Does he know it was you?" Mark asked. His heart was racing and he could hear it beating loudly in his ears.

"I don't know, but the way he acted makes me think he believes it was me."

"What did you say?" Mark asked, barely able to think.

"I said, 'Guess you caught me, Dad.' What do you think I said? Two words: 'No, Dad.'"

"My dad will ground me for the rest of my life if he finds out it was us. The part of my life that's left when I get out of reform school, anyway," Mark said, seeing his entire future destroyed by Tony's stupid prank. So much for thinking Tony could get away with anything. Then an even more terrible thought came to his mind.

"What happens when they find my dad's fingerprints on those cans? What were you thinking, just leaving them there, Tony? This time my dad could end up getting involved in this."

"Relax, don't count your dad in before we even get caught."

"You should've wiped the cans off or we could've worn gloves. Tony, we should have never left those cans behind. What am I going to do when my mom and dad find out about this?"

Mark read the paper every night for a week looking for anymore mention of the crime. He could not find a single word. Each night at dinner, Mark could hardly eat because he wondered if this would be the night the police came knocking on his door to take his dad to the police station for questioning. He nearly gagged every time he pictured that scene, especially when he envisioned himself, and not his dad, as the one the police took from the house in handcuffs.

By the time Christmas arrived, Mark was feeling a little less panic stricken every time the doorbell rang. Winter had settled in, and Mark gradually allowed the bitterness he'd felt for Tony to dissipate. Like all their other pranks, it seemed that Tony had in fact pulled this one off without a hitch, too. He and Tony liked the shorter days because the adults in the neighborhood spent the chilly evenings hiding in their houses. To the two boys, this early darkness meant a license to do whatever they wanted.

One night, shortly after dark, Tony called Mark.

"Hey, meet me up at the truck stop in ten minutes."

The truck stop was a couple blocks from Mark's house, half the distance as from Tony's. It was still early enough that Mark's mother had no objection when he said he was going to get a coke with Tony. Instead, he walked briskly to the truck stop and waited. It wasn't long before he saw his friend approaching through the darkness, a red glow intermittently lighting his face. Mark watched as the glow came and went until Tony reached the parking lot of the truck stop. Once Tony was under the lights, Mark saw his friend take a cigarette from his mouth and give it a toss. He wanted to ask Tony where he'd gotten a cigarette, but before he could open his mouth, Tony shoved him toward the truck stop's door.

"C'mon, I've got something to show you."

Tony walked to one of the booths along the windows and sat down as though he had been doing it for years. It surprised him when Tony acted as though he felt right at home, but at the same time it was so typical – Tony always seemed comfortable no matter where he went or what he did.

"You won't believe this. You can get a huge plate of hash brown potatoes with gravy on them for just twenty-five cents," Tony said as he flipped open the menu lying on the table. "And all the coffee you can drink for another dime." In a condescending tone, he added, "But don't worry, you can get a coke."

Tony told the waitress they both wanted hash browns with gravy, one coffee, and one coke. Mark tried to act at ease but realized he was looking around the inside of the truck stop like a tourist. He had ridden his bike around it for years delivering papers. One year he had delivered the newspaper to the truck stop's restaurant, but he had never gone beyond the counter where he laid the paper. When they finished eating and stood to put their coats on, Tony threw a dime on the table for the waitress.

"What are you doing?" Mark asked him quietly.

"Leaving a tip, moron. What do you think?"

Mark wondered why he had never noticed his dad leaving a tip when they had finished eating dinner at a restaurant, but then he realized the family had waited at the table while his dad went to the cash register to pay the bill. Maybe he paid the tip then. He was still mulling this situation over in his mind and feeling like a dumb little kid as he followed Tony to the cash register.

Tony dropped the change by the cash register and waved to the waitress coming around the corner.

"Thanks," he said, and when they got to the door, he shoved Mark through the doorway into the night air.

Mark was unprepared for Tony's manhandling and stumbled. He quickly regained his footing and, with a quick jab, cut his opened hand across Tony's face. It was not an attempt to cause pain or to get even for the shove, but he suddenly felt he needed to remind Tony that he could take care of himself. Tony just laughed as he zipped up his coat.

"So what's with the cigarettes?" Mark asked.

"Oh yeah, when I was in the truck stop with my brother last night, he asked for a pack of cigarettes when he paid for our coffee. They sold them to him without batting an eye. I'll bet they'd even sell them to me, but, if not, Kev says he'll get them for me." He pulled the opened pack from his pocket and casually handed one to Mark as though the two of them had been smoking for years.

"What are you doing?" Mark asked as he threw the offered cigarette on the ground.

"Hey, Sunday School boy, don't make me kick your butt. If you don't want it, just say so, but don't be throwing it on the ground." Tony picked it up and handed it back to Mark. "Just try it, it's kind of fun. You don't even have to inhale, but see if you can blow a few smoke rings. I spent last night trying, and I got pretty good at it."

Slowly, Mark put the cigarette to his mouth. Tony was already striking the match for him, and he touched it to Mark's cigarette. They started down the street and Mark cautiously sucked the smoke in and out a few times.

"See, it's not that big of a deal, is it?" Tony asked.

Mark found it strangely interesting that smoking a cigarette with his best friend actually didn't feel like that big of a deal. He was only a few blocks from his house, and he knew that any car that drove by could be someone who would recognize him from the neighborhood. Instead of being worried, a feeling of freedom began to grow within him, as years of restraint suddenly dropped from his shoulders. Who cared if someone saw him smoking? He could do whatever he wanted. It did surprise him, however, that he had a hard time ignoring the twinge of guilt he felt as they walked past the church.

"What're you doing for your birthday?" Tony asked Mark as they rode their bicycles to the municipal swimming pool.

"Not much, I guess. My parents are going to be out of town. My older brother and I are the only ones staying home, so I guess we'll just wait and do something for my birthday when they get back."

"Fifteen years old and you're going to have the house to yourself to celebrate, and all you're going to do is wait around for your parents to get home," Tony scoffed.

Mark could almost hear Tony's mind kicking into high gear.

"Follow me," Tony said as he suddenly turned 180 degrees on his bike. He quickly pedaled to the back of his house, which was only about a block from the swimming pool. He jumped off his bike, opened the little door that led to the storage area under the back porch, pulled a large bowl through the access door and set it on the ground.

"What's that?" Mark asked.

"I've been brewing this wine from a recipe my brother gave me. I was planning to keep it a secret until my birthday. Now we have a time and a place to use it. This is great." Tony pulled the balloon off the bowl that had been stretched over the top to seal it. He dipped his finger in the liquid and licked it. "Yep, still tastes like fruit juice, but it should be ready by the time your parents leave."

"So what are we going to do, sit around and drink some homemade wine and call it fun?"

"No, just listen," Tony said excitedly. "I was going to have pizza and beer for my birthday. Now we can have pizza, beer, and wine for your birthday. It's great."

"Beer, huh? I'm sure they won't notice you're not old enough to buy beer," Mark jeered.

"Kev is going to get it for me. We'll have him bring it over to your house, and we can have our own party. We'll be able to try the wine and if it's not good, we'll still have the beer. It's perfect because we won't have to worry about anybody catching us."

"Sure, that works. I guess it could be fun," Mark said.

By the time Mark's parents were ready to leave town, Mark and Tony were already imagining how much fun they were going to have. Everything was arranged, and this was going to be the party of their lives. After school on Friday afternoon, they headed to the back porch of Tony's house.

Tony pulled the bowl from the storage area and set it on the grass. He pulled the cover off and lifted the bowl above the Mason quart jar Mark was holding. Tony poured the precious liquid very slowly until the jar was full, and then he screwed the lid on with a final jerk to make sure it was tight. Once the bowl was rinsed out with the hose, the evidence was gone. They jumped on their bikes and headed for Mark's house.

"This place sure seems quiet with everyone gone," Tony said as he walked across the kitchen's linoleum flooring. "Hello, Hello," he yelled, and then abruptly stopped.

"What?" Mark asked, looking confused.

"Just waiting to see if I can hear an echo. With seven kids in your family, I've never been here when no one else was around before. You sure your brother won't be here any time soon?" Tony asked.

"No, he's working and won't be here until after midnight."

Tony opened the refrigerator and set his jar of wine on a shelf. "I'm sure it will taste better if it's cold."

"Now you're a wine authority, huh?" Mark laughed and then headed for his room. "Come on. I want to change clothes, so I'll be ready when Kev gets here."

"Why are you changing clothes?" Tony asked as he followed him.

"I'm a year older. I have to look cool." Mark put on a clean pair of Levis and went through his older brother's closet until he found a white tee shirt that had the local university logo across the chest. He always thought that shirt looked great when his brother wore it.

"Yea, you definitely look cool now," Tony snickered as Mark stood in front of the mirror.

"Shut up," Mark said as he turned and lunged toward Tony.

The two boys tussled for a few minutes and then Tony said, "I hear Kev's car," and he released Mark from a headlock. When they reached the car, they saw that Ricky, Kevin's friend, was sitting in the passenger seat.

"Where's the pizza?" Tony asked his brother.

"Yeah, I said I'd get it. Are you two little girls ready for a grown-up night?"

"Don't call me a little girl," Tony said defiantly as he slugged Kevin's shoulder.

"Ooo, you've got a ferocious little brother there, Kev. You better watch out or he's going to drink you right under the table," Ricky teased.

"We'll see about that," Kevin said.

"Who's your friend?" Ricky asked Tony.

"This is Mark."

"I think I know you," Ricky said. "Your brother's a senior, right?"

"Yeah," answered Mark. "Is he a friend of yours?"

Ricky laughed. "Well not exactly. We kind of hang with different people; if you know what I mean?"

"No," Mark said quickly. Then, about ten seconds too late, he added, "Oh, yeah, I know what you mean."

Everyone laughed at Mark, and the way they laughed made him feel exactly the same way he did when Tony called him Sunday School boy. Luckily, the conversation quickly moved on to a topic that didn't leave Mark feeling like he was in their cross hairs.

Kevin opened the trunk and pulled out the two pizza boxes. Ricky and Tony each took two six-packs of beer, and Mark grabbed the last one.

"Happy Birthday, kid," Kevin said as they headed to the kitchen.

Mark had not realized the older boys would be staying and he started to panic as Ricky popped the tops off a few of the bottles.

"Here you go," Ricky said as he held one out to Mark.

Mark took the bottle and started to put it to his lips, then stopped. "Hey, let's go outside and do this in the backyard."

"That's what I thought," Ricky hollered. "Your first beer!"

"Everybody has a first beer," Tony said as he nudged Ricky. Then he walked to the fridge and grabbed his jar of wine. "I'm not going to answer to his dad if I spill this stuff and ruin some carpet or something. C'mon, let's go outside." Looking at Mark, he winked.

While Kevin and Ricky dug into the box of pizza at the other end of the patio table, Mark turned his head away from them and said, "Thanks, Tony. I know what you did, and I just wanted to say that was great."

"Hey, what are best friends for?" Tony asked, in one of his rare displays of concern.

Mark and Tony had been friends a long time, but he was sure he had never heard Tony use those words before. Best friends. Such moments were what made Tony someone you would do anything for. If he was against you, heaven better be on your side, but if Tony was for you, he could be counted on to stop anyone from giving you crap.

"I guess I was almost your age when I had my first beer," Ricky said. He slapped Mark on the shoulder and laughed, but this time the laugh made Mark feel like he had been accepted as part of the group, rather than being the object of their derision.

By the time the first box of pizza was gone, Mark was feeling a little queasy. He had only downed two beers, and was determined to hold his own with Tony, who was now on his third.

"Time for the good stuff," Tony said. He picked up the jar of wine, unscrewed the lid, and handed it to Mark. Then he picked up his beer and raised it in the air. "Let's toast the birthday boy."

"Cheers!" they all said at once. They took a swig from their beers as Mark tilted his head back and took a few large gulps of wine from the jar. The three boys burst out laughing, and Mark could see they were looking at his shirt. When he looked down, he discovered a bright red stain covering most of the front of his brother's white t-shirt.

Mark laughed a little and marveled at how he thought the stain-covered shirt looked funny. Somehow, he knew he should be terrified of what his brother was going to do to him. He knew it should bother him that everyone was laughing at him, too, but after two beers none of that disturbed him in the least.

He raised the jar above his head and said, "Now that's some good wine. Here, Tony, time to enjoy the fruits of your labor." He handed the jar to Tony and laughed again, thinking what he had just said sounded very funny.

By the time the pizza and most of the beer were gone, Mark had moved from thinking everything was hilarious, to feeling very relaxed. Tony got up and walked to the edge of the grass. They all watched him, not sure if he was going to puke or take a leak. Suddenly, as if in slow motion, Tony dropped to the earth like a ton of bricks. Kevin was the first to reach him, and he leaned down to see if he was okay.

"Help me get him back onto the grass and out of the irrigation ditch," Kevin yelled. "He's still breathing – must have just passed out."

"Good thing the ditch is empty," Ricky said. It was nearly dark, but the three boys could still see well enough to position themselves where they needed to be without falling into the ditch themselves.

"Rick, grab one arm, and Mark, you take the other one. I'll get his legs," Kevin directed.

Mark bent down to grab an arm and instantly felt as though a burning arrow had been shot through his brain. He grabbed his nose and stumbled backward, falling onto the grass on his back. His eyes were watering so badly the star-filled sky above him was a total blur. Glancing around after the initial shock had worn off, Mark saw that a broken-off weed the size of a pencil had found its way up his nose as he bent over to help Tony.

Kevin stepped over Tony and kicked Mark in the side. "Get over here and help us, Birthday Boy."

Mark rolled to his side and pulled himself up. He stumbled toward Tony and helped pull his dead weight onto the lawn. "What should we do now?" he asked, looking at Kevin.

"Just let him sleep for a while, and he'll be fine. He scared me last month when we got drunk in our basement and he did the same thing. Come on, Ricky, we're out of here. Later, Birthday Boy."

The fun suddenly vanished from the party when Tony passed out. Mark went downstairs and grabbed a couple of sleeping bags since he wasn't going to take any chance on Tony puking all over his bedroom during the night. It was a perfect night to sleep outside, anyway. As he walked past the bathroom, he paused in front of the mirror. Sure enough, a little bit of blood was drying around his nostril. He could not believe the kind of bad luck it took to nearly run a weed through his brain. The fleeting thought of it going through his eye suddenly made him feel quite lucky.

Mark threw a sleeping bag over Tony, and then cleaned up the bottles and pizza boxes and threw them in the garbage can next door. He knew his dad and mom would find the remnants of his birthday party if he put it in one of their cans. Looking down, he pulled off his brother's stained t-shirt and stuffed it inside one of the pizza boxes. He would rather have his brother blame him for losing his favorite shirt than have to explain the stain to his mother. Finally, he returned to the back yard and settled into his sleeping bag.

As the night sky spun around him, he started to laugh. He could not believe he made it through the night without throwing up. He'd thought he was going to have to prove he could drink as well and as much as Tony, but he knew Tony would never remember how much Mark drank and probably wouldn't even want to talk about it. Mark drifted off to sleep feeling as though he had accomplished much more than just proving himself to his friend on his birthday – he felt like he had grown up.

INFLUENCES

When summer arrived, Mark found himself busy helping with chores at home and every volunteer project his mother could dream up. He helped mow his grandparents' lawn and picked their apricots. He helped the elderly couple who lived on the corner weed their garden and washed their windows. His dad dragged him along to help an elderly couple in their ward who needed some wood chopped, and he helped paint the entire exterior of his aunt's house. Somewhere amidst it all, Mark decided he would find a job before the next summer so he would be paid for all his work.

The little time he found to spend with Tony seemed to represent life on the opposite end of the pendulum. After watching Tony in action all during the school year, planning pranks that showed total disregard for other people or their property, Mark had begun to dread what his next escapade would be.

Under his parents' influence, Mark spent his time helping anyone his family felt needed help; Tony spent all of his time making people feel insignificant or demonstrating his total lack of concern for anyone but himself. Mark enjoyed the momentary thrill he shared with Tony, but afterward Mark always felt a little ashamed that he had laughed at someone else's expense. He realized Tony never felt any remorse. Some of Mark's other friends seemed to get caught every time they did the least little thing they shouldn't have. He wondered if it was just bad luck. Why did Tony always seem to come out smelling like a rose, no matter what he pulled? In the end Mark decided that so long as he stayed with Tony, he'd come out smelling like roses, too.

◆◆◆◇◆◆◆

"How do you like my new motorcycle?" Tony gloated one warm June afternoon the summer before their junior year.

Mark had talked about wanting a motorcycle ever since his older brother had given him a ride on his, but so far his only form of transportation was his bicycle.

"Wait a minute," Mark complained. "Neither one of us has a job. Where did you get enough money to buy a motorcycle?"

"It didn't cost all that much," Tony hedged. "Kev wanted a new bike. I just did a few things for him, and he let me have his old one."

"My brother won't even let me drive his, and your brother gives you his bike. Unbelievable!"

"We'll figure something out," Tony said, and in early July, his friend told Mark about an old motorcycle the car salvage yard was getting ready to sell. It seemed to run all right and after Tony dickered a little on the price, Mark was able to scrounge enough money to buy *his* first bike. After a few weeks of work and a little paint, it was ready to ride.

One afternoon, Tony whipped out a map and spread it across the seat of the motorcycle. "Here's where we're headed the last two weeks of summer break," Tony said as his finger settled on the Oregon coast.

"Are you kidding me?" Mark managed to say through an astonished chuckle. He knew Tony liked to push the envelope and usually managed to pull things off that he really shouldn't have, but a motorcycle ride to Oregon? He didn't dare share his doubts with Tony because he knew it would be taken as a personal challenge. Still, Mark was certain even Tony could not pull this idea off.

"Look, I have already laid the ground work," Tony assured him. "I told my parents that you and I planned to do this when we got your motorcycle finished. Their reaction was a lot like yours until I told them your parents were all right with it."

"You did what?"

"When they heard that, they said it would probably be all right, as long as we stayed with my uncle when we pass through Boise and stayed with my oldest brother in Portland. His place is only an hour or so from the coast, and we could stay with him a few days."

"Unbelievable," Mark gasped.

"I could never talk my parents into this wild idea. Tell you what, though, you're such a sweet talker, let's see you talk my folks into letting me go."

A few days later, Tony did just that. Mark watched in awe as Mister Smooth laid out the plan, using the same story that had worked on his own parents. Tony could sell anything to anyone, and this was just another challenge to him. There was no fear or hesitation in his voice. He hit all the positive points about staying with relatives and how excited his uncle and brother would be to see them. When Mark's own mother chimed in and said how great it would be if the two boys could stop and visit her brother as well at his farm near Boise, Mark was speechless.

"I cannot believe you pulled that off," Mark yelled into the air when they were a block from his house. "I would have put money against you on that one."

They found duffle bags at the surplus store and fit them to their bikes, then strapped sleeping bags, coats, and rain gear anywhere it would fit. By the time they were headed out of town, Mark fully embraced Tony's plan even if it had come from a lie. *There's not a thing wrong with living like this*, he thought as he watched his hometown fade behind him in his mirror.

In the end, however, the great escape to the Pacific Ocean was not quite as exciting as Mark had thought it would be. He certainly enjoyed being treated as an adult when they rented a motel room, and he loved the feeling of being able to do whatever he wanted without having to watch over his shoulder to make sure his parents did not catch him.

However, during the hours spent blasting down the highway on his new motorcycle, he realized the reason he did not want his parents to catch him was actually twofold. First, he did not want to be punished. Second, and perhaps more important, he did not want to see the disappointment in his parents' eyes. Now that he was far from them with no concerns about being caught, he found he still could not escape the sadness of knowing how disappointed they would be if they knew some of the things he was doing.

That night as he had just begun to doze off, Mark woke with an involuntary jolt. Deep within his heart he could feel how much his Father in Heaven loved him and was probably feeling even more disappointment because of his choices than his Earthly parents could feel. As Mark waded through the feeling of deep sorrow and regret that weighed so heavily upon him, he knew there was no hiding from his Heavenly Father. That night turned out to be the longest of Mark's life as he could not shake the feeling of gloom that surrounded him. For the first time, he felt far from home and began to miss his parents. Even more, he felt God was so far away that Mark may never find Him again.

His mind offered up the idea that he was just acting like a childish little boy on his first sleepover away from home. Just as he would almost begin to think his fears were humorous, the gloom would return and the whole thought process would begin again. Morning came, and still his mind debated on whether he could ever draw close to God or if it was too late.

Mark's junior year started, and his life settled into a routine of classes, chores, homework, and church on Sunday. He joined the wrestling team and gradually spent less and less time with Tony. who was increasingly occupied with other friends also; they shared his own interest in music.

As warm spring weather finally arrived, Mark decided that would be the last winter he'd depend on a motorcycle for transportation. He'd hated riding to school every day, in the snow, on his motorcycle. He had a little money saved but knew what he had would not be enough. Only one possibility remained if he hoped to ever be able to afford a car. He needed to find a job.

"I hate the thought of even looking for a job," Mark said to Tony one afternoon as they left the bowling alley.

"I'd rather steal a car than work to get one." At Mark's shocked look, Tony threw both hands up and pushed his palms toward Mark. "Just kidding!"

Ever since the motorcycle trip, Mark had begun feeling like he allowed Tony to make too many decisions for him. He decided this was one decision he wanted to make without his friend's advice, and besides, Tony's help was starting to make Mark feel as though he had two dads. As summer got closer, he decided to ask his mom for help.

"Hey, Mom, do you know anyone who might need help this summer? I'd like to save up enough to get a car before senior year starts."

"Well, I know that Mr. Walsh always needs summer help at his gas station. Why don't you stop by and talk to him, sometime?"

"That's a great idea. Thanks. In fact, I need to go get gas right now," Mark said eagerly.

As Mark pulled into the station, Mr. Walsh came out to pump the gas. The older man always had a smile on his face and was friendly to everyone. He had the look of someone who worked hard every day – evident strength and smooth agility – and his face and arms were deeply tanned. Even though he was always busy doing something, he was never in a rush with folks and was always very friendly. He asked Mark how things were going, just like he always did. The conversation turned to the subject of summer jobs so easily that Mark wondered if his mom had called the gas station before he got there. In the time it took to pump and pay for his gas, Mark found that he had a job.

Mark spent the first four weeks of the summer working the day shift with Mr. Walsh. He learned a lot about the entire operation, and it only took a couple days to get comfortable with pumping gas and checking oil. Occasionally, it would take him a couple seconds to find the dipstick – they seemed to be located in a different place on every car, but it wasn't long before he'd mastered fixing flat tires on the breakdown machine. Mr. Walsh was such a great boss, and he was so patient when teaching Mark something new, that in no time at all, changing oil and lubing cars felt like a breeze.

"Hey Mark, let me ask you something," Mr. Walsh asked one afternoon while Mark was lubing a car. "You've picked this up about as well as anyone I've had work for me. Do you plan on working here for the entire summer or are you going to get tired of this and quit now that I've shown you everything I know?"

"Oh, I don't think you could get rid of me." Mark chuckled. "Why are you asking?"

"Well, Dan signed up for some night courses at the college. I was wondering if you might be able to cover those shifts or if I need to try to find someone else. I know you can handle it, so I thought I'd ask you first."

"Wow, that's great. If you think I can handle it, I'll take your word for it, but yeah, I think I can do it."

"Great, we'll get you scheduled for next week. You can still come in during the day shift on the days you don't work in the evening."

Mark was a little nervous the first night after Mr. Walsh left. He had never been at the station all alone before. He soon discovered it was a lot like the day shift where he would sit in the office, bored, for twenty minutes without a single customer driving across the hose that rang the bell on the wall in the service bay. When one car finally came into the station, it seemed to be a signal for three more to drive in at the same time. During these moments, Mark frantically started the pumps on each car and tried to get the windshields washed before the pumps clicked off. But when someone only wanted two dollar's worth of gas, he had to pump it manually and that always ruined his rhythm. He'd have to run back and forth to the office to get change for each customer in the order the pumps finished, and it could be very hectic sometimes.

The first couple of nights were very stressful, and Mark almost regretted his decision to cover the extra night shifts, but soon Mark decided he actually liked them much better than the day shift. Sometimes he had flat tires to fix and oil changes that the day shift had saved for him to do during his slow times. This meant that Mark was never bored, and he found the time seemed to fly by each night. Mark loved it.

Never forgetting his goal to buy a car before senior year, he had been keeping his eye on a truck parked at the station. One afternoon he finally asked Mr. Walsh about it. "What's the deal with that old truck parked out back?"

"Well, it belonged to Sam Robinson, but he decided he didn't want it anymore, so I bought it from him."

"What are you going to do with it?" Mark asked, hoping he sounded casual and that his interest wasn't too obvious.

"I don't know. I thought it might make a nice fixer-upper for somebody. Why? Are you interested in it?"

Mark got a feeling the entire conversation had once again gone too smoothly to be coincidence. "Very interested. How much do you want for it?"

"Trust me, son, you can afford it. I can take some out of each paycheck if you want. Plus, you can put it up on the rack when you're working here at night, and as long as you don't make customers wait and you get all your closing tasks done, I don't care how much time you spend working on it."

"That would be perfect. Does it run at all?"

"Nope, but I'll help you until it will at least get you around town."

Mr. Walsh meant every word he said, and over the next few weeks, he helped Mark until the truck sputtered back to life. Mark loved that old truck. He was usually able to spend a couple hours every night working on it. He put it up on the rack and rebuilt the brakes, changed the oil, lubed it, and put new shocks and tires on it. Then he played with the engine until it was tuned perfectly. In just a few months, he learned so much from Mr. Walsh that he soon had it driving like a new truck, and true to Mr. Walsh's word, it didn't cost much, either.

Mark's job left little time for any pranks with Tony who came around the gas station occasionally at night and helped Mark work on his truck for an hour or so. Tony teased Mark for working too hard and not being around to hang out, but the underlying bond that had kept the two connected since elementary school didn't falter even as the boys' interests and time began to diverge.

Completing closing tasks each night before Mark left was one of Mr. Walsh's conditions for letting him work on his truck during the evening shift, and Mark tried very hard to make sure he performed those closing tasks correctly. Each morning when Mark got to the station after closing the night before, Mr. Walsh would quietly ask if he had gotten everything done before he left.

"Well, I thought so, but now I'm thinking I must not have or you wouldn't be asking me, right?"

"That's what I keep saying, you're a quick learner. Do you see those racks of oil by the front door? I had to come down last night when the police called and told me they were still out. Not a big deal, but try to remember next time, okay? "

"Sure. I'm really sorry. It won't happen again."

Every night Mark tried to remember what he had been taught. He wanted to show Mr. Walsh that he could do a good job. No matter how hard he tried, though, he always seemed to forget something; Mr. Walsh's patient, "Try to remember next time," only made him feel worse and increased his desire to improve and not forget anything during his next night shift. After forgetting a task yet again, he decided he needed some advice.

His first thought was to ask Tony, but even as he was considering that idea, he started laughing. If Tony learned he had left oil out overnight, he would probably start checking the place out after Mark left each night just to see what he could find that was free for the taking. He considered asking his dad, but that made him realize his dad was one of the very people whom Mark was trying to convince he was reliable and old enough to work at a job. *As reliable as my dad*, Mark thought. People always acted impressed when they learned who his father was; he had heard many comments about what a hard worker his dad was and how he always did such a great job. Sometimes Mark had seen people's attitudes change toward him as soon as they realized who his father was. He wanted to have that same kind of reputation, so he finally decided his dad was exactly the right person to ask for advice about how to do his job better.

One night after dinner, Mark said, "Dad, I know you have a lot of different houses your paint crews are working on all the time, and you assign guys to do various tasks at those jobs each day. How do you keep it all straight? I know it can't be easy, yet you seem to know the status of every job at any time. I can't even remember everything I'm supposed to do when I close the gas station. I don't want to lose this job, but Mr. Walsh won't keep me if I can't close right. Do you have any advice?"

"Do you have to do the same things every night?"

"Yes, there's a long list of things that have to be done every single night, and every night it seems like I miss something."

"Well, I can tell you what works for me. When I have to remember things that need to be done, I make a list. Then I follow the list and make sure I don't miss anything. Why don't you go in your room and write down the things you're supposed to do each night? Put them in the order they have to be done. Then tomorrow night when you're closing, follow your list. If you're interrupted, check the list again and continue until you get them all done. You might even discover something you forgot to put on your list."

"That's a great idea. It sounds simple, but I think it will work. Thanks, Dad."

"Glad I could help, Son."

Saturday night, Mark worked his way down the list and was amazed at how smoothly things were going with its help. He grabbed the garbage can by the pump and hurried toward the front door so he could empty the garbage in the office at the same time. Just before he got to the door, he tripped. Quick reflexes helped him break his fall before he hit the concrete with his face, but unfortunately, the stumble caused him to let go of the metal garbage can which sent it crashing through the glass front door.

After he made the call to Mr. Walsh, Mark swept up the glass and waited for the older man to arrive. He was certain this would be the last straw; Mr. Walsh would lose his temper and fire him for sure. When he arrived, he went around to the back of his pickup and pulled out a piece of plywood.

"Want to help me board up the door?" he asked with no hint of anger or disappointment in his voice.

Mark hurriedly ran inside the garage bay and grabbed a hammer and some nails. Mr. Walsh was silent while he boarded over the door for the night. When the job was finished, he turned to Mark and laid the hammer down. Mark took a deep breath and braced for the worst.

"Well, accidents happen, and I'm just glad you didn't hit the windows. I don't have a piece of wood that big. Can you put that away?" he asked, pointing to the hammer. "I'm going back home to bed."

Mark waved as Mr. Walsh pulled out of the parking lot. *What does it take to get that guy mad?* He wondered in awe. Even with all the mistakes he had made, Mr. Walsh had never raised his voice in anger or frustration, not even once. As he shook his head, he imagined what his dad would have done if he owned the place. As much as he loved his father, he knew from whom he had inherited his own quick temper. Mark's respect for and desire to be a responsible employee for Mr. Walsh deepened. If he was honest with himself, he didn't just want to be a good employee for Mr. Walsh, he wanted to be more like the man.

The following Saturday when Mark closed up the station, he stood at the cash register going through his list for the third time. He glanced at each area as he read the tasks aloud. There was no way he was going to let Mr. Walsh down, again. Finally, he turned out the light and pulled the door shut.

On Sunday morning, he was sitting on the couch in the foyer when Mrs. Walsh came into the church. She got a big grin on her face when she saw him, sat down next to him and put her hand on his knee.

"So, how did it go last night when you closed up?"

With all the confidence in the world, Mark puffed out his chest, "Well, I think it went quite well, if I do say so myself."

"I think George may have a different opinion since he's the one that had to go down and lock the front door when the police called him at midnight. Sure glad they happened to get out of their car and check the door instead of just rolling through the station. You might want to add that to the bottom of your list." She laughed good-naturedly as she stood and patted Mark's shoulder.

Mark had been totally confident about the job he had done. In an instant, he felt like a flop. He had let Mr. Walsh down again. He knew every single item on his list had been completed, but Mrs. Walsh was right. If it was not on the list, he could forget even a simple thing like locking the front door. He added "lock front door" to his list.

Mark worked at the gas station all summer, and his respect for Mr. Walsh grew with every interaction. Towards the end of the summer, he knew his boss had been sick for several weeks, but he didn't know any details. Then one day his mom sat down next to him at the kitchen table when no one else was around.

"Mr. Walsh has cancer, Mark. He's going through some treatments, and I know he'll never say anything to you, but I thought you should know what's going on."

Mark felt as though his world had shifted in an instant. One minute before, everything had been great – he had a job he loved and he was going to start his senior year in a week with a new truck. Now everything seemed off balance. He remembered going to his grandmother's funeral after she had died of cancer. "Is he going to die?"

"I hope not. All we can do is wait and see, and pray for him."

Mark realized his feelings for Mr. Walsh went far beyond appreciation for a job and help with his truck. The way his boss treated him was a lot nicer than he sometimes deserved. Not many men ranked up there with his dad, but Mark realized that Mr. Walsh was one of them. 'Pray for him,' his mother had said.

"I don't think my prayers are strong enough to help him much," he mumbled, nearly forgetting he was still sitting at the table with his mother.

"Maybe you should work on that. But I'm sure your prayers are much more effective than you realize."

More difficult news came when Tony's parents split up around Thanksgiving. While it was a shock to Tony, the news of the divorce seemed to shake Mark even more.

"I can't even imagine my parents splitting up," Mark said. "I've never even thought about that happening."

"It's not a big deal," Tony said.

"So you have to choose which one you want to live with?" Mark asked. He knew plenty of kids at school who lived with one parent because of a divorce, but he had never personally known the parents themselves. Tony's mom and dad were like second parents to him. He couldn't understand Tony's nonchalance while he felt so upset.

"I think I'm going to stay with my dad, not because I like living with him more, but Mom is moving to some little place twenty miles out of town. The school out there is puny; I don't even know if they have a music department. I'm getting established here, and my band might even get to play for one of the dances this year. I don't want to walk away from all that."

"Well, I'm so sorry, Tony. It's awful."

"Mark, it's not a big deal. Kev told me we might come out way ahead. If we make our folks feel guilty, it could be a good thing. Who knows?"

"Well, you can't be moving to another school. Not during our senior year."

"Don't worry," Tony answered again.

By the time the first snow fell, Mark was ready to park his motorcycle and start driving his truck. He still closed the gas station every Saturday night, and he was glad to have his truck back up on the rack – there was always something that could be improved. Mr. Walsh was not working any longer because of his declining health, but the kind man did manage to come to the station occasionally when Mark was working and was always interested in seeing what improvements Mark had made to the truck. Mark worried about Mr. Walsh and tried to not think about the possibility of him dying. He continued saying infrequent prayers for Mr. Walsh, trusting what his mom had said.

◆◆◆◇◆◆◆

One Saturday while Mark was at work, his mom drove into the station. "Fill it up?" Mark asked, very officially, when he reached her car.

"Sure," his mother answered with a small smile, but her tone was somber.

He got the gas pumping and washed the car windows. "What brings you out on a Saturday evening?" he asked, realizing this was the first time she had ever been there to get gas during one of his Saturday evening shifts.

"I have some sad news for you."

That got Mark's undivided attention, but before she could continue his mind began zooming through a whole list of awful possibilities. Was something wrong with his dad? Was he finally busted for some prank he had pulled with Tony? Were his parents getting divorced? Was it Mr. Walsh?

"I just learned that Mr. Walsh died this afternoon. I wanted to come and tell you before you heard it from someone else. I know how much you admire him."

Mark leaned against his mom's car. *Gone, just like that. Yesterday he was here, and now I will never see him again. I will never get to hear the admiration in his voice when he compliments me on something I have done on my truck. I will never get to tell him how much I appreciate all he has taught me or how much I admire him.*

"Are you all right, Mark?" his mother asked quietly.

"I'm fine," Mark said, sniffing and turning away from her. He heard the pump clunk signaling the tank was filled, so he removed the hose and placed it back on the pump. When he turned back, his mother was holding a ten-dollar bill out the window. He took it and slowly walked to the office to make change. He swallowed his tears and forced his thoughts to focus. As he walked back toward his mom's car, he had to focus on something other than his thoughts about Mr. Walsh or else he knew he'd start crying and not be able to stop.

"Thanks for coming to tell me," he said as he handed her the change. She nodded, her own eyes filling with tears.

"I love you, honey. Your dad and I are here if you need us." She reached out to squeeze his hand and then drove away.

Mark knew Mr. Walsh had lived a good life, and he imagined his mentor standing in front of God, now, feeling confident, welcomed, and loved. *How would I feel if I died today and had to face God?* It was a sobering thought for Mark, and weighed heavily on him for several weeks after the funeral.

GRADUAL SEPARATION

Mark continued making an effort to regularly say nightly prayers after Mr. Walsh's death. He often thought of the question that had come to his mind after his mom had visited him at the gas station, *"How would I feel if I died right now and had to face God?"* He began realizing that his regret would be greater if he was engaging with Tony or emulating his behavior, even when he wasn't around.

One of Mark's concerns at the top of the list was Tony's behavior toward girls. Tony and Mark had been seriously dating Cindy and Suzanne for awhile. As Tony was spending more time with his music buddies, Cindy and Mark ended up spending more time together. At first it was just a friendship in which Mark felt sorry for Cindy, as she was left alone by Tony so much of the time. A bond grew between them; however, they both refrained from letting it grow into something that would cause issues with Tony.

As Mark sat alone one evening he was thinking about Cindy. He wasn't sure if he and Cindy were keeping their relationship from evolving, out of fear or respect, for Tony. Mark snickered out loud as he realized, Tony finding out would result in a little more than the quick sparring or headlock reversals from their childhood days. But his mood went solemn as he remembered a recent conversation one evening with Cindy.

"I used to think there was a possibility of a fun and exciting future with Tony. But I have seen some changes in Tony that are really causing me to rethink our relationship." Cindy confided, with apparent reservation, not knowing what Mark may think.

Mark paused, picking his words with caution, "I've seen some changes that are causing me concern in several areas also. The area that bothers me the most seems to be impacting your relationship with Tony. I have feelings for you that"

Cindy sharply cut Mark off, "Wait, you can't begin telling me about feelings between us, before you finish telling me what it is that Tony is doing that causes you the most concern; especially since it is impacting my relationship with him."

Mark sat with a loss for words. 'Evidently I didn't choose my words carefully enough he thought to himself'. "Okay, you are right" he again began slowly. "It is sort of hard to say much; because of the way I have let feelings grow between us, you know, betraying my own friend. But I am not talking about a relationship like ours, that we have tried hard to not let it get out of hand. All I am going to tell you is that Tony is not being fair to you. You'll have to figure that out on your own. But I will tell you, that I am jealous that he has a perfect girlfriend like you and treats you like he does. Now back to my feeling for you. I have feelings for you that cause me conflict. I like you more than I have ever liked a girl. I have totally lost interest in Suzanne because all I can do is think of you. Tony and I aren't as close as we used to be; but I still feel guilty about sneaking around with his girlfriend. So as hard as it is for me to say this; I feel we should not see each other until we both get our situations figured out."

It was the last night Mark spent time with Cindy. After a long conversation, they parted ways as friends; however, both wished it was more.

Tony had been sleeping with girls for quite a while; which previously hadn't bothered Mark; but, now that he was cheating on Cindy, it felt personal. As with the others, Tony had begun talking like he was the only one who would be inconvenienced if Cindy got pregnant. Mark hated the vile way he talked about Cindy and all his girlfriends – he had no respect for anyone or anything.

The other thing that was high on the list of "Tony Annoyances", was that it seemed, music and notoriety were the only important things to Tony, now. His band had started performing in all the nearby towns. When they started playing songs Tony had written, their popularity grew even more. As the two friends continued drifting apart, Tony suggested that maybe Mark was jealous of his success. It was easier for Mark to let him believe that, than to tell him the real reason, "that he didn't like the kind of person Tony had become." Sometimes Mark wondered if that was how Tony had always been and he'd ignored it. After Mr. Walsh's death, though, he couldn't ignore Tony's selfishness anymore. It began to feel like Mark was seeing his friend through clearer eyes.

Occasionally, the two still ran into each other and out of habit spent an evening playing pool or going to a show, but rather than bringing the boys closer together, each time they hung out, Mark left feeling like they're interests and ideas were less and less alike.

"Quit being such a butt," Tony said to Mark one night while they were sitting in Tony's car talking after a movie. "I don't see you always staying on the straight and narrow, so don't tell me what I should do."

"I don't care what you do, but you have real talent, Tony. I hate to see you using hard drugs and then thinking that's what helps you write songs."

"You can't say it doesn't help. Oh, unless, of course, you have been experimenting around on your own without me. Have you?" Tony huffed insultingly at Mark and laid his head back against the seat. "So I guess as long as I just smoke a little weed, that's okay, huh?"

"Look, I'm not judging you, man; I just think you're getting in too deep."

"Don't tell me you still believe in all that stuff our Sunday School teacher taught us," Tony slurred. "Is that what this is all about?"

"No, you know I don't go to church much anymore, but that's only because I'm taking a little break. It's not like I don't believe it."

"Well, it sounds to me like you're a hypocrite. At least I am grown up enough to admit what I do, instead of sneaking around behind people's backs and pretending I am still a good little boy. Why don't you run home to mommy and daddy, and I'll find some grownups to hang with?"

Mark got out of the car without speaking another word. He walked all the way home, fuming inside at what Tony had called him. *Am I a hypocrite? Sure, I don't go to church much, no matter how many times my parents ask me, but I still believe what the church teaches, don't I? I still believe in God, right?*

Mark felt a little seed of self-doubt begin to grow in the pit of his stomach.

Then one evening, Mark got an unexpected telephone call from Tony. He was in town on a Friday night, something that hardly ever happened anymore, and he invited Mark to go get a pizza with him.

Mark felt uneasy as he sat down across from Tony. Even before they finished eating, it was apparent how far apart they'd grown. The spontaneous spark that used to keep each of them in stitches was gone. The only laughs they could muster up were short and forced. After they finished eating, they sat in Tony's car and talked, as they had many times in the past, but the conversation was anything but fun.

"Heroin isn't really as big a deal as everyone makes it out to be," Tony said flatly, as if he were thinking aloud.

"I don't really want to talk about this," Mark responded.

"So you know I use, have known it for a long time, probably; but, still want to pretend it's not happening. Unbelievable."

Mark tried to change the subject. "Have you ever thought about going back to church, Tony?"

Tony snickered, "I don't really believe all that stuff anymore."

"What is it that you don't believe?"

"I just don't believe that the magical ball described in the Book of Mormon guided Nephi's family to America or that two stones helped Joseph Smith translate languages. It just sounds phony. It's almost embarrassing to admit that I ever believed in those things."

A thought came to Mark. "Let me ask you something, Tony. Do you believe that a musical instrument can be amplified, recorded, sent across the country on a wire, then transmitted through the air and received by a car going down the road, allowing a driver to hear the sound as if the instrument was being played next to him in his car?"

"Well," Tony responded, "that's no big deal with our technology. That's just a simple radio broadcast."

"How unbelievable do you think that would have sounded to anyone in the nineteenth century?"

Tony thought for a moment. "I guess it would sound next to impossible to anyone back then."

"And have you ever heard of a compass, a GPS unit, or a text message sent to a phone?"

"Of course," Tony said, "and I even know how they work and what they're for."

"Do you think you could combine these technologies and make a ball that had a display that could give changeable instruction and direction?"

Tony just nodded his head, not wanting to admit it aloud.

"Okay, now imagine this. Have you ever seen an optical character recognition scanner that can scan a document, put it into a format that can be edited and even displayed in a different language?"

"Sure, there are things like that now because our technology has advanced."

"Not done yet," Mark said. "Do you think a person could put this same technology into a package that could be worn as a set of glasses?"

Tony sighed, and then nodded. "Sure, it's possible now. But that would be unheard of in Joseph Smith's time."

"Honestly, Tony, don't you believe that a God who created the Earth and every miracle in it could put together something equal, if not superior, to what we can build today? And wouldn't it be even more believable if a person described something in accurate detail that is currently possible, but was incomprehensible in his own day?"

"I know where you're going with all of this technology crap, Mark, but you still haven't actually proven anything."

"I can't prove it to you because it takes faith to believe it. Do you remember what faith feels like?" Mark asked, finding it hard to keep the tears from collecting in his eyes. It was even harder to swallow because of the huge lump that had formed in his throat. He felt like he was sitting next to a shell that had once contained his long-time friend.

After a few more attempts at shallow conversation and an awkward goodbye, they called it an evening.

It took Mark a long time to fall asleep that night because of the question that kept running through his mind: What do I believe?

When Tony asked him to go to the racetrack with a bunch of guys on Saturday night a few weeks later, Mark was relieved he could use work as an excuse to decline the invitation. Ever since their last conversation, things had felt even more strained between the two friends.

He was closing the station when Kevin's car sped over the cable and the older boy shouted hysterically that Tony had been in a serious accident. Mark quickly finished locking the gas station and jumped into his truck. He followed Kevin to the hospital and was shocked when he entered the small room to find Tony unconscious and hooked up to an intimidating row of beeping machines.

"What happened to him, Kev?" Mark asked when he could finally speak.

"We had a little mishap at the race track," Kevin answered, soberly. His face was pale, and Mark wondered if he was going to pass out.

"He looks like it was a lot more than a mishap."

"The race track was closed, but a bunch of us decided it was the perfect time to have our own race. We cut the chains on the gate and started taking turns on the track. Tony was standing with some of the other guys by their cars waiting for their turn to run. One of the other guys finished running the quarter mile track and started back up the return road. He was drunk and loaded and came racing back toward the cars. No one noticed him coming through the dark at full speed until it was too late."

Kevin stopped talking, and Mark turned toward him, eyes wide. "So he hit Tony?"

"No. The guy hit his brakes when he saw them standing by their cars, but his car spun around and slid sideways into Ricky's car. A few guys managed to dive out of the way just before the car hit. The back fender of Ricky's car caught Tony, and I thought he was a goner, too, but he made it. I mean he hasn't woken up yet, and they haven't determined all of his injuries, but he's alive."

"Where were you when it happened?" Mark asked without really wanting anymore details from Kevin.

"I saw it all. Tony flew through the air when that car hit him, and he landed in a heap. It was . . . "Kevin suddenly cut off mid-sentence.

"Where are my sons?" Kevin and Tony's dad rushed into the room and pushed past Mark as he grabbed Kevin's shoulders. "The police showed up at the house and said a bunch of kids broke into the race track and someone nearly got killed."

Kevin sobbed into his father's shoulder. "Tony is hurt pretty bad, Dad. They aren't sure . . ."

Mark backed slowly away from Kevin and his dad and glanced at Tony's mom who had come in quietly and was standing by Tony's bedside, holding his hand and crying. Mark turned and slipped out the door. He could not shake the feeling that if it were not for his job, Tony would probably have talked him into going to the track with the gang. Mark realized it then could have easily been his own mom standing by the bedside crying over him?

Mark stopped at the hospital to see Tony nearly every day even though Tony remained unconscious and was unaware of his presence. At the end of the third week, Mark was sitting next to Tony's bed when he suddenly had a powerful feeling that his friend would soon be leaving this life. Trying to overpower the lump that had formed in his throat, he reached over and grasped his dear friend's very still hand.

"Hey buddy, I know how hard you have been struggling lately, but I promise a better day awaits you whether you stay or go. If you need to go to find that better place, it's all right. And if you stay, I swear we will find a better place together. I know I will never find a better friend than you. Man, we have had an amazing time together haven't we? I know I would never have done so much or seen so many things if you hadn't been there shoving me along."

Mark chuckled quietly as his mind wandered back through the years starting with their first encounter at scout camp, to the many times Tony had manhandled him, times that were always followed by his endearing and contagious laugh. After sitting in the peace that had settled over the room, Mark said good bye to his best friend and left.

It was the last time he saw Tony, who slipped away that night. Mark was stunned and found it hard to breathe when he learned of Tony's death. He sobbed, feeling a greater sense of loss than he would have thought possible. Somehow, they were more than friends who had known each other since fifth grade. Something had always pulled him back to Tony and made him hope he could convince him that he was on the wrong path. Whatever that connection had been, it had not been strong enough to save his friend from such a senseless fate.

He wondered if he could have done more to help Tony. Could he have kept in touch a little more often or flat out told him he was making some bad choices? Could he have saved his friend?

Ribiab found Shroba working on a painting in the garden. "Hey, did you hear that Stephan has already returned from the New World?" Ribiab asked.

Shroba nodded. "I heard, but when I got to the Assembly Area, he had already gone. He must not have spent much time there."

"Yes, he returned not wanting to talk much about his experience, but I do know that Stephan's final days have been really difficult for Elias. In fact, Elias is kind of blaming himself for the way that Stephan's experience ended on Earth. Great Father has granted me permission to visit Elias and bring him some comfort. He told me He's granting this privilege because Elias is continuing to make changes in his life that demonstrate his desire to return to our Father. You made a wise decision in choosing him as your mortal father. I know he will be a huge help and blessing to you when you join his family not long from now."

The two friends shook hands and Ribiab turned to leave with a parting, "I'm headed to the portal now, take care."

"Thanks for taking the time to share your thoughts." Shroba called back. "I know I won't remember Elias, but I am glad that I will be with him again. I miss him. I'm glad Great Father is allowing you to go bring him some peace."

As Mark pondered on Tony's life and tragic death, a calming thought entered his mind as if someone was whispering in his ear, *"You know everyone has the right to make their own decisions when they come to Earth. Tony made his choices and you could not have made him do something he did not want to do. You did everything you could to help him, and he is responsible for his own actions."* Like that quiet moment in the hospital room, Mark's memory was again filled with all the wonderful times the two had shared when they were boys. He felt a wave of peace and truly believed he had done all he could to be Tony's friend. It was a relief to set down the burden of guilt over something of which he had no control.

Ribiab offered a prayer of thanks to Great Father for the opportunity to help his dear friend, Elias. It was so rewarding to see how his words of comfort instantly calmed Mark as the Spirit Ribiab brought from the Great Father filled him with peace.

Mark found himself unable to think of little else but Tony's death for the next several days. During the funeral, his eyes kept drifting to Tony's parents and his brother, Kevin, and he wondered how they would be able to cope with such devastating loss.

The tragic and sudden end of Tony's life and the powerful feeling Mark experienced when he said good bye to his best friend made Mark realize he needed to head to that better place he had promised Tony. After Mr. Walsh's death, he'd begun to make small efforts, but now he knew he had to begin to tackle some real changes in his own life. As he drove to work a few days after the funeral, he again thought of Tony being taken from the Earth so suddenly, and having to face God and explain what he was doing at the racetrack that night. Mark vowed he was going to start going to church again.

Even though Mark worked hard to make the necessary changes, sometimes late at night when he was drifting off to sleep, he would find himself wondering why Tony had always been able to pull him back into his life. It was like Tony had possessed some power to persuade Mark to overlook any resulting consequences to him or others. Tony's way had been fun and thoughtless. But Mark couldn't blame his friend. He had his agency and was responsible for his own actions and choices. He could see now that Tony's way had not been fun or easy at all. His friend had been a slave to drugs and alcohol, and it had led him to other people who shared those addictions. From now on, Mark would honor his friend by leading a different sort of life. He would choose the harder right.

FAREWELLS AND GREETINGS

Tony's death also reminded Mark how quickly life could end. There were no guarantees of a long life, and he wanted to be prepared to meet his Maker when his time came. He had no delusion that his choices had always been right, but he had always known right from wrong. Whenever he had chosen to do the right thing, it had been because he feared the consequences of doing the wrong thing. Now he found he wanted to do what was right because he loved God and realized all that He had done for him.

Mark continued to work at the gas station for a few months after he graduated. But after Mr. Walsh's death, the place felt hollow, especially in the evenings when it was slow; which, provided way too much time to recall the many hours he'd enjoyed being tutored by Mr. Walsh. Not just on mechanics, but about life in general. He also found himself often thinking about the night Tony's brother came to the gas station to tell him about his best friend's tragic accident. It had become an unhappy place for him, so after some thought, Mark decided to search for a new job. He loved working on his truck, and working on vehicles in general, but more as a hobby than as a career. A lot of his friends worked at grocery stores or restaurants, but he currently made almost as much as them while working at the gas station. He could see a career in that direction would probably not provide too much room for growth, either. Another group of friends from school had gone on to college. Mark couldn't see spending one more day in school now that he had graduated. His options seemed to be narrowing and he felt panicked. He went to the employment office and looked for other options. The most they could offer was a variety of laborer jobs at various plants. When he learned that the pay for those jobs was only a little better than packing groceries or flipping burgers, he knew it was time to confront the voice that had been whispering a solution in the back of his mind all along.

Mark had helped his father do some house and building remodels when he was growing up. He hadn't liked all the dirty cleanup and grunt work he had to do. It felt like freedom when he got his first paying job and didn't have to answer to his dad, but that little voice was very persistent. He knew his dad always needed help, and the pay for construction was better than almost anything out there. But would his dad actually consider him a real employee, or would he just end up working a bunch of hours and not getting paid for them like when he was younger? Mark decided it was time to find out.

"Dad, I have been looking for a new job, and I am not real happy with my options. I was wondering if you needed help on any of your crews."

"Well son, to tell you the truth, I am short of reliable guys right now. I have been impressed with how long you have worked at the gas station and how much integrity you have demonstrated by always showing up and learning as much as you could. I have thought about asking you if you wanted a job, but I wanted you to have the opportunity of deciding for yourself. It is important to find your own way, search it out, and then make it happen. That's part of becoming a man. I feel you have done that. Plus, it'd be hard to miss the blank job applications and blank forms from the employment office you have left lying around on the counter. I know what some of those places pay, and I am sure I can do better than that. I'm guessing that since they were blank, you have decided they really aren't for you, anyway. So, if you are asking for a job, I assume that must mean I am the best gig in town. If you want to work with Dan and Sam, I would love to have you as my newest employee." He slapped Mark jovially on the back.

"I thought I would have to do a lot more talking on a job interview. Guess I was wrong. This getting hired is a cinch," Mark joked as he laughed and returned the slap on his dad's back.

Mark spent the next few years working for his dad on a couple different crews. Dan retired, and many others were just not reliable employees. One afternoon, Mark's dad pulled up to the job site just before noon. With his iconic whistle, he quickly got Mark's attention. Mark set down his tools and jogged toward the truck.

"What's up?" he asked.

"Jump in. I think we can still catch the pizza buffet before it gets too crowded."

"I brought my lunch."

"Good, you can work late since you will be able to eat it for dinner."

Mark jumped in the truck, not really slowing his pace during the brief exchange. Lunch was something they often tried to do as work permitted. It was these times that Mark enjoyed so much. His dad would share stories he had never heard when he was growing up. He got to see a whole new side of his father. He learned about his childhood, his experiences in the military, how he met Mark's mom; and they often discussed all the historic church sites his father loved to visit so much. His dad had always been so busy working to provide for his large family, so Mark had never gotten to see much beyond the disciplinary task manager who came home exhausted at the end of the day.

They didn't just see each other for lunch either. Many mornings, Mark would go to his parents' house to begin the day. His dad would go over the status of the jobs and they would make a game plan for the crews, and of course he didn't mind eating the breakfast his mom prepared for them. It sure beat the other days when he just grabbed some chocolate milk and donuts in route to a job.

One particular morning Mark arrived to find place settings for two and freshly cooked breakfast sitting in the center of the table. Oddly, his mother was absent. Mark sat down with his dad who was already filling his plate. He answered the unspoken question. "She is in getting ready; we are going shopping this morning. She felt she ought to leave us alone this morning as there is something you and I need to discuss."

Mark suddenly felt a little uneasy. It was as though he'd come for breakfast and wandered into unfamiliar territory. Was this how Tony's parents had broken the news of their divorce all those years ago? Mark's dad must have seen the creased forehead that signaled the worrying thoughts running through his son's head because he burst out laughing.

"What is going on in that head of yours? You look like you're expecting a firing squad to step out from behind the fridge or something. Take a breath and put a smile on your face."

Mark started laughing, too, as he realized how transparent his thoughts must have been. "Ok, it just seemed a little odd this morning from the minute I got here. Now that you have had your laugh for the day, tell me what's going on."

"Well, your mom and I have decided it is time for me to semi-retire, and in a couple years we plan to go on a mission; then I'll retire completely. This morning, I want to talk to you about your plans and see if you are interested in taking over for me at running the business."

"Wow, Dad, I'm not really sure what to say, it sounds like you and mom have already settled on a plan, and you are just asking if I am interested in holding down the fort."

"You have it even before you've started to eat. That took a whole lot less explaining than I thought it would. We could have just done this on the walk to the truck and saved mom the time it took to prepare this breakfast."

"Hold on, I haven't agreed to anything. I still have plenty of questions." Mark felt the earlier discomfort creep back again.

"Of course you do. I am just kidding, son. I know this is a lot to consider, and we will have to work out a lot of details. I just wanted to break the ice this morning and see what your feelings are. There is no pressure here, but I think it would be a great opportunity for you, especially as you begin to consider starting a family."

Mark blanched, panicked, "No pressure?!" he cried. "Now we have the added expectation of me finding a wife and having a bunch of kids?"

Before his dad could speak, Mark took a deep calming breath that turned into a laugh at his own overreaction.

"No really, Dad, I am so excited for you two. This will be a whole new chapter in your lives, and you two deserve it. You have both worked so hard. Yes, I am very interested, and I don't need to take time to consider it. I am up for the challenge and will do whatever, whenever, and however you want me to do it. Just one clause: I'll find the wife and have the kids when I'm ready." With matching smiles, the two men reached across the table and shook hands.

Over the next few years, Mark put all his energy into stabilizing the business. When it no longer consumed all of his time and energy, he began contemplating his future. He had recently started attending the temple on a regular basis. One afternoon as he sat pondering, his mind recalled the conversation he'd had with his dad about retiring. What was once a joke now seemed to give Mark pause. He was ready. He wanted to get married and raise a family of his own, but he had never had a relationship that went beyond friendship. He began wondering if his mother was right – was he too picky?

He had dated girls during high school and in the years following. When Tony was alive, Mark had dated different types of girls than after his friend's sudden death. There had been some girls that he liked very much, but none of them caused him to wonder what marriage might be like with them. He was always careful to be a gentleman and not show disrespect, but he also never felt the kind of regard for anyone he dated that he was sure he would feel for his future wife. Mark realized that he had never been in love.

In his prayers, he began including a plea for help to find someone who was right for him. He briefly wondered if people got married and then let their love grow to what he was looking for in the beginning, but before the thought was even completed in his head, he dismissed it. He had a gut feeling that he just hadn't met the one who would end his searching.

A short time later, Mark had a vivid dream one night as he slept. He was sitting on a bench in a gorgeous garden with a beautiful woman. Both she and the garden felt familiar to him. As he looked at her face, he experienced powerful feelings of love for her. It felt familiar and comforting to hold her hand, as if it were a natural thing to do.

When he awoke, he knew this dream was unlike any dream he had ever experienced. It remained clear in his memory and each time he thought of the beautiful girl, he again experienced how strongly they loved each other. He lay in bed trying to determine what this dream meant. Was it a glimpse of something from his future? Did it hold any meaning at all?

Whatever the reason, he knew the feelings he experienced for the woman in his dream were much stronger than anything he had ever felt for anyone in real life. He tried to remember if the woman in his dream was his wife, but the only thing he was sure of was the love he felt for her. He tried to recall, without success, the location of the garden that had seemed so familiar to him, too.

As with all dreams, even those that seem vividly real, within a few weeks the feelings dulled and became buried within the forgotten chambers of his mind.

A few months later, Mark was shopping for a new pair of pants when he met an attractive sales clerk named Jenny. He felt very awkward during their entire exchange because he kept losing track of what she was saying. That afternoon, he discovered that the corny saying "lost in her eyes" became a reality every time her beautiful blue eyes looked at him. She smiled easily, and the long blond hair that framed her face and fell past her shoulders made the color of her eyes more prominent, more captivating. She was nearly as tall as Mark, about five foot seven, and her slender body moved fluidly, as though she was never in a hurry.

She was so familiar, and he felt sure he must know her from somewhere, but he could not recall where. He opted to avoid one of those "you look so familiar, have we met?" lines. Instead, he left the store feeling very disturbed, unable to shake the feeling. All the way home, he tried to place her face into any setting he had been in recently. As he pulled into his driveway, the dream of the beautiful girl in the garden came so clearly to his mind.

"Is that possible?" he asked himself.

Hurriedly, he drove back to the store. He had no idea what he was going to say, but he knew he had to see her again to determine if his suspicions were correct. As he walked up to where she stood folding clothes, he realized her face was the very face he had seen in his dream.

"Is something wrong?" she asked, obviously surprised to see him again.

Mark realized he was staring at her, but it seemed to take a long time before he could make his mouth form the words. "I liked the pants I bought so well, I decided to come back and get another pair before they're all gone."

He felt stupid as he uttered the lame excuse, and knew she must be thinking the same thing, but she simply smiled and pulled another pair from the double stack of pants.

"Thank you," was all he could say as he watched her ring up the sale. Soon he had no choice but to turn and leave the store.

His wardrobe increased considerably during the next week; he found himself back at the store each day in order to see her again. He was certain it was as obvious to her as it was to him that it did not matter what he bought, as long as she helped him. After repeating the visits Monday and Tuesday of the following week, his real intentions were revealed.

"Mark," Jenny said as she handed him the socks he had just purchased. "I am going on break. Would you like to join me?"

Mark laughed as he took the sack. "Yeah, I think that's probably a good idea."

Jenny led the way, amused at how shy this man seemed. It was obvious any woman would welcome his attention – he was the proverbial tall, dark and handsome. He wore his hair a little longer than many his age, and his hazel eyes were so intense it made her want to know what he was thinking. He did not seem self-conscious, and she would bet a month's wages that women did not intimidate him, but every time she caught his eye, he became flustered and embarrassed. She wondered if she would have to begin the conversation when they reached the break room, or if he would feel more comfortable when there was not a line of customers standing impatiently behind him. She pushed open the door and walked toward a worn couch.

"Now, would you mind telling me why you have come back to buy one new thing every day for over a week?"

"I've been trying to get up the courage to ask you out," he stated, not bothering to beat around the bush, and feeling a little amazed at how easy it was to talk to her, especially after constantly worrying how he would ever be able to begin a conversation that went beyond clothes.

"And have you done that?"

"Asked you out or worked up the courage?" Mark asked. He was not even the least bit nervous any longer.

"Worked up the courage. I already know you haven't asked me out yet," Jenny teased.

"Would you say yes if I did ask you to go out with me?" He hedged.

"I might. Why don't you try it and find out?" He certainly seemed a lot less uncomfortable, but she found it disconcerting that he never quite met her eyes while he spoke.

"Jenny," he began, "would you like to have dinner with me tonight?"

"Sure. I get off work at 6. We can meet and go from here if that is all right?" Mark's answering smile was bright, and Jenny's heart warmed even more to this shy man.

Mark was there 15 minutes early just in case she got off before their agreed meeting time of 6. He did not want to risk missing her. As he sat waiting, he realized he had butterflies that he had never felt before. He was so concerned that she may not find the spark that had instantly consumed him. He had never been as nervous in his entire life as he was waiting by the door for Jenny to come out.

"I was wondering if you would be out here when I opened the door. Thought maybe you might have come to your senses and run for cover." Jenny teased.

"Hardly. I have picked a quiet place, so we can get to know each other a little better. The food's pretty good too, you ready?"

The date went so well that four days later Mark stood at the back door of the store again. While waiting to begin their second date, he noticed he had far fewer nervous butterflies until they were in the car, and Jenny put her hand up, "Now, I don't want you to think this is some type of speed dating and I have advanced us to the point where we are meeting parents already. However, my parents are in town because my grandfather passed away and they'd like to see me sometime tonight. We can go by after dinner if you are all right with that or you can drop me off back here, and I can drive over there alone. I told them we have just started dating, so there's no pressure. I promise."

Mark began laughing, "Wow, I have never been asked to meet the parents on a second date before. You must really like me, huh? No, seriously that would be great. No better time than the present to meet my future mother-in-law." Their eyes met briefly and then darted away, and they both laughed nervously.

Jenny's parents liked Mark and the couple continued to date seriously for nearly three months before their relationship inexplicably shifted. Suddenly, their time together felt strained and rocky. Where there had once been ease and comfort, there were now awkward pauses and hurt feelings.

Sitting in the car outside Jenny's apartment one night, the mood in the car was nearly as cold as the snow lightly settling on the windshield. "I don't know Mark; it just feels like things have moved a little too fast. You say that you love me and want to marry me, but how do you know I am the one you want to be with forever? That is a huge commitment, and I think we should slow down and see if we feel the same after a little break from each other."

"Jenny, I don't need a break to figure out how I feel about you, but if a break is what you want and need, I will respect that."

"I'm not saying I want this to be the end of our relationship, Mark, I just think we need to regroup a little," Jenny said, trying and failing to soften the blow.

"Right, that's fine. Go have your break, and I will just talk to you later," Mark replied with uncharacteristic rudeness, as the feeling of rejection stung deeply.

Jenny waited a moment before opening her own car door for the first time since they'd begun dating, as Mark showed no intension of opening it for her or of walking her to her apartment. Almost to her porch, she broke down in tears as his tail lights disappeared into the darkness.

They each began dating other people, but the whole time Mark felt so concerned about who Jenny was dating. His worries astonished even himself; because, he had never been concerned like this about anyone he had dated. When it came to Jenny, he felt responsible and protective, and his feelings were much stronger than he could justify for a woman who was no longer his girlfriend. Mark tried to temper his feelings by reliving their last date in his mind, but just as he would begin to rekindle the anger he felt, he would remember the feeling he had when he had woken from the dream of sitting with her in that garden. He knew he was still hopelessly in love with Jenny and despaired that it was now only a one way relationship. He wondered if she still cared, but his pride kept him from picking up the phone to call her. He wasn't about to go looking for a second helping of rejection.

To distract himself from the void he felt, Mark began studying anything he could get his hands on about church history. His father had kindled his interest in church history years earlier after he had visited some of the sites with Mark's mom on an anniversary trip. Mark also spent a lot of time in the temple pondering the situation with Jenny. On one such occasion in the spring, an elderly sister sat down next to him.

"What is this great concern I see you struggling with young man?" she asked in a kind voice.

Reluctant to divulge how desperate he felt, he answered only somewhat truthfully, "I am just enjoying the solitude of the temple."

She smiled at him knowingly, and rephrased her question, "What problem brings such need for pondering?"

Deciding she was not going to be put off and a little relieved at the opportunity to finally share his feelings with someone, he told her everything. When he concluded, she smiled in such a warm and satisfied manner he wasn't sure if she was pleased because she had been successful at exposing his truly personal struggle, or if she found it amusing that anyone could be so desperate to find true love.

Reaching over, she gently put her hands around his. With a voice that soothed like the sound of a small rippling brook, she delivered the most pointed message he had ever received. "This very day I have been sealed to my deceased husband. I, too, waited for the right person my whole life and had totally given up, years ago. Then I met a man who had been single for a number of years after a failed marriage. We were married after knowing each other only a few months. Each of us felt we had known one another our whole life. Unfortunately, he passed away after we had been together, enjoying each other's love and companionship, for only a few short years. I was not a member of this great Church when we got married, but because of my dear husband's patient example I was baptized, and we set the date for when we would go through the temple and be sealed to each other. But he suddenly became ill." She stopped speaking, looked into Mark's eyes for a moment, and then continued. "If you feel you have found the right person do not settle for anything less. And above all, do not let your pride take a grand future from within your hands. Always seek God's desire for you, rely on the feelings He provides, and accept his will and timeline in all things. Life will then turnout better than anything you could create on your own even in your wildest dreams."

Mark's heart and eyes were both ready to overflow. The burning conviction within his heart made him sure the words were from his Heavenly Father, even if not spoken directly by Him.

"Thank you." It was all he could push through his lips before his voice began to break.

The change that occurred in Mark's heart that day in the temple was instant and complete. Over, the next few weeks he felt as if he were walking on air, and he no longer felt any concern or depression about Jenny and their future together, instead he continually thought of those sweet words of council he had received while in the temple. He found himself on his knees often, but now he was thanking his Father in Heaven for his newfound comfort, rather than asking for something to happen.

In this calm state of mind, Mark received a call from his mother one morning as he was preparing for work. She told him that his grandfather had unexpectedly passed away during the night. Mark sat silently as he took in the news. "I will call Dad tonight when he gets home and let him know how sorry I am. Thanks for letting me know, Mom. I will see you later this week."

Mark sat alone that night reminiscing on time spent with his grandpa. Slowly he began to feel a pain he had forgotten existed. His mind shifted and a gloom set in as he waded through the dark memories of Mr. Walsh's and Tony's passing. Again his mind shifted and he realized he'd had total control all along to stop the sadness of the last few months. He had been miserable without Jenny although he was trying to fool her, and himself, by dating others and acting like their break didn't bother him. His grandpa's death brought back the realization that the number of our days on this earth is uncertain, and at any time we may unexpectedly find we have been called home. His pride was responsible for him and Jenny not currently being together. He finally got up the nerve and called her.

"Jenny, do you remember our second date?"

"Of course I do, but are you asking about the dinner or meeting my parents?" she responded with a short laugh.

"Both. Listen, would you be willing to go to dinner with me on Wednesday and then to my grandpa's funeral on Thursday? My parents would really like to see you again," he paused. "But not nearly as much as I would like to see you." Mark managed to control his emotions until just at the end.

"I am so sorry to hear about your grandfather. Yes, I would love to come with you. Mark, I have wanted to pick up the phone so many times, but I wasn't sure how you felt."

"I'll tell you what, let's pretend this is our second date all over again and forget about anything bad that has transpired between the two second dates." Mark suggested as he tried to regain his composure. It was so good to hear her voice again.

"That sounds like the best idea I have heard in a long time. I look forward to seeing you on Wednesday. Good night."

And just like that, what had felt like an insurmountable wall was gone. They both knew they were responsible for part of the blame, but neither wanted to bring any memory of it back by even discussing it. It was over and gone. After their date on Wednesday, they headed back to Mark's parent's house as there was a lot of family in town for the funeral. Entering the kitchen it was evident that was where all the old people were. Seeing his mother's two brothers in the first two chairs on the right, made Mark almost turn around and leave. It wasn't that he disliked them, quite the opposite, but he knew as soon as they saw him he'd be in for one of their roasts.

"Well, who is this beautiful young lady, Mark?" the first uncle began.

Before Mark could even get Jenny's name out of his mouth, the second uncle jumped in, "Wow, she is a lot prettier than the one you brought over last night."

"I didn't bring anyone here last night," Mark said to Jenny, trying unsuccessfully to remain serious even as he burst out laughing. "They just always kid around."

The first uncle started up again, turning to his brother, "Oh, I don't think you should have mentioned the one last night. Hey, we're sorry Mark; we don't want to cause any problems." Then they both burst into laughter, obviously proud of themselves and their mischief.

"I don't know Mark, they sound pretty convincing." Jenny said as she squeezed his hand, and both headed toward the table to get something to eat.

After a few "new" dates their relationship felt strong and right. Only a month later they began talking about marriage. There wasn't really a formal proposal yet, more of a mutual understanding and excitement about getting married.

A few weeks went by before Mark and Jenny decided to drive to Salt Lake on Saturday morning. Jenny wanted to get some wedding ideas and they always loved shopping at the malls and finding good places to eat.

"Hey, do you mind if we stop in here?" Jenny asked, as if a magnet was pulling her into the jewelry store they'd just strolled past. Within minutes she found the ring of her dreams.

"How do you know this is it? I thought women had to look for hours for the ring before they knew they'd found the right one. Isn't there some kind of an oath you take about that when you're a teenager?" Mark joked.

"Lucky for you, I am a better shopper than most. This is it, I am sure." Her voice was hushed, and her face beamed with happy anticipation.

After a little more quiet whispering, Mark purchased the beautiful diamond ring and slipped the ring box into his pocket.

After finishing a seafood dinner that was unlike anything they could get back home, Mark suggested they stop by Temple Square. They passed through the large gates where Mark hoped to find the perfect view of the temple. He was pleased to see that the crowd was minimal due to the sudden chill and the time of day. Hand in hand they walked to the south east corner of the temple where Mark spotted an empty bench surrounded by flowers just to the right of the wide sidewalk. They sat down to enjoy the view of the temple and noticed how the evening sun caused the south granite wall to glow. Mark closed his eyes as the scent from the flowers floated around them. When he opened his eyes, Jenny was looking past him at the temple. Slowly, she turned her head and their eyes met.

Mark's mind was flooded with memories; first, the image from his dream when he had initially been shown Jenny's face, then a flash of the elderly woman as she convinced him to finally swallow his pride. Mark turned away and wiped at the tears that had begun streaming from his eyes.

"Mark, what's wrong?" Jenny asked with concern.

"Give me a minute," Mark chuckled as he stood and finished wiping at his eyes. He took a couple deep breaths and sat back down. Turning to face Jenny, he said, "That is not at all how I pictured this going." He pulled the ring from his pocket and slipped it on Jenny's finger, hoping to level the emotional playing field a little. As he had anticipated, her eyes instantly filled with tears, and just like that, he was wiping at his eyes again, too.

After a long comforting embrace, Mark made a formal proposal. As the mood lightened again, Mark teased, "I brought you here with the intention of giving you this ring and laughing as you made a spectacle of yourself in front of all these people. I guess the joke was on me." He pulled her close, and together they watched the temple shine brightly in the twilight.

On the day Mark married Jenny in the temple he wished very much that he could find the elderly lady who had given him the wonderful advice that had brought him to this moment. Looking at Jenny in her beautiful wedding dress felt like the beginning of Mark's life.

Unfamiliar with the need to make reservations at hotels during the summer months, Mark and Jenny traveled 50 miles before their first attempt to check into a hotel for their honeymoon. The hotel clerk was both blunt and amused at their naivety as he turned them away. After several more futile attempts, they drove back the 50 miles and hesitatingly approached the hotel desk where their wedding reception had been held earlier that evening.

"Do you happen to have a room available tonight?" Mark asked in what came out sounding a bit like an involuntary plea.

"We have been booked for weeks but you two are in luck, I just received a cancellation a couple hours ago. Can you fill this out for me?" After looking at the information Mark provided, the clerk's face filled with confusion. "Aren't those your names out there on the billboard right below the wedding congratulations?"

"Yes," Mark offered up with an embarrassed sigh as Jenny giggled, both too exhausted to provide more explanation because it was nearly 2 AM.

The next morning, while eating breakfast they both erupted into laughter when Jenny posed the obvious question, "Mark, why didn't we just go to your apartment last night rather than leaving ourselves at the mercy of yet another full hotel?"

"I guess it was the years of honeymoon programming or maybe just a total breakdown of reasoning at the end of a long but wonderful day." Their laughter continued and didn't stop until Mark leaned over and kissed his happy bride.

A few weeks later, in their tiny apartment, Jenny whispered in the darkness as she snuggled closer to Mark, "My mother told me that we needed to be sure we didn't have kids right away. That we should give our marriage a chance to work before we add the 'burden' of children to it."

Mark chuckled, "That's funny, the other day my mom said we shouldn't buy or build a house yet; we should just stay put in our little apartment for now rather than getting strapped down with a house payment. She said we should enjoy our lives a little before we become house poor. Gosh, between our mothers' advice I am beginning to think this marriage thing is not what they advertise it to be. Everyone acts like you need to get married to be happy, but then when you fall for it, they tell you how bad your life is going to be. I'm thinking we may have been conned, what about you?"

"I think we better look into how long we have before that 'I do' becomes permanently binding," Jenny grinned and punched Mark in the arm.

During the first two years of their marriage, Jenny and Mark both focused on working, so any free time they had together was highly valued. Some of their free time was spent alone together, but they also found time to camp and enjoy the outdoors with their siblings and friends.

On one of their infrequent solo campouts, Mark poked at the campfire and asked, "Jenny, what do you think about me changing my career? I have been feeling like we have no real security. Over the years I have gotten accustomed to the seasonal waves of construction, but last year's slow down took a heavy toll. Some say it was a recession, but whatever it was it has made me feel vulnerable. I'm considering going back to school and getting a degree. How do you feel about that?"

Jenny finished assembling her s'mores before she answered, "I think that would be great Mark. It will be a lot easier to do now while our family is still just the two of us. We have talked about how neither of us feels it is the right time for us to have kids yet, so your plan has my vote."

"But are you sure you're OK with supporting us financially for a couple years while I take a step backwards?" Mark asked with some guilt in his voice.

"I don't think getting your degree should be considered 'taking a step backwards.' I have a good job and it will sustain us for now, so let's take advantage of it. We won't have this option forever because we already agreed I won't be working outside the home after we start our family. Now is definitely the time for you to go back to school."

Mark watched Jenny lick the sticky marshmallow off her fingers, and his heart filled with gratitude for his kind and generous wife. "I have been struggling with this for a couple weeks and you make it so easy the minute I tell you. I think I can keep working part time while I go to school. One of the foremen has agreed to step up and eventually cover my duties running the company, so I'll still be able to contribute some. I still don't feel right about leaving you holding the load alone, but thank you, Jenny. I'll go check on getting registered for classes this week. Should we tell our parents we are putting off our family for awhile longer or just let them keep wondering when grandchildren are going to come?"

"Funny you should ask, Mark. While we've been talking, I was just wondering the same. I say we just let it ride."

"I am fine with that," Mark laughed.

The first few months of school were tough for Mark as he settled back into being a student. It wasn't so much the routine that was the adjustment; it was paying attention during class. During the last couple years, his construction job had been so mundane that his brain had become lazy. To pass the hours of driving and performing repetitive construction tasks, it had become natural and perfectly acceptable to let his mind wander. Now, sitting in class, he found himself constantly missing sections of the professor's lecture as his mind frequently lost focus.

He often met with a study group at the library on the evenings and weekends. When a study road block occurred, there was always someone in the group who could get them moving again. Mark found the group study sessions very advantageous. Sometimes members of his study group saved him from wasted time and frustration, and other times he was the one who helped the others in the group move along. The group was a little perplexed at first when he told them he would not be able to meet on Sundays. He vaguely explained that it was because of a commitment he had made before he began the school year.

Mark didn't really explain who the commitment was to at first, but some in the group made assumptions anyway. He missed Jenny so much during their hectic weekly schedule and felt it was important to have at least one day together; however, that was not the whole reason. His brother had told him about how he'd quit studying on Sunday while he was attending college, and his grades had improved dramatically. Mark had also read articles that indicated a brain thrived when allowed to rest, just like any other muscle. All those things individually made it worth a try, but viewed collectively not studying on Sunday seemed like the only option. As Mark grew more comfortable, he confided to some of his closer friends in the study group that when he was struggling with the adjustment of focusing and using his brain and being in a classroom all day, he had asked God for help. And at that time he had felt impressed to make a commitment to not study on Sunday as an indication of his dedication to following God's commandments. In the weeks following his confession to his friends, it was interesting to watch the Sunday study group attendance slowly taper off.

One Saturday evening, he sat alone on the couch relaxing while trying to find a movie to watch. There wasn't much on and the channel rested on a movie he had watched a month earlier. He found himself verbalizing the lines of each scene prior to the actor saying them and realized the change that had taken place to his memory and the ability to focus during the year. His eyes welled up as a burning within his heart confirmed that because of his sacrifice, God had turned his weakness into strength. Mark's successful commitment to not let school stall his quest for increased spiritual growth had been rewarded indisputably. In the following weeks, Mark also realized his tests had gotten much easier and he could recall exact wording of lectures while answering test questions.

As summer neared, Mark stood by the curb raking the grass after mowing the yard. Jenny pulled up and practically bounced out of the car.

"Well Mark, the rabbit died," she said excitedly.

"What?" Mark asked.

"Remember how I had an appointment to see the doctor today? Well, I'm pregnant!"

"OHHH" his voice trailed off and for a moment all he seemed to hear were the words, 'The sins of the children will be on the father's head.' His mind began rolling through many of the things he had ever done wrong, all the things he still needed to change, and how many corrections still needed to be made to become a good role model for his child.

"I am glad you are so excited," Jenny huffed, hurt by his silence. She was half way to the porch when Mark suddenly came back to the moment.

"I am. You don't understand." Mark shouted, running to catch Jenny and sweep her into a hug. He spun her around and then gently set her down and tenderly touched her stomach. "I am," he said again in a voice filled with wonder.

Later that night, Mark and Jenny carefully calculated their new plans. Jenny would work for another year until Mark graduated. She would take just enough time off to have the baby and then return to work for another six months. Her hopes of being a stay-at-home mom would have to be temporarily postponed. As soon as Mark began working after graduation, she would be able to quit.

"Well, I guess all the time we spent plotting out our lives was a bit of a waste. Do you ever get the feeling it is futile for us to make any plans when they often don't even resemble what actually happens?" Jenny asked with some frustration.

"I don't get that feeling sometimes; I get that feeling *all* the time. Then I remember God inks out the timeline and we are left just trying to guess at it. I can't say that it is a bad thing though. Sure, we are getting a baby a little sooner than we expected, but I have a distinct feeling it will all work out. It will make the last several months of school a challenge, but I am up for it."

Jenny stood and headed to the kitchen to check on dinner. As she went through the doorway, she called just loud enough for Mark to hear, "Sounds like someone is still working on damage control from earlier," and she began laughing.

The Great Father stood by Shroba in the Assembly Room and announced, "Shroba, you are one of the elect among my children. I am well pleased with thee this day as you leave us to begin your experience in the New World. Mighty works will result from thy actions as you earnestly engage in the events that will take place to usher in the beginning of a time of peace when My First Born will return again to the earth to begin His rightful reign of glory."

The tears of those who thanked Shroba for his untiring service toward them further testified of his complete dedication to serving his Father and those around him.

Father put His arms around him and said, "Please, come to me after you have said your farewells," then He turned and walked through the door covered by a silver-leafed vine.

"Are you still willing to talk to someone of my lowly state after getting such a public endorsement from Great Father?" Ribiab teased Shroba.

Shroba laughed and embraced his dearest friend. "Thank you so much for coming. I feel a little lost without Elias and Sarah here to support me. I guess it's pretty evident why I chose them to be my mortal parents; even from the New World, they are a source of strength and guidance to me. Still, having you here helps calm me, and I think I will be all right now."

"Did you ever get a chance to tell Sarah you had selected her to be your mortal mother?" Ribiab asked as his eyes scanned the others who were approaching to wish Shroba farewell.

"Yes, I told her a few days before she left for the New World. I didn't want to miss the opportunity again like I had with Elias. She sort of fell apart on me though. I still don't know if it was the right thing to do or not. I told her to be sure to tell Elias when she found him in the New World, and that caused her to smile, at least for a moment."

"You know, I have said goodbye to a lot of individuals on their departure days, and often I have done so with apprehension because I am not sure how they are going to fare during their experience in the New World, but Shroba, today I am filled with peace. You are going to do well my friend. I can feel the truth of it deep inside of me."

"Thank you, Ribiab. Your words mean the world to me." Shroba held his friend tightly, hoping to drain any remaining strength he could from him before Ribiab slowly backed away as other well-wishers approached.

Sometime later, Shroba entered the room to meet with Great Father; the sand colored walls with the green, gold, and gray tones made Shroba feel as if he had suddenly returned to his favorite place near the falls. The scene visible through the open doors at the top of the stairs captivated him, too. The majestic New World radiated with brilliance against the darkness of space.

"My son," the Great Father said, "Your character and personality will be unchanged in the New World. The mortal body and unfamiliar experiences that await you there will not alter your valiant character."

He asked Shroba to kneel before Him, and then administered a blessing upon him. "My son, I bless you with the rights and privileges you have earned through your obedience during your first estate. I promise unto you great protection in the New World from the evils that will be abundant around you during the days of your mortal life. You will have great power to lead others in truth and righteousness. As you know, your earthly parents are your dear friends Elias and Sarah, and they are very special souls. I bless you with the strength to care for and defend them."

After conferring several additional promises upon Shroba, the Great Father concluded the blessing. Shroba stood, and his Father softly uttered His final words of council regarding the last days before they embraced. Then it was time. Shroba walked up the stairs and turned for one final look at his Father before stepping through the open doors.

Mark stood at the front of the chapel to bless his baby son, Scott. As he waited the short seconds for those good men to gather to participate in the blessing, his mind flashed through the scenes of his life that had brought him to this point. He suddenly felt the worth of the valiant spirit he held in his arms. During the previous week as he had prepared to administer this blessing, he'd experienced nervousness, wondering if he would do an adequate job. He had offered prayers, begging for the help he felt he needed. As hard as he tried, he could not seem to collect his thoughts or prepare any words that he might say.

Now, standing in front of the congregation, he wondered if he could even say the words that were streaming into his mind while keeping the blessing to a reasonable amount of time. Wonderful words of guidance and promised blessings from on high came out of Mark's mouth— words that surprised even him. He concluded the blessing and held his son in the air for all to see. In that moment, Mark felt as if he was raising his son up as an offering to God to use for His righteous purposes. Tears of joy streamed down Mark's cheeks as he felt the Spirit burn within him. Looking out in the congregation, he could see Jenny's own tears running down her cheeks and into her joyous smile.

"I can't begin to tell you what a blessing you have been to my life," Mark said to Jenny later that evening when all their guests had gone.

"I have noticed all day that you were a little distracted. Care to share what's been going on in that head of yours?" she asked as she nursed baby Scott.

"Well, I've told you about Tony."

"Yes."

"It's been just over ten years since I attended his funeral. As I sat down after blessing Scott, today, I was overwhelmed with gratitude as I thought about where my life has brought me. The last several years have brought changes and a family that I once wondered if I would ever have. I've been blessed with the most wonderful wife, and today you heard a small portion of what I felt our son is going to accomplish during his life.

As I held Scott, I began thinking of Tony. It wasn't with the same sadness that I have struggled with in the past. It was like a whisper brushed that old sorrow from my mind, and then my thoughts were turned to how blessed I am for making the necessary changes in my life to get me to this very day. It was as if Tony's memory came only as a tender reminder, allowing me for a moment to see the stark contrast that can result depending on what I, or rather on what any of us, may choose to do with our individual experiences each and every day of our time on this earth. The impact and importance of enduring to the end, well became so very clear to me today.

Jenny snuggled baby Scott closer. "Tony seems to have been a driving force in your life, both for bad and good. You started down a path with him that wasn't great, but he was also the catalyst for where you are now."

"It's strange, isn't it? I don't recall him ever being happy. Not really."

"Maybe he just lost his way and couldn't escape the downward spiral he was in," Jenny suggested, trying to reason it out.

"Yeah, maybe. I used to wonder if Tony was angry because he did not want to do what we'd been taught in church when we were kids. But now I think that no matter how hard he tried to convince himself that he didn't believe in those things anymore, somewhere inside he still felt he was not doing what he knew he should, and that tore him apart inside every minute of the day."

"That sounds sad," Jenny said softly. "Do you think eventually he would have realized the truth and come back to the Church?"

"I don't know."

"It's not your fault, Sweetie."

Mark smiled at her. "I know. Since Scott's birth, I have been vividly aware that he lived with Heavenly Father until such a short time ago, and I think that's what made me start thinking about Tony again. I have always wondered what it was like for him when he got back to heaven. I feel so blessed that I found my eternal companion and now we have a son. My life feels perfect, and I wish so much that Tony's life had been better. I wish he could have experienced this same joy."

The following summer brought a number of changes. Mark graduated and secured a job within weeks. Jenny gave her notice and started her new job as full time mother. Both were excited for the changes, and after dinner on her first day home with baby Scott, Jenny glowed with excitement as she shared every detail of the day with Mark.

After she had taken him through a detailed account of Scott's evening bath time, she said, "Not to change the subject, but can I change the subject?"

Mark smiled. "Sure. What would you like to talk about?"

"Your new job! I think it is very exciting that you are going to be traveling all over the country. Have they told you where you're going on your first trip, yet?"

"Omaha. Real exciting, huh?" he smirked. "I just go where they have people who need to be trained, so Omaha it is. The one good thing is that I'll be able to visit Winter Quarters."

"What exactly intrigues you so much about the Church history sites?"

"I think it comes from when my dad and I would go to lunch, during those years I was working for him, and his stories would often turn to the historic sites he had visited. The ones that were most memorable to him were the historic sites of the church. Later, when we were taking our break, I began spending a lot of time reading about church history to distract me from missing you so much, and as I read about many of the sites it brought my dad's stories back to life in my mind. Up until then, studying history just seemed like words more or less, but as I studied about those sites it was like the people and locations came to life; they became real to me."

Jenny nodded thoughtfully.

Mark continued, "The more I studied, the more sensitive I became to the whisperings of the Spirit. For a time, I was obsessed with studying the history of Christians from the apostasy of the early gospel to its restoration and the trials and sacrifices of the early Latter-day Saints. The more I studied the history of the early pioneers, the more I wanted to see where it all happened. I can't even believe that now my job is going to pay me to travel to many of those locations I have always wanted to visit."

Mark paused and for a while the two young parents sat listening to the quiet breathing of baby Scott and the gentle squeaking of the rocking chair as Jenny slowly tilted back and forth.

"Jenny, while we're traveling down memory lane, there is something I want to tell you about. I have wanted to talk to you about it so many times, but the timing never really felt right. I want the words to do the experience justice because I feel it is the very reason we are here together tonight."

Mark knelt next to the rocking chair and told her of the frustration he'd felt during that period while they were separated. He told her of how he'd begun going to the temple and praying for God to help him find the person who was meant for him. He reached out and took Jenny's hand in his. He told her how even when they were apart he'd known that his search was over and that he had already found the woman who would become his wife. Finally, in reverent tones, Mark described the dream he had received all those years ago. Jenny began sobbing as he described the vivid details of the dream.

"Mark, I am so sorry I asked you to distance yourself from me during that time, the same time you received such a strong confirmation that we were meant to be together. I just wasn't ready, and I needed time to process everything. I can understand now how painful my words must have been for you and why you reacted the way you did. I think it was the only time you ever treated me rudely. It was so out of character for you and really painful."

Mark reached up to wipe the tears from Jenny's face. "I can now say that you probably did us both a favor by pressing pause on our relationship. We both still had a lot to learn and we needed to mature through some tough months. Honestly, I think that time apart helped us to gain an appreciation for one another." Jenny smiled through her dwindling tears and softly ran her fingers through his hair.

"I mentioned that during those months apart I spent a lot of time pleading to God to help me find the right person, but I was so filled with pride that I wouldn't even pick up the phone to call her! I had been given a dream that showed your face so clearly, yet I would rather ask God for another option because I didn't want to swallow my pride and make his gift to me a reality. I am surprised God didn't just say 'there is no hope for that young man' and send a dispatch to bring me home. Instead, through a huge act of mercy, God gave me another chance."

Mark took a deep breath and continued. "One afternoon as I sat in the temple, God sent me an angel. She sat by my very side." Mark struggled as he attempted to deliver every detail, word for word, that the dear little sister had told him while holding his hand. It was tough, but he managed to get through the message he wanted to deliver to Jenny. The two talked late into the night, and it was as if their eyes were opened to the reality that their lives together had begun long before their life on earth. Their marriage, they realized, was important enough to God that He had provided guidance and the opportunity for them to arrive at this wonderful moment, together.

HAND OF THE LORD

Baby Scott grew fast and within a few years was joined by a baby sister. Jenny gave birth to a daughter, Lynne, who from the very beginning was a curious little girl with her own unique personality. A couple years after Lynne's birth, Mark and Jenny were blessed with Jordan, their second little girl who surprised them all by possessing one green eye and one blue to match each of her siblings.

Like their parents before them, Jenny and Mark worked to create a world that evolved around their children. They took them on family vacations to Disneyland and drove them to dance classes after school. They taught them to ski during the winter and to swim during the summer. They made sure their children grew up with fond memories of time spent with their grandparents and their hordes of cousins. Although Mark continued to enjoy his job and the opportunity for travel it provided, he also looked forward to the time he was able to spend at home with his family. He was especially excited as he packed for a trip one October morning because he was going to be taking Scott with him. Mark's parents were serving a mission at Martin's Cove in Wyoming. Scott was going to spend some time with his grandparents while Mark went on to Denver for work. He only wished he could take Jenny and the girls, too.

It was late morning when Mark finally pulled out of the driveway. After situating Scott with books and other things to keep him occupied in the back seat, Mark assumed it would be a quiet evening of driving before they reached his parents' place.

They'd been traveling several hours when the short fall day turned to darkness. Within a few miles, the peaceful drive became an all-out battle with Mother Nature. The wind began to blow a light snow horizontally across the road. As the flakes got bigger, the road demanded Mark's entire attention. The vehicle's forward movement and the horizontal blowing snow made him nauseous. He slowed to fifty five miles per hour, but wasn't too worried; the snow was melting as soon as it hit the wet highway surface.

Mark drove for another hour and felt his consciousness drift into a semi-hypnotic state. His mind wandered as there was hardly any traffic and his speed was still moderate. The intense contrast of the darkness and vivid streaks of white, as the headlights seemed to ignite the blowing snow, made his geographic location indeterminable. The only thing he knew was that he was still headed toward Wyoming.

A thought drifted through Mark's mind. *I wonder where I am, I know there is a bridge over that large canyon ahead somewhere, but I haven't a clue how far.* He knew that the snow would probably be freezing to the road surface over the bridge section. He let the thought pass as his mind wandered to a new subject.

A few moments later; however, an image flashed before his mind's eye. In the image his vehicle had just slid through the bridge's guard rail, the passenger door flying open and the canyon floor visible beneath Scott, who was falling from the truck with a desperate hand outstretched to his father.

Mark instantly pressed the brakes, slowing to about twenty five miles per hour just as he passed onto the frozen bridge surface. Releasing and then gently tapping the brake again, he did everything he could to keep the vehicle from hitting the left guardrail, then the right, then left again, before finally regaining full control of the truck for the remainder of the way across the bridge.

After reaching the other side, he proceeded to a safe place to pull onto the shoulder of the road. Visibly shaken, he looked at Scott who slept peacefully in the back seat, oblivious to any danger. Mark gasped out a prayer to the God who had saved them as he knew there was no way they would have survived had he not received the vision and slowed the vehicle before hitting the icy bridge surface. His prayer flowed from thanks and gratitude for his blessings to begging for forgiveness.

"Why am I so slow to heed Thy voice?"Mark cried out.

He knew he had dismissed the first warning thought of the upcoming danger, requiring a second and extreme display which finally caused his compliance. His mind jumped to another time in his life when a second confirmation was needed. That time had required an elderly sister in the temple to remind him what God had already shown him in a dream.

Mark's prayer continued for some time as he covenanted with the Lord that he would listen and heed His first promptings in the future. He made vows to listen for the whispering voice and to not require a hammer to get his attention. He sat for some time as he quietly gave thanks and composed himself before pulling back onto the road and continuing his drive that night.

It was very late when they finally arrived at his parents' trailer, so they all headed to bed after a brief greeting and hugs all around. The next morning, after getting caught up on everyone's lives, Mark told them of his experience the night before. "Please don't say anything to Jenny, yet. I don't want her to hear it from anyone but me, but I am not sure how long it will be before I will be able to tell her." The image of his son reaching out for him was still too raw in his mind.

Mark left for Denver that afternoon and prepared for his training class the following day. He enjoyed his work and the opportunity to associate with so many people in the company, but each day of training drained him, and he was content to eat an early dinner and settle in his room.

When he first began traveling with the company, Mark had been excited at the novelty of spending time in hotel rooms and eating out. It didn't take long, however, to determine there was not much on television, at least not the types of things he felt comfortable watching. He had decided after the first few business trips that he would pretend there was no television in the rooms and use his time to read or study, instead.

Quiet evenings alone in his hotel room soon became his favorite time on the road. He would study the history of the areas he was visiting. If there was anything in the area pertaining to church history, he would go see it. If there was anything pertaining to history in general in the area, he would search that out, too. If there wasn't anything in the area to see, he would spend his time reading history books or the scriptures and writing about what he was learning. It made the time spent away from his family more tolerable.

At the conclusion of the second day of training, he headed back to Wyoming and his parents' trailer. He arrived just in time to eat the wonderful dinner his mother had prepared for them. Their conversation turned to the details of their mission at the historic Martin's Cove over plates of her homemade apple pie.

"You know I've always been so interested in early church history and love visiting these types of sites. I could not ask for a better place to serve our mission," Mark's dad began.

His mom jumped in, "My good friend is serving a mission in Salt Lake City at the Church History Center. I don't much like comparing notes because our mission is so much more physically demanding than hers. We spend our time moving dirt to put in trails and sanding and staining wood that we then use to make the handcart replicas. The hard work is a blessing though. We have seen so many miracles as this land has developed from an impossible dream into a place ready for the Prophet to come and dedicate to the Lord."

His parents proceeded to tell of the numerous occurrences on their mission that they considered miracles. His father shared, "The church was interested in purchasing this property from the owners, that is, the part that wasn't BLM ground, for several years, but the local church representative indicated there was probably no way the family would sell the multi-generation ranch. But after an amazing sequence of events, the family decided they would sell. In a conversation, one of the brothers indicated he had always known the land should belong to the church. Immediately, the other brother said, 'You have never told me that, yet I have felt the same.' After years of speculation, the sell was complete." Mark's father finished with excitement, as if he had been personally responsible for the sell.

Early the next morning, Mark headed up the trail to Martin's Cove. His mother had said she had some small jobs Scott could help her with that morning. After hearing all the stories his parents had told him of the Cove, he knew he could not go home without seeing it for himself.

Small scattered drifts of snow covered parts of the trail, left over from the storm that had passed through the night before. His light coat, perfect for the temperature he'd come from, was not sufficient for the frigid Wyoming morning air. The sun struggled to shine through the clouds. Mark walked quickly, occasionally breaking into a brisk jog in an attempt both to try and build up some body heat and to get back to his parents and Scott before they got too far into the morning activities. He paused at several locations along the trail to read the plaques that outlined the dreadful events that had claimed both lives and the future health of the survivors. The tragic scenes were vividly painted in his mind as he read each one. No one had been immune to the sorrow of that place. Young and old, male and female survived and young and old, male and female died. Every Saint on that trail had become acquainted with hunger, suffering, pain, and God.

On one plaque, Mark read how the starving pioneers formed a daily morning detail to bury the dead in ground frozen so hard that some bodies were only covered with rocks. Tents that had blown down during nightly storms remained that way until morning because those exhausted souls on the brink of death were just too weak to do anything about it.

Mark pondered in silence for a considerable amount of time, knowing that some of the individuals he'd read about that morning were his own ancestors. When he finally looked up, he saw that blue sky was now visible through the broken clouds. He noticed a passenger jet high above, the sun glinting off its metal wings. He shook his head in wonder over the contrast between the kind of travel experienced by early Saints and the kind experienced by those in the airplane high above Wyoming. One group had traveled for months, first through heat and then across a frozen wilderness filled with heartache and death; the other group, flying high above him, enjoyed a temperature controlled cabin, the comfort of reclined seating, shoes removed, and a refreshing beverage during a mere one hour flight. In this moment, with the biting wind blowing through his thin coat, and his nose and fingertips still numb, Mark developed a soul deep and lasting appreciation for all those early saints who'd given so much, in some instances, even their lives. Because of their sacrifices, he and his family now had the opportunity to partake of the blessings of the restored church of Jesus Christ and to continue their efforts by engaging in the final preparations for His promised return.

Mark stood, feeling different than he had before he'd set out on his walk that morning. He'd gained the feelings and perspective he had hoped for, by coming to that holy place. As he slowly began walking back, he noticed his legs were a little stiff from sitting in the cold and realized that at some point the temperature had no longer been a part of his thoughts.

After walking about twenty yards, he stopped. The presence of those courageous saints was so strong he could not help but pause' if even for just one more minute. Turning to look back, he almost anticipated seeing active scenes of those freezing souls trying to brave another day;

before a whisper came in his ear, "Why look ye for the living among the dead?"

A surprised laugh escaped from Mark. The voice had sounded joyous. His solemn mood of respect and sorrow was suddenly one of happiness. The few whispered words provided so much understanding. Those souls had given much and suffered much, but it was to a glorious end. They were now very happy and still actively involved in the great work they had helped to start. Their days were now bright and full of greater understanding. Their obscure little group was now actively helping their fellow saints worldwide. Mark arrived back at his parents' trailer to begin what felt like one of the brightest and most glorious mornings he had experienced in a long time.

A few days later, Mark and Scott returned home to Jenny and the girls. After he and Jenny got the kids settled for the night, they cuddled together on the couch. It was always extra nice to be close after Mark had been gone on one of his work trips.

"So, tell me about your trip. I know Martin's Cove is a special place to a lot of people and has a lot of church history associated with it. Your dad must be in heaven getting to be there for more than an afternoon."

"He is. It was so great, Jenny, at least once we got there. I am reluctant to tell you what happened on the way, but I guess I might as well now that it is over and no one was hurt."

Mark found he was able to talk about the frightening experience sooner than he thought, especially after thinking of it for much of the drive home.

"I knew Scott was going to have so much fun staying with my parents for a few days. Right after we left Salt Lake, we ran into the storm they had promised us. It was a lot worse than what they usually turn out to be."

Mark paused for a moment when he saw Jenny's forehead crease with concern, but as he continued telling of the amazing miracle of being saved from tragedy on that frozen bridge, her concern changed to wonder at how blessed Mark and Scott had been.

"I am so glad you stopped to thank God for the miracle he provided. The image of seeing Scott falling must have crushed you. Mark, I can't even imagine," Jenny gasped and hugged Mark tightly for a long time.

Eventually, Mark told of the morning trip to the Cove. The mood of his story followed the same pattern Mark had experienced that morning. There was solemn respect for the courageous pioneers and appreciation for the conveniences of living with modern day comforts. Even the humor seemed to touch Jenny as Mark told of his expectation of seeing pioneers still struggling with their tents, rather than now being engaged in a delightful eternal work.

A few months later, Mark was asked to go and train some new employees in Kansas City. It was something he thought would never come about--not the work assignment, but the opportunity to travel to the very places he had spent so much time studying. Evening after evening on earlier work trips, he had relived the life of Joseph Smith and the history of the early saints. Mark sat in silence in his generic motel rooms trying to envision years of events and places that had become so real to him that at times he'd almost been able to feel their weight. He had studied Independence, Far West, and the other locations where the early saints found such great opposition and also grew to know God as a tangible being. He studied the prophet Joseph Smith and looked forward to standing where the prophet had stood, hoping to gain true insights for himself rather than simply taking the words, good and bad, of others.

When he returned home from the trip, Jenny wanted to know everything he'd experienced and seen."Now, about Jackson County, or Independence, Missouri," he told her one night as he unpacked. "What I find especially interesting is the prophecies about what's in store for that area in the last days. Honestly, I had a hard time concentrating on the classes I was teaching, and by the time the weekend finally arrived, well, it's a miracle I didn't get a speeding ticket Saturday morning," he laughed.

"I doubt you could include that on your expense report," Jenny teased."So tell me, was it as wonderful as you thought it would be?"

"Oh, yes! But it was different, too. I was so grateful to be able to sit on the lawn where Joseph Smith indicated the temple of New Zion would be built, but then I got a strong feeling that I was missing the whole point of being there."

"I don't understand."

"I was a little confused, too. I went to the LDS visitor's center and watched the slide show, and one of those slides seemed to reach out and grab me. I felt a little rude for interrupting the show even though I was the only person there besides the two sister missionaries, but all I wanted to know was where the photograph on the slide had been taken and how could I get there. It looked like the most peaceful and tranquil place on Earth. They said it was at Springhill or what members of our church call Adam-ondi-Ahman."

"I've heard of Adam-ondi-Ahman before."

"I had, too, but I didn't really know much about it. While I was driving there, I started feeling the directing spirit I had felt before when visiting historic church locations, and I knew this visit was going to be special. When I finally found the place from the slideshow, all I could see was emptiness in every direction. It covers 2,500 acres that are owned by the Church, and I had no idea where to begin. I felt like a little kid in a huge toy store, unable to decide which way to go first. Since there were no buildings to tour, my only option was to study the plaques that designated specific things about the area. Jenny, even if I had never studied about Adam-ondi-Ahman, I would have known the area was sacred and important simply by the way I felt when I was there. There were only a few other people around, so it was easy to find a secluded place to sit. I closed my eyes and let my thoughts run freely."

Map 1 – Mark's Quest of Historical Locations

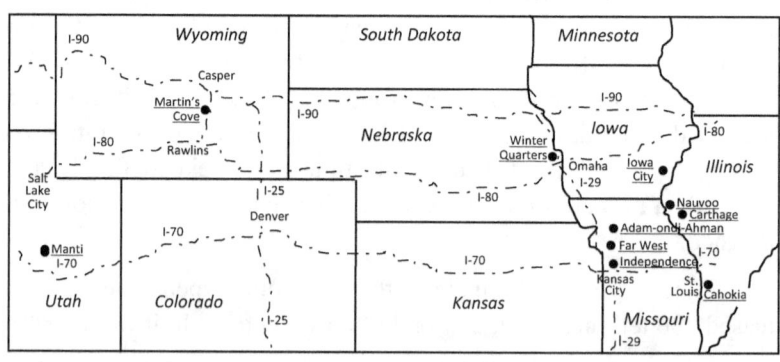

"I wish I had been there with you. Next time I hope I can be."

"I wish you could have been there too, that would have made the whole experience even better. After sitting for some time, I started walking. I found Tower Hill, and I could see the entire valley. I sat down again and closed my eyes, and the most amazing warmth washed over me; it was as real as if the sun were beating down on me. I was aware of a reverence there that, until that moment, I thought could only be felt in the most sacred buildings on Earth. I sat there and enjoyed the peaceful solitude.

"Pretty soon, a group of four men approached me. I found out later that the oldest man was the father of two and grandfather of the third. He began sharing experiences with us that one could never find in a book. It turns out he was one of the first missionaries called to that location by the Church to clean it up and make it a destination. He said that when he was doing some grading and planting trees on the small hill, he found three group-burial sites and some rocks that appeared to have formed some type of alter. As I listened to him share his experiences, the words felt familiar, as though someone had already told me those things. I waited until the men left, and then slowly worked my way down the hillside and walked a short way through the valley."

Mark reached out and took Jenny's hands in his. "It felt as if I were strolling with an old friend, rather than walking by myself. I enjoyed the solitude and peacefulness so much; there was a sort of reverent quiet to the place. The occasional sounds of birds and animals could be heard, but even my footsteps sounded hushed, as though I were walking in padded shoes through rain soaked leaves. The beating of my own heart seemed louder than anything around me."

"It must have been very special to make you tear up again as you tell me about it."

"It was amazingly spiritual. When I got back to my truck, I did not want to leave, even though I knew there was nothing else to experience or see. I had not exerted myself in any way, but I felt physically and emotionally drained – totally exhausted, as though I had played in a rugby tournament and at the same time listened to test results about a serious medical condition. I know I will never forget the feelings I experienced in that valley."

"I'm glad you took a recorder with you on this trip."

"I didn't use it while I was there, though. For some reason, it felt irreverent to talk or record anything while I was in that sacred valley. I did manage to record my thoughts as soon as I got back to the hotel that evening. As I recalled what happened in that special place, I found I again experienced those peaceful feelings. That valley is very interesting historically, but there is something more. I cannot pinpoint why, but I know there is some connection between that area and me. Does that sound strange?"

"Not coming from the man who saw me in a dream before we met."

Mark continued traveling often over the next several years. He felt blessed that so many of his trips were to areas of the Midwest, seeming to neatly follow the dots on a map of historic church locations.

On one trip, the locations he was scheduled to visit were close together, yet too numerous to complete in a single trip. He decided to lump the two work trips together and remain in the area over a weekend rather than travel home at the end of each week only to turn around and return on Monday. The schedule provided two weekends and several flexible travel days to spend visiting the sites he wanted to see.

Finally, the end of his trip arrived. Mark sat at the airport on a Thursday morning waiting to board his flight home. He was the first one to his gate, arriving early as was his habit. A calm feeling settled over him as he began recounting all his recent stops on the trip. The only thing that would have made it better was if Jenny could have shared all the many experiences with him. He could not wait to get home and see all the faces he missed so much. He had told Jenny the night before to line up a sitter because he wanted to share some quiet time together when he got back. She'd happily agreed.

Jenny and the kids picked Mark up from the airport, and the family headed for an afternoon at the zoo. It was so fun to see his children so excited and happy. He felt like they had visibly grown during the short time he was gone. After lunch and the zoo, they picked up the sitter. Stopping by the house, they got everyone situated before Mark and Jenny headed off together. They stopped by their favorite pizza place and got their go-to half and half pizza and salad. They then proceeded up to the place that had become their own little sanctuary from the world since moving to Salt Lake City a few years earlier. It was a little park high up on the bench that allowed a wonderful panoramic view of the entire valley. Seldom did they have to share it with anyone else especially in the early evening on a weekday. They ate and enjoyed the warm breeze coming up the hill to where they sat together catching up on the kids and the happenings at home during their time apart. Although the city was emitting volumes of noise, all that reached them was an occasional muffled horn or accelerating engine.

Jenny spread out the blanket and they moved from the table to stretch out on the grass. They both exhaled as if they had just run a sprint, then both started laughing.

"It's so nice to have you home. It feels like you were gone for months not weeks," Jenny began.

"I know. It was a great trip, but it was nothing compared to coming home and being with you and the kids again."

"So did you about go crazy with all that extra time on your hands? I think I would go nuts if I had to travel alone," Jenny squeezed Mark, as if the thought alone made her cringe.

"I have to admit I thought it was going to be the worst, being gone over a weekend, but it turned out to be okay. Not that I didn't miss all of you, but it gave me time to do some real soul searching and find some answers to a question that has been haunting me for some time. That is actually why I wanted some uninterrupted time to talk to you, because it is kind of complex and I am not sure if I can deliver it so you can get the whole meaning or understand the impact it had on me."

"It sounds daunting just from your intro. I am a little nervous for the shoe to drop. There isn't any trouble between us is there?" Jenny's voice was serious.

"No, I am sorry to open that way," Mark pulled her closer against him, lightly laughing to ease the tension he could feel emanating from her. "You and I are wonderful. This is totally about my own personal struggle and journey. I have been so excited, I could hardly wait to get home and share this very personal path I have traveled in finding my answer."

He felt Jenny relax, and a peace settled over both of them as Mark took a deep breath and began.

"Over the years we have discussed all kinds of things together as we've gained knowledge and our testimonies of God and our beliefs have deepened and become clearer. Yet something has nagged at me for a considerable amount of time, yet I haven't shared it with you. My testimony of God is unquestionable as is my testimony that Christ's church needed to be restored upon the earth. And I have had definite witnesses that the current prophets who lead and guide Christ's restored church are true prophets. Logic tells me there have always been prophets to testify or prepare the world for the coming of Christ from the beginning of time and will be until the end of time. Neither event of His coming to the earth is more important than the other. In the scriptures I find God always worked through his Prophets in each era of time, making it logical that He would provide Prophets for the two greatest prophesied events in history. However, a struggle has continued to grow within me."

Mark felt Jenny's hand involuntarily squeeze his leg. He was making her nervous again.

"Relax honey, this is a good thing." Jenny's grip relaxed, and Mark heard her sigh.

He continued, "Every time I saw a certain picture of Joseph Smith it bothered me. It was like that first impression you get of someone when you meet them. It was a gut feeling that he was not a good man. I knew you couldn't determine a man's character by the ability or inability of an artist, but I also felt I shouldn't be having these feelings if he was a true Prophet. I felt conflicted when anyone would mention Joseph Smith's name, and this internal debate led me on one of the longest and most extensive searches of anything I have studied.

I don't think it was a coincidence that about that same time my job provided the opportunity to visit many of the places significant to Joseph's life. I visited Independence where he and the early Saints experienced so much persecution and where many former members and friends became his greatest enemies. I sat at Far West and Adam-ondi-Ahman where he received inspiration and guidance from the Holy Spirit, and I visited places where he received priesthood authority. I sat and pondered at Nauvoo where the Saints found great joy when they were commanded to again build a temple, yet where they also experienced the return of disappointment and persecution. I visited Liberty Jail, where he was held through the freezing winter months in what is basically a crawl space with a dirt floor. I stood at the well located outside Carthage Jail where a mob viciously took his life.

After all those hours at these locations and the quiet time spent in hotel rooms recording my findings and feelings, I received a personal witness that Joseph Smith is a prophet called by God. It was like a long forgotten memory resurfaced. It wasn't that I remembered how the prophet Joseph looks or any time we spent together, it was more of a fondness in my heart and mind, a quiet confirmation that I knew him before I came to earth. Jenny, I know he is a man chosen to be the greatest of all the prophets, the one chosen to restore the gospel that Christ himself brought to this earth and to deliver the same truth that caused Christ his life. I finally have a testimony that Joseph Smith was one of the noblest of men and was one of the many prophets of God who sealed his testimony with his blood."

Mark broke his intense eye contact with Jenny and looked toward the beautiful red sky that was beginning to form around the setting sun. Neither said anything for several minutes as the spirit of truth and confirmation rested upon them.

It was Jenny who finally broke the calm silence, "I am not sure why you have never mentioned your struggle to me before. I didn't think we held anything back from each other, and now I find you have struggled for years with something fundamental to your testimony of the gospel. I am not sure how I feel about that. I appreciate you sharing that you have resolved it, but Mark, maybe you wouldn't have struggled for as long if we were working on it together."

Mark could see the hurt in her eyes fade as she concluded, "Either way, I am happy that you have been able to resolve your questions and concerns."

"I haven't ever thought of it as leaving you out. I knew how solid your testimony of the prophet was, and I felt I had a crack that I needed to fix. It always felt more like a mental rather than a spiritual thing. I've been too blessed to ever doubt what the Lord has proven to me. Mostly, I felt embarrassed. Now it seems almost as if God blessed me with a need to search deeper, and He provided the opportunities for me to do so. If nothing else, the experience has left me with a foundation that is unshakeable."

Jenny snuggled closer as the air around them chilled. "I guess I can't be too upset with you. Our family leans on you and your testimony, so I guess you better make real sure you are unshakable because your whole family depends on it," Jenny cautioned in a half serious half joking tone.

The need to travel began to dramatically decrease over the next couple years. New technology allowed classes to be conducted via the Internet, and Mark was at last able to stay closer to home. He was grateful he could spend more time with his family especially as Scott and the girls entered the challenging teen years. Soon, he wondered how he had ever been able to survive being away from them so much. Each workweek felt like a hurdle he had to get over until the next weekend arrived and he could spend time with Jenny and the kids. Their role as parents to three teenage children developed an emphasis on preparing their kids for the realities of the world they would soon live in, independent of their parents.

The night before Scott graduated from high school, Jenny and Mark stood at the kitchen sink washing the dinner dishes. The girls were at work, and Scott had gone to a graduation party with friends.

Mark pondered aloud, "I've been thinking about all the years I traveled for work and all the time I missed with you and the kids. I want you to know I think you did an amazing job of raising them yourself so much of the time. I appreciate all you have done over the years for our family. The work change a few years back and my being able to spend more time at home has felt like such a blessing.

I get the distinct impression that my whole focus in life is being redirected for the changing world that lies ahead for our family. I feel like those work trips made it possible for me to put my feet on the ground where important church events took place and where the Spirit could teach me. During those quiet moments, I gained something that can never be taken from me. In fact, I don't think I would ever have been strong enough for what I feel lies ahead for our family if I had not had those opportunities to travel. I would probably never have resolved the struggle I was having over Joseph Smith. I don't feel like it is a coincidence that the travel ended when it did. I had gotten my answers. The path we're on now is leading us somewhere new, I'm just not sure where yet. "

Jenny nodded but said nothing, only continued to dry the dishes.

"When did we become old enough to have a child graduating from high school?" Mark asked, handing her a soapy glass.

"Strange, isn't it," Jenny replied softly. "But the strangest part is, well, tell me honestly; when you look at yourself in the mirror and look into your own eyes, how old is the person looking back at you?"

Mark laughed. "If I only look at my eyes, I would say about eighteen – Scott's age. But if I look at anything else . . ."

"No, not allowed," Jenny poked him as she laughed. "Sometimes I don't even recognize this body. Does that seem strange?"

Mark passed her a plate. "We're a little older than most people are when their first child graduates from high school, because it took me a little longer to get you to settle for me," winking at her. "I do have a theory about why we hardly recognize our old bodies, though."

"Care to share?"

"Well, I think sometimes we can see our souls when we look into our eyes." He paused and took her damp hand in his. "And our souls don't ever get old. My theory is that the body gets older and older until it dies, but our spirit is always young and vibrant like an eighteen-year-old."

"It sounds like you've put a lot of thought into your theory, Sweetie," Jenny said with a smile.

"Yup. So, are you ready to watch our first child and only son graduate from high school tomorrow?"

"I think so. He's always been such a good kid. I think he'll do well out there in the great wide world," Jenny replied with motherly pride.

"When I graduated, I thought I knew it all, but now I see that I didn't really know very much at all. Scott's life is only beginning. It seems like just yesterday I gave him a name and a blessing and held him up toward heaven as a tiny infant."

Mark pulled his wife close. "We've done our best to raise him right. Now it's time for God to use him for whatever He has prepared."

A WORLD OF CHANGES

Life for Mark and Jenny was an enjoyable routine. Their role as parents to three children had always been focused on preparing their kids for the realities of the world they must live in, even while trying to isolate them just enough to preserve some innocence. That had become harder to do with each passing year. Scott left for college and both Jordan and Lynne were experiencing the added freedom a job and their own cars provided.

Mark was pleased when Scott became interested in the study of various historic cultures, and hoped his son's interest had grown from the seeds he had planted over the years as he shared stories of his travels. During graduate school, Scott had the opportunity to continue his studies in the Holy Land. It was a significant adjustment for Mark and Jenny to think of their son being half a world away. His interesting letters soon replaced their fears with fascination at the many exciting experiences he was having. They especially enjoyed his accounts of a new friend, Abram.

"You are difficult for me to understand," Abram said as he carefully watched the expression on Scott's face. "I know you will openly discuss any subject, and yet you seem guarded in your answers to my questions. That creates a confusing contradiction."

Scott threw back his head and laughed. "Then we are equally confusing to each other. I also get the impression that you never take offense at the questions I ask, and I like that. Sometimes you ask a question that makes me think you are more interested in the way I answer it than what the answer actually is, as though you're testing me to see if I will become angry when my beliefs seem to contradict yours."

This time Abram laughed aloud. "You have seen through me, my friend. I have always been told I am hard to understand and impossible to see through, and yet you see through me as though we had grown up together and you know me too well to be fooled by my actions."

Scott became very serious and leaned toward Abram. "It is so strange to hear you say the very thing I have been thinking ever since we met. From the first time I saw you, I felt I had to talk to you. It seemed we were old friends, and yet you were a stranger. That feeling made me seek you out until we finally became acquainted. Have you had any feelings like that?"

Abram again watched Scott's face, a habit that had become very familiar, and said nothing. Then after a moment, he sighed and looked away. "I think you are a mind reader. I have not felt something *like* what you describe. I have felt exactly what you describe. I am certain we have never met before. I've never been to America and you have just arrived in my country."

"So, am I correct that your questions are sometimes asked to find out how I will respond more than to hear my answer?"

Abram nodded and smiled. "When we are discussing things, such as our religion or our cultural differences concerning family relationships, I sometimes begin to feel as though we are teenagers and I want to tease you or make fun of your beliefs, but in a joking manner. My words do not correctly describe my feeling, but yes, I also sense that something strange exists between us."

"Well, now we can just relax and become better friends," Scott suggested. "I absolutely love learning about your country and seeing the places that I have studied about and heard of during my entire life. The fact that I get to see them is a dream come true, but having a friend who has lived here his whole life that is willing to share his feelings for these places is more than I even dreamed of hoping for."

"I wondered if the hesitation I sensed when you were visiting my family was because you felt uncomfortable, but now I think it may be because you are a little in awe of the places we go. I thought you regarded them as tourist spots that you could tell your friends you had seen, but now I believe you feel the sacredness of these places."

"Yes, I do feel the sacredness. My whole life I have listened to my dad tell me about sacred places in America that he visited, and the spiritual feelings he experienced there. He loves to sit in such places and ponder about what it was like when people lived there, and when I visit places here I have the same desire – to sit and soak it in."

"It is hard to tell what another person is thinking. I have seen that you gaze across a place and seem to be far away. I thought you were bored." Abram smiled and shook his head slowly.

"Never bored," Scott answered. "I love seeing all the places where the Savior walked or taught people, and I especially loved seeing where He was born. I often wonder if I would have been a believer if I had lived on the Earth when He was here."

Abram did not answer for a moment, and then he spoke without looking at Scott. "I often wonder if I would have been one of those who helped crucify Him if I had been alive then. No matter what He was, prophet or mortal man, I don't understand why He was crucified."

"That's strange," Scott said slowly. "I always assumed Jewish people thought it was fine that He was crucified because He claimed to be the Son of God, and they considered that to be blasphemy."

"I don't pretend to know what people who lived when Jesus was on the Earth thought, or why they did certain things," Abram said, sounding a little annoyed. "But I have never understood how anyone could crucify a man just because he taught things that didn't agree with accepted teachings."

"Interesting," Scott said. "Do you think Satan had a hand in getting the people worked into a frenzy so they would want Jesus to be crucified?"

"So you think the Jews were deceived by Satan and that's why they crucified Jesus?" Abram asked.

Scott thought carefully for a moment. "Would it make a difference if they crucified Him because they believed He was guilty of blasphemy, or because Satan had deceived them?"

"Yes, it would make a great deal of difference. If they did not believe He was the Messiah and He insisted He was the Son of God, they would have crucified Him for telling them their beliefs were incorrect. If they let Satan deceive them, that would be much worse."

Scott studied Abram's face and then proceeded very slowly, watching his reaction to each word. "I believe Satan can deceive anyone and convince them that something totally false is true. In *my opinion*, after Jesus was crucified, God sent many signs that they had just crucified the true Messiah. The Earth was dark for three days and there were terrible earthquakes, and yet the people remained convinced that Jesus was not their Savior. To this day, their descendants, like you, believe that Christ may have been a wise man, maybe even a prophet, but nothing more."

After thinking for a moment, Abram said, "I believe Jesus was a prophet."

"Okay," Scott ventured slowly. "If Christ was only a prophet, He would have been a false prophet, because He declared He was the Savior. He would have been deceiving His followers. Therefore, He was either the Savior or He was a deceiver. Satan is the father of deceit and deceit is contrary to all of Christ's doctrines. The only possible conclusion seems to be that if Christ was a deceiver, He was one of Satan's workers on this Earth, here to lead God the Father's children away from Him."

"I think I follow what you are saying," Abram slowly replied. "Continue."

"Okay," Scott said with a smile. "Knowing of Christ's mission on this Earth and acknowledging the love and light that He has personally poured upon me, I cannot imagine anyone not being able to determine which role Christ actually filled while on this Earth."

"It is hard to think of Jesus as a follower of Satan." Abram offered up.

Abram was not smiling, so Scott decided he was treating this as a serious conversation, and he continued carefully. "My dad had an experience when he was a teenager. One night he was praying and a light appeared in his room. There were three men standing within the light and my dad thought they had come to take him to heaven, and he screamed, 'No, I don't want to go with you yet.' The whole experience scared him badly. He said he never uttered another prayer for over a year. It took him thirteen or fourteen years to finally discover that the visitation had not been from God, but had been from Satan. It made him mad that he had allowed himself to be deceived for so many years. He taught me that no matter how successful Satan is in deceiving us, all we have to do is pray to God and ask a simple question: Is this true? When he finally prayed and asked God if the vision had been from Him, he received a strong answer that it had not been from God. He had spent years praying that he could understand what message he was supposed to have received from that experience and never got an answer. However, it was a very powerful lesson when he finally asked the right question, one that could be answered with a feeling of yes or no: Is this true?"

Abram finally did smile, a little. "Scott, my friend, I find your examples very interesting. Even when our opinions differ, I never feel you are criticizing my beliefs, and I hope you never think I am criticizing the way you believe. I thank you for sharing with me a lesson that took your father fourteen years to learn." Now Abram smiled and laughed. "I hope you have learned the importance of not waiting for fourteen years before you ask your questions correctly."

"Yes, I try to determine the correct question as quickly as possible."

They both laughed and knew their friendship was strong enough to allow sharing any opinion with each other, without fear of being offensive or being rejected. That was an amazing discovery for both of them considering how different their backgrounds and daily lives were. Scott felt he was blessed with additional learning that was not available to his fellow classmates.

Abram and Scott spent so much time together that people might have assumed they were brothers, except for the fact that they were complete opposites, physically. Scott was a few inches short of six feet, had a medium build, thinning blond hair that he kept short, and dark green eyes. He was physically competitive and anxious to try every sort of sporting activity he learned of. He had a passion for food, and even though he exercised and worked out regularly, he had a tendency to gain weight easily. Abram, on the other hand, was several inches shorter, stocky, had thick black hair, and a full beard, which he kept closely trimmed. His dark complexion and dark eyes made his extremely white teeth very noticeable whenever he smiled, which was often. He had never studied much about America, and he was surprised how Scott's stories about the history of his homeland had awakened a desire to learn more about the world he lived in. Abram did not share Scott's interest in trying new foods, and considered food only a necessary part of daily life. Abram had lived in Israel his entire life, and had a great respect and reverence for the history of his people, so study trips were very enlightening.

For eighteen months, Abram and Scott engaged in thought provoking discussions about both social and religious beliefs. Their cultures appeared to be very different on the surface, but the core beliefs and roots were similar. Some of their discussions focused on the differences, and after each of them emphatically expressed that their beliefs were correct, they always ended as friends and never compromised their individual positions in the slightest. However, the discussions that lasted well into the night were the ones that compared the similarities in their religious beliefs. Abram learned much about Scott's church and accepted some of the beliefs, but stood firm in his family's beliefs that had been handed down through the centuries.

When Scott graduated and returned to America, Abram joined his family's business, as his father was quite elderly. Modern technology allowed them to keep in touch – their friendship and deep respect for each other continued.

"I know I was only gone for a year and a half, but it's alarming to see the difference in the U.S. since I left," Scott told his dad one evening as they sat together in the living room. Moments like this had always been Scott's favorite sort of interaction with his dad, and he had missed it very much while he was in Israel.

"It's noticeable even if you haven't been gone for eighteen months. A single news program on TV can illustrate that. It's not just an increase in the amount of violence, but the cold-blooded things that people do to each other have become so awful it's hard to even listen to it being described."

Scott nodded in agreement. "And yet, at the very same time, it seems like more and more people are carefree, or unconcerned with the consequences of their behavior. Buying the morning after pill is as commonplace for some people as buying aspirins, and it wasn't like that when I left."

"I think you're going to notice a big change in people in general. It has always seemed like there was a group of people who had no morals and lived in their own reality, and then all the rest of the common folks like us were pretty much the same. That is not true anymore. Now, a few of us believe in following the Ten Commandments and trying to be honest and honorable. The vast majority, however, now act like Christ is no longer relevant, and He only meant that kids younger than twenty should abstain from sex until after they get married. The practice of living together without being married is so acceptable and widespread, no one even bats an eye."

"So the worldwide televised summer breaks and parties that seem to hop from one country to another, while hopping from one partner to another, are considered to be acceptable?" Scott asked. "You would be surprised to learn how many of the Jewish people think that kind of immoral behavior is totally despicable."

"Considering a slim majority of people in this country declare themselves to be Christians, it's shocking that here it is considered prudish and naive not to participate," Mark said. "Sometimes I wonder if the increase in violence has made people feel they need to increase the amount of partying and celebrating in their lives. Do they use it as a distraction from their increased fear and stress, or have they actually become more wicked. I don't understand why people can't see that today's events seem to run parallel to the horrible things described in the Bible and the Book of Mormon that are prophesied to happen at the end of time."

"Because they don't want to see that," Scott quickly responded. "They think they are sophisticated compared to those of us who still believe that God will hold us accountable for our actions. What I don't understand is why they lash out at anyone who dares suggest the people in this country are going down the same path as the ancient Romans or Egyptians, or any other civilization that has collapsed. The facts bear that out."

Mark nodded. "I know. Mankind is becoming arrogant. Not only do they think they are superior to former generations because of the many advances and discoveries of science and medicine, but they think they became superior when they stopped being deceived by old beliefs and doctrines that the less informed and less educated generations before them believed."

"I guess time will tell," Scott said. "And I'm betting it isn't going to be a long wait before that arrogance proves to be civilization's downfall."

♦♦♦◇♦♦♦

"Michelle and I would like to talk to you," Scott said to his parents. "Actually, I would like to tell you that Michelle has agreed to marry me."

Jenny jumped up and hugged Michelle, and then wrapped her arms around Scott and cried. "I'm so happy for both of you. We're so happy you are going to be in our family, Michelle."

"Congratulations, son," Mark said as he clasped Scott's hand and pulled him into a warm hug.

"Have you set a date?" Jenny asked as she wiped the tears from her face with a tissue she always carried in her pocket.

"Soon," Scott said as he smiled at Michelle.

Michelle smiled and moved close to him. "It all depends on how quickly I can find the perfect dress."

"I can't believe it's been twenty-five years since you came into our lives." Jenny sighed, looking at her son. "You were a fair-haired little boy who loved to play pranks on his friends, and then you grew into a sensitive young man who put your education on hold while you served a mission, and now you become more like your father every day." She turned and smiled at Mark and continued. "He's a few years younger than you were when we got married, but it sounds like his engagement will be as short as ours was."

"I figure I'll see her more once I get her to marry me because she has become such good friends with Jordan and Lynne I often feel I'm competing with them for her time."

"It's uncanny how much you and Lynne look alike, Michelle," Mark said. "People will think you're her sister rather than Scott's wife. You're both brunettes with dark brown eyes, and from what I've heard, you both like the same kinds of books and music."

"And we're both five foot four," Michelle added. "I do feel like they're my sisters, but I'm sort of glad they aren't. I'd much rather be Scott's wife than his sister."

Three months later, Mark and Jenny sat with their two daughters, eating wedding cake and reminiscing about each person's memories of Scott. Jordan and Lynne's memories became haunting fragments of a past life Mark and Jenny knew nothing about. Scott had been just enough older than the two girls to be a built-in baby sitter, and Mark and Jenny had always considered that a blessing . . . until now.

"Lynne," Jordan asked, "do you remember when Scott was watching us and he left that pop on the counter and went outside?"

"Like I could forget," Lynne said as her voice deflected a few octaves. "We couldn't believe he forgot all about the pop he left on the counter. We were going to each have a sip, but we each had to have another sip. And then before we realized it, the can was nearly empty."

Jordan obviously thought Lynne was taking too long to get to the incriminating part, so she picked up the story. "Then Scott comes in from outside and grabs the pop. We started laughing at the look on his face when he realized it was nearly gone."

"That look," Lynne interjected. "I'll never forget that look."

"Right," Jordan agreed. "His face turned to shock and he sounded terrified. He asked us if we had drunk the pop. Then we really started laughing and told him it was his own fault for leaving it on the counter."

Lynne sighed and continued. "We sure quit laughing in a hurry when he ran to the sink and filled two glasses with water and told us to drink it as fast as we could. He said he had put rat poison in the pop and was going to put it in the garage, because dad had told him he was having problems with mice. We started crying and guzzled glass after glass of water. Scott kept telling us we might be able to dilute the poison if we drank enough water, and he acted all afraid, like he was panic stricken that we might die."

"He kept it up for three hours," Jordan recalled. "Then he started laughing and told us there really wasn't any poison in the pop. I couldn't decide whether or not to believe him."

Jenny laughed but felt terrible that she had left her daughters alone so many times with their terrifying older brother. "I'm so sorry, girls. I cannot believe you kept all of that secret for so long. Why didn't you tell me then? You know I would have put him over my knee."

"Oh, don't worry, Mom," Jordan said as she and Lynne burst into laughter. "We evened up the score a little today. After Scott left his apartment to get his tux, we paid him a little visit. Well, we paid his apartment a visit."

This time Lynne was the impatient one. "Do you remember all the food Scott bought last week, Mom?"

"I remember," Mark said. "I'm the one that helped him haul all of it up to his apartment. We filled two full cabinets with cans of food."

"Well, he's really going to have fun when they get home from their honeymoon," Lynne said. "Every can looks the same now. All the labels are gone and now there are two cabinets full of nice shiny cans. There are a couple different sizes, so maybe that will help him decide what to open when he's cooking dinner."

"Can you imagine opening something and then trying to get yourself in the mood for it, rather than opening what you are in the mood for?" Jordan asked. "At least this helped to create a little balance in the universe."

"I do feel a tiny bit guilty," Lynne said. "It's not only Scott that will be suffering through all those crazy meals for the next year. Michelle really didn't do anything to us to deserve this, but that's the price for marrying someone like Scott, I guess."

They all laughed as they watched Scott and Michelle standing across the room, completely unaware of what awaited them at their new apartment.

I wonder if Scott will know this is revenge, or if he'll just think it's a prank," Mark thought.

When the training in St. Louis was scheduled, Mark was overjoyed that additional personnel issues made it necessary for him to do it on-site, especially since Jenny decided she could go with him. She found willing partners for all the shopping she could handle during the week since several other wives had accompanied their husbands. Early Saturday morning, Mark and Jenny drove across the river to explore the City of Mounds, an ancient city that preceded the era of the Native American Indians.

"How many mounds are here?" Jenny asked as she looked around in amazement.

"It says there are over eighty mounds, and the city is the largest archeological site in North America," Mark answered as he read the informational plaque.

"Cheater," Jenny said when she realized she could have found the answer for herself. "I know you've been studying about this place for years, Sweetie, so tell me what you know about it."

"Well, then, let me be your guide," he said with a flourish of his arm. "All the mounds were situated around the largest mound, where it is believed they built their temple. The rest of the mounds seem to be in a distinct pattern around the temple mound. Not much of any of the structures remain, but limited digging has uncovered artifacts and identified locations of large group burial mounds."

"There must have been a lot of people living here," Jenny said.

"Another interesting thing," Mark continued, "is that they have found remnants of protective walls that appeared to have been erected for protection from threatening enemies. A wall like that wouldn't keep out very many enemies these days, but there is evidence it worked for them."

"It's strange, but very beautiful. Do these mounds remind you of ruins in South America that we've seen on TV?"

"Yes, and they have another similarity with other ruins found in North and South America. The ancient civilizations that lived here seemed to have some type of influence from or connection to the early cultures of the Mediterranean area."

"They traded with each other? Is that what you mean?"

"Yes, and there's more. They were prosperous civilizations but they all seem to have disappeared from existence so rapidly that no one can even begin to speculate what happened to them."

"Why do you think you are so drawn to these areas?" Jenny asked as they walked among the mounds.

"That I don't know. I have spent many hours wondering why these specific sites have such a pull on me. Maybe it was just something I found to take up my time until I met you," he said.

"I'm glad you shared this with me. It's nice to meet my competition."

"You have no competition." He sighed, and then asked, "Do you think a place can be cursed? There must be a reason no one ever lived here again."

Jenny tilted her head and looked quizzically at Mark. "You think this place was cursed?"

"I don't know. There are places mentioned in the Bible that were cursed, then were destroyed or deserted. Sometimes it was promised that no one would ever inhabit the area again, or that it would never prosper."

"So would that mean that God cursed those places because the people who lived there were wicked?"

"Yes, and I've been wondering if places like this or the ruins in South America were cursed. I mean, if great civilizations lived there at one point, why are they now overgrown and totally abandoned?"

"The sacred valley you visited was completely empty. Do you think it was also cursed?"

"Well, I know there was a terrible battle there, and I remember reading that the ground was soaked with blood and covered with bones. Maybe a battle like that makes it cursed just because so much death happened there. I don't know. Maybe an area can become uninhabitable if God wants to preserve it because of some great sacrifice that took place there. Perhaps that's why Far West and Martin's Cove in Wyoming, and maybe even this place are empty. Significantly spiritual places, like Adam-ondi-Ahman, are empty, too, so maybe God wants them preserved for other reasons."

Jenny laughed. "Now I understand why these questions have remained unresolved even though you have studied them for many years. They are much too complicated for my poor brain to figure out. But I'm glad I got to share this special experience with you."

A large conference hall in Jerusalem, filled with noisy conversations, suddenly quieted when a man stepped to the podium and asked, "Would everyone please take your seat so we may begin?" Voices hushed and the only thing that could be heard was the shuffle of people moving into their seats and the ever-present stray cough. Then all noise ceased.

"Thank you." The man looked out over the group for a moment, looked down at the papers in front of him, and then again looked up. "I am certain most everyone in this building has just recently returned here to Jerusalem and that you have many, many questions and concerns. The purpose of this meeting is to answer some of those questions and let you know the details of our overall situation.

"As a matter of clarification, when we re-established this area as the land of our inheritance, it was named Israel, rather than Judah. This was done because this place is the homeland of the Twelve Tribes of Israel, not just the homeland of the lone tribe of Judah."

The speaker raised his hand, signaling someone, and immediately a large screen began lowering behind him and the lights slowly dimmed.

"The number of Jews arriving here every day requires extraordinary efforts at maintaining organization in order to meet everyone's needs. This map illustrates the entire area that has been legally returned to our control," and the speaker used a laser pointer to indicate the area he was speaking of. "As you are all aware, even though we have possession of the city, the surrounding land is filled with continual skirmishes and hostilities. We have regained our precious Jerusalem! We thought this was an impossible dream, but it has been accomplished. Our next goal is to build a temple on the sacred mount."

A wave of murmurs swept through the hall.

"Brethren, over many generations our holy records have been destroyed. We have lost the knowledge required to build a temple comparable to the temple our ancestors built so long ago. We have the writings of Ezekiel, but the words of Zenos and Zenock, and others, have been lost. We must understand the specific purpose for each room within the temple, and every detail about what is needed in order to worship and properly make sacrifices to the God of Abraham of old. We trust that God will guide us to the information we need."

A week later, another meeting was held – students who had recently returned from universities around the world were invited to attend. Although Abram had attended university in Israel, he felt impressed to attend the meeting and add his thoughts.

"I have heard many of the ideas being presented, and I would like to discuss something no one has mentioned to this point. When I was studying at the university, I met a young man from America. He and I spent many hours discussing the similarities and differences of our religious beliefs. He is a member of The Church of Jesus Christ of Latter-day Saints, but they refer to their church as the LDS Church. His Church has built temples in many places around the world, and those temples are used to worship Jesus Christ."

"Why do you mention the beliefs of that church when they believe their Messiah has already come to the Earth?"

"There are many similarities between the LDS Church and our beliefs. They believe in the teachings of the Old Testament that tell of events in the ancient world. Within their temple walls, they practice ordinances that they claim are the same as those practiced in the temples of Solomon, and the same as those practiced by other Prophets, such as Abraham and Moses. They claim to have the ceremonies that require fonts for baptizing, and that their ceremonies are for both the living and the redemption of the dead, just as in the temples of old."

"That religion has only been established for a couple hundred years, and does not even pretend to be passed down through the ages. I do not know why we are even discussing their beliefs, let alone comparing them to the teachings we have followed for thousands of years."

Abram slowly turned and faced the person who had spoken. "We all know the Jewish people are commissioned to build a temple where Elijah can return to herald the coming of the Messiah. We all know we do not have complete plans to show us how to build that temple. I share my knowledge of this church in compliance with the purpose of this meeting, which is to join as a group of students and share ideas. I apologize if this information is offensive to you."

"I apologize. All ideas should be welcomed and openly discussed."

Abram smiled warmly, nodded his head, and sat down.

Three days later, Abram was asked to meet with a group of Jewish leaders. He recognized Isaac, the person who seemed to be in charge of the group.

"Welcome, I am Moishe," one of the men said as he shook Abram's hand and motioned toward an empty chair. "Your suggestion that we meet with the leaders of the LDS Church has been discussed and it has been decided we will travel to Salt Lake City."

"And we invite you to go with us," the man sitting next to him said.

"Thank you David," Abram said. "I would be honored."

"Abram," Moishe said, "We will fly to Salt Lake City on Monday and meet with the leaders of the church on Tuesday. We will return on Thursday morning but if you wish to stay longer to visit with your friend we will make your reservations accordingly."

"Thank you," Abram said, as everyone stood. Several of the men shook Abram's hand and welcomed him to their group, then left.

"I'm glad you're going with us," David said. David and Abram had been friends in school, but David had left the country to go to college. Abram's family was not poor, but not affluent enough for him to study abroad. "I was afraid that when we both finished college, we would have changed and never be close friends again. I'm glad to see that wasn't the case."

"As am I," Abram responded as they embraced.

"Abram," Isaac said, "do you have a moment?"

"Certainly," Abram said as he sat in a chair near Isaac.

"I am familiar with the teachings of this church, and I have studied enough to know they share many of our basic beliefs. I wanted to inquire about your friend you mentioned in the student meeting. I am curious to know if you can describe his attitude about the differences in our two religions."

Abram laughed and then said, "I found it easier to discuss the differences with Scott than with other students here in Jerusalem. He asked questions about what I believed and was curious about our customs, but he never acted as though his beliefs were right and mine were wrong; quite the contrary. He usually tried to point out how similar our beliefs were, in spite of a few minor differences."

"Minor, as in their belief that the Messiah was Jesus Christ, and that we are still awaiting the arrival of our Messiah?" Isaac said sarcastically, but also making a point.

"Yes," chuckled Abram, "minor like that."

"And he now lives in Salt Lake City?"

"Yes, he was raised there and his family still lives there."

"I would like to meet your friend, if circumstances allow," Isaac said. "He sounds very interesting."

As soon as Abram returned to his room, he e-mailed Scott and told him about the planned visit.

The four delegates arrived in Salt Lake City on Monday evening, and went to the headquarters of the Church of Jesus Christ of Latter-day Saints the next morning. Exiting the elevator on one of the upper floors, they stood in front of large windows that faced southward, overlooking the entire valley far below. They were escorted into a large meeting room where three men were waiting for them, and introductions were made. It was apparent this meeting was important to both groups of men, but the visiting dignitaries from Israel were uncertain about what to expect.

After everyone was seated around a large conference table, Isaac spoke. "Thank you for taking the time to meet with us. We are interested in learning a little more about the purpose and function of the temples your church has built throughout the world."

The Prophet warmly smiled and replied, "We have been waiting for you with great anticipation." He nodded to an aid standing by the door, and then the aid left the room. "It brought so many around the world great joy as you have once again regained the legal rights to Jerusalem. We now feel so honored and blessed for the opportunity to share some things with you that may bring you great joy."

The door of the meeting room opened and the aid that had previously left entered the room pushing a cart. On it were rolls and rolls of drawings that were quickly transferred to the table. The lights were dimmed and a projection screen descended from the ceiling. Pictures of various LDS temples located around the world began appearing on the screen. Then a series of computer-generated pictures were shown. These images were of a temple that was quite different from the pictures of the existing temples previously shown. The external renderings were of various perspectives, and then the slide show stopped on one that depicted a view from afar. This temple was located in their native town of Jerusalem.

The Prophet stood and in a calm but direct tone said, "This is your temple that you are to build for your Savior."

Isaac, the senior delegate, suddenly stood and said, "I did not expect this from you. How dare you dictate that we build your temple in our home land; which, has been purchased through years of hardship and generations of death and spilled blood!"

No one spoke; no one even breathed. The Prophet quietly said, "Please, allow us to continue. We will show you what you have come to receive. We will show you the details of the rooms and explain their purpose. You can take the detailed plans back to your country to study and show your brothers," he said as he motioned toward the rolls of drawings on the table. "I would then ask you to pray to your God, the God of Abraham, and ask if this is what He desires of you. Then proceed as your hearts dictate."

Isaac slowly sat back down. There was a feeling of uneasiness in the room as the slides continued. They were stopped each time one of the visiting dignitaries indicated they had a question about something being shown. The distrust began to fade as the meeting continued. Dinner was brought in and discussions continued into the night.

"Abram," Isaac said as he leaned close enough to speak without interrupting the meeting. "Will you please call the airport and put our return flights on hold. We will make our reservations when it is known for sure when we will be ready to return."

"Certainly," Abram said, and then he left the room to make the call. To his surprise, even though it was nearly midnight, the secretary and several other staff people were still in the office. He explained what he had been asked to do, and the woman offered to help him in any way she could.

The following day the meeting continued and again lunch was brought in while they worked.

At 5:30 pm, the Prophet seemed to be ready for a break. "I do not know when you planned to return to Jerusalem, but we still have much to discuss. Will you be available to meet with us again tomorrow?"

"Yes," Isaac assured him. "We have cancelled our return reservations."

"Good, then would you be my guest for dinner?"

"Absolutely not," Isaac said, quite seriously. Then he smiled. "You have fed us for two days, and we insist that you be our guest for dinner."

"That would be fine," the Prophet answered. "Personally, I think we have talked long enough for today, after such a long day yesterday."

"Agreed," nearly everyone said, in one form or another.

After a very pleasant dinner, it was decided to meet again the next morning, and the delegation returned to their hotel.

Abram finally got to visit with Scott later that evening, and was able to introduce him to Isaac. After a very interesting discussion, Isaac invited Scott to come visit them in Jerusalem whenever he had the opportunity. As Isaac was leaving, he shook Scott's hand and said, "I am honored to know you. I am very impressed with those I have met of your church, and I am glad you became acquainted with Abram. You may very well be the answer to the prayers of more Jews than you can imagine."

After he left the room, Abram said, "My friend, I feel God provided the opportunity for the two of us to become friends. When I shared with the members of this delegation some of what you taught me, it was then that they made the decision to come listen to the leaders of your church."

"I totally agree with you. We did not meet by chance," Scott said with conviction in his voice. That conviction was offered again that evening in his prayer of thanks to his Heavenly Father.

On Friday, the elated delegates, laden with rolls of drawings and folders of pictures and notes, boarded a plane for home. They made no commitment to use any of the information, but were truly excited about the things they had learned. They had been taught the purpose of many sacred areas that had been discovered over the years in their home country. The mysteries of Masada and Qumran had literally been unfolded before their eyes.

The visit to Salt Lake City by the Jewish delegation had successfully been kept from the media. The state of affairs in Jerusalem following their return remained tense, but there was no escalation of violence toward the Jews. In fact, the Jews were hardly thought of at all for a short time.

NEW ZION STAKE

Michelle sat in the family room watching the news. She and Scott had returned from church a short while earlier, and had just finished changing into casual clothes. It had been a hectic week for both of them, and they were looking forward to a restful afternoon. Her mind wandered back to the incredible meeting between the Jewish Delegation and the leaders of the Church during the past week. Scott had told her about being introduced to Isaac, the head of the Jewish delegation, and how impressed he had been by Isaac's openness and faith. Scott had also told her about a discussion he had with Abram shortly before the delegation returned to Jerusalem.

"Israel has control of Jerusalem, but it is an empty victory," Abram had told him. "The Muslims presented a face of reconciliation to the world by conceding control of the temple to the people of Israel in exchange for Israel's withdrawal from Gaza. The peace agreement the leader of the Caliphate has brokered portrays your country as our ally, but it is a trap because America's leaders become less supportive of Israel every day. In reality, he has united the world against us. If a single stone of the temple is moved, we know the Muslim world will seek to destroy us, yet the temple must be rebuilt before the Messiah will come. The political climate in Jerusalem is as tinder awaiting a match. Even if we never touch the temple, the Imam will create a reason for the Caliphate to overrun our homeland."

"The Jewish people have always been persecuted, horribly, and I know the Lord will punish America if we withdraw our support of Israel, but I thought gaining control of Jerusalem brought you one step closer to building your temple. Now it sounds like that has only focused the eyes of the anti-Israel world upon you, making it impossible for you to move forward."

Abram slowly nodded his head. *"The Muslim armies have established small, temporary settlements all the way around Jerusalem. There have always been skirmishes and violence, but now there are so many who strive for our destruction that we have only God on our side."*

Scott hesitated, not wanting to assume their friendship allowed questions about Abram's personal feelings. *"I may have no right to ask this, but if the Jewish people believe so strongly that they need to build the temple, do you think the leaders will simply knock it down and move forward?"*

"You have every right to ask. We have openly discussed our religions' beliefs many times. I can tell you that our leaders do not believe we should take down the Dome of the Rock. We believe that if God wants us to build a temple there, He will knock down the obstacle that now prevents us from doing so. I think our leaders have been on hold, not willing to move forward, because there are still many questions that have to be answered." Abram looked down and inhaled slowly. *"My friend, what if our leaders have been on hold because God was waiting for us to be prepared before He removes the obstacle in our path?"*

"And you think the information you have received means you are now prepared?" Scott said, as if he were speaking to himself. He looked at Abram quickly and said, *"I do not mean to infer, not for a single moment, that we have the answers . . ."*

"Don't apologize. I believe Isaac was very clear about the situation when he said you might be the answer to the prayers of many Jews. So, for the sake of our discussion, if the information we have received from the leaders of your Church is what God was waiting for us to find so we would be ready to move forward...." Abram shook his head, unable to speak.

"Abram, if the Dome of the Rock is removed, whether by the hand of God or the hands of the Jews, what will happen?

"I believe the fear I hear in your voice tells me we are of the same mind. The tinder I spoke of? That would be the match."

The Breaking News Banner across the television screen instantly captured Michelle's complete attention.

"We have just received a report that a 7.2 earthquake has hit the area of Jordan and Israel. The epicenter is at Tiberius on the west shore

of the Sea of Galilee. We have no information regarding damage or injuries at this time. To repeat, a 7.2 earthquake has shook Tiberius."

Michelle scrambled to her feet and ran to the kitchen. "Scott, there's been an earthquake in Israel! Come listen."

Scott was standing in front of the open refrigerator, pouring a glass of lemonade. "In Israel?"

"Yes, they didn't say anything about damage, just that it was seven-point-two and it struck in Tiberius."

"I can't believe it." Scott pushed the refrigerator door closed with his hip, set the pitcher and the glass on the table, and then followed Michelle into the family room. "Are they still talking about it?"

"No, but let me switch to one of the news channels."

"...a little while after dark. We have some reports of damage but it will be morning before we can see what has happened. From the reports we have heard, the ground shook violently. We will break into our regular programming the moment we receive further information."

"It is two o'clock here, so that means it's eleven o'clock there," Scott said slowly. "It won't be light there for another six or seven hours. Maybe there will be more information on the ten o'clock news. I guess we might as well have dinner. Did I hear correctly yesterday that you were planning on frying some chicken for dinner today?"

They watched anxiously for more news during the evening but little was said about the earthquake. Then, shortly after 8:00 p.m., another Breaking News Banner flashed across the screen.

"Finally," Scott said as he leaned forward, grabbed the remote, and turned the volume up. "Maybe now we'll find out what's happening."

"There has been another earthquake in the Middle East. Even while officials were awaiting morning light to assess the damage from the quake after dark last night in Tiberius, another quake has hit north of the Dead Sea in Jericho. This massive 7.5 earthquake shook many walls to the ground. Though we have no pictures of damage from the previous quake, we have had reports that this was a catastrophic quake with major damage in Jerusalem. Reports during the night indicate the damage from the quake in Tiberius was experienced far to the south of that area, but we will not be able to confirm that until daylight returns to this region."

Scott and Michelle sat speechless, watching the screen of the television even though the regular programming had immediately continued. After several minutes, Scott said, "I don't get it. An earthquake in Haiti or Japan results in non-stop news coverage on every news channel for days. Now, two major earthquakes in the Middle East and all we are told is that they do not know what the damages are yet. What's going on?"

"It's not light yet. How can they report what they can't see?" Michelle said, as though Scott had forgotten about the time difference.

"No, even during the war in Iraq they had reporters standing in the dark with some dim light in the background, but they still reported every detail they had received, and they reported around the clock. Now two major earthquakes that are said to be violent, and it only warrants a news flash? They resume Sixty Minutes almost immediately? Something's not right."

"It should be getting light there, so maybe in an hour or so we'll hear more." Michelle scanned through several channels to see if there was any word of the situation in Jerusalem, but found nothing.

There was again only a passing statement on the 10:00 news, but then the 11:00 news anchor led with the statement that they had disturbing pictures from Jerusalem, after the commercial. Scott and Michelle braced themselves for terrible damage.

"I'm sure you're worried about Abram, aren't you," Michelle said.

"I guess I am concerned about him, but not because of the quake. I am thinking this earthquake could be the spark that ignites the unrest in the Middle East into a world war. I'm really anxious to see if the Dome of the Rock is still standing."

The newscast resumed, and they both watched the screen intently. Scenes of absolute destruction played across the screen, as the reporter spoke. *"As dawn approached here, the streets of many cities were filled with people crying and mourning. Panic has gripped the entire area, as the destruction is so great. It was as if the earthquake in Tiberius and the one that shook Jericho had communicated and focused their destruction toward each other. The border between Jordan and Israel has received heavy damage. Settlements and military strongholds have been reduced to a memory. Although damage is apparent, there is much conflicting information coming from all areas, and it will be some time before we can sort out what is happening in this area."*

"What?" Scott asked, as the newscast continued with another story. "What does that mean? Conflicting information about what's happening?"

The next two days, the news mentioned Jerusalem only to the degree that the Muslim settlements around the city had been destroyed, but there were no pictures of the temple or any mention of the Jewish casualties. Scott scoured the Internet for information, but again the only news seemed to be about destruction in Muslim settlements and cities. He tried in vain to reach Abram by telephone.

On Wednesday, Michelle had just put a pizza in the oven for dinner, and again flipped on the television to see if there was any news about the conditions in Jerusalem. The filmed report from Jerusalem astounded her. The scene was horrific. The Dome of the Rock was in ruins, with pieces of the gold dome strewn among the piles of debris, confirming what location was being filmed. There were pictures of heavy equipment leaving the area hauling away the rubble from the temple.

"Scott, you have to come listen to this," Michelle shouted.

"Is it news from Jerusalem?" Scott asked as he quickly came into the family room, pulling a sweatshirt over his head.

"You won't believe this!" she said without once looking away from the television. "This is unbelievable!"

"The Jewish people hauled away the wreckage of the Dome of the Rock most of the afternoon. Their heavy equipment entered the Temple Mount early in the morning hours and this film illustrates the result of their unthinkable acts. This is a most sacred site to Muslims all over the world, and the sacrilege carried out today by the Jews has ended months of stable but tense relations between the Jews occupying Jerusalem and the Palestinians in communities around the outskirts of the city. While Palestinians were sifting through the remains of their settlements and mourning the death of so many of their people, the Jewish people heartlessly took advantage of the chaos resulting from the two earthquakes that have paralyzed all Palestinian activities. As Palestinians watched helplessly, the big equipment began tearing apart the temple and removing it from Temple Mount. This structure was completed in 691 and it is the oldest Islamic building in the world.

"When the Crusaders captured Jerusalem in 1099, they used the Al-Aqsa Mosque, which is adjacent to the Dome of the Rock, as a palace and church. This site, known as Temple Mount, is the third holiest site in

Islam, and Muslims believe that the prophet Muhammad was *transported from the Sacred Mosque in Mecca to Al-Aqsa during the Night Journey.*

"The Dome of the Rock and the Mosque have been damaged or destroyed by earthquakes many times but always rebuilt.

"When the Israelis began clearing the site this morning, it caused a huge shock wave of anger and resentment to instantly spread through Muslim areas around Jerusalem, especially among those that had contended for the same ground, believing it was their sacred right to occupy the Mount. This act on the Temple Mount appears to be the ultimate act of sacrilege, and signals their intention to build a Jewish temple on the area believed to be so sacred by so many that despise the Jews."

"Can you believe that?" Michelle asked. "It's on every channel and it sounds like total propaganda designed to whip up the members of the Caliphate into action against the Jews."

"I'm shocked," Scott said. "I was happy that the Jews were going to finally build their temple because we believe that has to happen before the Savior will return. I knew it would not be well received by the Muslims. I am certain the earthquake, not the Jews, leveled the temple area. Especially after Abram told me they would wait until God destroyed the temple before making any move to build their temple. When I see this film showing them clearing that site and see how carefully the Muslim side of the story is being presented, I can see what's happening, and it's very sobering. This may be just what our government leaders are waiting for to withdraw their support from Israel."

"It has to mean war, right?" asked Michelle.

"I can't remember a time there wasn't war in the Middle East, but I think this is going to bring about some of those prophecies we've always heard about." Scott pulled Michelle close to him and hugged her tightly. "It makes me very afraid for the future. I want the Second Coming to happen, I'm just not looking forward to going through what is prophesied to occur before that happens."

The report of the Jewish people clearing the area where the Dome of the Rock once stood was shown around the world, repeatedly – heavy equipment scooping up pieces of the sacred Dome of the Rock. It made no sense to even entertain the notion that an earthquake could level Palestinian cities on the outskirts of the Old City and not destroy the

Dome of the Rock. However, the only destruction reported was that of the Palestinian cities and settlements, with scene after scene of rubble and dead bodies being hauled away. Not one word was uttered about any Jewish communities being destroyed, or any loss of Jewish lives.

The only people who knew the truth were the Muslim Caliphate that surrounded Israel. The earthquakes had reduced the temple to rubble; however, the leader of the Caliphate controlled the majority of what was reported as news globally, so the misleading story was shown repeatedly. The citizens of the world were carefully led toward a frenzy of hatred against Israel.

In spite of such horrendous events, life in Utah seemed to move forward unchanged, for the moment. When Scott arrived home the next afternoon, Michelle was waiting for him with an envelope in her hand.

"What's this?" Scott asked as she handed it to him.

"Something we received from the stake president."

Scott took the letter, walked with Michelle into the living room, and sat nextk to her as he read the letter. "I wonder what this is all about."

"I don't know," Michelle answered. "I've never received a written invitation to attend a special meeting at the stake center before. If it were just us, I think they would have *called* and told us to come visit with the stake president, but they sent a letter. That makes me think there were so many invited to the meeting, it was easier to notify them by mail."

"I guess we'll find out. Why would they ask us to not discuss this letter with anyone else? Maybe it is a new tactic to get meeting attendance up to one hundred percent. With all this mystery, would you just blow it off and go out for dinner instead?"

"No. Good point," Michelle agreed.

When they arrived at the stake center the following Saturday evening, they looked for others they might recognize. None of the families they knew with children were there, nor was anyone the age of Scott's parents. Everyone seemed to be a young married couple. There was no prelude music or visiting, as was usually the case while people waited for meetings to begin. There was only silence.

The stake president stood and welcomed everyone, and then offered an opening prayer. He asked that the lights be turned down, and the special broadcast began.

The Prophet appeared on the large screen at the front of the chapel. Rather than the usual backdrop of the conference center, he was seated at his desk in Church headquarters. "My dear Brothers and Sisters," he began. "Each of you has been invited to this meeting because you are worthy to volunteer for a very special assignment. This assignment will help further the work that must be completed before the Savior's return to Earth. I ask you to prayerfully consider if you could live the United Order as it was practiced in the early days of the Church. Ask yourself if you could leave your material possessions behind and embark upon a task for the Lord.

"If you can answer that question in the affirmative, please contact your stake president and let him know of your decision.

"I do not make this invitation lightly, and ask that you seek guidance from the Lord before you accept. This is a decision I ask each of you to make for yourself. I ask that you not discuss this decision with anyone but the Lord. A second meeting will be held with those who decide to participate. For those who decide their specific situation in life prevents them from making such a sacrifice at this time, I say you will have done nothing wrong in the eyes of the Church or the Lord.

"The events that have been prophesied since the creation of this world are unfolding around us, and I ask the blessings of the Lord to be with each of us during these perilous times. In the name of Jesus Christ, Amen."

The screen darkened as the light in the room was increased. The stake president again stepped to the podium and offered the closing prayer. There was no postlude music. No one spoke a word as they left the meeting. They had been there fifteen minutes, and it had been unlike any meeting Scott or Michelle had ever attended.

"What do you think about this?" Michelle asked after they were well away from the church parking lot.

"I don't even know how I feel about it. It's so routine to agree with anything that is asked of us by the Prophet that it seems strange to hear him ask us to make the decision about whether we will volunteer."

"And what exactly are we volunteering for? I think I have more questions now than I did before the meeting tonight," Michelle said.

"Can you walk away from everything we have worked so hard to get?" Scott asked. "I don't know what we're supposed to do with it, but the only real question he asked was whether or not we could walk away from our material possessions."

"True. So can we?"

Scott thought for a moment, and then said, "I can, but I won't even consider it if you don't feel the same way. And I certainly don't want you to feel . . ."

"I can, Scott. We agree about that."

When they pulled into their driveway, they both commented that after such a meeting, they certainly looked at their home in a different light.

"It's been ours since we signed on the dotted line, and it seems impossible to think of just walking away from it, but I can't say it makes me not want to participate," Michelle said as they settled onto the couch together.

"So what do we do? Sell it and give the money to our parents? Rent it out? Are we going to still be living here but working for the Church? I don't know how to make any decision until we know more about what we're volunteering for."

"Didn't the Prophet say the only decision we had to make was whether or not we could live the United Order?"

"And if we could leave our materials possessions behind and do the Lord's will," Scott reflected.

"Right. So, the only thing we have to decide is if we are willing. I guess if we say yes, then they'll tell us what to do next?"

"So what if we fast about this tomorrow and then pray about it?"

The following evening Scott called the stake president. "I would like to let you know that my wife and I have prayed about the questions the Prophet asked during the broadcast. We have decided we can do that."

"I am very pleased to hear that. I am instructed to tell you that on Sunday I will have an envelope for you. It will contain a questionnaire that asks about the abilities you and your wife possess, your family status, your overall health, and a few other things. When you complete the questionnaire, mail it to Church Headquarters in the enclosed envelope and that will be it. They think it will take a couple months to review the information, and if chosen, you will be invited to a special conference held here in Salt Lake. You will be notified whether or not you've been chosen to participate."

"Okay," Scott said as he took a deep breath. "Sounds good. Thanks."

"It has been a great undertaking to determine who will be invited to make this journey," the Prophet said to his counselors. "We have eliminated nearly four thousand applications on the basis of physical ability to complete the journey. The remaining three thousand applications have been separated into groups based on the skills each couple possesses. After we review these, and eliminate those who do not possess the needed skills, I feel we will be closer to selecting our core group. We must have a minimum of twelve people that are proficient in each required skill, and we will need an assortment of people with the other skills on the list in order to make a self-sufficient community." The Prophet took a deep breath and smiled. "This is an important endeavor, and I've explained our goal, but, as always if you receive some form of inspiration that someone less skilled is a person the Lord wishes to be included, just note that on their application and they will be included."

The Prophet pushed his chair back and sighed deeply. "I know we have worked long hours on this matter, but it is of the utmost importance that we seek the Lord's will in these choices. We will meet again, day after tomorrow. Is that agreeable?"

Both counselors voiced their agreement and the meeting was ended. When they reconvened, the Prophet shared an interesting moment of inspiration he had received regarding the Lord's guidance in their endeavor.

"As I considered the application of a young couple in Holland, the Lord's hand in this task became apparent to me. The young man had listed farming as a skill, but when I read his application, I learned he studied the effect the government had on farming in his country. I set that application aside, but when I began reading the last one in the pile, lo and behold, I discovered it was the one I had set aside. I wondered why it was again brought to my attention. When I more closely read his wife's information, I discovered she had a degree in agriculture. She has successfully helped farmers save their livelihood by teaching them to make adjustments for land types and weather. I believe the Lord wants this young couple included."

Similar experiences were shared by each of the counselors. They felt confident they were receiving continuing inspiration from the Lord while trying to make these difficult decisions. After several hours, the Prophet said, "We have now reduced the number of applicants from three thousand to seventeen hundred. We still have too many for our needs. I wonder if we could each take a third, review them, and meet again in two days."

The next time they met, the number of couples had been reduced to twelve hundred and ninety-two. "We have finished, at last," the Prophet said with a smile. "Was this a hard task?" he asked, looking at his first counselor.

"No, it was not," he replied. "When evaluating the young couples, it seemed the Lord directed my thoughts quickly and clearly."

"And you?" the Prophet asked his second counselor.

"The same. I am confident that the Lord has specific couples He has already chosen for this journey, and it seemed obvious to me what His choice was in each case."

"It was the same with me," the Prophet responded. "Thank you, Brethren. The Brothers and Sisters in charge of gathering the required materials for this endeavor will be here tomorrow morning to present a status report. I told them we just need an overview for now. They will present a detailed report in six weeks covering all items needed. They have worked on these preparations for many, many months, and I am certain the Lord is pleased with their work."

Scott and Michelle spent several weeks wondering what their future would hold. Each day they tried to continue with the routine that had been their life, as though things were unchanged. The hardest part was not discussing the situation with their families. After seven weeks, the waiting was over, they thought. The letter from Salt Lake was sitting on the table, unopened, when Scott returned from work. They sat across from each other and Scott held the envelope in his hands.

"Please open it. I have been trying to be patient all day long, and I can't wait any longer," Michelle said with a warm smile. "Please?"

Scott opened the envelope and unfolded the single sheet of paper.

Dear Brother and Sister,

We are pleased that you have decided you can live the United Order and are willing to embark on a journey for the Lord. You are invited to attend a special conference in the Tabernacle on the twelfth of April. After the conference, you will be asked to decide if you wish to continue with what is asked of you.

As requested after your attendance at the special broadcast, we ask your continued cooperation in not speaking of this matter with anyone.

"One more month of waiting," Michelle said with a sigh.

"Oh, well," countered Scott as he stood and pulled his wife close to him. "As long as we're together, we can endure anything."

"Agreed."

The month passed very quickly, and on a warm spring evening, they entered the Tabernacle along with a large group of people. A somber yet anxious atmosphere settled over the group as they sat in the building that had been at the center of Church gatherings for generations. Everyone understood this was more than just a request to come and listen to the Prophet, but no one was sure what would specifically be asked of them.

Scott leaned close to Michelle and said, "My hands are sweating and my throat is bone dry. How are you doing?"

"About the same," she whispered. "I think this is the first time I've been here without the Tabernacle Choir occupying the seats in front."

The Prophet was seated at the front of the room, along with the entire Quorum of Twelve Apostles. He stood and went directly to the pulpit. After offering a very stirring prayer, he stood before them in silence.

After several very long minutes, he said, "Do you believe Christ had the ability to walk on the sea? Do you have the faith of Peter to get out of the boat and walk to Him? Could you live the perfect law of pure love toward your fellow man, as did those of Enoch? Do you feel you have the faith and perseverance of our early Church pioneers?"

He had asked the questions as if he were addressing each person individually. Then he was again silent for a moment; some nodded their heads intermittently and some just sat in a confused stupor.

"If you can answer all these questions with an unwavering yes, please remain seated. If you have any doubt at all, I will excuse you with all our love and admiration for responding to our request to come here today."

He was again silent. Scott estimated that no more than 30 or 40 couples stood and quietly exited the room.

The Prophet began again. "Would you be willing to place your trust in God, leave your homes for an undetermined amount of time and turn them over to the Church to be managed by us during your absence?"

A mix of deflating lungs, sighs and gasps could be heard.

"You are all young married couples who have gained the necessary education to obtain stable employment or begin your own businesses. You are to be commended on your willingness to put the Lord first in your lives. We have called you to commence construction of New Zion and build the temple in Independence, Missouri. I am confident each of you is aware that the Church does not currently have possession of all the land where the temple will be built. I have drafted a letter that will be sent tomorrow to the governor of Missouri. It reads:

"Dear Governor. In consideration of the following Executive Order:

"WHEREAS, on October 27, 1838, the Governor of the State of Missouri, Lilburn W. Boggs, signed an order calling for the extermination or expulsion of Mormons from the State of Missouri; and

"WHEREAS, Governor Boggs' order clearly contravened the rights to life, liberty, property and religious freedom as guaranteed by the Constitution of the United States, as well as the Constitution of the State of Missouri; and

"WHEREAS, in this bicentennial year as we reflect on our nation's heritage, the exercise of religious freedom is without question one of the basic tenets of our free democratic republic;

"Now, THEREFORE, I, CHRISTOPHER S. BOND, Governor of the State of Missouri, by virtue of the authority vested in me by the Constitution and the laws of the State of Missouri, do hereby order as follows:

"Expressing on behalf of all Missourians our deep regret for the injustice and undue suffering which was caused by the 1838 order, I hereby rescind Executive Order Number 44, dated October 27, 1838, issued by Governor Lilburn W. Boggs.

"In witness I have hereunto set my hand and caused to be affixed the great seal of the State of Missouri, in the city of Jefferson, on this 25 day of June, 1976.

"(Signed) Christopher S. Bond, Governor.

"We accept the sincere apology that was expressed. And we take the opportunity to inform you that we consider the matter behind us in every aspect. This is to inform you that we are taking the liberty to resume ownership of what was possessed by LDS members at the time the extermination order was issued. Consideration was denied by the Governor at that time, but in view of the fact that the extermination order was officially rescinded, we feel it is open to reconsideration. Enclosed are copies of legal ownership of parcels of ground that the early members of the Church of Jesus Christ of Latter-day Saints had legally purchased. We again thank you for the correction of the injustice that Missouri has rectified and will be arriving in Missouri shortly to resume our legal possession of the subject land. Sincerely, The Brethren of the Church of Jesus Christ of Latter-day Saints

"The Lord has told us to proceed as though we are ready, and that is what we have done. We have no more idea than any one of you how this will come about, but we have complete faith that the Lord knows how this will occur, and we trust in His preparations. We have received instructions concerning the transportation that will be needed to get everyone involved to Independence, Missouri, and we have been told exactly what supplies will be needed. Everything we have been instructed to do has been prepared, and every detail has been completed exactly as we have been directed.

"It requires my complete faith in the Lord, and your complete faith in Him, also, for you to now go and do as we instruct. We ask that you return to your homes and set your affairs in order. We will meet here again in this facility two weeks from today. Please bring with you legal documents that will allow the Church to manage your homes while you are gone, and we want you to know that we feel there will be a need to let others live in your homes while you are away. We ask that you tell your family members you have been called on a service mission for the Church but have been asked to not disclose the exact location yet. Again, I invite you to think seriously on what I have said, and we will wait twenty minutes for you to decide if you can still commit to these expectations. We are expecting several of you to not be able to commit to such requirements for whatever personal situations exist in your lives.

Please leave if you cannot continue on with us, and be assured you are under no condemnation if you do so."

Several couples sporadically left during the next twenty minutes. Quiet, whispered conversations could be heard among some couples, but most sat in silence while holding hands and leaning close to each other. Scott and Michelle, though expressing to each other how unprepared they felt for such a task, remained seated. Michelle doubted anyone in the room felt prepared for such a task, while Scott somehow felt he had been preparing for this moment his entire life. The stories his father had told him since he was a small boy about the areas around Jackson County, Missouri, came flooding into his mind and he slowly shook his head and smiled.

During the rather lengthy meeting that followed, the Prophet unfolded how the huge task would be accomplished. "The leap of faith required by this group of pioneers," he explained, "will not be to walk across the plains and begin building Zion from scratch. You will have access to the latest technology available to make your lives as easy as possible. Hardships will be experienced, but before long you will not be using outhouses or washing your clothes on washboards, nor cooking over an open fire."

Several members of the group obviously thought he had spoken in jest, and soft laughter could be heard from the audience. The Prophet's lengthy silence convinced Scott he was not kidding.

Specific expectations were discussed and the group was divided into twelve smaller groups, each containing fifty couples. The organization was similar to a stake containing twelve wards. The stake leadership was announced and introduced – Colby Nelson was the President, Gary Stevens and Jack Fredericks were his counselors. After further instructions, the group was dismissed to return to their homes to make their final preparations.

The next morning found Scott delivering his rehearsed message to his family. "Michelle and I have been called to a very special service mission for the Church and will be leaving in two weeks. We have been asked to not yet indicate the exact location where we will be serving."

Tears were the first result of their disclosure, and hugs from Jordan and Lynne were next. "We're going to miss you," Jenny said.

"We'll miss you, too," Scott said as he took his mother's hands.

Michelle was softly crying with his sisters.

"It's especially hard to leave you when the world seems to stand on the brink of a global war." Scott stopped to force down his emotions. "We have to trust that the Lord and the members of your ward will look after you as we would if we were here."

"We'll pray for you every day," Jordan said, then broke into sobs.

"We have total faith in the Lord, son," Mark said. "We love you so much and we are so proud that you have made this difficult decision."

"Dad," Scott began, even though his voice kept breaking. "We are turning our house over to the Church. Not the deed, but papers that will allow them to manage it for us while we're gone. The Prophet said he felt there would be a need for others to live in it. That makes me think the last days are upon us."

"What do you mean?" Lynne asked, and then she quickly buried her face against Michelle.

"Dad," Scott said without looking at his father, "I have a power of attorney for you. If anything happens and we don't come back, the house is yours."

Tears that had nearly stopped were again renewed.

During the next two weeks, Scott and Michelle were busy following the Prophet's instructions. They gave copies of their will to their parents to eliminate any possible confusion that might arise. They kept an eye on the happenings in Jerusalem because each day the hatred against the Jews and their activities on Temple Mount became more volatile. One afternoon Michelle saw a home video on the Internet that showed Temple Mount the day after the earthquakes. Every structure in that area had been reduced to a pile of rubble, and the man making the film stated that it was obvious the Jews had not destroyed the Dome of the Rock. She was shocked that the news sources had been so successful in hiding this information. Given the frenzy that was building against the Jews, she doubted this new information would make any difference.

The young couple decided they needed to remove themselves from the political happenings in the world and focus on the task they had accepted. They spent much time fasting and praying that they would be worthy to fulfill what had been asked of them, and that God would watch over those involved in the circumstances in Jerusalem.

They spent as much time as possible with their families. Michelle's parents had come to Salt Lake to be with them, and were staying with Scott's parents. The last evening before Scott and Michelle were to leave for their mission was filled with overflowing emotions. There were many "remember when" moments shared, and tears spilled at each memory. When good-byes were being said at the end of the evening, Mark said, "The world we all remain in as you two venture to points unknown may be a little more familiar to us than your new home. However, if the Second Coming is as close as events predict, there may be things ahead in our own lives that will be life changing. We all have to trust in the Lord and pray for each other."

The historic hatred and distrust that had existed between so many countries in the Middle East seemed to disappear as their common hatred of the Jews forged alliances between them. The evening news became a narrative of the unbelievable audacity of the Jewish people in desecrating Temple Mount. Slowly, more and more of the destruction caused by the earthquakes was blamed on the Jewish people, further escalating the frenzy that was becoming more explosive by the day. Reports of violence that had become almost unbearable to hear during the wars in Iraq, Afghanistan, Libya, and Syria now seemed nearly civilized compared with what was being reported each night from Jerusalem.

The citizens of Israel continued with the preparations to build their temple as if oblivious to the hatred expressed by the growing masses that opposed them. For some unknown reason, the abhorrence and anger did not physically erupt in Jerusalem, but was directed toward any country of the world that supported Israel. The ultimate act, directed toward the United States, happened so quickly it was over before one word could be reported on the nightly news.

A barrage of nuclear warheads was simultaneously launched toward the United States. The military forces in the U.S. were able to intercept all of them, but one. A huge nuclear explosion erased Kansas City from existence in the blink of an eye. Immediate casualties were high and continued to grow as a large nuclear cloud spread across the Great Plains, driven by an unusual wind from the southeast; there was nothing to stop its spread until it reached the great wall created by the Rocky Mountains. The area of complete destruction was a circle 150 miles in diameter with Kansas City, Missouri, at the center point. The devastation created from the nuclear fallout spread from 75 miles east of

Kansas City to the Rocky Mountains in the western United States. It was immediately uninhabitable because the high levels of radiation killed all vegetation, polluted all water, and made the air toxic. The area was quickly renamed Desolation.

Disbelief spread through the world, as America had previously been immune to such destruction through centuries of global fighting. Americans felt very vulnerable, something they had not experienced since the creation of the United States. After the attack on the World Trade Center, it became apparent that terrorists could strike anywhere, but the country as a whole had remained untouched. Those living on both the east and west coasts had always feared they might be the first to be hit by a large-scale enemy attack. Even those living along borders shared by adjoining countries had sometimes feared that enemies might forge alliances with governments in Canada or Mexico to gain access from their borders. Those who lived in the center portion of the country had always felt it would be impossible for a predator to break through the impenetrable defenses of the United States to reach them. They were wrong.

Due to the pacts many countries had entered into, it was not clear who was responsible for the nuclear attack. The U.S. government committed every resource at their disposal to determine who had caused the catastrophe. However, the rest of the world seemed to quickly forget it had even happened as their focus returned to Jerusalem. Americans, quite unfamiliar with destruction on their own soil, seemed unable to resume their lives.

Martial law was immediately imposed on the entire country. The government shut down all communication capabilities in an attempt to stop further attacks. This was accomplished when the President issued an order for service providers of voice and data networks to suspend all service to their customers. The nation's commercial fuel was immediately dedicated to the military. There were no airplanes flying, no trains operating, no buses. Nothing moved that required gas or fuel to operate. No one knew if their relatives living in Wyoming, Texas or Illinois were still alive. Curfews mandated that everyone be in their homes after dark, and the police or military could stop anyone at any time and ask to see their identification. Grocery stores were empty and trash quickly piled up around homes and businesses.

The LDS Church was in a unique position in that they had an emergency preparedness communication network that allowed each surviving ward or stake to communicate with its members and work together to meet everyone's needs. Otherwise, the only information available from outside one's local neighborhood was that provided by government-controlled radio and television. Members of the Church were uniquely prepared as many of them had a year's supply of food and fuel to provide for their own needs; however, for others, basic survival became a full-time endeavor.

"Brethren," the Prophet began, "our hearts are heavy when we see the vast destruction that has occurred." He was speaking to his two counselors and the only member of the Quorum of Twelve Apostles who had been in Salt Lake when the missile attack occurred. Revelation received during the weeks before the attack resulted in an Apostle and his entire family being moved to each major area where the Church was established, and being prepared to direct the operations of the Church in that area of the world until the Savior returned to the Earth. "We can now see the reason for the preparations we have been directed to make during the past year or so. No mortal man could have imagined the scenes we have watched unfold so quickly, and without continual direction from the Lord we would not be prepared to proceed with the things He has commanded us to accomplish."

When the Prophet was overcome with sorrow and could not continue speaking, the brethren quietly waited until he could continue. "The revelations we received instructing us to purchase materials and build such unusual vehicles seemed so very strange at the time. However, we followed the directions we were given and now we are able to continue with our task. We did not know what lay ahead when we were commanded to gather such a specific list of supplies. We all knew the portent of stormy weather awaited the Church and the citizens of the world, but we see through the eyes of man and are blind compared to what the Lord can see."

He stopped to blow his nose and wipe the tears from his face. "It is such a miracle to watch the timetable of the Lord unfold. The new pioneers we have called arrived in Salt Lake two days before the bomb wiped much of the state of Missouri clean." Again, the Prophet broke down and cried openly. "No living thing has survived in that contaminated area, but the Lord has commanded this group of pioneers to enter that land and travel to Independence. It has been revealed that they will be blessed and the elements in that area will have no effect on their bodies. Their obedience in living the Word of Wisdom during their entire lifetimes will make that protection possible. The Lord knows they have great faith, and it will be tested, even as in the refiner's fire. That will prepare them to endure the presence of heavenly forces that will assist in building a glorious temple. We must set them apart and bless them. Our pioneers must be on their way before the government confiscates all sources of fuel and halts interstate travel."

The mood in the room was somber. Each one there felt the heavy responsibility they were required to bear to lead the Church during this time of chaos and tremendous losses on the American continent. The events happening in the world were those that had been prophesied as the precursors for the Second Coming of the Savior. Everyone impatiently awaited that grand event but dreaded the journey through hell that would be required before getting there.

The Prophet sat among the group of new pioneers in the Tabernacle, and because of the design of that unique historic structure, all those assembled could easily hear his voice without the use of a microphone. "I have received direction from the Lord as to how we must proceed. These are terrible times, but the Lord's work must continue as He directs. Each of you will be set apart and blessed before your journey begins. Great faith will be required on your part to set out from Salt Lake and travel to Independence, Missouri, through land that is filled with radiation and pollution. Even though the destruction and loss of life . . ."

The Prophet stopped as he began sobbing. He was unable to regain his composure for several minutes, and then he spoke through his tears with an occasional sob. "So many innocent people have been killed, but the Lord knows the intent of their hearts and they have now safely returned to the home they left before they came to Earth. We who are left behind must complete the work we have been commanded to do. During the next two days, all preparations will be completed and you will begin your mission. We ask that your stake president and his two counselors come forward so we can set them apart and pronounce a blessing upon them. You are the newest stake in the Church, the New Zion Stake."

The group stirred with quiet conversations as the three brethren walked to the front of the room. The Prophet, his two counselors and the Apostle now responsible for the Church organization on the west coast of the United States laid their hands on each person's head, set them apart to fulfill their new assignment, and blessed them with amazing promises.

Then the Bishops of the first twelve wards to be established in New Zion were called forward, set apart, and blessed. They were instructed to choose two counselors, a Melchizedek Priesthood Quorum Leader and a Relief Society President for their ward before the next day, so they could likewise be set apart.

Those who were members of Wards One through Six were instructed to remain at the Tabernacle until they were shielded from the dangers they would face. Those in Wards Seven through Twelve were instructed to go with the stake leadership so they could receive further instruction.

Scott and Michelle left the Tabernacle with other members of the Seventh Ward and walked to the street that bordered the west side of Temple Square. Several buses were parked street side; which they quickly boarded. The buses caravanned to the Little Cottonwood Canyon on the east side of the Salt Lake valley. Even though Scott lived in that area, he was not familiar with their destination – a cavern that seemed to be sculpted in the side of the granite mountain. As they disembarked the buses, they were ushered inside.

"It reminds me of an airplane hangar stuck in the side of a mountain," Scott said as he and Michelle walked with the crowd into the huge structure. Although there were nearly 600 people in their group, they seemed dwarfed inside the gigantic rooms they had entered. After walking for several minutes, Scott said, "What is that?"

That question was also asked by several others as the group passed through huge doors and entered another equally large area filled with the strangest looking vehicles any of them had ever seen.

"Brothers and Sisters," one of the men who had escorted them began. "You are looking at a vehicle that was constructed according to directions received from the Lord. Six vehicles identical to this one will be assigned to each ward, plus a seventh vehicle that will look similar but resembles a bus. I hope you can understand what miraculous directions we have received from the Lord for your benefit. I would personally like to say that you are like a band of pioneers who are about to set off on a journey that will determine the future of the entire world. We all know God has the power to command all elements, that He could create a temple, but instead you have been asked to build it for Him. We all greatly admire your faith."

"When you arrive in Independence, each of the vehicles will be totally dismantled and will serve as the building materials for your new homes and churches. The vehicle that resembles a bus will carry your entire ward to Independence. It will be roomy and comfortable for your journey."

"How fast will this truck go?" someone asked.

"It should average about fifty miles an hour. On top of each truck, we have stacked ten solar panels that have been wired to the electric motor of the truck. The solar panels provide enough electricity to power the vehicles on normal flat surfaces. For steep grades, a propane-powered engine kicks in to power the generators that provide additional electricity for the drive motor. When the vehicle gets back on flat ground, the propane engine shuts off and the vehicle shifts back to solar operation."

"That's amazing." One of the new pioneers commented.

"It has certainly impressed those of us who built it," the guide agreed. "All the vehicles have been built using panels made of a light-weight, honeycomb material covered with an extremely durable outer skin. The exterior side is coated with a solar liquid laminate that is so advanced it cannot even be referred to as the next generation product. Oh, and you will love this – each panel has battery type qualities on the inside. The panels have two sockets – one provides regulated AC electricity for normal household items, and one provides DC electricity so you can charge battery-operated items. These amazing panels will become the walls and roof of your houses and churches. The solar panels that are now the top of the trailers will provide temperature regulating properties that will automatically heat and cool the structures as needed, depending on the inside temperature. You'll learn more about these panels as you construct your houses and buildings."

"When you finish building and see how all this technology works together you will realize, as we have, that the best technology man has been able to come up with pales in comparison with what God can put together for us."

"How will a hundred people fit in one bus?" Another of the anxious pioneers asked.

"The bus has two halves, like all the trucks in your caravan. Each half will seat fifty people. There will be coolers on the bus filled with enough ready-to-eat food to last for your entire three-day journey, and some to spare for after you arrive. After your bus is dismantled, the coolers are designed to use the cold water in a river as a type of refrigeration. You'll have a supply of food staples for approximately one year, which should last until you can produce your own food."

"I have to ask about these tires," someone said from the back of the group. "And I can't wait to hear the techno-talk involved. They look like big black marshmallows, and yet they remind me of covered-wagon wheels."

"Funny you should say that," the guide answered. "We've all said that same thing. Maybe it's because they are positioned out to the side of the truck rather than underneath, like we are used to seeing. Well, not to disappoint you about the technical side, these tires are impervious to the toxic elements you'll be driving in, and they cannot go flat because they're not filled with air. We believe the roads are intact from here to about eighty miles west of Independence. Once the roads are gone, these tires will work just like those covered-wagon wheels to get you through any kind of terrain. You'll use these tires to start decontaminating the ground, as well as making a suitable surface for walkways and roads."

The guide was quiet for a moment. He turned to look at the vehicle, nodded his head and shrugged, and then said, "I think I've covered everything. Does anyone have any questions?"

The rumble of laughter that passed through the crowd indicated to Scott that most everyone felt like he did – overwhelmed, amazed, and completely confused.

"I have a question," Bishop Chandler said. "I haven't heard anything mentioned about the engine module and I just wondered if we were supposed to dig big pits and bury them to put iron back into the soil or what?" Bishop Chandler smiled and shrugged. "Just wondering."

"And I was so sure I had covered everything," the guide said, looking a little embarrassed. "Well, it's always good to save the best for last. When you arrive in Independence and dismantle the entire truck and frame, you will discover that the engine module is a freestanding, self-contained unit. And you'll say to yourself, 'I wonder why they did that?'" The guide smiled and shrugged, copying Bishop Chandler.

"Here's why. The chassis rails sit on the ground and provide a stable surface, and the radiator and SLL-coated sheet metal remain intact to provide a protective shell for the solar driven engine. Each ward will have seven of these babies, and several can be used to pump water from a river or lake, or a drill that can tap water from underground, so you'll have running water year round, even when the rivers freeze solid. That leaves four chassis. When you unpack the trucks, you will discover a blade and other agricultural apparatuses that require a motor, which you will just happen to have. You will be able to level ground or work the soil to plant crops, or even excavate building sites. The only question left is what to do with the other three. My advice would be to reserve one for a spare, if possible. So assuming you decide to take that advice, you now have two chassis that you can use as transport vehicles. Twelve wards can cover a lot of ground, so we think you will be very happy to have two transport vehicles to move your crops to a single processing area, or injured people to a central treatment area. I can think of a lot of reasons a group of twelve hundred people would like to have a couple dozen transport vehicles." The guide smiled. "Did that answer your question?"

Everyone clapped, whistled, and cheered. All fears, which had mostly been fears of the unknown, were gone. Humor and joy had been re-introduced into their rapidly changing daily lives, and peace was the resulting emotion.

"Thank you very much," Bishop Chandler said as he walked forward and shook hands with their guide.

"You're most welcome. You can look around, check things out, and ask any other questions you have," the guide said. "Anyone who's interested can check under the hood of this baby. Then when you are finished, head back to your bus and you will be taken back to the Tabernacle. There will be people waiting for you who will take you to their home and provide dinner and a place to sleep, and then bring you back to the Tabernacle in the morning."

Scott turned to Michelle and asked, "Do you suppose we could stay with my folks tonight?"

"Why don't we ask our guide?" she suggested.

Scott shrugged and they walked to where the guide seemed to be patiently waiting for everyone to leave the area.

"Excuse me," Scott said. "My parents live in town. Would we be able to spend the night with them rather than go with someone else to their home?"

The guide took a cell phone from his pocket. He pressed one button and after a very short time, he began conversing with someone. He explained the question Scott had asked. "What is your name, please," he asked Scott.

The guide passed that information on and paused while waiting for the answer. He smiled, ended the call, and said "Your parents will be waiting at the Tabernacle for you."

"Thank you very much," Scott said. He and Michelle left and walked toward the bus. "Too bad this kind of organization doesn't exist in the business world," he said as they walked.

"This whole thing is like being in a science fiction dream. In a few minutes I'm going to wake up and remember what it was I ate for dinner that caused such a strange dream," Michelle said, sounding completely serious.

During one last night spent with their families, as Michelle's parents were still visiting with Mark and Jenny, both families heard all about the amazing details, with the understanding they could not say anything they had been told for at least a week. The next morning a very tearful farewell was bid to Scott's sisters, and a second farewell to their parents; which, took place in the car parked at the West Temple Street entrance to Temple Square. Exiting the car, Scott and Michelle took a moment to calm themselves, then turned and walked toward the Tabernacle to await their blessing.

The members of the Seventh Ward sat together, patiently waiting. Many, many beautiful promises were pronounced upon their heads – promises that their bodies would be immune to the toxic elements they would be exposed to once they crossed the Rocky Mountains. These blessings, they were told, were granted to them from on high due to their previous strict obedience and adherence to the Word of Wisdom.)

While they waited, Scott said, "It seems like each blessing has some basic items about bestowing protection against the elements, but it's interesting to hear the specific and very unique things some blessings have contained."

Michelle nodded in agreement, but then added, "By the time we get our blessing, I don't think there'll be anything unique left to be blessed with."

"I'm sure they've reserved a special blessing just for you," he said as he gently squeezed her hand.

When their turn arrived, Scott watched as the Prophet, his counselors and the Apostle laid their hands on his wife's head. She was blessed that the harmful elements in the air, ground and water would not harm her body. Then surprise and shock rushed through him at the wondrous words he heard. "Your ability to have children will be preserved and your child will be the first to be born in New Zion. He will be the first child born on the Earth to never witness the corrupt world that currently exists. This child will be one of many that will be born in New Zion and will be one of the pure generation that will lead the final crusade at the end of the Millennium."

It was well into the night when the blessings were completed and each couple was taken to a nearby home for a night's rest. "I guess I was wrong about them running out of blessings," Michelle said as they were recording the words of their blessings.

Scott smiled. "This entire assignment now seems even more important because our son will also be depending on our success."

"How many women have been told by the Prophet that their first baby will be a boy?" asked Michelle through a giggle.

FINAL REQUIREMENTS

Very early the next morning, the caravan left the mountain structure. A prayer was asked that they would be blessed with safe passage until they were well into the radiation zone; those words caused more than one person to marvel that they now felt they would be safe only after reaching the toxic lands filled with radiation. They headed east on Interstate 80, and when they got into the mountains, they turned south toward Interstate 70. The effect of not being able to buy gasoline for the previous three days was clearly illustrated – the freeways were nearly empty. After several hours, they stopped at a rest area to stretch their legs.

Map 2 – Road to New Zion

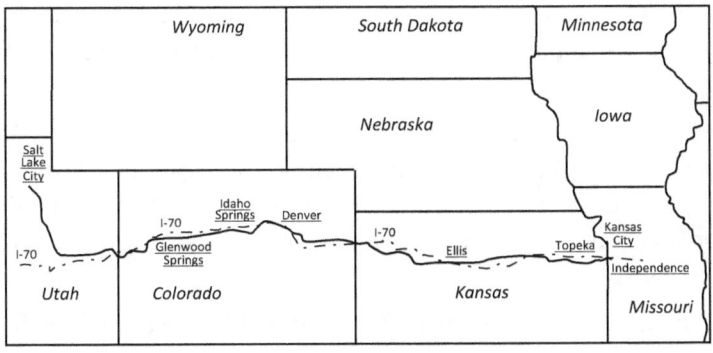

It's easy to understand why there are so few vehicles on the roads," Nancy Chandler, the Bishop's wife, said to Michelle. "What I don't understand is why no one seems to find our stranger-than-fiction vehicles unusual."

"They probably think these are freaky government vehicles and they're more *afraid* of us than curious," Bishop Chandler said.

Michelle found it interesting to watch how Evan had changed once he had been set apart as the Bishop. He and Nancy had been a quiet couple, blending in with the group so completely they rather disappeared, but now they were both making a visible effort to become acquainted with each of the 98 other people in their ward.

Although there were no visible changes to the landscape, the further east the caravan traveled, the easier it was to see the effects of the frenzied mass exodus west after the bomb had been dropped. Many homes and gas stations appeared to be empty. Still, most small towns looked like tourist towns during the off-season – some businesses were closed and they saw very few people. They drove late into the afternoon, stopping every few hours to rotate drivers. Each time a ridge was crossed that provided views of the land to the east, conversations grew quiet, as the reality of what lay ahead filled their thoughts.

The first day of travel passed uneventfully. They made several stops, ate their meals, and watched the sun travel across the sky.

"I think we're slowing down," Scott said as he leaned toward the aisle to see what might be happening.

"Brothers and Sisters," Bishop Chandler said as he stepped into the aisle, "we're going to stop for the night here. Because our vehicles are a bit oversized, and there are a lot of them, we will be spread out among the various recreational areas here in Glenwood Springs tonight. We'll gather with the folks riding in our trailer and have a group prayer before dinner."

Everyone gathered in a large grassy area. Bishop Chandler offered a sincere prayer and then asked that each person share their testimony of the importance of what they had been asked to do. By the time the last person had expressed their feelings, the Spirit was so strong no one felt even a tinge of concern.

A dinner was prepared from the food that had been sent with them, and the Seventh Ward sat together, talking quietly, as the sky darkened. Some chose to sleep in the bus and others took a small two-person tent from the truck and slept on the grass. Michelle and Scott escaped into a private cocoon within their small tent that sheltered them from the pressing closeness they were experiencing after only one day with no privacy. They had months ahead where privacy would not exist, and they had been counseled about that. However, the last night before that world became their reality they chose to spend alone together.

Michelle slowly became aware of the first rays of morning light beginning to pierce her eyelids. She heard Scott sigh, and knew when she rolled over to look at him his eyes would still be shut and that he would lay still, moving nothing but his lips, which would form one-syllable words to answer her early-morning questions.

"Are you ready to begin your new life?" she asked as she leaned close and softly kissed his eyelids.

"Yeah," he replied, and she could feel his cheek slightly move as a threatening smile made the corners of his mouth minutely turn upward.

"I've changed my mind. I want to stay here and miss the bus this morning," she said as she watched his face.

His eyes flew open and squinted part way shut again as the light was too bright to be tolerated by eyes accustomed to complete darkness. "What?" he asked as he started to sit up.

"Oh, nothing." She pushed him back down by leaning against him as she kissed him. "Just wondered if you were awake."

He rolled over so he was looking down at her face. "I'm awake. Guess we better get moving, huh?"

She nodded as she watched his face descend toward her.

When everyone gathered for breakfast, they noticed a commotion among the members of the ward camped near them. Word quickly spread that there had been a death in their group. Bishop Chandler and his two counselors went to find out if there was anything they could do to help. When they returned half an hour later, everyone gathered round to hear the details.

"We have sad news to report. This morning Brother and Sister Hanson decided to go for a swim. They were caught in the strong current and could not escape. Both of them drowned before anyone could rescue them."

The gasp that spread outward through the group was like a ripple spreading from a rock dropped in a pond. No one was prepared to hear the news that someone had drowned given the incredible miracle that protected each of them against elements that would normally be lethal to any human. The Bishop was silent for a long moment. It was evident he was struggling to control his emotions. During the silence, with the Bishop's sad news as the backdrop, the sorrow that plagued the earlier pioneers heading to Utah suddenly became a sobering reality for each of the modern pioneers.

"We will remain here until arrangements can be made to return the Hanson's to Salt Lake. I would counsel you, Brothers and Sisters, to remember that the Lord has promised us protection only against the elements and the radiation that is toxic to the normal human body. He has not guaranteed that we are immune to natural consequences of our actions. Please remember to be cautious. We need every member of our group to accomplish the things we have been commanded to do. We must work hard to avoid as many of the sorrows and setbacks the early LDS pioneers experienced. Putting our complete trust in God is our greatest tool, but we must remember to pray about new situations before we go forth. Without learning to be completely dependent on the Lord, without relying on inspiration from Him for every decision we make and every action we take, the consequences could thwart our strong faith and the best of our intentions. I pray that the sorrow of losing two members of our group will create a strong resolve to seek God's guidance in every aspect of our lives."

In a short time, with the assistance of the local Church leadership, the caravan was able to continue their journey. By the time they reached the eastern edge of the Rocky Mountains, they could easily see the brown parched valley below that stretched far to the east. The edge of the area contaminated by radiation was within sight.

The caravan pulled to the side of the freeway, and each ward gathered for prayer. When the Seventh Ward was assembled together, Gary Stevens, the Bishop's first counselor, was asked to offer a prayer. It was a lengthy request for protection and the Spirit could be felt so powerfully that no one was anxious for it to end.

By the time they began the descent from the mountains, Michelle found herself breathing deeply. Within minutes, the first contaminated air would be passing through her nose and entering her lungs. The dingy cloud that seemed to hug the valley floor was irrefutable evidence of the approaching test of their faith. When she turned to look at Scott, it was obvious his thoughts were the same. She smiled and said, "Do you want to see who can hold their breath the longest before we breathe in that polluted air?"

Scott leaned close to her ear and quietly said, "I'm afraid I would lose because my heart is beating so fast I can't hold my breath at all."

Michelle looked into his eyes. "You okay?"

Scott shrugged slightly and said, "I'm fine. I trust the Lord will protect us, but I feel like I did the first time my mom used no-tear shampoo to wash my hair. My eyes always burned so badly, and no matter how hard I squeezed them shut, they still burned. Then one night Mom started to wash my hair and I tensed up, but she said I didn't need to worry because the new shampoo would not burn my eyes. Did I believe that was possible? No. Did I trust my mother? Yes, but I still kept my eyes tightly squeezed shut while she washed my hair. I can still hear her voice saying, 'It's okay. It won't hurt you.' I mustered up every ounce of courage I could find and slowly opened one eye. That is how I feel right now. I trust the Lord, I trust my blessing, and I trust the Prophet, but right now, it is taking every shred of courage I have to draw in that first breath. That will *prove* they're right." Scott chuckled softly. "Do you think that means I don't have enough faith?"

"You have more faith than anyone I've ever known," Michelle said as she leaned close and kissed his chin. "Remember the picture I had above my desk at home? It said, 'You are not a human being having a spiritual experience; you are a spiritual being having a human experience.' That human instinct is telling you the contamination will destroy your body. God gave you that instinct and it's called self-preservation. But that spiritual being you are is the one that got on the bus in the first place."

When the cloud of pollution was very near, Michelle turned away from the window and asked Scott what he thought he would miss most about Utah. His answer resulted in several minutes of animated conversation. Then she turned to look out the window.

"Don't you find it strange that there's not a roadblock or any guards to keep people out of this area?"

"Not really. I doubt if anyone is going to accidentally wander into a contaminated area. After all, I think just about everyone is aware we've been nuked."

Michelle laughed. "I wondered if the air would smell differently, but I can't smell anything. Can you?"

Scott breathed in, slowly. "Nope. Just smells like air."

"It might *smell* the same, but the scenery doesn't look the same."

"Except for everything looking dead and scorched, I don't see any change at all," Scott kidded. "Oh, and the lack of people. I guess that is a change. They certainly chose a good name for this area. Desolation."

After riding for several hours, they stopped to rotate drivers. Everyone usually scurried to get off the bus so they could walk around for a few minutes, but people were slow to stand and walk toward the door of the bus. Nearly every person stood on the last step for a few seconds longer than usual. Then they looked down at the dirt before lowering their foot onto it. It seemed hard to comprehend that they were now standing on ground that was filled with radiation, and breathing air that should be burning their nose lining and lungs. The power of the blessings each one had received at the hand of the Prophet became a physical, tangible entity – a barrier between them and the elements.

When the caravan rolled through the quiet, abandoned streets of Idaho Springs, there was not one word of conversation. By the time they reached Denver, the sight of such a huge metropolitan city deserted and empty seemed to allow their minds to better comprehend the magnitude of the devastation. As if the city had refused to die peacefully, evidence of vandalism and looting made it seem the city had thrashed about madly before accepting its fate.

There were no major cities after they left Denver, only varying sizes of small farming towns. The degree of destruction the bomb had caused increased gradually as they progressed eastward. The disappearing sunlight dictated that they stop near what had been Ellis, Kansas.

The seven oversized vehicles that made up the Seventh Ward's caravan had seemed impressive when they were parked together the previous night, but when all eighty-four vehicles were parked in one area, it was evident they were part of a very large and well-organized endeavor. People began setting up tents, most for the first time – another test of faith. Somehow, the thought of sleeping on the contaminated ground produced more apprehension than walking on it. Another test of faith could be heard in conversations about water. Should they drink only the fast running water in a stream or could they drink any available source of water?

When the entire group had assembled before going to sleep for the night, President Nelson spoke. "When we actually arrived in this area of Desolation, I know many of us were pondering the exact meaning of being protected from the elements. Those words could cover a wide range of situations. Would we be protected just enough to keep us from dying or having permanent affects from the toxins? Or, would we not even be able to tell there was any pollution? Even though we are protected against the elements of this environment, we will be tried before we reach Independence. We need to remember that the Lord did not promise we could not get sick or have doubts. He only promised the radiation and pollution would not affect us. Did we think we could be called of God to cross a wilderness, as those that followed Moses or Brigham, and arrive in comfort with no proving of our merit, purging of our hearts, or tempering of our souls? We were chosen of God and called to do a work that has been prophesied for generations. Don't forget the shield of God that has been placed on our heads. Let's renew our desire to do what has been asked of us and continue eastward in the morning with complete trust in the Lord."

There was not a single murmur from the group. Being compared to a follower of Moses, or thinking of themselves as similar to the pioneers who helped establish the Restored Church seemed to galvanize their determination to endure any hardships they faced.

Scott and Michelle decided to stretch their legs and seek a little alone time. They walked along the slow moving river, holding hands, trying to comprehend the devastation that surrounded them.

"We are walking on radioactive ground and breathing toxic air," Scott said, "and yet so far most of us have only drunk the bottled water that was included as part of our supplies. That is beginning to run low. This may sound strange, but I feel as if there is a little voice inside my head asking, 'Are you going to put the Lord's promise to the test and start drinking the natural water before you're forced to?' It sounds silly when I say it out loud, but I promise it makes more sense when I'm thinking about it."

"Have you decided what you're going to do?"

"I'd like to drink the water in this river." He looked intently at the river – the fast moving water in the middle swirled into quiet eddies and calm pools along the bank

"It looks pretty inviting," Michelle said, watching Scott's face.

"Maybe we should take the ultimate step of faith and submerge ourselves in the water rather than just swallow a mouth full."

Michelle laughed as she sat down and began unlacing her shoes. "You can't fool me. You just want to go for a swim."

They took off their outer clothing and carefully stepped down the bank into the cool water. After standing in knee-deep water for a moment, they found a quiet pool along the bank and silently treaded water while facing each other.

"This feels so great," Scott said.

"I can practically feel my dry skin sucking in the moisture," Michelle agreed. "This brings back so many memories of skinny dipping with my sister in the old swimming hole at my grandpa's farm when we were kids."

They leaned their heads back to let the water wash the accumulated dust and dirt from their hair. Scott nodded slightly and smiled at Michelle. Then he lowered his face into the water and drank a swallow from the river. Michelle did the same and then they moved closer to the shore until they could stand on the bottom of the river.

"Do you feel okay?" Scott asked his wife.

"Yes, I feel great."

They talked to each other for some time, occasionally drinking the water until neither were thirsty any longer. They climbed out and sat on the riverbank until the warm air dried them, and then they dressed and headed back to the camp. Many couples were sleeping inside tents, but Michelle and Scott decided to sleep on a mat so they could see the sky. As they snuggled close together, they studied the breath-taking view created by the millions of stars now visible due to the total darkness that surrounded them for miles in every direction.

As soon as everyone was gathered for breakfast the following morning, Bishop Chandler said, "Our water supply is gone. Many of you are dehydrated from your obvious concern about drinking the polluted water. There is no choice but to begin drinking from any water source we can find. We have been blessed that our bodies will not be affected by the elements here, but we have not been blessed to live without water. We must all exercise our faith in this regard."

As the final day of their journey began, the devastation became greater with each passing mile. "Don't you think it's ironic," Michelle asked, "that we are leaving the civilization of the west that was developed by the pioneers' sacrifices years ago, and are proceeding to a wilderness in the east, that was once the civilization that the pioneers were forced to leave?"

"Yes, very ironic," Scott agreed.

When they finally reached Topeka, everyone was silent. They expected to find tall mounds of rubble where the multi-storied buildings had once stood. In reality, there was less indication a town had existed than in some of the small towns they had passed through earlier. All that was left behind were varying sized piles of unidentifiable rubble.

"My cousins lived here. We visited them at Christmas," the woman in the seat across from Scott said as she quietly sobbed.

"I'm so sorry, Honey," her husband comforted.

"There were over 123,000 people living in this city, and more than double that in the metropolitan area. Can you imagine? Over a quarter of a million people alive one moment, and all trace of their existence gone the next moment." She leaned against her husband and continued sobbing.

"And that is just one of the many huge cities," Michelle whispered quietly to Scott. "Kansas City and . . ." Her voice broke off and she, too, began sobbing quietly.

The caravan slowed and then stopped. When the members of the Seventh Ward had gathered together, Bishop Chandler said, "The devastation is hard for us to comprehend. I know some of you had relatives living in this area, and I'm sure this is disturbing to you. However, we know these people did not just vanish. They returned to the home we all shared before coming to Earth. They are probably very busy there, helping with the preparations for the Savior's return to Earth. We also must be busy with those preparations. We are about a hundred miles from our destination. I now understand the importance of our marshmallow tires, as we ran out of passable roads many miles back, and yet the bus has continued with hardly any noticeable difference. We will be traveling to the south in order to drop below the major rivers in the area. The next time we stop, we'll be at our destination."

Even though everyone was confident the Lord could guide them to Independence, they were openly grateful for modern technology. When they reached what had been Independence, there was no sign anyone had ever inhabited the land. It looked completely barren. The only way to describe the terrain was to say it appeared to have been swept clean. However, it was not flat enough to begin construction of any kind. The magnitude of the task they had been called to complete was vividly illustrated before their eyes.

Bishop Chandler offered a prayer to thank the Lord for delivering them to their destination. When he finished, his wife Nancy spoke quietly as she looked at the empty desolation surrounding them. "We were here a few years ago, and I can't believe it's the same place. I've read the temple site was west of town, but that's not very helpful when there's no longer any town."

"My dad had some very spiritual experiences in this place," Scott said, "but I seriously doubt that he could find it either. It looks like someone came in with a gigantic earth mover and just wiped everything away."

"Well," Bishop Chandler said, "we know we are in the general area, so for now we'll move ahead with the business of beginning to build homes for our group. That should keep us very busy for a while."

"What's the plan?" someone asked. "I'm ready to start right now."

"Great," Bishop Chandler said, "because I know there's a plan. Our group, our Ward, will be responsible to build homes for all of us, and to work the ground to begin growing food to sustain us. We will be responsible to help construct our ward building, also."

Everyone cheered and clapped when he spoke those words.

"It's May 4. Today is the first day in the life of the city we have been called here to build – New Zion. Even though we cannot recognize what this area looked like only a few days ago, I am confident that when this date arrives twelve months from now, none of us will recognize it as being the same area where we stand today. It will be a thriving town and the majestic temple complex will be under construction. We're making history, but before we get ahead of ourselves, I need to get some direction from President Nelson."

The Bishop walked away and most everyone returned to their bus in order to get out of the hot sunlight. When he returned, the entire Ward gathered around him.

"President Nelson is working with a group of men, even as we speak, to stake out the basic arrangement of New Zion. He is in contact with the brethren in Salt Lake, and they are using GPS to make sure the new city is designed in exact accordance with the plan we were given before we left. The design will provide space in the middle for a large stake center to eventually be built, and all twelve wards will be established in a circle around it. Our first priority is to get our tents arranged. The minute our ward's boundary is established, we will start getting settled. In the mean time, maybe we should eat and rest."

When everyone finished eating, it was announced that there was enough food in the coolers for one more easily prepared meal. That meant they would have to start using the food that had been sent with them. Within less than an hour, Bishop Chandler's hand-held radio squawked. He and his ten group leaders left shortly thereafter to find out where the Seventh Ward would be located.

When they returned, he showed everyone the diagram President Nelson had given him. Using the map, stakes were pounded into the ground where each circle of five tents would be located. The tents were arranged so the door of each opened toward the center of the circle, making it easier to communicate with each other. Tents, sleeping mats, and blankets were quickly unpacked and everyone went to work.

By nightfall, the area no longer looked barren. If one could view the area where Independence, Missouri, had once stood from an airplane, it would have now looked as though someone had dropped a very, very large donut out of the sky. An empty circle about a quarter mile in diameter was surrounded by twelve large camps that were narrow where they bordered the center space and fanned out in the shape of a slice of pie. Within each slice of pie was a ward, neatly arranged in a series of small circles that contained five tents per circle. Some distance away from the outside of each slice of pie sat the seven vehicles that had brought them from Salt Lake.

"Welcome home," Scott said as he lay next to Michelle near the opening of their tent.

"Yeah. The sky was never this ... dazzling at home. What more could we ask for?"

"A bigger yard and some privacy," Scott said quietly. "I'm glad to feel tired, especially after riding on that bus for three days. If we had made this trip on foot like the pioneers of old, I don't know if we would even be out of the State of Utah yet. We would be dirtier and our feet would be sore and blistered."

"When you look at it that way, we're pretty well off, huh?"

"Yes we are," Scott agreed. "Plus, I know how much you hate spiders, and there's not a single creepy crawler anywhere."

"That's a blessing! I'll be sure to thank Heavenly Father. Do you think our parents have received any word about how we're doing?"

"I would guess not. No one wants to broadcast the fact that we are out here. Not yet."

Shortly after breakfast the next morning, Bishop Chandler called the Seventh Ward together for a meeting.

"President Nelson reports that water has been found a little over a mile away from the center of our encampment, in both the north and south directions. From what Salt Lake has told him, before the destruction there were small reservoirs in both of those areas, but they now appear to be deep lakes that are fed from underground sources. Two wards have been assigned to get water to every ward by evening, and starting this morning underground water pipes will be laid so water can be pumped right to us.

"The area where our vehicles are now parked is where we will build the first of our houses. The plan that we used last night only included the portion where we put our tents, but this one," and he waved a sheet of paper, "has our entire ward laid out, very precisely. I have a list of five couples that will be in charge of staking out the area for our homes. As soon as each house is finished, we will start moving people out of the tent area, so just stay where you are for now. Building our houses and getting seeds planted are our two priorities. I will assign twenty couples to build houses and twenty couples to start getting our gardens planted, and this plan shows where the garden will be located. After we get settled into a routine, the brethren will be doing the heavy labor and the Sisters will be gardening and cooking, but for now, five couples will be assigned to cook for all of us, and that will be a whole new experience."

Work began in earnest. The genius behind having transport vehicles instantly became abundantly clear; they made it possible to unload all the trucks and create a separate area to store supplies. The Bishop's Storehouse was built with some of the spare panels from the dismantled vehicles, and Scott was called to oversee it. He knew their existing supplies were intended to last for a year, so he quickly inventoried and organized everything within the storehouse. Since it would take time before their gardens could produce any food to supplement their supply, Scott knew his assignment would require a great deal of guidance from the Lord.

The agricultural tools used in conjunction with an engine chassis were one of the first pieces of equipment to be assembled. Rather than trying to prepare the barren soil for gardening using shovels and hoes, they had equipment to level the ground and work the soil. Sites for building houses were prepared using the same piece of equipment. With forty people working, the garden was quickly planted, providing more people to help build houses.

Two transport vehicles were left intact and were used to bring water to their new garden. However, it did not take long for the underground water system to be completed and then watering their garden became a simple task.

As soon as the first house was under construction, the transport vehicles became invaluable. Although a single building panel weighed about three hundred pounds and could have easily been carried by five or six men, each house required ten panels. The transport vehicle carried all ten panels in one trip, probably saving at least eight or nine hours of work.

The forty people assigned to help build houses gathered to build Bishop Chandler's house. It took about thirty minutes for the Dirt Digger, as the multi-task vehicle had been nicknamed, to clear and level the area where the house would stand. Pylons that held the walls vertical were driven deep into the ground by the hydraulic rams fitted to the rear of the Dirt Digger. It took four men about an hour to complete that task.

A dozen rolls of metallic material were stretched across the area that would be covered by the house and was clipped to the inside of the pylons that would hold the sidewalls. The resulting configuration resembled a bed frame with evenly spaced support boards awaiting the mattress to be laid on it. The *mattress* turned out to be two panels that became the floor. They were made of the same lightweight material, but one side had the appearance of wide plank flooring. The five wall panels and one door panel were easily dropped onto the pylons, and the women worked from both sides to hold the walls upright while the magnetic strips that ran along the edges and sides of each panel were lined up. Once the connections were in place, a man standing on a ladder pinned a bracket in place over each joint to ensure the walls would not accidentally be separated if the house were ever bumped hard. The process took about two hours.

A lifting boom had been attached to the Dirt Digger just above the hydraulic rams. This boom connected to the hydraulic source and easily extended above the top of the houses' single level walls. Straps were attached to the four corners of the roof panel lying on the bed of the transport. A large hook collected the straps in the center and began to slowly lift the panel so it remained horizontal. One of the men held a rope attached to a single corner of the panel and helped to guide it to the final resting place over one half of the house. Strong magnetic strips on the bottom side of the solar panel snapped tightly against the strips on the edge of the walls and the roof was locked into place. The process was repeated on the opposite end of the house, and then two men, each standing on a ladder on opposite sides of the house, positioned and pinned down the bracket that fit over the middle seam of the roof panels, insuring the roof did not leak and the magnetic connection could not be disconnected.

"This is amazing," the Bishop said as he walked through the group, shaking hands with those who had helped assemble his house. "I can't believe the exterior of our house has been completed in about six hours. I'm certain we'll get even faster as we go along."

"I bet we could get it down to five hours each, or maybe four and a half," his first counselor added.

"Wow," the Bishop sighed. "That sounds to me like our homes might all be built in a couple weeks or so. I know we don't have any trees around here, but think back to the first pioneers who came to this area and had to build homes for themselves. They had to cut down the trees, strip the bark off, chop them to the correct size, and chisel out the notching. Then they had to use a team of horses to drag the logs up to the house. I bet it took a ton of work to put a roof on a log cabin. Then you have to chink it and cut out the places for the door and windows. What a job!"

The Bishop's wife chuckled as she put her arm around her husband's shoulder. "So that would mean maybe one house per summer?"

"If I was the one building it, it would have taken a lot longer than one summer," he said.

"And you can bet their houses didn't have heating, cooling, running water, toilets or stoves."

"Or couches," the Bishop added. "Speaking of which, look what's coming."

The transport vehicle was just pulling up to his new house. Within a few minutes, members of the work party had carried the furnishings inside. Even though the house was very small, all forty helpers were either standing inside or watching through the doorway.

"The stove goes in the corner and the sink unit hangs next to it," Nancy directed as she looked at a diagram. "The toilet goes in that corner behind the only door of privacy we have." That created a series of chuckles.

"We should probably double check that the drain flanges on the floor are secure," the Bishop said.

"Especially the toilet, please," Nancy added. "The table and four chairs go over here by the stove. The couch can go right between the table and where the bed folds down. When the water is hooked up, I will be able to stand right here, turn this handle, and get water. All the conveniences of home."

"Coming through," someone called from outside. Those crowded around the door moved so the cabinet being carried by two men could be brought into the house. Here's your dishes and cooking utensils," one man said as he quickly hung the cabinet on the brackets already mounted over the sink. "And, we found a little surprise that no one had mentioned." He held up a broom as though it were a prized heirloom. "Now all you have to do is drag your sleeping mats and blankets in here, stash your tent in the top compartment of the cabinet, and you're moved in. We have two more cabinets outside if someone will help bring them in."

Four men quickly stepped outside and brought the cabinets in. "This one is for kitchen things: towels, cleaning supplies, rugs, little things like that," the man explained. "This other cabinet is for storing your clothes. You will get your own supply of clothing from the Bishop's Storehouse. And," he said, and then took a deep breath, "I have one more thing to bring in."

He turned and walked back to the transport vehicle, lifted a lamp very carefully, then returned to the house.

"A light," Nancy said, almost reverently.

"And it plugs in right here," the man said as he plugged the light into the socket. "Mostly for mood lighting I guess." He spun on his heels like a butler and gave Nancy a remote. "I place this in your hands for safe keeping. If you select light, you can press one through seven to control the brightness of the recessed lights in the ceiling panels." Pointing to the east wall across from the couch, he announced, "Your communications center. For now, it is only a dark screen to stare at, but eventually that screen will be your favorite place to stare, because you will be able to communicate with your families. Eventually, we'll get a little more technology back into our lives. But for now, your journals and the batteries used in some of the hand tools can be charged in a couple hours in the battery charger that is built into each wall panel."

"Thank you so much," Nancy said as she shook his hand.

"Yes," the Bishop echoed. "I know there are other supplies that will be distributed once we get a few more houses up. We brought soap and laundry things, and a basic first aid kit for each house. There is rope for clotheslines and a supply of shampoo and stuff to keep us clean. As soon as we are settled and begin construction on the temple, we will be getting supplies from the east. They have designated a pick-up location where the supplies will be delivered, and then we will pick them up using our transport vehicles. Later, the big equipment and all the building supplies needed for the temple will get here the same way. Life will not be as easy as it was before we came here, but it will be an improvement over what it is now, and a lot easier than the pioneers who settled here while being pursued by angry mobs."

"Hooray," everyone in the group sang out.

"Does it feel like it's getting cooler in here yet?" Bishop Chandler asked.

"I don't think so," Nancy said, and then she laughed. "I'll bet the door has to be shut before the air in the house can be cooled."

The houses were soon completed and the tent city disappeared. The water and sewer pipes were buried below what would eventually become the streets. From that main line, a pipe ran to the side of each house and connected to the pipe extending out from underneath the coiled metal under the flooring.

"I was wondering how a plumber like me got a ticket to this vacation in paradise," Tyler said while working with the Bishop. "Running this sewer line is like what I did at home. But who plumbed the houses?"

"The indoor plumbing is built into the floor panels. More of your skills will be needed when we build the stake center. These floor panels have piping that zigzags back and forth. A chemical is injected in the pipe every time waste enters. All the waste is heated to a high temperature inside the pipe, so by the time it gets to the connection at the street, it is purified water. It's a treatment plant in the floor. That water is sent to the ward crop field."

"I didn't know you were a plumber, too, Bishop," Tyler said.

That brought a laugh from the Bishop, "I'm not a plumber, I just have to know how it works. While all of you are doing the real work, I have to study the plans and attend meetings where they teach us about all this stuff. As soon as you get the rest of these houses hooked to the sewer, you get to start on the sprinkler systems for the gardens."

"Where does the pipe I've laid in the streets end up?"

"Tonight after dinner, why don't you take your wife for a walk down to the north end of the ward crop field. A crew has been down there all day placing the water storage tanks underground. By tomorrow, they should be hooked up to the pipe you first dug in last week. Then it gets buried, so this may be your only chance to see it."

"Thanks, my first date with my wife since we arrived."

The entire building process was a major miracle to the people of the Seventh Ward. Within weeks, plants were growing in the toxic ground that had not even been able to produce weeds on its own. The transformation of New Zion was rapid and profound.

Scott and Michelle were one of the last to move. "No more tent," Michelle said the first morning they awoke in their new home. "And privacy. Not a single window and only one door. Absolute privacy."

"I think I'm looking out a window right now," Scott said as he looked up at the skylight through which sunshine was streaming into their new home.

"I guess you have me there," Michelle admitted as she stretched. "I sure wouldn't mind a bathtub, though. The thought of being immersed in water sounds very appealing. I can't even remember what it felt like to get out of the bathtub, lather on lotion, and then put on makeup and lipstick. It's like another life."

"I usually showered, so I feel pretty much at home," Scott said.

"All in all, I'm amazed at what conveniences we do have. When we first arrived, I didn't even dare to hope for running water."

"Do you regret giving it all up?" Scott asked.

"Not for one second. Sure, life was easier, but compared to how I feel about God and the purpose of our existence, I was so ungrateful and uninvolved then. I feel like I am part of something important, something worthwhile. That's a better feeling than I ever got from sweet-smelling lotion."

The entire population of New Zion had anticipated the arrival of Harvest Day. Each ward's garden area had been the source of many miracles: the food grew amazingly fast; each plant produced several times more than usual; and once the vegetables or fruit was picked, flowers again bloomed on the same vines, and a new batch grew. The growing season finally ended in October with a bountiful harvest. They were able to store enough food to easily feed them through the coming winter. With the arrival of their first holiday, frivolity filled the air.

Scott was just about to leave the house to help prepare for the festivities when he noticed a wonderful aroma.

"What are you making for the celebration?" he asked Michelle, as he inhaled deeply.

"Don't you recognize that smell?" she asked, shaking her head in disbelief. "Your mom gave me this recipe for skillet cookies."

"I knew it seemed familiar," he said as he came close to get a look. "Any chance of getting a taste?"

"It will cost you," she said, leaning close and waiting for a kiss.

"I could just take a spoon and sneak a taste while you're standing there with your eyes closed," he joked, right before he kissed her.

Women began carrying dishes filled with the last fresh vegetables of the growing season to tables set up for their harvest celebration. They also had cookies, cakes and other desserts. After living so closely together and working toward the same goal, it was fun to spend time simply enjoying each other's company.

The rest of the afternoon was spent at the lakes that supplied their water. Half of the wards gathered at each lake. Some actually swam in the beautiful blue water, but not for very long. It was, after all, October. Others stretched out on the sun-baked shore. Scott and Michelle found a spot along the water's edge and spread out their blanket.

"Michelle," Nancy Chandler said from a few blankets away. "Evan wants me to get your recipe for those skillet cookies."

"Sure," Michelle agreed. "I got the recipe from Scott's mom. She said it had been in their family for generations. I think his ancestors actually lived here in Independence at one time. Is that right, Scott?"

"Yes," Scott answered. "My family joined the Church in New York when it was first organized and moved west with them. They lived here, but were driven out by the mobs. They went to Nauvoo and actually went through the temple just a day or two before the saints were chased out of there. When they got to Salt Lake, my family went south to colonize in Oak City, but eventually my grandfather moved back to Salt Lake. We've lived there ever since."

Bishop Chandler stood and said, "And now here you are, back in the Independence area again." Then he spoke as loudly as he could. "Just as a matter of curiosity, if your family traveled with the original pioneers to the Salt Lake Valley, will you please stand?"

More than half of those gathered slowly rose to their feet.

"If we knew the location of each of your ancestor's homes while they lived here, I wonder how many of them were good friends with each other, exactly like those of you here in this group?" He sat back down and smiled at his wife.

"I wonder what everyone will be talking about the rest of the afternoon?" Nancy asked.

The next morning everyone was back to work. The Dirt Digger crew started at daylight and attached the tire shredder. Then, another group used chainsaws with specially designed blades to cut the tires into three foot slices. A third group of men threw the pieces up onto the Dirt Digger's flatbed.

Michelle ran to Scott's side when he finished helping cut the tires. "That looks like quite a contraption," she said as they joined the crowd.

The Dirt Digger lined up to start down the first row in the garden area. The shredder produced a high-pitched sound when it reached its running speed, much like a muffled jet engine. Two of the men on the flatbed began throwing strips of tires into the hopper that sat on top of the shredder. The driver slowly lifted his foot off the brake, and the beast rolled forward.

"That looks like suet," Michelle said as she watched the machine lay a moist layer of something on the ground as it moved along.

"That's the ground up tires. Look how it's leveling out the ground from the tilling we did."

"What did they spray on it?" Michelle asked.

Scott answered loudly to be heard above the noisy machine. "A fluid that starts a chemical process. Over the winter, the suet compound will cap the ground and work to neutralize the radiation in the soil. Every time we get rain or snow this winter, the moisture will act to dissolve the compound a little at a time. By spring, nearly all remnants of the black suet will be washed into the ground. What's left on top will act like a fertilizer, just as if a volcano had covered the ground with ash."

While the eyes of the world had been focused on the utter destruction of much of the United States, those living in Jerusalem continued to prepare to build their temple. Because of those plans, two hundred million people had gathered in a fertile valley 55 miles to the north. The mountains of Galilee were separated from the hills of Samaria and Judea by the Valley of Esdraelon, which connected the rich coastal plain with the Jordan Valley. This valley was anciently sacred to the Jews, as it was where King Saul was slain in a battle with the Philistines. Now the valley was home to people of many different cultures and beliefs who shared one common emotion – their hatred of the Jews – and they had joined the newly formed and very powerful Caliphate. The vast city of Megiddo provided a strategic vantage point since it was situated on the pass at the south end of the valley. Their black war flags easily identified the Muslim armies; their leader was referred to as Gog of Magog, and rallied countries from all over the world that craved the destruction of the Jews.

The Lord again blessed the Jews with Prophets, and they communicated God's desires to them. Jerusalem was fortified and the residents within the city enjoyed peace. Once again, it had become one of the great cities of the world. The Prophets taught them the true gospel of their Savior and much about the ordinances that would be available to them in their planned temple. Many miracles were performed among the people and their faith increased. After centuries of struggling to survive and patiently waiting for their Messiah, the Israelites began to flourish. The Prophets provided protection for Jerusalem, and thwarted all attempts of the Muslim armies to overtake the city, even though their armies greatly outnumbered those of Israel.

Abram had received a request from Isaac to meet with him at his office near the temple site. On the appointed day, when he entered Isaac's office, he was surprised to also see Moishe and David.

"This reminds me of the first time I met the three of you. I was a student and had just graduated from college. Even though I knew you, David, I was pretty intimidated by the fact that you were all three part of the Jewish Delegation. Very intimidated."

They all laughed and stood, in turn, to shake Abram's hand. "The past few years have brought many changes, have they not my dear friend?" Isaac asked as he embraced Abram. "Who could have foreseen the events of today back then, when we did not even know what our temple should look like."

"I am pleased to see all of you. What brings about this reunion?"

"Are you aware of the two Prophets who have begun teaching our people?" Isaac asked. "I am told that they represent themselves as followers of a Prophet named Joseph Smith and are themselves leaders of the church we visited in Salt Lake City?"

"I must admit," Abram confessed, "that I have listened to their teachings at length. At first, I was curious how anyone who was not a Jew had obtained entrance into the city. That was what I intended to determine, but when I approached them, they already seemed to know who I was and they talked about my friendship with Scott. I was dumb founded at the details they knew of our relationship, and they seemed to pick right up from where my discussions with Scott left off. They speak boldly and yet create no offense. It is a curious situation."

"Do you accept their words?" Moishe asked.

Abram's mind raced. He had not totally made up his mind whether or not he could accept their belief that Jesus Christ was, indeed, the Messiah the Jewish people were waiting for. However, he was certain he could not dismiss their teachings as incorrect. "I have prayed to God that I may know if their teachings are true. I cannot say I find them completely unacceptable. I know that sounds nearly blasphemous, but that is the truth."

Isaac smiled and said, "I knew I could count on you to speak your true opinion of their teachings. We have heard rumors and hearsay of what they teach, but none of us has heard them personally. I believe they have met with the government leaders, but I am anxious to hear their teachings for myself. However, I am not willing to allow my curiosity to subject me to questions from our leaders, so I am here to ask a favor of you."

Abram laughed and said, "What time would you like me to ask them to come here? That is what you want to ask me, correct?"

"Again, I am impressed with your willingness to help. All three of us would like to visit with them, in private. Would you be willing to ask them to come talk with us?"

"Is tomorrow at this same time all right, if they can make it?"

"It would be perfect," Isaac said.

As Abram walked toward his car, he wondered how he could find the two Prophets. He had seen them in every corner of the city but never knew where he would see them next. He quietly said a prayer that he would be able to find them. He drove along his regular route home, and as he drove past a beautiful fountain near the temple site, he saw the Prophets in the midst of a large group of people.

"We are the two olive trees, and the two candlesticks standing before the God of the Earth. And if any man will hurt us, fire will proceed forth out of our mouths and devour our enemies, and if any man will hurt us, he must in this manner be killed." The crowd understood the symbolism contained in their words and were amazed.

The second Prophet began speaking. "We have power to shut heaven, that it rain not in the days of our prophecy, and have power over waters to turn them to blood, and to smite the Earth with all plagues, as often as we will."

Abram had never heard such powerful speaking. Rather than sounding threatening or superior, as one would suppose, the crowd seemed to be stunned with the humble power of their words. Then their whole demeanor changed as they tenderly said that Jesus Christ loved each one of them and had waited patiently since He lived on the Earth for them to accept Him as their Messiah. Tears began falling as some were overpowered with a strong manifestation of the Spirit, and they fell to their knees. The Prophets reached out their hands to them, touching their arms as they bore witness to the truthfulness of their words, and invited them to pray and ask if the words they had heard were true.

Abram did not feel the Spirit to the degree that some had, but he had a strong feeling deep inside that these men were speaking the truth, even the same truth he had heard from Scott during their many conversations. He began wondering if he should have recognized that truth years ago or if his relationship with Scott was now making it easier to accept the words he had just heard.

"Abram, it is good to see you again."

Abram was startled to hear his name spoken, and looked up to see one of the Prophets standing near him.

"You wish to speak with us?"

Abram again felt a twinge inside his being that confirmed these were men of God and they spoke the truth. "Yes, I have sought you out. I wondered if you would meet with three of my friends tomorrow afternoon at their office. They have asked me to request this of you."

"You will be blessed for your acceptance of the truth," the Prophet said. "We will be there at the appointed time."

While Abram was wondering what exactly the Prophet had meant by his *acceptance of the truth*, the two Prophets disappeared into the crowds that mingled around the fountain. "But I didn't tell you where or when," he said aloud, to himself.

Abram sat in his car for quite some time, deep in thought about the two strange men. They had known what he intended to ask them. Then his mind pondered the things they had said. Was it possible that Scott had been right all along? Were the Jewish people waiting for a Messiah that had already lived among them thousands of years earlier? Then he laughed as a strange question popped into his mind. He wondered if the world would like the Jews better or hate them more if they were all converted and became members of the LDS Church.

That evening, Abram told his wife of the day's events. She listened quietly as he reviewed every detail of his strange and miraculous afternoon. "You can't imagine the power they conveyed in their voices, Rebekah. It was like a wind hit me in the face, but there was no breeze. It hit me with a force I cannot describe."

"Do you accept the symbolism of their words?" she asked her husband. "It seems strange for a Gentile to speak such words."

"I know, but if they are speaking the truth, if they are speaking for Jesus Christ, and if Jesus Christ really is our Messiah, then the symbols are unmistakable. The olive tree provides oil for the lamps of those who go forth to meet the Bridegroom. The lamp stand, or candlestick, signifies they shall reflect to men that light which comes from Him who is the Light of the World. Very bold words."

"You heard them," Rebekah said. "Did you believe them?"

"I was asked that same question today in Isaac's office. I cannot say I believe them, but I cannot say their words are not true. It sounds like a contradiction, but I must pray to God and ask Him to help me know if their words are true. What will you do if the answer to my prayers is that these men speak the truth?" Abram gathered his wife within his arms and kissed her neck softly. "I don't think I could ever accept their teachings if it created a separation between us."

"I am your wife, Abram. If you choose to accept their teachings, I will also accept Jesus Christ as my Messiah."

Abram looked at his beautiful wife and realized what a blessing it was that she had agreed to marry him. "If I choose to accept Jesus Christ, I would never expect you to accept Him on that basis alone. I would pray that you could find out for yourself and make the decision based on your own feelings. I *cannot* choose your God for you. That is too much weight to put on anyone," he said as his hand touched her soft cheek, "especially your husband."

The next morning, Abram began praying in earnest that he would know if the Prophets' teachings were true. Even as he prayed, a voice seemed to whisper in his ear that accepting such teachings would bring shame upon his family, upon his parents, and upon his ancestors. Still he did not stop praying. He was determined to receive an answer from God, and if he could not get an answer before he left for the meeting, he would continue to pray when he returned home later that day.

While he dressed, his wife sat on their bed and watched him. "What will you do, Abram, if you do not get an answer to your prayer?"

He smiled at her reflection in the mirror he stood before. "I will keep praying until I am an old man."

"I will pray for you while you are at your meeting," she said simply. He turned and pulled her up toward him. "You are the best wife any man has ever been blessed with, Rebekah."

"You flatter me with your words," she said.

During the drive to Isaac's office, Abram hoped he might see the Prophets since they had no way of knowing where the meeting was. When he could not find them, he decided to go to Isaac's office, inform him of his mistake, and then drive through the town until he found the prophets. When he parked his car and walked toward Isaac's office, he saw the two Prophets walking toward him.

"I was not sure you would know where to be," Abram said.

"Of course we knew where to be," one of them assured him.

"I think you are magicians."

"I don't believe that's really what you think," the Prophet said. "I believe you know we are telling you the truth."

Abram was hit with such a powerful manifestation of their authority to speak for God that he felt as though someone had poured warm sunshine over him, and it spread though his entire body. His chest burned with confirmation that what they were teaching was the truth. His eyes filled with tears and he could not speak.

One of the Prophets held his arm and spoke to his soul. "Your wife has also received a manifestation from the Spirit that our teachings are true. You will both need to be baptized for a remission of your sins and to become a member of His true church. You will then be blessed with the constant companionship of the Holy Ghost to guide and direct your decisions, and to manifest the truthfulness of all things to you."

Abram took out his handkerchief and wiped his eyes. Even if he could have spoken, he would not have been able to describe the unconditional acceptance he was feeling.

"Come," the Prophet said, as he guided Abram to Isaac's office. When Isaac saw them, he led the way to a private meeting room.

"You have asked us to meet with you today to answer your questions," one of the Prophets said. "We have been ordained with the authority to speak on behalf of Jesus Christ, having received this authority by the laying on of hands, in a direct line from the Prophet Joseph Smith who restored the Gospel of Jesus Christ in its fullness to the Earth. We have been given the power to successfully hold back the armies of Gog at Magog as long as the Savior desires. We have been sent here to teach you the doctrines of the only true church and invite you to be baptized and become a member of His church. You have your agency to accept the truth, but we would invite you to pray to your God and ask Him what He would have you do."

The last sentence the Prophet had spoken pierced Isaac to his very core. He recalled hearing the Prophet in Salt Lake City speak the same words. He looked at Abram, and realized his countenance had changed from the day before – he knew Abram had accepted the teachings of the Prophets as truth. He looked at David and Moishe and could see that they also could feel the spirit radiating from the two Prophets who stood in their midst. Could it be this simple, he wondered? Could a Prophet of God utter a single sentence and a person could know they were speaking the truth?

"Why has God sent you to Jerusalem?" David asked.

"You are His chosen people. He said the first shall be last and the last shall be first. He came to you first and you rejected Him. He came to us last and we were the first to accept His teachings. Now the last have come to teach His truth to you and invite you to accept His teachings and be baptized into His church. Thus, the last brings the truth to the first."

"He sent *you* to teach *us* rather than coming in person to His people who have waited for His arrival since the time of our first father?"

"He will come to Jerusalem as He has promised, and the world will kneel before Him and acknowledge He is the Son of God. Will you meet Him as a member of His true church or as a rebellious child who still refuses to accept His truth?"

"I will meet him as a member of His church," Abram said, again wiping tears from his eyes.

"As will I," Isaac said. There were no tears spilling from his eyes, but the emotion that was visible in his face could only indicate he had been moved by the Spirit.

"We will leave you now," the Prophet said. "We will meet at this address on Sunday." He removed a card from his pocket and laid it on the table. "We have baptized Jewish brethren and ordained upon them the authority to baptize you. Those who accept the truthfulness of our teachings will become missionaries to teach your brothers and sisters and will participate in the building of your holy temple. This temple must be completed before Jesus Christ will return to the Earth. Pray about what you have felt this day and ask God if you should be baptized as a member of His true church here upon the Earth."

Without speaking another word, the two Prophets turned and left the room. All four men sat in silence. Finally David spoke. "How can you two be so sure they are speaking the truth?"

Abram shook his head and smiled at David. "I spoke to them yesterday afternoon, and I have prayed that I would know if they speak the truth. I did not know until I saw them in the parking lot today, and then I knew. The truthfulness of what they are teaching came over me like a waterfall filling me with warmth and love. I pray that you have a similar experience after you pray about it."

"Is that what happened to you?" David asked Isaac, as his brow furrowed in visible confusion.

Isaac looked at David for a long time, and then slowly spoke. "No, I never felt anything like that, but I know they speak the truth. As they spoke to us, I became aware of many other people in this room, and my father was with them. He has been deceased for many years, but he came and spoke to me. He said he had been wrong in what he taught me, and that his strongest wish for me was that I would now follow his counsel and recognize that the words of the Prophets are true. He told me to be baptized so that we could be together as a family unit for all eternity. He was not a ghost, but as real as you are to me right now, and the love I felt from him was as real as when he lived. I will become a member of this church and I will teach my family and share my experience with them so they can feel the happiness I feel."

"I never saw visions or felt anything fill me from within," Moishe said quietly, "but I could definitely feel a strong power in this room, and I will pray about this when I get home. I think this has been a day we will never forget." With those words, he stood and left the room.

David stood also. "I'm leaving. I hope you do not think I will accept their teachings just because you do, Abram. We have been friends since we were children, but I must know for myself whether or not they speak the truth. I feel as though I am on a boat and everyone has left me alone, and now I am wondering where I can find safety. I will go home and pray that I can learn which decision will cause me to drown – the decision to stay in the boat and adhere to the teachings of our fathers, or the decision to leave the boat as you have. I am very confused, but I must admit that something extraordinary has happened here today. I wish you well in your new religion," he said as he shook hands with Abram and with Isaac. Then he, too, left the room.

"Abram, Abram, Abram," Isaac said. "Several years ago I asked you to come to my office because I thought you might have met someone who could answer our questions about building a temple to worship God. Then again, I ask you to come to my office because I thought you might be able to help us learn more about what the strange Prophets are teaching our people. Now, it seems you and I will be learning new things together as we accept their teachings as being those of our God. How strange it is that our relationship started so innocently and has led us to this moment, when we are about to abandon the teachings of generations of our people and accept Jesus Christ as our Messiah. This is truly a day of miracles."

Isaac stood and embraced Abram. "I will see you on Sunday."

When Abram arrived at home later that day, his wife was visibly changed. "You received an answer from God?" he asked Rebekah.

She nodded and began to cry – he could tell she had been crying for several hours. She always complained that she was not pretty when she cried, but he had never agreed with her. "Why are you crying?"

"I was praying that you would receive an answer to your prayers. You had prayed so hard and I wanted God to bless you with an answer. Suddenly I seemed to hear a voice that said, 'The things your husband has been taught are true. You will both need to be baptized.' It sounded as though someone was standing here in the living room and spoke to me, but I was not afraid when I heard the voice. I felt warm inside and I was happy. I could sense how you were feeling at that moment, as though you were feeling warmth spreading through your body and you were crying. I know it sounds strange, but that is what I felt."

"It's not strange at all. I felt exactly that way, and one of the Prophets told me that my wife was receiving a manifestation of the truth at that same time. Now I know he was speaking the truth. I am ready to be baptized into their church on Sunday, but if you need more time to think . . ."

"No, I do not need more time. I am anxious to learn about the teachings of this church, but I already believe they are true and I do not need to learn anything more before I am ready to be baptized."

He hugged his wife. "We have been greatly blessed this day."

Abram and Rebekah prayed many times, and each time they felt a stronger conviction that their decision to be baptized was pleasing to God. When Sunday arrived, they made their way to the address well before the appointed hour. The exterior of the building was simple with no indication of what activity took place inside, but the moment they entered the front door, they both felt as though they had stepped out of the world and into a place filled with peace and safety. The simple elegance of the building's furnishings was not typical Jewish decor, but made them feel comfortable.

A man stepped through double doors and extended his hand toward them. "Welcome. I am President Nebeker and I am glad you have come to join us this afternoon. Please come with me."

They stepped into a room that obviously served as a place of worship even though there were no religious icons visible. The room was filled with rows of pews. There were already other people seated in several of the rows.

Abram and Rebekah were led to an empty row and sat down. Although they had both received a strong spiritual witness that insured their attendance at the meeting, they were concerned about the repercussions their baptism would cause. As they sat in the peaceful silence, all fears dissolved and were replaced with overwhelming joy. They both seemed to realize, at the same moment, that the joy they were feeling was a gift they could share with their families and friends. The beautiful tune being played on the organ communicated to something deep within them, and the joy seemed to intensify until tears spilled down their cheeks.

The two Prophets and three other men, including President Nebeker, conducted the meeting. Those that chose to be baptized were taken to a changing room and given white clothing to wear. Everyone reassembled in front of the baptismal font, and waited their turn. When Rebekah's name was called, she walked to the stairs that led into the baptismal font, and slowly descended until she stood in the warm water. A Jewish Elder was already standing in the water and he took her hand. He recited the precise baptismal prayer and immersed Rebekah in the water. When he pulled her up, she was smiling.

The same process occurred when Abram's name was called, but when he came up out of the water and opened his eyes, he thought for a quick second that he saw a man dressed in white standing behind the man who was recording the names of those being baptized. In that quick flash, he saw that the man was holding what appeared to be an electronic handheld device, and touched his finger to the screen. The entire glimpse and revelation occurred between two beats of his heart, but was received as a strong witness of the correctness of his decision to be baptized. He knew he would never forget that moment.

After all the baptisms were completed, everyone returned to the chapel. The group was taught about the resurrection of Jesus Christ, and they learned that through His atonement all men would be raised from the dead. By accepting His sacrifice and following His teachings, every person could again dwell with their Father in Heaven. Receiving the incredible gift of the Holy Ghost and being confirmed a member of the Church of Jesus Christ of Latter-day Saints was explained.

One by one, each person was confirmed a member of the Church by the laying on of hands and given the Gift of the Holy Ghost. With each confirmation, the spirit in the room grew stronger.

Abram did not expect anything further as he had already received many strong impressions that his Heavenly Father was pleased with his decision to join the Church. Yet, when those who had the authority to confirm him a member of the Church laid their hands on his head, he felt such power flow from them into him that he could hardly concentrate on what was being said. He had not expected that the Gift of the Holy Ghost would be an actual force he would be able to feel and know he had received. Only one source could provide the feelings he experienced, and he knew it was God.

When the meeting ended, Abram and Rebekah were following the crowd as they slowly advanced toward the exit. Someone placed their hand on his shoulder and when Abram turned, he was surprised to see one of the Prophets standing next to him.

"Could you and your sweet wife please come with me?" he asked.

Abram looked quickly at Rebekah as he answered. "Of course."

They followed their guide into a row near the front of the room and sat down. "Please wait here. When the room is empty, we would like to visit with you for a moment." The Prophet smiled and left them.

Abram smiled at Rebekah. "We were so worried that our decision would bring disgrace to our family. Now I think we will bring joy to our family as we explain this gospel to them. I will pray that they experience the joy we are feeling when they are baptized and confirmed members of this great church."

As the room slowly emptied, Abram saw that several couples remained seated. He noticed Isaac and his family across the room from them. "Come with me," he said softly to his wife. "I would like to introduce you to Isaac, the man who is responsible for getting the plans required to build our temple."

"Isaac," Abram said when they stood next to him, "This is my wife, Rebekah."

Isaac stood and shook Rebekah's hand. "I am very pleased to meet you. This is a wonderful occasion to make your acquaintance. I would like to introduce to you my wife, Rachel. And these are my children, Eli, Hannah, and Leah." Isaac invited the young couple to sit with them.

"Do you have any idea why we have been asked to remain?" Abram asked.

"Yes, I do," Isaac answered, "but they are returning and you will quickly learn the answer to your question."

Abram turned and saw the two Prophets and the three men who had seemed to be in charge of the meeting, plus several other families coming to join them. Once all were seated, the two Prophets stood in front of the small group and began speaking.

"As people join the Church, we must form wards and stakes. Each ward contains about one hundred fifty families and ten wards are gathered together to become a stake. By bringing smaller groups together to become the responsibility of a larger unit, the Church is organized in a manner that allows the Prophet in Salt Lake City to receive organized reporting on the welfare of each member of the Church. Vast numbers are joining the Church here in Jerusalem, so it becomes necessary to organize new wards. We have asked Isaac to become the Bishop of our newest ward, and he has prayed and asked for inspiration from God about who would be the right brethren to become his counselors. As his first counselor, he has asked that Abram be called. Levi is the person he has asked to serve as his second counselor. We realize you are all new members of the Church as of this very afternoon, and we will provide all the training and guidance you will require. If you are all willing to accept these callings, we would like to ordain you and give you the authority to do this work."

After several minutes of silence, Abram stood and said, "I accept this assignment."

Levi quickly did the same. President Nebeker then explained that the new ward would become a ward in his stake. He and his counselors laid their hands on Isaac's head and ordained him a Bishop, and then pronounced many amazing blessings upon him.

"You will be instrumental in bringing together the needed skills to complete the holy temple here in Jerusalem. I bless you with the ability to lead the members of your ward to the Savior. You will be inspired to know the needs of your ward, and will be blessed with the knowledge required to keep them safe until that great day when the Savior places His foot upon the mount and saves His children here in Jerusalem. You will be blessed with the opportunity to see the Lord Jesus Christ and feel the scars of His crucifixion. You will witness many miracles as the last days come to a close."

Then Abram and Levi were also ordained and received the authority to fulfill their new callings.

In one day, the lives of all three men and their families were completely changed. There was no longer free time in the evenings when they wondered what to do. Nearly every evening was filled with teaching the Gospel to friends and family, or assisting those who were already members of their ward. Rather than feeling like a burden, every hour spent serving the Lord seemed to bring still more blessings into their lives. Rebekah quickly became acquainted with Rachel, and Levi's wife, and soon each of the women received responsibilities of their own in the new ward. Sunday became a joyous day when the members of the ward gathered to share their testimonies and help each other learn the principles of this new religion they had accepted.

NEW ZION'S FIRST CITIZEN

Everyone in New Zion looked like pioneers. There was no choice but to continue working when feet were sore and muscles ached. Skinned knees and elbows, and even bruises became so familiar they were no longer even noticed. Days were filled with the enormity of simply surviving – it took a great deal of work to live what everyone had formerly thought of as *the simple life.*

The cool weather that usually came with fall was held in abeyance, and work began on the ward meetinghouses. The 150 men in the Seventh, Eighth, and Ninth Wards assured the work on their building progressed amazingly fast. One afternoon Scott and Kirby were assembling pews when Scott suddenly laughed.

"What's so funny?" Kirby, the second counselor in his ward, asked.

"I remember when I built a storage building in my back yard. It took a couple months to get permits, then I had to hire certified workers, and the city had to inspect the entire thing when it was done. It took six months from the first permit to final inspection."

Kirby shook his head. "In comparison, doesn't this seem impossibly simple? Build fifty homes, find a lake and get water to make the garden grow, build a chapel. We've been here, what, five months? We couldn't have even finished the environmental study by now to determine if we were hurting anything by taking water out of the lake."

"Not to mention, all the water and ground are polluted so we would have been stopped right from the get go," Scott added. "I can sure see why making your home in a nuclear bomb crater makes things easier."

Both men were laughing when the Bishop walked in. "Well, I can see you're having fun, but how's the work coming, brethren?"

"We will be ready for services here this Sunday, Bishop," Kirby said. "I'm not sure if the padding for the pews or the carpet for the floors will be here in time, but I don't think they'll be missed."

"Sounds good. Scott, I just came by the Storehouse and my wife told me Michelle threw up when she first started working this morning. Maybe you should go check on her. I'll stay and help Kirby."

Scott handed the screwdriver he had been using to the Bishop and left. He ran to the Storehouse, but his wife was not there.

"I sent her home," Nancy told him. "She's not feeling well."

"Okay," Scott said, then he noticed Nancy was smiling. "Why the smile? Is this a joke? Is there a surprise party waiting for me at home?"

Nancy shook her head, but continued to smile. "No, I can promise you there is no party waiting for you at home."

"Okay," Scott said. He ran all the way to his house, and when he opened the door, Michelle was laying on the bed. "Are you okay?" he asked as he knelt next to her. "What's wrong?"

Michelle slowly sat up and swung her feet over the side of the bed, then patted the bed next to where she sat.

"I'm fine," she said and then drew in a deep breath and weakly smiled at him. "I went to see Doctor Branson this morning. I'm fine."

"You threw up this morning and you couldn't work in the Store-house. That doesn't sound like you're fine." Scott held her hand gently.

"We're going to have a baby boy. Remember?"

Scott jumped up and faced his wife. "Now? You are pregnant now? This is amazing. I'm going to be a father!" He pulled her up, very gently, and then hugged her loosely. "You're going to be a mommy."

Michelle pulled him close and hugged him. "And mommies don't break," she said as she squeezed him tightly.

"I have to tell the Bishop," Scott said.

"He knows," Michelle said.

"And Dennis."

"He knows."

"And Nancy?"

"She knows."

"And Kirby?"

"I'm sure he knows by now."

"Who can I tell, and why does everyone already know when I just found out?" Scott tried to look hurt, but could not stop smiling.

"My, let me tell you about living in a small town. There are a hundred people in our ward. The minute the doctor knew, his wife knew. I puked in front of Nancy and she told her husband. He told Kirby the minute you left."

"I get it. No one will be surprised. So when will our son be born?"

"In May. It will be spring." Michelle smiled and closed her eyes.

Scott was jolted back to the reality of the conditions in New Zion, and the blessing they had received at the hands of the Prophet so they could live in the toxic environment. "What about the radiation?"

"I don't know. My blessing included things about this child that indicated he would be born safely. I'm going to assume he will either be protected by my blessing or the Savior will return before he's born."

Scott looked at his wife's sweet face. Her complete, child-like faith enabled her to accept that Heavenly Father would not let her down. He slowly pulled her to him. "I am so blessed to have you as my wife. You fill every day with simple love and trust in God. I don't know what I ever did to deserve you."

"I don't have any more faith than you do, Sweetheart. Everything we were promised in our blessings has come true, in every detail. I am the first woman to become pregnant, just as my blessing foretold. That will make our son the first child born who will never see the corruption that exists in every corner of the world outside of New Zion."

"Wait," Scott said as he released her. "Are you positive you're the first woman in the entire colony to get pregnant?"

"Without a single doubt."

"But how can you be so sure?"

Michelle laughed and said, "Because even a town of twelve hundred people is a small town. I bet if you walked over to President Nelson's home right now, Patrice will already know I am pregnant. I haven't heard one word about anyone else being pregnant, so that's a pretty good sign no one is."

"You win. You win. I can live with that. In seven short months, I am going to be a father!

On Sunday, Scott finally realized his wife had been right about the rumor mill; every person he shook hands with congratulated him before he had a chance to tell them his good news. A few minutes before the meeting was ready to begin, President Nelson and his two counselors entered the chapel. "Congratulations, Scott. I hear you and Michelle are going to have the first baby in our new town."

Scott shook his hand and thanked him. He was tempted to ask how long he had known, but resisted. The stake leadership went to the front and sat next to the Bishopric. Their Sunday worship had become very focused; as a stake, they had begun praying earnestly that they would know where to build the temple – where the land was that Joseph Smith had dedicated for that purpose.

Michelle talked Scott into sitting on the back row of the chapel, just in case she had to leave quickly. After the Sacrament Service had been completed, the stake president stood and began speaking. "Brothers and Sisters, I don't have to tell you the importance of the Fast we are holding today. We are ready to begin construction on the temple, the very reason we were called on this mission. And yet, we have no idea where the land is that Joseph Smith dedicated for that purpose."

Scott heard the door behind him open and close. He waited for someone to walk past him and find a place to sit, but no one did. Then he realized President Nelson had stopped speaking. He looked toward the pulpit – the stake president was staring at him. He instinctively looked behind him to see if the person who had opened the door was still standing there.

Two men stood by the closed door. Without looking away from them, Scott reached for Michelle and pulled her toward him until she turned to look behind her. One of the strangers began to speak – his voice was filled with recognizable authority, and it seemed to cause the building and everyone in it to quake.

"Follow us and we will show you where the temple is to be built." The two men then turned and went out the door.

So many thoughts ran through Scott's mind in the time it took for him to take Michelle's hand and follow the two men through the door. How could two strangers just show up at a chapel in the middle of the land of Desolation? A voice in a very recessed part of his brain tried to tell him who the two men were, but it was so impossible he refused to listen. The entire chapel emptied in near-stampede mode. The two men were proceeding up the hill toward the risen morning sun. After walking nearly two miles, they stopped at the crest of a small rise.

As if every person in New Zion, whether at home or at church, had been notified of this amazing event, the entire town seemed to be following the crowd. When the two men turned to address the group, those closest to them froze in silence. Scott finally had to accept what his brain had been trying to tell him. He was standing so close to the man who had spoken in the chapel that he could feel warmth, gentleness and compassion radiating from him, and he was a little surprised at how large the man was – he had always imagined him to be a little smaller. He could tell Michelle knew who they were by the nearly painful grip she had on his hand. Speculations were whispered through the group, as those in the rear could not clearly see the men. However, all speculation fled, becoming reality, as one of them spoke.

"I am Joseph Smith and this is my brother Hyrum," he began. The crowd instantly hushed. "I want to express our love and appreciation to you for your great efforts. There are many people here with you, watching you, even though you cannot see them, and you have brought much joy to all of us. We have waited so long to see the work progress that we started. We who began the restoration of this Gospel were such a small group and we worked so hard. We suffered sickness, death, poverty, and persecution even to the point of murder. There were those who wondered if we could ever accomplish what the Lord had shown me in vision, or if our tiny voices would ever be heard outside this country. We wondered if we could ever really make a difference in this huge world. If you could see the multitude of angels who are here to help you, and who sing praise to you for your faith, you would understand how important your work is. You are beginning the final page in the last day of history before our Savior returns. Hold your heads high and gain strength in knowing that preparations for this day have been in motion since the Savior died for our sins. You will see the culmination of those plans as they come together to complete this great temple complex. Many years ago, I stood on this site and dedicated it as the location of the New Zion. It remains dedicated as such and here will stand the magnificent temple which you will build."

Hyrum handed Joseph a large flat folder, and Joseph then handed the folder to President Nelson. "This contains a plot map of the entire city of New Zion that will be built here. You received the portion of the map pertaining to the location of your houses, and it is pleasing to see how fast things are being accomplished. I also give you drawings of the temple, and call upon you to take extreme care in following the construction plans for the temple, even to the tiniest detail and exacting measurement. If you feel you perform a task that is not to the utmost preciseness, correct the work until it is perfect. You are building this complex for Christ, and He will visit when you have completed the exterior shell. Angels are here to help you. Listen for their still, small words of direction and encouragement. The eyes of all the righteous who have ever lived on this Earth are watching and waiting upon you."

Joseph and Hyrum smiled warmly at those gathered around them, and then turned and departed as quickly as they had arrived.

Joseph and Hyrum's visit to New Zion had a profound impact on the pace at which work was being completed – it nearly ground to a complete halt. The conviction each man felt in getting their ward meetinghouse completed had not diminished, but every time two individuals began working together on a project, they soon forgot about their work and started discussing the glorious experience of seeing Joseph and Hyrum, and how their words had made them feel. An hour would pass in discussion without one bit of work being performed.

President Nelson observed this phenomenon for several days. He had been set apart by the Prophet to preside over the building of New Zion. He had always been proud of his reputation as a man who accomplished what he started. His relentless attention to keeping work in New Zion on schedule had resulted in getting homes built for every member of his stake within weeks of their arrival. He had always been taught that the fastest way to get a group of people to work together was to become the obstacle they must overcome. When some wards had lagged behind in their construction schedule, he had pushed without compassion and watched as the other wards stepped up to help them. The Prophet had made it very clear how important New Zion's success was, and his responsibility weighed heavy on his shoulders.

After watching this lack of progress for two days without making any comment, he was more than ready to discuss the situation with the twelve bishops who requested a meeting with him. The bishops knew they would be the ones he held accountable for the continuing behavior and he was sure they would have already developed a plan to get things back on schedule.

When the meeting began, President Nelson thanked everyone for attending. Then he asked a question. "By a show of hands, how many of you have spent much of your time this past week in discussion and thought, rather than in performing the duties that you had set out to do?" He waited a moment and finally the majority of them pushed their hands up slowly, as if they knew they must, but did not want to.

"How many have felt a feeling of joy and excitement, rather than guilt, at your actions?" Again, he waited until the same hands slowly rose. President Nelson could see their dilemma. They felt they knew what would be said to them next, but they also had to tell the truth.

"This past week I was initially concerned by what I saw. I was concerned that we were not accomplishing much at all. I spent most of Wednesday evening on my knees. I prayed for many hours."

President Nelson scanned the faces that were focused on him. He had never seen it before, but it was plainly visible now. Every man in the room had an overwhelming desire to accomplish the tasks they had been assigned, but what was visible on their faces was the dread they felt as they waited to see what he would load upon their shoulders.

"I received a visitor," he continued. His voice caught as he recalled his miraculous visitation. "Joseph stood next to me as I rose from my knees. He stayed with me for hours and counseled me on my role in what we are doing here. After his visit, I spent all day watching the development of New Zion through very different eyes.

"Since we arrived here, we have lived in close contact with each other and everyone has struggled through required adjustments. There has been no contention. We worked together, and individual desires and needs were overlooked. Love, compassion and admiration grew for one another – things I didn't know could exist except between a man and his wife. Today I had to hide my eyes, as they flowed continually. Joseph taught me, and my Father in Heaven has allowed me to see that each of you has unleashed the true love that remains dormant in the natural man's heart. Many of you have had discussions with one another and shared how you felt about Joseph and Hyrum's visit. You have put your hands on each other's shoulders and have embraced one another for the simplest of reasons. I would assume that many of you wondered later why you did such things. In the last four days, there have been more witnesses born of Jesus and this great work among the members of our stake than within any other group of people since the City of Enoch was lifted off the Earth and taken to a better place. The only occasion that even comes close to rivaling what has happened here the last four days may be what happened in Kirtland immediately following the dedication of the Kirtland Temple. In Kirtland, however, that event was shortly followed by one of the greatest apostasies in the history of the Church. I have been warned of this, but I have also been assured that we can easily avoid such a thing.

"I give you the counsel I was given. We can avoid the problems of Kirtland and create something here that has never been experienced on this Earth. Joseph brought a special blessing and Spirit with him when he came last Sunday. That Spirit did not leave. The Spirit of Christ accompanied Joseph, and It will remain with us as long as we allow It to. And, we were told the Savior will visit us, when we are prepared.

"Now Brethren, I have been instructed to forget the ways I have led in the past. They are the ways of the world we have left behind, but we are in a new world. Everyone in our stake has proven they are dedicated to this cause, and willing to make the sacrifices necessary to be successful in this work. I ask each of you to follow the feelings in your heart at all times. If you are in the middle of a task and someone comes by, take the time to stop and visit. Find out as much as you can about them and about how they feel. If you are in mid-stride and someone comes to mind that may benefit simply from knowing you are thinking of them at that moment, turn and go find them. Share your impressions with them. Not only are we to strive to keep our hearts as uninhibited as they have been these few days, but we are to allow our words to be as innocent and open as a young child who tries to gather as much as he can from everyone and everything around them. This will make New Zion a place where the people of Enoch could visit and feel comfortable. This will make our Lord comfortable when He comes to visit.

"I have been taught that to hold your neighbor to a task or schedule that he does not agree with will create ill feelings. To speak of one another in any manner of criticism or complaint will allow a spirit to enter that should not be here. The measurement of success in the world we left behind was completing a task on schedule, but Joseph counseled us to perform a task to its utmost preciseness, and if we feel it is not exactly right, we were told to correct the work until it is perfect. In New Zion, the measurement of success is completing our tasks perfectly. We are not to dally about our duties, for they are urgent; however, we are to enjoy every minute of every day and take the time necessary to do those things that will help build ourselves and others, no matter how insignificant our actions may seem.

"I would now challenge all of you to take these words and feelings to your groups and cultivate what has begun to sprout this week. For it will truly grow into something beyond what this Church has ever known if we are diligent. I promise you blessings and spirituality you have never experienced. I know this is not what you expected to hear tonight, but I hope it is something you all understand and will try to live by. This I leave with you, with a heart full of more love and respect for each of you than I knew I was capable of feeling. Amen"

There were but few words shared after the meeting. Each bishop was anxious to return to his ward and convey President Nelson's message. The men that left that chapel had a new level of commitment they had not known before they heard President Nelson's words.

President Nelson was also a changed man. For the first time in his life, he had openly let his guard down and actually expressed what he felt in his heart.

It quickly became apparent the words were very favorably received. The visible concern and love demonstrated for each other continued as it had the previous four days. It was exceedingly heart-warming to watch people cast aside barriers they had accepted as normal their entire lives. As that happened, it was amazingly easy to love and appreciate the true person that had previously been kept hidden. It was a turning point, a new beginning, and a step closer to living as each person had before the veil was drawn over their mortal eyes, concealing memories of how they had always lived with each other.

Sometime later, President Nelson attended the Seventh Ward, and announced, "It had originally been planned to wait until the exterior of the temple complex was complete before work commenced on the stake center. Even though we meet together each week as ward groups I prayed that a way could be found to build our stake center so we could meet as one big family. My prayers have been answered, and I share this with you as my testimony of the power of prayer.

"From the time the Prophet was inspired to begin making preparations to build the temple here, everyone involved moved forward believing that if enough materials were shipped to build both the temple and the stake center at the same time, it would increase the possibility of drawing too much attention to our endeavor. Therefore, the plan was to build the temple first.

"All that has changed. The world beyond Desolation has known of our presence since seeing satellite photos of our caravans moving across the miles of radiation-filled wasteland. By some miraculous means, the only thing that interests them is a desire to know how we endure the radiation. They show no interest or concern in what we are doing here. Members of the press say they want to talk to us, but not badly enough to come get our story first-hand.

"As a result, we can now travel to the warehouse and get all the supplies for the temple and the stake center. I believe the anticipated completion date of the temple will not be compromised if we work on our stake center at the same time. I ask that we all work together to finish our ward buildings as soon as possible. While we are doing that, I would ask that each ward begin creating a plan in order to insure that we have as many people working on both the temple and the stake center as possible. Perhaps by May our stake center will be complete. That is seven months from now. It will be the anniversary of arriving here in New Zion, and it would be a great time to have a celebration.

"I want each of you to know how much I love you and how much I love Jesus Christ and my Father in Heaven. I want you to know how strongly I believe in the power of prayer. Both the temple and the stake center are righteous desires, and I believe we have found a way to accomplish both tasks. I have discussed with the Prophet my feeling that we need a place to meet as one group, one family, and he said to go ahead with our plans and see what happens. He cautioned, and I'm sure we all agree, that as nice as a stake center would be, if we find it interferes with work on the temple, the temple will be our top priority."

More than seven months had passed since the United States was attacked, but life still seemed to be at a standstill. It was predicted no one could safely enter the contaminated area for at least five years. At a time when people should be trying to help each other, the opposite occurred – the biggest problem society faced was lawless looting and vandalism. Larger cities along the east coast had been able to rein in most of the destructive behavior, but so much time and resources were spent trying to maintain some semblance of civility that little time was left to restore services and re-establish communications.

However, the western states were too rural for most areas to be policed. Salt Lake City seemed to function a little better than some metropolitan areas, even though life was far from what anyone would refer to as normal. Most people living there were prepared to handle such situations, and they willingly helped each other.

In the Church Office Building, the Prophet, his counselors and the Western States Apostle kept very busy, though to the public it appeared the LDS Church was as stagnant as other organizations in the area. Behind the scenes, they provided advice and needed supplies to the Jewish people who were preparing to build their temple in Jerusalem. They also managed the widely publicized activities in the land of Desolation, and inconspicuously assisted in relief efforts through their worldwide network.

"Brethren," the Prophet said to his counselors, "I wondered how the Lord would keep curious eyes away from New Zion when it became public knowledge that there was a town being created there. I never counted on the fact that the world would not care since there is nothing to gain by knowing what happens in a wasteland."

"I inquired of the Eastern States Apostle, as you requested," the first counselor reported. "He informed me that all supplies and machinery required for both the exterior of the temple and the stake center are already stockpiled. The delivery vehicles will be driven to a place inside the restricted zone, where the radiation levels are not a threat, and President Nelson will send drivers to retrieve the supplies."

"That sounds wonderful," the Prophet said. "Can you tell me what materials were obtained for the exterior walls of the temple?"

"Yes, we were able to get the same materials used in the St. Louis temple, the cast stone and Bethal white granite with the thermal finish. We have had that material set aside for quite some time."

"That's fine," the Prophet answered as he smiled.

"I have spoken with President Nelson about the additional supplies that will be included," the counselor continued. "How I would love to be there when those Brothers and Sisters receive new supplies of clothing, and washing machines to make life a little easier for them. The communication link has been established and there are a few supplies being sent which will allow them to activate the systems in each home so they can see and talk to their families. That will help calm the spirits of the parents of all those young couples."

"Please share with me how washing machines are possible where there is no sewer," the Prophet said.

His second counselor smiled and explained. "The water goes into tubing already in the floor panels, just like the other waste. Having washing machines will actually help provide the extra purified water needed to tend the yards around the houses. When water becomes available for such purposes, I have a feeling the Sisters in New Zion will decide each little house needs a flower garden outside the door."

The Prophet smiled as he envisioned the excitement of those faithful Sisters who had given up all the modern comforts of their homes to accept the calling to go into the barren lands of Missouri. "Are we sending flower seeds?" he asked.

"There is no need. A stake in Tennessee and one in Ohio has taken on the project of flowerbeds for our pioneers. Sisters have gathered flower seeds and pots to use around their homes, and border materials and hand tools for flower gardening. Relief Societies around the world are thinking of things they can do to make life more enjoyable for these young families. Several stakes are making quilts and others are desirous of making a more decorative cabinet for the new mothers and filling it with handmade baby supplies."

"Isn't it wonderful, brethren?" the Prophet asked. "In the midst of worldwide terror and conflict such as we have never seen, the sweet Sisters still find time to think of ways to make life better for others."

President Nelson looked at the twelve bishops sitting in his office. "Brethren, I have received word that the supplies from the east are ready to be picked up. We are getting everything we need to begin work on the exterior of the temple complex and our stake center. We will take one of the transport vehicles with enough men to drive all the trucks back to our city. The trucks and equipment will all remain here after the delivery. We cannot send contaminated vehicles back out to the world. You will be pleased when you see the new vehicles, because they look just like our own unique rides we have grown to love. I guess they built additional units and placed them in the warehouse before our country was bombed, just like they did in Salt Lake. That means we are going to have a supply of extra panels, generators, and tires, all things we need to build community buildings and expand our developing city. Remember, we won't always be in this building mode.

"I am so pleased that we will be ready to use these supplies as soon as they arrive. Our completed meetinghouses are beautiful, and they are impressive. I believe only one is not quite finished, but my wife informs me we will be attending a giant work party and picnic this afternoon, assuming it does not begin snowing."

"That's right, President. That's my ward and we are finishing up the last of the detail work," the Third Ward Bishop explained. "I believe the work can be completed in about an hour, but the Sisters use any excuse to have a party. It takes a lot of imagination to have a picnic near Thanksgiving, but none of us are complaining."

"That's wonderful," President Nelson said. "We have a surprise for every wife in our stake, and personally, I hope my wife does not hear about this until she receives it at her door. Small washing machines are on their way. I think that will be a big treat for each of our wives."

Each bishop agreed. Doing laundry as the pioneers had done was a lot of hard work, but not one sister had complained.

Early the next morning, the transport left with a substantial group of men. They arrived at the drop point without any trouble, as the GPS guided them to the abandoned column of vehicles. In minutes, they were all rolling westward, back toward New Zion. When they approached a specific coordinate identified by President Nelson, the last transport vehicle stopped; the rest kept moving toward home.

Randy Witherspoon had a background in communications before being called to serve in New Zion. He climbed out of the transport and walked to the back end. "This little rise in elevation is where they want us to mount the communications block," he explained to those helping him. "It's about half way between our homes and civilization. We just need to unload the skid with the boom and turn the unit on."

The men helped set the unit on the ground and made sure the indicator was pointing precisely north. Randy flipped the switch and the lights blinked on and off as the boot-up cycle ran. After a minute or so, all the LEDs turned green. "We're good," Randy said.

They climbed back in the truck and headed toward New Zion. Randy shook his head and said, "I've worked on communications all my life, but that is truly the easiest install I've ever done. Especially knowing absolutely nothing about the thing except that it's a communications block that hits satellites with the top side, the walls of our houses with the west side, and a Church feed somewhere near St. Louis with the east side. The radio signals will communicate both ways. The bandwidth is going to give us video communications, satellite feeds of programs from the Church and connection to the Church Internet site. I know all the guys will wish they could catch their favorite sporting events, but I already asked and was told that would not be on the list of things we get."

"It doesn't sound like we'll have time to watch much TV if we're building both the temple and the stake center."

"True," Randy agreed. "Besides, access to today's TV programming would definitely be detrimental to keeping the Spirit continually with us."

New Zion became a hive of activity, and the unexpected blessing of extremely mild winter weather was appreciated. To keep everyone busy, work was performed around the clock, six days a week – each person worked until they were tired, went home to rest and relax, and then returned to see if there was space for them to continue working. Even with both projects, there were always more workers than were needed at any given time.

Delivery of the washing machines provided a rare opportunity for each man to do something special for his wife – not one of them wanted to miss the look on his wife's face when she first saw it. Most husbands were not even surprised when their wife's happiness manifested itself in joyous sobbing. Within days, flowerbed borders began appearing around the front of each house.

Besides each Sunday, the only time work halted was Christmas Day. A light cover of snow made the morning perfect. Gifts exchanged were promised acts of service, baked goodies, or simple gifts of art. Everyone agreed it was the most spiritual Christmas they had ever experienced. In an evening gathering at the stake center, Christmas carols were sung in several languages. Those who had lived in countries other than the United States shared stories of how Christmas was celebrated in their homeland. About midnight, someone suggested they sing Silent Night as a group and continue singing as everyone returned to their homes. The spiritual feelings and manifestations were intense, and as each person reached their home and stopped singing, they stood outside listening to the others who were still singing. However, the music never stopped – angelic choirs continued singing throughout the entire night. The heavenly voices seemed to slowly fade as the pale pink light gradually dispelled the darkness at dawn.

By spring, the temple complex spread out over an area much larger than the quarter-mile space where the stake center was built. The vast structure towered majestically above any other structure. The spiritual experiences that occurred nearly daily created a tremendous incentive to spend as much time as possible working at the temple.

The arrival of spring brought vivid examples of life returning to New Zion. The ground bits of tires that had been spread over each garden spot had slowly decomposed and seemed to disappear except for a thin layer of dry ash-looking residue on the surface. Spring brought weeds – a definite sign that the soil was healthier than when they first arrived.

The highly anticipated birth of Scott and Michelle's baby boy added to the miracle of spring.

"Can you hear Benjamin?" Michelle asked as she looked at the image of Scott's parents in the communications screen on the wall of their house. "He doesn't cry much at all, and I don't know if you can hear the way he coos and seems to be trying to talk to us."

"I can hear baby noises." Jenny's voice came through the speaker as clearly as if she were only a few miles away. "It's like a miracle to see you, all of you. And you look so good."

"It's so amazing to see you sitting there in your living room," Michelle said. "It doesn't seem like we've been gone very long, but so much has changed." She could definitely see the recent signs of aging on Jenny's face, and thought how changed she and Scott must appear to them. "Even though we can't talk long, I'm so glad you can see your first grandchild."

"Are you crying, Mom?" Scott asked, certain she was.

"No," Jenny said, even as she sniffed and pressed a tissue to the corner of her eye. "Oh, it's just so good to hear your voices."

"It sure is," Mark agreed.

"Did you already know we were expecting?" Michelle asked.

"We were told early in October that we were going to be grandparents," Mark said. "We've received news about how you've been doing, just to let us know everything was going okay."

"Did you let my folks know?" Michelle asked.

"Yes, Dear, they were notified the same time we were. We have all been so excited about the baby. I'm sorry they don't live here in town, and that they could not be here today. But they should have their network up by this weekend."

"It's just nice to know they are aware of . . ."

"She's a little emotional these days, Mom," Scott said. "Please tell them that we both love them and wish they could have been there with you. Are Jordan and Lynne gone somewhere? I assume they would be there with you if they were at home."

"They're going to be heart broken when they get back from the gym and discover they missed your call. We all miss you both," Mark said. "We are very proud of you and know how much faith it took for you to go. Things are chaotic everywhere in the country these days, since the bombing, but we're not doing too badly here in Salt Lake."

"Being able to see you and keep in touch will improve everything about our daily lives," Jenny said with a soft laugh.

"We have to say goodbye, Mom," Scott said. "We can't talk for long, but we will call as often as possible. Tell the girls we miss them. We both love you and we can't wait to share some of the wonderful experiences we're having."

"Love you very much," Michelle hurried to add.

"We love you too and we'll continue to pray for you every day. Bye," Jenny said, abandoning the pretense that she was not crying.

"Love you," Mark added quickly.

When Michelle stopped crying, Scott wondered if she would actually run out of tears when she was able to talk to *her* parents. They decided to walk to President Nelson's house and personally thank him for the crib he and Bishop Chandler had made for their baby son.

President Nelson held the tiny baby in his arms and rocked him back and forth.

"Seeing the look on my parents' faces when they saw their first grandchild was amazing. I'm certain they would have preferred to hold him, but at least they got to see him," Scott said. "Dad told me that when I was a little boy he took me to visit my grandparents and he had a very spiritual experience that made him realize there is a thread that binds one generation to the next. He said that the love and acceptance I felt when I first saw my son was the same way he felt when he first saw me. He assumed he would experience that same feeling when his grandchildren came along, and he confirmed that he did feel that connecting thread when he saw Benjamin. I am so grateful for the ability to see our family members when we visit with them, because it allows us to share those feelings with each other."

President Nelson smiled. "Whenever I hold a newborn, I marvel at their purity. A few days ago they lived with Heavenly Father and probably were a little afraid to come here and leave all their brothers and sisters behind. Yet, we are overjoyed to see them and have them be part of our daily lives. It makes me realize that it is the same when we die. We're afraid to leave this world because we are not sure what it's like where we're going."

"I have something for you," Patrice said. "It's not much, but Nancy and I wanted to make something for Benjamin." It was a small, beautifully braided rug, sewn together with nearly invisible stitches.

"Oh, thank you," Michelle said as she held the small rug up for Scott to see.

"I can guarantee it will fit the cradle Evan and I made for you," President Nelson said. "I don't know who worked longer or harder, or who had more fun. Evan and I had so much help, sometimes more help than we wanted, but we finally got a crib made. Nancy and Patrice went to at least fifty homes to find enough work shirts worn to the point that the wearers were willing to donate them to the cause. Somehow they took those shirts and made that mattress for the crib."

"Thank you. Everyone has found special ways to let us know they're happy for us," Michelle said. "I'm glad there are other babies on the way, so Benjamin will have friends to play with, in a few years."

"Is the doctor taking good care of you?" Patrice asked.

"Very good care of both of us," Michelle answered.

When the braided pad was slid into the bottom of the crib, it fit perfectly. Several baby blankets were draped over the side of the crib –

not traditional receiving blankets, but warm and functional. Some gifts were clothing – tiny denim overalls lined with soft cotton material, and darling little flannel shirts. A simple sketch of him while he slept was a gift they would forever treasure.

Michelle's house became a favorite spot for Sisters to gather when they were not busy working. Many afternoons someone offered to take care of Benjamin so Michelle could work at the temple. Time spent working there was spiritually uplifting and helped immensely to balance the sadness and tears that seemed to overwhelm her when thoughts surfaced of how much she missed being able to share this special time with her mother. She wanted to share it with all of Benjamin's grandparents, but especially she missed sharing it with her mother.

PILLAR OF FIRE

Though the members of the LDS Church in Jerusalem were appreciative of the many blessings they continually received, they longed to see temple walls begin to rise. Since the day the earthquake had toppled the Dome of the Rock, the only work that had taken place was clearing away the debris of the demolished structures and improving the temple site by creating beautiful parks, fountains, and meeting places. When all the stakes in Jerusalem were invited to attend a combined meeting, everyone hoped to hear the long-awaited news.

When President Nebeker stepped to the podium, every sound ceased. "I am filled with joy as I announce we are ready to begin the actual construction of the temple." He waited for the sighs, quiet gasps, and soft utterances of gratitude to subside. "Our stake has been assigned the responsibility of providing security for the temple site and daily clean up of the construction debris."

Isaac and his two counselors were very busy organizing the members and monitoring their progress. The Jewish people who joined the Church were thrilled to finally be involved in building their temple. With so many men joining the Church, the work force continually grew and the diverse skills needed for the enormous project were found among the expanding membership. As the temple walls began to rise, so, too, did the anger and hatred of the armies that surrounded the city. Attempts to break through the wall around the city also increased.

Abram's life again crossed paths with his childhood friend David, who had been baptized shortly before construction of the temple began. David and Abram were in different wards, but both served as first counselor to their Bishop, and both were responsible for organizing security patrols at the temple site. The two of them spent many evenings watching the bank of security camera screens.

"No, I was not quickly converted as you and Isaac were," David explained. "I could never honestly say that I thought the Prophets were preaching lies, but I felt an anger inside of me that made me not want to acknowledge that it was the truth. Each time I heard the Prophets say something I knew was true, I felt the anger growing stronger. For a long time, I told myself that if Jesus Christ were the Messiah then He should have come to Jerusalem and told us in person, rather than sending two Prophets who are not even Jewish."

Abram laughed, and then quietly apologized.

"What did I say that seems so amusing?" David asked.

Abram laughed again. "Did you just say that if Jesus Christ was the Messiah then He should come to Jerusalem personally and tell us?"

"Yes," David said, looking quite stern.

"I'm sorry," Abram apologized as he again laughed, "but the last time He tried that, we crucified Him."

David seemed to melt a little as he slumped down in his chair. "I know. But at the time, that fact never occurred to me."

"So what happened that made you feel differently?" asked Abram.

Now it was David's turn to laugh, but his laughter was a little less animated. "One day I was listening to the Prophets as they spoke to a group of people, and I can quote verbatim what was said because it was if the words were written on my heart with fire. He said, 'One stands among us who wonders why Jesus Christ did not come in person to Jerusalem to announce that He is the Messiah. Jesus would like me to tell that young man that his own ancestors were among those who crucified Him, but that the young man knows at this very moment that Jesus Christ is, indeed, the Messiah.' Every fiber of my being felt the strength of that message, and I knew the Prophet was speaking directly to me. After everyone started to leave that day, the Prophets walked right up to me and asked if I heard what Jesus had said to me. I had no choice but to admit I knew all of their teachings were true. The anger I felt inside seemed to be overpowered. It felt like a real presence inside of me had finally been *forced* to leave, rather than just leaving because I heard the truth."

"That's incredible. When I was in college, my American friend told me many times about people who join the Church and how they rely on their faith that the teachings are true, and gradually that faith grows into a strong conviction that this is God's Church. Yet, the Israeli people who join the Church that I have talked to nearly all have a story similar to yours, or mine. We seem to have an experience that creates the conviction that what we are being taught is true, and then we need to cultivate the faith that keeps us going to church every week, reading the scriptures and saying our prayers."

David nodded. "I seem to be constantly reminded of the scripture that says Jesus will come to the Jews and they will reject Him, and then He will go to the Gentiles. They will accept Him and then they will come teach us. You know the one about the first shall be last and the last shall be first? That seems to also fit what you just said. We get the last thing first, the conviction, and then have to strive to get the first thing, the faith." David shook his head slightly.

Abram smiled. "It is not confusing to me because I also feel the same way. David, does it seem to you there is some sort of connection that keeps pulling us together? We grew up as friends and then went our separate ways when you left for college. When you came home, we met again, and worked together, and then when the Prophets arrived on the scene, we again seemed to take separate paths. I joined the Church and you did not. But that connection pulled us back together when you were baptized, and now we again travel the same path. Sometimes life seems very strange."

"I agree with that," David said. "Here's another strange thing for you. How many single men do you know in the Church?"

"Single *men*?" Abram asked. "Well, *you*. I think everyone else I know is married."

"Right. And how many single *women* do you know in the Church?"

"Lots," Abram answered quickly. "Lots and lots!"

"So why is it that I am not married? I know what the Church teaches about marriage and being sealed as a family unit for all eternity. However, every time I become acquainted with one of the single women in my ward, she becomes like a sister to me. I like them, but I have no desire to marry them. I am becoming very frustrated."

"Have you spoken with the Prophets about this? I know you spend a lot of time with them."

David shrugged and said, "Yes, and every single time they hug me and tell me that the Lord has a timeline for each person's life and that I should not be discouraged. I don't even know what that means."

"It means don't let this frustrate you. Just be happy that you've found the true Church and have accepted Jesus Christ as your Messiah, and leave the rest in God's hands."

"Easy for you to say as you spend every evening at home with your wife. But I do have faith that the Lord has a plan for my life and I continue to be patient."

Harvest time in New Zion was drawing to a close and nearly every sister's day centered on preserving food. The gardens provided even more abundantly after the tires had provided nutrients for the soil. Fresh vegetables and grains were so abundant that hardly any of the large supply of food that had been sent with them was required. The brethren worked a 24-hour-a-day schedule, and that usually included one nap and two shifts working on the temple or stake center.

One morning, as the Sisters moved through the gardens making sure every late growing pumpkin and potato had been harvested, snow began lightly falling. Halloween was only a few days away – they had been living in New Zion for eighteen months. After nearly a year of dedicated and painstaking work, the temple shell was complete.

President Nelson asked all twelve wards to meet at the stake center so they could pray as a group to thank the Lord for the many miracles and instances of help they had received. As people left their homes that Sabbath morning, they were stunned to see the glow of fire radiating from the temple. Panic set in and people began running toward the temple. Scott left Michelle holding Benjamin and ran as fast as he could to try to help. As soon as the first group was within a few hundred feet of the structure, they stopped short. They were not sure what caused the glow, but they were so filled with peace and love they knew nothing bad could be happening.

Scott was among those who were suddenly compelled to stop. A reverence washed over him as he slowly continued toward the temple. As he stepped through the doors, he immediately knew the person standing near the center of the room, slightly elevated above the floor, was the Savior. He fell to his knees as he gazed upon the most beautiful Being he had ever seen – He wore a simple white robe that seemed to float about Him. A warm glow seemed as if it were radiating from His being and yet seemed to also shine upon Him. He looked different than all the drawings Scott had seen of Him, yet there was no doubt in his mind that it was Jesus.

Within minutes, the entire temple structure was filled with people kneeling to worship Jesus Christ. There were still people trying to see inside to discover what was happening, but there was no more room. The Lord extended his arms and spoke. "Arise, and be not afraid."

His voice seemed to enter Scott's entire body, rather than only his ears. Slowly, hesitantly, they began to stand. President Nelson moved slowly toward the Savior and stood quietly looking into His eyes. Then he asked, "Is our endeavor acceptable to Thee?"

"If it were not, I would not yet have come to be among you." The Savior reached out and touched President Nelson's shoulder. "Well done. The light that brought you to mine house this day will become a pillar of light visible to all the inhabitants of the Earth. It will provide protection and cause fear in all that do not belong here, keeping them away. It will light the interior of the temple while you complete this edifice. The care and exactness that has made this structure beautiful will stand as a witness to your faith and dedication. All the hosts of heaven rejoice at your selfless service, and are grateful to you. I wish you to touch the wounds on My hands and feet that you may know I am Jesus Christ who dwelled on Earth to make it possible for you to return to live in the presence of your Father which is in Heaven."

He slowly began moving among the people and lovingly touched their arm or shoulder as they placed their hands on the imprints of His wounds. Scott felt Michelle nudge him as she tried to make room for her and Benjamin next to him. Without looking away from the Savior, he drew them close to his side.

When the Savior reached them, He leaned forward and took their son in His arms. He smiled at the baby as He softly rocked him. "His spirit is still as pure as the moment he left my presence. To you it has been five months; to me it is but a moment ago. Your son is among the valiant who will come to this Earth at this time, and he has chosen you to be his parents. You have prayed earnestly that he would be protected from the harsh elements that exist in this place. He is, even as are you."

Benjamin had been watching the Savior's face intently, as though he understood what Jesus was saying about him. Suddenly he opened his mouth and began speaking to the Savior. His words were melodious and distinct, even though neither Scott nor Michelle understood them. The Savior, however, did understand the words, and He smiled at Benjamin and spoke to him in the same language. Then, looking at Scott and Michelle, He said, "Memories of life with the Great Father have not been completely forgotten, and your son expresses his gratitude that he is privileged to come to Earth during this time. Even as Adam was the first mortal to inhabit the Earth, so your son is the first Spirit who will grow to adulthood without experiencing temptation from the Defiant Ones." He extended His hand toward them and repeated, "I wish you to touch my wounds that ye may know I am Jesus Christ."

Scott and Michelle timidly reached out to touch the imprints in His hands, even as He held their son. His skin felt the same as any other man's, and it was perfectly clear and radiant. Michelle noticed His beautiful hand and how dirty and rough hers looked next to His. She quickly pulled her hand back, feeling the touch of her hand would be uncomfortable to the Savior's skin.

Jesus returned Benjamin to Scott's waiting arms and reached out to take Michelle's hands in His own. "The purity of your spirit and the mighty faith you have shown by your willingness to come here is what I see. Your human exterior is visible only to yourself," He said as He smiled gently. He slid his hands along the length of hers as He slowly released her hands and moved on to others. When the Savior had personally spoken to each person in the temple, He moved through the door and continued to individually minister to those who had gathered outside. No one inside the temple moved for some time, and then those closest to the door slowly began to move out of the building. They silently mingled with each other until the Savior spoke to the group. "I am well pleased. The work can now move forward to complete the interior of Mine house. Those on both sides of the veil have much to do in these final days of the Earth." Then He bid them farewell.

Everyone proceeded on to the stake center, each commenting on the blazing sunset that made them realize the entire day had passed. As they walked, Michelle leaned close to Scott and asked, "Did you immediately know that was Jesus Christ?"

"I did."

"How did you know?" Michelle asked.

"I'm not sure," he replied. "I just knew it was Him."

"That was my experience also. I knew Him instantly, yet I have no idea how I knew that," Michelle said.

"This has been an amazing day. To hear our baby communicate with the Savior made me realize he knows more about our Heavenly Father and the Savior than we do, for the moment anyway. When Jesus likened him to Adam, it made me see him as more than an infant."

"Do you think we should call him Adam?" Michelle asked. "It seems like it would be a way to commemorate the day the Savior and our baby communicated with each other in an unknown language."

"Yes, I think that would be a constant reminder to us of what has happened today." Scott softly stroked Benjamin's cheek and said, "From now on, the name you will be known by on this earth is Adam."

When everyone had gathered in the stake center, President Nelson stepped to the podium and spoke.

"We are most blessed this day, and I can think of nothing to say or add. We have spent our Sabbath Day being fed directly by the Savior. I feel we should dismiss. Go to your homes if that is what you choose, or gather with friends. I know we will be talking of little else during the coming days. I encourage each of you to record the feelings of your heart in your journals. Your children will someday read your words and marvel at the sacrifices and miracles present in your lives."

He bowed his head and offered a prayer, on behalf of every member of the stake, thanking his Father in Heaven for allowing His son to visit them. It was a beautiful prayer and added even more to the rich blessing the day had been for those present.

The following Sabbath Day, the worship in each ward was unlike any that had previously occurred. The need to share their testimony with each other was so strong that the group remained together in the chapel for many hours as testimony after testimony of Jesus Christ was shared. Many felt driven to share their feelings as they had touched the Savior. Every individual's testimony illustrated how unique the experience was for each person. The newly practiced openness between each other was now taken to an even higher degree. People were much less inhibited about sharing their innermost feelings concerning the Savior. This confidence of unconditional acceptance created an even closer bond. The Spirit was poured out so abundantly upon those in attendance that no one wanted the meeting to end.

The glow that lit the temple from within remained. Every evening, the temple became a light that illuminated the entire city as a pillar of light stretched to the Heavens. The words of the Savior, that the entire Earth would see the pillar of light, were fulfilled perfectly. The world's media went into a full frenzy as they became aware of the new light. It could be seen night and day with the naked eye by those living on the east coast of the United States, and the images available via satellite made it visible to the inhabitants of the entire Earth.

"Have you seen these headlines?" Mark asked Jenny one evening. "Someone sure wants to spread fear and panic with such nonsense."

"It sells papers," Jenny answered as she carefully watched her husband. He had seemed nervous and frustrated for the past few days. "If a reporter wants to get anyone's attention away from Jerusalem these days, he has to find something pretty spectacular. What better than a huge underground source of nuclear energy that is so intense it projects a pillar of light that can be seen around the world. Sounds pretty impressive to me."

"But they're creating panic on the east coast, saying the radiation levels are getting higher and people should move further east. That's not true, and they probably know it."

"The people back east don't seem to believe it, either. I guess they put more stock in the tests the government conducts than what the newspapers print."

"The pictures on TV are so blurry it's impossible to tell what it is. Do reporters make up whatever they want to create more interest?"

Jenny moved closer to Mark. "You sound a little nervous. What is it about these stories that really bothers you, Honey?"

Mark breathed deeply and laid his head back against the couch. "I guess I felt better about Scott and Michelle being in New Zion when the rest of the world didn't know they were there. Now, well, what if some radical group reads these stories and believes them? I worry that the kids won't be safe."

Jenny leaned closer. "I know. I worry about them too."

Mark looked into Jenny's calming smile and breathed deeply. "In my heart, I know they're safe. The Lord has kept them safe for a year and a half, even Benja . . . I mean, even Adam. These headlines upset me, but I have no doubt that God is in charge and that they'll be safe."

"Sometimes, it's just hard to remember that's how we feel, right?"

"Yes, I guess so," Mark said as he slowly smiled at his wife.

"I know what's bothering you. You can't fool me," Jenny said.

"Is that right?"

"Yes, it's as plain as can be. You're frustrated that you have a grandson and have never even held him in your arms."

"I think you're right," Mark said. "I'm being very self-centered about this situation. I know how our parents enjoyed our children when they were babies, and I want to experience that for myself. Sure, knowing that our son and his family are helping build the temple that Christ will occupy is important, but compared to . . ."

"I know. I wish I could get my arms around all three of them."

Activities at Church Headquarters returned to a somewhat familiar routine, though routine was no longer a word anyone used.

"It appears that the sensationalism that passes for news coverage these days is going to end up helping our cause, Brethren." The Prophet shook his head slowly. "The world press did not seem all that upset to find a community of people living in a toxic radiation zone, and yet have talked of little else since the pillar of light appeared."

"It's nearly comical," his second counselor commented. "President Nelson informs us that the Savior said the pillar of light would make people afraid and they would stay away. Now the ridiculous stories created by the news agencies are ensuring His words will be fulfilled. Construction on the temple will continue without interruption."

"The next shipment of materials for the temple will be ready to pick up in a few days. All seems to be going even better than we had hoped," the first counselor reported.

"And I understand the clothing and food to sustain our pioneers for another year is included with this shipment?" the Prophet asked.

"It is, although President Nelson said they have quite a surplus left from the food we originally sent with them. In addition, quilts from several wards on the east coast will be included in the shipment. It will be a pleasant surprise for them, I believe," the counselor responded.

President Nelson and his counselors sat with the twelve bishops of his stake to discuss the status of specific work projects. The past two weeks had been such a spiritual high for everyone in New Zion, and many projects were on hold awaiting the arrival of supplies, so it was expected that little work had been completed.

"Bishop Chandler, can we begin with you?" he asked. "Tell us how the Seventh Ward has been doing."

The Bishop unfolded his notes. "Well, since we haven't had a meeting for two weeks, there is quite a bit to report. We completed our assignment to help clean the temple site. The Sisters have been busy raking and cultivating the soil around the temple so they can plant flowers next spring. Our Priesthood Quorum decided we had some extra time until the supplies arrive from the east, so we've gone through each one of our houses to make sure all the connections are still secure. We also surveyed each family in our ward to see what they need in the way of food and clothing and turned that report over to the Bishop's Storehouse."

"I am amazed," President Nelson said. "I had thought people would take this time to rest and enjoy having some leisure, and instead, they seem to have accomplished more work than ever. Please thank them for their efforts." After President Nelson had heard similar reports from each ward, he turned to Scott and said, "Do we have a report on the status of the Bishop's Storehouse?"

"Yes," Scott answered. "We made an inventory of the things in the Storehouse that were never used, things like lamps and baby cabinets. We distributed twenty baby cabinets to expectant parents and our storage area is ready for the new shipments when they arrive."

"You all make being your stake president a very easy job," President Nelson said as he smiled at the group. "And now I get to announce that the supplies we need to begin working on the interior of the temple are ready to be picked up. It seems our well being has become the focus of many Relief Society Sisters around the world, so we will also be receiving handmade quilts and a more diverse supply of baby things with this shipment. Let's keep that to ourselves so everyone can enjoy the surprises as they arrive."

The drivers left early the next morning to pick up the awaited supplies, and the long line of transport vehicles returned later in the day. Life in New Zion quickly returned to schedules that allowed work to continue around the clock. Many of the Sisters who, before coming to New Zion had depended on their husbands to take out the garbage and shovel snow off the sidewalks, were now becoming proficient in the use of table saws and belt sanders. Everyone had an overwhelming desire to help complete the temple.

Sundays continued to be the only day work was not performed. When Thanksgiving arrived, a common topic of conversation was the fact that progress on the interior of the temple was coming along much quicker than anyone had expected, and supplies would be exhausted again in a week or so. Everyone agreed that the finish carpentry and detail work could take longer than the entire project had taken so far.

Mark and Jenny sat together in their living room, contemplating their options. Mark held his wife close to him, his left arm around her shoulder, his right hand holding her hand. They had spent the past hour discussing the future they felt was inevitable.

"Do you remember a few years ago when the Prophet spoke about the prophecies concerning the future?" Mark asked Jenny.

"Funny you should ask that. I was just thinking about what he said and how it could apply to the chip," Jenny answered.

"What do you remember about that talk?"

Jenny thought for a moment and then said, "I remember how he compared Christ to freedom and anti-Christ to slavery. He said anything that Christ does for us involves freedom, personal freedom. And anything that is anti-Christ involves personal slavery."

"Strange, but that was exactly the part I was thinking about. Do you remember when he said that the leaders of the Church are not going to make every decision for us, but that we should be wary about anything we allow into our lives that limits our personal freedom in any way?"

"Yes, I do," Jenny answered. "I like the way our leaders do not tell us exactly what to do, but make us use our agency and faith to choose for ourselves. They don't tell us who to vote for, but tell us to study what the candidates stand for and choose the one that most closely follows what Christ taught us. When we heard that talk about keeping things out of our lives that limit our freedom, had there been any talk about the chip yet?"

"I think there were rumblings but nothing had been instituted. I don't think they had even tried the very first trial with the bracelets. What he said was truly prophecy. But even hearing that talk, and studying the events prophesied in the scriptures does not make the decisions regarding the chip any easier, especially for the girls."

"That's true. When Scott and Michelle told us they were going to ride a bus right into the middle of the radiated area, I was so afraid for them," Jenny remembered. "I trusted the Lord would protect them, but I wondered what kind of hardships they would be facing. Now, well, if we had the option to pack up Jordan and Lynne and all four of us go join them, I'd start packing right now."

"Things have certainly careened downhill at a furious pace since then. In less than two years, deadly radiation seems like a better option than what is happening right here in Salt Lake City. It's unbelievable."

"How are you going to tell the girls?" Jenny asked. "I'm more worried about how this will affect them than what it means for us."

"Of course you are," Mark said, squeezing her shoulder a little tighter. "You're their mother and you want to help them get through problems, not tell them you don't see any rosy scenario ahead. I think they're going to surprise us both and end up encouraging us."

"I guess we'll find out soon enough. The garage door just opened."

"Wish me luck," Mark said as he walked toward the kitchen. Jordan and Lynne came through the door, laughing and smiling.

"Hi, Dad," Jordan said as she quickly hugged him and headed for the living room. "We had so much fun, Mom. You have to come with us next time."

"Yeah," Lynne agreed as she hugged her dad and followed Jordan into the living room. "That was the best workout I've ever had. You are going to love it. All three of us can go on Saturday."

"I'm glad you had a good time, girls," Jenny said. The girls sat next to each other at the end of the couch. "Your dad and I have been discussing a few things, and would like to talk to both of you for a bit. Are you going to be home for a while or are you heading back out?"

"No, we don't have any plans for this evening," Jordan said, "unless you want to take us to the show or something." She smiled and laughed, and then seemed to sense the mood, and pulled her eyebrows together in confusion. "Is everything all right?"

"Yes," Mark said. "Nothing's wrong."

"Is something wrong with Scott or Michelle? Is Adam okay?"

"Everything's fine with them," Mark insisted. "We just wanted to talk to you about what's been happening lately, and the decisions we feel are ahead. Since those decisions affect you, we'd like to talk about it as a family."

"Is this about the mark of the beast?" Jordan asked. "Because if it is, Lynne and I have already talked and we don't want to do it."

Mark heard himself laugh and exhale at the same time. He looked at Jenny, who was slowly shaking her head and smiling, and then looked at his two wonderful daughters. "Well, decision made. Yes, that *is* what we wanted to discuss, but you have already talked about it? Tell me why you don't think it's a good idea."

"Well," Jordan began hesitantly, "I believe what you've taught us and what the scriptures say about it. I guess I really don't see much difference between getting a chip implanted in my wrist and swiping my credit card through some machine, but I know the prophecies tell us it's a bad thing." She shrugged. "Why is it so wrong?"

Mark settled into a chair where he could face all three of the women in his life. "It's about how technology has two faces."

"Oh, this sounds good," Jordan laughed.

"We used to buy and sell using cash, but as people found better and better ways to counterfeit cash, we moved to electronically transferring money. Soon, electronic hackers found ways to steal funds or make fraudulent purchases. Individuals, large corporations and banking systems were losing a lot of money by these schemes, and they were desperate for any technology that would provide greater security. A brilliant young individual worked out a solution to the problem, and leaders in the financial world agreed to try his plan in a small mid-west town to see if it would work.

"Each member of the community wore a bracelet that contained an electronic chip. The chip contained identification, bank account numbers, and insurance account numbers. People who used the bracelet didn't have to carry wallets or purses, and they eliminated all risk of fraud. Money was directly deposited into a person's bank account for any work they performed. Purchases they made were immediately taken from their account. If there was not sufficient money in an account, the service or purchase was not approved. The people of the community unanimously endorsed the experiment. They said it made their lives easier, made it safer for the buyer and the seller, and any problems were easy to resolve. The only weak link about the system was the bracelet, as it could be lost or stolen.

"The next step was to try it in a larger city, so they tried it in northeast Maine. Instead of the bracelet, they decided to have each person get a chip imbedded just under the skin on their wrist. This one-year experiment was even more successful.

"That was good technology, but then government leaders saw an opportunity to take control of the nation's money. When this country was established, the government was based on the premise that we had God-given rights, that the individual states were sovereign, and that the federal government was responsible only for defense and to ensure commerce between all the states. Over time, the government has made it seem that they are the source of our rights, and when the new financial plan was put in place nationwide, it eliminated individual sovereignty of the states. The new plan required banking facilities to update their equipment so they would be compatible with only the new technology, so any doorways that could be used for fraud or abuse were eliminated. It sounded fool-proof."

Jenny said, "I can remember a lot of people objecting to this new program when we first started hearing about it because of the requirements that everyone have bank accounts that had a prefix of six-six-six in order to participate. I didn't think it could ever become mandatory because there was so much opposition, but suddenly it's being implemented and the outcry seems to have evaporated."

"Exactly," Mark said. "The government promised everyone would be safe again, and no one would lose any money. What could be wrong with a plan that protects everyone?"

"Most of my friends don't think there's anything wrong with getting a chip or getting new bank accounts," Lynne said.

"We're definitely in the minority," Mark replied. "The reason your mother and I are opposed to the chip is because we believe a government program that requires us to get a chip and new bank accounts that begin with six-six-six is exactly what we are warned against in the scriptures about the mark of the beast in the last days. There is no commandment that says thou shalt not get the chip, but Christ's teachings are based on our personal agency, and once we get the chip, we relinquish that agency and allow the government to become our master. By taking the mark in order to survive, we may be subjecting ourselves to Satan's plan. These are troubled times and the Prophet has told us we are living in the last days. We have prayed about it, and we simply do not think it's right. We've decided not to get the chip."

"There are consequences for not getting the chip," Jenny said. "Your dad's employer threatens to terminate any employee who doesn't have an account insured by the federation, because paychecks will only be directly deposited into those accounts. Stores of every kind are saying they will stop accepting currency because it could be counterfeit, and no more checks because they could be forged or they might bounce. Besides, if they accept any form of payment other than withdrawals from federation insured accounts by using the chip, they have no way to deposit it in the bank because the financial institutions will only accept payments from a six-six-six account."

"Sounds pretty bleak," Jordan said. "Dad could lose his job and we might not be able to get food or gas? What about hair appointments and buying clothes?"

"It will affect everything we do. Do you both understand what the consequences can be from this decision?" Jenny asked her daughters.

Neither Jordan nor Lynne said anything. Mark determined to wait until they answered before he said any more. He wanted them to make their own decision in this matter rather than feeling as though he was trying to talk them into accepting his opinion.

"Dad," Jordan said quietly, pulling him from his thoughts, "I think we should follow what you and Mom think is right."

Mark smiled at her and tried to keep from looking at Lynne. He prayed she would at least let him know what she was thinking.

"Lynne, what do you think we should do?" Jordan asked.

"Are you waiting for me to tell you what I think? I was waiting for Dad to tell us what we do next. Of course, we should follow what they have decided. I've always assumed they had a direct line to God." With a laugh, she reached out and poked Jordan in the ribs.

Mark and Jenny both laughed. Lynne had exhibited that quality of absolute obedience since she was a baby, but both of them expected that someday she would become more questioning.

"Okay, then," Mark said. "I'll hold out as long as I can at work, and we'll just see what happens."

"All right. Come on, Jordan, let's go watch our new workout video. It'll probably be the last one we get."

Jordan shrugged her shoulders and shook her head. "Am I the only one who had to think about whether or not I wanted to get the chip? Lynne obviously didn't even consider it. Was it that easy for you to make your decision?" she asked her parents.

"No," Mark assured her. "Your mother and I have been discussing this situation for several weeks. I'm afraid this choice will cost me my job, but I don't feel right about making any of you get chips implanted in your wrists. Without the implant, we will not be able to shop at any store in our neighborhood, and we will probably lose access to our doctors and the hospital. This decision is going to affect each of us in every aspect of our lives."

"Dad, what other choice is there?" She hugged him quickly and then left to join her sister in the family room where the sounds of the new workout video could already be heard.

"We spent so much time worrying about how the girls would take this, Darling," Jenny said as she hugged Mark. "But it sounds like they didn't need any explanation at all. We've raised two very smart girls."

"They take after their mom," Mark said. "If they took after me they would still be trying to convince us how we could get the chips implanted and still be doing the right thing. I was easily led when I was younger, but never in the right direction."

"I'm not sure what our lives will become, but I am certain I feel amazingly peaceful now that we've made our decision," Jenny said.

The following day was Sunday, and Mark wondered if the talks and lessons would deal with the choice everyone had to make regarding the chip. He wondered if the Bishop would make any kind of announcement about changes required because of the chip. However, there was no mention of the situation at all. The talks given in Sacrament Meeting were about obedience, and although Mark thought the topic was perfect, there was nothing specific about whether refusing to get the chip would be demonstrating obedience.

When they separated for Sunday School classes, Mark thought for sure the lesson would include some mention of the chip, or at least the importance of seeking inspiration in making life-changing decisions. Again, he was wrong. The lesson was on the consequences early members of the Church endured by joining the Church.

"Do you think you would have had enough faith to join the Church, even if you believed it was true, if it meant you would lose your job?" the teacher asked. "What if everyone in your family told you it was a mistake and they would disown you if you joined the Church?"

She stopped and waited. Rhetorical questions were part of every lesson, and answers were to be pondered in your heart, but today the teacher seemed to have something else in mind. After what seemed like a very long silence, a timid voice spoke.

"I think I would have enough faith, even if it meant I lost my job. However, I think it would be very difficult if your family and friends did not support you in your decision. Friends should be accepting and supportive of decisions you make."

"Would your faith be strong enough to join the Church if everyone in your family and every one of your friends disagreed with you and said they could no longer accept you if you made that choice?" the teacher continued. Again, she waited while the silence stretched on. "Are the choices we have to make today any different?"

There was no silence after that question. The man sitting next to Mark stood and said, "I think the decisions we have to make today are very different. There was only one true church and people had to decide whether they wanted to join it, plain and simple. Today we have to face situations that are anything but plain and simple. Should I accept a job that will allow me to provide for my family if I have to work every other Sunday? Do I tell my son that he can join the football team but he cannot play in the championship game, which is always held on Sunday? Or should I tell him he cannot join any team that plays on Sunday? Does a farmer milk his cows on Sunday but not put out the milk for the dairy to pick up because that will cause them to work? What is more important, teaching my family to live by the letter of the law in every detail, or telling them to do the best they can within the framework of the world we live in?" He sat down as if the questions had been building inside him and he had no choice but to stand and let them out.

"Very good questions," the teacher said. "Does anyone else have a comment?"

"I wonder why we receive specific direction from the leaders of the Church for some things, and on other topics they are silent? Abortion? – absolutely not. Get married in the temple? – yes. Pay your tithing, even when you feel you can't afford it? – definitely yes. No tattoos, no body piercing except for one piercing per ear – very specific direction. Get the chip? – silence. Who to vote for? – silence."

"Have they been silent on this matter?" asked the teacher.

Mark slowly stood. "A couple years ago my wife and I went to a fireside at the Conference Center. It was about the difference between Christ and anti-Christ. We were told that anything that comes from Christ provides freedom, while anything that is anti-Christ involves slavery. I don't know if any of you heard that talk, but, to me, that concept provides specific direction that helps me decide what I should embrace in my life, and what I should not. The change in all of the Church curriculum years ago also seemed to set the stage for what we have faced since that time. We have been forced to make decisions as wards, organizations and even as individuals, with less guidance and direction from the Church. We have been taught to pray and seek guidance from the Spirit for answers. Our training has encouraged us to develop a closer relationship with God, that we can more clearly hear His voice and receive our own individual answers and confirmation to all of life's challenges. A stronger personal relationship with God enables us to receive the answer that is right for us individually; not relying on a world-wide answer, generic enough to fit everyone living in different situations and circumstances."

There were no further comments, and soon the teacher finished her prepared lesson and dismissed the class. Mark had barely walked into the classroom where the Elder's Quorum met before people began commenting about what he had said during Sunday School.

"Hi, Mark. I sure appreciated your comments," Allen Hunter said. "I've been having a terrible time trying to decide whether or not I should get the chip. You stated it so simply and clearly, I have no doubt which way I should go now."

"I don't really think it's simple or clear," another member of the Elder's Quorum said as he joined their conversation. "I work for the government and I have absolutely no choice about getting the chip."

Mark determined he would not respond because he had never intended to start a debate about the situation.

"I don't really understand how working for the government makes this decision any different than working in the private sector," Allen said, very slowly. He did not wait to hear if that comment caused any response, but turned and sat on one of the folding chairs.

Mark sat next to him. "It's a pretty hard decision, no matter how black and white it seems," he said quietly.

"Yes, it is," Allen answered. "I have absolutely no idea what we're going to do."

"You're a dentist, aren't you?" Mark asked.

"Yes, I am. Complete with an office staff and school loans to pay off. Not to mention three small children. My wife and I are actually considering moving in with my parents. They have a farm in Idaho, but all five of us living with them could really be a burden."

"Having small children would make that decision even harder," Mark said sympathetically.

"My wife has a little picture stuck on our bedroom mirror. It says 'I never promised life would be easy, I only promised it would be worth it.' That has pretty much become my mantra. I say it repeatedly to myself all day long. She keeps saying that something will work out for us if we stick to what we know is right. My wife has so much faith. That should be comforting to me, but sometimes it seems to add weight to my burden. Nothing seems to make much sense these days."

"This is definitely not an easy thing," Mark said. "I'm probably getting an ultimatum at work tomorrow – get the chip or lose the job. I already told my boss I won't get the chip so I'm hoping for a few more weeks to get as much money as I can before the job goes away."

"No telling when the ax will fall, but when the bank says no more service without the triple-six account, I'll be done," Allen said.

"Allen, why don't you and your family come over for dinner today. I know it's short notice, maybe you already have plans, but if not, I'd love to have a chance to talk to you more and get better acquainted with your family."

"I'll talk to my wife after church," Allen said. "Thanks very much. I think it would be nice to get better acquainted with those who are headed down this same road."

The two families visited during the entire afternoon. It was nice to be able to compare notes with them. Allen said the only person he knew for sure that was not going to get the chip was his next-door neighbor, Ken Goddard. He was a medical doctor and was still in residency, so he had loads of school loans to pay and no equity at all in his house.

TECHNOLOGY'S GRIP

Each day seemed to become more stressful and tempers were strained to the breaking point. Politeness on the road and in stores was nowhere to be found. Most discussions ended in frustration because no one could envision a sustainable way to make it through the loss of jobs and buying privileges at local stores. Yet, the news commentators on network television continued to insist this was the best of times. When the benefits of getting the chip implanted were repeated, over and over during every newscast, it was hard to remember that individual freedom was being jeopardized.

Mark and Jenny had closely followed the experiments of this system, and they remembered the *benefits* that had been discussed during the selling phase of the chip. But tracking people's movements, determining their spending history, gathering information about how they spent their free time and discretionary funds, and being able to compile better statistics about people's religious and civic affiliations were never mentioned on the nightly news broadcasts.

Mark heard approaching footsteps and held his breath as they got close to his office, but then exhaled slowly as they moved on and the sound slowly faded. He knew it was only a matter of time. On Monday, his boss had said a decision must be made by Friday. Today was the deadline. Ever since Mark and his family had made their decision, they had begun stockpiling food with any extra money they had. Each day Mark had been able to work meant Jenny could add more groceries to their food storage while their cash was still accepted.

Again, he heard footsteps coming down the hall, but this time they stopped in front of his office door. After a short time, there was a soft knock. Mark pushed his chair back and stepped around his desk to open the door.

"Come on in," he said to his boss. He sat in one of the chairs near his desk and motioned his boss to sit in the other. "You've been very patient, but you know I'm not going to change my mind."

"I know, Mark. I really respect you for sticking to your guns. I have to turn in the information today. If I do not receive a signed form from you, this has to be your last day. You know that, right?"

"Yes. My family has made our decision, but it's still hard to walk out the door and know I don't have a job anymore."

"What will you do?"

"I don't know. I've been trying to sell my house, you know, maybe try to buy something smaller so I would not owe anything, but nobody is buying. They all know if they wait a month or two they can step in and take over the payments on any house the bank has repossessed."

"Are you sure this decision is important enough to give up your career for, my friend? I simply don't see how you're going to survive."

Mark suddenly felt very calm. "You know, I think we're going to be just fine. Honestly." He felt the smile he had forced his lips to make become genuine, and actually heard himself chuckle. "Do I just give you my badge and keys, or do I have to go through personnel? What's the procedure, boss?"

"Uh, well, I have the check-out form right here that you'll need to sign and you can give me your company items. I believe you have a laptop, a cell phone, badge, keys, and your parking permit."

Mark walked around his desk and slid open the bottom drawer. "One laptop," he said as he took it out and put it on top of his desk. "One cell phone, my parking permit, and here's my keys and my badge. You can have this company pen just as soon as I sign the form."

"Sure sorry it's come to this, Mark. You are my most effective trainer, always have been. It will not matter how many security systems we sell. Without someone like you to train the technicians and users, I am going to have a lot fewer satisfied customers. I will never be able to find anyone else who can do your job as well as you have. I'll really miss you."

Mark extended his hand and said, "Thanks. That means a lot. Now I suppose you get to walk me to the front door, right?"

"Afraid so."

When Mark pulled into his driveway and pushed the remote to open his garage, he was surprised that he felt so calm. He had experienced a strong sense of well being while talking to his boss, but had totally expected that it would vanish the minute he left the office. However, he was still filled with calmness.

"I'm home," he called when he stepped into the kitchen.

"Hi, Sweetie," Jenny said. She was drying her hands and quickly put down the towel. She gave Mark a long hug. "How did it go?"

"Not bad. I did get my last check."

"Okay, ready to go shopping?" Jenny smiled and opened the coat closet to get her purse.

"Sure thing."

Knowing this was going to be Mark's last week of employment, Mark and Jenny had decided to pay the next month's utilities and bills, make their house payment, and then empty every checking, savings and credit union account they had. Even though they had their year's supply of food, they decided the wisest thing they could do with their money would be to buy as much non-perishable food as possible.

Mark's car was paid for, but the other three were not. They had talked to the bank that carried the loans, explained they would not be getting chips implanted, and wanted to know what they should do about the cars. The loan manager suggested they pay the loans in full before the end of the month. When they informed her that would not be happening, she said there would be no alternative but to repossess the cars. Mark had surprised her by offering to bring the cars to them. Jenny said it was for the best because having only one car in the garage would give them more space to store food.

They made two trips to the discount retail club that afternoon, but would have to make several more the next day.

"Was it awful to quit your job, Dad?" Lynne asked during dinner.

"Not too bad," Mark fibbed. "At least, not as bad as I had thought it might be. My boss said he was sorry to see me go and he would miss me. That part was nice."

"I'm guessing you don't want us to open the garage door from now on," Jordan said. "I mean, with all the food stacked in there."

"That would be helpful," Jenny answered. "Probably not a good idea to advertise our stash."

"I've been thinking," Mark said. "Our life is going to change drastically pretty soon, but I want you three ladies to have one last visit to the beautician this weekend. And then, how about going out to dinner with me?"

"Our last visit to the beautician?" Lynne asked quietly. "Then who's going to cut my hair?"

"The idea is to use barter," Jordan said. "We'll find someone who was a beautician and decided to not get the chip, and then we can trade. She can cut our hair and we will, uh, well, what can we barter with?" Jordan looked at her mother "What can I trade for a haircut?"

"You can baby sit," Jenny said. "You can clean house, and maybe you can start a fitness class. With no more manicures, going to the gym, or shopping at the mall, I think people will become very creative when it comes to bartering. Things are going to work out fine."

"I agree," Lynne said. She looked at Jordan and they both tipped their head and quickly shrugged their shoulder. Mark and Jenny recognized this gesture as a means of secretly indicating agreement with each other without actually saying a single word.

Mark had filled his cart and was waiting in line. He slowly realized that he recognized the man in front of him. "Grant, I take it you are no longer working either," Mark said. The man in front of him turned very slowly, as if stalling to think about what he was going to say.

"Mark. Did I hear you say *either?*"

Mark nodded and said, "Unless grocery shopping has become an event you love so much you're willing to use a day of vacation to fill that cart, I'm guessing you lost your job, just like I did."

"That's strange. I really thought I was just about the only person in the whole company who had decided to refuse the chip implant."

Mark shook his head slowly. "I'm betting the reason we were not allowed to discuss it on company property is because *someone* didn't want any discussion going on that might make people step back and think about what they were doing. I only know one other person who is not getting the chip. Do you know Ray Sinclair?"

"No, I don't recognize the name. Are you already involved in the barter group that's forming here in Salt Lake?" Grant asked.

"Uh, no. You mean like a formal barter group?"

"It's pretty formal. They have rules and suggested rates for services. I went to one of their meetings last night and it seemed like a good idea. At least it will get me in touch with people who are interested in barter as a means of commerce. I don't see any other valid option. What are you planning to do to get by?"

"This," Mark said, as he motioned to his filled grocery cart. "Convert money to food so I'll have something to use for trading. Many people in our Church have made the same decision we have, and they are attempting to get a little organized about trading services with each other. Oh, you might want to move your cart forward," Mark said as the line began to move.

Grant pushed his cart forward, and when he again turned to face Mark, he was holding a business card. "I don't know much about your personal life, but I do know mine. Years ago, I bought a sixteen-unit apartment complex. If you have to move and might be looking for a place to live, maybe you would be interested in taking a look. I nearly have it paid for, and unless I can find enough people to help me make the final payment, I will lose the whole thing. If you know anyone who might be looking for a place to live, maybe you wouldn't mind telling them about me." Grant looked down and shook his head, then looked back at Mark. "I hope I haven't offended you. I know I'm being very forward, but I will do whatever it takes to provide for my family. I'll stand on the street corner and pass out business cards all day long if that's what it comes to."

Mark took the business card from Grant and then put his hand on Grant's shoulder. "I totally understand. I have no problem with telling others about this. I'm not even close to owning my house. We just bought it about ten years ago and we'll probably lose it. Maybe my wife and I will drop by this evening and see your apartments so we can tell others more about them."

Grant smiled and shook Mark's hand. "I would appreciate that. It's going to be a rough ride for all of us CP's."

"CP's? Crazy People?" Mark guessed.

"Chipless People. My daughter's idea, and it sort of stuck."

"Line's moving again. I'm glad we ran into each other."

Mark thought about Grant as he drove home. "You might be the answer to my prayers, Grant," he said as he pulled into his driveway.

While Jenny helped him unloaded the car, Mark told her about Grant's situation. "I know we talked about trying to sell our house, but I talked to the realtor yesterday and he told me nothing is moving. He said the banks are on hold until their systems are revamped, which means they're not making loans right now. That will sink us for sure."

"Do you know how much Grant needs to pay off his loan?" Jenny asked. She shut the trunk and carried the last box into the garage.

"No, I wanted to think about it, and talk it over with you, before I asked a lot of questions. I wondered if you would like to run over and look at his apartments. Maybe it's something we might be interested in, maybe not."

"I know we talked about paying our mortgage and utility payments for the next few months, but eventually we'll have to leave anyway. If Grant's plan makes sense, it might be better to use that money to rent something from him."

"Wish I had a crystal ball to see if there's any possibility we could sell this place before we lose it." Mark slid his hand along the granite counter top in the kitchen. "It's a lot of house to just walk away from."

"If we can't sell it, eventually we will have no choice," Jenny said.

"Ray and Debbie are in the same boat," Mark said. "Maybe we should ask them if they'd like to go with us to look at Grant's apartments."

"I'll call them."

When they arrived at Grant's address, all four of them were impressed that it was clean and seemed to be well maintained. It was in a very different type of neighborhood; there were no high-end homes like Mark's and Ray's, and the single-family dwellings were at least eighty years old. However, it looked like a good neighborhood.

"What do you think?" Mark asked Ray.

"It actually looks better than what I thought we might be forced to live in once I didn't have a job. I say we take a look."

When Mark rang the doorbell, introductions were made and Grant led them to the second floor to look at one of the empty apartments.

"How many bedrooms are there?" Jenny asked.

"Three bedrooms. One on each side of the bathroom and then the master bedroom. Why don't I leave the four of you here to look around? I'll be back." Grant pulled the door shut behind him.

"Wow," Debbie said. "This reminds me of the apartment we lived in when Nathan was born."

"It's a lot like that place, isn't it?" Ray added. "We moved up slowly through the years, and now we would be right back where we started in one move." He laughed but did not sound very happy.

"Three bedrooms," Jenny said. "That's more than I'd hoped for. This isn't a bad size for a living room." She walked into the dining room, studying every detail of the rooms. "Looks like a nice enough kitchen, lots more cabinets than I would have thought."

Jenny opened the door into the master bedroom. When she opened the door to the walk-in closet, she laughed. "I have a nice closet, Sweetie, but I'm not sure where yours is."

"I can get rid of all my suits except one for church, so my clothes won't take much room. I am willing to settle for a whole lot less living space. I'm anxious to hear exactly what Grant has in mind. He said he needed to find people who would be able to help him pay off his loan. I'm guessing he'll want a few months' payment, at least, and I don't even know what he charges for rent."

As if on cue, the front door opened and they heard Grant calling. "I'm back." He spread a calculator and several papers on the kitchen cabinet and asked, "What do you think?"

"The apartment's pretty nice. What exactly are you looking for?"

"I'll tell you the whole, entire story. I already told you I'm desperate, so I'll just lay it all out and you can decide if you're interested." He pointed to a typed page of numbers and began to explain. "I still owe almost $50,000 on this place. I have put every cent I've made back into remodeling and upgrading the apartments, and now, if I don't come up with the rest of the money by the end of next month, I lose it all. I rent these apartments for twelve hundred a month, and I have seven empty units right now. Some people moved out because they decided to get the chip and I had no way to take their payments any longer. I have ten thousand that I can pay on the mortgage, but I've been waiting until I know what's going to happen. I have another five thousand from three of the existing people that said they could pay ahead on their rent. That leaves me thirty-five thousand short. What I am hoping is that I can find seven families who are interested in living here, and if they can each pay five thousand dollars, that would make the pay-off. I can apply that five thousand toward rent, and count it as five months rent. I am open to any suggestions. I just want to keep this place so those of us who do not have the chip will have a place to live. Plus, of course, I don't want to lose the past ten years of working evenings and weekends and putting every cent we could spare from our wages into this place."

"How are you going to pay the utilities and taxes if you don't have a chip?" Ray asked.

"I made an agreement with three of my existing tenants. They do have the chip and they will use the salary from their job to pay the water, power, garbage and taxes. I have given them a break on the rent for doing that. In fact, I am dropping everyone's rent to a thousand a month. I think that sixteen families could set up a small community, and trade services with each other."

"I'm a little confused," Jenny said. "How is having us do things for each other going to get rent for you?"

"I'm not looking to keep making money from this place. It will be in my name and if things ever change, I could sell it, or whatever. Right now, I want to have a home for my family and find a way to make life as pleasant as possible for us and fifteen other families. If we can get haircuts from someone who lives here, and if someone can do the repairs and work required to maintain this place, maybe someone else will be able to teach us things like cooking or a new language, or watch our kids while we go for a walk. I am hoping to create a haven that works for all of us. My main concern right now is finding the money so I don't lose the place back to the bank."

"Are there any storage units in this building?" Jenny asked.

"Not really," Grant answered, "but we have a huge space in the basement that used to be a laundry room, and next to it is a big unused space that may have once been a garage or a coal storage area. It's secure, but really dirty and spooky right now. Why do you ask?"

"I think you're going to need a big space to store all the food your new tenants have been stock piling. Maybe everyone could pitch in, clean up the space, and make it secure enough to store food."

"That sounds like a great idea. But before anything can even be considered, I still need to find seven new tenants with enough money to help pay this place off."

Mark looked at Jenny and smiled when she quickly tipped her head and shrugged her shoulder, indicating she was in agreement with him. How could she know he thought this was an answer to their prayers?

"I'm interested in your arrangement, Grant," Mark said. "I can't promise anything, but I'll talk to the people I know who've decided against the chip and see if any of them are interested. I have enough to help. We were going to make another month's payment on the house while cash was still acceptable, and pay our utility payments ahead, but if we decide to join with you, we will put that money toward your final payment. Let us see what we can do, and I'll get back to you tomorrow, to at least let you know what we're thinking."

Grant smiled and suddenly stepped toward Mark and wrapped his arms around him, hugging him tightly. He stepped away quickly, obviously embarrassed. "Sorry," he apologized. "I'm just so relieved that someone actually thinks this would be a good arrangement. Sure, think about it, and thanks for spreading the word. I am desperate; I might as well admit it. Any other questions, at all?" Grant asked as he looked at Ray and Debbie.

"No," Ray said. "It sounds interesting."

As soon as they were back in the car, Ray asked, "Are you seriously considering moving here?"

"I'm thinking it makes a lot of sense. I have to pray about it, but right now, it seems as though this is the answer to our prayers. What do you think?"

Ray slowly shook his head. "I think it's a great deal for your friend Grant. His loan gets paid off and we all stay there and give him food, clean his house, watch his kids, and help him maintain his apartment building. But what do we have to show for it in the long run?"

"Maybe I'm looking at this situation differently than you are, Ray. I am terrified that we will lose our house and have to move into a classroom at the church, if they would even allow that to happen, or some community shelter for the homeless. I would lose all my worldly possessions then because I would not have a home to keep them in. I've actually considered piling whatever we could in our car, hooking up a trailer to tow whatever food would fit in it, and heading for a climate that's warm enough to allow us to live in a tent for a few years. I have no idea how I am going to take care of my family. You must have something better in mind. Is it something I might be able to do that would allow me to provide for my family?"

"No need to get all wound up," Ray said as he ceremoniously leaned away from Mark. "I don't have any grand plan and I'm just as concerned as you. It's just that when I listened to Grant talking about how he had everything arranged to be sitting pretty when things get back to normal, it made me mad. Oh, I'm probably going to be begging him to let us live there. I have five thousand from my 401K that I emptied out when I lost my job. I have enough of a cushion that I was thinking I could pay things ahead and manage for a few months, but I had no options after that. The whole thing makes me pretty angry."

"I know. The whole thing makes me very angry, but not angry enough to get that chip. Maybe Jenny and I are a little more prepared for this change because we watched Scott and Michelle leave everything behind and head for Missouri. They actually seemed happy and were more concerned about us than they were for their own future."

"Do you know anyone else who might be interested in Grant's place?" Ray asked. "Maybe we should ask around?"

"Are you going to the Elder's Quorum Work Party at the church tomorrow?" Mark asked Ray.

"That's a great idea. Yeah, I was planning on going. We only need five more families."

Mark recognized the Lord's hand as things began to fall into place.

"These three men are members of the same church Ray and I belong to," Mark said as he began introducing them to Grant. "Randy Peterson, Ken Goddard and Allen Hunter. This is Grant Harrison."

"Nice to meet you all," Grant said.

"I've explained as much about the situation as I can," Mark said. "For our part, each of the five of us is willing to give you five thousand dollars to become involved, but I don't know if you've found two others who have the money to join in. Each of us will only give you the money when we get some legal documents drawn up and can see that you have the whole amount you need to pay off the loan. I think these men can offer some needed knowledge to your little habitat. Randy is an attorney, Ken was in the middle of his residency at the University Medical Center but is now unemployed like the rest of us. Allen is a dentist. He won't be able to open a dentist's office in one of the bedrooms in his apartment, but he has a few connections that will allow people to barter for dental care if it's needed."

"And what do you do for a living, Ray?" Grant asked.

"I'm not a professional like these guys," Ray answered. "I worked for the same company Mark did. I am an engineer and I helped put together big security systems for large corporations. I do have a marketable skill that might come in handy. I'm an electrician."

"Perfect," Grant said with a broad smile. "This is better than I had dared to hope for when you called me," he said to Mark. "I've found two people who have the money to help get this place paid off, but I doubted you two could find three more. That does it. If you can help us get the legal papers drawn up, we can all go to the bank together. I want to get this paid off today, or at least as soon as possible. I'm terrified that when I walk into the bank with the money, they'll come up with something that keeps the whole plan from working."

"Can I go through the agreements you already have with your existing and future tenants?" Randy asked Grant. "No offense intended, but I told these four guys that I would make sure we're not getting ourselves into some scheme that will leave us with no money and no place to live either."

"None taken," Grant assured him. "You can start going over things right now. I'll go get all the papers for this entire loan. I am so excited to think that it's actually going to work!"

"Grant," Mark said, "can you tell us what other professions or skills you have within the group?"

"Oh, sure, I was going to tell you about the two new tenants I found. One is a plumber. Can you believe that? We will have our own plumber and electrician. The other one is a man who had a construction company. He was on the verge of a huge deal that would have meant jobs for his entire crew for the next five years, plus provided enough work to hire about ten new employees. Now, because he refuses to get the chip, he's lost it all."

"Mark," Randy said, "I think we should go through the papers together. Grant, this is your show, but I would like to see all the tenants openly involved in every detail right from the beginning. Most of us are using the money we had set aside for next month's bills, so we need to be out of our houses by the end of the week, if possible."

Grant looked very relieved. "I agree. All those living in our complex should be included in every legal and financial arrangement, and I'll make a list of everyone's skills and abilities."

The world continued to keep their distance from the city of fire. Then one afternoon the residents of New Zion noticed a small caravan on the eastern horizon. The initial thought was that the press had found a way to minimize their personal risk. It was estimated that the caravan would arrive in about three hours, so a meeting was called to decide what they should do. It was unanimously decided they would not allow anyone into the city, and especially not within the walls of the temple courtyard. Each person vowed to lay down their life, if necessary – they would not be run out of Jackson County ever again. President Nelson left the meeting to call the Prophet for guidance.

Every one of the more than twelve hundred saints stood shoulder to shoulder about a mile east of the city, awaiting the arrival of the approaching caravan. Their only weapons were tools used for construction or gardening.

Soon a most unusual caravan rolled to a stop in front of them. It was made up of twelve older cargo trucks. Twelve young Native American drivers slowly got out of their trucks and gathered in a small circle next to the third truck from the front. They seemed quite reluctant to approach the large group who stood in a line before them. The pioneers, also nervous about the strange caravan, waited to see what danger might be hidden within the trucks.

The youngest driver started to walk toward the line of people. Two other drivers followed behind him. The three men stopped when they reached the back of the front truck. Neither group spoke or stepped closer to each other.

"It's all right," President Nelson said as he came running from New Zion. "I've been talking to the Prophet and he has received inspiration that those coming to our city are doing the will of the Lord."

"Come," the young driver said. "We have brought our work."

President Nelson stepped toward the drivers, and his two counselors moved forward with him. The three drivers extended their right hands, and President Nelson slowly shook hands with them. Instantly, he felt the warm spirit that permeated from the young men who were now smiling broadly. Warm feelings swept through each of them, along with the knowledge that they all shared the same belief and faith in Jesus Christ.

The youngest driver spoke timidly. "I am Alma." He opened the doors at the back of the first trailer. "We have prepared our work for Jesus and brought it to you."

President Nelson and his counselors were speechless. The trailer was completely filled with beautiful woodwork of every kind. There were railings, doors, door and floor moldings, tables, chairs, and all types of finished articles for the inside of the temple.

Alma began speaking. "I have been given the same name as many of my ancestors. A long time ago, Jesus visited my ancestors. He showed them His wounds of crucifixion. He taught them how to plant and irrigate, and how to build great architecture. Jesus taught them magnificent things of the heavens and the universe. He then called twelve disciples to represent Him and established a successful government, with each disciple being responsible for a branch of the government. Each disciple was replaced as necessary that our people might always have twelve disciples to lead us.

"Jesus gave my ancestors plans for a great temple that was to be built prior to His return to the Earth. The plans were very detailed and had specific drawings of great woodwork. They were instructed to complete the woodwork with the greatest of care. They were then to store it in the large caverns beneath the Earth. The plans called for twelve compartments, or rather twelve temples, to form one complex. Each wing of the temple had a very different design and purpose. Much of the work has been redone several times because the skill of my ancestors in working the wood improved generation after generation. As the level of skill improved, work previously completed was no longer felt to be good enough for the King's temple. Therefore, they took some of the work from the caverns and replaced it with even more beautiful and precise woodwork."

Alma climbed up to stand on the front of his truck, as so many from the city of light had gathered closely around. He spoke loudly so the entire group could hear his story.

"As very young boys, we were sent from our homes to a nearby town for schooling. We were educated through college and were schooled specifically in math and English. We were taught that it would be necessary for us to know English well enough to travel through the land without raising suspicion.

"Long ago, Jesus promised our people that a light would appear in the sky to signal that His new temple was ready for our work. When the light appeared that was talked about around the world, our Elders knew it was time for us to take the work our village had been preparing for centuries and deliver it to the distant city of light. We removed the woodwork from the caverns and loaded it onto the trucks the village had gathered. We have brought it to you, and also the plans that were given to my ancestors."

Alma climbed down from the truck, reached inside the cab and pulled out a set of plans. "These are the plans we have used."

President Nelson took them and said, "We will compare our plans to the ones you have brought, and I'm sure they will prove to be identical. Would you and the other drivers like to see the temple that is ready to receive the beautiful work you have brought?"

"We would like that very much," Alma replied. The drivers and many of the brethren walked toward the temple while most of the Sisters hurried to their homes to bring enough food to have a celebration.

During the next five months, the beautiful woodwork was installed into the specified areas of the temple. The beauty of the wood was unbelievable; everyone marveled that the wood fit in place so precisely it was as if the walls and woodwork had been formed from one piece of material. The phase that everyone thought would take the longest to complete was finished in the shortest amount of time

THE CRYING MAN

Most Sunday afternoons Mark took a nap after dinner, but today he had suddenly awakened after having a very strange dream. He sat in silence as he tried to figure out what to do.

In the dream Mark was standing on a dirt road; which, stretched across a barren landscape. The wind began to blow; he could not feel it, but could hear it. His focus was locked toward the wind that seemed to be coming from a nearby cedar covered hill. As the sound became louder, it became apparent that the sound was not wind, but was actually someone crying. Mark turned and noticed a man from his Ward, Greg Simpson, just up the road ahead. The noise he had thought was the wind was actually Greg crying. His cries became clear and Mark heard him pleading, "I don't know what to do." Greg's voice pierced Mark's heart; he could feel Greg's pain and sorrow, and his overwhelming sense of despair.

In a flash, Mark was talking to his brother who lived in Idaho, describing what he had seen while on that desert road. His brother commented, "These days a lot of people are feeling like they have no way out."

It was nearly four o'clock. In his mind, Mark could still hear Greg crying, as well as feel his fear and panic. He tried to figure out what any of it meant. It bothered him so much he actually got up and knelt by the side of the bed. He prayed that he might be able to relax and know what the dream meant.

As he pondered the dream, he thought back a few weeks when he had been home teaching Greg. He said his wife had gone to visit her folks. Then Mark realized he had not seen Greg at church earlier that day. He sat on the side of the bed wondering if he should call Greg and find out if he was all right. Before he knew it, he was picking up his car keys and heading for the garage. "I'm going to go visit Greg for a bit," he said to Jenny when she looked up from the book she was reading.

As he approached the door, he heard a sound from inside. As he stepped nearer to the door, Greg's voice became clear. "I don't know what to do. Please, help me. I don't know what to do." The voice was identical to the voice from his dream.

It took a couple minutes for Greg to open the door after Mark knocked. It was easy to tell he had been crying.

"Come on in. I've been trying to figure out some things that are going on in my life. I am sure everyone is going through the same kinds of problems these days because of the economy and the decision we all have to make about getting the chip. I'm sure you're going through a lot of the same problems too."

"Yes," Mark assured him. "I had to quit my job and we're trying to decide what to do. You have a contracting business so I'm sure you have a lot more worries than deciding whether or not to close up shop."

"Right," Greg said with a big sigh. "Things are not very good right now. I have been so upset about how I'm going to get through this. My wife, you probably already guessed, she has taken the kids and gone to stay with her folks for a while. I'm about at my wits end and I'm sure I haven't been very fun to live with lately." Tears were beginning to fall down his cheeks. "Sometimes I don't know who to be mad at: the economy, the housing market, God, my wife, myself? If I can't even support my own family what kind of a husband am I? Why hasn't God answered my prayers? I feel as if I've been abandoned, and I don't think I can get through this."

Mark asked Greg if he could say a prayer with him. Greg indicated that would be fine. Mark bowed his head and asked Heavenly Father to help Greg's mind clear so he could focus on his alternatives and seek God's help in making a decision.

"Thanks, Mark."

Greg seemed to have calmed down considerably. He began talking more to himself than to Mark. It was as if he was reasoning it in his own mind as Mark sat silently listening.

"My business was set to succeed big time," Greg said. "I had a great office manager and a wonderful crew chief and the work came in faster than we could get it done. I had just finished a huge house that took me a year to complete, and I had an offer on it. We were going to use the money from the house and build a bigger one, you know, keep the investment growing. I was also waiting for the checks to arrive from several other big jobs. Then the bottom fell out. The bank turned down the people who made an offer on my house, so then I had a mortgage payment to make. The big checks I was waiting for were delayed. In the meantime, my equipment costs and wages were stacking up, so I used the tax money to pay them. Then that made my taxes delinquent. I figured I would pay the taxes when one of the big checks came."

Greg stood and started walking back and forth in front of the couch as he talked. "The biggest project check arrived, and I ran right down to the bank and deposited it. I came home, wrote checks to all my employees, and paid my credit cards. It was amazing to know I was caught up except for the taxes. Then all hell broke loose. The government took the money out of my bank account to pay the taxes, but they had already put such big fines and penalties on what I owed that my entire project check did not even cover it all. Then the checks I had written all started bouncing. I kept trying to ride it out. I quit taking personal money in an effort to keep paying my employees. That's when my wife decided she could not take the stress any longer. Eventually things started getting behind at home because I was taking so little for myself from the company. Tensions are still growing between my wife and I because she wonders if I'm spending money I don't need to, and I'm wondering if she really needed something she bought for the kids."

Greg sat down on the couch again and dropped his head into his hands. "I don't want everyone knowing what's happening, so I find myself avoiding people, because they often ask how things are going. I don't want to lie when they ask, but it is my personal life. People want to help but I know they can't. They might help stop my fall if they could hand over a hundred thousand dollars. When people offer help, they are talking hundreds or less. A business can swallow up thousands in days, and shortly I'm going to need two hundred thousand to pay the bills that will be due. Daily my integrity is questioned, and honesty is no longer a quality that people associate with me. My mind seems so occupied with all the stress and how I am going to resolve things that I can't function. I see someone laughing and I cannot remember the last time I found anything funny enough to make me laugh. I feel so responsible for my family and wonder if my decisions have been a disservice to them. There are days that I would hold my breath until I died if that would actually work. I know suicide is not the answer and is so wrong that I don't dare let it reside in my mind for more than a millisecond. If it stays longer I might actually find a way to justify it."

Greg seemed to have talked himself out and leaned back against the couch.

"Have you considered bankruptcy?" Mark asked quietly.

"I've considered every possible solution, but none of them solve all the problems."

"Greg, what is the most important thing in your world right now?"

"My family," Greg said without any hesitation.

"Are you going to get the chip implanted in your wrist?"

"No. I have already decided that most of my problems have been created because the bank or the government felt they had more right to run my company and spend my money than I did. Once they pulled that first check and made things start bouncing, I was doomed. I have to do whatever it takes to get my family back together, and that can't happen if I try to hang on to my business."

"I can't begin to know what's involved, but if you walk away and drive to Idaho to be with your family, what would happen?"

Greg turned and looked at Mark. "Well, I'd lose this house and the big house I've worked on for over a year. My employees will no longer have jobs. My credit is ruined and the IRS will probably put me in jail. I'll default on my bank loans, credit cards, and personal loans." Greg actually smiled ever so slightly.

"Is there anything I can do to help you, and I have to tell you I don't even have a hundred dollars to give you. I do have enough to pay for the gas it would take to drive to Idaho, and I would gladly give that to you."

Greg smiled for real and seemed to relax. "I just may take you up on that. I know I could work with my father-in-law and make enough to feed my family. He belongs to a neighborhood group that has already formed a little community where they barter. He has been trying to talk me into moving there and getting back to the basic things in life. He told my wife to bring the kids and move into the other half of their duplex. Everything he owns is paid for so nobody can touch him. I should have gone with my wife, but I felt so responsible for my employees, and I don't feel right about walking away from my debt. You are a good friend, Mark. It seems so clear now. The only thing that will be important when I die is my family. I cannot save my employees, as much as I wish I could. I can't even save my business."

"Get your coat, Greg. You're coming home with me for dinner. It's just Jenny and me. The girls are gone to some youth activity this evening. We can talk about this more after we eat. Why don't you call your wife and tell her you're coming to Idaho, and then come over?"

"Thanks, Mark. I'll do that, and I'll be over in ten minutes."

When Mark stood, Greg hugged him warmly and thanked him again. All the way home, Mark was grateful he had listened to the prompting he had received. He was certain Greg would still have difficulties to work through, but the indecision and inability to move forward seemed to be gone. It brought back so many memories of times when he was young and never thought to ask God to help him work through problems. When he got home, he told Jenny he had invited Greg to join them for dinner.

"I knew if you were gone this long there must be problems. A good Sunday dinner is always a great idea when a person has problems."

"His wife has already gone to Idaho and is living with her family. He is going to join them. I think he just needs a little extra friendship until he can get things resolved and get out of here."

"You're amazing," Jenny said. "You've just lost your job, and you're worried about someone else. I think you are pretty wonderful."

Mark hugged his wife but did not tell her that the only reason he was anything close to wonderful was because she loved him.

◆◆◆◇◆◆◆

"Are you taking your laptop?" Lynne asked Jordan. "I don't think we're going to have any Internet connection once we move."

"You're probably right," Jordan agreed. "But I have several boxes of DVD's that we can play. That might be useful if you're going to be babysitting. Plus, we can still use our workout videos. I think Mom was joking about us teaching fitness classes, but it might be fun to get all the girls our age together to work out."

"I guess I better get my DVD's out of the *donation* box then."

"Lynne, we're not going back in time, we're just moving to a different part of town. I know there will be lots of changes in our lives, but life in our bedroom will pretty much remain unchanged."

"Did you forget we won't have cell phones?"

"Okay, so that will change," Jordan agreed.

"No more shopping trips to the mall, either."

"I don't agree with that one," Jordan said stubbornly. "The only thing that's really going to be different is that we'll have to ride with one of our friends that still has a car."

"That might work," Lynne agreed. "But are you sure you'll be wanting to go to the mall when you have ugly hair and no makeup?"

"Mom said one of the women in the apartment building is a beautician, so at least we'll be able to get haircuts."

"And all we have to do is clean her house and watch her kids and maybe cook dinner for her family, right?"

"You've got it," Jordan beamed.

"How are you girls coming along?" Jenny asked as she walked into the room. "Ray will be here in about an hour and we can fill his pickup with things from your rooms, if you're ready. The plan is for the three of us to get the beds moved this afternoon and our bedrooms set up, and then spend tomorrow moving the kitchen things. The guys will be moving the furniture tomorrow afternoon."

"Who's moving all that food in the garage?" Jordan asked, certain she did not want to hear the answer to that question.

Jenny just smiled at her.

"That's what I thought," Jordan said. "And what is happening to all the stuff we can't fit into the apartment?"

Jenny took a deep breath and then crossed her arms tightly in front of her. "We're going to put some of it in Scott's garage, but most of it is going to charity. We have to downsize, so make sure you take the things that mean the most to you, but not so much that you can't enjoy what you do take. Anyway, that's my motto." She looked around the room and then offered, "What can I help with?"

"I almost threw away my DVD's," Lynne said, "so maybe you could help me decide what I can take with me."

"Okay, let's go see." She put her arm around Lynne's shoulders and headed out of Jordan's room. "Be ready in an hour," she said to Jordan as she left. When they got to Lynne's room, Jenny looked at her youngest daughter and said, "Are you all right? I know this isn't the most fun thing our family has ever done, but it won't be so bad."

Lynne sat down on her bed and looked up at her mom. "I'm not worried about this *stuff*. It's just, well, I thought this whole thing of not getting a chip was going to make a huge difference in my life, but every time I think I know what the difference will be, I find out I'm wrong. I just can't figure out how it will really affect me."

"That's a fair concern. Let's just go through your day and think of what will change."

"Good idea," Lynne said, pulling her mom down until she was sitting next to her on the bed. "So I get up and eat breakfast. Then I take a shower and get dressed. I get ready for work. But now I don't have a job."

"That will be a change. You'll be busy during the day helping me bake because we'll have to cook everything from scratch and find ways to use all those cans of food we bought. Then you'll have to find ways to earn the things you want."

"Like cleaning house and watching kids in exchange for haircuts?"

"Yes, and you can offer to do other things for the beautician so you can get makeup she may have access to. You could ask her if she would let you sanitize her combs and brushes, or sweep up between customers. You'll still be able to do things with your friends, but if they want to go somewhere, they will have to pick you up since you don't have your car any longer. That will be different. And you'll have to find things to do that don't cost money. You can still play tennis, but you'll have to do it at the park rather than the tennis club. You can still work out, but you can't go to classes at the gym."

"Mom, all that sounds fine, but people act like this is going to be terrible. I want to know the terrible part so I can get prepared."

Jenny laughed and hugged her daughter. "You know something, Sweetie? I don't think there is going to be a terrible part for you. Some people act like their whole world would end if they had to give up their job and their car and their charge cards. You've already done that and it hasn't seemed to even bother you. You're incredible."

"You wouldn't say that if you knew that I really don't see anything wrong with getting a chip. I never have. I'm going along with this because I know you and Dad believe it's important, but I really don't see anything wrong with it."

"That's what makes you so incredible. You have always accepted our advice, and that shows that you respect us, and you have faith in the answers that you get from praying. I love you so much."

As if the moment of revelation was over, Lynne wiggled out of her mother's hug and said, "So, if I can take everything in my whole room, want to help me pack?"

"Are you ready for a break? I need a breath of fresh air."

"Sure, Ray," Mark said. "Let's go sit under the trees in the back."

The two men left the basement where they had been working most of the morning. The unused laundry room in their new home had been emptied and they were in the process of gutting the old, moldy room. Spiders, cobwebs and musty basements had never been inviting for Mark, but he knew the space was badly needed to store everyone's stockpiled food.

"Manual labor gives my brain way too much time to think. I still keep going right back to where I was. You know, feeling like Grant is going to benefit by our arrangement," Ray said as they sat down. "We pay off his loan and now we're fixing up his building. For free."

"I'm surprised to hear you say that. I thought this was really the only viable option for either one of us."

"Yeah, that's the rub. I feel as though I have been backed into a corner and there is no way to get out. I know the counsel from the Prophet was to not put ourselves in a position where we no longer could exercise our free agency, but that feels exactly like what I've done. The only thing I see in my future is playing monopoly with my kids and doing manual labor for my keep. It's infuriating when I see people from our old neighborhood still living like we used to. No lightning strikes hitting their houses yet."

"Ray, you made this decision, same as I did, and we both made it for the same reason. So why are you now doubting your decision?"

"I guess it's watching my kids and how hard it is on them. Nathan had one year of college left and he was on his way. Now he can't even get a job. His fiancé was not happy when he decided to not get the chip, and within a few months, she dumped him. Last Thursday was supposed to have been his wedding day, and now he just seems to drift through the day, totally uninterested in anything going on around him."

"Oh, man. I hadn't heard he was having such a hard time. I can't imagine losing my wife, even when we first met. It would feel like half of me, or maybe all but a tiny part of me was gone. How is a person supposed to function when the one person who made them visible to the rest of the world is no longer around? What can I do to help?"

"I don't know," Ray admitted. "That's the problem. No matter what I say or do he just seems to be getting more and more depressed."

"Tell you what, Ray. Let's start a tennis league. I know he used to play with us at the gym a lot. There's a court at the park a few blocks from here. We could find out how many men in our building would be interested. Heck, Ken and Allen used to play sometimes. I'll talk to Grant and find out if he knows anyone else that might be interested, and we'll drag Nathan along with us. A good workout might help give him something else to focus on for a bit."

"Talk to Grant about what?" their manager said as he walked into the back yard. "Can I join you?" Grant gave both men a cold bottle of water and sank down beside them. "I was just looking inside and you've got a lot of work done. What can I do to help you?"

"This was a good first step," Mark said, holding his half-emptied bottle up. "If you could find some way to make mold smell like sunflowers, that would be good, too."

"Maybe we could market that," Grant said, and then he snapped his fingers. "Oh, I forgot, we can't market anything. Oh, well. So, what did you want to talk to me about?"

"We were talking about starting a little tennis competition among the guys in this complex. Do you know anyone living here that might be interested in joining us?" Mark asked.

"That's a great idea," Grant answered. "Yeah, quite a few people would probably be interested. How about making it couples? I know my wife would be interested."

"That's an even better idea," Mark said. "My wife and daughters would probably all be interested, but I think we should start out with only men. You see, Ray's son was supposed to have been married last week, but his fiancé dumped him because he's a CP. He's pretty down in the dumps and we thought maybe a little diversion might help. After a couple weeks or so, if he takes an interest in it, maybe we could have his mom coax him into letting her play and then we could open it up to the other women."

Grant looked at Mark with a strange expression on his face for a moment. Mark finally shook his head and said "What?"

"I think this is a great idea, but not for the reason you may think. I'll help you get in touch with all the men in the complex to see who is interested. Maybe we should start having meetings or parties that everyone in the building is invited to so we can start getting better acquainted. That way we can become more than just a group of people caught up in a similar situation." Grant stopped speaking but, after a short silence, continued. "Would you be as interested in helping someone in the building who is not a member of your Church?"

"Grant," Mark asked, "do you honestly think we're only interested in people who belong to our Church? I can't understand what we've done to give you that impression."

"It's not you, so much," Grant answered. "Just others I've known before that belonged to your Church. They acted like I wasn't good enough to talk to because I wasn't a member of your Church."

"I'm sorry to hear that. But I can assure you that our Church teaches exactly the opposite. We are taught to follow the teachings of Jesus Christ and that involves loving everyone, members or not, and being of service when we can. I hope your opinion of us improves a little bit as we become better acquainted. Is there someone else living here that you think we might be able to help?"

Grant sighed deeply. "It's my daughter, Gina. Sometimes I wonder if I made the right decision by refusing to get the chip because she seems so unhappy. She was a cheerleader and had a scholarship for school next year. Now her so-called friends treat her like she suddenly came down with leprosy. They not only abandoned her, but made rude comments to her when she tried to get in touch with them. One of them started calling her a religious fanatic, and she does not even go to church. She just hides in her room most of the day, and it's about to tear my heart out."

"Maybe she would like to do something with my girls," Mark offered. "They're trying to get the kids in the entire complex together and have fun. I'll have Jordan invite her to join in."

"Good luck with that. I have to practically drag her out of her room just to eat dinner."

"Well, I'll talk to Jordan and Lynne and see if they can think of a way to get acquainted with her."

"I have a question for you," Grant said, sitting up and facing Mark. "If you and your friends are members of the LDS Church, why are you living here? I always heard that your Church had a great welfare program that took care of their own."

"They do have a welfare program for members in the ward that can't take care of themselves. We are taught to be self-sufficient and fend for ourselves, then, if needed, we should seek help from our families. Only as a last resort should we reach out for help from the Church. Your apartment complex saved us from having to do that."

"That's all well and good, but why does your Church only help those that are members rather than helping the whole community, like the people who set up food banks?"

Mark thought for a moment. "I think the big difference is that we have several types of relief organizations. One type helps people in their own ward when they need food or assistance to pay bills, and then allows them the opportunity to work for that help. The other branch is called Humanitarian Aid and it provides emergency relief and development projects around the world. The Church sends supplies, and uses volunteers to help with the distribution. Hundreds of full-time volunteers serve as teachers, farm workers, nurses, doctors, or whatever is needed."

"Why haven't I ever heard about this?" Grant asked.

"Most of the help our Church provides is totally behind the scenes. They don't seek or want any publicity for helping. Have you ever been to a Deseret Industries store?"

"Sure, lots of times," Grant responded.

"Well, that's part of the Church's welfare program. People who have disabilities or cannot find work elsewhere are hired and trained to repair things, to organize the store, or to clerk. Sometimes they move on to better-paying jobs after they've been trained."

"I've never heard one word about any of this." Grant said.

"The Church even has a job placement service that teaches people how to look for a job and where to find work. And I'm certain the jobs they find don't require people to get a chip."

"So maybe that's why you guys never acted desperate, like me. I was terrified that I would not be able to provide for my family but I was even more afraid to have a chip put under their skin. Some days I thought I was going to go insane because I could not think of any solution. When I lost my job, I really wondered if I had made the right choice. My wife and I had the most horrible fights and then I started worrying about whether or not I was going to lose my family."

"You're not alone, Grant. These are very trying times, especially if you don't follow the crowd. My next door neighbor, in my former neighborhood," Mark said with a smile, "was in business buying fixer uppers and had an investment group working with him. They bought houses and fixed them up, but instead of selling them, they went the rent-to-own route. It was a huge success because people with marginal credit were able to get into a house and use a portion of their monthly rent toward their down payment. They were doing great and then he decided not to get a chip. His whole business fell apart and they could not get people financed. His investors dried up and the properties sat empty until the bank took them over. He's lost everything."

Ray, who had been silent during the conversation, spoke up quietly. "Don't you find it hard to stay positive about things when everything you've worked for is falling apart? How do you do it, Grant? I've watched you act like this is one big windfall for you, but that's just a cover isn't it?"

"I have to work hard at being optimistic," Grant said. "Even now, it may look like I'm going to come out on the winning end of this stick. I don't believe that for one second. I feel like this is a waiting game, and I've managed to get through the first hurdle. Every day I wait for a letter that tells me the government has found a way to confiscate my property because I refused to get a chip. I have a hard time trying to convince my kids that they should work hard and try to improve their lives when I hardly believe it myself most days."

Ray's eyes suddenly filled with tears. "That's the hardest part," he said with a sob. "My daughter feels like her life is totally ruined and I can't help her. How can I try to teach her to be thankful for the life we still have when I feel like staying in bed and hiding, just like she's doing? I did resent you, Grant, because I thought somehow you were coming out ahead in this situation. I see now that I was wrong. We are all in this together and it is totally up to us to make our lives worth living. Even though I know not getting the chip was the right decision, I feel like a huge loser because I can no longer provide for my family."

"We all feel the same way, Ray," Mark said, trying to comfort his friend. "There's not a single day that I don't question all the decisions I've made. All day long I wonder which thing I maybe could have changed to have my house paid for or been successful enough to maintain my family's way of life."

"I can identify with that," Grant said. "I've worked so hard for the past ten years to make this complex work. In the space of a few hours, I can go from feeling like a failure because I nearly lost it all, to feeling lucky because I was able to find tenants. I try to be positive. It feels phony, but it's the only way I can make myself move forward."

No one spoke for a moment, and then Grant continued. "What I hate is when I wake up during the night and a wave of intense fear comes over me. I have already lost all my retirement accounts and our savings. If the chip went away today, I could never recover. Most of my tenants kicked in money to help pay this place off, so I would not have any income. I could never work enough hours for wages to pay the utilities and keep up with the maintenance. I'm trapped, and I have no cushion to fall back on."

"We're all in the same situation," Mark said, "but I think we're heading the wrong way with this discussion. I'm not saying I don't have all those same feelings because I do, but when I start wondering if our decision to not get the chip was right, I think of my son and his wife. They left everything they owned behind and accepted a call from the Prophet to go to the radiation zone and build a temple. They have sacrificed every material possession they ever had and have never uttered one word of doubt or complaint. They have a little boy that was born out there and they seem so happy. How can I complain about *my* life? I can't. Or at least I try to remember that I shouldn't."

"Are you talking about the crazies on the news? The ones who went to Missouri in a caravan?"

"Yes," Mark said. "They've built a temple in preparation for the second coming of Jesus Christ."

"How are they surviving that radiation? Or is there really no radiation at all?" Grant was very interested, and Mark knew it was the perfect opportunity to share his testimony with his new landlord.

"They received a blessing from the Prophet before they left Salt Lake. The radiation is real, but it doesn't affect them or their son."

"You're serious? They don't have a magic protective chemical?"

"No, Grant. It is faith that keeps them safe. Do you believe the prophecies about Jesus Christ coming back to the Earth?"

"The same prophecies about needing the mark of the beast to buy or sell anything?" Grant rolled his eyes. "I never thought I believed in that stuff, but for some reason I just couldn't go along with the chip. Maybe I need to study a little more and see if I can figure out exactly why I didn't think the chip was a good thing."

"I would be happy to discuss any of that with you any time. In fact, your family could join with the five of us that believe in that stuff. We meet together every Monday evening, study the scriptures, and discuss those prophecies. You are welcome to join us anytime. But right now, I hear a moldy laundry room calling my name."

"Thanks, Mark," Grant said as he stood and followed him to the unfinished task that waited. "I think I would like to hear more about your church. They seem organized and prepared for things before the rest of us even know what's coming. Plus, I watch how you guys act. You all have the same concerns and fears that I do, but you are not scared like I am. Something is helping you feel peace in your heart while the world is falling down around us. I would really like to know more about that."

"Grant, your family is welcome to go to church with my family any time. It would be a great way for your daughter to meet some other kids her age."

The hardest adjustment for either Jordan or Lynne was the attitude of some of their friends.

"Forget them. If they were really your friends, they would never talk to you like that," Lynne told her older sister. Jordan had always been Lynne's protector, and it felt awkward to be consoling her.

"I had it all figured out, remember," sobbed Jordan. "They all said things would stay the same, and we'd find ways to work around the system. They said we could still go shopping and hang out together at the mall. Now they tell me they thought Dad would change his mind and we would be moving back home."

"I'm sorry," Lynne said quietly.

"I told them the chip is exactly what God described in the Bible. They really got mad when I told them I didn't see how they could go to church every week and not understand that. They actually said that having a bank account number beginning with six-six-six had not changed their beliefs or how they lived."

"Forget about them," Lynne said.

"I asked them why they didn't want to be my friend any more if the chip didn't make any difference. I didn't care if they had the chip, but it sure seemed to be a big deal to them because I didn't have one." Jordan's voice was rising in both tone and volume.

"Jordan, don't get so worked up. I'm sure they are still your friends. Maybe one of them was just having a bad day."

"My best friend said I acted like I thought I was better than her. Can you believe that? Does that sound like she was having a bad day?"

"Okay, but don't tell me she's still your best friend. I think I'm even a better friend than that," Lynne said, trying to console her sister.

"No, I can clearly see she's not my best friend any longer." Jordan said amidst a fresh round of sobbing. "It's just, well, she was my last link to our old life. For nearly as long as I can remember I've had the same girl friends, and now the last one is gone, the one who said we would be friends forever, no matter where I lived or what happened."

Lynne waited patiently while Jordan sobbed, and smiled when her sister finally lifted her head. "You know what? There is a girl our age that lives in our building, and she hates this new system, too. Dad said she stays in her room all the time and that's why we've never met her. I think we should go talk to her. She is the owner's daughter, her name is Gina, and maybe she'll be your next best friend."

Jordan shrugged in total defeat. "Okay. Let's go get acquainted."

"Not even. Look at your face. Go put some cold water on your ugly red eyes, and then we can go visit. Maybe we should visit Betsy

Sinclair, too. She is close to our age, and Dad mentioned she is pretty depressed these days."

When the two girls knocked on the manager's apartment, Grant's wife answered. "Come in girls," she said. "What can I do for you?"

"We actually came to see Gina, if she's here," Lynne explained.

Her face lit up so quickly, Lynne had a hard time keeping a straight face. "Yes, of course she's home. This way."

Lynne and Jordan followed Gina's mother, and waited while she knocked on the door, announcing she had visitors. The door slowly opened and Gina looked at them, showing absolutely no emotion.

"I like your room," Jordan said as she stepped through the open door and into Gina's bedroom. "My name is Jordan and this is my sister Lynne. I've just been totally dumped by my so-called friends, and we wondered if you would like to hang out with us for a while? What do you like to do?"

Gina's mother slowly closed the bedroom door. Gina had not said a single word, but Jordan kept talking.

"Lynne and I like to work out, play tennis, and listen to music. By the way, what kind of music do you like? Oh, I see you have some of the same CD's as I do. I guess that gives us something in common."

Gina finally spoke. "I don't think I've ever seen you around here. What apartment do you live in?"

Lynne smiled. "We live on the second floor right next to the stairs. We wondered if there are any other girls our age living here."

Gina shook her head slowly and said, "I don't know. About half of the people moved out when we became CP's. I haven't met any of the people who moved into their apartments. My friend used to live here, but her family moved, and then she said my whole family were fools because we brought hardships on ourselves for no reason at all. I haven't heard from her since."

"Like my sister just told me," Jordan said, "she probably wasn't a very good friend anyway. So how about if we just forget about those people who don't want to be our friends anymore and make our own fun right here?"

Gina smiled and was surprised how strange her face felt. She had not smiled in a long time and was getting pretty tired of feeling so sad. "Why not?"

"So what do you like to do for fun?" Lynne asked.

"I don't know. Everything I liked to do, I can't do any more. Shopping and hanging out at the mall. I was taking some body jam classes but that ended. I was a cheerleader, but now I can't afford the outfits or the special camps. My life is crap."

"Your dad owns this place, right?" Jordan asked.

"Yeah."

"Let's find out if there are other girls our age, and then we can decide what we want to do. I would love to learn body jam," Jordan said. "We were taking slide board classes at the coolest gym, but we can't do that anymore. We have lots of exercise videos, so we could work out together."

"Mom will know if there are other girls living here. Let's go ask her," Gina suggested as she opened her bedroom door.

SURVIVING ISOLATION

"We have a new situation to deal with," Jeff Solomon said to the members of the neighborhood watch group. "When I went to get crime updates from the CBC yesterday, I was told we should be careful about helping people who may seek refuge in our complex."

"What's the CBC?" Ray asked.

"Oh, sorry," Jeff said. "It's the Chipless Barter Community. I go there to get the latest news of what's happening to people like us who are trying to live without having the chip." Jeff looked like the poster child for a neighborhood watch group leader. His demeanor conveyed he was ex-military, and he never let his guard down for a second, even when he was playing tennis. The bulk of his six-foot-four muscle-bound body was intimidating enough, but the way his gray eyes always seemed to look right through a person, and the maturity his silver-gray hair provided made most people think twice before questioning anything Jeff suggested.

"Are you saying we would be in trouble if we help someone trying to get out of the system?"

"I'll get to that. Let me just tell you what I was told. People started cutting the chip out of their arm when they decided they wanted out. That was happening so often, the chip company made a modification to the programming, and then they were able to track a person's whereabouts. They could tell where a person was when they had the chip cut out. So, next thing you know, the doctor who cut the chip out is suddenly in jail, or dead, or his whole office just accidentally burned to the ground."

"And that's happening a lot now?"

"Yes. We can still let people join our group; we just have to make sure they don't remove their chip anywhere in our neighborhood. Otherwise, the authorities will come down on our entire group."

"It sounds like some of our fears are now reality," Grant said. "Did he say why people are trying to get the chip out of their wrist?"

"Yes. It's because of the changes that have been made. The dollar has now been replaced by a worldwide currency, and when the New World Order leader broke the peace agreement that has been in place for several years, that threw the entire world economy into a mess. Now there are rules that regulate how much of your money you can donate, and who you can donate to. If the *authorities* decide a religious speaker should not be supported, he becomes a blocked vendor and is instantly out of business. Sounds exactly like what we were afraid of."

"So, we can still let new members in?" Mark asked.

"If we're careful. We cannot let them remove their chip on our premises. I was told many new neighborhoods are starting up, big ones and little ones, and we should be very careful about accepting new people because spies are being sent out to infiltrate neighborhoods and then report back who lives there." Jeff shook his head and said, "I think we were smart to not get a chip in the first place, but it's easy to see those in charge have no intention of just letting us be."

Mark stood and said, "My church has its own communication system, and last week we were told that even though the states are no longer sovereign entities, several states have gone bankrupt and been completely absorbed by the federal government. The government takes over their hospitals and every aspect of health care, jails and transportation systems. The state government is disbanded. And not one word about any of it is ever reported on the regular news." Mark walked back and forth while he continued to talk. "What the federal government is doing really scares me. The constitution has always been the one thing that made America different from any other nation in the world. I've always believed it was written by men inspired by God, and now the government acts like it's totally irrelevant."

"You know I'm not a religious person like some of you," Jeff said, "but I was willing to live like a third-world refugee rather than let the government tell me what I could or could not do. I thought being an American still meant something. But, after talking to the CBC today, I don't know that the United States is even considered a separate country any longer. All anyone talks about now is the world government and what's good for the *world*. There's never any mention of what's good for America."

"There is no news any more, just propaganda," Ray said. "It sounds like the radio broadcasts after World War Two that said we had to have the big work programs from the government or our country would fail. Only now, they're saying how smart people are to have recognized that the chip is the best thing that has ever happened to them because they don't have to carry money around, so no more fraud or corruption."

"I think brainwashing everyone is corruption. On the *news* yesterday, one of the *authorities* said that anyone who doesn't have a chip is a religious fanatic and is guilty of forcing self-inflicted hardships on their children, so it may become necessary to remove the poor innocent children from their homes in order to insure their safety."

"Well," Jeff said, "I don't think they're powerful enough to take our kids away from us yet, but if they're successful in keeping the truth out of the news media, it's not hard to imagine that they'll soon start trying to do that very thing."

"When I lost my job," Mark said, "my wife and I took all the money we could find and stockpiled food. Now that's not possible any longer. The six-six-six accounts prevent people from taking out large sums of money. They say it's to prevent a run on markets and to help insure stabilization. But it certainly makes it difficult for anyone already in the system to walk away from it."

Ray slammed the table with his fist, and then said, "And now they track where people go?"

"Right. They claimed that was necessary for terrorist control," Jeff said. "But now you can't do anything without the government knowing your every action. That's even worse than cameras on every corner."

Ray sighed and then said, "So when people remove their chip they will become enemies of the government, with no money to get help, and the only ones who would consider helping them are the ones who already walked away from the establishment and have no money. Pretty good strangle-hold, I'd say."

Mark stood and said, "I, for one, have no stomach for talking about how terrible things are. I have a lovely wife, I am free to worship as I choose, and I have a very nice place to live, thanks to you, Grant. And, speaking of my wife, I can think of lots I could be doing with her that would be more fun than sitting around here getting all depressed. I hope this meeting is about finished!"

"Finished, it is," Jeff said.

"I may never be able to wire a power box again. I think all my fingers are permanently molded into a giant 'C' from holding a sledge hammer," Ray said. "I'm just glad we're finally done."

"I'm feeling a few muscles that I've never noticed before," Mark said. "Still, it's worth it if it keeps vandals out of our neighborhood."

Mark and Ray sat in the cool grass to rest.

"What is it about anyone who tries to buck the system that incites people to begin the abuse?" Ray asked. "I know it's been happening forever, but it reminds me of the early members of the Church. They just wanted to be left alone to practice their freedom of religion that was guaranteed by the constitution, but never seemed to be able to do that without having mobs snapping at their heels. Now here we are, determined to make our own way without the chip and that seems to bother a lot of people."

"Strange, isn't it?" Mark asked. "Especially since we've totally removed ourselves from their world. We barter to meet our needs, we don't ask anyone to help take care of us, and yet they seem unable to just let us be. And now we have to create our own security."

"Having a fence around our entire neighborhood with a single entrance makes it easier to monitor who comes and goes. I don't suppose there's any guarantee it will keep everyone out, but it will make it harder to drive a car through this fence again. And all the new lighting should help intimidate intruders."

"I'm going to sleep better tonight," Mark said as he slowly stood.

At the next neighborhood meeting, Jeff announced there were several issues that needed to be resolved. "There's a sheet coming around and each man needs to sign up for at least two nights a week to stand guard at the new security entrance. We'll meet in this corner after the meeting to answer any questions. Next on our agenda is our kids' schooling."

Jenny stood. "For those of you who do not have a child in school, I would like to tell you what it's like for our students there. They are not allowed to ride the bus to school. They are not allowed to use any of the supplies provided at school. They're not protected from the bullies who feel they have the right to pick on them, knock them around, and take anything they can from our kids. The school cannot legally forbid them from being there, but they do not have to do anything for them because they are not in the system. So, a few of us here in our neighborhood have been talking about forming our own school. Please raise your hand if you've been a teacher, worked in a school in any function, or ever been taught how to teach anything?"

Nearly half of those in the room raised their hand.

"That's wonderful! If you're interested in getting involved in teaching our kids, please meet me in that corner after this meeting is over," Jenny said as she indicated the corner farthest away from where the security people would be meeting. "If you have no experience or training, but are interested in helping or want to know what's happening with this project, please feel free to join us."

Jeff stood and said, "All right, is that it? Anybody else want to say anything before we leave?"

"I would," Jordan said from the back of the group.

"Tell us who you are," Jeff said.

"I'm Jordan. Mark and Jenny are my parents."

"Okay, then," Jeff stated. "Come on up here so we can all see you."

Jordan walked to the front of the room, catching her mom's eye as she walked past her. "I would just like to ask if anyone would be interested in forming our own group to exercise and work out together. My sister and I have lots of DVDs. It's always more fun to do that together, and maybe we could use this room. It's about the biggest room in our neighborhood. Is anyone interested?"

"Is it just for girls?" an obviously male voice asked.

"Nope, for anyone interested in working out and having some fun."

Lynne's hand shot up as high as she could possibly raise it. "I'm interested." As if no one wanted to be first, once Lynne's hand was raised, ten or fifteen others indicated they were interested.

"I see no reason you can't use this room," Jeff said. "It's used by some folks off and on, but I'm sure we can schedule a time for you."

"Thanks." Jordan smiled and sat in an empty chair by Jenny.

"Anybody else?" Jeff asked. He waited about ten seconds, and then said, "Okay, we're done. Let's meet again a week from now so we can see how the patrols and school things are coming along."

Hardly anyone left the room; they simply migrated to a group gathering in one of the corners. The young people decided to go outside and discuss their plans.

"Wait a minute," Jeff's voice boomed over the lively conversations beginning. "I just want to ask if everyone agrees that the young people can use the electricity to run their DVDs in here. I hadn't thought of that earlier and I think we should all have a say about that."

"Let's take a vote," Grant offered.

"Okay," Jeff agreed. "If you think it's okay for the kids to run their DVD for one hour each day for exercising, raise your hand."

Jordan held her breath as she looked back at the group from the doorway. Every hand was raised and most were smiling at the group of young people ready to leave the room.

"Okay, Jordan," Jeff said, and then he smiled. "Please limit your viewing to no more than one hour each day, seven days a week, or maybe two hours on Saturday if you don't think you'll be getting together on Sunday. Will you please be aware of what the young people are watching, Jenny, since Jordan is your daughter?"

"I will," Jenny said.

"Thanks, everyone," Jordan shouted, and then hurried through the door with Lynne. "That sounds to me like we can exercise five days a week and maybe get together and watch a movie on Saturday. Do you think that's why he told Mom to be aware of what we're viewing?"

"That's what it sounded like to me. This will be a lot of fun!"

During dinner that evening, Jenny said, "I never thought I'd be involved in teaching kids. The group of people that met after the meeting was so excited about being able to teach our kids here, where it's safer. There are seven teachers that have taught in regular schools, and there are enough people like me to provide one helper for each teacher. That will allow more of us to be involved and probably be a better environment for the kids to learn in. More individual help."

"Where will the school be?" Mark asked.

"In the community room. Not ideal, but I think the kids will be happy they don't have to go to school outside our little neighborhood. It's scary for most of them. I'm going to meet with the principal and the School Board to see what we need to do to make our little school official. It's the same as home schooling, and there are materials and curriculum already set up that we can use as a guideline."

"Are you going to be in the community room all day during the week?" Jordan asked.

"Yes," Jenny said, but then smiled at the expression that suddenly covered her daughter's face. "We're going to have school from eight in the morning until two in the afternoon. You can have your turn in the room at three o'clock each afternoon if you want. Will that work?"

"Yes," Jordan said, looking very relieved. "Mom, do you think Jeff thought we would be exercising for two hours on Saturday?"

"I asked him about that after the meeting," Jenny said. "The way he worded that seemed funny, so I asked him what he meant by *viewing*. He said he figured that as long as I monitored what you were watching, he didn't care if it was workout tapes or movies. However, he really did not think you should watch movies every day. Sounds like you got a bonus. Exercise during the week and movie time on Saturday."

"I told you," Lynne said. "He did a good deed for us. Did you see him smile? We should do something nice for him in return."

"And how did your security meeting go?" Jenny asked Mark. "Did you get a lot of volunteers?"

"We did, and each person only has to do it once a week, from ten in the evening until six in the morning. There will be three men on patrol each night. I don't know what we can do if someone tries to get in, but we have to try to protect our little neighborhood."

"I know it's legal here in Utah to carry a gun," Jenny said. "Will you be armed?"

"Yes, but we're determined to not use our guns. We are afraid that if we actually shot anyone the police would come down on us, and maybe even take our guns away. We cannot take the risk of losing our guns in case we really need them some time to defend our families' lives. Right now we're just talking about property being damaged."

Jenny started laughing, and when she tried to speak, she laughed even harder. Finally, she calmed down enough to talk. "It's like we've gone back a hundred years, only science fiction style. On one side of the street is this little country town where we have a one-room school for all the grades." She started laughing again, but continued after a minute. "We have our militia that keeps watch over our town. We have our little general store like on 'Little House on the Prairie' where we take our food and trade for other things we want to buy. But right across the street is the twenty-first century house with modern cars driving around, and every house has a satellite dish on their roof, and they go shopping at the mall." She laughed again, and for a moment, it sounded like it had nearly turned to crying. She took a deep breath and said, "If it wasn't so sad and ironic, it might be funny."

"We're ready to start our meeting," Jeff said, and the low rumble of conversations stopped instantly. "Our first report is from Jenny."

Jenny stepped to the front of the group and smiled. "We're having so much success. We have seven teachers, an aide for each teacher, and three other women who have taken on the challenge of keeping required records for the school district. Now that we have declared ourselves as a home school organization, we have access to last year's supplies from the official home schooling association. As much as people are against those of us who do not have the chip, no one wants our children to suffer because of our stupidity, so they are willing to help us a little. Everything's going great."

She sat down and the group spontaneously began clapping. That had never happened in one of their meetings before, and Jenny stood back up and thanked them.

"Any other business?" Jeff asked.

"Just a quick little announcement. I am Nathan, and Grant is my dad. I was wondering if any of the kids in the exercise group would be interested in joining the men who have been playing tennis for several months. If you are interested, we practice at the two courts we built on the south end of our complex and we will be there Saturday morning.

We'll determine what skill level everyone has and divide into teams. Please join us if you are sixteen or older and interested in playing. Oh, and if any of you don't have a racket, talk to me after this meeting so we can find one for you before Saturday. Several folks in our neighborhood have rackets they would be willing to loan you."

"He's kind of cute, don't you think?" Jordan said quietly to Lynne.

Lynne made a sound that clearly indicated her disagreement. "He's got to be at least twenty-five years old."

"I know," Jordan answered, watching Nathan return to his seat.

Several nights later, Mark was awakened from a deep sleep by strange noises. He could hear cars speeding by the neighborhood, honking their horns and squealing their tires. He was out of bed in a flash and pulled on a pair of jeans and his shoes, then grabbed a sweatshirt as he headed for the front door.

"What's going on?" Jenny asked as she sat up. "Mark?"

"I'll be right back," he called as he pulled the door shut behind him.

He ran the short distance to the main entry gate and found the three men who were on patrol standing in the shadows of the community building. "What's all the commotion?" he asked as he joined them.

"Not certain yet," Jeff answered. "Cars keep rushing the gate but nobody's broken through. Looks like a lot of commotion down at the other end of our neighborhood, but we don't dare leave here because they keep buzzing this end of the fence. It looks organized. Now that you're here, we could go check it out. That will leave two here."

"Do you want me and Ray to go?" Mark asked Jeff."

"Sounds like a good idea. We'll stay here."

Mark and Ray moved cautiously away. When they had gone about six blocks, they could see an orange glow big enough to suggest at least one house was on fire. They moved through the back yards of the houses closest to the fence and road. After sneaking through the darkness for another block, they saw people running in and out of houses, screaming and shouting.

"We have to get closer so we can see what's happening," Ray said.

"I agree," Mark whispered. "It doesn't look good."

They crept forward through two more yards and came to the end of the block. What they saw looked like a war zone.

"Look at the fence along the road," Ray said as he stood up and began running across the street.

"Ray, what are you doing?"

"Come on, Mark. The people that did this are gone. Look at the hole in the fence."

Mark followed Ray, still unsure of what was happening. The fence was completely gone in front of three houses. Two houses were on fire and the windows were broken in the two houses between him and the fires. There was a large group of people gathering near the blazing houses, and several people were lying on the ground nearby.

After a few minutes, Ray spoke into his walkie-talkie. "The guys that did this left a few minutes ago, but they've killed several people and . . . and raped some women. Two houses are burning."

Mark saw five bodies on the ground and someone began covering them with sheets. A man standing close to him said, "They cut down the fence and then ran into those two houses and shot the people that lived there. Cold blooded murder. No reason. Just vile, evil people."

Mark turned to console the man. His face was bloody and his cheeks were streaked from his tears. "Are you all right?"

"Don't worry about me. I tried to stop them. When I tried to pull one of them off of a woman he was raping, he got a little upset."

"Do you live in one of those houses that are burning?" Mark asked.

"No."

"Come with me," Mark encouraged as he led the man a few steps closer to the group of people. "Sit down here." He helped the man to the ground and then shouted, "Do any of you know this man?"

The people in the group turned – one woman's face was also bloodied, and Mark felt as though he were in a nightmare.

"Henry," the woman said. "This is my neighbor." She knelt beside him as she spoke to Mark. "He ran right out of his house after them. I thought they were going to kill him. I'm so sorry," she said, looking back at her neighbor. The woman totally broke down and cried aloud. "They shot my son when he tried to help." Her sobs filled the air as she wept.

Mark heard the sound of feet running toward him, and he jumped to his feet and turned, ready to fight.

"It's just me," Jeff shouted. "Help's on the way."

Jeff immediately moved to the group of people still standing like statues, watching the houses burn to the ground. "Who lives in that house?" he shouted, pointing at the house furthest away from them.

"They're dead, right over there," a man said flatly, pointing at the covered bodies. "A man and his wife. They shot them both."

"Who lives in the house next to it?" Jeff continued.

"They're dead, too," the same man said, again pointing to the bodies on the ground.

"And who lives here," Jeff said, pointing to the house they were all standing in front of.

"I do," the same man again answered.

"Are you okay? Is anyone still in your house?"

The man slowly moved his head to look at Jeff for the first time. "I didn't think she was home. They both went to help with the party for the kids. I thought she was still gone, and then I heard her screaming."

"Your wife? Did they hurt your wife?" Jeff asked.

"They were on top of her, in the front yard. Mike ran after them when he heard her screaming, but they shot him. I tried to help her, too, and they shot me."

Jeff put his arm around the man's waist and walked toward Mark. A wound was visible on his arm, near his shoulder. "Sit here, against the tree," Jeff instructed. "Mark, can you put a pressure dressing on this man's arm. He's been shot, and his son was killed. I think, excuse me," Jeff said to the woman Mark had been helping, "is this your husband?"

"Yes, he tried to help Mike but they shot him. Then they..." and she again began sobbing. "Why did they do that? I never did anything to them. Why did they do that to me?"

"Mark," Jeff said, "can you make sure he stays sitting against the tree. Don't let this wound get lower than his heart, okay?"

"Sure," Mark said. "This man over here looks like his head got hit pretty hard. What should I do for him?"

"Just keep him warm, if you can. We've got a few folks notifying everyone about what's happened and we should be getting some medical folks here to help pretty soon."

Jeff knelt down to talk to the woman who was now consoling her husband. "Do you know if this man you were just talking to had any other family members in the house?"

She looked at him for a moment without speaking, and then said, "Just him and his wife. All the kids were at a sleep over down the block. Everybody went there. Our two girls are there. They never got hurt. His girls are there, too. His wife is still helping, we were both helping, but I came home early. I should have stayed there longer."

"You just rest. I think you'll be fine," Jeff comforted. He left the three in Mark's care and moved back to the group to see if he could learn what had happened. One young man seemed less traumatized by the scene everyone was watching. Jeff touched him on the shoulder and asked, "Can you tell me what happened?"

The young man stepped away from the group and Jeff followed him. "Yes, I can tell you what happened. We organized a sleep over for all the young kids in this block, and some of us went over and cooked dinner for them. We tried to make it a fun night. We watched a movie after dinner and then they danced for a while. I was just coming back to go to bed, and when I stepped outside I could hear the commotion. Three cars were parked along the fence and the fence had been cut down, just like you see it. There was screaming and I could smell the fire. When I ran around the corner of the house, I could see the men running from the houses. They took whatever they could carry and threw it in their cars and left. The two houses on the end were on fire, and the people that lived there were laying in the front yard. From what I've learned, they broke into the two houses on the end, actually pulled the women outside and raped them, and then when their husbands came out of the house, they shot them."

"So four of those bodies are the husbands and wives from the two burning houses?" Jeff asked, trying to remain distance from the senseless violence displayed all around him.

"Yup. While that was going on, the rest of the despicable creatures went into these two houses and started breaking the windows. They pulled the woman out that lived in the house next to the burning one, pulled her right out on the front lawn and raped her." The man's voice caught and he was overcome with the emotions. "They raped . . ." He was now sobbing and his continuing story was delivered in broken sentences. "Sylvia here," he said, pointing at the woman sitting with her husband, "and when her son came out of the house to help her, they killed him. Then her husband came running out and they shot him. He fell on the front porch. That's where I found him."

"I'm sorry to make you keep talking," Jeff said quietly. "But I'm one of the security patrol and I'm trying to piece it all together."

"Well, this house on the end, Jeremy lives there. He was alone in the house when they started looting. He had his own gun and started shooting at them from his bedroom, but they managed to hit him with a pipe. He seems to be okay. His wife was not here and I have no idea if she even knows what's happened. It's unbelievable that they would come in here and do this. Like spawn of the devil. There is nothing to be gained by hurting these people. None of us have anything worth stealing, and certainly nothing worth killing for."

"I don't think they need a reason," Jeff said quietly. "Are you all right? Is there anything we can do for any of these people?"

"No," the young man offered. "The houses will burn to the ground because the firemen will never come to help put out the fires. Luckily, the houses are far enough apart that nobody else's house will catch on fire. We'll go get the kids from the party and make sure everybody has a place to stay tonight. What can we do but try to pick up the pieces and move on? Those men will probably be back again. I mean, they have raped three women and killed five people and no one will ever charge them for any of it. Burned two houses down, and nothing. Stolen everything they could carry and no one will ever punish them."

"I know," Jeff said. "We're going to help you fix the fence and maybe tomorrow we can get together and talk about how we can all join together to protect our entire neighborhood. We have a neighborhood group organized, but not everyone participates. Men patrol every night and I think it's time every person gets involved so we'll all be better protected." Jeff patted the young man's shoulder and said, "I'll come see you tomorrow. We will be safer if everyone works together. Where do you live?"

"Right there," he said, pointing to the house across the street.

"Okay, I'll be back tomorrow." Jeff walked toward Mark. Several neighbors had arrived and were beginning to help their injured friends. They found Ray and then headed to their end of the neighborhood.

"This is serious," Ray said. "I'm beginning to think the guys that crashed through our fence awhile ago were just testing the waters. I remember we had bats and shovels to fight them off with, and they probably saw that and decided this area was easy pickings."

"They learned a few more things tonight," Jeff reminded Ray. "They learned that there were only three guards, so as long as all three of us were stuck down here waiting for them to break through, they knew there was nobody guarding the other end of the fence. Tomorrow I am going from house to house and get every single man involved in our patrols. Even though our neighborhood is small, we don't really know the people who don't already participate in our group, and we all need to share responsibility for protecting each other."

"I can't even imagine how those men felt when they saw their wives pulled out in the front yard and raped. What has this world come to?" Mark could not get that image out of his mind. "They're like animals, not humans."

"Mark," Jeff said, "I don't know how you can even be surprised by any of this after living here all this time. You've seen how they treated our kids in school and how the police ignore us. How long did you think it would be before the thugs decided this was a safe playground for them? We have to wise up and get ourselves armed and trained. We need to learn how to strike the first blow when punks break into our neighborhood. Either that or you might as well take your family to the park across the street and spend the night camping out on the lawn. We are easy targets, and the only thing that stands between them and us is that puny security fence, which they can drive through or cut down. Not a big deterrent."

"I know, Jeff. I just never realized how vulnerable my wife and daughters are. I have never sat down and figured out whether or not I could protect them from men who have no conscience. Now there are five people dead. I have to take a step back and rethink what's required of me, what I have to do to better protect my family, physically."

Jeff put his arm around Mark's shoulder and continued walking. "Hey, man, I'm way too mouthy. It just eats me up inside when I see what is happening these days, and what gets ignored. You're all right,

Mark. We all contribute what we can to make life work around here. You don't have to be superman." They never spoke for a time, and then Jeff said, "As long as you keep feeding me, I'll try to be superman." He laughed, and even though it sounded hollow and wrong, Mark and Ray laughed with him.

When Mark got home, Jenny was anxiously waiting for him in the living room. "What's going on out there?" she asked as she stood and hurried toward him.

"I'm so upset right now that I don't think I can tell you about what happened." Mark hugged Jenny and fought to keep from losing control of his emotions. "There were some guys that got into the other end of the neighborhood and hurt some people. Can I ask you to let me try to get some rest and we can talk about it in the morning? I want you to know that I love you and our girls so much, and I'm very concerned about my ability to keep you safe."

"Yes, of course."

"I'm going to sit here on the couch and try to clear my mind. Why don't you go back to bed and I'll be in soon."

Jenny hugged him, kissed him gently, and returned to the bedroom.

Mark sank down on the couch and tried to come to grips with everything that had happened. He found himself starting to pray but then his mind toggled between praying and trying to find a solution that would better protect his family and the community. Eventually, his mind drifted into a dream...

A village had barely survived the latest attack, and as Mark walked along a street he could see people digging through the rubble of their destroyed houses looking for their family members who had been killed. This was not the first attack the village had experienced, but he knew that each one was more devastating than the one before, and he knew it would be a miracle if the village could withstand even one more. Mark was aware this village was not his home, but what he was looking at reminded him of pictures he had seen of the ruins discovered in South America. Even though he was a stranger, no one seemed to even notice his presence as he walked along.

Suddenly, he was aware the night had passed and it was morning. Now Mark found himself inside a large stone-walled room filled with the men of the city who were frantically discussing how to protect their wives and children. The fear and vulnerability were apparent on every face Mark looked at, but again it was as though he were an invisible spectator rather than a participant in the meeting. A man who could only be described as a majestic warrior stood and raised his hands slowly in front of him, and every conversation quieted. He looked stronger than anyone else in the room, and when he began speaking, his confidence was apparent. He described cities in other parts of the country where he had designed fortifications to help protect the inhabitants from invading armies. Explaining how it had been successful in those cities, he said he would be more than willing to help them.

Everyone gathered around the warrior and he began describing in detail how to move the people into the center portion of the city and fortify it with secure walls. That would make it easier for the men to defend their wives and children, and having everyone together in a smaller area would make their resistance more effective. As Mark watched the warrior speaking, he found he was no longer standing outside the group and observing their actions. Now he was sitting close enough to the warrior to make eye contact. When the warrior finished talking, he looked directly at Mark and nodded, as though he were indicating he had finished his explanation and Mark now had all the information he needed.

Time seemed to quickly advance and again Mark became a spectator. He watched as the ancient warrior taught the men of the village, and then he continued to watch as they built great walls that included shooting or archery towers with a platform that ran along the inside of the entire wall. Time seemed to slip forward again, and now Mark was watching the same village in the midst of another attack from an invading army. From some distant vantage point, he could see that the fortifications were successful in protecting those inside, and he knew he had to seek out the ancient warrior and thank him.

Mark awoke with a start. The dream had seemed so real he was surprised to find himself back in his apartment. He looked around the room for the mighty warrior, disappointed that he could no longer feel the calm assurance that had emanated from him. He tried to separate his mind from the dream, but the terrible events he had seen a few hours earlier seemed more unreal than the dream. He realized there was something more to the dream, something he needed to understand, and he dropped to his knees and began to pray. "Please help me understand why I feel such a connection and regard for the warrior. What am I supposed to gain from this dream?"

After some time, he went in the bedroom and found Jenny was just waking up. He lay down next to her and pulled her close to him. He was again overwhelmed with his awareness of how vulnerable she and his daughters were in their present environment.

"What happened last night?" Jenny asked. "You're trembling. Can you tell me what happened?"

"It was worse than terrible. Three men were shot and killed. Three women were raped and two of them died. It made me face the fact that I am not capable of protecting you here."

The sound that escaped from Jenny's lips echoed the fear and uncertainty Mark was feeling, and they hugged each other tightly.

"I had a dream after I finally went to sleep on the couch and it seems to weigh as heavily on my mind as what I saw last night. My mind keeps going in circles and I don't know what it all means."

"I can't imagine how a dream could be worse than what happened. Would it help if you told me about the dream?"

"The dream wasn't worse than what happened here, but it plays in my mind as much as those terrible scenes from last night. I saw a village that resembled the ancient ruins in South America. After the village was attacked, it was modified with structured walls that withstood the next attack. I watched as the warfare strategy and the purpose of the protective walls were explained by a warrior."

"And you think something from that dream will help us?"

"Maybe. Right now everything is going around and around in my head. I'm way too wired to sleep, so how about you trying to get a little more rest and I'm going to try to put some of this stuff down on paper. Maybe that will help me understand it better."

"Okay, but you look so tired," Jenny said.

"I'll be fine, at least as fine as anyone else in our neighborhood."

Mark kissed his wife and then went back into the living room, grabbed a notebook, and began sketching what he had seen in his dream. As he sketched, he vividly remembered the ancient warrior nodding at him, as though every word he had spoken was meant specifically for Mark. The same feelings of regard and gratitude returned, and his mind cleared.

"It wasn't just a dream," Mark said to himself. "This will work for us. Thank you. I don't know who you are, but thank you."

Mark sat looking at his notes, grateful for the information he had been given. Suddenly, as though someone had actually spoken words to him, he received a thought. *The Book of Mormon was written for your day and contains the information the Lord knew you would need.* The gratitude he had been feeling faded after realizing he should have already known what had just been whispered to him. He was grateful but slightly embarrassed that he had not recognized that the needed answer was already available.

Words from the Book of Mormon seemed to pass in front of his eyes, descriptions of the conditions in the world in the last days before the Savior returns to the Earth. The world was filled with extreme corruption and the wicked threatened to annihilate all the righteous. The story of Moroni described the same types of situations that currently existed, as well as what would be required to overcome it – only the names and places were different. A wicked man named Amalickiah made false promises and flattered the people. Moroni became angry and tore his coat to make a flag. On it he wrote: "In memory of our God, our religion, and freedom, and our peace, our wives, and our children." He fastened the flag to a pole and called it the title of liberty. Then, dressed in his battle armor, he prayed to God, asking Him to allow the people to keep the freedom they had. When Moroni finished praying, he went among the people, waving the title of liberty in the air. He cried out, "Whosoever will maintain this title upon the land, let them come forth in the strength of the Lord, and enter into a covenant that they will maintain their rights, and their religion, that the Lord God may bless them." The people came running, dressed in their armor and tearing their cloaks as a symbol of the covenant they were making to obey the Lord. They gathered around Captain Moroni, ready to defend their freedom.

No wonder we are told to constantly read the Book of Mormon. Everything that was experienced in Moroni's time is pertinent to what is happening in the world today. That is why the Lord preserved those records for us.

As soon as Mark thought Jeff might be awake, he walked to his apartment and knocked on the door. When Jeff opened the door, it was obvious he had not slept much either. "Sorry to bother you, Jeff. You look as worried as I feel about this entire situation."

"Yes," Jeff said as he opened the door, motioning Mark to enter. "If we can't come up with something that provides more security for our entire neighborhood, we won't survive another attack like that one."

Mark could not help but smile when Jeff's words seemed to echo the feelings he had heard expressed by the inhabitants of the village he had seen in his dream. "I may have an idea for you."

The expression on Jeff's face was easy to read: *You could hardly cope with what was happening last night, and now you think you have an idea that will help us?* Mark knew he probably should feel more fearful, but he was suddenly filled with confidence as he handed his notebook to Jeff.

"I know this is going to sound as though I've gone entirely mad, but I had a dream last night about a village in some ancient civilization that was being attacked by an army. They were exactly where we are – one more good attack and it's over. But a warrior taught them how to build fortifications to protect themselves, and I saw that they worked."

Jeff was slowly turning the pages of Mark's notebook, and finally looked up. "You dreamed this stuff?"

Mark nodded and smiled. "Do you think it will work?"

Jeff nodded, stood and walked toward the door. "Come on, Mark. We're going to call a meeting of the men in our village."

Mark found it easy to explain the concept to the group that later gathered in the community center. After explaining how the fortifications would help, he said, "What we need to do is vacate all the houses on the outside perimeter of our neighborhood and relocate those families into houses that have extra room. Then we remove everything except the outside wall of each house on the perimeter, and connect them with the building materials we remove. We'll end up with a secure wall around the entire perimeter of our neighborhood. Any single-story house will be built up to the level of the two-story buildings, and we'll build a platform on the upper level so we can keep watch through the windows. We'll build stairwells to provide access to the platform at several locations along the wall."

Mark was put in charge of overseeing the construction. The fact that he received the instruction in a dream did not seem to bother anyone. In fact, it seemed obvious to everyone that the dream had been more than fantasy, that it had been Divine guidance to help them protect their families. The work continued day and night, especially at night, to let any intruders know they would face a large group of men if they attacked again.

As soon as the continuous walkway was completed, the men gathered in the community center. By now, members from every household in their entire neighborhood were working together as a single unit. Jeff explained how the watch patrols would work, but he sensed there was some confusion.

"Does everyone understand the importance of being able to see the guard to your left and the guard to your right every minute during the night?" he asked. He waited for a moment and when no one spoke, he continued. "So far, each time someone attacks our neighborhood, they gain a little more information about us. They learned that if they could find out where the patrols were, they could break through the fence someplace else and there wouldn't be anyone guarding there."

"So, maybe I'm dense," someone stated, "but when there were three men standing watch together, we had safety in numbers. Now you want us to stand by ourselves, far enough away from another person that we can just see them? That sounds to me like we'll be easier to pick off."

"Fair comment," Jeff said. He closed his eyes and was silent for a moment and then he smiled. He reached behind him and picked up a cup filled with dice that had been piled with other games in the corner of the counter. He dumped the dice into one hand and turned the empty dice cup upside down on the table. "This is our neighborhood." He laid the dice on the table and said, "These are the members of our security patrol." Everyone chuckled at his visual aid and he grimaced.

He arranged the dice in groups of three and set them on four sides of the dice cup. "This is how we've been operating. You can see the wide spaces where there is no protection. Now if we spread the dice out so they are evenly spaced around the cup," he said as he rearranged the dice, "there are no spaces left without protection. Each guard can see the person on his left and the person on his right."

"Oh, I get it," the lone dissenter agreed.

"Okay, now if each guard has a gun and shoots anything that tries to come through the wall, what do you think the gangs will do?"

"Shoot us before they try to break through the wall."

"You may be right, but at least when they shoot one of us, there will be two other guards who see it happen and will shoot back. All we have to do is shoot anyone who tries to get inside our wall. If we do that every single time someone tries to get in, they'll stop trying."

Grant stood. "It's this simple. We shoot them or they shoot us."

"There's one other thing to consider," Mark said as he slowly stood. "When those families were killed a while back, I saw their bodies laying in their own front yards. I saw the woman they raped, the one whose son was killed when he tried to come to her aid. I have not been able to forget the look on their faces. If these gangs get through our perimeter wall, if they kill us, it will be our wives and our daughters that are drug outside and raped. Picture that clearly in your minds, my friends. Picture your wife being raped by some animal. Is that worth standing at this fence every other night, gun in hand, to try to prevent?"

Mark sat down and there was complete silence in the room.

"I was there that night, with Mark," Jeff said. "I don't want that scene to ever be repeated in our neighborhood. They torched two houses and looted two more, just for fun. We win, or they win."

Within days, all the stairs needed to provide access to the shooting platform were completed. The next night Mark stood between Ray and Jeff for eight hours. Several times cars rushed the fence, but gunshots fired from the windows encouraged the drivers of the cars to leave the area. Those inside the cars could be heard laughing as they drove away. Every other night Mark took his turn guarding the fence.

Outside the isolated neighborhood, the government continued its downward spiral. Utah's state government collapsed, and the state became an inseparable part of the federal government. Any state employee the federal government chose not to keep was unemployed.

"It won't be long before the entire country is run by one central government. If the Constitution is not completely irrelevant, it's barely hanging on by a thread," Ray lamented one night while on guard duty.

"That could never have happened if people had refused to get the chip," Mark said. "Soon we'll be hearing how the federal government has given control of our country to some one-world order government. How much longer will it be until the Savior returns and ends this madness?"

"I don't know," Ray said. "How many people died trying to reach the Salt Lake Valley? How many struggled and sacrificed their whole lives to help Utah become a state?"

"How many were now rejoicing because the people of Utah are just a drop in the bucket of the one-world power that looms on the horizon? Life has become a fight for survival, just as Jenny described it. She described the security patrol as the militia that kept watch over the town. Now we truly have evolved into a gun-toting, night-patrolling, ever protecting militia."

Four cars sped by, their engines racing and then stopping a short distance away. Mark's heart raced and he pulled the gun from his jacket pocket. Would he really be able to shoot a person, end their life, if they tried to get through the perimeter wall? The men climbing out of the parked cars immediately made their intentions clear.

"We're coming in," one of them shouted. "So if you don't want to die, back off. Run home!" A dozen men were running toward the wall in two separate groups, axes and hatchets in hand, and some were waving guns above their heads.

"Leave, or we'll shoot you," Jeff's voice boomed in the darkness.

The gang members laughed and continued toward the wall. When one of them reached his destination, he raised his ax and prepared to break through the wall. A shot rang out and he fell backwards.

"You're dead!" another gang member shouted as he aimed for the window Jeff had fired from. Another shot rang out and he fell, a bright red spot visible in the middle of his forehead.

"They shot him!" members of the gang shouted. They aimed and shot at the windows along the wall.

When the third member of their group fell onto the street, dead, the rest ran for their cars. The screech of squealing tires filled the air.

No one moved. They had just killed three men. Mark's voice rang out clearly. "No one is going to get to my wife unless I am dead!"

The same sort of attack occurred again nine days later, and two members of the gang were left behind, lying dead in the street. After that, there were no additional attacks for a long time.

ADAM-ONDI-AHMAN

With the neighborhood now more secure, the men in the apartment complex found time for minor repairs.

"Do you remember your concern that Grant was going to be sitting pretty after the world got back to normal?" Mark asked Ray.

"Yeah, seems like a different lifetime, doesn't it?" Ray tightened the last screw on the circuit box cover. "Now it's easy to see how foolish it was to even try to make plans for the future. There is no way we could have ever dreamed our lives would play out like this. Why do you ask?"

"I was just looking at the headlines in this paper from last week. A tsunami wiped an entire island clean. No survivors. It's unbelievable how the Earth seems to be tearing itself apart."

"Right," Ray said as he shut the lid of his toolbox. He sat down across from Mark and turned the newspaper so he could read the headlines. "My wife was telling me last night that some of the major insurance companies have gone bankrupt and shut their doors because of the huge storms that have hit here in the U.S."

"Do you think they collapsed because of the number of claims or because of the huge reduction in the number of people who can afford to pay their premiums? I know many people thought getting a chip embedded in their wrist would guarantee a secure future for them and their families. Now they seem to be facing huge cuts in pay with absolutely no recourse."

Ray laughed. "And having a chip doesn't guarantee there will be food to buy. I guess it was a bad idea to import so much of our food from other countries. When they have problems, we don't eat very well."

"I find it quite amusing that man is so arrogant he thought he could control the entire world. What good is it to control the money when the land your empire sits on slides into the ocean?"

"You know, the hardest thing I've gone through so far was watching Nathan's whole life fall apart in front of my eyes. It was almost more than I could take." Ray chuckled and then added, "I guess watching him start living again has helped a lot. How do you feel about him dating your daughter?"

Mark answered with a smile. "I think Nathan is a very nice young man. Jordan seems to be happier, too. The world must seem claustrophobically small to all these kids when you compare it with what their lives were like before the chip. The Internet and cell phones put the entire world at their fingertips, and then it was reduced to one square mile. Nathan really helps the kids keep busy and stay positive."

"Do you really like Nathan?" Lynne asked her older sister. "I think he's an okay kind of guy, but he just doesn't seem to be your type."

Jordan was making a list of all the DVDs the kids in her exercise group owned so they could be checked out and watched at home. She looked up at Lynne and asked, "What's my type? Ever since Nathan started asking me out you've seemed a little bothered, so tell me what's bugging you."

"I don't care who you date," Lynne responded. "I find it strange that you're interested in Nathan. He is quiet and seems content to follow the crowd. Every guy you have ever been interested in takes charge of things – a real enterprising sort of person. Nathan doesn't seem to fit that mold."

"I think he's a leader, but in a quiet sort of way. He started the tennis league, but he doesn't always have to be the boss. I kind of like that. If I have an idea, he helps me make it happen without taking control of the project."

"Oh, this sounds serious," Lynne said. "So pretty soon I'll be on my own to find a social life, huh?"

"Is that what's bothering you? You think I'll quit doing things with you? Come on, Lynne. Think back to when Scott first got serious with Michelle. Did he quit doing things with the family?"

"No, in fact Michelle became like a sister to us and he seemed to be tagging along lots of times," Lynne recalled, laughing.

"Right, and if you give Nathan half a chance, he'll be as good a friend to you as Michelle is." Jordan suddenly became very serious. "I miss her and Scott so much. Seeing them occasionally on a screen is nice, but Adam is already a little boy and we've never even held him." She sighed deeply. "We can't ever let anything come between us because I'm afraid Scott and Michelle will never come back to live with us. We have to stay close. Promise?"

"Promise," Lynne said as both girls stood and hugged each other. "I try to not think about them, but I still do. I saw Mom crying Sunday night after we talked to Scott. I know she misses them a lot, too."

"I'm sure Mom and Dad both do. I think it's different for us. Scott and Michelle are our brother and sister, but for Mom and Dad, it's their son and his family, their grandson. We should start having a game night on Sunday evening and invite some friends so Mom and Dad will have something else to focus on besides missing Scott and his family."

"That's good advice," Lynne said. "I have to stop thinking about myself and try to make life happier for the rest of our family. I'm sorry I've been a drag about Nathan. I'll try to get better acquainted with him. You could bring him to the game night."

"Okay." Jordan looked at her watch. "Oh, man, I'm supposed to meet Nathan in ten minutes. Do you want to come?"

"Thanks for the invite, but Terry and I are going to work on a new routine for our next exercise class." Lynne opened the bedroom door and then turned back and said, "Have a good time."

Life passed from one day to the next without too much violence or disruption. Still, the fact that Jordan felt her relationship with Nathan was indefinitely on hold created an occasional need for a good cry, in private.

"I'll be back in a while," Jordan told her mother.

"Wait," Lynne called from the living room. "Can I go with you?"

Jordan felt her shoulders rise and fall from the involuntary sigh that escaped her lips as she turned toward her sister's footsteps. "Okay."

Lynne sensed Jordan was upset and said, "Are you going to meet Nathan? Just tell me if you don't want me to come."

"No," Jordan said quickly. "I'm not going anywhere special and you're more than welcome to come with me." They began walking down the sidewalk at the back of their apartment building. "I'm just having a pity-party today and I thought maybe I would take a walk."

After walking in silence for a couple blocks, Lynne asked, "Did you and Nathan have a fight?"

"No, why?"

"So what's wrong, then?" Lynne pressed.

"Nothing in particular," Jordan said. "You know, once you start a pity-party, all kinds of things come to mind to make you sad."

"I see. So, is being in love with Nathan making you happy or sad?"

Jordan could not help but laugh at her sister's perceptiveness. "Both. He is such a wonderful man, and knowing he loves me makes me happy. The way he tries to make life better for all the kids makes me happy. However, there's absolutely no way we can get married, and even if we could, there's no place for us to live."

"You could move into his bedroom."

Jordan laughed but Lynne could easily hear the sadness.

"Jordan," Lynne said quietly, "Do you think you're happier in any way with less things in your life? I mean, I know we all miss satellite TV and fast food, but are you happier with a slower life?"

"There's one thing I like much better now," Jordan answered after thinking for a moment. "The commercialism that made so many things seem necessary in our lives is gone, and we seem to be more aware of the true value of an item, or of a person. What's inside is more important than how something looks. I like that a lot."

"Like there's no more status based on the clothes we wear or the car we drive or where we live?"

"I think there's still status, but everyone in this complex is the same status: no jobs, no cars, no new clothes. Not much at all from the outside world."

"Is that part of what's making you sad?" Lynne asked.

"No. What upsets me is that Nathan and I are both adults, yet we live at home with no prospect of getting married or having a baby. Time keeps sliding by, and today it feels like there is no hope of that ever happening. And I know I can't keep thinking like this, so . . ."

"I know," Lynne said excitedly, "let's go find Nathan and one of his friends and play tennis!"

Jordan laughed, and this time it sounded like she was happy. "Great idea! Come on, this pity-party is over!"

On May 4, two years to the day after the pioneers had first arrived at New Zion, the temple was completed. The young men who had delivered the woodwork stayed to see it installed so they could tell their people how the temple looked when it was completed. They shared many stories about their people, including how they had been able to come into the land of desolation without being affected by the radiation.

"Before we left," Alma told them, "our entire village fasted and prayed for three days. At the end of that time, the leader of our people gave all twelve of us a marvelous blessing. He blessed us that we would be safe while we traveled, and would have no accidents or problems delivering our precious cargo. He asked the ancestors who had helped make the woodwork to go with us and watch over us on our journey. We never doubted that we would be safe, even when we heard stories about the temple being built in a poisoned land."

Although of monumental importance to the world, the temple was completed without its awareness. Also unbeknownst to the world were hundreds of thousands of emigrants who visited and passed through Salt Lake City. Members of the Church temporarily housed them, but the commotion happening in the Middle East at the time was so intense this grand gathering did not even draw the attention of the local press. The Conference Center was packed to overflowing when the leader of each of the ten tribes of Israel presented their history and records to the Prophet of the Church. Each of their Prophets, in turn, received blessings and was endowed with priesthood keys and rights that had been restored through the succession of Prophets since Joseph Smith. No one noticed that the many meetinghouses in the Salt Lake area were operated day and night for many weeks as the masses were baptized and became members of the Church, even though they had previously been baptized to gain a remission of their sins. Every temple in the entire Intermountain Area was operated around the clock to perform baptisms for the ancestral names the emigrants carried with them, and other ceremonies for the redemption of both the living and their ancestors. Still, no one noticed.

In contrast, the sons of Judah completed their temple in full view of the world, in spite of the escalating opposition and hatred brought to bear against them. It had taken two years of dedicated work by the new members of the Church in Jerusalem. During that time, Isaac and Abram grew closer to the Lord and became righteous leaders. Isaac began classes in his ward to teach the members about the prophecies concerning the events that would occur before the Savior returned to rule the world. It was sobering work, but as they studied the prophecies and prepared as best they could, they were blessed with calm hearts.

President Nelson and his two counselors, Gary Stevens and Jack Fredericks, sat together in his office. "While we're waiting for the phone call, I have news to share. When I talked to the Prophet earlier this morning, he said that the temple in Jerusalem will be dedicated in two weeks."

"That's amazing, considering the violence that surrounds them," Jack said. "The Lord must be very busy protecting them these days."

"Any word when the temple here will be dedicated?" Gary asked.

"No, and I asked the Prophet about that. The way he worded his answer seemed a little odd, but I did not ask for any explanation. He said those who had been assigned to dedicate our temple were not available yet, but as soon as they were, they would come here immediately."

"At least we know it's sort of being planned, right?" Jack asked.

"I decided the only thing I had been told was that more than one person will perform the dedication, but they are not yet available."

"Any idea what this phone call is about?" Gary asked.

"None," President Nelson answered. "The Prophet just asked that the three of us be in the office to receive a call from him. Who knows, maybe he's going to tell us when the dedication will be scheduled."

When the panel sitting on the President's desk indicated an incoming call, all three men sat up a little straighter.

"Hello," President Nelson answered.

"Greetings," the Prophet returned. "How nice to hear your voice. Are your two counselors with you?"

"Yes, they are," President Nelson answered.

"Good. I have a special assignment for your stake, Brethren. This assignment is momentous regarding the coming of the Savior, and I think it will be a well-deserved reward for our faithful pioneers. They have endured a great deal to complete the temple. I would like you to select a group of thirty-six men from your stake, three from each ward, and have them ready to leave Wednesday morning for a special work project. It will take several days to complete this assignment, so please take the necessary provisions."

"All right," President Nelson replied. "Do we need to take certain tools? Are you looking for particular skills or abilities?"

"No. There are no particular skills needed for this assignment."

"Is there anything I need to know before selecting them?"

"No," the Prophet answered, and he chuckled softly.

"So, my first thought is to take the three men in each bishopric. That would give us the thirty-six men we need."

"The only thing needed is physical strength, and I believe every man in your stake would meet that requirement."

President Nelson was a little confused. The Prophet's directions had always been precise and exact; however, he now sounded unconcerned about who was chosen to help. "Very well, President. We'll gather the needed men."

The Prophet was still chuckling. "Brethren, thank you so much for your efforts, and I will call you at six a.m., your time, at the stake center on Wednesday morning. Please have the brethren you select assembled in the chapel at that time."

"Thank you for your call, and we will be ready on Wednesday morning," President Nelson said, and then he disconnected the call.

"Well, I guess we could put everyone's name in a hat and draw out three names from each ward. Any thoughts on the matter," President Nelson asked as he turned his chair toward his two counselors.

Jack cleared his throat. "I wonder what sort of momentous assignment regarding the coming of the Savior takes only thirty-six men to complete."

"We'll soon find out," President Nelson stated. "I suggest each of us contact four bishops and ask him to bring two men with him to the stake center on Wednesday morning. We'll let *them* choose."

When Wednesday morning arrived, Gary was at the stake center at 5:50 a.m. He made sure the signal was strong and all was ready for the meeting to begin. By the time the video portion of the broadcast flickered to life, everyone was seated, talking quietly.

"Good morning everyone," the Prophet said as he smiled from the screen at the front of the room. "I thank you for your dedication and for being here this morning. Each of you have helped complete the magnificent temple, and the Savior's return is imminent." The Prophet stopped speaking and the quivering of his chin made everyone aware that this subject stirred deep emotions within him.

"Brethren, three years before Adam died, he called together all who were high priests amongst his posterity and blessed them. Mighty men such as Seth, Enos, Enoch, Jared, and Methuselah were in that group. That incredible gathering was held at Adam-ondi-Ahman, which when translated means *place or land of God where Adam dwelt*. The Savior Himself attended that gathering and administered comfort to Adam. That multitude knew Adam's true nature and called him Michael, the archangel. Adam was filled with the Holy Ghost and he foretold the events that would occur in this world, even to the last generation." The Prophet stopped speaking and wiped the tears from his eyes. "Now there will be another gathering in this same place, the valley of Adam-ondi-Ahman. Adam, the Ancient of Days, is the father of the entire human family, and he will preside over this gathering, even as he did at the first assembly, and all who have held the keys of any dispensation must stand before him in this grand council, for he holds the keys of salvation. This will be a day of judgment. It will be a day of preparation for the Savior's return to the Earth. In this council, Christ will take over the reins of government, officially, on this Earth.

"You will be traveling north this morning to that sacred place to begin preparations for this grand council. The special vehicle and trailer you received in the last supply pick-up months ago will be driven and left there, so you will need to take one of your transport vehicles to carry everyone back on your return trip."

The Prophet was again silent for a moment, allowing the reality of his words to be realized. Then he smiled and said, "President Nelson, use your GPS to locate what used to be I-35 going northeast. Type in Far West and continue until you get there. Please call when you arrive."

When the broadcast ended and the group was exiting the building, President Nelson caught up to Bishop Chandler, Scott, and Dennis, all members of the Seventh Ward. "Bishop Chandler, can you three drive the vehicle and trailer parked behind the storehouse? The rest of the group will ride in the Second Ward's transport."

"Of course," Bishop Chandler answered. "By the time everyone gets aboard, we should be right behind you."

The three men hurried to the storehouse. "I wonder what's in this truck and trailer," the Bishop said as he started the engine.

"I hope we get to find out when we get to Far West," Scott said.

"That was quite a sobering talk from the Prophet," Dennis said as he looked from the Bishop to Scott.

"Yes, very," the Bishop answered. "It's one thing to know the temple has been completed, but to hear the Prophet say that the meeting we've read about all our lives is now about to take place, well, it makes me suddenly realize that the Millennium is upon us."

Scott sighed and then said, "I had a funny impression the whole time we were listening to the Prophet. I kept thinking that I already knew the Savior was

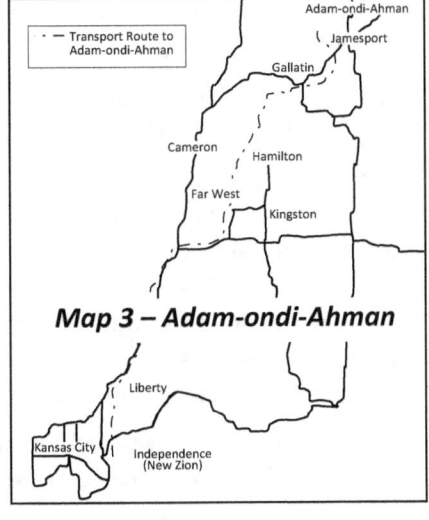

Map 3 – Adam-ondi-Ahman

coming soon, and when He does, the Millennium will arrive. As I listened to the Prophet talk about the Savior returning to the Earth shortly, I suddenly realized I had not quite grasped the magnitude of those words. The time for repenting and improving ourselves is nearly over. My son is going to grow up without knowing what it feels like to be tempted by Satan. It's not a prophecy about something in the distant future, it's happening now."

"Yes, it is," Bishop Chandler agreed. They traveled north in silence. The terrain remained unchanged – desolate, flat and barren.

Dennis sighed loudly, "I can see we didn't miss much by never getting out of town. The quick trips east to pick up supplies offered better views than this."

"I don't know," Scott said. "The shock factor when we first left Salt Lake and headed for Independence is gone, so that's an improvement. Plus, since we're following what used to be I-35, it actually feels like we're driving on a road every once in a while."

"Oh, look out," Bishop Chandler shouted. He held the GPS screen up high enough for Dennis and Scott to see. "Sharp turn to the east ahead. Oh, wait, another turn to the north. Wait for it . . . we missed it. How can you say this is just like our trip from Salt Lake? That trip *was* boring, but this time the roads turn every few miles."

Dennis laughed in spite of himself.

"What's that?" Scott asked. "There's something on the upper edge of the GPS display."

Bishop Chandler looked at the screen. "There it is," he said excitedly. "Far West. We're here!"

The vehicles rolled to a stop and all three men were laughing as they walked to where the other men were gathered. President Nelson was speaking into his satellite radio. He slowly walked a short distance ahead of the vehicle and turned in a circle, his eyes fixed on the horizon. "No, there are no trees or any signs that man ever existed here. It looks the same for as far as I can see." He lowered the radio from his ear, turned and walked south down the small knoll.

The group of men watched President Nelson walk a short distance, and then he slowed and seemed to study a small pile of dust and debris.

He seemed sad, and sat down on a flat rock. Slowly he brought the radio back up to his ear.

"I found it, just north of where I'm sitting. It's just dust." He was silent for a moment and then said, "I was here several years ago and it was such a beautiful little oasis of trees and shrubs. I remember it was a short drive back into Kansas City from here. There were so many people, so many people." He stopped as his voice broke. He was overwhelmed by emotion and lowered the radio from his ear again as tears began rolling down his cheeks.

He dragged his sleeve across his eyes and raised the radio to his ear again, "I'm sorry, this is harder than I thought it would be." He listened to the Prophet for several minutes and then stood and began walking. "Okay, I'm walking to the west. How many steps?" He walked a short distance and then stopped and began kicking at the dust. "Yes, I found it." Nodding his head, he walked to the south and began kicking in the dust again. "Here it is." Then he traveled to the east and again kicked around until he uncovered the last of the four cornerstones of the Far West Temple site. "Okay, I'll call you when we get there."

Almost as if President Nelson had totally forgotten he was not alone, he seemed surprised when he looked up and saw thirty-eight men patiently waiting for him. He smiled and said, "Well, I don't suppose you caught what the Prophet was saying, but this is the Far West Temple site. The Saints dedicated it before they left Missouri. We will get to develop this area, but not today. The Prophet just wanted to know if we could find it and determine where the temple was to be built." He began walking toward the transport vehicles as he continued speaking. "From here we're going to travel north to Adam-ondi-Ahman. That's where we'll spend the next few days. So, let's head out and see what lies ahead."

Dennis and Scott visited quietly while the Bishop continued driving, following closely behind the other vehicle. Suddenly, both trucks slowed down, and each person sat up a little taller and looked around. They rolled down the windows as an old familiar scent came streaming in – the smell of life! As they slowly drove across what appeared to be the remains of a bridge, they saw a wide, slow moving river below, but nothing that could create such a wonderful aroma. When they crested the next ridge, the trucks ground to an immediate halt. It was as if a dream materialized before their eyes. A valley that stretched in front of them for miles was in full summer bloom. The vegetation itself was enough to cause them to stop and stare, but the fact that the barren land changed to a bountiful garden in one step astounded them. The growth did not begin as sparse vegetation and gradually thicken to a lush landscape. It was as if an imaginary wall existed that held death on one side and preserved life on the other. They drove a short distance before reaching a point that overlooked the entire valley below. A crystal blue river flowing along the western side of the green vegetation could be seen from their vantage point, but it was obvious the river would drop out of sight behind a ridge once they reached the valley. Everyone exited the trucks and reverently let their eyes wander over the magnificent view.

"This must be what the Prophet was talking about," President Nelson said. "Seeing what God has created for us in the midst of all this destruction fills my heart with joy. Or perhaps He merely protected what we took for granted, so we could partake of it after living in such ugliness for so long."

"I wish everyone was here to enjoy this with us. I can't even imagine trying to describe this amazing view to my wife and seeing the disappointment on her face because she didn't get to see it," the Second Ward Bishop said.

President Nelson laughed and turned to look into the Bishop's eyes. "Maybe we should not mention this to our wives. The Prophet has sent us here to set up the contents of this truck and trailer, and leave them here. And sometime next week our whole stake will be returning to this place to assist and serve those that will be visiting this area. Maybe our wives should enjoy the surprise of seeing this beautiful valley, just as we have." President Nelson continued smiling as his meaning registered with the Bishop.

"Are you telling me that the Great Gathering that has been awaited since the days of Adam, the meeting that is to take place at Adam-ondi-Ahman, is going to be next week?" the Bishop asked, slowly enunciating each word.

"Those exact words were not spoken to me," President Nelson said. "What I heard was that we have a lot of work to do. So, my friend, unless you want this radio so you can call the Prophet and ask him your questions personally, maybe we should get started." The laughter from the entire group grew as President Nelson slapped the Bishop's back warmly.

The two sections of the transport vehicle were separated and parked, one half at the north end of the luxuriant valley and the other half at the south end.

"The Prophet said we should get out the three large tents first, and try to get them set up today," President Nelson said. "One tent goes in the middle of the valley, one will be located at the north and one at the south ends of the valley, right by the transport vehicles. Wards One through Six, would you please help in the north end? The tents should be placed so the front faces toward the east, and each transport vehicle will be parked behind the back or west wall of the north and south tents. If the rest of you will please come with me, we will work in the south end. These tents will remind you of tents you've seen in Hollywood movies, not the kind you slept in when we first arrived in New Zion."

The two groups worked the rest of the afternoon. Each tent was made using vast amounts of a material that resembled canvas but looked smooth and shimmered like silk. The square tents measured over 300 feet on each side. When the first two tents were finished, everyone worked together to erect the center tent. When they finished, the orange hues of the sun were sinking into the pale haze that hugged the horizon, and everyone gathered on the grass near the center tent to watch the sun set.

"Quite a sight," President Nelson said. "I've never seen anything like it. The glorious colors of the sunset reflected by three huge palaces gently swaying in the breeze, palaces made of iridescent material fit for a king. Good job, everyone."

"President," someone asked, "do you have any idea what these three tents are going to be used for?"

"My imagination and remembering what the Prophet said to us this morning, and what I have studied about Adam-ondi-Ahman are my only sources of information," he admitted. "But while we were working I've been picturing Jesus Christ sitting in this tent in the center, and perhaps Melchizedek in the tent to his right and Aaron in the other tent. I can imagine several million Priesthood holders facing the tents and some form of ceremony going on as the keys are returned to Adam, and then to Christ. Can you imagine the sound of millions of men voicing their agreement that the Savior rule the world?"

After a long silence, Gary Stevens said, "It makes my hair stand on end to think that we will be allowed to be here, while the likes of Adam and Moses and Noah are sitting right where we can see them. Can you imagine speaking to Moroni or Nephi? I think I would reach out and touch their arm, just to see if they were real. I don't know how we can possibly be of service to them, but being allowed to see them is unbelievable."

"Most of those attending this gathering will be resurrected beings," Scott said. "But the present leadership of the Church will be here, and that alone will be a huge group of people. We've been isolated from something as routine as General Conference ever since we left Salt Lake, so just being around the apostles who lead the Church today will be incredible."

President Nelson stood slowly and looked around at the group of men laying or sitting on the grass. "I don't know what we'll be asked to do when we all come back. Maybe we will be in charge of running errands or fetching water. I don't know. It is fun to speculate what will be happening here next week, but try not to let your mind wander with imaginations. Let's just concentrate on getting our assigned task done, and then going home and getting the rest of our group to come back here and do whatever it is the Prophet has in mind for us. Does that sound reasonable?"

Everyone nodded in agreement.

"Great! Am I the only one who's hungry?" The murmurings that started to grow was answer enough. "Let's go find something to eat."

Eventually, everyone returned to the grass in front of the central tent and settled down to speak quietly with those close around them. The conversations became fewer and fewer and finally everyone slept on the thick grass that seemed as comfortable as a velvet bedspread.

When the sun rose the next morning, everyone was refreshed and eager to continue the work. President Nelson spoke with the Prophet on his satellite phone while the group ate breakfast. He was smiling when he walked into the midst of the group to explain their assignments for the day.

Specific containers were unloaded from each of the two transport vehicles, and the contents were moved into the tents at the north and south end of the valley. Ultra-modern electronic and communication equipment was arranged on tables in one portion of each tent. Computers, scanning and fax machines, and dozens of telephones were organized. A satellite communication dish was mounted behind the center tent, far to the west side of the valley. The data network from each of the two tents was connected to communicate to the wireless networks located in each vehicle, and the connection between the satellite dish and the network located in Salt Lake was confirmed to be working. Inside the transport vehicles were two large banks of batteries powered by the solar panels that created the walls of the transport. President Nelson commented that solar panels like these were probably not available to the public – everyone agreed.

President Nelson stood looking at the batteries, watching several men connecting cables of every size and unrolling more cable as they walked into the back of the massive tent. He listened to the sounds of men, working together in teams, checking connections and verifying satellite frequencies were operating. He turned and walked the length of the valley toward the other tent that was being equipped in the same manner. He thought back to the early days of New Zion when he tried to force the members of his stake to do things according to his schedule. The love that filled his heart for each man he passed swelled his being until he felt he might burst. He thanked God for the events that had changed him and was filled with gratitude that he and his wife had been blessed with a calling that strengthened their faith and filled their lives with blessings.

When the sun began to set, everyone gathered near the transport vehicles to eat their dinner. Nearly every conversation reflected the feeling that the sacredness of the valley seemed as tangible as the thriving vegetation. After a second night of undisturbed rest, the men arranged vast numbers of small tents in row after row behind the three tents, as well as between the center and south tent. A large area between the center and north tent was left conspicuously vacant. The last two assignments were to set up thousands of tables and chairs on the east side of the valley, and then arrange large lights throughout the area. The fact that the lights had no cords did not even seem strange to this group of men; they had been continually amazed with solar-powered technology since their arrival in the area.

Work continued until every detail of each task was completed in a manner that made them comfortable presenting it to the Savior for His use. As they left the green valley, they realized how quickly they had become accustomed to God's intended nature. Within minutes after leaving the green vegetation, all conversation ended. The silence created by the lack of birds, locust, or any of the sounds of nature that had filled their ears for the past few days was depressing. While each person privately tried to reach deep within himself to find a reserve of strength they felt would be needed to deal with the total desolation they had returned to, their eyes fixed on the southern horizon. The pillar of light began to bring joy back into their hearts. It banished the longing for the vegetation they acutely missed and seemed to fill their souls with the fondness they associated with home.

Before anyone left the transport, President Nelson said, "I would like each of you bishops to take time in your Sacrament Meeting to teach the prophecy of the last days; specifically the Great Priesthood Gathering at Adam-ondi-Ahman. And let the two brethren that went with you each talk about the sacred feelings that exist in the valley, and that it will soon be experienced by everyone." President Nelson then stepped off the transport and everyone quickly headed home.

When the call finally arrived from Salt Lake several days later, each ward boarded their transport amidst excited chatter and the trip north began. The twelve vehicles rolled without difficulty as their previous tracks were still very visible in the powdery dust and sand. Each bishop spoke briefly as they passed Far West, describing their experience on the previous trip. Scott sat next to Michelle, trying to watch her every expression without awakening her curiosity. He wanted to see her face the first moment she sensed the presence of vegetation. They had been discussing how Adam would react to a gathering of millions of people when Scott noticed Michelle was no longer hearing what he said. Her eyes seemed to glaze over and he could almost read the thoughts on her face. When she moved her eyes to look at him, he could no longer hide his amusement.

"Is that grass I can smell?" she asked, with the most puzzled expression he had ever seen on her face.

"Grass?" he asked. "Does grass smell?"

She leaned close to the open transport window and breathed deeply. "Yes, grass smells like childhood and summer and cool evenings. You have to be able to smell that," she said in undisguised bewilderment.

He tried to keep up the charade, but failed and started laughing. Leaning close to Adam, he said, "You are going to see the most amazing sight in just a minute. Grass that is so thick you want to lie down on it and bury your face in it. And it's so warm here you don't even need a blanket at night."

Michelle grabbed a pinch of skin on Scott's arm between her finger and thumb, which immediately got his undivided attention. "Why didn't you tell me?" she asked.

"Because it would have ruined the total surprise," he said, as the fertile valley suddenly came into view.

"Ohhh," Michelle sighed. "Adam, look."

The transports pulled onto the west end of the fertile valley and excited passengers poured out into the fragrant air. Everyone began hugging each other and it looked more like recess on a grade school playground than a group of pioneers who had just completed building a temple. Years of carefully contained emotion rose, unchecked, as their senses drew in the beauty before them – beauty they had washed from their memories in an effort to cope with the desolation that surrounded them. For the first few moments, they seemed to question whether they had ever seen this level of beauty – if it had ever really existed at all. Then, in the next moment, they felt so at home in the vivid landscape they wondered if the last few years living in Desolation had only been a bad dream.

The days of planning, which had taken place since the initial group's return, kicked into gear and each ward's assigned tasks were begun. Michelle was on a committee in charge of organizing the area where meals would be prepared.

Scott worked diligently with the other brethren of the Seventh Ward organizing stacks and stacks of materials – check lists, genealogical pedigree charts and family group sheets. They set up areas identified as Information Gathering Stations, and were told they would staff these areas during the Gathering.

A large group of people were involved in preparing areas for tired travelers to eat and rest. When other assigned tasks were completed, everyone became part of this group since it required the most work. By Saturday afternoon, the tasks were completed and the grassy area in front of the middle tent became a gathering place. Scott and Michelle sat with several other couples that had small children.

"Is that another vehicle?" Michelle asked when she noticed a small dust cloud in the distance coming closer and closer to the valley.

Everyone turned to look and then watched in silence as a vehicle drove right up to the edge of the green grass where they were sitting.

"Any ideas?" Scott asked, and then saw the entire stake presidency walking toward the small transport. "Maybe we're the only ones who don't know what's happening," he added, nodding in their direction.

"Maybe the gathering has begun," someone suggested, "but if we're expecting millions, they must be arriving by some other mode. There can't be more than a dozen people, at most, in that vehicle."

As the group watched, the stake president opened the vehicle's door and the Prophet emerged. His counselors followed. Everyone started walking toward the transport, but President Nelson redirected them to the large tent in the middle of the valley. The Prophet and his counselors also walked toward the tent, and embraced each pioneer once everyone was inside. The Prophet then walked to the front of the congregation and began speaking.

"I know there has been much speculation as to what will happen here. You have not been alone in your lack of information. We have each come to some conclusions about what will take place, but we have no agenda or detailed plan of the events that will occur. We are as excited as you at the possibilities of what we may see during the next week here, but we try to control *our* speculation, as well. I do want to thank you once again for your dedicated service and willingness to perform any task placed before you. There has been no thought of self or rumblings amongst you. You are truly a remarkable example of living the true United Order. Many in the world know you are here, but few know what you have accomplished. As we . . ."

The Prophet stopped mid-sentence and stared beyond the congregation. Everyone turned to see what he was looking at.

Jesus Christ stood with two other men at the door of the tent. The power and intense brightness of the three beings pierced through each person as a blast furnace of heat and light, sweeping through the entire tent.

Scott fell to his knees, filled with exquisite joy that was so intense it seemed to consume his entire being. Suddenly, everything around him became brighter, as though a dark film had been removed from his eyes – colors became more intense and vivid. The joy he had felt when he saw the Savior at the temple in New Zion paled in comparison to the feelings that burned through him at that moment. He had been holding Adam and that awareness returned to his mind. When he looked down at his son, he appeared to be sleeping, peacefully and calmly. The contrast between what Scott was feeling and the serenity on his son's face was overwhelming, but at that same instant, he easily accepted the difference. The radiant glow from the three Beings seemed to fill those who stood in the tent until every person appeared to radiate a lesser version of the same glow. Scott did not know if it had been only a few seconds since he had turned and beheld Jesus, or if a long period of time had passed. As he watched, the three Beings slowly walked through the midst of those standing in the tent, toward the Prophet. Each of the three embraced the Prophet in turn. Then turned and each embraced his counselors.

Scott wanted to look at Michelle to see if she was experiencing the same indescribable emotions he was, but he found it impossible to look away from the Savior embracing the leaders of the Church. Finally, he was able to turn his head, and he quickly saw that Michelle was visibly changed. Her skin was smooth and radiant, the way it had looked when he first met her. The beauty of her smile and twinkling brown eyes that had always mesmerized him had now become more intense, as though an inner light was shining through her physical features, and he could see the intentions of her heart and her goodness as easily as he could see the vibrant color of her hair. The tired determination that all the women in New Zion had worn nearly from the first month they had arrived was gone, and in its place was calm acceptance and joy.

A sound he could only describe as rushing wind filled the tent, and yet there was not the slightest breeze. Suddenly, the tent was filled with an army of angels. The roof of the tent no longer blocked the visible skies above – a conduit encircled by heavenly beings extended toward the heavens with no end to the glorious escort.

Jesus spoke of one of the angelic personages near him, and His voice reverberated through each person's being. "This is the beloved Father Adam, the father of all the Earth. Through his loins, the family of man was created. He received the authority to act in the Father's name and stands as the presiding High Priest over all the Earth for all ages. He passed precious keys from generation to generation, to the time of Moses. Some have been lost from the Earth through the ages. Wickedness has tried to frustrate the great role of man and capture the glory that could not be purchased. Time has come to an end on this Earth where the mortal life of man has been played out. Father Adam will now call all to his footstool and they will render up their stewardships to the first Patriarch of the race, who holds the keys of salvation. The keys that he has entrusted to others since the first ordination he performed will now be returned to him."

Then Jesus turned to Aaron and said, "This is Aaron who first received his priesthood from God. When Moses was taken from the Earth, the fullness of the priesthood was also removed. From then until the time that I came to dwell on the Earth as the Son of Man, the most prevalent priesthood upon the Earth was the Aaronic Priesthood. Those who received keys of authority through this priesthood will return them to Aaron during this great gathering. Aaron, in turn, will return those keys to their source."

Adam then began speaking. "When the reports of stewardship have been completed, I, as holder of the keys for this Earth, will report to the Savior of this world, even Jesus Christ, Our Lord. He will then assume the reins of government and direct the Priesthood, and He, whose right it is to rule, will be officially pronounced the ruler by the voice of the Priesthood here assembled. This Grand Council of Priesthood will be composed of not only the faithful who now dwell on this Earth, but also the Prophets and apostles of old, who have had directing authority. This council will attend to the greatest matters concerning the destiny of this Earth."

Jesus again spoke to the group. "The vast number of people attending this Gathering and the information that will be gathered and conveyed to the leaders of the Church on the Earth will be as prophesied. Your efforts and service are greatly appreciated and accepted. Your faithfulness has enabled you to endure My presence. Your bodies are now transformed to terrestrial bodies that will continue until your appointed days on the Earth are completed. Then you will be translated in the twinkling of an eye and become a resurrected Being. The veil that was placed before your eyes when you came to the Earth will be lifted. As we visited with each other in New Zion, here also will we visit, one with another."

The way the Savior smiled at each person in the tent seemed to convey a personal greeting and feeling of friendship. They marveled that they could feel such overpowering awe and respect for the Savior at the same moment that they felt love and acceptance from Him.

As they watched, Jesus, Adam and Aaron ascended upward through the conduit made from a multitude of angels singing His praises. The angels remained, as though to guard the connection between the Sacred

Valley and Heaven. The Prophet directed everyone to rest, as they would be very busy for the next several days.

When Michelle and Scott left the tent, they observed something so unexplainable. While inside the tent, they had been able to view the angels who escorted Jesus and the two Beings, and saw them ascend into the heavens. Once they stepped outside the tent, the vision was no longer visible. Scott stepped quickly back inside the tent to confirm his observation, and he could clearly see the army of angels. When he stepped back out to join Michelle, he could not see them.

"I guess no one on Earth realizes this event is happening. That makes it even more of a blessing that we have been allowed to be here to observe this event," he said to Michelle.

"I can't get over the fact that we have seen Jesus again, and now Adam and Aaron," Michelle said as they walked toward the grassy area where many others had gathered. Adam had been asleep through most of the spectacular appearances and Scott laid him on the grass between them.

"This has been an evening unlike anything I have ever experienced," Scott said. "Can you even imagine what it will be like when Noah and Moses and Nephi and Lehi are part of the group?"

"And we're supposed to rest and sleep well tonight, huh?" Michelle said with a laugh. "We need to include in our prayer tonight that we will be able to sleep, because I'm so wide awake I can't imagine being able to."

After they prayed, Scott and Michelle laid closely together, with Adam nestled securely between them. "Do you remember the night after our first conference in Salt Lake? The one where we were asked to decide if we could walk away from all our material possessions and live the United Order?"

"Yes, I remember that night very well," Michelle answered.

"We could have missed all this if we had decided we couldn't do it. That would have been a terrible loss," Scott said softly as he bent and kissed Adam's forehead.

"But we made the right decision," Michelle reminded him. "And we've been blessed every day since then.

CONVERSING WITH ANCIENTS

Isaac stood in the temple yard, looking at the magnificent edifice that was ready to be dedicated. He had prayed unceasingly for this day to arrive. His heart overflowed with gratitude; his family would now be sealed together for all eternity. Living in a place as volatile as Jerusalem made that blessing even more precious.

Three years had passed since the Prophets first began serving in Jerusalem, and Isaac and his family were among the first that had accepted Jesus Christ as their Messiah. He briefly felt ashamed for all the years he had refused to accept Jesus Christ as his Savior, but that shame was quickly pushed aside when he realized how many people he had been able to introduce to the Church, and that they now shared the great joy he had found when he was baptized. He felt the familiar warmth wash over him as he pondered the magnitude of the many blessings he had received.

For the past two years, completing the temple had been his first priority. Rachel had unwaveringly supported him when responsibilities received from the stake president consumed many evenings each week.

Great banks of fog had begun forming around Jerusalem early that morning, making the scene dark and oppressive. Isaac felt a burst of wind that seemed to push down from above, thickening the fog. The *weather* could not dampen the elation felt by those quietly filing into the temple to participate in the dedication. Again he looked up at the glorious edifice they were about to present to God and dedicate as a House of the Lord. When he lowered his eyes, he saw his shadow, and quickly looked up. He gasped at the beauty he beheld. A hole had opened in the fog; the entire temple yard was now bathed in warm sunshine. Around the opening, long feathers of solid white clouds seemed to be spilling over the top of the gray mass and sliding down toward the ground like a waterfall. A breeze blowing down through the opening filled the entire area with the sweet smell of blossoms. Isaac closed his eyes and breathed deeply, letting the warm fragrance fill him – it was easy to imagine God had opened a portal to view the proceedings.

Isaac sat beside his wife during the first of four dedicatory sessions and listened to the beautiful prayer offered by one of the Prophets. The day was filled with spiritual manifestations and increased testimonies of the importance of linking eternal families to their ancestors in a chain that continued back to Father Adam.

During the following days and weeks, the miracles performed by the two Prophets could no longer be rationalized as coincidence or lucky breaks. Jews from around the world flocked to their homeland to help preserve it from the constant war waged by the armies of Satan. The city had expanded to the west, and the area became fertile; crops grew at a miraculous rate and in great abundance, even while drought and famine ravaged the surrounding region.

The miracles, coupled with the outspokenness of the Prophets toward the people who fought against the Jews, became known throughout the world. Earthquakes, volcanoes, hurricanes, and drought were common occurrences in the countries that opposed the Jews, and the Prophets openly took responsibility for the misery caused by the elements. With boldness, the Prophets promised to continue this punishment until those fighting against the Jews softened their hearts, or were no more. The great hatred directed toward the Jews grew to such violent proportions that the armies sometimes seemed unable to contain their anger and fought against each other.

The armies also fought an invisible tide that defeated them before they could even advance on the Jews. One well-planned attack against Jerusalem was met with a sand storm of unequaled magnitude that immobilized all vehicles. Guns and artillery jammed and proved useless. The next attack dissolved before it began when all the soldiers became deathly sick from spoiled food eaten the day before. Sickness and disease swept through the ranks and millions were forced to retreat to distant areas in search of aid from doctors and hospitals. Years of this pattern of defeat caused many to become superstitious and fear the magicians helping the Jews. In vain, the armies seeking the destruction of those protecting the Jews called upon their gods – with no success.

Leaders of the armies of Magog recalled their most skilled tacticians from the countries where they led attacks against those who supported the Jewish people. Overtaking Jerusalem became the top priority and the Valley of Esdraelon swelled with troops.

"I believe I have a plan which will not only get us inside the walls," one tactician explained, "but will convince the Jews themselves to help us." The excitement his words produced erupted in a loud outburst that took several minutes to quiet. "A few of our chosen soldiers will become martyrs, and we will rejoice at their victory. The unholy Jewish temple *must* be destroyed, but we are prevented from doing so until their false prophets who use the power of the devil to control the elements are killed. Then we will eliminate the Jews and destroy everything they have ever built. We will erase every trace of them, as though they never existed."

The plan was secret. Not one soldier or commander in the Army of Magog that stood watch at the wall surrounding Jerusalem was aware of it. On the chosen day, those that were willing to become martyrs traveled from Megiddo, but they did not look like soldiers; they looked like foreign visitors, friendly to the Jews. They gathered near the armies and their leader uttered the final words of instruction.

"We must advance unnoticed to the edge of our troops, and then make a dash for the wall surrounding the city. Our greatest risk is that our own soldiers will be successful in killing all of us before we can make it to the wall. Once the Jews see that we are being fired upon, they will open the gates and fight in our defense to protect us. When we enter the city, their prophets will be at our mercy. May Allah be with us."

Suddenly the tightly bunched group crouched low and ran toward the wall. Materials to create bombs were carefully protected under bulletproof vests that each person wore, but the risks were many. Once their own troops began shooting at them, they returned fire, being careful to aim high. When several of their group fell to the ground, they ran faster, determined that at least one of them would reach the gate to the city that had been opened slightly. The Jewish troops began firing at the troops outside the wall and swung the gate open to offer sanctuary to the approaching men.

"Come in, quickly!" the Jewish soldiers on duty at the gate called.

Once the six remaining members of the group made it through the gate, the Jewish soldiers pushed the gate closed. Many soldiers gathered around the *businessmen* who had dropped to the ground in exhaustion.

"Thank you," they said between gasps for air. "Thank you. We knew it would be dangerous, but we wanted to get into the city so we could hear the teachings of the Prophets. The entire world is talking about them. We have traveled far to hear them."

The soldiers helped them to their feet. "I will bring cool water for you to drink," one soldier volunteered. "Rest. The Prophets will be informed that you would like to visit with them."

The disguised soldiers were led to a room that provided shade from the hot sun. The back wall of the room was the wall that surrounded the old part of Jerusalem. The men sat comfortably in the shade, studying the structure. They realized they could give their own troops the exact locations to fire rocket propelled grenades and mortars, and the resulting destruction would provide access into the city.

"Their stupidity is unbelievable," one of them said after shutting the door, ensuring privacy. He quickly took out his cell phone and called his leaders. "We have succeeded. The infidels have given us refuge in a room that is against the wall. They are bringing their Prophets to speak with us, and their search of us was so incompetent they have not taken any of the weapons we believed they would find, let alone the ones we took great care to hide. Their foolishness will ensure their destruction." He provided the GPS coordinates for the attack that would begin immediately after the explosives they were now preparing were detonated. "We go to receive our rewards."

The soldier ended the phone call and began the final preparations of double-checking the connections between the charges and the remote detonator. Then prayers were recited and necessary rituals were performed as the six men prepared to offer themselves as a sacrifice to ensure the annihilation of the Jewish people. "They will pay for the blasphemy they have perpetrated on our holy mosque. They will finally be wiped from the face of the Earth!"

One of the soldiers opened the door of the room they had now converted into a death trap. "We need a breath of fresh air," he said as he smiled at those standing nearby. From the open doorway, he would be able to see the Prophets as they approached. Pitchers of cool water and trays of fresh fruit were brought to the guests while they patiently waited.

Meanwhile, in a park near the temple, David sat with a large group of people listening to the Prophets. He was usually too busy to spend the afternoon enjoying the spirit that radiated from the Prophets, but today he felt compelled to spend a little time listening to their teachings. He knew he would need to leave soon in order to be on time for his shift at the temple site to watch the security cameras. He glanced at his watch and decided he could only stay five more minutes.

Suddenly a man ran into the midst of the group and began talking to the Prophets in a frenzy of excitement. "Come with us. A group of men has just broken through the enemy's defenses, and they came here to listen to your teachings. We will take you to them."

The messenger's words caused David to stand, instantly uneasy. "That must have been the gunfire we heard a while ago. Who are these men?" he asked.

The messenger turned to David. "Yes, the armies outside the wall tried to kill them before they could reach the gate. I don't know who they are, but they have risked their lives to hear the Prophets. Some members of their group were killed before they could get to the gate. They were willing to die just to listen to the Prophets."

"I'll go with him," David told the Prophets. "I'll find out who they are and if it's safe for you to go talk to them. Something's not right."

"No, David," one of the Prophets said, as they both stood. "We know what is happening. You do not need to worry about our safety. For this purpose have we come to Jerusalem."

Both Prophets shook hands with the messenger and then began to follow him. "They entered at the Lion Gate," the messenger said, "and we have taken them to the room that is built against the wall north of that entrance. They are very anxious to see you."

"And we have waited for them to arrive," one of the Prophets said, smiling warmly at the messenger.

David watched as the Prophets walked away. The uneasy feeling he had experienced when the messenger arrived was growing stronger by the moment. He ran to catch up with them. "Are you sure you won't let me at least talk to them first and find out a little more about them?"

One of the Prophets turned and smiled at him. "David, why do you worry for our safety? God has sent us here to teach His truths. We have done as He commanded us. Many here can now provide strong leadership for the Church, and we are no longer needed."

"What do you mean?" David asked. The Prophet's words pierced his soul. "Why do you think you're no longer needed?"

The Prophet put his hands on David's shoulders. "We were sent here by God to fulfill a mission. That mission is complete. It does not matter what happens to us now. We appreciate your caution, but do not concern yourself on our behalf, David. You do not need to accompany us if you feel uneasy about the newcomers. Do you recall our many conversations concerning the Lord's timetable for each of our lives?"

"Yes, I remember them well," David answered.

"Do you have faith that God protects each of us until the mission we have been sent to Earth to accomplish has been completed?"

"Yes, I have come to understand and believe that principle."

"Then, be of good cheer. If it is the Lord's will that we teach those that come to this city, He will keep us safe."

David smiled as he felt a warm sense of calm and peace wash over him. "I guess I'll always be a worrier," he said. "Thanks for being patient with me. I strive to be accepting of what comes into my life as being from God, but sometimes I need to be reminded."

The Prophet embraced David and then the group walked toward the wall.

From within the room, the soldiers watched the small crowd approaching the open doorway. "That must be their Prophets coming now," one of the soldiers said. The other men inside the small room stood and gathered close to the entrance. When the Prophets were close enough to see the faces of the men inside the room, they smiled and extended their hands toward the new arrivals. One of the soldiers stepped through the doorway and immediately pulled the trigger of the automatic weapon he had concealed under his clothing, spraying back and forth, killing not only the Prophets but everyone in the group that had accompanied them. Then he stepped quickly back into the room and activated the remote switch.

The explosion was powerful. The walls of the room, as well as the section of wall that formed the back of the room, were blown outward, instantly creating a gray cloud that could be seen for miles. Large chunks of rock and debris crashed to the ground, and before anyone could comprehend what had occurred, the roar of approaching rockets preceded more explosions, expanding the hole that had been created in the protective wall. Even before the dust settled, enemy troops began pouring into the city. There was so much confusion it was easy for the invading troops to overtake and secure that portion of the city. The soldiers were overjoyed that the despised Prophets were dead, and ordered their bodies remain where they lay so the Jews could watch them decay in the streets.

Michelle realized she had been awake for some time. The sun had not risen yet, but the stars were no longer visible overhead. Without moving, she opened her eyes and saw Scott smiling at her. Adam was still asleep between them.

Nearby, Bishop Chandler stood and filled his lungs with air. "I trust everyone is ready to begin our assignments?" he asked. "I didn't mean to infer you had to begin work without breakfast though. The idea of eating breakfast was inviting, but especially because he loved the smell of pancakes in the morning. "I guess it's up to you whether or not you want to eat," he added, slowly shaking his head.

As each woman walked toward her assigned work area, Michelle noticed a plume of dust on the horizon, approaching from the north. It was the same as what they had seen the evening before, except that rather than a single plume of dust coming closer, it appeared to grow wider as it approached. That meant a long string of vehicles would soon be arriving.

By the time the first of the unending line of all-terrain vehicles arrived, the food was ready for them. They appeared to have been traveling for a long time, and were very appreciative of the Sisters' efforts on their behalf. When they finished eating, they walked toward the place to rest or sleep.

"If this pace continues, it won't be difficult to feed everyone," Michelle said.

"Especially since they all seem to know exactly where to go. Someone has organized this gathering precisely, down to the smallest detail."

"So much for arriving slow enough for us to keep up," Michelle said as she pointed east at another large cloud of dust.

Nancy Chandler put her arm around Michelle and said, "I hate to burst your bubble, but just take a look around, all the way around."

Michelle slowly turned around in a circle. Plumes of dust were approaching from every direction. "I'm glad I won't be getting tired as quickly as I did yesterday," she said and then chuckled.

"Do you suppose our fathers will be here?" one of the Sisters asked. "Many of them are High Priests, right?"

Michelle nodded and then turned to look at the dust plumes arriving from the west. "What are the odds that we could even find our fathers? There's a lot of tables to choose from and we'll only be working half the time."

"Plus, here's another snag," Nancy said. "Not one of them will have a clue we're here. Even if they see there are women here cooking food for them, what would make any of them think their daughter might be here. Our parents all think we're in New Zion."

The group of women sighed as they looked across the horizon at the dust clouds. "Do you think we could make signs and stick them to all the food tables?" Michelle asked with a grin. "You know, '*Food Prepared by Sisters from the New Zion Stake. If your daughter is in that stake, she's here.*'"

"I'll make the signs if any of you want to ask President Nelson what he thinks of that idea," Nancy said. No one volunteered.

Scott and Dennis had been assigned to work immediately inside the entrance to the Melchizedek Priesthood tent. They gave each man who passed by a small hand-held device and asked them to provide the requested information and then put the device in a large basket. When the basket was filled, they took it to another work area located behind the tent where each device was plugged into a panel that retrieved the information and reset the device.

"What happens to this information?" Dennis asked one of the men who worked in that area.

"It's sent to Salt Lake via satellite. The information is added to the Book of Life the Church has been building. Remember when all the temple work went online? That's when this project began."

"Isn't their information already in that Book?" Dennis asked.

"Probably. All these people are active in the Church and most have access to a temple. However, some are from areas that have just recently been opened to our missionaries so they probably have never been to a temple. Plus, there will be resurrected Beings in attendance and the information they provide could be something that is missing or has been recorded incorrectly."

"Sounds like a huge undertaking," Dennis said. "Do we need to provide our personal information, too?"

"Nope. The mission papers we filled out before we left Salt Lake contained the same questions, and that information has already been entered."

"Just one more question," Dennis said, "if you have time?"

"Sure, what is it?"

"What happens when people arrive who can't understand English? What should we do?"

"Not a problem. No matter what language is spoken, the message is received in each person's native language. The Gift of Tongues is being poured down upon everyone in this valley. Do you remember when you listened to Adam and Aaron speaking in the tent last night?"

"Yes. I never thought about it, but I guess Adam wouldn't be speaking American English, would he?" Dennis asked.

"Right, but you heard him in your own language. I do know that somehow the information fed into the computers and communicated to Salt Lake will make sense to the machines and everything will work out smoothly. Anyway, that's what we were told when we started our shift this morning."

"Well, thanks for the info. Makes you wonder how many years have been spent planning this meeting and organizing all these details," Dennis said.

"I think probably ever since the first meeting here," the man said, more to himself than to Dennis.

By the time the sun had set that evening, the members of the New Zion Stake were ready to stop work and rest for a time. They gathered on the eastern edge of the valley where many members of the stake had slept the night before. Scott and Michelle sat near Bishop Chandler who was sharing an experience from earlier in the day.

"He was the President of the Church when I was a kid and he's always been one of my favorites. He was talking to a man who must have been one of Alma's ancestors, the Alma who brought the woodwork to us for the temple, because he thanked him for the work he did during his lifetime to help build the interior trim for the temple in New Zion. The man explained how he had been taught to do the work when he was very young, and then taught those skills to his sons so the work could continue. Every person who had made some of the woodwork was at the temple when Alma's caravan arrived, and they were allowed to watch as their contribution was put in place."

"They were watching us. I remember how we all felt there were others there, helping us. Now we know who they were."

Nancy put her hand on her husband's shoulder and said, "Thanks for sharing that with us. Everyone we have served meals to seems to be dressed like people living on Earth now. Was Alma's ancestor dressed like that?"

The Bishop and Scott exchanged a quick look, and then the Bishop said, "I'm sorry. I did not realize the Sisters had not witnessed the arrival of the resurrected beings. Do you remember the conduit between heaven and Earth we saw in the tent last night?"

Nancy nodded.

"They're arriving, or descending, through that conduit."

"Oh," Nancy said. "Have any of you brethren seen the Prophet Joseph Smith?"

This time Michelle and Nancy both noticed the look that was exchanged between their husbands.

"I guess the resurrected Beings don't need to eat, so none of the Sisters would be aware of their arrival," Scott said.

"And you might want to catch a glimpse of some of them, right?" Dennis asked his wife. "Let me work on that."

In the morning, everyone was quickly involved with the increased number of people arriving in the valley. About noon, people in very unusual attire began arriving. Some appeared to be from civilizations that were unexposed to modern clothing. They were very humble people and seemed to be amazed by everything they saw; they acted as though they had never used silverware or sat at a table to eat. They smiled every time anyone did anything for them, and were extremely appreciative.

Late that afternoon, Dennis Bigelow stepped in front of Michelle and told her the women of the stake had been requested to meet in the center tent.

"What about the people who are waiting for food?" Michelle asked.

"Don't worry. Someone will take your place until you return."

From all over the valley, women began walking toward the tent. President Nelson was there to meet the group, and he patiently waited until every woman in his stake had arrived.

"Sisters," he began, "yesterday afternoon, Bishop Chandler brought to my attention that none of you were aware of the resurrected Beings assembled for this momentous occasion. I want to assure each of you that there is no reason you cannot see them. None of them have yet ventured out of this tent because they have been very busy. I spoke with the Prophet this morning and expressed your desire to see the Prophet Joseph, specifically, and he thought it would be fitting if you could spend time with some of the those you might know from reading the scriptures. For the next hour or so, you are welcome to visit with them. Please come with me."

The tears were already falling as the group of women followed their stake president into the tent and toward a large group of resurrected Beings. The Prophet Joseph Smith walked directly to President Nelson and began greeting the women. With him were his brother Hyrum and Brigham Young. The spirit was so intense it made it difficult for any of the women to speak. However, within a very few moments, they began moving through the group, stopping to visit with specific individuals.

Michelle was listening to a conversation between Nancy and Brigham Young, marveling that such a conversation could be taking place. Then she found herself thinking of her favorite person from the Book of Mormon. She had a painting of him standing at the railing of a great ship as he and his family traveled to the new world, and she had always wondered what it would have been like to stand in his presence and hear him speak. Someone touched her arm and as she turned, she saw Nephi, instantly recognizing him even though he looked nothing like the man in the painting on her living room wall.

"Nephi," was all she got out before her voice broke and she could not speak.

"Yes. I heard your thoughts and I would like to ask you a question."

"Sure," Michelle managed to say. She tried to wipe the tears from her face so she could see him clearly.

"As you read the many great accounts my people wrote for your generation, what made you identify with my words?"

"Many great events were recorded in the Book of Mormon, but I always marveled that you could be so forgiving when your brothers continued to, well, continually tried to kill you. I always admired that about you."

Nephi smiled at Michelle and said, "I am amused. Preserving the teachings of Jesus Christ and the traditions of our fathers was an immense responsibility for each person who had charge of the records during their life. The beautiful story of my people when Jesus visited them following His resurrection or the plight of Moroni would have been my choice for the most memorable events recorded in the book. But now I hear that forgiving my brothers is what impressed you?" Nephi smiled and shook his head slightly. "I was embarrassed to record that my brothers were unwilling to follow the teachings of our father, and I felt even worse about recording that they tried to kill me. I was certain it revealed that I was a poor influence on them. Your words are very special to me. I had no choice but to forgive them. I was mortal, even as you are, and I was in need of Jesus Christ's atonement, which required that I forgive those who trespassed against me."

"You sound so human," Michelle said. "I mean, your reasoning sounds like what my husband or my father might say. *I simply tried to do what the Lord expected of me.* I have read about you my whole life, and it is so amazing to talk with you, and to hear that you had insecurities, just like I do. Thank you so much for speaking with me."

"You are the person I wrote that record for, Michelle," Nephi responded. "All the years I engraved the words on the plates, I wondered if anyone would ever find value in the record. I remember wondering if people who would live on the Earth in the last days would be interested in anything about our lives. Now I know we are the same. We are both children of the Great Father, and have been sent to Earth at different times, but we are all brothers and sisters."

Nephi moved a step closer to Michelle and hugged her lightly, then stepped back. "Is there anyone else you would like to speak to? I don't know if they are here, but I will try to help you find them."

"There is one person I would love to talk to. But the questions I would ask him would probably sound like I am jealous of him, even though I greatly admire his faith . . ."

"Mosiah is right there. Maybe he could help you find the answers you seek," Nephi said.

Michelle shook her head, again surprised that Nephi had heard her thoughts. "Okay." She walked with Nephi toward a man who appeared to be watching them approach.

"Mosiah," Nephi said, "this is Michelle and she would like to visit with you."

"Thank you, Nephi," Michelle said. Then she turned to Mosiah and found herself looking into the gentle eyes of a man who was larger than she had imagined. For some unexplainable reason, she had imagined Mosiah to be about Scott's size.

"Am I not what you expected I would be?" Mosiah asked, and Michelle could not help but smile as she noticed how his eyes twinkled with amusement.

"I don't know why I imagined you as I did, but now that I see you, it seems that you could look no other way. I know that probably sounds strange, but it is as though I recognize you. I hope you do not mind my questions. I only wish I had enough faith to know the answers without asking the question."

"You have great faith, Michelle. You have trusted God to keep you safe in the midst of a poisonous atmosphere. I do not believe my faith is any stronger than yours."

"Maybe faith is not really the right description of what I would like to talk with you about. I have prayed for my brother many times, prayed that his heart would be softened and that he could understand how much God loves him." Michelle could not continue talking, as the heartache she felt every time she thought of her brother seemed to overpower her.

"You love your brother very much. You can identify with how much I loved my son and wanted him to realize the danger he faced in following his chosen path. I know you have prayed long and often for your brother's eternal well being. I also know that each time you have prayed for your brother to feel God's love for him, you have become the recipient of those prayers. God has sent those experiences to you as a witness that He has heard your prayers."

Michelle dropped to her knees, overcome with emotion and the powerful faith she could feel emanating from Mosiah. "Am I not praying hard enough for my brother? Why did God send an angel in answer to your prayer and yet my prayers do nothing to change my brother's heart?" she begged to know. "What more can I do? I would do anything if an angel would stand before him and reprimand him in such a way that caused a great change within him. I would not expect him to become one of the greatest missionaries who ever lived, as your son did. But if only he could let God into his heart enough to find the peace that he searches for." She could hardly speak as her inability to help her brother tore at her heart. "If only you could tell me what else is needed to be able to do such a great thing for someone you love."

Mosiah knelt and tenderly embraced Michelle. "You have done all you can. Only God knows the heart of each of His children. I cannot tell you why an angel has not stood before your brother and personally reprimanded him for his behavior. But you must never cease praying for him and never allow your faith to falter; God loves your brother even more than you do."

"I'm sure it was your great faith that brought about such an amazing miracle," Michelle said between sobs.

Mosiah gently pulled Michelle to her feet and studied her tear-streaked face. "My dear sister, do you believe that each person who comes to this Earth has the freedom to choose for himself?"

Michelle nodded as she sniffed. Tears streamed unchecked down her face but she did not care.

"Perhaps an angel has appeared to your brother. Perhaps his heart was softened, but he refused to accept the restrictions accepting the gospel would bring into his life. Perhaps your prayers have been answered exactly as were mine, but your brother has used his personal agency to make his own decision about whether or not to listen. Our Great Father in Heaven will never force any of His children to accept His teachings. Do you believe that, with all your heart?"

Again, Michelle nodded.

Mosiah continued to speak quietly. "Your prayers on behalf of your brother have reached your Father in Heaven. Remember, He has experienced the same thing you are going through, inasmuch as a third of His children rebelled and decided they did not want what He had to offer. However, they were not content to walk away; they have tried ever since to thwart the Father's plan for the rest of His children. Take comfort in knowing how much your Heavenly Father loves you and understands what you are going through. Continue to do all you can for your brother. Have faith, find peace in the knowledge that Father knows your brother's heart, and can truly judge his intentions." Mosiah smiled down at Michelle and asked, "Have I helped you?"

Michelle was filled with peace and her tears stopped. "Yes. I'm sorry I am such a crybaby, but I love my brother so much. Thank you for talking with me."

"You are very welcome and I am extremely pleased that you sought me out. We know each other better than you realize, and I will see you again."

Michelle managed to smile and said, "Thank you." She gave him a warm hug and thanked him again. When she turned around, she saw Nancy and Marie watching her. She smiled and walked toward them. "Who have you talked to?" she asked Nancy.

"Brigham Young and Noah. It has been amazing."

"How about you, Marie?" Michelle asked.

"Isn't this wonderful?" sighed Marie. "I talked to Jeremiah and Enoch, and I listened to Patrice Nelson's amazing discussion with the Three Nephites."

When the women left the tent, they returned to their assigned tasks. It was fortunate the visits with the resurrected Beings had not occurred at the beginning of the day's work assignments because the Sisters thought of and talked about little else the rest of the afternoon.

Michelle was very excited to share her experience with Scott, so as soon as they were both finished with their work shift, they took Adam and headed for the grass on the east side of the valley. Not surprisingly, everyone who worked the same shift as they did was also seeking a quiet place to talk. Rather than individual conversations between husband and wife, small groups of friends assembled to share their experiences. Michelle started to describe her visit with Mosiah, but found she was quickly overcome with the same strong emotions she had experienced during their conversation, and had to be content to listen to others for the time being.

Nancy was sharing the details of her conversation with Noah and it seemed very amusing to the group gathered around her.

"I wanted to know how he got the animals into the ark, but the first words that came out of my mouth were, 'Was it hard to convince your family that they needed to get on the ark or they would perish?' I was surprised to hear myself ask that question, which Noah answered, but then he also answered the question I had been thinking."

"Wow," Beth said. "And what was his answer to the question you asked, about getting his family onto the ark?"

"Well, he said his wife never questioned his actions and just started getting ready to do it. But then he smiled and added that in those days wives did not question their husbands without great cause."

"All right," Nancy's husband added, as though he had won a personal victory. "Did you catch that, brethren? Wives never questioned their husbands. Way to go, Noah!"

Nancy laughed quietly and then cocked her head and watched her husband until he stopped the little victory dance he had decided to perform.

"Okay," the Bishop said, as he sat down. "I apologize." Then he smiled broadly and said, "I just never expected such profound words to be spoken to my own wife by a Prophet of God."

"I can wait if you want to entertain us further," Nancy said to her husband as she tried to look obedient and subservient.

"No, go right ahead, my unquestioning wife."

"Oh, thank you." Nancy lowered her head as though bowing to her husband and then laughed. "Noah did say that his youngest son thought he was crazy, at least at first. But, after praying about it, his son received confirmation that what his father was saying was true. Noah said he thought it was ironic that his son then had an equally difficult time convincing his own wife that she should believe him. But in the end, all of his family were in the ark."

"Now tell us how he got the animals on the ark," Beth said.

"He said he didn't."

"What?" more than one person asked.

"He said he didn't get any of the animals on the ark, all he did was open the doors and let them in. God directed them and they obeyed. He said there was no enmity between them, and they conversed with Noah and his family, just like they did in the Garden of Eden. So, all but the fish in the sea just walked in the doors and found a place to sleep."

"That's amazing. Simple, just the way it should be if God is in control," the Bishop answered. "Nancy, did you get the feeling that Noah would be just like our present Prophet if he were to wear the clothes we are used to?"

"It's funny you should ask that," Nancy said. "We sort of had that very conversation. I did get a distinct impression while I was talking to him that if he dressed like we do today, he would fit right in. When I mentioned that he seemed like one of the Church leaders of today and that rather surprised me, he said I was a pleasant surprise for him, too. He said he has watched the spirits of those returning from Earth, and many of them arrive with a proud and arrogant attitude, almost as if they should be in charge rather than feeling remorseful about disregarding our Father in Heaven's teachings. He said it caused great sorrow to realize that the sacrifices that had been made by so many during their life on Earth could be of such little value to those who followed the whisperings of Satan. He said it was wonderful to see people like us who had shown such great faith to come into the land that was filled with poison. I found it interesting that he seemed as pleased to visit with us as we were to visit with the resurrected Beings."

"I was surprised at that, too," Marie said. "I thought people like Enoch and Jeremiah would think it was rather a waste of time to talk to mortal women. However, when I talked to Enoch, he did not act like that at all. I didn't even have to ask him any questions. I told him how amazing it was to be standing in his presence when he was so righteous he was removed from the wicked environment of the Earth, and then he told me that he was impressed that we could live among those who were so unrighteous and still have such strong testimonies and faith. Then I was wondering what it would be like to live where there was never any temptation from Satan. He said that I would know how that felt very soon, because when the Savior returned to the Earth, Satan would cease to have any influence over the people on the Earth. I think I will always remember every second spent with such amazing men."

"Even Brigham Young was a big surprise to me," Nancy said. "I always thought he was a stern leader who just told people to step up and do what the Lord wanted them to do. When I stood looking into his eyes and could feel the absolute faith he had, and how his whole demeanor softened when he spoke about his wives and children, I felt the same way I do when I am close to the Prophet. His love and concern emanates from him, and I felt it pass through me when I was close to him. I agree with Marie that this was the most amazing day I have ever experienced."

"You said you talked to Jeremiah, Marie. What was he like?" Michelle asked.

"It was amazing. Since he and Lehi were both in Jerusalem at the same time, I asked him why there were two prophets in the same place. He said that even as there are two Prophets in Jerusalem now, so there were two Prophets in Jerusalem then. I asked him why he didn't leave Jerusalem when Lehi and his family did, especially since Lehi was prophesying that the city was going to be destroyed. He said that we know Lehi's dealings with God because of the record his posterity recorded for our time, and that was according to God's plan. However, Jeremiah's responsibility was to call the people of Jerusalem to repentance and that was what he did. I felt his faith, just like Nancy was describing. I felt very privileged to be able to speak with him and see that he was a child of God, just like me, who did what he was sent to Earth to accomplish, the same as we have done by coming out here to build the temple. You know, even though we did not really discuss that, the impression I got while we were talking was that we both accomplished what we were sent here to do. I'll never forget that feeling."

Scott broke the short silence that had followed Marie's words when he said, "I find it interesting that the women in our group wanted to know how the Prophets of old felt when they were doing what they had been sent here to do, and sometimes they wanted to know how they accomplished the great works recorded in the scriptures. That really points out to me the difference between our spirits. If it had been the brethren invited to speak to that same group of men, I for one would have asked very different questions. I would have wanted to talk to the Three Nephites and ask them if I had ever met them or if certain events in my life had ever been influenced by their work. I would have wanted to know how involved they are or have been, and how visible they are to the public. I don't think I would have asked the same questions of them as the Sisters did."

"I agree with what you're saying," Bishop Chandler said. "I am so grateful our wives have had this opportunity. I know if I had the opportunity to speak with Mosiah, I would have wanted to know how it felt to be so inspired that he could give a single sermon that would cover everything a person needs to know – everything. His sermons were a huge factor in my personal conversion, when I became certain the Church is true. How can mere words written about what one man said be strong enough to convert someone more than two thousand years after they were written?"

"I wonder if we will someday have the opportunity to meet the person who is powerful enough to change the heart of anyone and everyone in the entire world." Dennis asked. "We all read about the Holy Ghost, but we are never told anything about Him. Yet I sometimes wonder how amazingly positive His influence must be in order for Him to confirm righteous things. It seems to me God must hold him in the same regard as our Mother in Heaven, and I think Heavenly Father has never allowed anyone to record anything about them or even know their names because they are so revered by Him." Dennis looked at his wife and said, "I'm actually thinking you and the rest of the Sisters were given this opportunity so you could bring back these wonderful experiences and share them with us hard-boiled guys. Sometimes we get caught up in the *how* and forget to cherish and seek the *why* or relish the feelings involved in the *doing* of events that have shaped the world."

President Nelson spoke from behind Dennis and said, "I have certainly enjoyed walking among the members of our stake this evening and listening to the amazing blessings we have received this day. I'm sure we'll be sharing these experiences for many weeks to come."

The next morning there was a noticeable difference in the attitudes of the members of the New Zion Stake. It was a visible change in the expression on their faces. When they first arrived at Adam-ondi-Ahman, the general attitude had been one of willingness to do whatever was needed. When Jesus arrived, their attitudes had exhibited total dedication to their duties. After the Sisters' incredible opportunity to visit with resurrected Beings, the love they felt from their visitors changed them even more, and now that love motivated their every action. Their service to those attending the gathering and their relationships with each other moved to a higher level that resulted in even greater joy being experienced from the service given.

Scott and the Bishop were in the Melchizedek tent, helping the steady stream of newcomers. Suddenly, they were alone – the arrivals seemed to end.

"Scott, has Michelle been able to tell you what she discussed with Mosiah? She seemed so emotional last night when we were all talking, and Nancy told me she had sobbed nearly uncontrollably during her conversation with him."

"She still gets emotional when she tries to describe her experience, but she did say they were talking about her brother. He is inactive and she loves him so much. It hurts her that he seems to be searching for something he feels is missing in his life, and looks everywhere but in the teachings of the gospel. He always tells her that he never felt anything spiritual when he was a member, and he thinks she is brainwashed into thinking the teachings could be true. She cries so many nights when she prays for him."

"Well, Mosiah must have said something that brought her a little understanding because Nancy said she was totally peaceful when her conversation with him ended, and yet she was still too emotional to share it with us. Many of our group has family members that have been deceived by Satan. I hope she will be able to share her experience with us at some point. Perhaps it will help all of us who desperately want to share our love of the gospel with inactive family members."

"I think she'll be able to, eventually," Scott said. "Michelle has such a tender heart that she has a hard time controlling her emotions when something so spiritual occurs in her life."

Preparations were complete. Cleaning the entire valley of Adam-ondi-Ahman in preparation for Jesus' return for the final ceremony involved everyone in attendance. With so many helping, the process resembled a cartoon. They swept across an area filled with chairs, tables, lights, and supplies. The area was emptied nearly as fast as they could walk, leaving only the grass and vibrant foliage behind. Before mid-day, the transports were reloaded and all the men participating in the final ceremony began moving to their assigned places.

Scott walked with Michelle and Adam to the transport that would take them back to New Zion. "I'll be back before you even get Adam settled down," Scott said as he embraced Michelle. "You be a good boy," he said to Adam.

"Good boy," Adam repeated.

"Yes, good boy." Scott watched through the window while Michelle situated Adam in his seat, and then stepped away.

"Ready?"

Scott turned to see the Bishop and Dennis approaching him. "Yeah. Ready." He turned to wave at his wife and son one more time, and then followed the two men. They had been asked to stay behind and drive the transport back to New Zion.

"Can you believe we get to witness this world-changing event in person?" Dennis asked.

Bishop Chandler had been quiet as they walked, and suddenly he seemed to experience a small explosion of excitement. He let out a quiet whoop, and his entire body seemed to shiver. "Unbelievable! I thought for sure President Nelson and his two counselors were going to stay and bring back the transport. I think I would have done that if I were the stake president."

"Where are we supposed to go?" Dennis asked as they neared the area where everyone was assembling.

"President Nelson told me that we should stand with the men in the Melchizedek group, in front of the tent in the south end of the valley. He told me to follow the lead of the men in the group, but to remember that it was all part of a ceremony. He said we would know what to do."

"Okay," Scott said. "I find great consolation in the fact that I can make a mistake or two and not be noticed. One advantage of being part of a group that numbers in the millions."

The men joined the group waiting in front of the southern-most tent. The grandeur that was to be the final phase of the Grand Gathering at Adam-ondi-Ahman began to unfold. In spite of the vast number of men assembled, it was so quiet the soft rippling of the tents caused by the slight breeze could be heard. The front edge of the tent they were standing by had been gracefully folded up and the massive number of resurrected Beings that were assembled inside was now visible. They began to move out of the tent to join the men standing on the grass.

The sounds of the angels singing praises to Jesus Christ began as a quiet melody that made everyone strain to hear it. The volume increased gradually as the army of angels descended through the conduit that had remained connected between heaven and Earth during the gathering. They quickly spread out until they filled the entire valley. The emerald green of the grass made their dazzling white robes seem even brighter. It was hard to estimate how many angels were in the group; the grass and vegetation covering the 3,000 acres used for the Great Gathering was completely covered, except for the areas that were occupied by the three massive tents.

The rhythm of Scott's heartbeat quickened and he felt himself breathing harder, as though his entire being was preparing for the ceremony to begin. Even though the front wall of the center tent had not been raised, it was obvious to everyone when Jesus Christ returned to the valley from His home in heaven and was again in their presence.

Adam moved from where he had been standing in the center of the southern tent, and walked through the vast gathering in front of his tent. He stopped when he reached the northern edge of the group; everyone turned to face north. Scott could see the tent on the north end of the valley. The front wall had been folded up and the men standing in front of it were now facing south. A lone horn could be heard heralding the beginning of the event. The sound seemed to waft through the entire valley. Both Adam and Aaron began walking toward each other, leading their group of men in a slow, rhythmic step. The millions of men, walking in unison, made the Earth tremble with each step, and the music from the horn was joined by an ever increasing number of additional horns and instruments never heard on Earth before that were somehow hauntingly familiar. When the two groups met in front of the center tent, Adam and Aaron walked forward. The volume of the heavenly choir increased as the front of the tent was raised in wide sweeping folds, revealing a golden throne resting on a floor that appeared to be made of solid gold. Jesus Christ, no longer the meek servant that had come to Earth as a sacrifice for mankind, sat in regal glory upon the throne and looked out at the gathering in front of Him.

Adam stepped forward until he stood directly in front of the Savior. Scott could not hear the words being said, but he could see that Adam stood very formally in front of Jesus and the movement of his body made it seem that he was giving a report to the Savior. After speaking for a considerable amount of time, he knelt before Jesus, who stood and stepped forward; He put His hands on Adam's head and pronounced a blessing upon him, and then pulled Adam up from his knees and embraced him warmly.

Adam stepped back away from Jesus and remained standing, facing Him.

Aaron stepped forward and spoke to Jesus for some time, as though he was also presenting a report, and then he knelt before Jesus. The Savior laid His hands on Aaron's head and blessed him, and then pulled

Aaron to his feet and embraced him. When Aaron stepped back near where Adam was standing, both men stepped further away from Jesus and stopped, still facing Him.

Scott, for the first time, allowed his eyes to look around at the grand gathering. He noticed the large area to the south of the center tent that had been left vacant was now completely filled with crates and tables full of scrolls, plates, and other artifacts. He wondered when they had arrived, as he could not remember having looked at that area within the last twenty-four hours. Suddenly, his attention was again focused on the proceedings.

From among the groups that were assembled, the Prophets of the last dispensation, from Joseph Smith to the current Prophet, walked to the area where the records and scrolls were located and retrieved their personal writings. Then they slowly assembled in a line before Jesus. The Prophets individually presented their writings to Jesus and gave a verbal report. The group concluded with Joseph Smith presenting the scripture he had written. He did not present any of the Book of Mormon, as those were words written by other Prophets. When he concluded speaking, that group of Prophets knelt before Jesus. He laid His hands on each of them individually, gave them a blessing, and then embraced each as He pulled them to their feet.

Groups of Prophets continued to come forward, but Scott was not familiar with who these men were. Each Prophet retrieved his writings and presented them to Jesus. As each group finished, Jesus repeated the same actions as they knelt before Him.

Scott saw that as each record was given to Jesus, He then gave it to an individual who took it into the tent. This continued until all the Prophets of the Earth's history had presented their words to Jesus.

Jesus looked over the multitude assembled before Him and spoke. Scott was surprised that His voice could be clearly heard by everyone in attendance; he had not been able to hear Christ's words during most of the ceremony, and he was now certain that was intentional.

"I commend each of you for faithfully fulfilling your stewardship. The writings that have been presented to me are a record of the warnings each of you delivered to the inhabitants of this Earth during your lifetime. These records stand as a witness of the innumerable opportunities mankind has been given to turn from sin in every dispensation of time, and they will stand for or against each man at the day of his final judgment. Your records provide a witness of the goodness and mercies that have been bestowed upon the children of God, throughout the history of this world. These records have now been delivered to heaven. The accountability I have to my Father for this creation is nearly complete."

Jesus turned and again sat upon the golden throne. Adam and all those in the long row of Prophets turned to face the assembly and shouted to the men. As Scott watched, some ritual that seemed to be known to the Prophets unfolded. The ritual was unfamiliar to him, but he found it easy to follow the lead of the men standing around him. Adam shouted a word of praise, and the millions of men shouted the same word in return, then Aaron shouted the word of praise, and the millions of men shouted it back in return. Jesus then shouted to the entire group and His voice actually did cause the ground to tremble; His authority to command the elements of the Earth was apparent as He waved His hand in a wide arc around where He sat. The vegetation everyone had been so grateful for during the past four days seemed to become more vivid in color and intricate in texture in a circle around Him that quickly spread away from Him. The ground that had been barren outside the 3,000 acres designated as Adam-ondi-Ahman instantly changed to match the land inside the boundary, and the change spread out in an ever-spreading circle in every direction from where Jesus sat, until it spread over the horizon in every direction. The toxic, barren landscape that had been the result of a nuclear explosion was healed and returned to the pristine condition that existed when Adam and Eve first dwelt on the Earth.

No one moved or said anything for a long moment. Scott found himself weeping for joy, as was everyone around him. The prophesied day had finally arrived and Jesus Christ was now the ruler of the Earth. He had performed the ordinance and was given the reins of leadership for governing the whole Earth by the voice of the Priesthood. Angels began to encircle Jesus and the Savior rose in their midst until He disappeared into the conduit that could not be seen except by those standing close to the center tent, and the majority of men who had been standing before Him followed.

In less time than it would take to retell the miracle, the multitude took the three massive tents down and packed them into the waiting transport. The valley was returned to its original splendor. Not one visible thread of evidence from the great gathering was left behind, and everyone seemed very anxious to begin their individual journey home.

The three brethren of the New Zion Stake quickly drove south toward New Zion. "I still can't make my mind believe that we just saw Jesus assume the reigns of leadership for the government of this world," the Bishop said, eventually breaking the silence that had existed since their departure. "And even as we speak, Jesus and His army of angels are preparing to come to Earth. I wonder if we will get back before He arrives in New Zion."

Dennis spoke, more as though he were continuing the Bishop's thoughts than addressing the other two men. "And now every person on the Earth will know He is the Savior of the world. Soon, or maybe already, He will depart from Heaven, clothed in glory, and proceed to Earth to assume His rightful place as ruler. Today. Not some distant time in the future, but today He will visit the temple we have built for Him, and receive it unto Himself."

"So this is the great and dreadful day of the Lord," Scott said quietly. "Dreadful does not even begin to describe what I have experienced today, and great is too weak and insufficient to describe what happened. I wonder if this is how people feel when they retire after working all their life. Yesterday I had a job and I loved it, but now it's over and I'm wondering what I will be doing every day for the rest of eternity."

After several moments of silence, Bishop Chandler said, "I remember hearing mention of a temple that will be built in Far West.

A COMET

Abram stopped speaking to Isaac when he heard the gunshots, and before either of them could voice a single question, the explosion was heard. They instinctively ran to the entrance of the building to determine if they should take shelter inside or leave to help fight. What they saw was hard to comprehend. A large plume of smoke rose above the northeast corner of the old part of the city. Off-duty troops raced toward that area of town and the sound of gunshots and small explosions continued.

"I'm going home," Abram shouted as he ran toward the parking lot. His mind toggled between fearing that the enemy troops would damage the temple and having concern for the safety of his wife. It took every ounce of resolve within him to stay in his car rather than abandoning it and joining the majority of Jerusalem's citizens who were running through the streets.

When he finally reached home, his wife ran from the house to his arms. "I have been so scared! I knew the attack was close to your office and I was so afraid."

"I am safe," he said, hugging her tightly.

"Could you see what is happening?" she asked, before burying her face against his chest.

"The enemy troops broke through the wall in the northeast corner of the city. I saw smoke and heard explosions. We'll stay here until we learn what's happened."

They stayed inside their home, huddled in safety, watching the local news reports on television. Muslims gathered in Megiddo reported the victorious annihilation of the Jewish prophets. Celebrations began in the Valley of Estraelon and spread through the cities of Hadera, Netanya and Tel Aviv. In Jerusalem, Muslims joyfully danced around the bodies of the Prophets that lay where they had fallen.

Their ward had developed and rehearsed plans to reach areas of safety if the armies broke through and overran the city. So far, the Jewish army was able to hold back the Muslims, so all they could do was pray and try to be patient until the will of the Lord was revealed.

"I can't believe these people get so much satisfaction from seeing two people they have killed laying in the street," Abram said. "What would happen if we killed their religious leader and then never allowed them to show proper respect for his body?" He quit speaking because his anger increased with each thought he expressed.

When Rebekah spoke, Abram noticed there was no emotion in her voice. "These evil people intend to leave the bodies of our Prophets laying in the street for three and a half days to symbolize the three and a half years they have been protecting Jerusalem."

Abram could easily see the anguish in her eyes. "Are you afraid they will overrun Jerusalem?" he asked.

"Yes, I am. They have gained access into our city and the number of Muslims who have congregated outside the city swells by the hour, with a steady stream of new arrivals. How will we ever protect ourselves or our temple?"

"The only thing we can do is pray to God that He will deliver us. We have been doing that since the beginning of time."

"I know. I just thought we would have many more years to spend with one another," Rebekah answered as tears began to roll down her face. "My one consolation at this time is that we will be together for all eternity, no matter what happens."

"Can we please do that last line again?" Ruth asked timidly. "I can't quite seem to get it right."

"Certainly," the conductor said. "The last line again, please."

After they sang the last line again, the conductor said, "There doesn't seem to be a problem that I can hear. You are all free to go. I do not think we even need another practice because this choir sounds perfectly beautiful. As soon as Jesus is ready to leave and go to Earth, we will all be ready to join Him."

When Jacob quietly laughed, Ruth asked, "Why are you laughing?"

Jacob looked up at her beautiful smile. "It's ironic. Your voice is one of the prettiest in the entire choir and you sang every note perfectly, even though you didn't feel you got it right. I'm still getting used to the idea that I will be participating in His glorious return. I've only just arrived back home from Earth, and if things had happened a little differently, I would have been standing on Earth watching His arrival, wondering what was happening."

"I don't believe things happen in any way other than the way God planned them to happen," Ruth said, and Jacob smiled, just as everyone who ever heard her voice had done.

"Some of the last words I heard on Earth were in complete agreement with what you just said," remembered Jacob. "I was walking with one of the Prophets in Jerusalem, and he asked me if I believed God had a plan for each person's life. I told him I did, and then I died. Doesn't that seem strange to you?"

"How old were you when you expired?"

"I wasn't old; but, was an adult. I had only been a member of the Church for a very short time and I was not married. I had been baptized and received the ordinances in the temple and am so thankful I was there long enough to do that."

"Then you are very blessed," she said. "I lived on the Earth when the truth was nowhere to be found. I lived in Russia and only lived for two years. No one on Earth even knows I ever lived. I have been waiting and hoping that someone will find my name and my Earthly parents' names and then complete our Earthly ordinances so we can be an eternal family."

"I don't understand. I thought you didn't need to be baptized if you expired before you were eight years of age."

Ruth smiled and her eyes sparkled as she said, "That's right. But my parents are waiting for someone to be baptized for them, and then marry them so we can be sealed as a family."

"Oh, I see," Jacob answered, now feeling sorry for her. "Do you even remember living on the Earth?"

"Oh, yes. I remember everything about the time I was on Earth. I know my parents loved me. My older brothers, my sister and I are all waiting to be sealed together as a family."

"Do you have relatives on Earth now who could do the Earthly ordinances for you?" he asked.

"Yes. I watch them and I know they believe in God, but they have never even heard the gospel message."

"That must be very frustrating for you," Jacob said. "I was very fortunate to live in Jerusalem and be taught about the gospel."

"You lived in Jerusalem. Were you a Jew?"

"Yes, do you know about Jews?" Jacob asked, quite surprised.

"I believe everyone knows about the Jews. Jesus was a Jew, and they are the ones that crucified him."

Jacob looked away and sighed. "That's very true. Were you here or on Earth when that happened?"

"I was here," Ruth answered quietly.

"As was I. I remember how I felt when we watched that terrible event in disbelief. It's hard for me to fit life with the Great Father and life on Earth into the same picture."

"That feeling will pass quickly. Are you happy that you lived in Jerusalem?" Ruth asked.

"Would you like to walk with me?" Jacob asked. "I like to be outdoors."

"As do I."

Jacob slowly walked toward the door. "To answer some of your earlier questions, I did love living in Jerusalem. I loved being a Jew. I loved our traditions and I was proud of the history of my people. The only involvement I had with the United States was that one of my friends met an American when he was in college."

"Are Americans different than the Jews?"

"Yes. Abram's friend was different, in a very good way. They had many discussions about their religions, and Abram said he came to realize that the teachings of his friend's religion contained many similarities to the Jewish beliefs. Later, after they finished school, Abram got to visit his friend in Salt Lake City, and he always talked about how special that trip was."

"Is your friend Abram still living on Earth?" Ruth asked.

"Yes, he and his wife live in Jerusalem. There is a war going on there. In fact, I died during an attack from the enemy armies."

"Have you asked for permission to see your friend's life?" Ruth asked as she slowed her stride.

"No, I should do that... I am so happy to be back home and also want to visit the places I loved so much. What's your favorite place?" Jacob asked, suddenly hoping this girl enjoyed spending time with him.

"A beautiful waterfall. Would you like to see it?"

"Very much," Jacob answered. "When I lived here, I was never in this area except to bid farewell to friends when they left for Earth. Do you know of the area past the river of sand?"

"I know of it, but I seldom went there. Is that where you lived?"

"Yes. I will show it to you sometime, if you like."

"What about the central gardens?" Ruth asked, as she walked through the green grass. " Have you been there?"

"Afraid not. What kind of gardens are they?"

"Flower gardens. All colors, all kinds, the most amazing flowers. I'll show that to you someday, if you're interested."

Jacob nodded and walked in silence next to Ruth as she led the way to the edge of the cliff that overlooked the magnificent falls that fell into the lagoons far below. "This is beautiful."

"I used to come here with my friends before I went to Earth. I find it interesting that all my friends, both the men and the women, lived in the Americas, except for me. My friend Elizabeth lived on the Earth until she was an old woman, and Bethany lived until she was married, but Sarah is still there, like your friend. Do you think they will be surprised when Jesus returns?"

Jacob paused for a moment while he seriously considered her question. "They know the Second Coming is close at hand. The two temples that had to be completed before the Messiah returned are both done, and the prophecy about the Prophets who were killed in Jerusalem has now been fulfilled."

"Our wait is nearly over also. Soon my family will be able to go to the temple and have the Earthy ordinances performed for us."

"So, what do you like best about this place?" Jacob asked as he looked at the thundering falls and the mist that rose up from the water.

"The lagoon at the bottom of the falls. I like swimming there, and then laying on the rocks and letting the sun dry me. I sometimes feel as though I am being absorbed into the beauty that surrounds the area. I can be content there for hours."

"Would you take me there with you some time?" Jacob ventured.

"Yes. When we return from escorting the Savior to Earth, all those who cannot abide His presence will expire and return here. That will keep us very busy for a time, but when we again have free time, I will be happy to show it to you."

They talked for a while, and then agreed to meet again the next day, Ruth watched Jacob as he walked away. She wandered slowly toward the place she loved to be, and found her friend there.

"Elizabeth, I'm glad you are here."

"What is it? Is something bothering you?"

"No," Ruth answered, smiling. "I just met someone new while the choir was rehearsing. He has just returned from Earth, and we spent some time together this afternoon."

"That's wonderful. You have many friends, so what is different about him?"

"He is intriguing to me." The smile faded from her face and she said, "But that's not why I wanted to talk to you. He told me about his friend who is still on Earth. He and his wife are working on the temple in New Zion, and the man was friends with a Jewish man named Abram that he met while he was in college."

"Okay," Elizabeth said slowly.

"Do you think there is any chance that his friend is the son of Elias?"

Elizabeth laughed and hugged Ruth. "He could be, but there are many people working on the temple in New Zion. Why don't you ask your friend what his friend's name is? If he says Scott, then maybe you are right. That would be nice. I have watched Sarah from time to time, and I know she has been concerned about her son."

"I'll ask him."

"Ruth, are you ever sad that you don't yet have an eternal companion?"

Ruth looked at her friend and shrugged. "I watch you with your companion and I know Sarah has found Elias on the Earth. I have always been happy so I don't know if I will be happier when I find an eternal companion." She smiled and then looked away from her friend. "I did have a good time this afternoon, though."

Jacob sat alone replaying the events of the day in his mind. He smiled when he thought of Ruth. He liked this pixie-like woman who made him smile every time she spoke. Her eyes sparkled when she talked, and she seemed different from anyone he had ever known. She seemed interested in knowing more about him. He smiled, knowing she would soon be able to see the temple in Jerusalem first hand when they trailed behind Jesus as He arrived on Earth in glory and majesty. Perhaps he had finally met someone he could enjoy being with who did not make him feel like her brother.

The barricades the Jewish armies had erected kept the Muslim armies contained in one corner of Old Jerusalem, but it was only a matter of time before vast numbers of troops would overrun the entire town. The Jewish people trapped inside Jerusalem knew their only possible salvation would be through divine intervention from God. After a tumultuous night of skirmishes and occasional explosions from rockets launched into several residential areas, the sun finally rose. For the third day, extreme Muslims continued to celebrate the murder of the two Jewish religious leaders.

Abram and Rebekah watched the limited news being broadcast within Jerusalem. About noon, they were stunned when Muslim soldiers suddenly attacked the commentator. In horror, they watched as a soldier beheaded the commentator, and then casually sat in front of the camera.

"We want the residents of Jerusalem to know what lies ahead, and we have decided to tell you the schedule for the coming few days. Your despicable religious leaders will remain in the street until tomorrow at three. During that time, our celebrations and gift giving will continue as we honor those who sacrificed their lives to kill these wicked men. The magicians will spend three and a half days rotting in the sun and each

day will represent a year that they held our forces at bay by their trickery. Maybe you who live inside the city of Jerusalem, you Jews, thought the past three and a half years passed quickly, but I can guarantee you that they did not pass quickly for those of us who are the rightful possessors of this holy city. It has grown increasingly long as we suffered outside the walls of this oasis in the desert.

"If these so-called prophets were your long-awaited Messiah, then their ministry was the same length as when Jesus Christ lived among you, and it will end equally bad for every Jew in the world today. Our celebrations will end tomorrow at three in the afternoon. At that time our armies will flow out over the entire city of Jerusalem and rid the world once and for all of every Jew now living here. We will destroy the sacrilege you call a temple. It will be torn down and not one stone will be left intact. At the same time, our armies around the world will seek out and destroy every government and citizen that has supported the Jews in any way. There are no neutral entities in this final battle to rid the world of the scourge the Jews have brought upon us. If you are not actively supporting our cause, you will be annihilated along with the Jews. By nightfall tomorrow there will be no Jew or any person who supports their cause, left alive on the Earth!"

The television screen went black and Abram and Rebekah sat in silence for many minutes. They held each other tightly and both softly cried. "No one ever told me that if I joined the one true church of God and was baptized I would be saved from this fate," Abram said. "However, deep in my heart, that is what I believed. Now I realize that ever since Jesus was crucified, we as a nation have been waiting for Him to come save us. I believe He has already saved us, Rebekah. We have been bound together for all eternity, and our death will not change that. It's not pleasant to think that tomorrow we will be killed, but it is not unpleasant to think that tomorrow we will enter the gates of Heaven together and live in peace for all eternity."

"I have never lived in peace," Rebekah said. "I will like that."

"Imagine, no more soldiers seeking to kill us. No more hatred from people we do not even know. No more fear that each day might be our last. We could try to flee with the members of our ward, but I am at peace. I cannot explain my feelings. Please tell me what you would like to do, because, if you wish, I will leave with you right now and we can seek a place to hide."

"I would like to see the Prophets one more time before I die."

Abram tried to speak, but his voice caught. After a moment he said, "Then you shall see them. Tomorrow at noon, we will leave our home and walk to the Temple Mount. Then we will walk close enough to see the Prophets and wait for our fate." Again, his voice broke, but he continued. "I would rather be killed in the first wave of annihilation than wait like a caged animal for them to find us."

Abram had no choice but to chuckle when Rebekah said, "That way we will arrive in Heaven before it gets too crowded."

Ribiab sat on the bench he had always thought of as Elias' bench. He went there often when he wanted to think of his friend. Ribiab remembered the day Elias left for his test on Earth. He had kept track of him as much as he was allowed, and had even been permitted to visit him on Earth when Stephan had taken his own life. Elias had felt such guilt and was filled with sadness. Those were dark times for Elias; Ribiab being blessed to have whispered words of encouragement into his ear.

Watching Elias travel along his path in life, Ribiab had helped inspire Elizabeth to speak words of encouragement to Elias as he sat in the temple. It had been a glorious day when Sarah finally came into Elias' life.

"Why are you sitting by yourself?" Phebe, Ribiab's Earthly sister, asked as she sat down on the bench next to him.

"I am enjoying this beautiful day. I sit here often because one of my closest friends met his eternal companion one afternoon while she was sitting right here."

"Do I know this friend?"

"I don't think you've met." Ribiab sighed and smiled. "It seems strange to me that we could be brother and sister on Earth, and that I've known you forever, and yet you and Elias do not know each other. He is on Earth, and has earned great honor by his obedience."

"You seem very calm compared to everyone else these days. Aren't you even a little excited about Jesus returning to the Earth again?"

"Yes, I am. I guess thinking about that is what brought me to this bench today. Elias and his wife, Sarah, are nearly finished with their Earthly test and I can't wait to visit them."

"My dear husband and I have been assigned to work in the temple in New Zion and I wanted to tell you before we left."

"I have long admired how you and your husband have helped those seeking their ancestors. Do you know specifically what you will be doing there?"

Phebe smiled and rubbed her hands together, fairly bursting with excitement. "Yes, we are going to help people correct errors caused by using incorrect records. I think it's going to be amazing to help unravel the confusion and connect families together."

"Our Earthly sister told me she will be working from this side of the veil making sure people are at the temple in New Zion when their earthly ordinances are performed. So that means someone could have been waiting for hundreds of years because their records were lost, and as soon as you get things straightened out, she will bring them to the temple to witness their earthly ordinances being completed. Is that right?"

"That could happen, and I'm excited about helping. Do you know what you will be doing during the Millennium?"

"Yes. Bethany and I have been assigned to work in the Salt Lake City Temple. We will escort those being sealed together as eternal families to the ordinance rooms where the work will be performed. Elias, my friend," he said, waving his hand to indicate the bench they were sitting on, "will be the mortal conducting the sessions. He will be able to see me and we will be able to become good friends again, even before he becomes a resurrected being and the veil is lifted. He knows Bethany, also, so we are both looking forward to seeing him again."

"It sounds like we'll all be busy. Mother and Father will be working in one of the temples in the eastern United States," Phebe said. "It's nice to visit with you for a moment, Ribiab. These are exciting times. I will tell my husband all the news you have told me. I love you." She leaned close and kissed Ribiab on the cheek and he hugged her.

"I love you," Ribiab said. He watched her walk away and was amazed, as always, that the love he had felt for her and the other members of his family on Earth had intensified since they returned to live with the Great Father. He again thought of Elias and realized that the love he felt for him was equally strong, but very different. He had always been an entity unto himself that interacted with Elias, Marash, and Shroba. They had become friends and grown very close, sharing their innermost feelings and views. However, he was part of the entity that included his two sisters and their families, and his Earthly parents. Generations that had seemed so distant from one another while his family lived on Earth, like his great uncle he had been named after, were very close when they had completed their mortal lives. The family unit included every generation from the present to the beginning of Earth's existence, and they moved as a unit through time.

Ribiab stood and looked down at the bench. "I'll see you soon, my friend."

"I'm pretty concerned about you. You've been distant all day and now I find you here talking to Sarah's bench."

Ribiab turned and smiled at his companion, then took her in his arms and hugged her. They slowly walked through the flower garden.

"I've been thinking about Elias and Sarah most of the day. I think they had a much harder trial on Earth than I did, but they have survived it. The Savior will shortly return to Earth and their test will be finished. And," he said, turning to smile at Bethany, "we'll get to work with them. Well, at least with Elias. I'm very excited to see him again."

Ribiab took Bethany's hand. "Soon you will be my eternal companion. I can honestly say I have waited forever for that to happen. I hope you are half as happy as I am."

"There is not any possible way I could be one bit happier," she said as she stood on her tiptoes to kiss him.

When the long-awaited day arrived that Jesus Christ would return to Earth in glory, everyone gathered at the Departure Building. The assembled children of the Great Father seemed innumerable, but nearly every mind reflected back to the great council when many more had gathered together with them. Those that had been cast out had organized and plotted, lied and deceived, and brought so many down to the depths of sorrow and despair. Finally, the time of had arrived, pausing the ability of the Defiant Ones to exert any influence upon Great Father's children.

When Jesus was ready to leave, the Great Father approached Him and hugged Him warmly. "You have been diligent in teaching and preparing your brothers and sisters for this day. I give you this gift in honor of your service, and as a token of my love for you."

Jesus accepted the gift and then let it unfold before Him. It was a beautiful scarlet robe. He pulled it on over the white robe He was wearing and hugged the Great Father. "Thank you, Father."

Jesus walked to the Departure Building and myriads of Father's children followed behind Him. They would now proceed to Earth through the departure portal as one flowing entity. When Jesus arrived on Earth, He would usher in the beginning of the Millennium.

"Do we have a telescope tucked away in some closet?" Mark asked Jenny. "I know I used to have a great telescope but I haven't even thought of looking through it for years."

"What sparked your interest now?" Jenny asked. She had just finished folding a batch of laundry and was in the process of putting the clean towels in the linen closet.

Mark had gone to their bedroom closet and was pulling things off the top shelf. "I know I've seen that telescope since we moved in here."

"I hope you're planning to put all that stuff back on the shelf when you're through playing in the closet," Jenny said as she stood with folded arms, watching Mark.

"This morning, several of the guys at our neighborhood meeting were talking about some comet they spotted last night. They said it was something new and people are really panicked about it because it's approaching Earth very quickly and seems to be on a collision course."

"That sounds serious," Jenny said. "It's times like this that I really miss satellite TV. I loved how I could flip on the TV and find out what was going on all over the world. By the time the local channels here in Salt Lake start broadcasting information about some comet, it will probably have already hit us."

"You're wrong this time, Honey," Mark said as he patted her arm on his way out of their bedroom. He went to Lynne's bedroom next and immediately opened her closet door.

"Don't you respect your own daughter's privacy?" Jenny asked from the hallway. "And what did you mean about me being wrong this time? Wrong about what?"

Mark's muffled voice came from the closet as he answered. "Turn on the TV and you'll see. I think every channel in the world is talking about little else."

"Don't forget that you have to put everything back, in both closets," Jenny said, and then she went to the living room to find out if he was right about the news. She waited impatiently for the picture to appear on the screen. "Wow," she said as she sat down.

"...land impact, it can be said in general that an asteroid approximately 75 meters in diameter can destroy a city, a 160 meter asteroid can destroy a large urban area, a 350 meter asteroid can destroy a small state, and a 700 meter asteroid can destroy a small country.

"If this asteroid were to impact the Earth over an ocean, the destruction would be much greater. The effects of an ocean impact are felt much further away than the effects of a land impact because the water's waves result in propagation that is more effective."

Jenny was not interested in the projected damage the asteroid could cause. She wanted to know if it was going to hit Earth for sure, and when. She flipped to another channel.

"The appearance of this asteroid has allegedly caught the scientific community by surprise. They monitor all major bodies in the galaxy, and yet this comet seemed to suddenly appear out of nowhere. What we know for sure is that every hour this asteroid becomes more of a concern, as it has been determined it is headed directly toward the Earth. We have received no reports of specific size or the expected impact site, so there are no confirmed reports of projected damage. We do know that this event has captured the attention of the world and it will only be a very short time, perhaps a day or two, before everyone's questions will be answered, probably with more clarity than we would prefer."

Jenny clicked the television off, as if she could erase from her reality the report she had just heard.

"Pretty sobering, isn't it?" Mark said from behind her.

Jenny was determined to not let the news create panic in her heart. "I take it that's why you wanted to find your old telescope."

"Yes, but from the sounds of that, we'll probably be able to just go outside and watch it arrive."

Jenny concentrated on making her voice sound calm and forced herself to speak slowly. "Has anyone heard when it is expected to hit the Earth?"

"No, just the same reports, repeated over and over, that no one knows for sure when it will arrive, where it will land, or how much damage it will create."

Jenny stood and walked to where Mark was standing. She put her arms around him and held him tightly. "We've seen all the prophecies come to pass. We know the temple is ready to be dedicated. The temple in Jerusalem has been completed. The Jews have gathered to their homelands. Is it time for the Savior to return to the Earth?"

Mark was overcome with emotion. He briefly tried to tighten his throat so no sound could reach his lips, but it was futile. "This is so hard, even with complete faith in Jesus Christ and knowing that this fulfills the purpose of Earth's creation. How do we stand here and patiently wait for things to end? Should we gather our daughters into the house and spend our last hours with each other, or do we let them go about their routine activities until they decide to seek out our company?" Mark's voice broke and he softly sobbed with Jenny.

Nearly everyone who had gathered to watch their eldest brother depart began moving to their assigned areas. Those living on the Earth that had failed to live in a manner that would allow their bodies to endure the presence of their Savior would immediately return to their former home when the Millennium began. The Great Father loved each of His children unconditionally, and each would be welcomed when they returned, even though He would be filled with sorrow at the eternal state those returning had achieved.

For two days, everyone in New Zion had been watching the sky. The comet that was headed toward the Earth could be seen with the naked eye, and each day those awaiting its arrival grew more excited. While the rest of the world seemed to be captured in a quickly disintegrating world, those that were prepared for the Savior's return were not afraid.

"It looks so close, surely it will arrive today," Michelle said.

Scott tried to keep Adam's attention focused on the approaching mass of brightness. "I wonder if our little boy will remember any part of today? I can't remember anything before I was about three years old."

"That's sad, isn't it? He will be one of the first people on Earth to witness the Savior's Second Coming, and he probably won't remember it."

As the group waited and visited, the white cloud grew closer and closer. Soon it became apparent the cloud was Jesus standing amid a group of angels, and those angels seemed to extend back to Heaven itself.

"Look," Michelle said. "The last time we saw Him, His robes were white as snow. Now He's wearing red robes."

"I've read the scriptures that said He would come in great power and glory wearing scarlet robes. You know, I thought since we had been so blessed to see Him and visit with Him at Adam-ondi-Ahman, this time it would be a little less overwhelming. I was wrong." Scott fell to his knees as the Savior came close to them. Jesus stopped, then as He had done each time He was close to Adam, reached out to take him in His arms.

"I am always so happy to see you," He said. "You will be a great leader to those like yourself who will grow up not knowing any influence from the Father of All Lies. I bless you, Adam, with the power to lead with great strength and humility."

He kissed Adam's forehead and returned him to his parents, smiled at Scott and Michelle, and moved forward into the temple. Many members of the multitude that arrived with the Savior followed Him into the temple. After a short time, the Savior emerged from the temple alone. He stopped to address the group of pioneers who had built the temple in preparation of His return.

"The air that has been polluted since you arrived is now pure once again. This place has been cleansed from the effects of any wickedness that could not endure my presence."

He stretched His arm out and moved it in a wide circle around Him. Immediately the ground began to change and green shoots could be seen pushing through the soil. Scott and Michelle were close to where the Savior was standing and they could feel the authority He was exercising over the elements of the Earth as vividly as they could feel His love and concern for them. Jesus was the same as He had been when He visited with them at Adam-ondi-Ahman. However, an added element of authority made everyone who gazed upon Him certain He was completely in charge of the events that were taking place. He walked to other couples that had babies, and in each case, He took the child in His arms and gave it a blessing. The demonstration of power strong enough to transform the Earth and loving concern that caused Him to bless newborn babies overwhelmed everyone in the group and the tears flowed freely.

"I wonder if we will ever get used to being around Him?" Scott said quietly to Michelle. "I always feel like throwing myself on the ground and kissing His feet. I wonder if we always felt that way about Him even before we came to Earth?"

"Personally, I think it will always be obvious that He is accepting of us and we love Him, but He is so perfect I feel the need to worship and adore Him."

Jesus had finished blessing the babies and stood looking at the group around Him. "The faith and dedication you have shown in building this House, even an Holy house unto me, has already allowed you to endure my presence and the change brought to pass upon the Earth which will cause it to become a terrestrial world. Those who have not kept the commandments and have listened to the voice of the Father of All Lies will be burned as stubble, as they will not be able to abide these changes. Two of my Prophets who have died in my service in Jerusalem will shortly come here and dedicate this House to fulfill the purpose of its creation. People from both sides of the veil will work together to complete the work that will be performed in this temple. Many who have come with me will remain here to aid with that work. Soon people will begin to arrive and the temple will be filled with those awaiting their endowments and sealings. This work must all be completed before the end of the thousand years, in which I will reside here and rule the world. I leave you now and say unto you, well done, thou good and faithful servants."

Then He turned and moved away from New Zion, the massive group following behind as if gliding on a cloud.

Everyone watched the group that departed. Their hearts overflowed with love and appreciation for the many things the Savior had done for them. They watched the procession until it disappeared from view. The dry, toxic land they had become used to had been changed; grass covered the ground, flowers, shrubs, and small trees now provided additional landscaping around the temple, and the flowers that had been carefully planted and tended increased in beauty and vigor. By the time everyone's attention was returned to the present, they could scarcely believe their eyes. The blossoms that filled the air with sweet fragrance were everywhere they looked. Trees filled with ripened fruit and berries of every type dotted the landscape. The gardens they had tended were overflowing with abundance, and were now only a small part of the vegetables and fruits that seemed to be ready for harvest.

There was silence as the awareness was accepted that the Savior's arrival had ushered in the Millennium. Thoughts of the devastation that had been prophesied to occur at this time in every part of the world tempered their joy.

"Jesus," Adam said.

Michelle and Scott smiled at each other, and then Scott seemed to think of something that made the expression on his face become one of concern. "I have wondered many times about Abram. There could be terrible things happening in Jerusalem right now. He was receptive of the teachings of the Church, but he always remained faithful to the religion of his fathers. So many times, I wanted to bear my testimony to him and beg him to pray about whether or not the Church was true, but I always felt strongly that I should simply be a good friend to him. He was one of the best friends I ever had and yet I never was able to share the joy that membership in the Church brings into our lives. That has always made me feel sad."

"The fate of so many, many people is being made known at this very moment as the Millennium arrives. Now our land of desolation seems like the very best place to be in the whole world."

◆◆◆◇◆◆◆

The news agencies in every country of the world had talked of little else but the approaching comet, but suddenly no one cared. Instead, the only story being discussed was the announcement from the organized joint military forces of the Muslim population in Jerusalem promising the death of every Jew by the following day.

Christian nations around the world quickly put into action their respective emergency plans. Although the United States, as a country, had withdrawn their support of the Jews several years earlier, it was well known that financial support was sent to Jerusalem on a regular basis by a Jewish underground movement. What was less known was that another underground organization was actively seeking to destroy anyone who was sympathetic with the Jewish underground movement. Those who had refused to accept the embedded chip were also on the list of targets.

On the same day the Jews were to be finally and forever eliminated from the face of the Earth, a group using the global communications network planned to infiltrate and destroy every person who refused chip implantation.

Quietly, and with no public announcement, word had gone out from Church Headquarters in Salt Lake City that righteous people throughout the world seeking refuge from God's wrath and final destruction upon the wicked should gather to the stakes of Zion early in the morning. It was pointed out that secured neighborhoods, no matter how well fortified, would not provide adequate protection. Once inside the stake centers, all doors and windows were to be locked, all curtains were to be closed, and any view to the outside was to be blocked.

In the pre-dawn hours of the following day, secured neighborhoods across the United States became empty as those living in them, for the most part, made their way to the nearest stake center. Each building became a cocoon that securely held those who had chosen to heed the Prophet's directions. They sat quietly and prayed. Some hummed or softly sang a hymn. Some read scriptures as they held their children in their arms. The mood was sober but calm.

When Abram and Rebekah finished their noon meal, they washed the dishes and replaced them neatly in the cupboard. They tidied the tablecloth and swept a few crumbs from the counter into the garbage can. They slowly wandered through the rooms of their small home, straightening a pillow or centering a vase on a table as they walked. Then they hugged each other, remaining in each other's arms for several minutes.

"I love you, Abram," Rebekah said. "I have loved you since the first time I saw you. I've never told you that because I was sure you would think me bold, but I want you to know."

"Thank you for telling me," Abram said. "I am afraid it took me longer to know I loved you. I was becoming content to live my life alone, and then I slowly realized that my life was empty when you were not with me. I knew I loved you and had to propose. I was so afraid you would turn me down. Now we will be husband and wife for all eternity. That is the best blessing I have received from God in my entire life."

They shared one last kiss of farewell, and then walked out their front door. They remained on side streets and in residential areas as long as possible. When they finally approached Temple Mount, they entered from the southwest corner, farthest from the area that had been infiltrated. All was quiet, and they slowly moved from one structure or object that would keep them hidden to the next.

"The temple looks unharmed," Abram said with a deep sigh.

"I can see our soldiers," Rebekah said as she looked toward the blackened hole in the city wall. "Oh, Abram, look at the mass of Muslim troops gathering outside the wall!" Rebekah squeezed Abram's hand and pressed herself against the building in hopes they had not been seen.

"I am amazed!" Abram said as he pointed at a large monitor mounted immediately behind the barricades of the Muslim soldiers. Pictured on its oversized screen was the image of the Prophets' bodies. "I guess they want to be sure we see that they are still laying where they died. I don't know how our soldiers can watch that screen all day and not rise up and shoot every enemy soldier he can kill."

Rebekah squeezed Abram's hand; he closed his eyes, and inhaled slowly and deeply. Hatred would not make his final hours on Earth any more enjoyable. He tried to focus on the task he hoped to complete – providing an opportunity for his wife to view the bodies of the Prophets before she died.

"We'll wait here until shortly before the hour of their announced advancement, and then we will try to get close enough to see the bodies before we die." He heard the words he spoke, and felt as though he were an actor in a play. He could not possibly utter such words so calmly.

Isaac gathered his family around him and offered a prayer to God asking for guidance and direction in protecting them. The children then took turns praying to God for deliverance from the promised extermination.

"Heavenly Father, please bless us that we can find a place to hide from the armies," prayed Leah, his youngest daughter. "And please bless Daddy that he can remember where the hiding places are."

Isaac's heart ached as he thought of the fate awaiting his precious children. He forced his mind to dwell on the trust his family had in the Lord.

"Heavenly Father, thank you for helping us learn that Jesus is our Savior. Please bless the armies that they will understand that, and that they will stop hating us. Please watch over all the people who live in Jerusalem." Hannah's voice caught and she buried her head in her folded arms.

Eli quickly began his prayer so his sister would not feel self-conscious. "Dear Father in Heaven. We love thee so much and we know miracles happen every day. We saw so many miracles while the temple was being built and we are so happy that we could live here in Jerusalem when the temple was finally finished. We are thankful that we will be together as a family forever. Please help us, Heavenly Father. Please help us find a way to escape from the soldiers."

"Thank you, my children," Isaac said, his voice deep and husky from the emotion his children's words had invoked.

Rachel caught Isaac's eye to let him know she was ready to take her turn. She bowed her head and spoke softly. "Our Father in Heaven. We are so grateful for the wonderful children Thou hast entrusted to our care. We are grateful for the priesthood that their father holds and we are grateful for him. We are grateful for the callings Thou hast extended to him, and grateful for the opportunities we have had to show our support and love for him by supporting him in those callings. We are grateful for the knowledge we have of the Plan of Salvation that allows us to feel calm and peaceful at a time such as this. We are grateful to know that no matter what happens tomorrow we will be together, united as a family through all eternity. We pray that Thy spirit will help us be accepting of whatever comes into our lives and trust in Thy love for us. We thank Thee for the many blessings we receive from Thee each day. In the name of Jesus Christ, our Savior, Amen."

Isaac looked at his children. The complete trust they had in him was plain to see on their faces. He wondered if such trust was evident when God looked into his own heart. "I love you all very much. We have to trust God to deliver us."

Rachel spoke softly to her children and said, "I have a feeling, a very powerful feeling, that tells me we will be fine. The feeling that we will be happy takes control of my mind every time I start to worry about what will happen. I know these feelings come from God and He is telling me that I should trust Him."

The silence inside the stake center where Mark and Jenny sat was suddenly shattered by the sound of a small explosion somewhere close by. Several similar explosions were heard a few minutes later. Soon, sirens could be heard approaching from one side of the building, only to fade in the opposite direction as the vehicles sped to some unknown location. Prayers became more urgent and families drew closer together. Lynne sat on one side of Mark and he held her tightly, while holding Jenny close with his other arm. Jordan sat next to Jenny and leaned toward Nathan who had an arm around her shoulders.

Several blocks away, the looters broke through the locked gate at the entrance into their neighborhood. The vandals did not try to be quiet because they were hoping the residents would rush out into the street to fight. The neighborhood remained silent. "Come out and fight like men!" someone called loudly. When there was no response, several men kicked in the doors, but that brought no response. "I know where they went! They went to church! Let's destroy this place!"

The sounds of shattering glass and breaking wood filled the air. Furnishings were thrown out through windows or slashed with knives. Anything that was breakable was broken; items that were not were submerged in filled bathtubs or vandalized in any manner available. The expected excitement seemed hollow with no one protesting their antics, and soon they were off to find another secured neighborhood to destroy.

Strangely, the thought of going to the stake center never occurred to any of them.

Abram and Rebekah had one hour left before the announced killings would begin. Suddenly, the invading army began firing upon the Jewish troops. Grenades flew through the air, and rocket launchers were aimed into Jewish neighborhoods. Wave after wave of hatred-filled soldiers swarmed into the city, killing every Jewish person they could see. Abram and Rebekah were among the first civilians to die.

Soon the army spilled into Jerusalem. Wives were ravished, children were dashed to pieces before the eyes of their parents, and every structure was destroyed. It seemed as though the gates of hell had been opened.

At the very moment the wicked attackers thought their victory was inevitable, the two Prophets of God were resurrected. As they rose to their feet, the glory of their resurrected bodies blinded all that looked upon them. The fear the two Prophets had instilled into those that wanted to destroy the Jews was dwarfed by the wave of panic and hysteria that now swept over them. Heat, like that from a furnace, spread through all who were near them. The large screen that had been filled with the image of their dead bodies now showed the undeniable power and glory of the resurrected Prophets, and it was seen on every screen receiving the images throughout the world. Those watching were pierced to the core, as with a flaming arrow.

A great voice was heard from heaven. "Come up hither." The two Prophets ascended to heaven in a cloud as their enemies throughout the region helplessly watched from below. A deafening silence followed the realization that they had been fighting God's anointed. They immediately fell to the Earth, then rose and began running to and fro, as if trying in vain to find a hiding place. Cries of fear and defeat rang out. After a time, their desperation turned to extreme anger as bloodthirsty hatred filled their hearts. Armies numbering in the millions began killing one another as memories of past culture clashes flooded their minds.

The horrendous sounds of death reached Isaac as he sat with his family. "The only thing wrong with our emergency escape plan is that it depends on chaos or some diversion that would create a lot of confusion for the soldiers," he explained. "If they are advancing toward us in an organized manner we will have no way to escape, but there is still a little while until three o'clock. We will give God at least that long to send us help."

"What could He do to help us?" Hannah asked. "Will He kill all the soldiers so they can't hurt us?"

"That would help us a lot, wouldn't it," Isaac said. "But he could also cause another big storm to keep the soldiers from finding us, or he could . . ."

Isaac felt the ground shake beneath his feet, and knew their prayers had been answered.

"He could send us an earthquake so the soldiers would be too busy to look for us," shouted Rachel, excitement filling her voice. "Grab your backpacks and let's go," she encouraged as she pushed her arm through the strap of her own.

"Father in Heaven has answered our prayers," Isaac shouted as he picked up Leah and ran for the front door. It felt as though the ground under the floor was rolling like the surface of the ocean, and he leaned against the walls as he moved. He grabbed the baseball bat he had placed by the front door, just in case he needed it. Once he got outside, he could see his neighbors fleeing their homes. He waved his bat in the air and called to them. "Run for the hiding places! Come on!"

Even as the news of the Prophets being raised from the dead spread through every corner of the Earth, a great earthquake began to shake the planet with a force that had never before been experienced. Mountains shook until they began to fall and the firmament began to crumble. Every island on the Earth disappeared as the landmasses were joined together into one continent.

Large cracks opened in the Earth, swallowing huge groups of people, then slammed shut like a giant monster devouring its prey. People around the world, desperate to find logical explanations for the worldwide destruction, declared the comet hitting the Earth was to blame.

Isaac shouted directions as he ran through the neighborhood, banging his bat on doors as he passed. "Come on, come with us," he shouted. The convulsing ground made their escape frustratingly difficult. "Come on, we have to get to the refuge. Think about what we rehearsed!" He saw his wife trip and fall, but she was quickly up and running. "You will die if you don't get to the hiding spots. There is no other refuge!"

Eli shouted encouragement to those around him, even though the increasing violence of the earthquake made it hard for him to stay on his feet. Amid all the confusion and fear, it was obvious the many hours spent preparing for this escape had paid off; the people seemed to be heading in the right direction as if on autopilot, even while the Earth battered them from every direction.

In the midst of the earthquake that was quickly changing the entire surface of the planet, Jesus Christ set His foot upon the Mount of Olives. It split in half, and the elements obeyed His word as half of the mountain moved east and the other half moved west. The myriad of angels with him moved to the entrance of the valley that had formed.

As he ran, and fell, and got back up to run again, Isaac decided that even if this attempt to find safety was not successful, the hope he could hear in the voices of those shouting words of support to people still joining their group was easier to abide than sitting quietly at home waiting for certain destruction to arrive. The ground shook violently, but everyone seemed able to keep together. Soon they had left the Jewish quarter behind and began heading for the southwest corner of Old Jerusalem.

Isaac could hear noises from the north – the troops had advanced further south than he had expected. "They began advancing through the city much sooner than announced or they could not possibly have traveled this far already," he shouted to Eli, who was running close by him.

"What are we going to do now?" called Eli, looking around frantically.

"Head back home," Isaac shouted. "We'll be overrun by the soldiers if we go any further west." He turned into the crowd and began shouting. "Troops ahead! Head back home! Follow me!"

The group turned back toward their homes. *You should go east*, Isaac heard, but he quickly dismissed the thought. The Dung Gate was close to their homes, but the invading armies had blocked it days earlier. The protective wall that encircled the east side of Old Jerusalem joined the Temple Mount, creating a dead-end trap. He forced himself to think of possible alternatives even as he was running and encouraging those with him.

As they re-entered their neighborhood, they found many of their homes had already toppled to the ground. Groups of people wandered amid the rubble seemingly unsure which way to run. *This is no good,* Isaac told himself. *We will be butchered right here in our own neighborhood.*

You should go east, the quiet voice again suggested.

Isaac was quickly approaching the section of wall that connected to the south end of the Temple Mount. Even as his mortal logic told him this was a terrible mistake, something inside filled him with hope. He nearly stumbled when he saw the wall had been destroyed and realized they could escape. Without even slowing down, he grabbed his wife's hand and pointed at the newly discovered escape route.

"God has provided a miracle for us!" Isaac called to those around him. To those escaping through the demolished fence, the only explanation was intervention directly from God. The group ran east across the ruined roads and into the cover of trees. This, too, had become an obstacle course as trees had been uprooted and were flung in various directions like toys a child had tired of and thrown to the ground. Instinct, or God, told him to turn and travel northward, keeping his group in the shelter provided by the trees. He knew that directly north from where they were was the main gathering place of the Alliance Armies, so they would have no choice but to turn east very quickly. When they reached the Church of All Nations, they stopped running and stood in awe at the pile of rubble – all that remained of the great structure. Each person uttered gratitude to God that, with His help, an earthquake strong enough to crumble ancient walls and modern buildings had not seemed to impede their escape.

"We must head for the Mount of Olives," Isaac said. "I don't know why, but we must go there."

The group accepted his counsel without question and followed him, carefully crossing the huge, jumbled, jagged pieces of asphalt, all that remained of the road to Jericho. They quickly gathered near the Church of Mary Magdalene and were again stunned to see the building had been destroyed.

"Look!" Eli said as he pointed toward the Mount of Olives. "The entire mount looks like it has been torn to pieces."

"Run," Isaac said as he felt a sudden urgency to reach that area. Soon he could see that a valley now existed where the Mount of Olives had once stood. Isaac knew for a certainty at that instant that the Spirit of God had led them to this valley, and it would be a place of refuge for them. "Run into the valley!"

Isaac looked behind him, while continuing to run, to see if he could spot the armies that were surely close behind them. All he could see were members of his group, panic and hope mingled in the expressions on their faces, running for their very lives. When he returned his eyes to the landscape ahead of them, hoping to see a place that might serve as refuge, time stopped for him. He immediately wanted to stop running and fall to his knees. His brain tried to convince his body to stop, but his legs were so committed to carrying him to safety they were slow to listen. At the same time, he wanted to put his arms around his wife and pull her close to him. It was impossible to separate individual thoughts, let alone actions, but somehow he found himself on his knees, with his wife and children close by, but the tears that filled his eyes made it nearly impossible to see the scarlet robes of the person he had nearly crashed into.

The Savior stepped forward and gently lifted Isaac and his wife to their feet. Looking out over the multitude, He began to speak. "Rise and fear not. I am He whom was cast out from mine own people. I am your Savior, and I come to break the bands of death and usher in your long awaited peace. I am come to destroy your enemies, that they will never again harm or scatter my beloved people. Come, that you may see the wounds from the sacrifice that I endured for your sake, that my people might be saved, that they might not be burned in their disbelief. You are greatly blessed because you hearkened unto the words of my servants, the Prophets, and have listened to the whisperings of the Spirit and recognized the truth of my Church here on Earth. Now I transform you that you may enter into a world filled with peace."

Isaac touched the Savior's palms and felt the impressions left from spikes long ago hammered through His hands and wrists. He fell to the Earth and caressed the Savior's bare feet exposed below the crimson robes. Isaac's tears dropped to the scars on the top of His feet. His fingers traced the ridges where the spikes had been nailed. He knew where the crucifixion had occurred; he had visited that place many times. The sounds that must have been heard that day, long ago, filled his ears – the day his own ancestors had rejoiced as Jesus Christ was lifted up on the cross and crucified. If he had lived on the Earth in that day, would he have been one of those guilty of such a horrible crime?

How could the Savior ever forgive those who betrayed Him and rejected His teachings? Isaac sobbed uncontrollably.

He felt the Savior pulling him to his feet. "You have been washed clean through your baptism and have completed the Earthly ordinances that will unite your family through all eternity. So many of my people have been led to the truth through your faithful service. Well done." As Isaac felt the Savior's arms gently enfold him, the unbearable sorrow he had felt only seconds before was completely replaced with the overwhelming love and acceptance he felt for and from Jesus Christ.

Time appeared to stand still as those that had fled into the valley now filed forward and individually felt the wounds on the Savior's hands and feet. They acknowledged their very survival depended on His mercies, without which they faced certain death from the pursuing armies.

The passage of time slipped into fast-forward as Isaac and the members of his ward suddenly became aware of the approaching armies. As if a flash of lightning had crashed to the ground and deposited a wall of light, a blinding glare formed in front of the pursuing army, completely stopping their advancement. The veil was lifted. What the armies saw overwhelmed them with unspeakable fear and they fell to the Earth. Before them loomed a massive group from heaven – a great and terrible army of light. Fierce and powerful strength radiated from them. As they advanced toward the army of puny mortals, each step caused the Earth to shudder. Weak with terror, the army turned to retreat. They instantly discovered their escape was blocked by an even greater army of light. The Earth began to swallow those who were determined to kill the Jews, as the waters of the Red Sea had swallowed the armies of Pharaoh when God protected those that followed Moses. The Savior spoke to the elements – fire, torrential rain, wind and destruction poured down upon the places where the Alliance Army had been dwelling, quickly obliterating every person and building from sight.

All prophesy that spoke of this great and dreadful day when the Savior would return to the Earth, all the years of enduring scornful attacks, the hatred of most of the people of the world, and years of fighting to regain possession of their sacred city now seemed a small price to pay for the experience of having Jesus the Christ return and claim them as His chosen people.

♦ ♦ ♦ ◇ ♦ ♦ ♦

The anger among the wicked of the world increased at the same pace as their fear. The armies around Jerusalem turned on each other, killing their own people. They ran hysterically, as if to outrun the consequences of their years of defiant, deplorable actions. They darted from one direction to another as if they could avoid their fate, but mother Earth opened her mouth and consumed all the wretchedness she had withstood for so long. Jesus Christ poured out fire, brimstone and great hailstones on the wicked in all the nations of the world.

Those who survived the horrendous earthquake felt blessed, but the destruction they had feared from the approaching comet and the dawn that inexplicably arrived without the rising sun had stretched their emotional and mental capabilities to the breaking point. Suddenly some of the people around them and several buildings and homes began to ignite like dry weeds. There was no noticeable increase in temperature. There were no bolts of lightning crashing down from the heavens. Things burned so completely there were not even ashes left behind. The people who witnessed these things were overwhelmed and fell to the Earth as they were consumed with a brightness that pierced them to their core and filled them with peace.

A brilliant white cloud drifted across the face of the globe. From the midst of the cloud a comforting but thundering voice called all from their hiding places and directed them to rise to their feet and fear not.

THE MILLENNIUM

"It's safe to leave the building," the Stake President said as he walked past the room where Mark and his family had spent the day with others who had heeded the warning to gather at the Stake Center. The somber mood that had consumed nearly everyone since early that morning was immediately replaced by tear-producing gratitude.

With one arm around Lynne and the other holding Jenny close to his side, Mark followed Jordan and Nathan out the door.

"What is that?" Lynne asked.

What at first appeared to be a brilliantly bright cloud covering the entire city caused Mark to drop to his knees. "Jesus Christ has returned! The Savior is here!"

The unconditional love he felt wash over him confirmed what his heart already knew – the beautiful being dressed in flowing scarlet robes, surrounded by an innumerable group of angels singing His praises, was ushering in the Millennium. Trailing angels extended toward heaven until they disappeared from sight. Mark bowed his head and thanked his Father in Heaven that he and his family had been kept safe.

His heart was filled with shame as his mind recalled every opportunity he had disregarded to serve his fellow man. Every unkind word he had ever uttered to or about others passed through his memory, and he was filled with sadness. He vividly relived every time he had remained silent, rather than standing up and speaking out for the truth.

A building across the street from where he stood with his family burst into flames and within a few minutes was gone. There were no smoldering remains – only empty ground. It was made known to Mark that the Earth was being prepared for the presence of Jesus Christ, and any structure or person that possessed qualities contrary to the teachings of God was consumed.

"I always thought it was Jesus who would cause the wicked to burn as stubble when He returned to the Earth," Mark said to his family, "but now I realize it's the condition or state of those who do not follow His teachings that makes them unable to withstand His presence."

"This is unbelievable," Nathan said. "The corruption that enforced the six-six-six accounts is gone. We don't have to live in hiding any longer." He wrapped his arms around Jordan and swung her around in a circle. "We made it!"

For several hours, Mark and his family sat together on the sweet smelling grass and shared their feelings. Each person's thoughts helped the rest of the group realize how much their life had changed in the twinkling of an eye. Satan's influence had been removed from the Earth – that affected nearly every aspect of each moment of their daily lives.

After Jenny and her daughters left to look at their apartment complex, Mark and Nathan sat together on the lawn at the stake center. "I think it's going to take some time to get used to this new world," Mark said.

"It sure is. For one thing, we no longer have a home, but that's not a concern. Now there will be room to spread out and start our own life . . ."

"Our own life?" Mark asked, staring intently at Nathan. "Would that *our* include my daughter, by any chance? I noticed you two were inseparable the whole time we were in the stake center." Mark had to stop speaking in order to not laugh. This was the only time he would ever have Nathan totally at his mercy so he decided to enjoy it. "Would you mind telling me exactly what's going on between you and my daughter?" He continued to stare at Nathan, without speaking. When Nathan offered no reply, Mark said, "Well?"

"Well, I care a great deal for Jordan. We have been seeing each other for quite some time. Well, of course you know that. She is wonderful. We have never tried to hide anything from you. How could we, I mean, we all live so close together and there's no place two people can be alone, ever. Not that we have ever wanted to be alone together. That's not what I meant. I think your daughter is a wonderful person. I have a high regard for her. She's wonderful and I care for her a lot . . ."

Mark found it increasingly hard to not laugh aloud as he watched Nathan take a deep breath and silently tense his entire body.

"Mark, I love Jordan very much. I have for a long time. She feels the same way about me, but we knew we could never get married while we were all living in such cramped quarters in the apartment complex. Things have changed now. I would like your permission to marry Jordan. Sir."

Mark smiled and extended his hand toward Nathan. "That's the best entertainment I've had in a long time. Of course, you can marry her. I have been expecting you to ask that for quite a while. Welcome to the family."

"Thanks," Nathan said shyly. "I'm glad you enjoyed my, uh, misery."

Mark shook his head and laughed. "If Jordan is anything like her mother, your biggest job now will be to convince her you're interested, and I mean *interested* in every detail involved in the wedding. When you cannot keep up the pretense any longer, just tell her you are late for a game of tennis we planned, and then come find me. I'm always willing to be your excuse."

When the sky began to dim, Mark's family wandered back to the stake center to retrieve the blankets they had taken with them early that morning. They had no house to go to, so they sat down and began talking.

"It's hard to put into words," Mark said, "but I just realized that since Jesus was here, I've not had a moment of fear. It's as though I can feel the peace."

"I've felt the same way," Jenny said, "but I thought it was just because I'm a woman. I've always spent every minute being afraid of something, whether for myself or my family."

"I'm sure none of you will be surprised at what I've been thinking of," Jordan said. "My life can move forward now. Nathan and I can be married and become adults, instead of children still living at home."

Lynne jumped up and hugged her sister. "Congratulations! No more pity-parties." She moved away from Jordan and said, "There has been one huge change today and no one has even mentioned it. We forgot to eat."

Everyone laughed and then Jenny said, "I guess we were all too excited to think about food. I suppose all of you realize that our food storage is gone, but we can deal with that issue tomorrow."

"It's been a very long day and I'm ready for some sleep," Mark said. "I think I'm going to take my blanket outside and sleep under the stars like I did when I was a kid. I was never afraid to do that when I was growing up. Well," he admitted, "maybe I was a little afraid of what my friend Tony might think of doing to me while I was asleep, but I was never afraid of anything else. It feels so good to know we are safe. Anyone else want to join me?"

"Us three girls would love to join you," Jenny said as she pulled her daughters close to her. "I can't even believe it was just this morning that we came to this very building wondering what the day would bring. It was only today that we saw Jesus Christ. It seems like this day has lasted for a week. I'm so ready to find a place to sleep."

As his family slept peacefully on the church lawn, Mark's thoughts turned to the days ahead. He was filled with overwhelming gratitude for the Savior. As his tear-filled eyes blurred the brilliant stars overhead, he was overcome with gratitude that Christ's atonement had compensated for the huge imbalance of wrong over right that had comprised his life.

When Mark awoke on the second morning of the Millennium, he lay still without opening his eyes, listening for the sounds that would tell him if Jenny was still sleeping or was already up preparing breakfast. He heard birds chirping and felt the warm sun on his face at the same moment, and then opened his eyes to make sure he was awake. He was outside, not in his bed. He looked around and saw his entire family sleeping. He jumped up and frantically turned about, trying to figure out where he was. The stake center? On the lawn?

The events of the day before flooded his mind and he smiled as he inhaled a sweet smelling fragrance. He sat back down on his blanket and patiently waited as each member of his family woke up. He saw that their first few moments of awareness were the same as his. Once they were all awake, they started discussing what to do.

"Mark, how are you today?" his Bishop asked. "Did your family sleep here last night?"

"Bishop Mallery. Good morning," Mark said. "Yes, we all slept right here on the grass. It was amazing!"

"It's rather like waking up in the Garden of Eden, isn't it? At least, that was my impression this morning."

"That was exactly my impression, too, Bishop."

The Stake President began addressing all those that had gathered at the Stake Center. "I received some information during a very lengthy meeting this morning and am so eager to pass it on to each of you. To begin, temples will now be operated twenty-four hours a day in order to complete the required proxy temple ordinances by the end of the Millennium. Everyone but the children will be involved."

Mark smiled as he looked at those around him. He and his family had gathered with the other members of their stake. It reminded him of his childhood when summer days were warm and cares were non-existent.

"And although we no longer need homes for protection from the elements, or for our safety," the stake president continued, "I think you will all be happy to hear that we will soon begin building homes for each family. You are going to be amazed at how simple it will be to build a home. Everything about our daily life has changed. Living the United Order means that each person contributes what they can and receives what they need."

"This sounds like a dream. Somebody, pinch me before I grow too content. I don't want to be all depressed when I wake up." A random voice involuntarily projecting what nearly everyone was thinking.

"I know. It does seem too good to be true," the stake president responded. He smiled as he looked over the group gathered around him. "We'll divide our stake center into groups of twenty families, and each group will work together to build a house for each family."

The stake president stopped speaking and lowered his head. After a moment, he looked up as he wiped a tear away with the back of his hand. "From now on, when you get up in the morning, you will help with building homes for four hours a day, four days a week. When the houses are completed, those four hours will be spent in whatever type of service you choose. I know you can each sense the change inside that makes you not think of this assignment as a job. It's more like you want to do something for anyone you can help, and if you need help you know others will be equally willing to help you."

Everyone in the group was nodding their heads as they reflected on their own feelings.

"After the houses are completed, we will build community buildings and meeting places. Let me point out one more thing that will take some getting used to. It will not matter if you teach a class, lead a building crew, design new types of structures, sand a wooden table, or help bring a new baby into the world. Every hour spent in service of others is of equal value."

"Who will be in charge of the building crews?"

"Those with the most experience will naturally take the lead," the stake president explained. "Our entire community will consist of homes, meeting places and churches, and farms where crops will be planted and harvested. There will never again be a need for police stations, courthouses, jails, hospitals, or doctors' offices. No government buildings, or military bases. You'll never again need an attorney."

What began as a sigh of relief grew to outright shouts of happiness, and then became laughter mixed with tears of joy. Everyone finally began to comprehend what it meant to be living in the Millennium.

"Does this look like a good place to build our new home?" Mark asked his family. "This is like choosing which part of a manicured park is the best place for a picnic."

"And no yard work," Lynne added. "Imagine that! We'll live here for a thousand years and won't have to mow the lawn once."

"That means my children will never have to mow the lawn or weed the garden. What will they do for chores?" Jordan asked.

Jenny hugged her daughter and said, "I am so happy for you. We will actually get to hold your babies while they are still babies!" Mark smiled and shook his head as he realized he would never grow old. He would be able to play tennis with his great-great-great grandchildren.

When Jordan and Nathan decided on the date they wanted to be married, they made a reservation at the temple. More than once, when preparations for their wedding were being discussed, Nathan would begin glancing at his watch and then inform his fiancé that he had to leave in a few minutes to help her father with something they had previously planned. Since thoughts were communicated as effectively as spoken words, this routine always caused everyone but Jordan to chuckle. Jenny always assured her that Nathan's lack of interest in wedding preparations did not mean he would not be a good husband and father.

One evening when the family was together in their new home, Jenny said, "It doesn't really seem like you two are getting married. When Scott and Melissa got married we were all busy for months."

Jordan gently squeezed Nathan's arm. "I remember that there used to be so much stress, expense, and frustration involved in planning a wedding, that the ceremony itself was almost unimportant and insignificant. Now that's the most important thing and everyone can concentrate on the sacredness of getting married."

"I was a little worried you might feel bad because your wedding will be so different than what you were used to," Mark said to his daughter and future son-in-law. "But it's easy to see that you think perfect is better than stressful. Every time I think it's impossible to be any happier than I am, an evening like this happens and I find even more happiness in being together as a family."

When everyone's home was completed, new temples were built in an amazingly short time. The moment a temple was dedicated, it was scheduled to full capacity. Mark and Jenny worked in the Salt Lake Temple two days each week. Even though there was no longer any evil in the world, the singularity of purpose within the temple resulted in an intense feeling of peace.

During the prayer meeting that began each shift, everyone was reminded that the temple was filled to overflowing with resurrected beings that came to witness the proxy work being done for them. The magnitude of completing proxy ordinances for everyone who had ever lived on the Earth, in only a thousand years, was explicitly apparent.

Mark officiated in a sealing room, where husbands, wives, and families were vicariously sealed together for eternity. After he picked up the folder containing the names of the deceased individuals whose work would be performed that day, he always went to the empty sealing room and thanked his Father in Heaven for the opportunity to serve in the temple. He never tired of the way the beauty of the room seemed to increase the intensity of the Spirit that filled his entire being. The marble alter in the center of the room was covered with pastel apricot-colored velvet. It also covered the step surrounding the alter, where people knelt as they participated in the ceremonies.

One morning, when he opened the folder he discovered the page that contained the names for the first session was blank. He flipped through the pages for the three other sessions he would conduct that day, and there were names listed on each page. Since the patrons would be arriving shortly, he knew he only had a few minutes to return to the sealing office and resolve the situation.

When he stepped into the hall, he saw an unusually large group coming toward him. They seemed to be in a hurry and their demeanor revealed their excited anticipation. When the couple at the front of the group, hand in hand, stood before him, Mark was overwhelmed and leaned against the doorway of the sealing room.

"Hi, Mark," the woman said as she embraced him.

"Cindy, is it really you?" Mark exclaimed.

"Yes, it's so wonderful to see you. I would like to introduce you to the man I will be sealed to this morning, Ribiab."

Mark shook the powerful hand that was extended to him, and experienced a sudden wave of familiarity. "Have we met before?"

"We certainly have, but no matter how hard you try you'll not find any memory of our relationship. But, believe me, we are friends."

Mark smiled at the man. He felt a closeness that could not be explained, but was satisfied to accept Ribiab's explanation.

Ribiab continued. "It was another time and place, and some day we will once again be very dear friends. As you are aware, by now, we are from the other side of the veil, our entire group. We have all looked forward to this day for a very long time." He handed the list of names to Mark and said, "The information is all correct and you are to include this list in your folder when you turn it in at the end of your shift." Then he pulled Mark toward him and spoke softly. "Don't make a fool of yourself today. I know you're a crybaby, so try to stay in control."

Mark smiled at the easy friendship Ribiab offered. He looked at Cindy and was suddenly saddened as he recalled her days on Earth with his troubled friend Tony.

Hearing his thoughts, Cindy took his hand and held it softly. "Mark, you don't need to feel badly about Tony. He said to be sure and tell you hello when we saw you. You always were and still are his dearest friend. He was a very sad individual when he returned; but, he has worked hard and reclaimed some of his former strength and character. He still has a long way to go, but you can be assured that he is once again happy and doing well."

Not sure how she had known of his concern, Mark welcomed the words of comfort. "Thank you, Cindy. I have worried about him so much. Will you please tell him how happy I am to hear this news? Even though he had some problems, there was just something about him that always kept me coming back, wanting to see him happy."

"I'll tell him," she said.

Mark went into the sealing room and the large group followed him. They stood any place there was not a chair or piece of furniture, and their excitement increased as the patrons came into the room. Mark did find it difficult to keep his emotions under control, but Ribiab's smile helped. The routine words he uttered at the beginning of each session seemed insufficient in explaining how special this day was. His eyes blurred and his voice cracked as he spoke.

"Those individuals from the other side of the veil having ordinances performed for them are in attendance today." He struggled to think what he could say to convey his absolute knowledge that today they were there. Embarrassment came upon him, as he realized people had been present in each session. He remembered times when he had let his mind wander to earthly concerns during a sealing session. Surely, those from the other side of the veil had known, just as Cindy had been able to read his thoughts earlier. He raised his eyes and looked at those standing around the room, and they smiled back at him, as if confirming his thoughts.

After Mark completed the first session, he was surprised how sad he felt when those from the other side of the veil left the sealing room. When his shift ended, he sat in the empty sealing room, contemplating his amazing experience during the first session. He was just standing to leave the room when Cindy, Ribiab and their entire group again entered the sealing room. He wondered if they had waited to make sure he took the list of completed work to the sealing office. Cindy immediately said, "No, we just wanted to personally thank you for your service to us this day." Then, each person individually embraced him, and thanked him for his diligence and dedication that made this day possible for them. When they departed, he followed them into the hall and watched them leave. Their pace was slower than when they had arrived, and he could feel the great contentment that radiated from the group.

After that day, each time Mark opened his folder and found a blank page for one of the sessions, he was blessed to see the group that entered the sealing room. He thoroughly enjoyed and appreciated each opportunity to visit with Cindy and Ribiab, and looked forward to each update on Tony's progress.

"Are you nervous?" Jenny asked Jordan as she stood behind her, looking at their reflection in a large mirror. Jordan moved slowly from side to side looking at the reflection of her dress – the soft material shimmered each time she moved. The wide beaded satin waistband accentuated her tiny waist. Seed pearls adorned the scalloped neckline and bottom of each sleeve, and the A-line skirt fell softly to the floor.

"No, I'm not nervous," Jordan answered. "I'm just happy. It seems like there should be another word that better describes how I feel, but that will have to do."

A daughter's wedding day is a precious event to any mother, but Jenny had many additional reasons to treasure each moment. Scott and Michelle had arrived several weeks earlier after being gone for more than three years. It was the first time Adam had met his aunts or grandparents, and he had quickly chosen Grandpa Mark as his favorite person. It was also the first time any of the family had met their newest grandchild, Elizabeth, who was nearly a year old.

"You look like an angel. I think Nathan is very lucky to have you for his wife, but then I suppose I might be just a wee bit prejudiced."

"Thanks, Mom."

"Are you ready," the matron asked as she entered the room. "You look perfectly beautiful."

"Thanks," Jordan said. "I think we're ready."

Jenny and Jordan followed the matron to the sealing room where Jordan and Nathan would be sealed as a family for all eternity. Jordan quickly sat next to her future husband on a bridal chair that sat against a mirror-covered wall.

"I love you," Nathan said quietly. "Look straight ahead. You can see us disappear into forever."

Their reflection in the mirror across the room from where they sat repeated continually because of the mirrored wall behind them until their image became a small speck in the midst of innumerable reflections.

"It does look like seeing into forever," she agreed.

"Do you know all these people?" Nathan asked.

"Not everyone. I have never met the man Scott's talking to, but I think I know everyone else. Are there people you don't know?"

"Oh, yes. I don't know anyone that isn't in our ward. I take that back. I know your grandparents and your aunts and uncles, but for example, I don't know the couple sitting next to Michelle."

"That's her parents. They're staying with Mom and Dad."

"Okay. Looks like we're ready to start," Nathan said as Mark stood and walked toward them.

"It's a wonderful blessing when a man gets to perform his daughter's wedding ceremony. Are you ready to begin?"

Nathan looked at Jordan and then they both nodded.

"Very well." Mark closed the door of the sealing room and then returned to his chair behind the writing desk. "Brothers and Sisters, it's wonderful to see such a large group here to celebrate Jordan and Nathan's wedding." After a beautiful explanation of the responsibilities Jordan and Nathan were entering into by being sealed together for time and eternity, he counseled them in several areas that were unique to their personalities and experiences. When the ordinance was completed, Nathan kissed his new bride and then friends and family members of the new couple offered their congratulations. When people slowly began to leave the room, Jordan and Nathan walked to where her brother was sitting.

"Congratulations," Scott said as he hugged both Jordan and Nathan. "I'd like to introduce you to Isaac. He was instrumental in teaching the gospel to the people in Jerusalem before Jesus Christ came to rule the Earth."

"I'm very honored to meet you," Nathan said as he shook Isaac's hand.

"Thank you," Isaac said, "but I can assure you, I have done nothing compared to what Scott and his wife did. I do find it interesting that we were both involved in building the last two temples that had to be completed before the Savior could return."

"And he's very modest," Scott said. "When you two get back from your honeymoon, I'll try to convince Isaac to spend an evening with us and share some of his amazing experiences."

"That does sound interesting. I hope you will," Jordan said.

After the newlywed couple had left the sealing room, Scott walked with Isaac toward the elevator. "Let's take the stairs," Isaac suggested.

"Sure," Scott said, following him through the doorway to the stairs. Rather than turning to descend, Isaac began climbing to the next floor.

"We have to go down to leave the temple," Scott said with a smile.

"I think you should come up to the next floor with me," Isaac said with an even larger smile. "There's someone waiting to visit with you." He never offered any clue as they walked down the hallway lined on both sides with office doors. When he stopped at one and opened the door, he stood back so Scott could enter ahead of him.

Scott watched Isaac's face as he walked past him, and when he turned to look into the room, he stopped in his tracks. "Abram?"

"Have you so quickly forgotten what I look like?" his old friend said as he stepped forward and threw his arms around Scott. "Of course it is I."

"But, you are a resurrected being. How is it that I can see you?"

"This is even more amusing than I thought it would be. You are correct. My wife and I were killed on the day the Savior returned to Jerusalem, but we were resurrected that very day. I am so happy to see you again.

Scott sat next to Abram. "I can't tell you how happy I am to see you."

"I have been given special permission to visit with you. Has your father told you about being able to see his friend Cindy and her husband, also resurrected beings?"

"Yes, he has. He's amazed that he's allowed to regularly visit with them."

"You will also receive that opportunity. There are more proxy ordinances to perform for the Jewish people than we can possibly complete before the end of the Millennium in the temple at Jerusalem, so I have been assigned to bring some of those people to this temple. I have been given the opportunity to come here and ask that you begin serving in the sealing area, even as your father. Then we can visit with each other."

Scott was speechless. His mind was filled with questions even as he tried to concentrate on what Abram was telling him. "The man my father communicates with has told him they were friends in the pre-existence."

"True," Abram said as he closely watched Scott's reaction.

"We were friends on Earth." Scott stopped. Only one question filled his mind at that moment. "Are you telling me we were friends in the pre-existence? That we met here but already knew each other?"

Abram slowly smiled. "Over time, I will be allowed to share with you details of the bond that exists between you and I, and Isaac. It is a thread that has bound the three of us together from the beginning of time, and will always keep us close."

Memories of the days he had gone to college with Abram flashed through Scott's mind, as well as his impressions of Isaac when they first met. Then he remembered Isaac's words when they had been in Salt Lake. *You may be the answer to the prayers of more Jews than you can imagine.*

Abram put his hand on Scott's shoulder and Scott's focus returned to the present moment. "You never understood how important your role was in regard to the salvation of the Jewish people. When we were in college together, we both wondered if there was more involved than mere chance that brought us together. Scott, before you left your Heavenly Father's presence, you made covenants that would become as important to the Jewish race as Moses was to their liberation from the Egyptians. You think of yourself as only an ordinary person who loves to serve others, but you are much more."

Scott was unable to speak. He hugged Abram and allowed the tears to fall freely. After a long time, Abram spoke quietly. "I must leave. But I will return when it is time to bring those who are ready to accept the Earthly ordinances that will be done for them in this temple." He turned to Isaac and embraced him. "Thank you for helping make this visit possible. I will see you again when you return home."

Abram again hugged Scott and then left the room.

"I don't even know what to say," Scott said. "It sounds like you and Abram communicate regularly, but I'm confused how that can be."

"The veil of forgetfulness concerning our pre-Earth life can be lifted for any purpose our Father chooses. Abram and I worked closely together before he died, and we have been blessed with the opportunity to continue that work. This blessing is the result of covenants we made before coming to Earth, and we have been allowed to finish that work together."

"Are you saying that I made that same covenant with both of you?"

Isaac smiled and nodded. "Today is a glorious day for you because your sister has been sealed to her eternal companion, and you have learned of the eternal nature of covenants made before we came to Earth. Go now; join your family in celebrating the wedding. I will be here for some time and we will have many opportunities to discuss the needed preparations to continue with our work. I will visit you and your family as your sister has requested. It is good to share the experiences we remember from the day the Savior returned to Earth.

PEACE IS ENDED

Over time, Mark had many opportunities to visit with Ribiab. Eventually, he learned of their relationship in the pre-existence. Mark's memory of those events was not restored, but Ribiab's explanation helped Mark understand why they were allowed such interaction. Ribiab told him about places that had become precious to him during his mortal life, and Mark realized he had also experienced very moving spiritual experiences in some of the same places. When he explained that, Ribiab smiled with a sheepish grin.

"My friend Marash and I sat with you as you visited the valley of Adam-ondi-Ahman. Your ability to sense our presence is partly responsible for that experience being special to you. We were also with you at winter quarters in Omaha, and Cahokia, the mound city across the river from St. Louis. Do you remember the words I whispered to you as I sat with you at Tony's funeral?"

"You were there?" Mark's mind flashed to each of those scenes. "Thank you. You know, I felt your presence when I visited those places, but sometimes I thought it was my imagination because I tried to visualize what had occurred in those locations."

"Do you remember the lady that gave you words of direction in the temple, when you were so troubled about finding a mate?"

"I remember," Mark said. "I will never forget what happened that day. She knew so much about me, I was certain she must have been an angel sent from heaven to speak to me."

Ribiab smiled and put his hand on Mark's arm. "Even though she was a stranger to you on Earth, she was a very dear friend in the pre-existence. Her name is Elizabeth and she has been your friend for as long as I have. Many of our friends came to the Earth at different times and places. Jenny, Elizabeth, you and I were all friends before being sent to Earth. Many of the people who have crossed your path during your Earthly life, especially those who seemed familiar to you, were close friends when you lived with your Father in Heaven. You felt compelled to reach out and help some, others were reaching out to help you. Many of those situations were agreed upon by both of you before you came to Earth. I can assure you such agreements were made with great joy as both parties vowed to help each other in every way possible to return to our Father in Heaven."

"That sounds amazingly simple and seems easy to understand. But if we can't remember our life before coming to Earth, how did Elizabeth know enough about my life to offer encouragement?"

"She was only days from returning to the Father's presence herself. The veil was very thin for her at that time, especially as she sat in the temple. She knew when she saw you sitting there alone that you had not yet found Jenny. As she sat with you, she was assured that it would not be long before you would find her, and she knew you would know she was your mate as soon as you saw her. Have you ever considered that friends from the other side of the veil would be allowed to attend your wedding in the holy temple? She and I were there, and it brought her great joy to see you sealed to each other for all eternity."

Mark was grateful that the insight Ribiab was able to share with him answered questions and resolved things he had wondered about for many years. Mark's life seemed more joyous and rewarding with each passing day. The weeks faded into months, and the months blurred into years. With no evil to cause conflict in people's lives, the time seemed to float by.

Mark was very impressed with the children who were born during the Millennium. They flourished and their dedication to the Lord seemed to be incredibly strong. They never experienced Satan's influence, so none of their time was wasted in recovering from the effect of sins committed, as had happened during Mark's life. He grew old, and he divided his free time between working in the temple and teaching those born during the Millennium how to overcome the temptations they would face when Satan was loosed at the end of his thousand-year bondage.

When he reached the age of an ancient, Mark's physical body, previously changed to a terrestrial state when Jesus returned to the Earth, cast off all restrictions and limitations. The veil was lifted inasmuch as he instantly remembered everything about his life with the Great Father before he came to Earth. He had been called Elias. He remembered falling in love with Sarah and promising to find her. He remembered Tony, when he was called Stephan, and how close they had been. On earth Cindy had been with Tony, but now he remembered she was called Bethany and was now sealed to his friend Ribiab for all eternity. His friendship with Marash came to his memory, and he remembered the trials he had faced while he lived on earth and was known as Daniel. An especially sweet memory was the time he spent with the Great Father right before he departed to begin his life on Earth, and the unconditional love he felt while listening to His words of counsel.

Elias felt strengthened by the returned knowledge. The next week when he entered the temple for his weekly session, he was excited to see Ribiab, who he now remembered. When they greeted one another later that morning, Mark was surprised to feel rejuvenated when they embraced. Always before, when Elias worked in the temple, he had returned home greatly weakened by his contact with the resurrected beings.

During the next while, Elias tried to share with Scott some of the differences he had experienced since his memory of the pre-existence was restored. It was like trying to tell his newest grandchild how wonderful it would be when he could talk. Saddened, he struggled to be content with the treasured conversations they had while they were at the temple. The veil seemed to be very thin there for Scott also, and they were able to share many exquisite experiences while serving in the House of the Lord.

The next time Scott worked at the temple, he prayed while he was waiting for Abram and his group to arrive. He asked that he would be able to understand the things his father had tried to explain. More than for himself, Scott wanted this blessing so he could maintain the close connection he had always felt with his father. No matter how hard he tried to comprehend the difference having a memory of his pre-existence would make in his life, he needed help from his Heavenly Father to do so.

When Abram arrived, those he brought with him quickly filled the room. Scott became absorbed in the joy he witnessed as temple ordinances were completed. Each time he read a person's name he watched as the couple being married for all eternity quickly stepped close to the alter and listened intently to the words being spoken. When he read the name of Abram's dear friend David who had been killed when the Prophets were killed in Jerusalem, he watched to see which couple stepped closer to the altar. He saw David, known as Jacob before he came to Earth, walking hand in hand with a beautiful woman who was close to five feet tall and resembled the image Scott had always pictured when he thought of Tinkerbelle. She was tiny and impish looking, and he could clearly see how much she and David loved each other by the way they looked into each other's eyes while listening to the words he spoke. He wondered when David's eternal companion, Ruth, had lived on Earth and how she and David had met.

Scott worked very hard to give each of the remaining couples in the room as much attention as he had given Jacob and Ruth. The spirit had been so strong during the entire session that Scott was a little sad when it ended. After his shift was over, Scott found Abram still waiting in the hallway for him.

"I could tell you knew who Jacob was," Abram said.

"Yes," Scott assured his friend. "I was so happy that he had found his eternal companion. I wondered if he had any idea I was also one of your friends. Not that it mattered at all. This was his wedding day and I would not have wanted to detract from that. But it was strange to watch him and wonder if he knew you and I were friends."

"There were more connections involved than you know. Can we sit in the sealing room?"

"Absolutely," Scott said. "Another group will be arriving in about half an hour, but for now it's empty."

They went in and sat in the chairs near the door. "I know you are aware that you and I were friends with Isaac before we came to Earth. Have you ever thought about the people you have met during your life on the Earth? Your family members and people you met in school? Acquaintances that seemed to click and you became close friends? Your sphere of influence consists of a relatively small number of people when you consider the population of the world as a whole."

"Yes," agreed Scott. "I have thought about that at times."

"And now you know that some of the people you associate with on Earth are the same as those you associated with before you came here."

"Yes," Scott said.

"The relationships you form on Earth are limited to people who live on the Earth at the same time you do, but the relationships you formed before you came here had no such limitations."

"That makes sense," Scott said, carefully watching Abram's expression.

"So you could easily understand how Jacob's wife was one of your mother's friends in the pre-existence?"

Abram sat quietly as Scott sorted out what he had heard. "So," Scott began, "my mother, Jenny . . . and Jacob's wife Ruth . . . were friends in Heaven before Mom was born?"

"Yes." Then after a moment Abram said, "And your mother and her friends knew your father and his friends."

Scott's eyes narrowed as though he was trying to shut out all distractions. "So Ribiab, my dad's friend who brings names to the temple, and his wife Bethany, and Bethany's Earthly friend Stephan were also part of that group of friends?"

"Yes, exactly. The reason I am telling you this is that, even though it is not the case for every person, you, your wife, and your children all knew each other in the pre-existence. Your children chose you to be their parents, even as you chose your parents. Many of the people you became friends with while you were in New Zion you have known most of your existence."

"Wow, that's a lot to think about. I guess I've always thought of Heaven as a place where everyone who came to Earth lived, and everyone knew everyone. Then we come to Earth, have this Earthly experience, and return to the place where everyone knew everyone and we were all friends, one big happy family. However, this makes more sense to me. Just as we only know a few people on Earth, we also know only a few people in heaven, and you're telling me that most of my friends here were also my friends there?"

"Yes. I know your father has been trying to explain some of the changes that have come into his life since he became a resurrected being, and he feels frustration at his lack of success in that endeavor."

"Well," sighed Scott, "I'm sure his frustration is caused by my inability to grasp what he's saying."

"Ribiab asked me to help you understand what your father is trying to tell you."

"Ribiab's friendship with Dad in the pre-existence must have been very strong if he's asked you to help me better understand him. I am so moved by that demonstration of love between two friends. Even after working in the temple and serving with the people in New Zion, that touches my heart." Scott was filled with an awareness of how strong the bond of love would have to be before that kind of concern would be present. He wept unashamedly. "I feel like I've been making light of what Dad has been trying to explain. He won't find that kind of attitude in me again."

"Try to remember one little fact, and I think it will change much for you," Abram said gently. "You chose your father from among all those that you knew because you respected him and were certain of his love for you. That is why Adam chose you to be his father. This is a great blessing, because that was not the case for everyone as they came to Earth – situations may have prevented desired choices for some. On Earth, we develop the bonds of love that tie us to our family for all eternity, but we don't see the extreme respect and admiration we felt for those we chose as our parents until we remember our life before coming to Earth. Your father has just now remembered that life, and that is a powerful revelation. He's trying to share the appreciation and gratefulness he feels toward you now that he remembers the feelings you shared before you chose him to be your father."

Scott cried freely as the strong feelings of love he felt for his father filled his heart. Each time he caught a glimpse of the magnitude of the feelings he and his father had shared in the pre-existence, his emotions again spilled over with tears.

"Thank you, Abram. I am so thankful you have taken the time to share this with me. There are no words to describe what I'm feeling right now, and I'm pretty sure that's how Dad must have been feeling recently when he tried to communicate his newly understood feelings with me."

"Yes," Abram nodded. "Ribiab convinced me that you may be better able to understand this concept if it were explained to you within the walls of the temple where spiritual things are more easily communicated. He will be happy to learn he was correct."

Scott wrapped his arm around Abram's shoulder and said, "Please tell him thank you. He was absolutely correct."

◆◆◆◇◆◆◆

Preparing those born during the Millennium for the day they would be subjected to the final attack from Satan became a priority. Elias was very concerned for the souls he taught, and he used scriptures from every civilization and dispensation of the earth's history to help teach them. He prayed that his first-hand knowledge would provide extra insight to help prepare the students for what lay ahead. However, each new class of young spirits treated Elias' real-life experiences more like unbelievable stories of fiction, presented for entertainment rather than survival. He never let their disbelief dim his determination, and many came to love him nearly as a father.

One afternoon when Scott and his family were visiting his parents, an amazing phone call was received. Elias and his grandson Adam were asked to come to the Prophet's office.

"Why do you think the Prophet wants to see me?" Adam asked his grandfather.

"I don't know," Elias answered. "You're unique. You were the first person to be born on the Earth during the Millennium. Perhaps the Prophet needs something that only you can offer."

"I remember when you were a tiny baby," Michelle said as she smiled at her son. "When we were in New Zion and the Savior came to the temple, He took you in his arms and blessed you that you would be a great leader in the final days."

"I love to hear about your experiences while you were building the temple," Adam said. "But you're changing the subject, Mom. About this phone call from the Prophet. I have heard many people thank you, Grandpa, for what you have taught them. I can think of many reasons why the Prophet would want to see you, but can you think of one single reason he would want me to come with you?"

Elias laughed and quickly hugged his grandson. "The Prophet probably thinks if he calls me to serve in a position with you, some of your great faith will rub off on me. But I guess we'll both have to wait and see."

When their appointment time arrived, they sat together, looking across the desk at the Prophet. "We know the Millennium is drawing to an end," the Prophet said, "and we know the Father of All Lies and his followers will soon begin one final assault to deceive as many souls as they can. We have been instructed to create an army of missionaries to contend with the approaching onslaught." The Prophet stopped speaking and smiled, and then he nodded at Adam and continued. "I can feel the strength of your faith, and you can provide a great service to others like you."

Then the Prophet turned to Elias and said, "We are aware of your frustrations and fears that the innocent ones no longer seem to value your first-hand experience. You are a greater influence than you realize, and we ask that you continue to serve in this capacity. The need for your great service grows with each passing day. As soon as students finish your classes, we would like them to immediately be taught by someone like Adam who may be able to present the same information from a different point of view. Adam, we would like you to be in charge of creating the army of missionaries, and determining how they can help instruct those born during the Millennium. The Lord has directed us to better prepare our innocent souls to withstand the fiery darts of the Defiant Ones."

Elias patted Adam's shoulder warmly and said, "This new direction truly feels like an answer to the prayers of all of us who teach these classes."

The Prophet stood and walked around his desk to shake hands with them. "We are confident you will fulfill the Lord's desire in this endeavor."

After Adam had been introduced to Elias' fellow teachers, he presented his ideas about what might be beneficial in strengthening the faith of the innocent ones. He accepted the responsibility to find and organize teachers, and then traveled to each mission in the world to gather all the innocent ones that were willing to teach such classes. It was nearly miraculous how quickly a powerful army of missionaries was gathered together, missionaries that were willing to dedicate their entire existence to preparing for the final conflict. They had great faith and instinctively knew how fierce the final battle would be.

For several years, Adam and Elias led the preparations for the final conflict. One evening Elias sat next to Jenny in their living room, while both of them read.

"Do you ever wonder if you will get tired of spending a quiet evening with me, year after year after year?" Sarah asked.

"No, I never wonder about that."

Sarah laughed and said, "Do you remember when Adam was born and you joked about not minding becoming a grandpa, but you weren't too sure about sleeping with a grandma?"

Elias laughed at that memory.

"And now," she said as she continued to laugh, "we are great, great, many-times-great grand parents, we've both become resurrected beings, and yet I feel as though I am still thirty years old."

"You look as though you are still in your twenties," Elias said. A sudden wave of darkness swept over him and he found it hard to breathe. Not wanting to startle his wife, he smiled at her and lovingly patted her leg as he stood and left the room.

He went in the bedroom and dropped to his knees beside the bed. Feelings of alarm and urgency engulfed him and he prayed fervently. The room seemed to darken, almost as if a stench-filled vapor was removing the light.

"Elias, you must hurry, there is no time to lose!" came a familiar but disturbed voice from behind him.

He jumped to his feet and saw that Ribiab's expression was one he had not seen for over a thousand years.

"Has it been so long you do not recognize the horrible presence of old? Satan and his angels have been released for a short time. You must immediately gather those you have been teaching and begin warning them, as you have never done before. Tell them of the final days before Jesus Christ returned to the Earth and warn your students of the dangers about to overwhelm them. It is not just the young you must help, but also all that have been born since the Millennium began. Go immediately!" Ribiab was instantly gone from before Elias.

Then Elias saw Sarah standing in the doorway.

"And now the generations of our grandchildren we were just discussing are going to be subjected to the deceptions of Satan? How will they ever be able to withstand?" She rushed to his waiting arms and buried her face against his shoulder. "We had years to fail and repent, many times over, and still some we know were deceived. What of these unsuspecting generations?"

"Pray for our family, Sarah. Contact as many as you can and ask them to pray unceasingly. I am going to contact the leaders in our community and ask for their help in gathering everyone; our combined numbers will give us additional strength. Pray as hard as you ever have. I am so afraid for our family. I will be back as soon as I can, but don't worry if I am gone for a long while. I want to help as many as I can."

Elias encouraged his students and their family members to gather with him. Many attended his class to find out what was so important.

"We have tried for years and years to prepare you for the day when Satan and his angels would be unleashed upon you. That time has arrived and we hope we can impress upon you the danger of the force that is about to become a daily part of your life."

"This is a joke, right?" someone yelled from the group.

"Please don't think for one minute that this is a laughing matter. I assure you, that is one of Satan's greatest tools. If he can get you to laugh at something, you will not realize the power of what is truly planned for you. Are you willing to risk losing this peaceful way of life by treating Satan as something funny enough to laugh about?"

"Let's listen to what our teacher has to say," another person shouted.

"I have seen with my own eyes the result of following the whisperings of the Defiant Ones. People kill themselves after becoming extremely depressed because of their own actions. Armies who serve him become so filled with hatred they begin killing everyone they meet, and then turn on their own ranks and kill each other."

"Nothing could ever make someone sad enough to kill themselves," someone else yelled. "Why do you tell us such unbelievable stories?"

"You cannot see the love that your Father in Heaven bestows upon you, but each day you can feel it. Each day you benefit from the blessings He pours down over you. It is the same with Satan. You cannot see his evil deceptions, but you will soon begin to see the grief and sorrow that come into your lives if you follow his whisperings."

"You should write fairy tales because your imagination is working overtime." Several people stood and began leaving, pulling their friends behind them.

"Please, please, don't leave," Elias called. "Please stay with us. We have more power to withstand his evil if we face him as a group, encouraging and lifting each other up with prayers."

"We've learned what you've taught us, and we know how to pray. You make it sound like we have to depend on the older generations to survive, but we have just as much faith as you do," another said.

"I know the horrible stories of carnage caused by the evil presence are hard to understand or accept. I am more sensitive to the darkness that has arrived with the evil ones because I experienced it before."

"And somehow you survived! How bad can it really be?"

"Satan is incredibly clever. He knows that if he comes at you head on, full force, you would be scared and cling tightly to your beliefs. So he slowly entices you to follow him, he convinces you that your attitude toward evil can be altered slightly with no harm done. He tells you that you are tolerant when you accept others and their differences."

"Are you saying we should not accept the differences in others? God has taught us to accept everyone unconditionally!"

"You could safely do that while Satan was bound, but he has been set free. When Jesus Christ lived on the Earth, He lived among the sinners, but he never accepted their actions when they did not follow the teachings of His Father in Heaven."

"He forgave those who sinned."

"Yes, He did. And He told them to go and sin no more. If you accept those who perpetrate evil acts, you will soon find it easy to accept a few of their behaviors. Little by little, you will slide down that slippery slope until you dwell with Satan. It is but a short season that he will be allowed to tempt you. Please, kneel down and ask God to help you resist Satan's influence so that you can remain here with your family and friends, living in peace and happiness. Please, don't let him deceive you."

"I think your own fears are the basis for such talk rather than the reality of the situation. We love living in peace. Why do you think we would ever do anything that would prevent us from being free?"

Elias bowed his head and his arms fell against his sides. He knew that even though their eternal status was at risk, they were unable to grasp the seriousness and finality of the consequence of their actions.

When Elias met with his students at their next class, he could see that the attitudes of some had changed, ever so slightly, and he encouraged them to tarry longer with him.

"I think you have no faith in our judgment," one student accused.

"Why do you act like you're the only one smart enough to keep us safe?" questioned still another.

Elias' fellow teachers told him they were receiving the same type of insults. The change was gradual, and then some students stopped coming to class. Each new dropout found those eager to share what they had found to fill their spare time. Experiences many had never before even known about were described and offered. A missing quality came into their lives – fun! All they had ever been taught was to seek joy in life through serving others. They soon discovered that serving their own wants offered a temporary feeling that was exciting to them.

No one born during the Millennium had ever experienced a single thought of being alone with someone they were not married to. It had never occurred to anyone to leave the group and sneak off to spend a few exciting hours exploring each other's body and reveling in the feelings that could be experienced. Forbidden pleasures were now available for the taking.

Resentment began to grow against people like Elias. Many voiced their opinion that teachers had lied to them for generations in an attempt to keep them from enjoying such things, the same kinds of things the teachers themselves must surely have enjoyed in some past age. More voices joined theirs and discussed at length how superstitious teachers had created fictitious characters to represent good and evil because they thought they had the right to decide what was right or wrong.

Elias felt he was failing to do as the Prophet had requested. Many he thought would never be deceived fell prey to the old game and more of his students fell away from correct principles. He began to focus on those who had left the class, concentrating his efforts on convincing them that they needed to return, and soon those efforts caused him to miss classes himself.

One afternoon Elias learned where the newest additions to the ranks of the nonbelievers were meeting. If he could save even one single soul from choosing the path that prevented them from enjoying eternal life he thought he could regain a little of his wavering self worth. A block before he reached his destination, he suddenly found Ribiab standing directly in front of him.

"What are you doing here?" Elias asked.

"Elias," Ribiab said with deep concern evident in his voice, "have you stopped to think how many faithful you may have lost since you began missing your daily classes?"

"What?" asked Elias, thoroughly confused.

"The lines have been drawn, and many have fallen from innocence. Tarry no longer with those that offer a doubtful harvest, but go and strengthen the faithful who grow weary, who fear you have abandoned them. They are filled with fright that the surrounding darkness will consume them. Close your eyes that you might see."

Elias closed his eyes. He felt Ribiab's hand gently rest upon his shoulder. Suddenly his ears were filled with the prayers of his trusting students. He heard the terror in their voices and saw the familiar dark vapor encircle them, even as they called upon God for help. He listened as the Defiant Ones tried to convince them there *was* no defense against the darkness that had been unleashed upon them.

Elias's eyes flew open as he gasped for air. He stood alone, wondering if Ribiab had actually been there. His heart was pierced with the ache of a parent that watches helplessly as their child suffers fear and uncertainty.

Immediately, he turned and hurried to his classroom. He was not sure what he had expected to find when he entered the classroom, but he was positive it was not what met his eyes. A large group had gathered, but they sat in their chairs as if in a daze. No one spoke. It was apparent they had come to the classroom hoping to find the security they had prayed their teacher could provide.

Ribiab had spoken the truth. In his efforts to retrieve souls who had already decided to leave, Elias had forgotten those who looked to him for support. He prayed for inspiration to know how he could help his students, and immediately felt strength begin to fill his body.

"I am so sorry," he apologized. "I feel the fear you are experiencing. I promise you it *is* possible to overcome Satan. I have already done it once before. I had forgotten the overwhelming fear I experienced then, fear that made it hard for me to believe I could successfully overcome my trials."

Elias walked among his students and touched each shoulder as he passed. "Satan can be defeated. I have seen him totally defeated. I remember the day he was bound by Jesus Christ. God is stronger than Satan. The Defiant Ones are mere children in the eyes of God. Satan has been unleashed so you can have the experience of resisting his influence, for that is knowledge you must gain before your mortal trial is complete. Remember that God is in control. This is only a test to see how you will handle Satan's temptations. When you decide to never allow even a single crack in the armor of God's protection, Satan has no power over you."

The class members began to smile at Elias.

"Please join me in prayer," Elias said as he dropped to his knees. He then asked his Father in Heaven for strength and understanding, on the behalf of his students. After concluding the prayer, Elias rose to his feet and began to talk of a time of old – a time when the world seemed to be filled with wickedness and corruption, and everyone feared they were on the brink of annihilation. He described seeing the wicked totally consumed. Then he told of the beautiful experience of witnessing the first resurrection as the saints went forth to meet the Lamb of God.

"Prayer is the only way you can tell if something comes from God or Satan," Elias said slowly. The words had flowed into his mind, and even as he spoke them aloud, he recalled the experience that proved those words were true. He slowly inhaled while looking at the trusting faces watching him.

"I had an experience when I was quite young. I learned a powerful lesson about Satan's ability to become anything he wants to be, appear to us as anything he chooses, and how easy it is for him to deceive us. I have never shared this story with any of my classes before because it seemed too personal, too private. Nevertheless, I think I should share it with you.

"One night I laid in bed saying a prayer." Elias smiled and nodded his head. "I hate to admit I was laying in bed, rather than kneeling on the floor. My eyes suddenly focused on a small dot of light in one corner of the ceiling. That light suddenly began to grow as it came closer toward me. In that circle of light, I could see three men dressed in white and they were reaching out to me. It was as though they were reaching through a window and I could only see the upper part of their bodies.

"It all happened very rapidly, and by the time I realized what it was, they were right by my bed. I suddenly yelled, 'I don't want to go yet.' I remember how surprised I was when I heard those words come out of my mouth. It was almost as if someone else had spoken – I realized the reason I had said that, was because I thought I was dying and those three men had come for me."

Elias stopped and studied the faces of his students. Sharing this precious experience exposed a very sacred part of himself to those in the room. If anyone treated his words lightly, he determined he would not continue. What he saw were looks filled with hunger to know how to identify and resist Satan. Therefore, he continued.

"The instant I spoke those words, the light vanished. I laid in my room that was once again dark and tried to figure out what had just happened. I remember I started trembling, uncontrollably.

"Now I want you to realize that this happened late at night. In the house where I grew up, everyone went to bed well before eleven o'clock, and this was after midnight. However, as I lay there in my bed, I heard my father come downstairs and begin working on the plumbing in the bathroom right next to my bedroom. He told me later he had been in bed and got so restless he had decided to come downstairs and finish a project he had not had time to finish. I was so glad when I heard him come downstairs and I wanted to run into that bathroom and tell him what had just happened, but I did not have the strength to get out of bed for about ten minutes.

"When I did go into the bathroom, he was sitting on the floor working on some pipes, and then he looked up at me. I will never forget how shocked his voice sounded when he asked if I was all right. He said my face was as white as if I had seen a ghost. He had no idea how correct he actually was.

"After I had gained some strength and explained what had happened, we went upstairs to tell my mother. They asked me several questions. My mother asked if I recognized any of the people that had appeared to me. I didn't. We talked for a long time, but in the end, no one had any idea what had just happened. It was decided that we should kneel and say a prayer, and my father prayed that we might know the purpose of the experience.

"I had no idea why I had that experience. However, it had a huge effect on me. I quit praying. I was afraid to pray for a long, long time, especially when I was alone, and certainly when I was in the dark.

"Years passed and, from time to time, I would wonder what I was supposed to have learned from the visitation that night. I fasted and prayed several times that I would know what message I was supposed to have received, or if my life really had nearly ended that night. Like most people, there are times in my life when I feel closer to the Spirit than at other times. During the times I felt closest to God, I would ask for an answer. Then there were times when I would do something contrary to the Spirit of God, and my dad would ask me how I could do such things when I had received such a powerful visitation. I wondered that myself. But, time has a way of dulling experiences, whether they are good or bad.

"Many years after the visitation, I was married and had a little boy. I had been transferred to a new job in a new town, and I had moved there ahead of my wife so I could find a place for us to live. It was a very lonely time for me because I did not like being separated from my family. I became very diligent in reading the scriptures and praying several times a day. I think I started doing this in hopes that it would help fill the void in my life that resulted from being away from my wife and son.

"I knew that prayer and scripture reading were the key elements to having the Spirit as a constant guide and companion. I knew that was what matured and developed missionaries and made them strong and successful. I did not go on a mission when I was young, so I decided to use that time when I was alone to try to bring that strength into my life. It worked. The time I spent alone, waiting for my family to join me, turned out to be a time when I felt closer to the Lord than I ever had.

"One evening, I started reading a genealogy of my grandmother's family that my sister had compiled and sent to me. As I turned the pages, I came to a photograph of my grandmother's grandfather. As I viewed this picture, it was as if someone shouted in my ear, with great excitement. "It's him!" That is all I heard, but I immediately knew it was in reference to the visitation I had received so many years before.

"My eyes filled with tears and my heart pounded wildly. I was excited that I had finally learned who had visited me that night. I still had no idea why he had come, but at last, I knew his identity. Even though I felt this revelation had finally solved my dilemma, I knew I needed to get confirmation from God. I knelt down and began to say a prayer. I asked one question. Was this the person that visited me that unforgettable night in my room? At that moment, every bit of excitement left me. I do not remember hearing the word no, but I felt it. There was no disappointment, or any other question in my heart. I stayed on my knees for probably another minute, trying to think of something else to say. My mind was blank. I could not even find an Amen to close my prayer. I no longer wondered what is meant by a stupor of thought.

"That inability to find words instantly made me realize that the original visitation I had received while in my teens had not been a visit from God. Without saying another word or even closing my prayer, I sat back up on the couch and continued to read the family history. After I read for a short time, my mind began to ponder what I had just experienced.

"As I thought about the original visitation, and also that current experience, I gained some very powerful insight that has helped me in a number of situations throughout my life. It helped me understand the power of prayer. I also gained a first-hand knowledge of the importance of using the correct method while praying.

"When we are taught to pray, we are told to ponder our question and make a decision, and then go to the Lord and ask if the decision we have reached is correct. We are not told to ask the Lord to tell us what to do, but we are to ask Him if the decision we have made is correct. If the answer is yes, we'll feel excited and good about our decision. If it is the wrong decision, we will have a stupor of thought.

"The night of my original visitation, to the best of my knowledge, my father prayed that we might know the reason for the visitation. I do not believe he ever asked the Lord if I was to have been taken that night, which was my belief and fear for a number of years. But, I never asked that question either. For years, I fasted and prayed that I might know what message I was supposed to have gained that night. I do not ever remember asking if that visitation was from God. That probably should have been the very first question any of us asked. However, I may not have been living worthy enough to receive an answer prior to that night.

"I am not saying that God can only answer us if we word things just so, because I know that He is capable of doing anything He desires. However, if we ask questions in a manner that requires a whole conversation to respond, what are the chances we will receive an answer? We would need a visitation like Joseph Smith received, or a detailed dream to receive that type of an answer. In contrast, if we ask questions that require a simple yes or no, how much more likely are we to receive an answer? With that type of question, we can receive what is described in the scriptures as a burning within our heart that tells us something is true, or a stupor of thought that tells us it is not true.

"I later called my sister and told her I had finally gained some insight about my original visitation. She told me she had always felt it was an evil visitation because of two factors. First, the visitation scared me so badly that I ceased praying for over a year. Second, it left me confused. She believed that if God had a message for me that was important enough to send a messenger through the veil, I would have understood the message.

"It was almost comical to hear her say, 'I don't think a messenger from God will turn around and leave because you say no. Can you picture someone going back and reporting that his mission didn't go well because the person didn't want to return with him?'

"The original visitation certainly did confuse me, and it took years for me to figure out what the purpose of the whole thing was. After receiving an answer that night, after viewing my great, great grandfather's picture and praying about it, I was not disappointed or afraid. I had gained valuable knowledge that increased my awareness about how Satan works. He will go to any measure to get one individual to follow him. He will entice us and deceive us in any manner he can. The only feeling he cannot provide for us is peace, but he will play on our fears and the things that are most important to us. He is very patient and has a long-range plan. It does not matter to him how long it takes if he ends up securing someone's future for eternity.

"Satan is the master of deceit. The men who visited me that night were dressed in white, something we associate with men of God. Satan did not fill me with radiance that my father could see; my face was white because I was so frightened. Even though I was filled with great joy and excitement when I saw that picture of my great, great grandfather, those feelings were not from God. They left the second I asked God to confirm the conclusion I had reached because of those feelings.

"I have learned that Satan can make us believe we are having a religious experience. He is capable of creating the same feelings within us that God does, except for peace. However, if you sincerely pray and ask if a vision or feeling is from God, Satan is not allowed to confound or confuse you. Only God can cause you to have the burning in your bosom that tells you it is of God, or the stupor of thought that tells you it is from Satan.

"This makes it clear to me, that even when searching for truth in religion, it is necessary to gain some knowledge about the subject so we can make our own decision. You are all familiar with the promise in the Book of Mormon. When you have read the book, then you can ask God if it is true or not. That is our example. Get the information, study it, and then ask God if it is true or not. The only way to ask God a question is to pray to Him. If you seek answers to questions in any way other than prayer, Satan has the means to intervene."

Elias knew sharing the story of his visitation with the members of his class had been the right thing to do. He could visibly see peace on the faces that still intently watched him. He knew those in the room did not want to leave and go back out into the world. He stayed with them for hours, and told stories of what it had been like when Christ came to the world and ushered in the Millennium. He told them about how quickly the ugliness had been eliminated. He told them how hearing Christ speak had removed all fear, and those who had followed his teachings were armed with knowledge and determination.

"Satan will try to convince you that his power is great. He will even try to convince you that he can utterly destroy all the Saints and gain God's glory. When Jesus Christ returned to the Earth, Satan's followers believed his lies, and during the final battle his armies greatly outnumbered the Saints. Then it became abundantly clear that sheer numbers and perceived power were no match for God. They could not even prevail against a much smaller group of Saints endowed with God's strength. You know that God prevailed as He had promised in days of old, and that His people rose up and were victorious. In this final battle, you are His warriors. You possess the armor of God, and you are ready to withstand the battle."

As had happened when the Millennium was ushered in, the gap widened between those who remained true to the teachings of God and those who had succumbed to the temptations of Satan. It took only a few short years to polarize the opposing groups to the same degree that had previously taken generations to accomplish. The familiar scenario played out as Elias and Sarah watched, unable to fathom that it had been one thousand years since the last conflict. It was apparent to Elias that the most valiant spirits had been saved to come forth in the end of time. When Satan deceived one of them, they fell under his power and became vigilant in their fight against God.

As the final battle raged on, it seemed to become a continuation of the war that was fought in heaven before anyone had been sent to Earth. If the wicked killed someone, they passed through death in an instant and remembered their life before leaving their pre-earth experience. In addition, the wicked knew they could not kill anyone who had already been resurrected.

Satan endeavored to capture as many souls as possible, fulfilling his threats of long ago. Those that understood Satan knew his true goal was to cause his Father as much sorrow as possible, and he knew every single individual he convinced to turn their back on the Great Father would increase His sorrow considerably. Victory was not part of Satan's plan, for he knew he could not win. He knew the Great Father would strip him of his power when He determined the battle had gone on long enough.

The season of Satan's influence passed quickly. Once again, Elias and Sarah stood with the righteous and waited for the wicked to fall upon them. Elias felt no fear; he knew Satan had no power to harm him or his wife. He knew there was no temptation Satan could use that would entice the saints to give up their eternal happiness with the Savior.

Elias began quietly singing a song he had heard in a dream the night before. He sang louder as he noticed others were beginning to sing with him. It was a tune he had never heard before and he was not sure how he had learned the foreign words, but it had been etched into his mind so vividly during his dream that he now boomed it out with confidence and great volume. As those around him joined in the song of praise to their God, in His pure undefiled language, it caused the wicked to fall to their knees with the same power that had leveled the walls of Jericho.

As if sleep were clearing from the eyes of the faithful saints, the veil began to deteriorate. Michael the Archangel and countless angels from heaven encircled the wicked and securely bound them. Adam drove the wicked before him until they reached the prison that had been prepared for them. The righteous were caught up in glory and returned to the place they lived before their trial on the Earth.

From afar, every soul that had populated the Earth, from its beginning to its end, watched as mother Earth passed away. Her cycle of life was the last of Father's creations associated with the Earth to expire. The Earth's magnificent diversity turned to gray sand. Then, as had happened with each of God's creations, the Earth was resurrected, and the original beauty of the Earth was restored. The change continued until the Earth began to glow, and the glow intensified until it became brighter than the sun itself. The sun was no longer needed and the Earth moved to where it had come from when life was first placed upon it by Jesus Christ. Earth would become the celestial home of the righteous who had been tested there. As prophesied, there would be three heavens, and the Earth would be the greatest of the heavens..

ELIAS' FINAL JUDGMENT

When the final conflict ended, there was no more fear or sadness. There were no more trials. There would never again be any doubt about who controlled the elements and every living thing. The leaders of the Earth were God the Father, Jesus Christ, and The Holy Ghost. All power had been removed from the Evil One and his angels, and they would never again be able to influence those who had lived on the Earth.

All the righteous once again had a full knowledge of the complete plan of salvation, and a full memory of the process that had earned them their eternal place in God's kingdom. All were equal, with only the knowledge and experience gained during their earthly existence making each one unique from another.

Friends who had been separated for long periods were once again reunited. Elias, Marash, Ribiab and Shroba were together once again. Many things had changed since they innocently spent their time on the cliffs wondering what lay ahead of them. Stephan was destined to live in a world his four friends could visit, and he was extremely happy.

"I will never be able to explain how I feel," Stephan said one afternoon when they were together for a time. "The day I returned from Earth, I wanted to cease to exist. I was so ashamed of what I had done that I could not even look my Heavenly parents in the eye. I wanted to sink into the ground when I saw Bethany, knowing how horribly I had treated her on earth. Yet she still looked upon me with love and sympathy apparent in her eyes. Now I am able to accept it, and I have learned to be happy for her happiness. I have found a place where I am comfortable, where I am with others who are like me. We made poor choices," he said, and then shrugged and rolled his eyes. "All right, we all made a mess of our lives, but we are comfortable and truly happy living with others like ourselves. You can all come to visit me any time and you will always be welcome."

"Can I ask you something?" Ribiab asked.

"No, I am not unhappy that Bethany is married to you," Stephan said, again laughing. "She deserves someone who can make her happy, but I'm not that person. She possessed the same level of light that all four of you possess, and somehow even when we were on Earth I was aware of that. I always felt I was trying to be something I was not when I was with her. I wanted to be like her, but I could not make myself change, so I constantly tried to drag her down to my level. That only made her miserable. Now that she is with you, she has found someone who is her equal."

"How is it that you seem to know where you are going to spend eternity when we have not yet gone through the final judgment?" Ribiab asked.

Shroba laughed at his friend and asked, "How is it that you are not aware you have achieved the highest level of eternal life? Just look at the light that emanates from your body. It's the same as these other three characters," he said, motioning to Elias, Shroba and Marash. "I don't have that same light, so it's obvious I would not be comfortable living with all of you. I know where people who possess my level of light will be assigned, and that is where I will feel comfortable. In addition, I already know that it is filled with much more beauty than anything I ever expected or hoped for while living on Earth. If you all promise to visit me occasionally, I will have everything I need to be happy forever."

Elias put his arm around Stephan. "You can bet on that. Regular visits forever."

"Good," Stephan beamed. "Well, I hate to run off, but I have promised a certain young woman I would join her for a few hours and I'd better be going."

"Whoa," Elias said. "Young woman? Let's hear it!"

Shroba laughed and his friends noticed that he sounded genuinely happy. "She's someone who had a life on Earth very similar to mine," Stephan said as he slowly backed away from the group. "We have a lot of fun together and I'm pretty sure we will be in the same place following the judgment. In the mean time, we're having a good time getting better acquainted."

"When do we get to meet her?" Ribiab asked.

"When you come to visit me," Stephan shouted as he turned and ran toward the place he was certain she was waiting for him.

"I spent so many years feeling bad about Stephan and wondering if I could have done something else to help him," Elias said. "It's amazing to see him so happy and looking forward to a new relationship. Best of all, he truly seems happy about his eternal state. Exceedingly happy!"

One step remained in the Plan of Salvation. Each person who had ever lived on the Earth would now stand alone before the judgment bar of the Lord. This included every person from Adam to the very last soul that was sent to the Earth to gain a mortal body.

A schedule was once again posted, reminiscent of the list that had informed each person of their appointed time to dwell on Earth. The judgments were in the same order as the departures had been. All the chronological events that took place on Earth were to be considered during each person's individual judgment. The wait to go to Earth had filled each person with curiosity and excitement. Waiting for the final judgment was much more difficult.

Everyone had a unique way of looking at what the final judgment would mean to them. Some were filled with regret and anxiety, knowing they could have done so much better while they were on Earth. Some were confident they would be happy wherever they were assigned, and others seemed to be going through the motions as though the outcome did not matter to them.

Elias and Sarah sat together on their favorite bench. Even after living for a thousand years on Earth, their bench in the central garden was their favorite spot. Elias was so content to just be with Sarah. Each day he tried to trust that he had done his best while on Earth and would be satisfied with whatever judgment his life had earned for him. Then he would think of the possibility that he would not be with Sarah for eternity, and he was unable to stop the panic that seemed to cause his breathing to become erratic.

"What are you thinking about right now?" Sarah asked, looking closely at her eternal companion.

"I was thinking that our time on Earth, even with the thousand years during the Millennium, seemed to pass as quickly as the blink of an eye. And yet our eternal lives depend on what we did during that time."

"So, are you worried about something involved with that? Every time we sit quietly together, you seem unable to catch your breath, and I know your perfected body is not experiencing problems with your lungs. So tell all, what's bothering you?"

Elias breathed deeply and pulled Sarah's hand to his lips. "I try not to think of what will happen if I am not worthy to live on the celestialized Earth. I know you will live there, and I wonder how I could endure a single minute if I were not there with you."

"Elias, you have done everything you could to be worthy of such a judgment. I have known you longer than just your lifetime on Earth, and you have always been worthy of living on the new Earth. Since the first moment I saw you, which was right here, I knew I had to spend my life with you. Your heart has been pure, always."

"You are extremely prejudiced, I fear." Elias said.

"Do you have any doubt that your three children will be dwelling on Earth?" Sarah asked very seriously.

"No, I don't. They have been valiant both in this life and in their life on Earth. I was worse than rebellious when I was growing up on Earth. I was raised knowing the truth and I not only took it for granted, I tried every single day to see how closely I could walk to the edge of the abyss and still keep from falling in. It was like a game. Stephan seems to be confident he will be required to pay the price for his actions, and sometimes I feel like a hypocrite that still hopes he is worthy of living with you."

"You are not, nor have you ever been, like Stephan. I believe you were his one great hope and you enabled him to achieve as much as he possibly could. You continually tried to get him to understand the importance of God's teachings. You nearly let him drag you down to his level, as he tried to do with Bethany, but you were only there to help him, not there because you were like him. You have never seen that about your relationship with him, have you?"

"No, I can't agree with you. I willingly followed where he led me. If I had been half as persuasive and persistent as he was, he would have followed me."

"Elias, I have complete faith that we will spend eternity together, and you will know that for a certainty much sooner than I. When you enter the Departure Building for your final judgment, I will never know where you ended up until I go through my own judgment. I pray every day that when I step through the portal after my judgment, you will be waiting there for me. And I'm not worried that I will step into the celestialized Earth and not find you, I'm worried that I will step through and be somewhere else, and you will have been sent to Earth."

"Not a chance," Elias comforted her.

When each person's scheduled time for the final judgment arrived, they went into the Departure Building alone, and immediately to the Judgment Hall. An individual's sins were not made public unless they sinned openly against God, in which case, their open defiance was made known to all.

Ribiab was the first to leave, as he had done when he went to Earth. Bethany walked with him to the entrance of the Departure Building and kissed him farewell. As agreed, she turned and walked away from the building and Ribiab did not turn to enter the building until she had disappeared from his view.

Marash was the next, and he went to the Departure Building with his eternal companion. Deborah stopped and kissed Marash goodbye before they entered the grounds of the area, and then she watched Marash turn and walk away from her without a backward glance until he entered the building.

Each parting had been simple and there seemed to be no great show of emotion or fear. It was as if one were leaving for the day and the other would join them soon. Their farewells definitely seemed to feel temporary.

Elias would depart before Stephan, so he would never know if he approached the Departure Building alone or with a friend, but he did know he needed Sarah at his side as he walked to the building. He constantly tried to convince himself that their separation would be temporary, but his emotions were visible to anyone who saw him. He was exceedingly concerned. It was almost a relief when he stepped away from his long embrace with Sarah and turned to enter the building. He did not look back because he could not bear to look at her again, wondering if it would be the last time he would ever see her.

Elias slowly walked to the Judgment Hall, in no hurry to step through the doorway and face the council that would judge his life, a council made of men so great they could look into his very heart and mind. He was not sure he could bear the look on his Great Father's face when He looked into his heart and saw the many mistakes he had made.

He stood at the door, knob in hand, thinking of all the times during his mortal life when a tiny bit more effort could have reaped eternal benefits. He recalled the small acts of kindness he thought of but had never performed, acts that would have cost him nothing, but might now have eternal implications.

He breathed deeply, trying to stop tears that were flowing freely. He thought of Shroba's contentment and genuine happiness at having earned a place where he felt comfortable.

A smile actually formed on his lips as he realized that regardless of all the levels of inequality that existed on Earth, a person who had lived with the *least* amount of temporal possessions now had the opportunity to live in a palace far better than anything that had ever been available to the inhabitants of Earth. For some unexplainable reason, he remembered the people he had known on Earth who thought the only thing that mattered was their physical appearance, and how surprised they had been when they left Earth and found that their inner qualities were more visible and adored than their physical characteristics.

He turned the knob and pushed the door open. How he wished he could have Sarah by his side to help him shine. He had always felt invisible when she was not with him. He was now to be judged strictly on his own merit.

As Christ entered the room, Elias felt as if he were suddenly stripped naked. Not of clothing, but of pride. Every weakness and character flaw he had let develop within himself was totally exposed. He could not raise his eyes from the floor as every moment of his life flashed before him. It was not a quick momentary flash of a few events. Instead, it was every moment and event from his birth. The secrets he had hidden from everyone were now exposed to sacred, righteous entities, who now stood directly in front of him. In some miraculous way, his knowledge that there was no way he could achieve eternal exaltation through his own efforts alone came to mind. He prayed fervently that Jesus Christ would find the decisions he had made while on Earth qualified him to receive the mercy offered through His Atonement.

The review of his life continued. As he viewed a misdealing with a partner, or a lie he thought he had gotten away with, the images stopped. The individual he had wronged entered the room. He had to confess what he had done, how he had wronged them, and what he gained by his own misdeed, all while looking directly into that person's eyes, and then he had to ask for their forgiveness. If no one on Earth witnessed a sin, the Book of Life was opened and a member of the Judgment Counsel read what those on the other side of the veil had witnessed. Once he had confessed his sin, the moments of his life again continued forward from that point.

Throughout his judgment, he found it extremely difficult to continue standing in the presence of his Great Father, Jesus Christ and those on the panel. He looked at the scars still visible on the Savior's hands and feet, and felt total and complete sorrow that his sins had added to the suffering the Savior had been forced to bear. He was grateful that the terrible things he had previously repented of were now absent from the activities he saw replayed from his life. He was grateful that each sin he had repented of increased the possibility that he might spend eternity with Sarah. He wished he had the ability to rewind the hands of time, live a moment of weakness over again and make the right decision.

The images of his life ended. The witnesses had all come forward, allowed him to admit his guilt, and left the room. Now he was alone standing before his judges. He forced himself to slowly raise his eyes from the floor. The nervousness that had nearly consumed him when he first entered the room was gone. For the first time he actually looked around. All of God's chosen were now sitting in a semi-circle in front of him on beautiful white thrones. Christ sat in the middle upon His throne. The walls were a beautiful weave of white material different from any fabric he had known before. The floor was one continuous piece of white marble stretching from wall to wall.

The entire room appeared luminescent. Although no direct source of light could be detected, the room glowed with brightness. The light was so pure and warming that it felt as if it embraced and soothed him. The left and right ends of the room appeared to have no visible walls. The room itself seemed to be floating between the two realms – the one on the right and the one on the left. The light visible from the left side of the room reminded him of a heavily overcast day. Streaming into the room from the right was golden light that carried sweet fragrances and sounds that reminded him of the falls he loved so much.

The difference between the two areas, right and left, was immense – much greater than the difference between being below the clouds on a dark, dreary, rainy day, and being above them where the sun warmed everything it touched and made the clouds glow bright and white against the deep blue sky.

Suddenly he was pulled back to the reality of what was taking place when Christ called him by name. In a very gentle, understanding, and caring voice He asked, "Viewing all that you have said and done throughout your life, knowing the talents and blessings you were given, did you help to benefit or destroy your fellow man and all my creation? Your decision will determine if you pass to your right or left."

The decision had fallen upon his shoulders, and the weight of it drove him to the floor. As he knelt there, hands and knees pressed against the floor, every fiber of his being wanted to run through the entry to the right, but he knew what he deserved. The regret of every mistake and sin he had made during his life on Earth seemed magnified a thousand times, totally overwhelming him. He tried to confess that he knew he had been foolish and could have done so much better, but the words would not come. He sobbed uncontrollably, knowing that it all ended at that moment, and he would never have another chance to change anything he had done during his test on the Earth.

Suddenly, he felt himself being helped to his feet. Christ embraced him and Elias let his sorrow flow freely. He could feel warm energy radiating from his Savior and spreading through every cell in his own body. He wanted to stay right there and never have to face the moment that loomed ahead.

Christ slowly helped Elias move toward the end of the room and then said, "Our Father said it would be very difficult and we would lose many of those dear to us. You fell often, but you struggled until you got back up. Although you wandered from side to side, you always walked in my direction. You have a long time to work on your weaknesses. But without going to Earth you would not have gained compassion and understanding for your fellow man."

Elias opened his eyes and looked at the Savior, not able to see Him clearly because of the tears that filled his eyes. He tried to stand on his own and forced himself to turn and look at the portal he would now be required to step through.

"Well done, Elias," the Savior said softly.

The sight of the beautiful flowers that were visible through the portal caused Elias to cry loudly and again turn to embrace the Savior. He sank to the floor and kissed the Savior's feet, overcome with the realization that when Sarah stepped through the portal and into the flower garden he could now see, he would be standing there – waiting to take her in his arms.

INSPIRATIONAL RESOURCES

Books:

- ❖ Behold I Come Quickly, The Last Days and Beyond, Hoyt W. Brewster, Jr., Deseret Book Company, 1994
- ❖ Discourses on the Holy Ghost, comp. N. B. Lundwall, Bookcraft, Inc., 1959
- ❖ Handcarts to Zion, LeRoy R. Hafen and Ann W. Hafen, The Arthur H. Clark Company, 1960
- ❖ History of the Church of Jesus Christ of Latter-day Saints
- ❖ Levi Savage, Levi Savage's Diary, typescript copy, Church Archives.
- ❖ Scriptures: The Holy Bible (King James Version)
- ❖ The Book of Mormon, Another Testament of Jesus Christ
- ❖ The Doctrine & Covenants
- ❖ Sons of Utah Pioneers.org, volume 53, No. 3
- ❖ T.B.H. Stenhouse, *Rocky Mountain States* (New York, 1873), later printed in *Among the Mormons* Eds. William Mulder and A. Russell Mortensen (New York, 1967) pages 282-290.
- ❖ The Coming of the Lord, Gerald N. Lund, Bookcraft, Inc, 1971
- ❖ The Father is Not the Son, Ramon D. Smullin, Envision Pub Services, 1998
- ❖ Those Gold Plates, Mark E. Petersen, Bookcraft, Inc., 1979

Audio/Visual Information:

- ❖ Joseph Smith the Prophet, Truman G. Madsen, 2007
- ❖ Music and the Mind, Michael Ballam, 1994
- ❖ Secret Burial Mounds of Prehistoric America, A&E Home Video (VHS)

Locations:

- ❖ Adam-ondi-Ahman, Mormon Historic Site, Davies County, Missouri
- ❖ Cahokia Mounds State Historic Site, administered by the Illinois Historic Preservation Agency, near Collinsville, Illinois
- ❖ Carthage Jail- Carthage, Illinois
- ❖ Liberty Jail- Liberty, Missouri
- ❖ Mayan Ruins: Chichen Itza, Tulum, Xcaret, Xel-ha Coba - near Cancun, Mexico
- ❖ Mormon Handcart Visitors' Center, Alcova, Wyoming
- ❖ The Church of Jesus Christ of Latter-day Saints and The Reorganized Church of Jesus Christ of Latter-day Saints Visitor's Center and Grounds, Nauvoo, Illinois

- ❖ The Church of Jesus Christ of Latter-day Saints, Far West Visitor's Center - Far West, Missouri
- ❖ The Church of Jesus Christ of Latter-day Saints Visitor's Center - Independence, Missouri
- ❖ Winter Quarters Visitor's Center and Cemetery - North Omaha, Nebraska

ABOUT THE AUTHORS

Richard Green

Growing up in Idaho provided a childhood that many would believe to be fiction. As a youth I bounced back and forth between what was right and trying to walk the edge of destruction; leaving me very acquainted with both forces present on this earth. As an adult, my family has lived in many locations, yet Salt Lake City has been considered home for more than twenty years.

Being interested in tearing apart and putting together my bikes as a child grew into a life long hobby of building and painting custom motorcycles and cars. My work career has been as diverse and evolving as every other aspect of my life. The recession of the 80's caused me to move from construction to the security of Telecommunications. Later, again finding myself back in construction, the recent recession sent me scurrying for my former career in Telecom.

My life has often been full of turmoil and amazing experiences, providing a vast library from which to pull stories. However, the desire to create this book came from living in a family that has been threaded together through generations. My wife and three daughters added a dimension of love and memories that have given my life true purpose. Another driving force has been my spiritual experiences and the search to gain the knowledge of what it all means. God has granted me an amazing experience on this earth, and even greater, the ability to see that it is an amazing experience.

Anita Johnson

I grew up in Idaho, and was very blessed that all my friends were also active members of the Church. However, I had gone through the motions but never developed a testimony of my own. As a young adult, I became inactive. Several years passed before I returned to Church. The sweet Spirit I felt that day made me realize how much I had missed, and awakened within me a desire to develop my own testimony of the Gospel's truthfulness.

I know many of my trials have been of my own making. A very short marriage blessed me with a son; when I spend time with his growing family, I realize what a rich blessing our posterity brings into our lives. I know my Heavenly Father has a specific plan for each person's life. Many of my trials have helped me better understand that precious gift, and value it enough to listen to the Spirit more closely – and be more obedient.

My eternal soul mate came into my life after I had given up hope of ever finding him. We made our home in Poulsbo, Washington, for 26 years. Although he has completed his earthly test, being sealed together for all eternity is a glorious blessing. This book was written during the last years of his life, and it helped make the other side of the veil as tangible as this mortal existence. I cannot imagine being able to endure his death without that blessing. The precious spiritual experiences with which I have been blessed leave no doubt whatsoever that our love for each other continues after death, and I hope this book will bring similar comfort to others facing comparable situations.

Heavenly Father desires that we find joy in every phase of our life, even during difficult times when we might see only "enduring to the end" ahead. This painful period passes also: my present husband is daily proof of that blessing.

OTHER BOOKS BY THE AUTHOR

A collection of poems and thoughts written by brothers, Richard and Jon Green. Realizing they had each unknowingly been writing similar themed material for decades, they decided to combine their work that focuses on the Savior, family, and life experiences.

LIFE'S PURE WATER
Available on Amazon
ISBN 9780991516322

Years of unanswered prayers and a fear of praying, caused me to wonder if even Jesus Christ could save me. I share the event that caused me to confirm and verify every experience through prayer. A gained understanding of the depth of Christ's atonement.

A LIFETIME OF CONVERSION
Available on Amazon
ISBN 9780991516377